Praise for these nationally bestselling authors:

LINDA HOWARD

"Linda Howard makes our senses come alive...
She knows what romance readers want."
—*Affaire de Coeur*

"You can't read just one Linda Howard."
—*New York Times* bestselling author
Catherine Coulter

FERN MICHAELS

"Her characters are real and enduring,
her prose so natural that it seems you are
witnessing the story..."
—*Los Angeles Sunday Daily News*

DEBBIE MACOMBER

"I've never met a Macomber book I didn't love!"
—*New York Times* bestselling author
Linda Lael Miller

"Debbie Macomber can always be counted on for
first-class entertainment..."
—*Affaire de Coeur*

Linda Howard

New York Times bestselling author Linda Howard says that books have long played a profound role in her life. She cut her teeth on Margaret Mitchell, and from then on continued to read widely and eagerly. In recent years her interest has settled on romance fiction, because she's "easily bored by murder, mayhem and politics." After twenty-one years of penning stories for her own enjoyment, Ms. Howard finally worked up the courage to submit a novel for publication—and met with success! Happily, the Alabama author has been steadily publishing ever since.

Fern Michaels

This *New York Times* bestselling author has a passion for romance that stems from her passion for the other joys in her life—her family, animals and historic homes. She is usually found in New Jersey or South Carolina, where she is either tapping out stories on her computer or completing some kind of historical restoration. Legions of fans around the world thrill to the romantic stories Ms. Michaels creates in every one of her novels.

Debbie Macomber

Debbie Macomber always enjoyed telling stories—first to her baby-sitting clients and then to her own four children. As a full-time wife and mother and an avid romance reader, she dreamed of one day sharing her stories with a wider audience. In the autumn of 1982 she sold her first book, and that was only the beginning. Debbie has been making regular appearances on the *USA Today* bestseller list—not surprising, considering that there are over forty million copies of her books in print worldwide!

LINDA HOWARD

FERN MICHAELS

DEBBIE MACOMBER

THROUGH *the* YEARS

Silhouette Books

Published by Silhouette Books

America's Publisher of Contemporary Romance

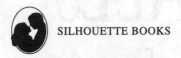 SILHOUETTE BOOKS

ISBN 0-373-48403-8

THROUGH THE YEARS

Copyright © 1999 by Harlequin Books S.A.

The publisher acknowledges the copyright holders of
the individual works as follows:

TEARS OF THE RENEGADE
Copyright © 1985 by Linda Howington

GOLDEN LASSO
Copyright © 1980 by Fern Michaels

BABY BLESSED
Copyright © 1994 by Debbie Macomber

This edition published by arrangement with Harlequin Books S.A.

® and TM are trademarks of Harlequin Books S.A., used under
license. Trademarks indicated with ® are registered in the United States
Patent and Trademark Office, the Canadian Trade Marks Office and in
other countries.

Visit us at www.romance.net

Printed in U.S.A.

CONTENTS

Tears of the Renegade
Linda Howard

To Vanessa and Gail
for their dedicated nagging.

Chapter 1

It was late, already after eleven o'clock, when the broad-shouldered man appeared in the open French doors. He stood there, perfectly at ease, watching the party with a sort of secret amusement. Susan noticed him immediately, though she seemed to be the only one who did so, and she studied him with faint surprise because she'd never seen him before. She would have remembered if she had; he wasn't the sort of man that anyone forgot.

He was tall and muscular, his white dinner jacket hugging his powerful shoulders with just enough precision to proclaim exquisite tailoring, yet what set him apart wasn't the almost dissolute so-phistication that sat so easily on him; it was his face. He had the bold look of a desperado, an impression heightened by the level dark brows that shadowed eyes of a pale, crystalline blue. Lode-stone eyes, she thought, feeling their effect even though he wasn't looking at her. A funny little quiver danced down her spine, and her senses were suddenly heightened—the music was more vibrant, the colors more intense, the heady perfume of the early spring night stronger. Every instinct within her was abruptly awakened as she stared at the stranger with a sort of primitive recognition. Women have always known which men are dangerous, and this man radiated danger.

It was there in his eyes, the self-assurance of a man who was willing to take risks, and willing to accept the consequences. An almost weary experience had hardened his features, and Susan knew, looking at him, that he would be a man no one would lightly cross. Danger rode those broad shoulders like a visible mantle. He wasn't quite...civilized. He looked like a modern-day pirate, from those bold eyes to the short, neatly trimmed dark beard and moustache that hid the lines of his jaw and upper lip; but she knew that they would be strong lines. Her eyes traveled to his hair, dark and thick and vibrant, styled in a casual perfection that most men would have paid a fortune to obtain, just long enough to brush his collar in the back with a hint of curl.

At first no one seemed to notice him, which was surprising, because to Susan he stood out like a tiger in a roomful of tabbies. Then, gradually, people began to look at him, and to her further astonishment a stunned, almost hostile silence began to fall, spreading quickly over the room, a contagious pall that leaped from one person to another. Suddenly uneasy, she looked at her brother-in-law, Preston, who was the host and almost within touching distance of the newly arrived guest. Why didn't he welcome the man? But instead Preston had gone stiff, his face pale, staring at the stranger with the same sort of frozen horror one would eye a cobra coiled at one's feet.

The tidal wave of silence had spread to include the entire huge room now, even the musicians on the raised dais falling silent. Under the glittering prisms of the chandeliers, people were turning, staring, shock rippling over their faces. A shiver of alarm went down Susan's slender back; what was going on? Who was he? Something awful was going to happen. She sensed it, saw Preston tensing for a scene, and knew that she wasn't going to let it happen. Whoever he was, he was a guest of the Blackstones, and no one was going to be rude to him, not even Preston Blackstone. Instinctively she moved, stepping into the middle of the scene, murmuring "Excuse me" to people as she slipped past them. All attention turned to her as if drawn by a magnet, for her movement was the only movement in the room. The stranger turned his gaze on her, too; he watched her, and he waited, those strange lodestone eyes narrowing as he examined the slim, graceful woman whose features were as pure and serene as a cameo, clothed in a fragile cream silk dress that swirled about her ankles as she walked. A three-strand pearl choker encircled her delicate throat; with her soft dark hair drawn up on top of her head and a few tendrils curling about her temples, she was a dream, a mirage, as illusive as angel's breath. She looked as pure as a Victorian virgin, glowingly set apart from everyone else in the room, untouched and untouchable; and, to the man who watched her approach, an irresistible challenge.

Susan was unaware of the male intent that suddenly gleamed in the depths of his pale blue eyes. She was concerned only with avoiding the nastiness that had been brewing, something she didn't understand but nevertheless wanted to prevent. If anyone had a score to settle with this man, they could do it at another time and in another place. She nodded a silent command to the band as she walked, and obediently the music began again, hesitantly at first, then gaining in volume. By that time, Susan had reached the man, and she held her hand out to him. "Hello," she said, her low, musical voice carrying effortlessly to the people who listened openly, gaping at her. "I'm Susan Blackstone; won't you dance with me?"

Her hand was taken in long, hard fingers, but there was no hand-shake. Instead, her hand was simply held, and a slightly rough thumb rubbed over the back of her fingers, feeling the softness, the slender bones. A level brow quirked upward over the blue eyes that were even more compelling at close range, for now she could see that the pale blue was ringed by deep midnight. Staring into those eyes, she forgot that they were simply standing there while he held her hand until he used his grip on her to pull her into his embrace as he swung her into a dance, causing the skirt of her dress to wrap about his long legs as they moved.

At first he simply held her, his strength moving her across the dance floor with such ease that her feet barely touched down. No one else was dancing, and Susan looked at several people, her level gaze issuing a quiet, gentle command that was obeyed without exception. Slowly they were joined by other dancers, and the man looked down at the woman he held in his arms.

Susan felt the strength in the hand on her lower back as the fingers slowly spread and exerted a gentle pressure that was nevertheless inexorable. She found herself closer to him, her breasts lightly brushing against his hard chest, and she suddenly felt overwarm, the heat from his body enveloping her. The simple, graceful steps he was using in the dance were abruptly difficult to follow, and she forced herself to concentrate to keep from stepping on his toes.

A quivering, spring-loaded tension began coiling in her stomach, and her hand trembled in his. He squeezed her fingers warmly and said into her ear, "Don't be afraid; I won't hurt you."

His voice was a soft, deep rumble, as she had known it would be, and again that strange little shiver rippled through her. She lifted her head and found how close he had been when one of the soft curls at her temple became entangled in his beard, then slid free. She was almost dazed when she found herself looking directly at the chiseled strength of his lips, and she wondered with raw hunger if his mouth would be firm or soft, if he would taste as heady as he looked. With an inner groan, she jerked her thoughts away from the contemplation of how he would taste, what it would be like to kiss him. It was difficult to move her gaze higher, but she managed it, then wished that she hadn't; staring into those unusual eyes was almost more than her composure could bear. Why was she reacting like a teenager? She was an adult, and even as a teenager she had been calm, nothing like the woman who now found herself quaking inside at a mere glance.

But she was seared by that glance, which surveyed, approved, asked, expected and...knew. He was one of those rare men who knew women, and were all the more dangerous for their knowledge. She responded to the danger alarm that all women possess by lifting her head with the innate dignity that characterized her every movement, and met that bold look. She said quietly, "What an odd thing to say," and she was proud that her voice hadn't trembled.

"Is it?" His voice was even softer than before, deeper, increasingly intimate. "Then you can't know what I'm thinking."

"No," she said, and left it at that, not picking upon the innuendo that she knew was there.

"You will," he promised, his tone nothing now but a low rasp that touched every nerve in her body. As he spoke, the arm about her waist tightened to pull her closer, not so close that she would have felt obliged to protest, but still she was suddenly, mutely aware of the rippling muscles in his thighs as his legs moved against hers. Her fingers clenched restlessly on his shoulder as she fought the abrupt urge to slide them inside his collar, to feel his bare skin and discover for herself if her fingers would be singed by the fire of him. Shocked at herself, she kept her eyes determinedly on the shoulder seam of his jacket and tried not to think of the strength she could feel in the hand that clasped hers, or in the one that pressed so lightly on the small of her back...lightly; but she had the sudden thought that if she tried to move away from him, that hand would prevent the action.

"Your shoulders look like satin," he murmured roughly; before she could guess his intentions, his head dipped and his mouth, warm and hard, touched the soft, bare curve of her shoulder. A fine madness seized her and she quivered, her eyes drifting shut. God, he was making love to her on the dance floor, and she didn't even know his name! But everything in her was responding to him, totally independent of her control; she couldn't even control her thoughts, which kept leaping ahead to more dangerous subjects, wondering how his mouth would feel if it kept sliding down her body....

"Stop that," she said, to herself as well as to him, but her voice was lacking any element of command; instead it was soft and shivery, the way she felt. Her skin felt as if it were on fire, but voluptuous shivers almost like a chill kept tickling her spine.

"Why?" he asked, his mouth making a sleek glissade from her shoulder to the sensitive hollow just below her ear.

"People are watching," she murmured weakly, sagging against him as her body went limp from the flaming delight that went off like a rocket inside her. His arm tightened about her waist to hold her up, but the intensified sensations of being pressed to him only made her that much weaker. She drew a ragged breath; locked against him as she was, there was no mistaking the blatant male arousal of his body, and she lifted stunned, drowning eyes to him. He was watching her through narrowed eyes, the intense, laser quality of his gaze burning into her. There was no embarrassment or apology in his expression; he was a man, and reacted as such. Susan found, to her dazed astonishment, that the deeply feminine center of her didn't want an apology. She wanted instead to drop her head to his shoulder and collapse into his lean, knowledgeable hands; but she was acutely aware not only of the people watching him, but also that if she followed her very feminine inclination, he was likely to respond by carrying her away like a pirate stealing a lady who had taken his fancy. No matter how he made her feel, this man was still a stranger to her.

"I don't even know who you are," she gasped quietly, her nails digging into his shoulder.

"Would knowing my name make any difference?" He blew gently on one of the tendrils that lay on her temple, watching the silky hair lift and fall. "But if it makes you feel better, sweetheart, we're keeping it in the family."

He was teasing, his teeth glistening whitely as he smiled, and Susan caught her breath, holding it for a moment before she could control her voice again. "I don't understand," she admitted, lifting her face to him.

"Take another deep breath like that, and it won't matter if you understand or not," he muttered, making her searingly aware of how her breasts had flattened against the hard planes of flesh beneath the white jacket. His diamond-faceted gaze dipped to the softness of her mouth as he explained, "I'm a Blackstone, too, though they probably don't claim me."

Susan stared at him in bewilderment. "But I don't know you. Who are you?"

Again those animal-white teeth were revealed in a wicked grin that lifted the corners of his moustache. "Haven't you heard any gossip? The term 'black sheep' was probably invented especially for me."

Still she stared at him without comprehension, the graceful line of her throat vulnerable to his hungry scrutiny as she kept her head lifted the necessary inches to look at him. "But I don't know of any black sheep. What's your name?"

"Cord Blackstone," he replied readily enough. "First cousin to Vance and Preston Blackstone; only son of Elias and Marjorie Blackstone; born November third, probably nine months to the day after Dad returned from his tour of duty in Europe, though I never could get Mother to admit it," he finished, that wicked, fascinating grin flashing again like a beacon on a dark night. "But what about you, sweetheart? If you're a Blackstone, you're not a natural one. I'd remember any blood relative who looked like you. So, which of my esteemed cousins are you married to?"

"Vance," she said, an echo of pain shadowing her delicate features for a moment. It was a credit to her strength of will that she was able to say evenly, "He's dead, you know," but nothing could mask the desolation that suddenly dimmed the luminous quality of her eyes.

The hard arms about her squeezed gently. "Yes, I'd heard. I'm sorry," he said with rough simplicity. "Damn, what a waste. Vance was a good man."

"Yes, he was." There was nothing more that she could say, because she still hadn't come to terms with the senseless, unlikely accident that had taken Vance's life. Death had struck so swiftly, taken so much from her, that she had automatically protected herself by keeping people at a small but significant distance since then.

"What happened to him?" the silky voice asked, and she was a little stunned that he'd asked. Didn't he even know how Vance had died?

"He was gored by a bull," she finally replied. "In the thigh…a major artery was torn. He bled to death before we could get him to a hospital." He had died in her arms, his life seeping away from him in a red tide, yet his face had been so peaceful. He had fixed his blue eyes on her and kept them there, as if he knew that he was dying and wanted his last sight on earth to be of her face. There had been a serene, heartbreaking smile on his lips as the brilliance of his gaze slowly dimmed and faded away forever….

Her fingers tightened on Cord Blackstone's shoulder, digging in, and he held her closer. In an odd way, she felt some of the pain easing as if he had buffered it with his big, hard body. Looking up, she saw a reflection in those pale eyes of his own harsh memories, and with a flash of intuition she realized that he was a man who had seen violent deaths before, who had held someone, a friend perhaps, in his arms while death approached and conquered. He understood what she had been through. Because he understood, the burden was abruptly easier to bear.

Susan had learned, over the years, how to continue with everyday things even in the face of crippling pain. Now she forced herself away from the horror of the memory and looked around, recalling herself to her duties. She noticed that far too many people were still standing around, staring at them and whispering. She caught the bandleader's eye and gave another discreet nod, a signal for him to slide straight into another number. Then she let her eyes linger on her guests, singling them out in turn, and under the demand in her clear gaze the dance floor began to fill, the whispers to fade, and the party once more resumed its normal noise level. There wasn't a guest there who would willingly offend her, and she knew it.

"That's a neat trick," he observed huskily, having followed it from beginning to end, and his voice reflected his appreciation. "Did they teach that in the finishing school you attended?"

A little smile played over her soft mouth before she glanced up at him, allowing him to divert her. "What makes you think I went to a finishing school?" She challenged.

His bold gaze slipped down the front of her gown to seek out and visually touch her rounded breasts. "Because you're so obviously...finished. I can't see anything that Mother Nature left undone." His hard, warm fingers slid briefly down her back. "God, how soft your skin is," he finished on a whisper.

A faint flush colored her cheeks at the husky note of intimacy that had entered his voice, though she was pleased in a deeply feminine way that he had noticed the texture of her skin. Oh, he was dangerous, all right, and the most dangerous thing about him was that he could make a woman take a risk even knowing how dangerous he was.

After a moment when she remained silent, he prodded, "Well? Am I right or not?"

"Almost," she admitted, lifting her chin to smile at him. There was a soft, glowing quality to her smile that lit her face with gentle radiance, and his heavy-lidded eyes dropped even more in a signal that someone who knew him well would have recognized immediately. But Susan didn't know him well, and she was unaware of how close she was skating to thin ice. "I attended Adderley's in

Virginia for four months, until my mother had a stroke and I left school to care for her.''

"No point in wasting any more money for them to gild the lily,'' he drawled, letting his eyes drift over her serene features, then down her slender, graceful throat to linger once again, with open delight, on her fragrant, silky curves. Susan felt an unexpected heat flood her body at this man's undisguised admiration; he looked as if he wanted to lean down and bury his face between her breasts, and she quivered with the surprising longing to have him do just that. He was more than dangerous; he was lethal!

She had to say something to break the heady spell that was enveloping her, and she used the most immediate topic of conversation. "When did you arrive?"

"Just this afternoon." The curl of his lip told her that he knew what she was doing, but was allowing her to get away with it. Lazily he puckered his lips and blew again at the fine tendril of dark hair that entranced him as it lay on the fragile skin of her temple, where the delicate blue veining lay just under the translucent skin. Susan felt her entire body pulsate, the warm scent of his breath affecting her as strongly as if he'd lifted his hand and caressed her. Almost blindly she looked at him, compelling herself to concentrate on what he was saying, but the movement of those chiseled lips was even more enticing than the scent of him.

"I heard that Cousin Preston was having a party,'' he was saying in a lazy drawl that had never lost its Southern music. "So I thought I'd honor old times by insulting him and crashing the shindig.''

Susan had to smile at the incongruity of describing this elegant affair as a "shindig,'' especially when he himself was dressed as if he had just stepped out of a Monte Carlo casino…where he would probably be more at home than he was here. "Did you used to make a habit of crashing parties?" she murmured.

"If I thought it would annoy Preston, I did,'' he replied, laughing a little at the memories. "Preston and I have always been on opposite sides of the fence," he explained with a careless smile that told her now how little the matter bothered him. "Vance was the only one I ever got along with, but then, he never seemed to care what kind of trouble I was in. Vance wasn't one to worship at the altar of the Blackstone name.''

That was true; Vance had conformed on the surface to the demands made on him because his name was Blackstone, but Susan had always known that he did so with a secret twinkle in his eyes. Sometimes she didn't think that her mother-in-law, Imogene, would ever forgive Vance for his mutiny against the Blackstone dynasty when he married Susan, though of course Imogene would never have been so crass as to admit it; a Blackstone didn't indulge in shrewish behavior. Then Susan felt faintly ashamed of herself, because Vance's family had treated her with respect.

Still, she felt a warm sense of comradeship with this man, because he had known Vance as she had, had realized his true nature, and she gave him a smile that sparked a glow in her own deep blue eyes. His arms tightened around her in an involuntary movement, as if he wanted to crush her against him.

"You've got the Blackstone coloring," he muttered, staring at her. "Dark hair and blue eyes, but you're so soft there's no way in hell you could be a real Blackstone. There's no hardness in you at all, is there?"

Puzzled, she stared back at him with a tiny frown puckering her brow. "What do you mean by hardness?"

"I don't think you'd understand if I told you," he replied cryptically, then added, "were you handpicked to be Vance's wife?"

"No." She smiled at the memory. "He picked me himself."

He gave a silent whistle. "Imogene will never recover from the shock," he said irreverently, and flashed that mocking grin at her again.

Despite herself, Susan felt the corners of her mouth tilting up in an answering smile. She was enjoying herself, talking to this dangerous, roguish man with the strangely compelling eyes, and she was surprised because she hadn't really enjoyed herself in such a long time...since Vance's death, in fact. There had been too many years and too many tears between her smiles, but suddenly things seemed different; she felt different inside herself. At first, she'd thought that she'd never recover from Vance's death, but five years had passed, and now she realized that she was looking forward to life again. She was enjoying being held in this man's strong arms and listening to his deep voice...and yes, she enjoyed the look in his eyes, enjoyed the sure feminine knowledge that he wanted her.

She didn't want to examine her reaction to him; she felt as if she had been dead, too, and was only now coming alive, and she wanted to revel in the change, not analyze it.

She was in danger of drowning in sensation, and she recognized the inner weakness that was overtaking her, but felt helpless to resist it. He must have sensed, with a primal intuition that was as alarming as the aura of danger that surrounded him, that she was close to surrendering to the temptation to play with fire. He leaned down and nuzzled his mouth against the delicate shell of her ear, sending every nerve in her body into delirium. "Go outside with me," he enticed, dipping his tongue into her ear and tracing the outer curve of it with electrifying precision.

Susan's entire body reverberated with the shock of it, but his action cleared her mind of the clouds of desire that had been fogging it. Totally flustered, her cheeks suddenly pink, she stopped dead. "Mr. Blackstone!"

"Cord," he corrected, laughing openly now. "After all, we're at least kissing cousins, wouldn't you say?"

She didn't know what to say, and fortunately she was saved from forming an answer that probably wouldn't have been coherent anyway, because Preston chose that moment to intervene. She had been vaguely aware, as she circled the room in Cord's arms, that Preston had been watching every move his cousin made, but she hadn't noticed him approaching. Putting his hand on Susan's arm, he stared at his cousin with frosty blue eyes. "Has he said anything to upset you, Susan?"

Again she was thrown into a quandary. If she said yes, there would probably be a scene, and she was determined to avoid that. On the other hand, how could she say no, when it would so obviously be a lie? A spark of genius prompted her to reply with quiet dignity, "We were talking about Vance."

"I see." It was perfectly reasonable to Preston that, even after five years, Susan should be upset when speaking of her dead husband. He accepted her statement as an explanation instead of the red herring it was, and gave all of his attention to his cousin, who was standing there totally relaxed, a faintly bored smile on his lips.

"Mother is waiting in the library," Preston said stiffly. "We assume you have some reason for afflicting us with your company."

"I do." Cord agreed easily with Preston's insult, still smiling as he ignored the red flag being waved at him. He lifted one eyebrow. "Lead the way. Somehow, I don't trust you at my back."

Preston stiffened, and Susan forestalled the angry outburst she saw coming by placing her hand lightly on Cord's arm and saying, "Let's not keep Mrs. Blackstone waiting."

As she had known he would, Preston shifted his attention to her. "There's no reason for you to come along, Susan. You might as well stay here with the guests."

"I'd like to have her there." Cord had instantly contradicted his cousin, and in a manner that made Susan certain he'd spoken merely to irritate Preston. "She's family, isn't she? She might as well hear it all first hand, rather than the watered-down and doctored version that she'd get from you and Imogene."

For a moment Preston looked as if he would debate the point;

then he turned abruptly and walked away. Preston was a Blackstone; he might want to punch Cord in the mouth, but he wouldn't make a public scene. Cord following him at a slight distance, his hand dropping to rest lightly on Susan's waist. He grinned down at her. "I wanted to make sure you didn't get away from me."

Susan was a grown woman, not a teenager. Moreover, she was a woman who for five years had managed large and varied business concerns with cool acumen; she was twenty-nine years old, and she told herself that she should long ago have passed out of the blushing stage. Yet this man, with the dashing air of a rake and those bold, challenging eyes, could make her blush with a mere glance. Excitement such as she had never felt before was racing through her, setting her heart pounding, and she actually felt giddy. She knew what love was like, and it wasn't this. She had loved Vance, loved him so strongly that his death had nearly destroyed her, so she realized at once that this wasn't the same emotion. This was primitive attraction, heady and feverish, and it was based entirely on sex. Vance Blackstone had been Love; Cord Blackstone meant only Lust.

But recognizing it for what it was didn't lessen its impact as she walked sedately beside him, so vibrantly aware of the hand on her back that he might as well have been touching her naked body. She wasn't the type for an affair. She was a throwback to the Victorian era, as Vance had once teased her by saying. She had been lovingly but strictly brought up, and she was the lady that her mother had meant her to be, from the top of her head down to her pink toes. Susan had never even thought of rebelling, because she was by nature exactly what she was: a lady. She had known love and would never settle for less than that, not even for the heady delights offered by the black sheep of the Blackstone family.

Just before they entered the library where Imogene waited, Cord leaned down to her. "If you won't go outside with me, then I'll take you home and we can neck on the front porch like teenagers."

She flashed him an indignant glance that made him laugh softly to himself, but she was prevented from answering him because at that moment they passed through the door and she realized that he had perfectly timed his remark. He had a genius for throwing people off-balance, and he had done it again; despite herself, she felt the heat of intensified color in her face.

Imogene regarded her thoughtfully for a moment, her gray eyes sharpening for a fraction of a second as her gaze flickered from Susan to Cord, then back to Susan's flushed face. Then she controlled her expression, and the gray eyes resumed their normal cool steadiness. "Susan, do you feel well? You look flushed."

"I became a little warm during the dancing." Susan was aware that once again she was throwing out a statement that would be regarded as an answer, but was in fact only a smokescreen. If she didn't watch it, Cord Blackstone would turn her into a world-class liar before the night was out!

The tall man beside her directed her to a robin's egg blue loveseat and sprawled his graceful length beside her, earning himself a glare—which rolled right off of his toughened hide—from both Preston and Imogene. Smiling at his aunt, he drawled a greeting. "Hello, Aunt Imogene. How's the family fortune?"

He was good at waving his own red flags, Susan noticed. Imogene settled back in her chair and coolly ignored the distraction. "Why have you come back?"

"Why shouldn't I come back? This is my home, remember? I even own part of the land. I've been roaming around for quite a while now, and I'm ready to put down my roots. What better place for that than home? I thought I'd move into the cabin on Jubilee Creek."

"That shack!" Preston's voice was full of disdain.

Cord shrugged. "You can't account for tastes. I prefer shacks to mausoleums." He grinned, looking around himself at the formal furniture, the original oil paintings, the priceless vases and miniatures that adorned the shelves. Though called a library, the room actually contained few books, and all of them had been bought, Susan sometimes suspected, with an eye on the color of the dustjackets to make certain the books harmonized with the color scheme of the room.

Preston eyed his cousin with cold, silent hatred for a moment, an expanse of time which became heavy with resentment. "How much will it cost us?"

From the corner of her eye, Susan could see the lift of that mocking eyebrow. "Cost you for what?"

"For you to leave this part of the country again."

Cord smiled, a particularly wolfish smile that should have warned Preston. "You don't have enough money, Cousin."

Imogene lifted her hand, forestalling Preston's heated reply. She had a cooler head and was better at negotiating then her son was. "Don't be foolish...or hasty," she counseled. "You *do* realize that we're prepared to offer you a substantial sum in exchange for your absence?"

"Not interested," he said lazily, still smiling.

"But a man with your…lifestyle must have debts that need settling. Then there's the fact that I have many friends who owe me for favors, and who could be counted on to make your stay unpleasant, at the least."

"Oh, I don't think so, Aunt Imogene." Cord was utterly relaxed, his long legs stretched out before him. "The first surprise in store for you is that I don't need the money. The second is that if any of your 'friends' decide to help you by making things difficult for me, I have friends of my own who I can call on, and believe me, my friends make yours look like angels."

Imogene sniffed. "I'm sure they do, considering."

For the first time Susan felt compelled to intervene. Fighting upset her; she was quiet and naturally peaceful, but with an inner strength that allowed her to throw herself into the breach. Her gentle voice immediately drew everyone's attention, though it was to her mother-in-law that she spoke. "Imogene, look at him; look at his clothes." She waved her slender hand to indicate the man lounging beside her. "He's telling the truth. He doesn't need any money. And I think that when he mentions his friends, he isn't talking about back-alley buddies."

Cord regarded her with open, if somewhat mocking, admiration. "At last, a Blackstone with perception, though of course you weren't born to the name, so maybe that explains it. She's right, Imogene, though I'm sure you don't like hearing it. I don't need the Blackstone money because I have money of my own. I plan to live in the cabin because I like my privacy, not because I can't afford any better. Now, I suggest that we manage to control our differences, because I intend to stay here. If you want to air the family dirty laundry, then go ahead. It won't bother me; you'll be the only one to suffer from that."

Imogene gave a curious little sigh. "You've always been difficult, Cord, even when you were a child. My objection to you is based on your past actions, not on you personally. You've dragged your family through enough mud to last for four lifetimes, and I find that hard to forgive, and I find it equally as hard to trust you to behave with some degree of civility."

"It's been a long time," he said obliquely. "I've spent a lot of time in Europe, and too long in South America; it makes a man appreciate his home."

"Does it? I wonder. Forgive me if I suspect an ulterior motive, but then, your past gives me little choice. Very well, we'll call a truce…for the time being."

"A truce." He winked at her, and to Susan's surprise, Imogene blushed. So he had that effect on every female! But he was a fool if he believed that Imogene would go along with a truce. She might appear to give in, but that was *all* it was: appearance. Imogene never gave in; she merely changed tactics. If she couldn't bribe or threaten him, then she would try other measures, though for the moment Susan couldn't think of anything else that could be brought to bear on the man.

He was rising to his feet, his hand under Susan's elbow, urging her up also. "You've been away from your guests long enough," he told Imogene politely. "I give you my solemn promise that I won't cause any scandals tonight, so relax and enjoy yourself." Pulling Susan along with him like a puppy, he crossed the floor to Imogene and bent down to kiss his aunt. Imogene sat perfectly still under the touch of his lips, though her color rose even higher. Then he straightened, his eyes dancing. "Come along, Susan," he commanded.

"Just a moment," Preston intervened, stepping before them. Imogene might have called a truce, but Preston hadn't. "We've agreed to no open hostilities; we haven't agreed to associate with you. Susan isn't going anywhere with you."

"Oh? I think that's up to the lady. Susan?" Cord turned to her, making his wishes known by the curl of his fingers on her arm.

Susan hesitated. She wanted to go with Cord. She wanted to laugh with him, to see the wicked twinkle in his eyes, feel the magic of being held in his arms. But she couldn't trust him, and for the first time in her life, she didn't trust herself. Because she wanted so badly to go with him, she had to deny him. Slowly, regretfully, she shook her head. "No. I think it would be better if I didn't go with you."

His blue eyes narrowed, and suddenly they were no longer laughing, but wore the sheen of anger. He dropped his hand from her arm. "Perhaps you're right," he said coldly, and left her without another word.

The silence in the library was total, the three occupants motionless. Then Imogene sighed again. "Thank heavens you didn't go with him, dear. He's charming, I know, but beneath all of that charm, he hates his entire family. He'll do anything, *anything*, he can to harm us. You don't know him, but it's in your best interest if you avoid him." Having delivered her graceful warning, Imogene shrugged. "Ah, well, I suppose we'll have to suffer through this until he gets bored and drifts off to hunt other amusements. He was right about one thing, the wretch; I do have to get back to my guests." She rose and left the room, her mist gray gown swaying elegantly about her feet as she walked. Imogene was still a beautiful woman; she hardly looked old enough to be the mother of the man who stood beside Susan. Imogene didn't age; she endured.

After a moment, Preston took Susan's hand, his ingrained sense of courtesy taking control of him again. His confrontation with his cousin had been the only occasion when Susan could remember seeing Preston be anything but polite, even when he was disagreeing with someone. "Let's relax for a moment before we join them. Would you like a drink?" he suggested.

"No, thank you." Susan allowed him to seat her on the loveseat again, and she watched as he poured himself a neat whiskey and sat down beside her, a small frown puckering his brow as he regarded the glass in his hand. Something was on his mind; she knew his mannerisms as well as she knew her own. She waited, not pushing him. She and Preston had become close since Vance's death, and she felt strongly affectionate toward him. He looked so much like Vance, so much like all the Blackstones, with his dark hair and blue eyes and lopsided smile. Preston lacked Vance's sense of humor, but he was a formidable opponent in business. He was stubborn; slower than Vance to react, but more determined when he did.

"You're a lovely woman, Susan," he said abruptly.

Startled, she stared at him. She knew she looked good tonight; she had debated over wearing the cream silk dress, for her tastes since Vance's death had been somber, but she had remembered that the medieval color of mourning had been white, not black, and only she knew when she put on the white dress that she did so with a small but poignant remnant of grief. She had dressed for Vance tonight, wearing the pearls that he had given her, spraying herself with his favorite perfume. But for a few mad moments she had gloried in the knowledge that she looked good, not for Vance's sake, but because of the admiration she had seen in another pair of eyes, strange lodestone eyes. What would have happened if she had gone with Cord Blackstone tonight, instead of playing it safe?

Preston's eyes softened as he looked at her. "You're no match for him. If you let him, he'll use you to hurt us; then he'll leave you on the trash pile and walk away without looking back. Stay away from him; he's poison."

Susan regarded him steadily. "Preston, I'm a woman, not a child; I'm capable of making my own decisions. I can see why you wouldn't like your cousin, since he's so totally different from you. But he hasn't done anything to harm me, and I won't snub him."

He gave a rueful smile at her firm, reasonable tone. "I've heard that voice in enough board meetings over the past five years to know you've dug in your heels and won't budge without a good reason. But you don't know what he's like. You're a lady; you've never been exposed to the sort of things that are commonplace to him. He's lived the life of an alley cat, not because he had no choice, no way out, but because he preferred that type of life. He broke his mother's heart, making her so ashamed of him that he wasn't welcome in her home.''

"Exactly what did he do that was so terrible?'' Deliberately, she kept her tone light, not wanting Preston to see how deeply she was interested in the answer, how deeply she was disturbed by Cord Blackstone.

"What didn't he do?'' Sarcasm edged Preston's answer. "Fights, drinking, women, gambling...but the final straw was the scandal when he was caught with Grant Keller's wife.''

Susan choked. Grant Keller was dignity personified, and so was his wife. Preston looked at her and couldn't prevent a grin. "Not this Mrs. Keller; the former Mrs. Keller was entirely different. She was thirty-six, and Cord was twenty-one when they left town together.''

"That was a long time ago,'' Susan pointed out.

"Fourteen years, but people have long memories. I saw Grant Keller's face when he recognized Cord tonight, and he looked murderous.''

Susan was certain there was more to the story, but she was reluctant to pry any deeper. The old scandal in no way explained Preston's very personal hatred for Cord. For right now, though, she was suddenly very tired and didn't want to pursue the subject. All the excitement that had lit her up while she was dancing with Cord had faded. Rising, she smoothed her skirt. "Will you take me home? I'm exhausted.''

"Of course,'' he said immediately, as she had known he would. Preston was entirely predictable, always solicitous of her. At times, the cushion of gallantry that protected her gave her a warm sense of security, but at other times she felt restricted. Tonight, the feeling of restriction deepened until she felt as if she were being smothered. She wanted to breathe freely, to be unobserved.

It was only a fifteen-minute drive to her home, and soon she was blessedly alone, sitting on the dark front porch in the wooden porch swing, listening to the music of a southern night. She had waited until Preston left before she came out to sit in the darkness, her right foot gently pushing her back and forth to the accompanying squeak of the chains that held the swing. A light breeze rustled through the trees and kissed her face, and she closed her eyes. As she often did, she tried to summon up Vance's face, to reassure herself with the mental picture of his violent blue eyes and lopsided grin, but to her alarm, the face that formed wasn't his. Instead she saw pale blue eyes above the short black beard of a desperado; they were the reckless eyes of a man who dared anything. A shiver ran down her spine as she recalled the touch of his warm mouth on her shoulder, and her skin tingled as if his lips were still pressed there.

Thank heavens she had had the good sense to ask Preston to bring her home instead of going with that man as he had asked. Preston was at least safe, and Cord Blackstone had probably never heard the word.

Chapter 2

The Blackstone social circle ranged in a sort of open arc from Mobile to New Orleans, with the Gulfport-Biloxi area as the center of their far-flung web of moneyed and blue-blooded acquaintances. With such a wide area and so many friends of such varied interests, Susan was amazed that the sole topic of conversation seemed to be Cord Blackstone's return. She lost count of the number of women, many of them married, who drilled her on why he was back, how long he was staying, whether he was married, whether he had been married, and endless variations on those questions, none of which she could answer. What could she tell them? That she had danced two dances with him and gotten drunk on his smile?

She hadn't seen him since the night of his return, and she made a point of not asking about him. She told herself that it was best to leave well enough alone and let her interest in him die a natural death. All she had to do was do nothing and refuse to feed the strange attraction. It wasn't as if he were chasing her all over south Mississippi; he hadn't called, hadn't sought her out as she had half feared, half wanted him to do.

But her resolution to forget about him was stymied at every turn; even Preston seldom talked of anything except his cousin. She decided that all Cord had to do to irritate Preston was to breathe. Through Preston, she learned that Cord was working on the old cabin at Jubilee Creek, replacing the roof and the sagging old porch, putting in new windows. Preston had tried to find out where Cord had borrowed the money to repair the cabin, and found instead, to his chagrin, that there was no loan involved. Cord was paying for everything in cash, and had opened a sizable checking account at

the largest bank in Biloxi. Preston and Imogene spent hours speculating on how he had acquired the money, and what his purpose
was in returning to Mississippi. Susan wondered why they found it
so hard to accept that he had simply returned home. As people grew
older, it wasn't unusual for them to want to return to the area where
they had grown up. It seemed silly to her that they attached such
sinister motives to his smallest action, but then she realized that she
was guilty of the same thing. She'd all but convinced herself that,
if she had allowed him to drive her home that night, he would have
taken her to bed over any protests she might have made...if any.

If any. That was the hard part for her to accept. Would she have
made any protest, even a token one? What had happened to her?
One moment of her life had been as serene as a quiet pool on a
lazy summer day, and she had been satisfied, except for the hollowness left by Vance's death. Then Cord Blackstone had walked in
out of the night and everything had shifted, the world had been
thrown out of kilter. Now, suddenly, she wanted to run away, or at
least smash something...do anything, anything at all, that was totally out of character.

And it was all because of Cord. He was a man who lived by his
own rules, a man who lived recklessly and dangerously, but with a
vital intensity that made every other man seem insipid when compared to him. By contrast, she was a field mouse who was comfortable only with security, yet now the very security that she had
always treasured was chafing at her. The priorities that she had set
for herself now seemed valueless in comparison with the wild freedom that Cord enjoyed.

She had been a quiet child, then a quiet girl, never according her
parents any of the worries that most parents had concerning their
children. Susan's personality was serene, naturally kind and courteous, and the old-fashioned, genteel upbringing she'd had merely
reinforced those qualities. By both nature and practice she was a
lady, in every sense of the word.

Her life hadn't been without pain or difficulty. Without resentment, she had left school to help care for her mother when a stroke
left the older woman partially paralyzed. Another stroke later was
fatal, and Susan quietly supported her father during their grief. Her
father remarried within the year with Susan's blessing, and retired
to south Florida; she remained in new Orleans, which had been her
father's last teaching post, and reorganized her life. She took a
secretarial job and dated occasionally, but never seriously, until
Vance Blackstone saw her gracing her desk at work and decided
right then that she should be gracing his home. Vance hadn't swept

her off her feet; he had gently gained her confidence, gradually increasing the frequency of their dates until she was seeing no one but him; then he had proposed marriage by giving her one perfect rosebud with an exquisite diamond ring nestled in the heart of it.

Imogene hadn't been thrilled that her son had selected his wife from outside the elite circle of their social group, but not even Imogene could really find fault with Susan. Susan was, as everyone phrased it, "a perfect lady." She was accepted as Vance's wife, and for three years she had been blessed with happiness. Vance was a considerate lover and husband, and he never let her forget that she was the most important thing in his life, far more important than the Blackstone empire and traditions. He demonstrated his faith in her by leaving everything to her in his will, including control of his share of the family businesses. Devastated by his sudden death, the terms of the will had meant nothing to Susan. Nothing was important to her without Vance.

But time passed, and time healed. Imogene and Preston, at first furious when they learned that she intended to oversee her share of the businesses instead of turning them over to Preston as they had expected, had gradually forgotten their anger as Susan handled herself well, both privately and publicly. She wasn't a woman on an ego trip, nor was she prone to make irresponsible decisions. She had both feet firmly on the ground...or she *had* had, until another Blackstone had entered her life.

As the days passed, she told herself over and over how silly she was being. Why moon over a man who hadn't shown the slightest interest in her since the night they had met? He had just been trying to irritate Preston by playing up to her, that was all. But as soon as that thought registered in her mind, a memory would surface, that of a hard, aroused male body pressing against her, and she knew that Cord hadn't been playing.

She couldn't get his face out of her mind. Odd that she hadn't noticed the family resemblance, but for all the blue eyes and dark hair, nothing about Cord had seemed familiar to her. When she looked at Preston, she was always reminded strongly of Vance; Cord Blackstone resembled no one but himself, with his black brigand's beard and wicked eyes. His personality overshadowed the similarities of coloring and facial structure.

Stop thinking about him! she told herself sternly one night as she dressed to attend a party with Preston. She had been looking at herself in the mirror, checking to see if her dress fit as it should, and had suddenly found herself wondering if Cord would like the dress, if he would find her attractive in it. With rare irritation, she whirled away from the mirror. She had to get him out of her mind! It had been almost three weeks since she'd met him, and it was obvious that she was in a tizzy over nothing, because in those three weeks he'd made no effort to see her again.

It was just as well; they were totally unsuited. She was a gentle spring shower; he was thunder and lightning. She had let a simple flirtation go to her head, and it was time she realized that there was nothing to it.

Glancing out a window at the gloomy sky, she reached into the closet for a coat. The capricious weather of the Gulf states had reminded everyone that it was still only March, despite the balmy weather they had been enjoying for most of the month. The temperature would be close to freezing before she came home, so she chose the warmest coat she owned, as well as wearing a long-sleeved dress.

Preston was always exactly on time, so Susan went down a few minutes early to chat with her cook and housekeeper, Emily Ferris. "I'll be leaving in a few minutes; why don't you go home early today?" she suggested.

"I might at that." Emily looked out the window, watching the wind whip the giant oak tree at the edge of the yard. "This is the kind of day that makes me want to wrap up in a blanket and sleep in front of a fire. Do you have a coat?" she asked sternly, looking at Susan's slender form.

Susan laughed. "Yes, I have a coat." Emily watched over her like a mother hen, but mothering came naturally to Emily, who had five children of her own. The youngest had left the nest a year ago, and since then, Susan had received the full intensity of Emily's protection. She didn't mind; Emily was as steady as a rock, and had been in Susan's employ since she had married Vance. It was in Emily's arms that Susan had wept her most violent tears after Vance's death.

"I'll leave the heat on, so the house won't be cold when you come in," Emily promised. "Where're you going tonight?"

"To the Gages'. I believe William is planning to run for governor next year, and he's lining up support and campaign contributors."

"Hummph," Emily snorted. "What does a Gage know about politics? Don't tell me that Preston's going to support him?"

Susan lifted one elegant eyebrow. "You know Preston; he's very cautious. He'll have to look at every candidate before he makes up his mind." She knew from experience that every politician in the state would be burying the Blackstones under an avalanche of invitations. Susan had tried to stay out of politics, but Imogene and

Preston were heavily courted, and Preston invariably asked her to accompany him whenever he attended a party with either political overtones or undertones.

She heard the doorbell at the precise instant the clock chimed the hour, and with a smile she went to greet Preston.

He helped her with her coat, arranging the collar snugly around her throat.

"It's getting really cold," he muttered. "So much for spring."

"Don't be so impatient." She smiled. "It's still only March. It's just that these last few weeks spoiled everyone, but you knew it wouldn't last."

It began to rain as they drove to the Gages' house, a slow, sullen rain that turned the late afternoon into night. Preston was a careful, confident driver, and he made the thirty-mile drive in good time. Caroline Gage met them at the door. "Preston, Susan, I'm glad you could come! Would you like a drink before dinner? William's playing bartender in the den."

Despite Caroline's easy manner, Susan caught a hint of tension in the older woman's expression and wondered if Caroline wasn't enthusiastic about her husband's foray into politics. Following Preston into the den, she found the room already crowded with friends and acquaintances, the usual social crowd. Preston was promptly hailed by William Gage, and with a smile for Susan he allowed himself to be drawn aside.

Susan refused anything to drink, since she hadn't eaten anything, and wandered around talking to her friends. She was popular with both men and women, and it took her quite a while to make a circle of the room. It was almost time for dinner and she glanced at her hostess, frowning when she saw Caroline watching the door, anxiety clearly evident on her face. Was some special guest late?

The doorbell chimed and Caroline paled, but didn't pause as she went to greet her late-arriving guests. Susan watched the door curiously, waiting to see who it was; Caroline was usually unflappable, and it must be someone really important to have her so on edge.

Her brows rose when George and Olivia Warren came into the room; the Warrens were part of the social hierarchy, but Caroline had been friends with them for years. Cheryl Warren followed them, her ash blond hair a mass of carefully disarranged curls, her svelte body outlined in a form-fitting black dress...and behind her, towering over her, his bearded face sardonic, was Cord Blackstone.

So that was why Caroline was nervous! She'd known that Cord would be with Cheryl Warren, and she was on pins and needles at having Cord and Preston in the same room.

She needn't have worried, Susan thought, glancing at Preston. He wouldn't like it, but neither would he make a scene in someone else's home. If Cord just behaved himself, the evening would go smoothly, though she was acutely aware that Cord would behave himself only if it suited his own purposes.

But, surprisingly, he was a perfect gentleman throughout the long dinner. He was politely attentive to Cheryl, a fact which made Susan's stomach knot. She tried not to look at him, and told herself wryly that she shouldn't have been surprised to see him with another woman…any other woman. He was a man who would always have a female companion. She *was* surprised, however, by the jealousy that jolted her whenever she heard Cheryl's clear laughter, or caught the dark murmur of Cord's voice under the noise of the general chatter.

Caroline had cleared the large living room for dancing, and after dinner she put a stack of easy-listening albums on the stereo, keeping the volume low so her guests could dance or talk as they wished. Susan danced a few dances and talked with her friends, wishing that Preston would cut the evening short and take her home, but he was effectively caught in a group of men earnestly talking politics, and she knew that it would be hours before he was free. She sighed and absently watched the slow-moving couples swaying to the music, then stiffened as her gaze accidentally locked with Cord's pale, glittering eyes. Cheryl was held securely in his strong arms, but he wasn't paying any attention to her as he stared at Susan over Cheryl's bare shoulder. He didn't smile; his gaze slid down her body in a leisurely journey, then returned to her face, staring at her as if he could pierce her thoughts. She paled and looked away. Why had he done that? He'd made it plain by his silence these past three weeks that their flirtation hadn't meant anything to him; why look at her now as if he meant to drag her away to his lair? How *could* he look at her like that, when he held Cheryl in his arms?

Susan pushed her thoughts away by entering into a conversation about vacation cruises, and kept her back turned to the center of the room. It was a tactical error, but one she didn't realize until she felt the fine hairs on the back of her neck standing on end, the age-old warning of danger nearby, and she knew that Cord was behind her. She tensed, waiting for the contact that she knew was coming. His hand touched her waist at the same time that his dark, husky voice said above her head, "Dance with me."

A variation of the same tune, she thought dazedly, allowing herself to be turned and taken into his arms. *Taken*… that was the operative word. She felt taken, as if the simple closing of his arms around her had sealed her off from the rest of the world, drawn her deeply and irrevocably under his spell. She was crazy to dance so close to the flame, knowing that she would be burned, but she felt helpless to resist the temptation of his company. As his arms brought her close to his body, the virile scent of his subtle cologne, mingled with the intoxicating smell of his male flesh, went straight to her head and she all but staggered. His hand was burning through the fabric of her dress and scorching her skin; her breasts throbbed and tightened in mindless response, completely out of her control, and she closed her eyes at the powerful surge of desire. Her heart was thumping heavily in her chest, almost painfully, sending her blood zinging through her veins like electrical charges.

There seemed to be nothing to say, so she didn't try to make conversation. She simply followed his lead, intensely aware of the fluid strength of his body, the animal grace of his movements. His warm breath was caressing her temple like the fragrant spring breezes that she loved, and without thinking she opened her eyes, lifting her misty, dreaming gaze to meet the laser intensity of his.

Something hard and frightening was in his gaze, but it was swiftly masked before she could read it. The hard planes of his face were taut, as if he were under some sort of strain. He muttered, "I've tried to stay away from you."

"You've succeeded." Confused, she wondered what he meant. *He* was the dangerous one, not she. Why should he want to stay away? She was the one who should be running for safety, and the fact that she wasn't had her almost in a panic.

"I haven't succeeded at all," he said flatly. The arm at her waist tightened until she was pressed into his body, his hard thighs sliding against her, making his desire firmly obvious. Susan pulled in a wavering breath as her fingers tightened on his shoulder. He dipped his head until his mouth was against her ear, his voice a low rumble. "I want to make love to you. You're responsible for this, sweetheart, and I'm all yours."

The words should have frightened her, but she was beyond fright, already oblivious to anything beyond this man. Her senses had narrowed, sharpened, until he was the only person in the room who was in focus. Everyone else was blurred, distant, and she danced with him in an isolated glow. She closed her eyes again at the thrill that electrified her from head to toe.

He swore softly under his breath. "You look as if I'm making love to you right now. You're driving me out of my mind, sweetheart."

He *was* making love to her, with his words, with every brush of his body against hers as they moved in time with the music. And if he was tortured, so was she. She had been utterly chaste since Vance's death, not even kissing another man, but now she felt as if Cord possessed her in the most basic sense of the word.

"Cheryl came with me, so I'll take her home," he said, placing his lips against her temple as he talked. "But we're going to have to talk. Will you be at home tomorrow afternoon?"

Dazedly, she tried to recall if she had made any plans for the next day; nothing came to mind. It didn't matter; even if she had, she would cancel them. "Yes, I'll be there." Her voice sounded cold, she noted dimly, as if she hadn't any strength.

"I have some business to take care of tomorrow, so I can't nail down an exact time when I'll be there, but I *will* be there," he promised.

"Do you know where I live?"

She could feel his lips curving in a smile. "Of course I know where you live. I made a point of finding out the day after I met you."

The song ended, and she automatically moved away from him, but his arm tightened around her waist. He grinned, his teeth flashing whitely in the darkness of his beard. "You're going to have to shield me for a few more minutes."

A delicate rise of color tinted her cheeks. "We shouldn't dance. That would only...prolong the situation."

"We'll find a corner to stand in." A twinkle danced in the glittering depths of his eyes. "We'll have to stand; I'm incapable of sitting down right now."

She felt her blush deepen, and he chuckled as he moved with her to the edge of the room. She was aware deep inside herself that her heightened color wasn't from embarrassment, but from a primal excitement. She wasn't shocked that he was aroused; she was proud!

He positioned himself with his back to everyone else, his broad shoulders effectively blocking her view of the room. His eyes roamed slowly, intently over her face, as if he were trying to read something in the serenity of her expression. "Did you come with Preston?" he asked abruptly.

"Yes." Suddenly she wanted to launch into an explanation of why she was there in Preston's company, but she left the words unsaid and let her simple reply stand on its own. Preston was her brother-in-law, and she was fond of him; she wouldn't apologize for being with him.

The magnetic power of Cord's eyes was frightening; tiny prisms of light seemed caught in them, holding her gaze captive. Her breath caught in her throat and hung there, swelling her lungs, as she waited for him to release her from his spell. "Am I horning in between you and Preston?" he finally asked in not much more than a whisper. "Are you involved with him?"

The breath that she'd been holding was released on her soft answer. "No."

A smile lifted one corner of his hard mouth. "Good. I just wanted to know if I have any competition. It wouldn't stop me, but I like to know what I'm up against."

No, he didn't have any competition—in any sense. He stood out like a cougar among sheep. The thought of him turning his single-minded attention on her was alarming, but at the same time, she already knew that she wouldn't say the words necessary to turn him away. She knew that she should run like crazy, but her body refused to obey the dictates of common sense.

A tiny frown flickered across his brow as he stared down at her, as if he had seen something that he hadn't expected. He couldn't be wary of her, or alarmed by her femininity; he had known far too many women for there to be any mysteries left for him. Perhaps he was surprised to find himself flirting with her, because she certainly wasn't his type. Perhaps he was looking at her quiet face, her becoming but unspectacular dress, and wondering if he'd temporarily lost his mind. Then the frown was gone, and he smiled faintly as he brushed her cheek with the tips of his fingers. "Tomorrow, sweetheart."

"Yes."

Susan both dreaded and longed for the next day to arrive, but with outward calm and practiced self-discipline, she made it through the remainder of the evening with her usual dignity, chatted normally with Preston on the drive back home, and even went through her nightly routine without missing a beat. Once she was in bed, however, lying alone in the darkened room, she couldn't keep her thoughts from swinging dizzily around Cord, picturing his saturnine face, his incredible lodestone eyes, the black beard that was as soft as a child's hair.

He had a black magic that went to her head like the finest champagne, but how could she be so foolish as to let herself be drawn into the whirlpool of his masculine charm? She'd be sucked so far under the dark waters that she'd have no control over herself or her life; she'd be his plaything, as other women had been, toys that interested him intensely for a short while before they were discarded in favor of a new and more intriguing amusement. Could she really let herself become one of his toys? She'd known real love with Vance, a love that had endowed their physical union with a deep and satisfying richness. Having known that, how could she settle for anything less?

Her mind, her heart, the very core of her being—all said no. Her body, however, lying warm and quivering, yearning for the touch of his strong, lean hands, rebelled against the common-sense strictures of her mind. She was learning now how primitive and powerful desire could be, how disobedient the flesh could be to the demands of conscience. Her soft, feminine body had instinctively recognised the touch of a master, a man who knew far too many ways to bring pleasure to her.

She lay awake for several long, tormented hours, but at last her quietly indomitable will won out over her fevered, longing body. She was not now, never had been, and never would be, the type to indulge in a shallow affair, no matter how physically attractive a man was. If he wanted her company for something other than sex, then she would be happy to be his friend, but the thought of sex without love was abhorrent to her. Making love with Vance had been spiritual and emotional, as well as physical, and her knowledge of the heights had left her dissatisfied with the lower peaks that could be scaled without love.

Not once, during the dark hours, did she have any doubts about the nature of the relationship that Cord wanted with her. He'd told her bluntly that he wanted to make love to her; she sensed that he was always that honest about his desires. His honesty wasn't the courageous openness of honor, but merely his lack of concern over what anyone else thought or had to say about him. He was already an outlaw; why worry about ruining his reputation further?

If only the forbidden weren't always so enticing! Her mind darted and leaped around his image, held so clearly in her memory. He was wickedly attractive; even talking to him gave her the sense of playing with fire. She had to admit that Cord had certainly captured her imagination, but it was nothing more than that, surely, except for his obvious physical charm. The ways of the wicked have always held a fascination for those who walk the bright and narrow path of morality.

But that bright and narrow path was where she belonged, where life had placed her, where she was happy. The shadows where Cord Blackstone stood weren't for her, no matter how intriguing the weary knowledge in his crystalline eyes.

She slept little, but woke feeling calm and rested. Her inner surety of self often masked such physical weaknesses as tiredness or minor illness; her features might be pale, but there was always a certain calmness that overlay any signs of strain. It was Sunday, so she dressed and drove her eight-year-old blue Audi over to Blackstone House to attend church with Imogene and Preston, as she had always done. To her relief, Preston didn't mention that Cord had been at the party the night before; he was too interested in relating to Imogene the details of William Gage's infant political career. Susan commented little, entering the conversation only when she was addressed directly. She sat quietly through the church service, accepted Imogene's invitation to lunch, and maintained her mood of strong reserve all through the meal. Her in-laws didn't try to draw her out of her relative quiet; they had learned to accept her occasional silences as they accepted her smiles. Susan didn't run to a comforting shoulder to unburden herself whenever something troubled her; they might never know what made her deep blue eyes so pensive, and they didn't ask.

They had just finished lunch and were moving into the den when Mrs. Robbins, the housekeeper, appeared with a visitor at her elbow. "Someone to see you, ma'am," she told Imogene, and went about her business. Mrs. Robbins had been with the Blackstones for five years, but she had evidently not heard the rumors and wild tales that had circulated about Cord Blackstone, because there hadn't been a flicker of recognition in the woman's features as she admitted him.

Susan's eyes swept over his face, and she surprised a look of irritation that drew his level brows together in a brief frown when he saw her. Then the frown was gone, and he crossed the room with his easy grace to kiss Imogene, bending down to touch his lips to her cool, ageless cheek. Once again that astonishing colour pinkened Imogene's face, though her face was as controlled as always when she spoke. "Hello, Cord. We've just finished lunch, or I'd invite you to eat with us. Would you like something to drink?"

"Thank you. Whiskey, neat." His mobile lips quirked at the iron-clad Southern manners that demanded she offer him food and drink, even when he knew that she despised him. Watching him, Susan surprised herself by reading exactly the thoughts that were only hinted at in his expression. She would have thought that Cord would be more difficult to read.

He chose one of the big, brown leather armchairs, and accepted the short, wide glass of amber liquid that Imogene extended to him, murmuring his thanks in a low voice. Totally at ease, he stretched his long legs out before him and sipped the whiskey.

The room was totally silent, except for the rhythmic ticking of the antique clock perched on the massive oak mantel. Cord seemed to be the only one who was comfortable with the silence. Preston was becoming increasingly red in the face, and Imogene fidgeted with her skirt before she caught herself and commanded her hands to lie calmly in her lap. Susan didn't fidget, but she felt as if her heart were going to bruise itself against the cage of her ribs. How could he have this effect on her by simply walking into the room? It was insane!

He was dressed with fine disregard for the capricious March weather, wearing only impeccable black slacks, creased to a razor's edge, and a thin blue silk shirt through which she could see his darkly tanned flesh and the curling black hair on his chest. Her eyes drank in the details of him, even as she tried not to look at him. For the first time, she noticed the small gold band that he wore on the little finger of his right hand, and she wondered if it was a woman's wedding band. The thought jolted her. What woman had been so important to him that he would wear her ring?

Behind her, Preston had evidently reached the end of his patience. "Did you have a reason for coming here?" he asked bluntly.

A level brow rose in mocking query. "Do you have a reason for being so suspicious?"

Preston didn't even notice the way his words had been turned back on him, but Susan did, and she lifted her head just a fraction of an inch, only a small movement, but one that signaled to people who knew her well that she wasn't pleased. Preston and Imogene knew, and Preston gave her a look that was abruptly apologetic. He had opened his mouth to apologize aloud, a concession that Susan knew didn't come easily to him, when Cord cut smoothly across him.

"Of course I have a reason for coming, and I'm glad that you're smart enough to know that you aren't going to like hearing it. I wouldn't enjoy knowing that I have an idiot for a cousin."

Cord was being deliberately argumentative, Susan realized, and her eyes narrowed just a tiny bit as she stared at him, but she didn't say anything.

Again silence reigned, as Preston and Imogene seemed to stiffen, waiting. After a moment's surprise, Susan realized that both of them seemed to know what Cord was getting at, and she looked from her in-laws back to Cord's faintly amused expression. He let the quietness draw itself out until the room fairly reverberated with tension; then he negligently crossed one booted foot over the other.

With an air of idle musing, he said, "I know you've probably thought that I've spent the past few years bumming around the world, but I've been gainfully employed most of the time since I left Mississippi. I work for an oil company, as a sort of trouble-shooter.'' His pale eyes gleamed with amusement as he watched the parade of astonishment marching across the features of his cousin and aunt. He didn't look at Susan at all.

"I...smooth things out for them," he continued silkily "I don't have a title; I have contacts, and methods. I'm surprisingly good at my job, because I don't take no for an answer.''

Imogene was the first to recover, and she favored Cord with a polite smile. ''I appreciate that you're very well suited for your job, but why are you telling us about it?''

"I just wanted you to understand my position. Look at it as honor among thieves, if you prefer. Now, let's get down to business.''

"We don't have any business with you," Preston interjected.

Cord flicked an impatient glance over him. ''The Blackstones own a lot of land in Alabama, southern Mississippi, and Louisiana. I inherited my share of it, so I should know. But the land that I'm interested in isn't part of my inheritance; if it was, I wouldn't be here now. I know that several oil companies have approached you in the last ten years for permission to drill in the ridges, but you've turned them all down. Newer surveys had indicated that the reserve of oil or gas in the ridges could be much larger than originally projected. I want to lease the ridges for my company.''

"No," said Preston without hesitation. ''Mother and Vance and I talked it over when we were first approached years ago. We don't want any drilling on Blackstone property.''

"For what reason, other than a vague idea that it's too money-grabbing for a blue-blooded old Southern family like the Black-stones?''

Susan sat very still, nothing in the room escaping her attention. A cold chill was lacing itself around her body, freezing her in place. The ridges weren't exactly ridges; they were only ripples in the earth, clothed in thick stands of pine. She liked the ridges, like the peacefulness of them, the sweet smell of pure earth and pine. But why was Cord asking Imogene and Preston about them? Didn't he know?

"It was nothing as silly as that," Imogene explained calmly. ''We simply didn't feel that the chances of a significant oil find were great enough to justify disturbing the ridges. There aren't any roads into them except for that one Jeep track; trees would have to be cut, roads made. I've seen the messes that drilling sites make.''

"Things have changed in the last ten years," Cord replied, carrying the glass of whiskey to his lips. ''A lot more care is taken not to disturb any area, and, as I said, it looks as if there's a lot more oil in the ridges than anyone thought at first.''

Preston laughed. ''Thank you for the information. We'll think about it; we might decide to allow drilling in the ridges after all. But I don't think we'll use your company.''

A slow, satisfied smile began to move Cord's lips. ''I think you will, cousin. Or you can face criminal charges.''

Susan didn't know what he was talking about, but she knew that he had led Preston to exactly that point. He had played the scene as he had wanted it, knowing what Preston's reaction would be, and knowing all the time that he held all the aces. Cord Blackstone had a streak of ruthlessness in him, and her chill deepened.

Preston had gone pale. Of course, she thought absently. Cord wouldn't have made a statement like that without being very sure of himself. She noted that Imogene was also as white and still as a china doll, so Imogene also knew what was going on.

''What are you saying?'' Preston asked hoarsely.

''My inheritance.'' Cord smiled lazily. ''I'm a Blackstone, remember? I own stock in all the Blackstone companies. The funny thing is, I haven't been receiving my share of any of the profits. Nothing has been deposited into my accounts at any of the banks we use. I didn't have to dig very deep before I found some papers that had my signature forged on them.'' He took another sip of whiskey, slowly tightening the screws. He knew he had them. ''I believe forgery and theft are still against the law. And we aren't talking about pin money, either, are we? You didn't think I'd ever come back, so you and Aunt Imogene have been steadily lining your own pockets with my money. Not exactly an honorable thing to do, is it?''

Imogene looked as if she would faint. Preston had been turned into stone. Cord looked at them, totally satisfied with the effect he'd had. He smiled again. ''Now, about those leases.''

Susan stood, her movements slow and graceful, drawing all attention to her. She felt curiously removed from them, as if she were swathed in protective layers of cotton. Somehow she wasn't surprised, or even shocked, to learn that Preston and Imogene had been taking profits that were legally Cord's. It was a stupid thing to do, as well as illegal, but they had a different view of things. To them, what belonged to one Blackstone belonged to all of them. It was a feudal outlook, but there it was. The most trouble she'd ever had with Imogene had been when Vance died and it became known that he'd left everything to Susan, instead of returning it to the family coffers. That was the one mistake Cord had made, in assuming that

Vance had left his mother and brother in control of his share. It was an uncharacteristic mistake, and one that he had made because he was a Blackstone himself, with all of their inborn arrogance.

"You're bullying the wrong people," she told Cord remotely, her low voice cutting through the layers of tension and hostility. She felt the lash of his suddenly narrowed gaze, but she didn't flinch under it. "If Preston and Imogene are guilty, then so am I, by association if not actual knowledge. But they can't get you the leases to the ridges. The ridges belong to me."

Chapter 3

She didn't remember driving home. She'd walked out, pausing to get her coat, but hadn't felt the cold in her detachment. The house was empty, when she got home, without any welcoming smells emanating from the kitchen, because Sunday was Emily's day off. Susan knew that she'd find something in the refrigerator already prepared, if she was hungry, but she didn't think she'd be able to eat again that day.

She changed clothes, carefully hanging the garments in the closet, then immediately took off the casual clothing she'd just put on. She needed a hot bath, something to take away the coldness that had nothing to do with her skin, but was rather a great lump inside her chest. She threw some sweet herbs into the hot water and eased into the tub, feeling the heat begin to soothe away her stress.

Why did she feel so stunned? Preston had warned her that Cord was ruthless; why hadn't she believed him? It wasn't even what he had done, as much as the way he had done it. He had a right to punish Preston and Imogene for taking what was, essentially, his birthright. If he had wanted to trade that for the leases to the ridges, that was also his right. But he had played with them, leading them step by step to the point where they would feel the shock the worst, and he had enjoyed the effect his words had had on them. There was obviously no love lost between them, but Susan didn't believe in inflicting unnecessary pain. Cord had wanted them to squirm.

When the water had cooled, she let it out and dried herself, sighing as she dressed again in the dark brown slacks and white shirt she'd chosen. The bath had helped, but she still felt that inner chill. She checked the thermostat and found that it was set at a comfortable level, but she didn't feel comfortable. She lit a fire under the logs that had already been placed in the fireplace in the den, then wandered into the kitchen to put on a pot of coffee.

The fire was catching when she went back into the den, and she sat for long, increasingly peaceful moments, staring at the licking blue and orange flames. There was nothing as calming as a fire on a cold day. She thought about the needlepoint she was doing, but discarded the idea of working on it. She didn't want to sew; sewing left her mind free to wander, and she wanted to wipe the day from her mind, occupy her thoughts with something else. She got up and went over to the bookshelves, then began to run her finger across the spines of the books, considering and rejecting as she read the titles. Before she could choose a book, the doorbell chimed, then was followed promptly by a hard knock that rattled the door.

She knew instinctively who it was, but her steps didn't falter as she went to the door and opened it.

He was leaning against the door frame, his breath misting in the cold air. His blue eyes were leaping with a strange anger. "I didn't want you involved in this," he snapped.

Susan stepped back and waved him into the house. He had made some concession to the weather, after all, she noted, as he shrugged out of the lightweight jacket he wore. She took it from him and hung it neatly in the coat closet. She was calm, as if the shock of seeing his cruelty had freed her from the dizzying spell of his sensuality. Her heartbeat was slow and steady, her breathing regular.

"I've just put on a pot of coffee. Would you like some?"

His mouth thinned into a hard line. "Aren't you going to offer me whiskey, try to get me drunk so it'll be easier to handle me?"

Did he think that was why Imogene had offered him something to drink? She started to ask him, then shut her mouth, because it was possible that he was right. Imogene could have offered coffee, because there was always a fresh pot made after every meal. And neither Imogene nor Preston drank very much, beyond what was required socially.

Instead she treated his question literally. "I don't have any whiskey in the house, because I don't drink it. If you want something alcoholic, you'll have to settle for wine. Not only that, I think it would be difficult to get you drunk, and that being drunk would make you harder to handle, rather than easier."

"You're right about that; I make a mean drunk. Coffee will do fine," he said tersely, and followed her as she went into the kitchen. Without looking, she knew that he was examining her home, seeing the warmth and comfort of it, so different from the formal perfection of Blackstone House. Her rooms were large and airy, with a lot of windows; the floors were natural wood, polished to a high gloss. A profusion of plants, happy in the warmth and light, gave the rooms both color and coziness.

He watched as she took two brown earthenware mugs from the cabinet and poured the strong, hot coffee into them. "Cream or sugar?" she asked, and he shook his head, taking the cup from her.

"There's a fire lit in the den; let's go in there. I was cold when I got home," she said by way of explanation, leading the way into the other room.

She curled up in her favorite position, in a corner of the loveseat that sat directly before the fire, but he propped himself against the mantel as he drank his coffee. Again he looked at his surroundings, taking in her books, the needlepoint she'd been working on, the television and stereo system perched in place on the built-in shelves. He didn't say anything, and she wondered if he used silence as a weapon, forcing others to make the first move. But she wasn't uncomfortable, and she felt safe in her own home. She drank her coffee and watched the fire, content to wait.

He placed the mug on the mantel with a thud, and Susan looked up. "Would you like more coffee?" she offered.

"No."

The flat refusal, untempered by the added "thank you" that politeness demanded, signaled that he was ready for the silence to end. Susan mentally braced herself, then set her cup aside and said evenly, "I suppose you want to talk about leasing the ridges."

He uttered an explicit Anglo-Saxon phrase that brought her to her feet, her cheeks flaming, ready to show him the door. He reached out and caught her arm, swinging her around and hauling her up against his body in a single movement that stunned her with its swiftness. He wrapped his left arm around her waist, anchoring her to him, while he cupped her chin in his right hand. He turned her face up, and she saw the male intent in his eyes, making her shiver.

She wasn't afraid of him, yet the excitement that was racing along her body was very like fear. The false calm she'd been enjoying had shattered at the first move he'd made, and now her heart was shifting into double time, reacting immediately to his touch. He wouldn't hurt her, she wasn't afraid of that. It was her own unwilling but powerful attraction to him that made her uneasy, that brought her hands up to press against his chest as he bent closer to her.

"Stop," she whispered, turning her head aside just in time, making his lips graze her soft cheek. His grip on her chin tightened, and he brought her mouth back around, holding her firmly, but instead of taking her lips he let his mouth wander to her ear, where his teeth nibbled sharply on the lobe. Susan caught her breath, then forgot to let it out as the warm slide of his lips went down the column of her throat and nuzzled her open collar aside, to find and press the soft, tender hollow just below her collarbone. She felt his tongue lick out and taste her flesh, and her breath rushed from her lungs.

"Cord, no," she protested frantically, alarmed by the tingling warmth that coursed through her body, spreading like wildfire from the touch of his mouth on her. Her pushing hands couldn't budge him. All she succeeded in doing was making herself deeply aware of the powerful muscles that layered his chest and shoulders, of the wild animal strength of him.

"Susan, honey, don't tell me no," he murmured insistently into the fragrant softness of her shoulder, before licking and kissing his way up her throat. Her fingers dug into his shoulder as every tiny flick of his tongue sent her nerves into twitching ecstasy. He finally lifted his head and hovered over her, their lips barely separated, their breaths mingling. "Kiss me," he demanded, his voice harsh, his eyes narrowed and intent.

Her body was quaking in his arms, her flesh fevered and aching for greater closeness with him, but her alarm equaled her physical need. The look in his pale eyes was somehow both cold and fiery, as if his body were responding to her but his actions were deliberately planned. Horrified, she realized that he knew exactly what his touch did to her, and if she didn't stop him soon, she would be beyond stopping him. He'd actually done so little, only kissing her shoulder, but she could feel the hardened readiness of his body and the tension that coiled in his muscles. He was a fire waiting to consume her, and she was afraid that she didn't know how to fight him.

"No, I can't—" she began, and that was all the chance he needed. His mouth closed on hers, and Susan melted almost instantaneously, her body telegraphing its need for him even though her mind rebelled. Her lips and teeth parted to allow the intrusion of his tongue; her hands slid up to lock around his neck, her fingers clenching in the thickness of his hair. As a first kiss, it was devastating. She was already at such a high level of awareness of him that the growing heat of the kiss was inevitable. She gave in without protest to the increasing pressure of his arms as he gathered her even closer to the heated need of his body.

The warning voice of caution was fragmented into a thousand helpless little pieces, useless against the overwhelming maleness of him. Too many sensations were attacking a body that had been innocent of sensuality for five long years, turning her thoughts into chaos, her body into a dizzying maelstrom of need.

She'd never before been so aware of a man's kiss as a forerunner to and an imitation of the act of sexual possession, but the slow penetration and withdrawal of his tongue sent shudders of pure desire reverberating through her. Mindlessly she rose on tiptoe, and he reacted to the provocation of her movement, his hands sliding down her back to curve over and cup the roundness of her buttocks, his fingers kneading her soft flesh as he lifted her still more, molding her to him so precisely that they might as well have been naked for all the protection their clothing afforded her from the secrets of his body. A moan, so low that it was almost a vibration rather than a sound, trembled in the air, and after a moment Susan realized with shock that it was coming from her throat.

No.

The denial was, at first, only a forlorn whisper in her own mind, without force, but some portion of her brain heard and understood, accepted that she couldn't allow herself to sample the lustful delights this man offered her. With the age-old wisdom of women, she knew that she couldn't offer herself casually, though he would take her casually. It would be nothing to him; a moment of pleasure, good but unimportant and swiftly forgotten. Susan, being the woman she was, would have to offer her heart before she could offer her body, and though she was dangerously attracted to him, she was still heart whole.

No! The word echoed in her mind again, stronger this time, and she tensed in his arms, oblivious now to the seduction of his mouth. The protest still hadn't been voiced aloud, she realized, and with an effort she pulled her mouth free of his. She was suspended in his arms, her toes dangling above the floor while he cupped her hips to his in a position of intimacy, but her stiffened arms held her head and shoulders slightly away from him. She met his glittering diamond eyes evenly. "No."

His lips were red and sensuously swollen from their kiss, and she knew that hers must look the same. His dark beard had been so soft that she hadn't been aware of any prickles, and a rebellious tingle of desire made her want to nuzzle her face against that softness. To deny herself, she said again, "No."

His mouth quirked, amusement shining like a ray of sunshine

across his face. "If people learn through repetition, then I have that word engraved on my brain."

Under any other circumstances, she would have laughed, but her nerves were too raw to permit humor. She increased the pressure of her hands against his heavy shoulders, desperately trying to ignore the heat of his flesh searing her through the thin silk of his shirt. "Put me down. Please."

He obeyed, slowly, and his obedience was almost as provocative as his sensual attack. He let her slide with excruciating slowness down the hard length of his body, turning her release into an extended caress that touched her from her knees to her shoulders. She almost faltered, almost let her hands leave his shoulders to slide up and clasp around his neck again. Alarmed, determined, she stepped back as soon as her feet touched the floor, and with a wry smile, he let her go.

"You weren't so wary of me last night," he teased, but he watched sharply as she carefully placed herself out of his reach.

That was nothing less than the truth, so she agreed. "No, I wasn't."

"Do I look more dangerous in the daylight?"

Yes, infinitely so, because now she'd seen a ruthlessness in him that she hadn't realized was there. Susan regarded him seriously, not even tempted to smile. She could try to put him off with vague excuses, but they wouldn't work with this man. He was still watching her with the deceptive laziness of a cat watching a mouse, letting it go just so far before lashing out with a paw and snatching it back. She sighed, the sound gentle in the room. "I don't think I could trust anyone who did what you did today."

He straightened from his negligent stance, his eyes narrowing. "I only went as far as I had to go. If they'd agreed to lease the ridges, the threat wouldn't have been made."

She shook her head, sending her dark hair swirling in a soft, fragrant cloud around her face. "It was more than that. You set it up, deliberately antagonized both Imogene and Preston from the moment you walked in the door, pushing them so hard that you *knew* they wouldn't lease the ridges to you, *knew* you were going to hit them with your threats. You led them to it, and you gloated every inch of the way."

She stopped there, not voicing the other suspicion that was clouding her mind. Even without really knowing him, she felt as if she knew enough about him to realize that he seldom made mistakes; he was simply too smart, too cunning. But he had either made a mistake in not completely investigating the ownership of the ridges, or he had known all along that she was the owner, and hoped to use his threat against Imogene and Preston as a means of forcing her to sign the leases. It was common knowledge in the area how close she was to her in-laws; even an outsider could have discovered that. Cord might not have the means of threatening her personally, but he would see right away that she was vulnerable through her regard for her husband's family. And even worse than that, she had another suspicion: Was he bent on seducing her for some murky plan of revenge, or as a less than honorable means of securing the leases on the ridges? Either way, his attention to her was suddenly open to question, and she shrank from the thought.

He was still watching her with that unsettling stare. "Guilty as charged. I enjoyed every minute of making the slimy little bastard squirm."

Shaken by the relish in his tone, she winced. "It was cruel and unnecessary."

"Cruel, maybe," he drawled. "But it was damned necessary!"

"In what way? To feed your need for revenge?"

It had been a shot in the dark, but she saw immediately that it had been dead on target. The look he gave her was almost violent; then he turned and took the poker in his hand, bending down to rearrange the burning logs in the fireplace, expending his flare of anger on them. Straightening, he returned the poker to its place and stood with his head down, staring into the hypnotically dancing fire.

"I have my reasons," he said harshly.

She waited, but the moments stretched out and she saw that he wasn't going to explain himself. He saw no need to justify himself to her; the time had long passed when he needed anyone's approval of his actions.

The question had to be asked, so she braced herself and asked it. "What are you going to do about the money Preston owes you, now that you know he doesn't control the ridges?"

He gave her a hard, glinting look. "I haven't decided."

Chilled by the speculation in his eyes, Susan resumed her seat, an indefinable sadness overwhelming her. Had she really expected him to trust her? He probably trusted no one, keeping his thoughts locked behind iron barricades.

It had to be due to a streak of hidden perversity inside her that, even though she'd rejected the idea of having an affair with him, now she was hurt because she thought he might have an ulterior motive for pursuing her. If she had any brains at all, she'd not only keep the mental distance between them, she'd widen it. He'd made a pass at her, but she couldn't attach any importance to it; he probably made passes at a lot of women. If his kisses were anything, they were a subtle means of revenge. She was a Blackstone by name, and automatically included in his target area. Besmirching the reputation of Vance Blackstone's widow would be a scheme likely to appeal to Cord, if he wanted the Blackstones to squirm.

Because she couldn't stand the horror of the thought, her tone was abrupt when she spoke again. "I can't give you an answer about the ridges. I won't say no, but I can't say yes, either. I'll have an independent geological survey made, as well as gather several opinions about the ecological damage to the area, before I can reach a decision. And the decision I make will be based on the results of the survey, not on any blackmail you may try to use."

"I don't remember asking you about the ridges," he murmured, smiling coldly.

"That's why you're here, isn't it?"

"Is it?"

"Oh, please." She waved her hand tiredly. "I don't feel up to playing word games. I know the ridges are what you're after."

His eyes sharpened, and a certain tension invaded him, giving him a stillness that reminded her of an animal poised to attack. "I've never prostituted myself for an oil lease yet," he drawled, yet anger lay beneath his lazy tone like a dark shadow.

Susan darted a glance up at him. "We both know I'm not your usual type."

"Hell, no, you're not! I'll agree to that!" He glared at her, his lips compressed into a grim white line. "You sit there as cool as a cucumber and accuse me of something pretty low, but you never even raise your voice, do you? Tell me, lady, is there anything that gets a rise out of you? Do you have feelings, or are you just a china doll, useless but nice to look at?"

She almost recoiled in shock, feeling the force and heat of his anger. "Yes, I feel," she whispered. "I don't want to be hurt. I don't want you to use me."

Suddenly he crouched down until his eyes were on a level with hers, and he leaned forward, so close that she pressed herself back into the cushions to relieve the sensation of being swamped by him. "I don't think you feel anything at all," he rasped. "Or rather, you're afraid of what feelings you do have. You want me, but you're too afraid of what people will say to reach out and take me, aren't you? You're too tied to the security of your network of leeches, all of you pretty, useless people who live off the work of others. You're pretty, sweetheart, but you're nothing but a bloodsucker."

His words hit her like blows, but she lifted her chin proudly. "You don't know anything about me," was all she said.

"I know enough to know that trying to get passion from you is a hopeless cause," he returned caustically. "Look, I'll be in touch about the leases, but don't save any dances for me."

She sat there for a long time after he left, wishing he would come back so she could spill out her fears and uncertainties to him, but knowing that it was for the best that he'd gone. He was right; she did want him, and she was afraid that if he knew just how weak she was, he'd play on those weaknesses and use her in any way he wanted, even as a means of revenge. If nothing else, she couldn't let that happen.

How quickly he had destroyed the peace, the even tenor of her days! She spent another night lying awake, twisting under a mantle of unhappiness. When dawn finally came, revealing a low gray sky, she wanted to do nothing more than lie in bed all day as a refuge from the thoughts that whirled around in her tired mind. But with her usual determination she forced herself out of bed; she would maintain her regular schedule if it killed her! She wasn't going to let Cord Blackstone tear her life to pieces.

She went to the offices in Biloxi every day; Preston ran everything, but since Vance's death she had become more immersed in the daily details of running a corporation with a myriad of interests, and Preston had long ago gotten in the habit of talking everything over with her. He had the training, but she was quick and knowledgeable, and had good instincts about business. After Vance's death, taking over his office had been a means of keeping her sanity, but before long she'd found herself enjoying the work, enjoying the flood of information on which decisions were based.

She arrived early, but Preston was even earlier. Having seen his car in the parking lot, she went straight to his office, knocking softly on his door. Their mutual secretary hadn't arrived yet, and the building echoed with sounds not usually heard during the busy days.

He looked up at the interruption, and a welcoming smile eased the shadow of worry that had darkened his face. "Come on in. I've already put the coffee on."

"I could do with an extra jolt of caffeine," Susan sighed, heading straight for the coffeepot.

They sipped the hot brew in companionable silence for several minutes, then Susan put her cup down. "What are we going to do?"

He made no pretense of misunderstanding. "I went over the old books last night, trying to nail down exactly how much we owe him. It's a lot, Susan." He rubbed his forehead wearily.

"You're going to try to replace the money, aren't you?"

He nodded. "What else can I do? The hell of it is, we don't have that much ready cash right now. We've invested heavily in research that won't pay off for another couple of years, but you know that as well as I do. I'm not going to touch anything that you have an interest in; Mother and I agreed on that last night. We're going to liquidate some of our personal assets—"

"Preston Blackstone!" she scolded gently. "Did you think I wouldn't be willing to help you?"

"Of course not, honey, but it wouldn't be fair to you. Mother and I did this, and we knew that we were taking a chance. We gambled that Cord wouldn't come back until we'd been able to replace the money, and we lost." He shrugged, his blue eyes full of wry acceptance of his own mistake. "It didn't seem so wrong at the time. We didn't use the money for anything personal; every cent of it was invested back into the corporation, but I don't suppose that would make any difference in a court of law. I still forged his signature on some papers."

"Will you be able to raise enough?" He might protest, but if they couldn't cover the amount they owed Cord, then she would insist on helping them. She didn't want to do anything to jeopardize the corporation, so she agreed that its assets shouldn't be touched, but Vance had left her a lot of personal assets that could easily be liquidated, including some highly valuable property. She also had the ridges, she realized with a sudden start. How badly did Cord want them? Badly enough to take the land in exchange for not pressing charges against Imogene and Preston? Two could play his game!

"I have an idea," she said slowly, not giving Preston time enough to answer her question. "I have something he wants; perhaps we could make a trade."

Preston was a smart man, and he knew her well; he leaned back in his chair, his blue eyes narrowing as he stared at her and sorted out the options and details in his mind. He didn't waste time on unnecessary questions. "You're talking about the ridges. You know that even if you lease the ridges to him, he can still file charges, don't you? He might swear that he wouldn't, but I don't think his word of honor is worth much. Not only that, you'd be giving in to his blackmail."

"Not quite," she said, thinking her way through the situation. "I'll have to have those surveys made, and estimate the worth of an oil lease on the ridges, but if he accepts the leases as restitution for the amount you owe him, then he doesn't have a case any longer, does he?''

Preston looked thunderstruck. ''My God, you're talking about letting him have the oil leases for free? Do you have an idea what a rich field could be worth?''

''Millions, I'd imagine, or he wouldn't be so determined to have it.''

''A lot more than what we owe him! He'd jump at the deal, but you'd be losing a fortune. No, there's no way I can let you do that.''

''There's no way you can stop me,'' she reminded him, giving him a tender smile. She'd gladly give up a fortune to keep her family intact and safe. Preston had his faults, as did Imogene, but she knew that they'd never turn their backs on her, no matter what happened. They weren't easy people to know—the stiff-necked Blackstone pride and arrogance was present in abundance in both of them—but they also had a loyalty that went all the way to the bone. When she married Vance Blackstone, she had been taken into the family and guaranteed its protection. Preston had been a life-saver for her when Vance died, pushing his own grief for his brother aside to comfort her and protect her to the best of his ability. Even Imogene, whose proud head had never lowered even on the day of Vance's funeral, had helped Susan by showing her a gritty courage and determination that wouldn't falter.

Preston's frustration was evident in his eyes as he glared at her. ''I don't like it when you use that soft, sweet tone of voice. That means you've dug in your heels and won't budge, doesn't it?''

A sound in the outer office alerted them to the arrival of their secretary, Beryl Murphy. Knowing that they both had a lot of paperwork to handle, Susan got to her feet and used that excuse to escape to her own office, even though she knew Preston wanted to try to talk her out of letting Cord have the ridges. Blue fire was in his gaze as he watched her leave the office, but Beryl was already approaching with the first of the day's crises, and he groaned in momentary surrender.

Susan had a stack of reports left on her desk from the Friday before, and she dutifully began reading them, but before long she'd lost the thread of meaning as her mind worried at every angle of the deal she'd be offering Cord.

She really needed to know the monetary value of the oil leases on the ridges before making a deal, but on the other hand, she didn't want to wait before approaching Cord about it. Though he could file charges immediately, she didn't think he would; he would wait, as much to worry everyone as to make up his mind. He probably had already made up his mind, she realized with a burst of panic. Should she wait, or should she tell him right away about the deal? Finally she decided to approach him immediately, before he could take any legal action. If any formal charges were ever made, there would be no way of keeping them from becoming public knowledge, and that would hurt her in-laws enormously.

The realization that she would have to see him, that day if possible, sent a chill down her spine. Just the thought of being close to him again made her blood tumble madly through her veins, whether in dread or anticipation she couldn't say. The way he had kissed her the day before was still seared into her mind, and she couldn't get the taste of his mouth from her lips, or rub from her skin the lingering sensation of the soft brush of his moustache and beard. He was a dangerous animal, but he appealed to her on a primitive level that she had never before suspected existed within herself. She wanted him, and her body's longing made every meeting with him hazardous, because she wasn't certain of her mind's ability to retain control.

But how silky his beard was! Not bristly at all, but soft and sensuous. Was the hair all over his body as soft as that? An image of his nude form sprang into her mind, and a wave of heat washed over her, forcing her to take off the suit jacket she was still wearing.

My God, what was she thinking?

It was useless to entertain daydreams of him. Oh, he'd willingly use her sexually, but for reasons that had nothing to do with being attracted to her personally. Her feminine spirit couldn't take that, nor could her conscience allow her to so abandon her morals.

She got through the day, and somehow avoided Preston when he tried to pin her down at lunch. He didn't want her to sacrifice anything, and Imogene would also object. She'd have to stay one step ahead of both of them, and she meant to do that by seeing Cord as soon as possible. She made the necessary phone calls to get the geological survey in progress and grimly ignored the thought that now she couldn't let any ecological damage to the area matter.

By afternoon a weak sun was trying to break through the cloud layer, and a brisk wind had sprung up. Would Cord be working on the old cabin at Jubilee Creek? If he wasn't, she had no idea where to find him. She'd deliberately tried not to listen to all the gossip about him these past few weeks, and now she wished instead that she'd absorbed every word; at least then she might have an idea of where he was. She could ask Preston, but she knew what fireworks that would set off, so she decided simply to try her luck at Jubilee Creek.

She left early, because she wasn't certain of her memory of the location of the cabin. Secondary roads wound through the region like grape runners, criss-crossing each other and meandering in no particular direction, it sometimes seemed. Vance had taken her to the Jubilee Creek area a few times, early in their marriage, but that had been years ago.

Suddenly the sun brightened, as the wind pushed the clouds away, and she squinted against the sudden glare of sun on the wet highway. Reaching above the visor, she grabbed her sunglasses and quickly slid them on. Perhaps the sun was an omen; then she made a face at herself at the frivolous thought. She didn't believe in omens.

She was nervous, her stomach queasy at the thought of dealing with him, and to take her mind off of it she tried to concentrate on the passing scenery. The weather might be chilly, but there were signs of spring after all, even discounting the stubborn jonquils. Oak trees had that fuzzy look conveyed by new leaves, and patches of green grass were shooting up. In another week, two at the most, colour would be rioting over the land as shrubs and trees bloomed, and it couldn't happen soon enough for her. It was already what she counted as a late spring.

She almost missed the turn onto the narrow road that she thought was the correct one. It was only a roughly paved secondary road, without benefit of a painted center line or graded shoulders. She slowed down, looking for the next turn, and just when she had almost decided that she'd taken the wrong road, she recognized the turn she was supposed to take. It was an unpaved lane that was really only two tracks, crowded on both sides by tall, monolithic pines and sweeping oaks that rapidly hid the secondary road from view. The lane made a long curve; then she found herself rattling across an old wooden bridge that spanned Jubilee Creek itself.

The rain had filled the broad, shallow creek, and the muddy water tumbled over the rocks and around the meandering curves as the creek snaked its way south to empty eventually into the Gulf. She could see the cabin now, a small structure dwarfed by three massive oaks behind it, capping the crest of a small rise. Even from where she was, it was evident that the porch that ran the length of the cabin was completely new, and as she drew closer she could see that the roof was also new, shingles replacing the rusted tin that had been there before.

She didn't know what kind of car he drove, but it didn't matter anyway, since there was no sign of any vehicle. Her heart sank. She slowed her own car to a stop in front of the cabin, staring at the curtainless windows in despair. Where could she find him?

She was just about to put the car in reverse when the door opened and he stepped onto the porch. Even from that distance she could see the icy glare of his eyes, and she knew that this wasn't going to be easy. She drew a deep breath to brace herself, then cut the ignition off and got out of the car.

Walking up the steps was like running a gauntlet; he leaned against the door frame and watched her in nervewracking silence, his arms crossed over his chest. He looked huge, she noticed; perhaps it was his clothes. He wore only a pair of faded jeans and a black T-shirt, and scuffed brown boots on his feet. The short sleeves of the T-shirt revealed his brawny forearms, sprinkled with dark hair and corded with veins that pulsed with his hot, life-giving blood. From the way the thin cotton clung to his torso, she knew that the image she'd had of his nude body had been remarkably accurate, and her mouth went dry. He was lean and hard and muscular, and his chest looked like a wall.

His glacial eyes swept her from her neat spectator pumps to her head, where her dark hair had been swept into a simple chignon. "Slumming?" he drawled sarcastically.

She controlled the quiver that wanted to weaken her legs, and ignored his opening salvo. "I want to make a deal with you," she said firmly.

Amusement, and a savage satisfaction, glinted in his eyes. He stepped away from the door and waved her inside with an exaggerated bow. "Come inside, lady, and let's hear what you have to offer."

Chapter 4

Their steps echoed hollowly as she entered the cabin and he followed, closing the door behind him. The smell of newly cut wood struck her nostrils, and fine particles of sawdust floated through the air. Through an open door she could see a couple of sawhorses with a length of wood lying across them, and she realized that she had interrupted his work. She wanted to apologize, but the words refused to leave her thickened throat. To give herself time to recover, she looked around the empty cabin; despite the improvements, it still had an atmosphere of being old and still felt incredibly solid anyway. The new windows, large and airtight, let the light in but kept the damp chill out. An enormous fireplace, laid with logs but unlit, gave the promise of cozy fires. The open door to the right of the fireplace indicated the only other room, and except for it, she could see all of the cabin from where she stood. Beneath her feet, the floor was pine, treated and polished, then left alone to glow with its natural golden color. In spite of her nervousness she was charmed by the old cabin, as if she could feel at peace here.

He stepped past her and leaned down to strike a match and touch it to the old newspaper in the fireplace. It flamed with tongues of blue, which quickly caught the kindling, and soon the fire was licking at the big logs. "I don't feel the cold much while I'm working," he said by way of explanation. "But since you've interrupted me—"

"I'm sorry," she murmured, feeling incredibly awkward.

There was nowhere to sit, but he looked perfectly comfortable as he wedged one strong shoulder against the mantel and gave her a sardonic look. "Okay, lady, you wanted to talk turkey. Talk."

He wasn't going to give an inch. She didn't waste time pleading with him to be reasonable; she lifted her chin and plunged in. "Have you filed charges yet?"

"I haven't had time today," he responded lazily. "I've been working here."

"I—I want to make you an offer, if you'll agree not to file charges."

His ice blue eyes sharpened and raked down her slim, tense body. "Are you offering yourself?"

The thought jolted her, and she wondered what would happen if she said yes. Would he take her now, on the bare floor? But she said, "No, of course not," in a low voice that disguised her reaction.

"Pity." Nonchalantly, he surveyed her again. "That was the one offer you could have made that might interest me. It might have been fun to see if you get mussed up when you're having sex. I doubt it, though. You're probably starched all the way through."

Susan curled her fingers into her palms, and only then did she notice how cold her hands were. "I'm offering you that lease on the ridges."

He straightened, his hard mouth curving in amusement. "Let me remind you that that was my original offer. But I've thought about it since then, and I've changed my mind. And didn't you tell me yesterday that you couldn't be blackmailed into selling me the lease?"

She stepped closer, to get nearer the fire as much as to read his eyes better. "I'm not offering to sell you the lease; I'll *give* you the lease, as restitution for the amount owed to you by Preston and Imogene."

He laughed, throwing back his dark head on the rich sound. "Do you have any idea how much money you're talking about?"

Preston had asked her the same thing, and her answer was still the same. "More than what they owe you. I realize that; I'm asking you to accept the lease as restitution."

He stopped laughing, and his eyes narrowed on her. "Why should you pay their debts? Why should I let them off scot-free?"

"They're my family," was all she could offer by way of explanation.

"Family, hell! They're pit vipers, sugar, and I should know better than anyone else. I don't want *you* to pay; I want *them* to pay."

"Like you said last night, you want them to squirm."

"Exactly."

"You're turning down an oil lease worth a fortune just for your petty sense of revenge?" she cried.

Anger darkened his face. "Easy there, lady," he said softly. "You're pushing me."

Susan swept an agitated hand across her brow. "You need pushing! How can you be so stubborn?" He wasn't going to agree, and desperation clawed through her stomach. "Why don't you take the lease as payment?"

He grinned, but it wasn't from amusement; his grin was one of grinding rage and grim anticipation. "Because if I accept the lease under those conditions, then I no longer have a case against them, as you well know. Did Preston talk you into this? Well, it won't work. I'll pay you for the lease, and I'll pay you well, but I won't let Preston hide behind your skirt. It's no deal."

Tears stung her eyes as he turned away from her to kick the burning logs into better position. She clutched at his arm, feeling his warm flesh, the steeliness of the muscles underneath. "Please!" she begged.

He swung around, looming over her, the red flames of the fire reflected in his pale eyes and making them glow like a devil's. "Damn you!" he spat from between his clenched teeth. "Don't you dare beg for them!"

Wildly she reached out with her other hand and grasped the fabric of his T-shirt, trying to shake him, but unable to budge him. She had to make him understand! How could he destroy his own family, his own blood? The thought was so horrible that she couldn't stand it. She had to do something, anything, to convince him how wrong and futile revenge was. "Don't do this, please!" she cried frantically. "I *am* begging you—"

"Stop it!" he ordered, his deeper, darker voice completely overriding hers. He jerked her hands off him and held her, his long fingers wrapped around her upper arms. Anger made his fingers bite into her soft flesh, and she gasped, twisting in an effort to free herself. Immediately his grip relaxed, and she jerked away. In the silence that fell between them, her breathing was swift and audible as she gulped in air, her breasts rising and falling. His eyes dropped to the soft mounds as they moved, lingered for a long, heart-stopping moment, and when he finally looked back up to her face, black fury had filled his gaze. "You begged—for *him*. Get out of here. You can tell him that his little scheme didn't work. Go on, go back to him, and to his bed."

Susan came apart under the tension and the lash of his words. She, who never lost control, whose nature was serene and peaceful,

suddenly found herself flying at him, thrusting her face up close to
his and yelling, "It was *my* scheme, not his! He tried to talk me
out of it! You fool! You're so wrapped up in the past, in your sick
need for revenge, that you can't even see how self-destructive you
are! If this is how you were fourteen years ago, no wonder you
were run out of town—mmmmph!''

He had reached out, his hard hands closing on her waist, and had
jerked her against him with enough force to knock the breath out
of her. She threw her head back, gasping, and his mouth came
down, attacking, fastening on hers, forcing her lips to part and mold
themselves to his. There was nothing gentle or seductive in his kiss
this time; he forced her response, his arms locking around her and
holding her to him, one hand going up her back to fasten in her
hair and hold her head back for him to drink as he willed from her
mouth. Dazed, dizzied by his sudden sensual attack, she made no
effort to wrench away from him.

He kissed her again and again, his tongue making forays that
brought her onto her tiptoes, straining against him, forgetting the
anger between them, forgetting the reason she was there. The feel
of him, so hard and warm, so strong, was all she wanted in the
world, the source of every comfort she could imagine. His kisses
became deeper, longer, sweet-tart with the passion that turned their
embrace into pure fire. His hand went under her jacket, sweeping
up to close over her breast with a sure touch that didn't allow her
to deny him the right to touch her so intimately. Her blouse was
opened so roughly that she was dimly surprised when the buttons
didn't fly off; then his hand was inside, sliding between her bra and
the soft, satiny flesh beneath it, her nipple stabbing into his rough
palm.

She whimpered into his mouth as his hand stroked and kneaded,
his demanding man's touch swamping her with a sensual delight
that turned her body into pure molten need. Her breasts were very
sensitive, and his expertise made them harden with desire, turned
the velvet nipple into a taut, throbbing point. She was throbbing
everywhere, her entire body pulsating, her own hands digging into
the deep valley along his spine, then pulling frantically at his
T-shirt until it came free of his pants and she could slide her hands
under it, running her palms up the damp, muscled expanse of his
back. He quivered under her touch, telling her without words that
he was as aroused as she. He had the raw, musky smell of sweat
mingled with his own potent masculinity; and she wanted to spend
the rest of her life locked in his hard arms, breathing in that scent.
It was mad, but oh, it was sweet.

When he released her and stepped back, she was as shocked as if a bucket of icy water had been hurled in her face. Disoriented, lost without the heat of his body, the hard security of his arms, she stared up at him with bewildered blue eyes grown so huge that they dominated her face.

He wasn't unaffected; he was breathing hard, and color was high in his face. When he looked at her open blouse and his pupils dilated, she swayed on her feet, thinking for a moment that he was going to return to her. Then he thrust a rough hand through his hair, ruffling the silky strands. "Is this Plan Two to get me to agree to your deal?"

Susan stepped back, her face losing its color. "Do you really believe that?" she choked, anguish twisting her insides.

"It seems possible enough. You don't have the guts to admit that you want me; you have to cling to your spotless, genteel reputation. But if you sacrifice yourself to me to save your family, why, then you're a noble martyr, and you get to enjoy the sin without sinning. I admit, it sounds like something out of a Victorian novel, but that's what you make me think of."

"A coward," she said painfully.

A hard smile twisted his mouth. "Exactly."

She stood poised, uncertain if she should go or try again to convince him not to press charges against her family. She badly wanted to leave; she was afraid that if he threw any more harsh words against her, her dignity and self-control would be totally destroyed and she'd begin crying, and she didn't want that. She swallowed to force control on her voice, and said quietly, "Please reconsider. How can you turn down a fortune? You know what those ridges are worth if the geologists are right, and what the lease would normally cost you."

"You're offering to save my company a fortune," he pointed out coolly. "I wouldn't get any of the money personally. What's in it for me?"

Confused, she stared at him. How stupid of her! Her great plan had been to offer him personal gain, and he had let her make a complete fool of herself before reminding her that giving the lease to him would benefit the company he worked for, not him personally. Mortified, she turned and walked quickly to the door, wanting nothing more than to leave. A deep chuckle followed her, and as she opened the door and stepped onto the porch, he called, "But it was a good try!"

Susan kept her pace steady as she went to the car, trying not to run even though she wanted to get away from him as fast as she could. What a colossal blunder she'd made! And how he must be laughing at her! When she thought of the way she'd returned his kisses, she blushed, then turned pale. Good Lord, how could he think she was anything but cheap, after she'd virtually offered herself to him? He'd thought that she was just part of the deal, and she couldn't blame him for that; what else could he think, when she'd kissed him back so hungrily?

When she pulled into her own driveway and saw Imogene's Cadillac in front of the house, she groaned aloud. The last thing she felt like right then was facing Imogene's drilling; she wanted to take a long bath and pamper herself in an effort to soothe her ragged nerves. She knew that Preston would have called Imogene and talked to her about Susan's ploy, and now Imogene was here to discover how things had gone. Why couldn't she have waited just a few hours more?

There would be no easy way to dash Imogene's hopes, and the strain was evident in Susan's face as she entered the house and walked to the den, where she knew her mother-in-law would be waiting. The older woman rose to her feet when Susan entered, and her shrewd gray eyes examined every nuance of expression in Susan's face. "He turned you down, didn't he?" It wasn't like Imogene to give in to defeat, but now her discouragement gave a leaden cast to her eyes, dulled her voice.

He'd turned her down in more ways than one, Susan thought wearily. Her mental and physical fatigue muted her voice as she sank down in one of the chairs. "Yes."

"I knew he would." Imogene sighed and resumed her seat, her patrician face still with effort. "It would be too easy to let you pay; it's Preston and me that he's after."

Remembering the cold contempt in his eyes when he had looked at her, Susan couldn't agree fully with Imogene. A hard knot of pain formed in her chest; why did it have to be like that? When she remembered the intense magic of their first two meetings, she wanted to weep at the harsh words that had passed between them since then. She felt as if she had lost something precious, without ever having held it in her hands. He was a hard man, yet inexplicably she wanted to get closer to him, to get to know him, learn his moods and his laughter as well as his anger, delve into his protected personality until she found some inner core of tenderness. When he had kissed her the first time, it had been with a tender consideration for her soft flesh. But today— Susan raised her fingers and touched her lips, still a little swollen and sensitive from his hard kisses. He hadn't been gentle today; he had been angry, and he had punished her for daring to try to protect Preston.

Suddenly she realized that Imogene had followed the tell-tale gesture with knowing eyes, and she blushed.

Imogene sat upright. "Susan! He's interested in you, isn't he? How perfect! Thank God," she said fervently.

Susan had expected a subtle scolding, not Imogene's almost rapturous joy. "What's perfect?" she asked in confusion.

"Don't you see? You're in a marvelous position to find out what he's planning and keep us informed; that way we can take steps to counteract anything he does. Why, you might even be able to talk him out of staying here!"

Stunned, she stared at Imogene, not quiet able to believe what was being asked of her, what Imogene automatically assumed she would do, without protest. After all, she was family, and her first allegiance was to that family. It was the same sort of thinking that had allowed Imogene and Preston to use Cord's money illegally in the first place; it wasn't as much Cord's money as it was Blackstone money, and therefore available for their use.

She strove for an even tone. "He's not interested in me. If anything, I'm tarred with the same brush he's used to paint you and Preston."

Imogene waved that thought aside with a brisk movement of her hand. "Nonsense." She examined Susan critically, her gray eyes narrowed. "You're a lovely woman, though of course not his usual sort. It shouldn't be difficult for you to get around him."

"But I don't want to get around him!"

"Dear, you *must!* Don't you see that the only way we can protect ourselves is to know in advance what he's planning?"

Agitation tumbled Susan's insides with a restless hand, and she got to her feet, unable to sit still. "It's impossible," she blurted. "I'm not a—a slut. I can't sleep with him just to *spy* on him!"

Imogene looked affronted. "Of course you wouldn't, but I'm not asking that of you, Susan. All I'm asking is that you see him, talk to him, try to find out what he's planning. I realize that it may cost you a few kisses, but surely you're willing to give that in exchange for our protection."

A few kisses! Did Imogene really know so little about her own nephew? Susan shook her head slowly, denying the idea to herself, as well as to Imogene. "A few kisses isn't what he wants," she said, her voice muffled. And even if she went to bed with him, he still wouldn't divulge any secrets to her. All he wanted from her was a good time in bed, physical release, a momentary pleasure.

Imogene didn't give up easily; there was steel in her spine, in her character. Sitting very upright, her chin lifted proudly, she said firmly, "Then it's up to you to keep him under control. You're not a teenager, to be seduced in the back seat of a car to the theme of 'but everyone does it.' You can string him along."

If Susan had been less shocked, she would have laughed aloud, but as it was she stood frozen, staring at Imogene as if she were a stranger. What her mother-in-law was telling her to do struck her as little less than prostitution, and she felt chilled by the realization that Imogene had so little regard for her feelings, her morals. She was simply supposed to do whatever was asked of her.

"No," she refused in a low voice. "I can't—I *won't* do it."

A cold fire began snapping in Imogene's eyes. "Really? Do you care so little for me, for Preston, that you'll simply stand and watch while that wretch destroys us? We won't be in it by ourselves, you know. You'll suffer, too. If he decides to sue us for damages, he could bankrupt the company, and there would go the standard of living that you currently enjoy. People will talk about you just as they would about us; everyone will believe that you knew about the money from the beginning. You've made a big show of 'working' at the company since Vance died, so people will assume that not only did you know about it, you approved."

Susan had seen Imogene in action before, and knew that few people could stand up to her when she lashed out with her lethal tongue, when she stared at someone with those cool, hard eyes. Most people gave in to her without even a hint of resistance. Vance had had the strength to soothe her, agree with her, and calmly go about his own business in his own way, smiling at her and charming her whenever she realized that he'd ignored her directions. Preston wasn't that often at variance with her, though he was a lot warmer, a lot more human. Because she had been challenged so seldom in her life, she didn't expect anyone to disobey her openly. The quiet determination Susan had shown in becoming Vance's wife, then in taking up the reins of his business interests at his death, should have told her that Susan wasn't like most people, but still she wasn't prepared for a refusal.

Susan stood very straight, very still, her expression calm, her dark blue eyes quiet and level. "Regardless of what anyone says, I'll know that I haven't done anything wrong, and that's what's important to me. I'll help you anyway I can, except for that way. I'll sell everything I own, but I won't play the whore for you, and that's what you're asking me to do. You know as well as I do that Cord isn't a man who can be controlled by any woman."

Imogene got to her feet, her mouth tight. "I expected more loyalty from you than this. If you want to turn your back on us when we're in trouble, I can't stop you, but think very carefully about what you stand to lose."

"My self-respect," Susan said dryly.

Imogene didn't storm out of the house; she swept out, regally, in a cold rage. Susan stood at the window and watched her drive away, her chest tight with hurt and sadness because she hadn't wanted to damage the relationship she had with Imogene. Since she'd first met Vance's mother, she had carefully cultivated a closeness with the older woman, knowing how important the ties of family were to a marriage, and how much Vance had loved his mother despite her reserve. Imogene wasn't a villain, even though she was autocratic. When she loved, she loved deeply, and she'd fight to the death for those she cared about. Her blindness was her family; anything was acceptable to her if it protected her family. Until now Susan had been wrapped in that fierce blanket of protection, but now she felt that she'd been cast out as Cord had been cast out. Dues had to be paid if someone expected to benefit from that protection; conformity was expected, and a willingness to sacrifice oneself for the well-being of the whole. Cord had been cast out because he hadn't conformed, because he'd left the family open to gossip. His reputation hadn't been up to par, and he'd been forced out of the closed circle.

Had he felt like this? Susan wondered, running her hands up her chilled arms. Had he felt lost, betrayed? Had he been alarmed to be without the support that he'd known since birth? No, he hadn't been alarmed, not that man; instead he would have thought with grim delight of punishing them for turning their backs on him. Wasn't that what he was doing now?

Cord. Somehow all her thoughts these days returned to him, as if he had become the center of her world. She hadn't wanted him to, but since the moment he'd walked in from the night, he had eclipsed everyone else in her every waking thought, in her dreams, had invaded even her memory, so that she constantly had the taste of his mouth on her tongue, felt the hard warmth of his hands on her flesh. *I could love him!* she thought wildly, and shuddered in half-fear, half-excitement. Loving him would be the most dangerous thing she'd ever done in her life, yet she felt helpless to deny the effect he had on her. If it wasn't love yet, it had nevertheless gone beyond mere desire, and she was teetering on the edge of an emotional chasm. If she fell into it, she'd be forever lost.

The emotional strain that she was under was visible on her face the next morning when she walked into the office, later than usual for her because she'd spent a restless night, then overslept when she finally did manage to fall asleep. Because she felt so frazzled, she'd attempted to disguise her emotional state by hiding behind an image that was sterner than the one she usually projected. She'd pulled her soft dark hair back into a tight knot and applied makeup carefully, hoping to divert attention from the lost expression in her eyes. The dress she had chosen was sleekly sophisticated, a black silk tunic with narrow white vertical stripes, cinched about her slender waist with a thin black belt. It wasn't a dress that she wore often, because it had always seemed too stark for her, but today it suited her mood perfectly.

She told Beryl good morning, then went straight through to her office and closed the door, hoping to submerge herself in the reports that she hadn't finished the day before, because she'd been in a hurry to see Cord. A wasted effort, she thought with a painful catch in her breath. Resolutely she pushed away the thought of her failure and picked up the first report, only to replace it when someone knocked firmly on her door.

Without waiting for an answer, Preston let himself in and sauntered over to ease himself into the chair opposite her desk. He sprawled in it and pressed his fingers together to form a steeple, over which he peered with blue eyes alive with curiosity. "What did you say to Mother?" he asked with relish. "I haven't seen her so angry in years?"

Susan caught the grin that twitched at his mouth, and against her will she found herself smiling at him. Preston had a little bit of the devil in him at times, a puckish sense of humor that he seldom allowed to surface. Whenever he did, it made his eyes sparkle in a manner that reminded her strongly of Vance. Now was one of those times. Despite the pressure he was under, he was being eaten alive with curiosity, wondering what Susan could possibly have said to his mother to put her in such a snit.

She wasn't certain just how much to tell him, if anything. She decided to stall. "Did Imogene tell you that Cord turned down my offer of the ridges?"

He nodded. "I'm glad, too. I know it would've been the easy way, but I don't want you to pay for something that was our fault. You know that." He gave a graceful shrug. "Mother didn't agree; she thought that it would be worth it if we stopped any trouble before it began."

Yes, head off scandal, at any cost. Deciding to tell him the truth in the hope that he would support her, she took a deep breath and braced herself. "She wanted me to see Cord—play up to him—and try to find out what he was planning so you could counteract it. I refused.''

Preston's eyes had widened, then narrowed as he realized the scope of her simplified explanation. He swore softly. ''Thank God for that! I don't want you around him. Mother shouldn't have suggested anything like that.''

''She'd do anything to protect her family,'' Susan offered in Imogene's defense.

''Telling you to play up to Cord is like throwing a lamb to the wolves,'' he snapped. ''You wouldn't have a chance. What in hell ever gave her the idea?''

A faint blush crept into Susan's cheeks, and she looked away from him. ''She knows that he kissed me—''

Preston bolted upright in his chair. ''He what?''

''He kissed me,'' she repeated steadily. Did Preston think that was something to be ashamed of?

He'd turned pale, and abruptly he surged to his feet, running his fingers through his neat hair in an uncharacteristic gesture. ''I thought, the night he first showed up, that he was just playing up to you to get back at me. Is that all it is?''

Susan bit her lip; she honestly didn't know. Her body told her that Cord Blackstone's interest wasn't limited to her name, but her mind worried over the issue. A man's sexual instincts could be aroused even when he had another motive for seducing a woman, so she couldn't let herself be confused by the physical responses he'd shown. Yet, he'd responded to her from the very beginning.... Just when her heart was beginning to beat faster in faint hope, she saw herself stretching out her hand to him, and heard herself saying, ''I'm Susan Blackstone....'' No, he'd known from the first that she was a Blackstone, married to either Vance or Preston. Unhappily, she looked up at Preston. ''I don't know,'' she said miserably.

He began to pace around the room. ''Susan, please, don't have anything else to do with him. Don't see him at all, unless you have to. You don't have any idea of the type of man he is.''

''Yes, I do,'' she interrupted. ''He's a hard, lonely man.'' How could he not be lonely? He might have built an emotional wall to guard him, but he was all alone behind it.

Preston gave her a derisive, unbelieving look. ''My God, how can you be so naive? You've got to stop seeing good in everyone! Some people are bad all the way through. Will you promise me not to see him again, and protect yourself before he has a chance to really hurt you?''

There was a very real chance that *he* wouldn't want to see *her*, but suddenly she knew that if by some miracle he gave her another opportunity, she'd seize it with both hands. She wanted to be with him. She wanted to kiss him, to try to discover if what she felt for him was a fleeting sexual magic, or if the seeds of real love had been sown. For five years she'd grieved for Vance, and though her love for him would never die, neither would it grow. Vance was frozen in place in her heart, but he didn't occupy all of it. There was still so much love in her to give! She wanted to love again; she wanted to marry again, and bear children. Perhaps Cord wasn't the man who would be able to touch her heart, but she already knew that she had to take the chance. If she let the opportunity pass, she'd always wonder about it, and mourn for lost chances for the rest of her days.

She looked Preston in the eye. "I can't promise that."

He swore softly, and suddenly his shoulders hunched. "All of these years," he muttered. "First you were Vance's wife, then his widow. I've waited, knowing you weren't over Vance, that you weren't ready to become involved with anyone else. Damn it, why does it have to be Cord?" The last sentence was a harsh cry, and his chest welled with the fury inside him. He gave Susan a look so tortured that tears welled in her eyes.

She found herself on her feet, unable to calmly sit there while he bared his deepest secret to her. "Preston—I didn't know," she whispered.

His clear blue eyes were a little shiny, too. "I know," he said, taking a shuddering breath. "I made sure I kept it from you. What else could I do? Try to steal my brother's wife?"

"I'm sorry. I'm so sorry!" What else was there to say? Events couldn't be altered. Perhaps, if their lives had been allowed to go on undisturbed, she might one day have come to love Preston in the way he wanted, though she rather thought that instead she would always have seen him as Vance's brother, and looking at him would always have been like looking at a slightly altered photo of Vance. But the even tenor of her life had been disrupted from the moment she'd seen Cord, and crossing that dance floor to take his hand and shield him from the scene that had been brewing had forever altered her, in ways that she hadn't yet discovered.

"I know." He turned his head away, not wanting her to see the depth of his pain. He was a man of pride and patience, and his patience had gained him nothing. All he could do now was cling to his pride. He walked to the door and left, his shoulders square, his gait steady, but still Susan knew what the effort cost him, and her vision blurred as she watched him.

Would Cord be glad that, even involuntarily, he'd managed to hurt Preston? She winced at the thought. She'd certainly never tell him that Preston had hoped for a deeper relationship. What he'd told her today would go no further; it was the least she could do for someone she loved as much as she could, even though, for him, that wasn't enough.

Chapter 5

By Friday her emotional turmoil had taken its toll on her, and the price she'd paid was evident in an even more slender waistline, and a fragility in her face that was startling. She and Imogene had made up, in a way. They had spoken to each other on the phone, never making reference to their difference of opinion, but their conversation had been stilted and brief. Imogene had simply asked her if she would be attending Audrey Gregg's Friday night fund-raising dinner for a local charity. Imogene had a prior commitment, and she wanted Susan to go, since Audrey was a very good friend. Susan had agreed, reluctant to face an evening of having to smile and pretend that everything was all right, but acknowledging her family duty. At least it wasn't formal, thank God. Audrey Gregg believed in keeping her guests entertained; there would be dancing, a generous buffet instead of a sit-down dinner, and probably a night club act brought in from New Orleans.

Spring was tantalizing them again with marvelous weather, though only the day before it had been cold and overcast. Today the temperature had soared to eighty, and the forecasters had promised a mild night. With that in mind, Susan dressed in a floaty dress in varying shades of lavender and blue, with a wrap bodice that hugged and outlined her breasts. She was too tired and depressed to fool much with her hair, and simply brushed it back, securing it behind each ear with filagree combs. The sun was setting in a marvelous skyscape of reds and gold and purples when she drove over to Audrey's house, and the natural beauty lifted her spirits somewhat. How could she keep frowning in the face of that magnificent sunset?

The brief lifting of her spirits lasted only until she glanced over the crowd at Audrey's and saw Cord, casually sophisticated in gray flannel slacks and a blue blazer, dancing with Cheryl Warren. Cheryl again! Though Cheryl was a likeable person, unexpectedly kind despite her chorus-girl looks, Susan felt an unwelcome sting of jealousy. It was just that Cheryl was so...so sexy, and so *together*. Her tall, leggy body was svelte, with a dancer's grace; her makeup was always a little dramatic, but always perfectly applied, and somehow right for her. Her ash blond hair looked wonderful— loose and sexy, tousled.

Compared to Cheryl, Susan felt nondescript. Her simple hairstyle suddenly seemed childish, her makeup humdrum, her dress the common garden variety. She scolded herself for feeling that way, because she knew the dress was becoming to her and was perfectly stylish. It was just that Cord made her feel so insecure, so unsure of herself that she did know what she wanted: She wanted Cord. But she couldn't have him; he was all wrong for her, and he didn't want her anyway.

Suddenly Preston was at her elbow, his strong hand guiding her to the buffet. With a pang, Susan realized that normally she would have been here with Preston, but this time he hadn't even asked her. Cord had managed to drive a wedge between her and Preston, whose friendship she had depended on for so long. How pleased he would be if he only knew what he'd done!

Preston's blue eyes were worried as he looked down at her. "Relax for a minute," he advised. "You're wound up like a two-dollar watch."

"I know," she sighed, watching as he automatically filled a plate for her. He knew all her favorite foods, and he chose them without asking. When he had two laden plates in his hand, he nodded over to a group of empty chairs and they made their way across the room to claim them, with Susan stopping enroute to fetch two glasses of champagne punch.

He watched as she nibbled on a fresh, succulent Gulf shrimp. "You're lovely," he said with the blunt honesty of people who know each other well. "But you look as if you're going to fly into a million pieces, and that isn't like you."

She managed a wry smile. "I know. You don't know how I wish I could do more than catnap. At least Imogene's speaking to me again."

He grinned. "I knew she wouldn't last long. She's been so restless, it was almost funny. Honey, if it's such a strain on you, why don't you take a vacation? Forget about all of this and get away from all of us for a while."

"I can't do that now." The look she gave him was worried. "I can't leave you not knowing if...if..."

"I know." He covered her hand with his, briefly applying pressure before removing his touch. "I'm handling it, so don't worry so much. In another week to ten days, I'll have the money repaid into Cord's account."

She bit her lip. She knew that he would have had to liquidate a lot of assets to raise that much money so quickly, and she felt guilty that he hadn't allowed her to help. Perhaps she hadn't known anything about it, but she had profited by the use of the money because it had made the company stronger.

By sheer willpower, she kept her gaze from straying too often to Cord as the minutes crawled past, but still she somehow always knew where he was. He'd stopped dancing with Cheryl, and she was surprised by the number of people who engaged him in conversation, despite how wary most of them still were of him. Why was he here? She couldn't imagine that Audrey Gregg had invited him, so he had to have come with someone else, probably Cheryl. Was he seeing Cheryl often?

For a while he stood alone, off to one side, slowly sipping a glass of amber liquid, his dark face blank of any expression, his eyes hooded. He was always alone, she thought painfully. Even when someone was talking with him, he had a quality about him that set him apart, as if he were surrounded by an invisible barrier. He'd probably had to become hard and aloof to survive, but now that very protection kept him from being close to another human being.

It was too stressful to watch him. To divert herself, she began talking to Preston, and resolutely kept her gaze away from Cord. Good friend that Preston was, he talked easily of many things, keeping her occupied. She knew that he had to be under a strain himself, even more so than she was, but he was handling it well, and his concern was all for her.

Suddenly Preston looked past her, his blue gaze sharpened and alert. "It's in the fan now," he muttered. "Grant Keller is about to tie into Cord."

Susan whirled, and gasped at the hostility of the scene. Grant Keller was a picture of aggressive, bitter hatred, standing directly in front of Preston, his fists knotted and his jaw thrust out as he spat some indistinguishable words at the younger man. His handsome, aristocratic face was twisted with hate and fury. Cord, on the other hand, looked cool and bored, but there was an iciness in his eyes that warned Susan that he was on the verge of losing his temper. His stance was relaxed, and that too was a signal. He was perfectly balanced, ready to move in any direction.

Her breath caught in her chest. He'd never before seemed so aloof, so unutterably alone, with only his natural pride and arrogance to stand with him. Her heart was stabbed with pain, and she felt as if she were choking. He was a warrior who would die rather than run, standing by his own code, loyal to his own ideals. Oh, God, couldn't they see that only pain could force a man into such isolation? He'd been hurt enough! Then, out of the corner of her eye, Susan saw Mary Keller watching her husband, with distress and a wounded look evident on her quiet face.

Suddenly Susan was angry, with a fierce swell of emotion that drove away her depression, her tiredness. That old scandal had already caused enough trouble and pain, and now another woman was about to be hurt by it. Mary Keller had to sit there and watch her husband try to start a fight over another woman, something that couldn't be pleasant. And Cord...what about Cord? His youthful love affair had caused him to be driven away from his family, and the hard life that he'd lived since then had only isolated him more. Grant Keller was the wronged husband, true, but he wasn't the only one who had suffered. It was time for it to end, and she was going to see that it did!

People who had never seen Susan Blackstone angry were startled by the look on her face as she headed across the room, and a path was cleared for her. Her eyes were a stormy indigo, her cheeks hot with color, as she marched up to the two men and put her slender body gracefully between them. She was dwarfed by their size, but no one had any doubt that the situation had been swiftly defused. She was practically sparking with heat.

"Grant," she said with a sweetness that couldn't begin to disguise the fire in her eyes. "I'd like to talk to you, please. Alone. Now."

Surprised, he looked down at her. "What?" His tone indicated that he hadn't quite registered her presence.

Cord's hard hands clamped about her waist, and he started to move her to one side. She looked up, smiling at him over her shoulder.

"Don't...you...dare," she said, still sweetly. She looked back at Grant. "Grant. Outside." To make certain that he obeyed her, she took his arm and forcefully led him out of the room, hearing the buzz of gossip begin behind her like angry bees swarming.

"Are you crazy?" she demanded in a fierce whisper when they were out of earshot, dropping the older man's arm and whirling on him in a fury. "Haven't enough people already been hurt by that old scandal? It's *over!* It can't be undone, and everyone has paid for it. Let it die!"

"I can't," he returned just as fiercely. "It's burned into my head! I walked into my own home and found my wife in bed with *him.* Do you think he was ashamed? He just glared at me, as if she were *his* wife, as if I had no right to be there!"

Yes, that sounded like Cord, able to stare down the devil himself. But she brushed all of that aside. "Maybe you have bad memories, but you're just going to have to handle them. Are you still in love with your first wife? Is that it? Do you want her back? You have Mary now, remember! Have you given her a thought? Have you thought of how she must feel right now, watching you start a fight over another woman? Why don't you just walk up and slap her in the face? I'm sure it wouldn't hurt her any worse than she's hurting right now."

He blanched, staring down at her. Perspiration broke out on his face, and he wiped his brow with a nervous hand. "My God, I hadn't thought," he stammered.

Susan poked him in the chest with her forefinger. "It's a dead issue," she said flatly. "I don't want to hear about it again. If anyone...*anyone*... wants to fight Cord over something that happened fourteen years ago, they're going to have to go over me first. Now, go back in there to your wife and try to make it up to her for what you've done!"

"Susan—" He broke off, staring at her pale, furious face as if he'd never seen her before. "I didn't mean—"

"I know," she said, relenting. "Go on now." She gave him a gentle push, and he sucked in a deep breath, obviously preparing himself to face a wife who had every right to be hurt, humiliated and angry. Susan stood where she was for a moment after he'd gone, drawing in her own deep breaths until she felt calm seep back into her body, replacing the furious rush of adrenalin that had sent her storming across the room to step between two angry men.

"That's a bad habit you've got." The deep drawl came from behind her, and she whirled, her breath catching, as Cord sauntered out of the shadows. Abruptly she shivered, no longer protected by her anger, as the cooling night air finally penetrated her consciousness. Quickly she cast a glance at the crowd of people visible through the patio doors, some of them dancing again, going about their own concerns. She had stepped in too soon for anything exciting to happen, so there wouldn't even be much gossip.

"They all know we're out here, but no one is going to intrude," he said cynically. "Not even Preston, the Boy Wonder." He touched the soft curve of her cheek with one finger, trailing it down to the graceful length of her throat. "Didn't your mother ever teach you that it's dangerous to get between two fighting animals?"

She shivered again, and when she tried to speak she found that her voice wouldn't work right; it was husky, strained. "I know you wouldn't hurt me."

Again his finger moved, sliding with excruciating slowness over her collarbone, then stroking lightly over the sensitive hollow of her shoulder. Susan found that the touch of his finger, the hypnotic motion of it, somehow interfered with her breathing; the rhythm of her lungs was thrown off, and she was almost hyperventilating one moment, then holding her breath the next. She stared up at him, seeing his lips move as he spoke, but her attention was focused on his touch, and the words didn't make sense. She swallowed, licked her suddenly dry lips, and croaked, "I'm sorry. What—"

One corner of his mouth lifted in a strange almost-smile. "I said, you'd be a lot safer if you didn't trust me. Then you'd stay away from me, and you wouldn't get burned. I can't decide about you, honey."

"What do you mean?" Why couldn't her voice be stronger? Why couldn't she manage more than that husky whisper?

His finger moved again, making a slow trek over to her other shoulder, touching her in a way that made her heart slam excitedly. She'd never noticed her shoulders being so sensitive, but he was doing things to her that were rocketing her into desire. "I can't decide whose side you're on," he murmured, watching both his finger and the way her breasts were heaving as she struggled to regulate her breathing. "You're either the best actress I've ever seen, or you're so innocent you should be locked up to keep you safe." Suddenly his pale eyes slashed upward, his gaze colliding with hers with a force that stunned her. "Don't step in front of me again. If Grant had accidentally hit you, I'd have killed him."

She opened her mouth to say something, but whatever was in her mind was forever lost when he trailed his finger downward to her breasts, stroking her cleavage, then exploring beneath the cloth of her bodice to flick over a velvet nipple. She caught a moan before it surfaced, gasping in air. With a slow, sure touch he put his hand inside her dress, cupping her in his palm with a bold caress, as sure of himself as if they weren't standing on the patio where any of fifty people could interrupt them at any time. He looked at her face, soft, drowning in sensuality, and suddenly he wondered if she looked the same whenever Preston touched her. She was either the most sensual woman he'd ever seen, or she was fantastic at faking it. At the thought of Preston, he removed his hand, leaving her dazed and floundering. "You'd better get back inside," he muttered; then he turned and walked away, disappearing into the night shadows, leaving her more alone than she'd felt since Vance's death.

Her body burned from his touch, yet she was shaking with something like a chill. It was like a fever, she thought dimly, burning hot and cold at the same time. He *was* a fever, consuming her, and she reached the horrified realization that the way she felt about him was no longer under her control. Without wanting to, she cared too much about him. She was playing Russian roulette with her emotions, but it was far too late to stop.

She stood there in the cool night for several minutes longer, then slipped quietly inside to rejoin the party. Preston came over and touched her arm gently. "Are you all right?" he asked with tender concern, and in his eyes she saw the love that he couldn't quite hide.

She was calm enough now to give him her most reassuring smile, one that made most people feel that everything was right with the world. "Yes, I'm fine."

"Grant and Mary have gone home. What'd you say to him? He looked like he was in shock when he came in, and he went straight to Mary."

She shook her head, still smiling. "Nothing, really. I just calmed him down."

His look said he didn't quite believe her, but he kissed her forehead lightly in tribute. It was inevitable that when Susan glanced around she saw Cord standing across the room, staring at her with cold, unreadable eyes, and a sad pain bloomed in her heart. He'd never trust her, she thought, and wished that it didn't mean so much to her.

Audrey Gregg found the opportunity to thank her for averting a scene, and after that Susan made her excuses and drove herself home where she fell into bed in mental exhaustion, then got up ten minutes later to restlessly pace the house. Finally she turned on the television to watch an old Jerry Lewis and Dean Martin comedy, letting their antics clear her mind. She was engrossed in the movie, chuckling to herself, when the doorbell rang. Frowning, she glanced at the clock. It was almost midnight, the witching hour.

"Who is it?" she called through the door, tying the sash of her robe tighter.

"Cord."

She unlocked the dead-bolt and opened the door to him. He straightened from his slouch against the door frame and walked inside. Her eyes dropped to the whiskey bottle he carried in his hand. A half-empty whiskey bottle.

"Are you drunk?" she asked warily.

"On my way." He smiled at her and took a drink from the bottle. "It's hard for me to get drunk, but champagne does it to me every time. Something about my chemistry. I'm just trying to finish it off with this."

"Why do you want to get drunk?" He was walking toward the den, and she followed him automatically. If he was drunk, or even high, he was certainly handling it well. His walk was steady, his speech clear. He sat down on the couch and stretched his long legs out before him, sighing as his muscles relaxed. Susan went over to the television and switched it off in the middle of a Jerry Lewis pratfall.

She repeated her question. "Why do you want to get drunk?"

"It just seems like the thing to do. A sort of tribute to the past."

"So you lift a glass...excuse me, a bottle...to auld lang syne."

"That's right." He drank again, then set the bottle down with a thud and pinned her with his glittering eyes. "Why did you have to get between us? I wanted to hit him. My God, how I wanted to hit him!"

"Another tribute to the past?" she asked sharply.

"To Judith," he corrected, smiling a little. "Do you know what he said? He came up to me and said, 'So the little whore didn't stay with you, either.' I should've broken his neck on the spot."

Susan hadn't heard the name before, but she knew that Judith had been Grant's first wife, the woman caught in bed with Cord. She sat down beside him and folded her robe around her legs, waiting. Her attitude was calm, her entire attention focused on him. People often talked to her, telling her things that they'd never tell anyone else, without really understanding what it was about her that inspired such trust. Susan didn't understand it herself, unless it was that she truly listened.

He leaned his head back, and his eyelids drooped to half-mast. "She was pure fire," he said softly. "A total mismatch for Grant Keller. She had red hair and slanted green eyes, just like a cat's. She sparkled. She liked to laugh and dance and have a good time, do all of the things that Grant was too stodgy to enjoy. He wasn't the type to go skinny-dipping at night, or dance in the streets during Mardi Gras. But, as far as I know, she was entirely faithful to him." He felt silent, staring into the past.

When several moments had passed, Susan prompted him. "Until you."

He glanced up and gave her a wry look that held a curious overtone of pain and guilt. "Until she met me," he agreed harshly. With a deft movement he seized the bottle and tipped it to his mouth. She watched in amazed fascination as his strong throat worked, and when he set the bottle down it was empty. He looked at it savagely. "There wasn't enough."

Warily, she wondered if he would still be able to say that when his body began to absorb the alcohol he'd just consumed, if he would be able to say anything at all.

A fine sheen of perspiration had broken out on his face, and he wiped it away with the back of his hand. "We'd been having an affair for almost a year before we were caught." His voice was gruff, strained. "I'd asked her over and over to divorce Grant, leave with me, but beneath all of that flash, Judith was strongly conventional. Her reputation meant a lot to her, and she adored her kids. She just couldn't break all her ties. She didn't have any choice after Grant found us together."

Susan swallowed, trying not to imagine the scene. What would it do to any of the three people involved in a triangle for a husband to walk in while his wife was in bed with her lover?

"She was crucified." He heaved himself off the couch and walked restlessly around the room, and what she saw on his face frightened her. "She didn't have a friend left; her own children wouldn't speak to her after Grant threw her out of the house. My dear Aunt Imogene was the leader in ostracizing her. Preston doesn't know that I know what *he* did, because he made certain he wasn't in the group, but he organized a sort of mob scene; a group of teenage toughs danced around Judith one afternoon in the parking lot of a grocery store and called her 'Blackstone's Whore.' It sounds almost Victorian, doesn't it? I caught one of the kids that night and...ah, *persuaded* him to tell me who'd set it up. I hunted for Preston, but he flew the coop, and I couldn't find where he'd gone."

So that was why he hated Preston so fiercely! She could understand his bitterness, but still she stared at him, troubled. Couldn't he see that revenge so often had a backlash, punishing the avenger as cruelly as his victim?

His fists were knotted whitely at his sides, his lips drawn back over his teeth. Alarmed, Susan got up and went to him, putting her soft hands over his fists. He'd removed his tie, and his shirt was open at the throat, revealing the beginning curls, and for a moment she stared at them, entranced, before she jerked her thoughts away from the dangerous direction they were taking and looked upward.

"Where is she now?" she asked, having a vision of Judith in some sleazy bar somewhere, middle-aged and despairing.

"She's dead." His voice was soft now, almost gentle, as if he had to put some distance between himself and his memories. "My wife is dead, and that bastard called her a whore!"

Susan sucked in a quiet breath, shocked at what he'd just told her. His wife! "What happened?"

"They broke her spirit." He was breathing deeply, almost desperately, but his hands had unknotted, and now his fingers were twined with hers, holding her so tightly that he hurt her. His face was pulled into a grimace of pain. "We were married as soon as her divorce was final. But she was never Judith again, never the laughing, dancing woman I'd wanted so much. I wasn't enough to replace her children, her friends, and she just faded away from me."

"She had to love you, to risk all that she did," Susan said painfully.

"Yes, she loved me. She just wasn't strong enough not to have any regrets, not to let the hurt eat away at her. She came down with pneumonia, and she didn't want to fight it. She gave up, let go. And do you want to know the hell of it?" he ground out. "I didn't love her. I couldn't love her. She'd changed, and she wasn't anything like the woman I'd loved, but I stayed with her because she'd given up so much for me. Damn it, she deserved more than that! I did my best to make sure she never knew, and I hope she died thinking that I still loved her, but the feeling was long gone by then. I'm guilty, too, in what happened to Judith. As guilty as hell!"

His eyes were dry, burning like wildfire, and Susan realized that though he wasn't able to weep for his dead wife, he was about to fly apart before her. She forcibly tugged her hands away from his death grip and cupped his face in her palms, her cool, tender hands lying along his hot flesh like a benediction. His soft beard tickled her palms, and she stroked it gently. His eyes closed at her touch.

"She was a grown woman, and she made her choice when she decided to have an affair with you," she pointed out softly. "The stress was too much for her, but I can't see that it's any more your fault than it was hers." She wanted to ease his pain, do anything to take that look of suffering off his face. My God, he'd been little more than a boy, to bear so much!

He put his hands over hers and turned his face to nuzzle his lips into her left palm, then rubbed his cheek against her hand. His pent-up breath gusted out of him on a long, soft sigh, and his eyes opened.

"You're a dangerous woman," he murmured sleepily. "I didn't intend to tell you all of that."

Looking at him, Susan saw that the whiskey was hitting him hard and fast. Cautiously, she eased him back over to the couch, and he dropped heavily onto it, sighing as he relaxed. For a moment she stood indecisively, then made up her mind; he was in no condition to drive, so he would have to spend the night there. She knelt down and began removing his shoes.

"What're you doing?" he mumbled, his eyelids drooping even more.

"Taking off your shoes. I think you'd better stay here tonight, rather than risk driving home."

A faint smile quirked his lips. "What will people say?" he mocked; then his eyes closed and he sighed again, a peculiarly peaceful sound.

Susan shrugged at his question; what people would say if anyone knew he'd spent the night here was almost beyond her imagination, yet she really couldn't see that she had a choice. He was mentally and emotionally exhausted, as well as drunk, and if anyone chose to gossip about that, she couldn't stop them. She wouldn't risk his life for that. She completed her task and set his shoes neatly to one side, then swung his long legs up on the couch.

He grunted and adjusted his length to the supporting cushions, dangling one leg off the side and swinging the other one over the back of the couch. Sprawled in that boneless position, he went to sleep as quietly and easily as a child.

Susan shook her head, unable to repress a smile. He'd told her that he was a mean drunk. Looking at him as he slept so peacefully made her doubt that. She went upstairs to get a pillow and blanket, returning to drape the blanket over him and place the pillow under his head. He didn't rouse at all, even when she lifted his head.

Lying alone in her own bed, she was aware of a deep feeling of contentment at just knowing he was under the same roof. The warm aching of her body told her that she wanted more from him than just his presence; she wanted the completion of his lovemaking. She wanted to be everything to him, every dream he'd ever had, every wish he'd ever made. She wanted to ease him and comfort him, and make him forget his black past. Knowing that he stood too much alone to allow anyone to mean that much to him didn't lessen the way she felt. How odd it was that, when she loved again, she loved someone so different from herself!

Yet Vance had been different. Unlike Cord, Vance had conformed, at least on the surface, but she had always known that
Vance could have been a hard, dangerous man if anything or anyone
had threatened those he loved. Circumstances had been different for
Vance than they had for Cord, and that part of his personality had
never developed, but the potential had been there. With Vance she
had felt utterly protected, utterly loved, because she had sensed that
he would have put himself between her and anything that threatened
her, without counting the cost to himself.

The way I love Cord! she thought, shocked, her eyes wide in the
darkness. It stunned her to think that she could be stirred to violence, but when she thought of the anger that had surged through
her that night, she knew that she'd have done anything she could
have to keep Grant Keller from punching Cord. She didn't fear for
Cord; he was far too capable of taking care of himself. It was simply
that she couldn't bear the idea of him suffering the least hurt. She
would gladly have taken a punch on the jaw herself rather than let
it land on Cord.

She fell asleep quickly and woke before her alarm clock went
off. The sun coming in her window, bright and warm, told her that
it was going to be another gorgeous spring day. Humming, she took
a shower and put on fresh lacy underwear and chose a bright summer dress that reflected her rise in spirits. The pure white fabric,
with its fragile lace trim and scattering of brightly colored spring
flowers, made her feel as fresh as the new day, as full of hope. Still
humming, she went downstairs and peeked into the den, where Cord
still lay sprawled on the couch, sleeping heavily. He'd rolled over
on his stomach, and his head was turned to the back of the couch,
revealing only his tousled dark hair. Quietly she closed the door
and went to the kitchen.

Emily was already there, quietly and efficiently making breakfast.
When Susan entered, the older woman looked up with a smile.
"Who's your guest?"

"Cord Blackstone," Susan replied, returning the smile and pouring herself a cup of fresh coffee. While the coffee cooled, she got
the plates and silverware for setting the table.

"Cord Blackstone," Emily mused, her eyes softening. "My, my,
it's been a long time since I've seen that boy. He even spent a few
nights under my roof, when he was younger."

"He was drunk last night," Susan explained as she arranged the
plates on the table, absently placing the napkins and silverware just
so, moving them around by fractions of an inch until she was satisfied.

"I don't remember him as being much of a drinker, though of course that was a long time ago. I'm not saying that he couldn't put it away, but it just never seemed to affect him. My boy would be passed out, and Cord would be as steady on his feet as ever."

After pouring another cup of coffee, Susan carried it into the den and carefully placed it on the coffee table, then knelt in front of the couch. She put her hand on his blanket-covered shoulder, feeling the warmth of his flesh even through the fabric. "Cord, wake up."

She didn't have to shake him. At her touch, her voice, he rolled over, tangling himself in the blanket, and his eyelids lifted to reveal pale, glittering irises. He smiled, then yawned, stretching his arms over his head. "Good morning."

"Good morning," she replied, watching him with veiled concern. "Do you feel like having a cup of coffee?"

"H'mmmm," he said in a rumbling, early-morning voice, a noise that could have meant anything. He heaved himself into a sitting position, raking his fingers through his hair. He yawned again, then reached around her for the coffee, holding the cup to his mouth and cautiously sipping the steaming liquid. He closed his eyes as the caffeine seared its way to his stomach. "God, that's good! Do I smell bacon cooking?"

"If you think you can eat—"

He grinned, opening his eyes. "I told you, I don't have hangovers."

Susan couldn't help the laughter that bubbled out. "Yes, but you also told me that you're a mean drunk, and you weren't anything but a big pussycat! A big, *sleepy* pussycat!"

He reached out and caught her hand, his gaze on her radiant, laughing face. "It depends on my company when I'm drunk. I can be mean if I have to." He finished the coffee and set the cup down, then slid back into a reclining position, closing his eyes, her hand still held loosely in his.

She shook his shoulder with her free hand. "Don't go back to sleep! It's time for breakfast—"

Without opening his eyes he tugged on her hand, and Susan found herself on the couch with him, sprawled over him in a very undignified position. Her eyes widened to huge blue pools, and she began squirming in an effort to push her skirt down, but her efforts were hampered because her feet had somehow become tangled in the blanket and she couldn't get her legs straight.

He sucked in his breath sharply, and his hand caught in her hair, holding her still. "I'd rather have you for breakfast," he muttered huskily, his fingers exerting just enough pressure to ease her head forward slowly, an inch at a time, until he could put his mouth to hers. Susan quivered, her lips opening to his like a soft spring blossom, her mouth being filled with the coffee taste of his. Like a welcome, familiar friend, his tongue entered lazily and explored the tiny serrated edges of her teeth, the softness of her lips, the sensual curling of her tongue as it met his. His hand left her hair and moved down her back, searching out the slender curve of her spine, as slow and inexorable as the seasons.

Susan forgot about breakfast. She wound her arms around his neck, her hands clenching in his hair, meeting the open hunger of his kiss with her own. It was so sweet and good, and it was all she could ask of life, to be in his arms. She felt his hands on her body, experienced, calm hands, as they sleeked down her sides to the graceful curve of her waist, then down to the roundness of her hips. He cupped her buttocks, grasping, filling his hands with the smooth mounds and pressing her to him. The raw sexuality of his gesture left her reeling with pleasure, unable to rein in the hot sparks of desire that were shooting through her body. She was a woman, and he knew exactly what to do with her woman's body. With a few swift movements he had her skirt up, and his hands were under the material, burrowing under the elastic waistband of her panties to brand the coolness of her buttocks with the heat of his palms.

Susan moaned aloud, and the sound was taken into his mouth. He began nibbling at her flesh, his teeth catching her lower lip, the tender curve of her jaw, the delicate lobe of her ear. Her breath was rushing in and out of her lungs, her heart racing out of control. The feel of him was driving her mad, and she wanted to sink down on him in boneless need. Now he was biting at her neck, his teeth stinging her skin; then he soothed it with tiny licks of his tongue. Her hands had made fists in his hair, pulling at the thick, vital mane mindlessly. She wanted to give him everything, every part of her, blend the softness of her body with the hardness of his.

"Two minutes!" Emily sang out from the kitchen.

Susan heard the words, but they didn't make any sense to her. Cord groaned, and his hands tightened on her buttocks in momentary denial; then he reluctantly withdrew his touch from her enticing curves. "I thought a two-minute warning was only in football," he grumbled, easing her to one side.

She sat up, dazed and aching with frustration, wondering why the narcotic of his touch had been so suddenly withdrawn from her feverish, addicted flesh. He looked at her face, so soft and vulnerable in her passion, and his jaw went rigid with the effort he had to make not to reach for her again. She was too much woman to be so prim and proper, and he was becoming increasingly fascinated by just how prim and proper she wasn't. She was forbidden fruit, and probably deceitful into the bargain, but logic had nothing to do with the way he wanted her.

Susan willed herself to be calm, forcing her shaky legs to support her when she stood, forcing her voice to a deceptive evenness. "You'll probably want to wash before eating," she murmured, and showed him the way to the downstairs bathroom. "Come through to the kitchen when you're finished."

But for all her surface serenity, it was several moments after she entered the kitchen before she had collected her thoughts. After staring blankly at the small table in the breakfast alcove, set with three places, a vase of cheerful shasta daisies in the center, she was overcome by the thought that for the first time in five years she would be sharing her breakfast with a man. And not just any man! She would be eating the first meal of the day with a man who made every other man of her acquaintance pale in comparison. A quiver of desire ran through her body again, and she blushed hotly at the thought that she would have let him take her a few moments ago, sprawled on the couch like a wanton, with Emily in the kitchen. Muttering an excuse about collecting his coffee cup, which she'd left in the den, she escaped for a few minutes of necessary solitude.

She had returned with the cup and had a refill of fresh, steaming coffee sitting by his plate when Cord paused in the doorway, assaulting her senses with his size, overpowering everything in her feminine house. He had an aura of hard vitality about him, and for a moment she could only stand and stare at him helplessly. It didn't make it any better to know that he affected every woman that way; not even Imogene was immune to him, and now Emily turned to greet him, a flush of pleasure pinkening her features. "Cord Blackstone, I swear, you're even handsomer than ever!"

He searched her face for only a second, his ice blue eyes sharp; then he grinned and his white teeth flashed. "Mrs. Ferris!" Without pause, he moved across the kitchen to take her firmly in his arms and press a kiss on her flustered mouth, a warm and friendly kiss that had Susan envying Emily for even that small moment.

Emily was laughing and patting his cheek. "That beard! You look like an outlaw for sure! Sit down, sit down. I hope you still like your eggs over easy?"

"Yes, ma'am," he replied, his inbred Southern courtesy not allowing him to address her in any other manner. He seated Susan and Emily before taking his own chair, his long legs fitting under the table with difficulty, but Susan didn't mind the way their knees bumped. His presence at her breakfast table was as natural as if it were an ordinary occurrence, and the sun was shining for her after an absence of five years. She could feel Emily's glance on her, but she couldn't control the radiance of her smile.

She wasn't the only one who was smiling; Emily was clucking around Cord, chattering at him and fussing over him, and he was eating it up with a look of pleasure that told Susan it had been a long time since he'd known the subtle delight of being cherished in the small, all-important ways. Susan didn't talk much, just listened to their conversation. She learned that Cord and Emily's eldest son had been inseparable companions during their teen years, and that Cord had eaten a lot of meals that Emily had cooked. Emily brought Cord up to date on Jack's life, but Susan noticed that Cord didn't divulge any information about himself. His past was a closed book; she realized that she didn't know anything about what he'd done or where he'd been since he'd left Mississippi, not even where he'd been immediately before returning.

She hated to see the meal end, but all too soon the table had been cleared and the kitchen cleaned, the last cup of coffee drunk. She walked with him to the door, her heart beating slowly, heavily. It was either bright sunlight or the darkest shadows, she realized painfully; there was no middle ground in loving him. She stopped in the middle of the foyer, her heart in her eyes as she looked at him.

Chapter 6

His eyes were hooded and unreadable as he watched her, but his hand smoothed over her shoulder as if he couldn't prevent himself from touching her, his fingers heating the cool silk of her skin before sliding upward over her throat to cup her chin and lift her face. He hadn't said a word, but he didn't need to; the burning possession of his lips told her all she needed to know. With a silent gasp, she melted against him, her hands going up to lie along his jawline, where the silkiness of his beard tickled her palms.

He lifted his mouth and simply held her close for a moment. Susan kept her hands on his face, stroking her fingers lightly over his beard, drowning in the enjoyment of being cuddled by him. His strong, warm throat beckoned, and she stood on tiptoe to press a light kiss onto the skin above his collar. "What do you look like without a beard?" she asked dreamily, for no other reason than that her hands were on his beard and it was the first sentence that popped out.

He chuckled, a husky, male sound that rippled over her like warm water. "Like myself, I suppose. Why? Are you curious?"

"M'mmmm," she said, letting him interpret the sound as he chose. "How long have you worn a beard?"

"Just for this past winter, though I've had a moustache for several years. I was stranded for a week or so without any way of shaving, short of scraping my face with a dull knife, and I realized just how much time I wasted in scraping hair off my face when it promptly grew back, so I kept the beard."

She trailed one fingertip over his bearded chin. "Do you have a cleft chin? Or a dimple?"

Suddenly he laughed, pulling away from her. "Well, see for yourself," he teased, catching her hand and pulling her after him as he started up the stairs with a swift, leaping stride. "Where's your bathroom?"

Susan laughed too, and tried to stop him. "What're you doing? You're going too fast! I'll fall!"

He turned around and scooped her up in his arms, and kissed her so hard that her lips stung. Holding her securely against his chest, he opened doors until he found her bedroom, then walked into it and let her slide to the floor. He looked around at the completely feminine room, the lace curtains, the cream satin comforter on her bed, the delicately flowered wallpaper. His face changed, became curious, surprised. "Vance didn't sleep in here," he said. "This is a woman's room."

Susan swallowed, a little surprised at his perception. "This was our room," she admitted. "But I changed everything when he died. I couldn't sleep in here with everything the way it had been when he was alive, so I bought new furniture and had the room redone completely. Not even the carpet is the same."

"A different bed?" he asked, watching her narrowly.

Susan shivered. "Yes," she whispered. "Everything. New mattress, new sheets...everything."

"Good." The single word was a low growl of satisfaction, and his gaze was so heated that she rubbed her hands up her bare arms, feeling a little singed. He looked around and indicated a door, releasing her from his visual force field. "Is that the bathroom?"

"Yes, but why—"

"Because," he answered maddeningly, catching her hand and pulling her with him again, into the bathroom. He began unbuttoning his shirt, opening it down to his waist, then pulling the fabric free of his pants and finishing the job. He shrugged out of the shirt and handed it to her; she took it automatically, folding it over her arm.

"You aren't going to do that," she said in disbelief, having realized what he intended.

"Why not? Do you have a fresh blade for your razor? And I'll need a pair of scissors to start off."

"There's a small pair in the drawer there," she said, pointing. "Cord, wait. I wasn't thinking for you to shave off your beard."

"It'll grow back, if you don't like my naked face," he drawled, opening the drawer and taking out the scissors. "Why don't you just sit down and enjoy the show?"

Because there was nothing else to do, she closed the lid on the toilet and sat down, her eyes wide with fascination as she watched him snip the beard as short as he could get it with the scissors. He asked again for her razor, and she indicated the left-hand side of the built-in medicine cabinet. He extracted the razor, new blades, and shaving gel from the cabinet, then deftly changed blades.

He wet his face with warm water and worked the gel into a lather, covering his face with enough foamy white soap to make him look like a wicked Santa Claus. Susan almost winced when the razor sliced into his beard and left a smooth streak of skin in its path. Half of her was trembling with anticipation at seeing his face, but the other half of her hated to see the beard go; it had been so soft and silky, and made her skin tingle wherever it touched.

He went through the contortions that men put themselves through when shaving, arching his neck, tilting his head, and Susan sat spellbound. It was the first time she'd seen him without his shirt, and her eyes drifted down over his muscled torso. She'd known he was strong, but now she saw the layered muscles that covered him, and her mouth went dry. His broad shoulders gleamed under the light, the skin as taut and supple as a young boy's. With every movement he made the muscles in his back bunched and rippled, then relaxed, flexing in an endless ballet that riveted her attention. His spine ran in a deep hollow down the center of his back, inviting inquisitive fingers to stroke and probe.

Susan noticed that the rhythm of her breathing had been broken, and she wrenched her gaze away from his back. Determinedly she again looked in the mirror at the reflection of his face, and the complete concentration she saw there started an ache deep inside her. That frown was so completely male, and it had been so long since she'd seen it. Vance had frowned just like that. For five years her life had lacked something because she hadn't been able to sit in the bathroom and watch her man shave; a simple pleasure, but one of the lasting ones. Cord was giving her that pleasure again, as he had given her his presence at breakfast, and somehow the simple act of watching him shave was seducing her more completely than his heated kisses could have done.

Slowly her gaze dipped, and she inspected his mirrored image. His chest was covered by a triangle of black curls that looked as incredibly soft as his beard had been; she clenched her hands to prevent them from reaching out to touch him and verify the texture. His nipples were flat circles, small and dark, with tiny points in the center of them, and she wanted to put her mouth to them. The curve of his rib cage was laced by bands of muscle, and the solid wall of his abdomen rippled with power. The tiny ringlets of hair on his chest became a straight and silky line that ran down the middle of his stomach and disappeared into the waistband of his pants. He raised his arms and his torso stretched, giving her a glimpse of his taut, shallow navel, and the thin scar that began on the right side of it, angling down out of sight.

Susan almost strangled, and this time she couldn't stop her hands; they flew out, touching the scar, tracing it lightly. Now her fevered gaze roamed over him again, anxiously, and she found other marks of other battles. A small, silvered, puckered scar on his right shoulder had to be from a gunshot wound, and her spine prickled with fear for him. Another line ran from under his left breast, around under his arm, and ended below his left shoulderblade. Obviously he hadn't always ducked in time.

Suddenly she noticed that he was very still under her hands, and she let them fall to her side, swiftly looking away from him. She was aware of his slow movements as he splashed the remnants of lather from his face and patted it dry, but she couldn't look directly at him.

"There's nothing wrong with touching me," he growled harshly, dropping his words into the sudden canyon of silence. "Why did you stop?"

She swallowed. "I was afraid you'd think I was prying. My God!" she burst out rawly. "What happened to you? All those scars..."

He gave a short, mirthless laugh. "Just a lot of hard living" he answered obliquely. "I was tossed off the lap of luxury a long time ago."

She glanced up at the harshness of his tone, and for the first time since he'd finished shaving, she saw his face. Her mouth went dry again.

She'd never before seen anyone who looked as hard and cool as he did. He'd left his moustache, thank God; she couldn't imagine his face without it. His jaw was lean and clearly cut, his chin square and impossibly stubborn. His lower lip had taken on a fullness that she hadn't noticed before, a new sensuality. He lacked the classic perfection of handsomeness, but he had the face of a warrior, a man who was willing to fight for what he wanted, a man who laughed at danger. The hard recklessness of him was more apparent now, as if he'd torn aside a veil that had hidden him from view. She'd thought that his beard had made him look like more of a desperado than he really was; now she realized that the reverse had been true. The beard had disguised the ruthlessness of his face.

He was looking down at her with mockery in his eyes, as if he

had known that the beard had been a camouflage. The years and
the mileage were etched on that hard, slightly battered countenance,
but she wasn't repelled by it; she was drawn, like an animal from
the depths of a cold night to crouch by the warmth of a fire. In a
fleeting moment of despair, knowing herself lost, she realized that
the more attractive the lure, the higher the risk, and she would be
risking her entire way of life if she allied herself with him. She was
by nature cautious and reserved, yet as she stood looking at him in
silence, she accepted that risk; for her heart, she would disregard
the past and the future, and count the reward well worth the danger.
With an inarticulate murmur, she lifted her arms to him.

An odd look of strain tightened his feature; then with a harsh,
wordless sound, he picked her up and carried her into the bedroom,
lying down on the bed with her still in his arms, twisting until he
was half on top of her. His left hand buried itself in her hair, holding
her head still, and his mouth came down to imprint his possession
on hers. She parted her lips willingly to the demanding thrust of his
tongue, giving a tiny sigh of bliss as she curled herself against him,
twining her arms around his neck and shoulders, pressing her
breasts into the hard, warm plane of his chest. She kissed him with
fire and delicacy, offering herself to him with gentle simplicity. He
lifted his mouth a fraction of an inch from hers, his breath coming
in fast, irregular gulps. "I think...I think I'm going to lose my head
over you," he muttered. "Why couldn't you be what I'd expected?"

Before Susan could ask what he meant, before it even occurred
to her to wonder at it, his mouth was on hers again, and his arms
were tightening about her with a force that would have bruised her
if she hadn't been boneless with need. Everything combined to
overwhelm her senses. She was aware, with every pore of her body,
of the warm fragrance of the new day, the slight breeze drifting in
the open window, the sweet trilling of the birds as they darted about
among the huge trees; then there was nothing, nothing but the touch
of his hands and mouth.

He unzipped her dress, pulling it down to bare her breasts to him,
and he took them hungrily, first with his knowing hands, then with
the furnace of his mouth. She cried out as the strong suckling sent
shock waves of primitive pleasure crashing along her nerves, and
she arched into his hard frame.

The phone beside the bed began ringing, and he lifted his head,
muttering a violent curse under his breath, then settled himself more
fully on her, his muscular legs parting hers and making a cradle for
him. Her nipples were buried in the curly hair of his chest, her

hands clutching urgently at him; she wanted all the layers of clothing between them gone, but she hated to release him long enough to remove them. She twisted against him, wanting more, more...

"Susan! Telephone!"

Emily's voice wafted up the stairs, startling them as much as if a bucket of cold water had been dashed over them. Susan drew a sobbing breath, unable to answer. No, no! Why now?

"Susan?" Emily called, raising her voice in question.

She bit her lip, then managed to call out, "Yes, I'll get it. Thanks, Emily." Her voice didn't even sound like her own, but Emily must have been satisfied.

Cord rolled off of her with a sigh. "Go ahead, answer it," he said gruffly. "She'll be up here checking on you if you don't." He lifted the receiver and handed it to her, stretching the cord across his chest, then relaxing against the pillows.

Susan wet her lips, and took a deep breath to steady herself. "Hello."

"Hello, dear," came Imogene's brisk voice. "I wanted to congratulate you on your quick thinking last night. I knew you wouldn't let us down."

Susan frowned in puzzlement, her thoughts still too fogged by desire for her to understand what Imogene was saying. How could she think when she was lying half on Cord's chest, his heady scent rising to her nostrils like an aphrodisiac. "I'm sorry, I don't understand. What do you mean?"

"Why, playing up to Cord," Imogene replied impatiently. "Remember, you have just as much to lose in this as we do. String him along and find out all you can. Last night was a brilliant move—"

Susan darted a quick, agonized look at Cord, and her blood congealed in her veins when she saw the iciness of his eyes and realized that he'd heard every word; how could he not, when she was practically on top of him? A cold, cruel smile curved his mouth as he gently took the telephone receiver from her nerveless fingers and cradled it on his shoulder. "You jumped the gun on the congratulations, Aunt Imogene," he purred with silken menace. "That was a tactical error; you should've let Susan call you when the coast was clear."

With a deliberate movement he dropped the receiver back onto the hook, then turned back to her. The smile on his face was deadly, and she could do nothing but wait, her breath halted, her heart stopped.

"My God, you're lovely," he murmured, still smiling, his eyes dropping to her bare, creamy breasts. "And so willing to give me anything I want, aren't you? No wonder you let me talk so much last night; did you think I'd spill my guts to you, tell you everything I'd planned?''

A fine trembling invaded her limbs. ''No,'' she whispered. ''You needed to talk; I was available.''

She was so close to him that she could see his pupils dilate, the inner blackness expanding until only a thin circle of blue remained. ''Are you available?'' he drawled, deliberately covering her breast with his hand. ''Are you as available for me as you are for Preston?''

She felt as if he'd kicked her, and she tried to jerk away, but he locked his other arm around her and held her to him. His fingers kneaded her soft flesh with a slow precision that frightened her, and tears stung her eyes. ''I'm not available for Preston! Except as a…a friend. I'm not a sexual release valve for anyone!'' She could feel her cheeks burning with mortification, and she tried to pull away again, an attempt that was useless against his effortless strength.

''Sure you're not,'' he crooned. ''That's why you're on this bed with me. You offered yourself to me, darling, for a little fun and games. But dear Aunt Imogene, bless her nosy soul, couldn't stay off the phone, and she blew it for you. Now what are you going to do?''

''It's not like that!'' she cried desperately, pleading with him to understand. ''Imogene wanted me to sleep with you so I could try to find out what you're planning to do, but I refused—''

He laughed, a low, harsh sound of disbelief. ''It really looks like you refused,'' he taunted, stroking her breast. He adjusted her squirming body to his in a way that branded her with his male heat. ''For once, she had an idea that I like. We shouldn't let a little phone call interrupt us—''

''No!'' She wedged her arms between them and braced her hands on his chest, pushing against him in a useless effort to create more of a space between them. It took a tremendous effort to prevent herself from bursting into tears, but she refused to give in to that weakness and blinked her eyes fiercely.

''Why not? You'd enjoy being—''

''Used?'' she broke in bitterly.

''Now, darling, I wasn't going to be crude. I was going to say that you'd enjoy being with a man again, because I don't count Preston as a man. What do you say? I promise that when I…*use*… you, I won't leave you unsatisfied.''

''Stop it!'' she almost shouted, horrified at what had happened, at how swiftly something that had been so *right* had deteriorated into something so ugly. "I've never had sex with Preston. Let go of me!"

He laughed and recaptured her as she almost wriggled free, his hand going to her buttocks and cupping them, pressing her into him. "Settle down," he advised, still laughing, though how he could laugh when she felt as if someone had torn her heart out was more than she could understand. "I'm not going to attack you. Though, my God, woman, if you don't stop squirming against me like that, I may change my mind!"

She stilled. After a long moment she said rawly, "Please, let me get up."

With a mocking lift of his eyebrows, he opened his arms and released her. She sat up away from him, fumbling with her dress, trying to straighten the fabric over her breasts. He got up from the bed and sauntered into the bathroom, returning with his shirt. He pulled it on and buttoned it, then unzipped his pants to tuck the shirttail in, standing nonchalantly before her. Susan sat in frozen horror, too miserable to do anything but stare numbly at him.

"Don't look so unhappy, darling," he advised in a mockery of tenderness. "I probably wouldn't have told you anything, anyway." He strolled over to where she sat on the bed and leaned down over her, his weight braced on his arms. Briefly, firmly, he kissed her, a little rough in his anger. When he straightened, a tiny fire was burning in his eyes. "Pity she couldn't have waited another half hour before she called," he said, touching her cheek with his finger. "See you around." With that nonchalant goodbye he was gone, and she sat in paralyzed agony, listening to his sure steps going down the stairs. Then there was the sound of the door, and a moment later the throaty roar of a powerful, well-tuned engine.

After a long time she managed to slide stiffly off the bed, but that was all she could force her body to do. She leaned against the wall, her eyes closed, while she tried to come to terms with what had happened. She almost hated Imogene for coming between her and Cord, even though it had been unintentional. No, if Imogene had known that Cord had been there, she wouldn't have done anything to rock the boat! She simply couldn't believe that Susan would balk at prostituting herself for the good of the Blackstones, namely Imogene herself and Preston. To her mind, if Susan had anything to do with Cord, it was based on ulterior motives.

It was particularly painful because, for a little while, he had seemed to be lowering his formidable barriers just a bit. Their kisses had been building a frail bridge of understanding between them, until Imogene's heavy touch had shattered it. For a few hours Susan had been on the verge of an ecstasy so deep and powerful, so wide in scope, that she had difficulty in believing the richness that had hovered just beyond her fingertips.

Black despair engulfed her, a depression so deep that only Vance's death compared to it. After Vance's burial, when she had been forced to admit to herself that there was no miracle that would restore him to her, for a time it had seemed that there was nothing worthwhile left in her life. If it had been possible, she would have died quietly in her sleep during that time, so bitter and helpless had she felt at the irrevocable chasm of death. Time had healed her, time and the gentle steel of her own nature, but she hadn't regained the utter delight in being alive, capable of experiencing pleasure again, until Cord had walked into her life and touched her with his hard fingers, bringing fires that had been banked for five years back into full blaze.

It was an hour before spirit began to return to her numbed brain. She had learned at Vance's death that even the most precious life could be extinguished, and she had also learned that death was final. But she was very much alive, and so was Cord. She couldn't let him just walk away from her like that! If you truly loved someone, then you had to be willing to fight for them, and she was willing to fight the entire world if need be. Thankfully, it wasn't necessary that she take on the world, but the one stubborn, dangerous man she had to face was bad enough. If it hadn't been so necessary to her life that she make him listen, she would never have been able to summon the courage. She could face down almost anyone, but Cord could intimidate the devil himself.

Without giving herself time to think, because if she paused, she'd stop altogether, she told Emily that she'd be gone for the rest of the day, then grabbed her purse and ran to the car. She broke the speed limit getting to the cabin, not daring to rehearse what she would say to him, but knowing that she had to make him listen.

She thundered across the old bridge over Jubilee Creek, and the car fishtailed when she slung it around the long, sweeping curve of the incline going up to the gentle rise where the cabin sat. A bright red Blazer with enormous tires was parked at the front steps, and she pulled up behind it, scattering rocks and dust. Before the wheels had stopped rolling, she had the door open and was out of the car, bounding up the steps in a very unladylike manner. She had pounded on the door twice with her fist when a piercing whistle reached her ears, and she spun around. Cord was standing down at the creek, about a hundred yards away. He lifted his arm, beckoning her to come to him, and she was in too much of a hurry to use the steps; she jumped off the end of the porch and headed down the slope at a fast walk.

He went back to work, his powerful arms swinging a slingblade with easy rhythm, sending showers of rioting greenery flying into the air as he sliced through a section of heavy overgrowth. Her pace slowed as she approached, and when she reached him she stood to one side, well out of the way of the slicing blade. He stopped after a moment, leaning on the handle and giving her an unreadable glance, a little smile pulling at his lips. "The honeysuckle is out of hand," he drawled, wiping his forearm across his sweaty face. "If we ever decide to conquer the world, all we have to do is ship out some cuttings of honeysuckle and kudzu, then wait a year. Everyone else would be so worn out from fighting the vines that we could just waltz in."

She smiled at the whimsy, but to Southern farmers, it wasn't that much of an exaggeration. Now that she was standing before him, she couldn't think of anything to say; for the moment, it was enough to simply be there, staring at him, drinking in the sight of this magnificent masculinity. He was glistening with sweat, his dark hair wet and stuck to his skull, and he'd twisted a white handkerchief into a band that he'd tied around his forehead to keep the sweat out of his eyes. His shirt had been discarded and was lying on the ground; his jeans were dirty. None of that mattered. He could have been wearing a tuxedo, and he wouldn't have looked any better to her.

When she didn't say anything, he tilted his head in question, a devilish gleam entering his eyes. "Did you come here for a reason?"

She swallowed, trying to conquer her voice "Yes. I came to make you listen to me."

"I'm listening, honey, but you're not saying much."

She searched for the perfect words to use, the ones that would make him believe her, but with a sinking heart she knew that there weren't any. He was still watching her in amusement, letting her squirm, and suddenly it was unbearable. She blurted out, "When Imogene asked me to spy on you, I refused, and she's not used to anyone telling her no. Someone must have told her what happened last night, and she assumed that I'd changed my mind. I haven't."

He laughed aloud and shook his head in amazement. "So what were you doing on that bed with me? My ego isn't so big that I'll fall for the line that you just have the hots for me. I know your reputation, lady, and it's the straight and narrow all the way, as far as anyone knows. I have my doubts about Preston—"

"Shut up!" she cried, knotting her hands into fists. "I've told you and told you—"

"I know," he interrupted wearily. "You haven't slept with Preston."

"It's the truth!"

"He's in love with you."

Startled by his perception, she admitted, "Yes. But I didn't know until a few days ago. That doesn't change anything. I'm very fond of Preston, but I'm not in love with him; there's never been anything sexual between us."

"Okay, say there's nothing between you," he attacked sharply, changing positions. "That means there's been no one in your life, romantically speaking, since Vance died, which makes it just that much more unlikely for you to suddenly take up with me. There has to be a reason."

Susan turned pale. "There is. When I met you, I realized that I'm not dead. I've mourned Vance for five years, but he's never coming back, and I'm very much alive. You make me *feel* things again. I'm not like you; I've never been brave or adventurous, or taken a gamble on anything, but when I'm with you I feel just a little braver, a little more free. I want to be with you for *me,* not for Imogene or Preston or any amount of money."

His eyes had darkened as he listened to her, and now he stared at her for a long, taut moment taking in the tension of her slim figure, the almost desperate earnestness in her eyes, eyes of such a dark blue that they looked like the deep Pacific. Finally he untied the handkerchief from his forehead and began using the square of cloth to wipe the rivulets of sweat from his face and arms, then rubbing it across his chest. He was silent for so long that Susan could bear it no longer, and she grabbed his arm. "It's very simple," she said desperately. "All you have to do is not tell me *anything!* Since you're forewarned, how can I possibly find out anything? How can I possibly be using you?"

He sighed, shaking his head. "Susan," he finally said, his voice so gentle that she shivered at the sound of it, "you said it yourself: We're nothing alike. I've lived a hard life, and it hasn't always been on the right side of the law. You look as if you've been carried around all of your life on a satin pillow. If you think you want pretty words and pretty flowers and hand-holding in the moonlight, you'd better find some other man. I'm not satisfied with hand-holding."

She shivered again, and her lashes drooped to veil her eyes in a sultry, passion-laden manner. "I know," she whispered.

"Do you?" He moved closer to her, so close that the heady scent of his hot, sweaty body enveloped her, tantalizing her senses. "Do you really know what you're asking for?" His hands closed on her waist, his fingers biting into her soft flesh. "I'm not much on genteel gropings in the dark, on schedule every Saturday night. I'm a lot rawer than that, and a lot hungrier. I want to take your clothes off and taste you all over," he rasped, hauling her close to him so that their bodies touched. A fire alarm of pleasure began clanging inside her, and she let herself flow up against him like a tide rushing to shore. "I want to take your nipples in my mouth and suck them until they're hard and aching for more. I want to feel your legs wrapped around my back, and I want to go so deeply into you that I can't tell where I stop and you begin. That's what I want right now, and what I've wanted every time I've seen you. And if that's not what you want, too, you'd better run, because you're about to get it."

Susan sighed in delirium. Her body was alive, aching, throbbing, wanting to do those things he'd described, and more. She wanted to give her heart to him, and with it, the soft, burning ardor of her body. She couldn't give him the words; she sensed that he didn't want love, that he'd feel burdened if she admitted that she loved him, so she would bite the words back and instead content herself with the offering of her body.

"I'm not running," she said into the damp refuge of his neck.

"Maybe you should," he said roughly, releasing her. "But it's too late for that. You had your chance, honey. My sense of honor doesn't go that deep!" He leaned down and lifted her into his arms, his brawny back and shoulders taking her slight weight easily. He began walking up the slope with a determined stride, and when Susan dared to slant a quick look up at his face, she quivered at the fierceness of his expression. The thought of the risk she was about to take in giving herself to him made her feel faint with apprehension, and she turned her face into his warm shoulder. Only one man had made love to her in her life, and that with love, with deep tenderness. Cord didn't trust her; he would take her in lust but not in love, and she didn't know if she was strong enough to handle that. On the other hand, she knew beyond doubt that she had to try to reach him, that she had to try to show him with the gentle offering of herself that she wasn't a treacherous or mercenary person. She had to show him what love was, because he'd never known it.

Her sheltered life had not prepared her for this, but neither had it prepared her for the reality of her husband dying in her arms, with his blood soaking through her clothing. Since Vance's death, she had held a small part of herself sealed off from the world, protected against hurt, allowing even those closest to her only the shallowest portion of her love. The seal had remained intact until she'd met Cord. He had awakened her to a deeper knowledge of herself, an awareness that she wasn't such a creature of convention as she'd always thought. She wasn't as wild as Cord, as free, nor had she ever been a gambler, but she was willing to take a chance that she could make him care for her. She *had* to take that chance. There were many things she didn't know about him, but that made no difference to the essence of her, the combined power of heart and soul and body, which had recognized him on sight as the mate of her lifetime, the one man who could mean more to her than anyone else could even begin to imagine. She had loved Vance, loved him deeply, and yet that emotion now seemed as mild when compared to the way she felt about Cord as a light spring shower compared to the thunder and fury of a towering electrical storm. She would gladly follow this man anywhere on earth that he wanted to go, because there was no physical discomfort that could rival the hell she would endure if deprived of his presence.

His long legs ate up the distance as he moved up the slope, showing no sign that her weight in his arms was hampering him in the slightest. He leaped up the steps and shouldered the cabin door open, then turned sideways to enter with her. His boot heel collided with the door and sent it slamming back to the frame. He carried her straight through to the bedroom and set her on her feet, his narrowed eyes on her pale, strained face. A cool, cynical smile touched his face as he dropped to the bed and sprawled on its surface, dragging a pillow over to crumple it into a ball which he placed behind his dark head. He crossed his booted feet and let his gaze rake over her. "All right," he drawled. "Strip."

Susan put out a hand to steady herself as she swayed. The room was dipping crazily, and a sudden roaring in her ears made her think that she might not have heard him correctly. "What?" she asked soundlessly, then swallowed and tried it again. The second time, her voice was a weak croak.

In an insultingly casual manner, he eyed her breasts. "Strip. Take your clothes off. Since you're so all-fired anxious to try me out in the sack, I'm giving you the chance. You may have been planning on a quick flip of your skirt, but what I have in mind will take longer than that."

He didn't think she'd do it. She suddenly realized that as she stood there trying to regulate her breathing. He hadn't believed anything she'd said. He probably thought that all he had to do was push her a little and she'd run crying back to Preston. What had made him so wary that he couldn't trust anyone?

Slowly, with trembling fingers, she reached behind herself and tried to grasp the zipper of her dress. She found the tiny tab, but couldn't manage to hold it. After it slipped out of her jerky fingers for the third time, she took a deep breath and let her arms drop, turning her back to him and sitting down on the edge of the bed beside him. "I can't manage my zipper," she said thinly. "Would you do it for me, please?" For a long, silent moment, he didn't move, and she felt his eyes boring into her back. Then the mattress shifted, and he touched the zipper. Slowly, like thickened molasses, the zipper moved down, and her dress loosened. When he released the tab, she stood up before she lost her nerve and turned to face him again.

His face was expressionless, his black lashes dropping to shield anything his eyes might have told her. An insidious quiver began in her legs and spread upward, turning her insides to jelly. She stepped out of her sandals and caught the straps of her sundress, dropping them off her shoulders and pulling her arms out of them. The cloth dropped to her waist, baring her breasts. She hadn't worn a bra with her little-nothing dress, and a fragrant spring breeze wafted in the open window, touching the pale brown of her small nipples and puckering them into soft, succulent buds. Though Cord hadn't moved, she sensed the tension that pervaded every muscle of his body. Still his eyes were veiled, but she felt them on her, visually touching the creamy slopes that she offered to him. Her breasts were high and firm, deliciously rounded, and she was suddenly, fiercely glad that her woman's body could entice him.

Deep inside her, welling up from the bottomless reservoir of her love, was the inborn need to belong to him. She was woman, and he was man. She was *his* woman, in any way he wanted her, if only he'd take her. There was nothing else as important to her as the time she had with him; that time might be fleeting, and she would have to carefully garner every precious second of it. Circumstances might separate them, or he might leave without notice, his restless spirit leading him on. He'd spent too many years wandering the dark corners of the earth to ever completely settle in one place. For whatever time she had with him, she would take each day as it came, enjoy it totally, as if that were all there was, all there would ever be. She couldn't set a limit on how much of herself she would give to him. She had to give him everything, every ounce of her love.

With precise, graceful movements she pushed the dress down

over her hips and dropped it into a billowy puddle around her feet. She stepped out of it, her body completely bare to him now except for her lace panties, letting him see her sleek, shapely legs, her flat tummy and rounded hips, the graceful curve of her waist. She stood motionless before him, letting him look all he wanted, sensing the coiling need that was beginning to throb through his body.

If time still existed, she wasn't aware of it. It could have been seconds or minutes that she stood there, waiting, hearing nothing but the cheerful songs of the birds in the trees outside the window, the drone of insects. When he didn't move, she slid her fingers inside the waistband of her panties and began sliding them down over her hips, baring the final mystery of her womanhood. Her heart was slamming so wildly in her chest that her ribs hurt. What if he didn't do anything? What if he just lay there and looked, then got up and walked out? She thought she'd die on the spot if that happened. Taking a deep, wavering breath, she pushed the panties down her thighs and dropped them to the floor.

Perhaps he hadn't meant for her to realize his reaction, but she heard the audible intake of his breath, and that gave her the courage to continue standing there before him, vulnerable in a way only another woman could understand. By offering herself this way she was exhibiting a deep, enormous trust in him as a human being, taking it on faith that even though he possessed the strength to hurt her badly, if he were cruel or careless, he would instead treat her tender flesh and heart with the care they deserved. She stood motionless in the bright morning sun, yet she was a statue with warm, supple skin, and the coursing warmth of her life's blood gave her a faint, rosy glow. Her eyes were deep pools of midnight blue, beckoning him, enticing him to enter the world of sensuality and love that was waiting for him.

He was still stretched out on the bed, but every muscle in his body was taut, the tight fabric of his jeans doing more to outline his arousal than conceal it. Burning color had flared on his high, chiseled cheekbones, and his tongue edged along his lower lip in an unconscious move, as if he were already tasting her sweetness. Finally he began to move, sitting up in slow motion, his eyes never leaving her body, glittering hotly as he explored every inch of her with visual hunger. He reached down to take off his boots and socks, tossing them to the side, where the boots landed with muffled thuds. Then he stood, unfolding his tall frame to tower over her. All moisture left her mouth. Without her shoes, she was suddenly aware of the differences in their sizes, their strength, the very shape and texture of their bodies. He was male, powerful, and aggressive.

She was completely feminine, soft and satiny, yet capable of taking all of his aggression and power and turning it into an expression of love. She hoped, oh, how she hoped!

His lean hands were pulling at his belt buckle, releasing it and stripping the belt free of his pants with one firm tug. When he moved to unsnap his jeans, Susan came to life and reached out to cover his hands with hers. "Let me," she whispered. His arms fell to his sides, and he sucked in another deep, shuddering breath.

Slowly, drawing the time and the moment out, she released the snap and slid down the zipper, her tender hands moving inside the opened garment to trace his hipbones, explore the tight little cavity of his navel, then move around to palm the hard, taut roundness of his buttocks. Gently she ran her hands down his thighs, taking the jeans with her, delighted as she realized that he wore no underwear. When the jeans were below his knees, he moved suddenly, as if his patience had abruptly worn out. He stepped out of the entangling denim and kicked it away, seizing her simultaneously and falling back on the bed with her in his arms, cradling her against his chest.

Like a willing sacrifice on his sensual altar, she entwined her arms around his muscled neck and lifted her lips to his, her body writhing against him in a slow, delicate dance. His mouth closed over hers with hard, fierce possession, and he pulled her more fully into him, mingling his legs with her as he mingled his breath with hers, his tongue with hers, his taste with hers. The tartness of desire lay like a heady wine on his lips, and she sipped it eagerly. She was alive, soaring, her entire existence focused on him and exulting in the intensity of her being. She trembled in his arms, her entire body quaking.

He released her mouth to slide his lips like a burning brand along the curve of her jaw, then down the soft column of her neck. As if he'd discovered a rare treasure, he pressed his face into the tender hollow of her shoulder. His tongue darted out and tasted her, and Susan shivered in blind delight, her fingers lacing into his hair and pressing him to her.

"My God," he muttered thickly, nipping at her flesh with his sharp white teeth, leaving little stinging points of sensation that stopped short of pain and instead raised her internal temperature by several degrees. "You make me crazy. Sometimes I think I'd kill to get to you, even knowing that Preston has had you."

For a moment pain so intense that it blinded her tore at her insides, and she inhaled sharply. Then she managed to push it away, accepting that she would have to prove to him that he could trust her, in all things. She moved against him in a way that wrenched a groan from his lips. With a lithe, powerful twist of his body, he rolled and placed himself above her, his muscled legs controlling hers.

With one shaking finger, he outlined the small circles of her nipples, watching as the velvet flesh puckered into succulent buds. "Sweet Susan," he breathed, and lowered his head to offer homage with his mouth. Like fire, his lips burned over the soft mounds of her breasts, and he teased the quivering slopes with his devilish tongue. Susan moaned, a sound unnoticed except perhaps by the deeper, primal instincts of the man who bent over her. Her insides were molten, her body liquid with the flow of desires that urged her relentlessly onward. He suckled strongly at her breasts, and the moan became whimpers, little sounds of pleading.

But he lingered over her, as if determined to enjoy everything about her. With hands and mouth he explored her, discovering the different textures and tastes of her body, searching out her most sensitive places with probing fingers and a curious tongue. She writhed under his touch, her hips undulating as she arched higher and higher toward the sun, her skin breathing the perfume of passion. She cried out in hoarse, mindless reaction when his hand moved with sure, heartstopping intimacy to discover the degree of her readiness, and he sucked in a deep breath. "Now," he said with fierce intent, his hand moving her thighs apart, opening her legs to him. Susan obeyed the demanding touch instantly, unable even to think of not doing so, opening herself to him like a vulnerable flower, chaining him with her trust more surely than he could chain her with his strength.

He moved over her, his eyes feverish with desire, his strong body shaking as he covered her softness with the hard power of his own frame. He slid his hands under her, cradling the satin curves of her buttocks in his palms and lifting her up to his thrust. Susan whimpered softly, wanting him so much that she was aching with it, and she arched invitingly. He took her with a powerful surge that drove him deeply into her, sheathing himself completely in the searing velvet of her flesh. The whimpers in Susan's throat caught as a shock wave thundered through her body, her chaste body that hadn't known a man's passion since Vance's death. A reflexive cry of pain slipped from her lips, and her fingers dug into his biceps, feeling them bulge with the strain as he reached desperately for control.

He hung over her, staring down at her with astonishment freezing his expression. "My God," he muttered hoarsely.

Her lips were parted, her breath moving swiftly in and out between them, as her body struggled to accept him, adjust to him.

"Cord?" she gasped, asking for reassurance, a little frightened with an instinctive, feminine fear.

He held himself very still. "Do you want me to stop?" he asked. "I don't want to hurt you."

"No, no! Don't stop! Please, don't stop." The words turned into a moan as they trailed out of her mouth. She felt as if she would die if he left her now, as if a vital part of her would be torn away. But he didn't pull away; he lay motionless atop her until the tension had eased out of her body and he felt the inner relaxation, until she began to move under him with little instinctive undulations of her hips. She clung to him, her arms around his neck, her legs locked around his waist when at last he began to answer her movements with his own. He was slow and gentle, taking incredible care of her, making certain that she was with him every step of the way as he pushed his body toward satisfaction. His hands and mouth buried her conscious thought under a flurry of hot caresses that intensified the fire in her loins, pushing her out of control, past any semblance of serenity or decorum. In his arms she wasn't the quiet, demure Susan Blackstone; she was a wild thing, hot and demanding, concerned only with the riptides of pleasure that were sucking her out to sea. She clutched at him with damp, desperate hands, and her heels dug into his back, his buttocks, the backs of his thighs. He was no longer gentle, but driven by the same demons that drove her, pounding into her with a wild power that had only one goal.

"I can't get enough of you," he gritted, his teeth clenched. It was a cry that erupted without conscious thought, and he heard it but scarcely realized that he'd said it. But it was true; he couldn't get enough of her. He couldn't get deeply enough into her to satisfy the burning need that was torturing him; he wanted to blend his flesh with hers until the lines of separateness faded and he absorbed her into himself. He wanted to bury himself so deeply within her that she could never get him out, that her body, the very cells of her flesh, would always have the imprint of his possession.

While he was branding her with his touch, Susan branded him with hers. She'd never realized how incomplete she felt until this moment when she knew the shattering satisfaction of being whole. She tried with her hands, her mouth, the undulant caress of her body, to show him how much she loved him, giving him everything she had to give, declaring her love with every movement, mingling herself with him in an act of love that transcended the physical.

There, on a sun-washed bed, she gave her heart to an outlaw and found a heaven that she hadn't known existed.

In the silent aftermath of passion they lay together with their bodies slowly cooling, their pulses gradually resuming a normal rate. Time drifted past, and still they lay together, reluctant to move and break the spell, reluctant to face the moment when their flesh would no longer be joined. Her fingers threaded through the tousled softness of his dark hair, stroking gently, and he settled his full weight on her with an almost soundless sigh of contentment. Susan stared at the ceiling, so happy that she felt she might fly into a million little pieces of ecstasy. Her lips trembled abruptly, and the image of the rough, timbered ceiling blurred. She bit her lip to stifle the sob that rose in her throat and demanded voicing, but she couldn't prevent the identical tracks of moisture that ran out of the corners of her eyes and disappeared into the hair at her temples. He was relaxing into sleep and she tried to keep from disturbing him; it was silly to cry because the most wonderful thing in her life had just happened to her!

But he was a man who had stayed alive by paying attention to his senses and gut instincts, and perhaps he felt the fine degree of tension in her body. His head lifted abruptly, and he surveyed her brimming eyes with sharp attention. He levered himself up on one elbow and lifted his hand to wipe at the tears with his thumb, the callused pad rasping across the sensitive skin of her temples. He was frowning, the dark, level brows lowered over narrowed eyes that searched her delicate features so intently that she felt he could see inside her mind.

"Is it because I hurt you?" he rumbled.

Quickly she shook her head and tried to give him a smile, but the stretching of her lips wobbled out of control and vanished. "No. You didn't really hurt me. It was only at first...I wasn't expecting..." She couldn't get the words out, and she swallowed, forcing her will on her voice. "It was just so...so special." Another tear escaped her eye.

He caught that one with his lips, pressing an openmouthed kiss to her temple and darting his tongue out to cleanse the salty liquid from her skin. "Susan," he breathed almost inaudibly, saying her name as if he could taste it, as if he savored the sound of it. "I want you again."

Golden sunlight washed the room with brightness, allowing no shadows to hide their passion, and no shadows at all on her heart. Her lips trembled again, and she reached for him, drawing him into the tenderness of her embrace. "Yes," she said simply, because she couldn't deny her heart.

Chapter 7

There were isolated moments, during the hours that followed, when she was able to think, but for the most part she was overtaken by the unstoppable tidal wave of desire. He knew just how to touch her, how long to linger, how to bring her time and again to the heart-stopping peak of pleasure. His hard hands learned every inch of her as he taught her to accommodate his desires, and she gave herself to him without reserve. She was incapable of holding any part of her heart back, all thoughts of protection left behind in the dust of the past. She had to love him with all the strength and devotion she could, because she could give no less. He'd known too much coldness, too much pain, and she sought to heal him with the soft, searing worship of her body. He was wild, hungry, sometimes almost violent, but with her love she absorbed the bitterness from him, soothing away the loneliness of his isolation. A combination of many things had made him a loner, a man without hearth or home, who lived on the razor's edge of danger and stayed alive by his wits and his finely honed body. Without words she accepted his passion and gentled it with her unquestioning trust. She tried to show him that he was safe with her, that he had no need for the wall that he'd built to keep himself apart from the rest of the world.

The sun was past its zenith and sliding down to the horizon when he relaxed abruptly and fell asleep, as if a light had been clicked off. Susan lay beside him and almost cried again, this time in thankfulness. He *did* trust her, at least a little, or he wouldn't have been able to sleep in her presence. She somehow had a mental image of him taking his pleasure with innumerable women, faceless and nameless; then, when they slept sated in his arms, he wound slip away from them to find his solitary bed. She watched him as he slept, his powerful body sprawled across the bed, his mouth softened under the black silk of his moustache. He had long, curling lashes, like a child's, and she smiled as she tried to imagine him as a toddler, with his cheeks still showing the chubby innocence of a baby.

But the innocent child had grown into a hard, wary man whose body was laced with scars, evidence of the battles he'd fought just to stay alive. He'd told her about Judith, but other than that he'd kept his past locked away in the depths of his mind. Other men would have had tales to relate of their adventures, or at least mentioned the different cultures and lands they'd seen, but not Cord. He was a silent warrior, not given to rehashing past battles, and when he was wounded, he crawled away to lick his wounds alone.

The thought of him being hurt made her heart clench painfully. She couldn't bear it if he were ever hurt again; just knowing that he had already borne wounds was almost beyond bearing. She leaned forward in blind desperation and touched her mouth lightly, tremblingly, to the round, silvered scar on his right shoulder. His skin twitched under her touch, but he didn't awaken, and she drifted to the long, thin line that ran down under his left arm, trailing her lips along the length of the scar, with aching tenderness trying to draw from him even the memory of those wounds. She found every scar on his body, licking and kissing them as she crouched protectively over him, guarding him with her slender, delicate woman's body, healing him. She felt him quiver under her mouth and knew that he was awake, but still she roamed over his body, her gentle hands caressing him. He began to shake, his body taut and ready.

"You'd better stop," he warned hoarsely. She didn't stop, instead turning her loving attention to a scar that furrowed down the inside of his thigh, then moving on to a newer, still-angry scar that snaked down his abdomen. He groaned aloud, his hands clenching on the sheet. She lingered, more intent now on the tension that she could feel building in him, intensifying to a crescendo, wanting to make him writhe with need as he had done to her.

He endured her loving torment until he was a taut arch on the bed, then his control broke and he reached for her, a primal growl rumbling in his throat as he swept her over him, thrusting up to bury himself in the sweet comfort of her body. His movements were swift and impatient, his hands grasping her hips so tightly that tiny smudged spots would mark the placement of his fingertips for a week. He held her still for his sensual assault, rotating his hips in a manner that drove her to a fast, hard culmination, then followed

her while she was still submerged in the powerful waves of satisfaction.

Afterward he cuddled her against his side, and she curled into
his hard, strong body with a sigh that reflected her bone-deep exhaustion. His hand stroked over her hair, smoothing it away from
her damp face. "I'm sorry I hurt you, that first time," he murmured,
his thoughts turning lazily to the morning, remembering the shock
he'd had at how *virginal* she'd felt. "But I'm glad as hell that
Preston hasn't had you."

So he'd realized what her difficulty in accepting him had signi-
fied. She wished that he had trusted her enough to take her word
in the matter, but he'd learned the hard way not to trust anyone,
and it would take time for her to teach him that he didn't always
have to guard his back. She ran her hand through the dark curls on
his chest in an absent manner. "Since Vance—" She stopped, then
continued so softly that he had to strain to hear her. "You're the
only one."

She didn't look up, so she missed the expression of almost savage
satisfaction that crossed his hard face. She knew only the momentary tightening of his arms before his embrace relaxed and he shifted
his weight, coming up on one elbow to lean over her. His hand
settled proprietarily on her soft stomach, a little gesture that said a
lot. "I don't want you going anywhere else with him," he informed
her in a voice so darkly menacing that she looked up at him in
quick surprise.

She hesitated, wondering if she dared presume that this day of
naked passion had established any sort of stable relationship between them. Very steadily she asked, "Are you offering your services as an escort if I need one?"

A guarded look came over his face, and he stroked his jaw in a
restless manner, as if missing his beard. "If I'm available," he
hedged.

Susan slowly extricated herself from his arms and sat up, feeling
a little chilled by his answer. "And when will you be unavailable?"
she queried. "When you're with Cheryl?"

Surprise pulled his brows together, but she couldn't tell if it was
the thought itself that surprised him, or that she'd thought she had
a right to ask the question at all. Then his face cleared, and amusement began to sparkle in his pale eyes. Very deliberately he let his
gaze wander over her, noting the tumbled dark hair, the soft flush
that his lovemaking had left on her creamy skin. Her lips were
swollen and passionate-looking, and he remembered the way they'd
drifted over his body. Her breasts, high and round, fuller than he'd

expected, also bore a rosy glow from his caresses and ardent suckling, and as he stared at them he noticed that her pert little nipples
were hardening, reaching out as if for another kiss. Swiftly he
glanced at her face, and his amusement deepened when he saw the
way she was blushing. How could she still blush? For hours she'd
lain naked in his arms, totally unselfconscious, allowing him the
complete freedom of her body, yet now it took only a slow, enjoy-
able visual tour of her nakedness to have her blushing like a virgin.

Then he had still another surprise as he felt the lower hardening
of his body in response to her. How could he even think about sex
again right now? Five minutes before, he'd thought that the day had
been fantastic, the most sexually satisfying day of his life, but that
he probably wouldn't be able to respond again for a week. Now his
body was proving him a liar. He wanted her, again and again. The
sensual pleasure he felt with her was staggering, but no sooner had
his pulse calmed than he began to feel the nagging need to possess
more of her. From the moment he'd seen her, he'd wanted to lie
on her tight and deep, immerse himself in her tenderness. He'd
never been jealous of a woman in his life, until he'd met Susan. It
knocked him off balance, the fury that filled him whenever he
thought of her dancing with Preston, kissing Preston, letting him
put his arms around her. He'd wanted to hurt her because it drove
him crazy to think of Preston making love to her. Now he knew
that she'd been chaste, yet still there was the possibility that her
loyalty was to Preston. Women were hard to read, and a treacherous
one was deadly. If he were smarter, he'd keep this one at a distance,
at least until everything was settled and he wouldn't have to watch
every word he said to her, but he couldn't force himself to say the
words that would send her away, just as he hadn't been able to
resist her rather innocent striptease that morning.

Susan watched him, waiting for his answer, but his eyes had gone
opaque and his face was a blank wall, his thoughts hiding behind
it. She was aware that he was becoming aroused by looking at her
body, so why should he suddenly lock himself away? Was it because he didn't think she had any right to question him about his
relationships with other women? Well, if he thought she'd sit quietly home while he danced the night away with Cheryl Warren,
he'd just have to think again! She balled her fist and thumped him
on the chest.

"Answer me," she demanded, her blue eyes darkening with fire.
"Will you be out with Cheryl? Or any other woman, for that
matter?"

He jack-knifed to a sitting position and swung his long legs off the bed. "No," he said shortly, getting to his feet and leaning down to scoop his jeans from the floor. "I won't be with any other woman!"

Did he resent having to give her that reassurance? Suddenly she felt embarrassed at her nakedness, and she snatched up a corner of the tumbled sheet to hold it over her breasts. Until then she had felt protected by the closeness she'd shared with him, but now he was suddenly a stranger again, and her bareness seemed much more vulnerable.

He gave the sheet a derisive glance. "It's a little late to try to protect your modesty."

Susan bit her lip, wondering if it would be better simply to get up, get dressed, and leave, or if she should try to talk him out of his sudden ill-temper. Had she gotten too close to him today? Was he reacting by trying to push her away with hostility? Looking at him worriedly, she thought that he looked uncomfortable, the way a man looks when a woman is making a nuisance of herself and he doesn't know how to get rid of her. She paled at the idea.

"I'm sorry," she heard herself say in swift apology, and she scrambled off the bed, abandoning the flimsy barrier of the sheet in favor of dressing as quickly as she could. Without looking at him, she grabbed up her panties and stepped into them. "I didn't mean to push you. I realize that having sex doesn't mean anything—"

"Whoa, lady!" Scowling, he dropped his jeans to the floor and grabbed her arm, pulling her upright as she bent to retrieve her dress, then drawing her into the circle of his arms. Her soft breasts flattened against his chest, and she quivered with enjoyment, her thoughts instantly distracted. How could she want him again? Her legs were distinctly wobbly after the day's activities anyway, and she was already feeling achy in various places, but she knew that if he wanted to tumble her back on the bed again, she would tumble gladly and worry about her aches tomorrow.

He frowned down at her. "Don't try feeding me that free-and-easy hogwash, because that isn't you, and I know it. I'm just feeling uneasy. Things are getting complicated all of a sudden." He stopped without explaining any further and cupped her face in his warm fingers. "Are you sorry it happened?"

She put her hand over his, rubbing her cheek against his palm. "No, I'm not sorry. How could I be? I...I wanted it, too." She'd started to say, "I love you," but at the last moment she'd choked the words back and substituted others that were true, but lacked the depth of what she felt. He didn't want the words, didn't want to be burdened with her emotions, and she knew it. As long as she didn't say the words aloud, he'd be able to ignore the true depth of her feeling, even though he had to know how she felt after these past hours spent in his arms, when she had given herself to him completely in a way that only a woman in love could give. He had to know, yet until the words were spoken, the knowledge didn't exist.

"I don't want you to get hurt," he muttered.

She leaned against him, wrapping her arms around him. He was warning her, letting her know that she shouldn't expect anything permanent from him. Pierced by a stiletto pain at the thought of one day watching his back as he walked away, she was also grateful for his honesty. He wasn't going to hit her with a blow from behind. And maybe, just maybe, she could change his mind. He wasn't used to being loved, and it was obvious that, even unwillingly, he felt more for her than he was comfortable with. She had a chance, and she would risk everything on that.

"Everyone gets hurt," she murmured against his warm skin. "I'm not going to worry about what might or might not happen some day in the future. I'll worry about someday when it gets here."

Someday she might have to do without him, a little bit of her dying every day of emotional starvation. But that was someday, and she had today. Today she was in his arms, and that was enough.

Later that night, facing Imogene across the width of the kitchen, she tried desperately to hold on to the memory of what she'd shared with him. Imogene's first words to her had been of concern, but that had quickly faded when Susan told her flatly that she wasn't going to play spy. "I told him what your plan was," she confessed remotely. "Then I told him to make certain he didn't tell me anything, so he couldn't think I was with him just to whore for information."

Imogene whitened with fury. She drew herself up to her full height, her anger making her seem six feet tall. Imogene in a rage was a formidable sight, but Susan stood her ground, her soft mouth set in a grim line, giving back stare for stare.

"Susan, my God, are you a fool?" Imogene shouted. "Haven't you realized yet that we stand to lose everything?"

"No, I haven't realized it! Cord hasn't made any move at all, other than threatening to press charges if the ridges aren't leased to him. I've agreed to that, and he's waiting for the geological surveys. Stop painting him as the devil, Imogene!"

"You don't know him like I do!" Suddenly Imogene realized that she was yelling, and she drew a deep breath, visibly forcing herself back under control. "You're making a big mistake if you take him at face value. He's planning something; I *know* it. If I just had some inkling, so I'd know what to protect! You could have found out," she said bitterly. "But instead you've let him turn your head and make you forget about where your loyalty lies."

"I love him," Susan said quietly.

Imogene gaped at her, her eyes going wide. "You...what? But what about Preston? I thought—"

"I *do* love Preston, as a friend, as Vance's brother." Susan groped for the words that could explain. "But Cord...makes me feel alive again. He gives me something to live *for*."

"I hope you're not banking too much on that! Susan, where's your common sense? He'll willingly take you to bed, but if you expect more from him than that, you're a fool. When he gets tired of you, he'll drop you without thinking twice about it, and you'll be left to face everyone you know. You'll always be Cord's leftovers."

"If I'd gone along with your plan, I would have been, anyway," Susan pointed out. "I won't stab him in the back, even if it means I lose everything I own, but I don't think he means to do anything else at all. I think all he wanted was the oil leases."

"You're not the only one who's involved here! You're not the only one who's at risk. Preston and I also stand to lose everything. Doesn't that mean anything to you?"

"It means a great deal to me. I simply don't think he's a threat to you."

Imogene shook her head, closing her eyes as if in disbelief at Susan's blindness. "I can't believe you're so blind where he's concerned. You love him? Well, that's just fine! Love him if you have to, but don't be fool enough to trust him!"

Susan went white. "I have to trust him. I love him too much not to. I'd trust him with my life."

"That's your decision, I suppose," Imogene snapped sarcastically. "But you're also trusting him with ours, and I don't like that at all. He must really be something in bed, to make you so willing to turn your back on the people who love you, knowing that all he'll ever offer you is sex."

Susan felt as if she were staring at Imogene from a great distance, and a faint buzzing sound in her head warned her that she might faint. Dizzily she groped for one of the kitchen chairs and almost fell into it. They were tearing her apart! The awful thing was that she could see Imogene's side of it. Imogene fully expected Cord to take some sort of revenge against her, and she was frightened, as well she should be. Imogene was lashing out, reacting to a driving need to protect her own, and in her desperation she was willing to hurt people if they got in her way.

Imogene hesitated for a moment, staring at Susan's pale, damp face as she slumped in the chair; then her face twisted, and for a moment tears brimmed in her pale gray eyes. She blinked them back fiercely, because Imogene Blackstone never wept, and moved swiftly to the sink, dampening several paper towels and taking them to Susan. She slid her arm around the young woman and gently blotted her face with the cool, wet towels. "Susan, I'm sorry," she said, her voice steady at first, then wobbling dangerously. Imogene never apologized. "My God, he's got us fighting among ourselves."

The damp coolness of the paper towels banished Susan's momentary dizziness, but it couldn't banish the ache in her heart. She wanted to run to Cord, to throw herself into his arms and let his kisses make her forget that there was an outside world. But despite the hours she'd spent in his bed, she wasn't entitled to dump all her worries on his shoulders, even though all her worries centered around him.

She clasped her hands on the table, entwining her fingers so tightly that they turned white. "I haven't turned my back on you or Preston," she said with hard-won steadiness. "I simply can't do something that's so completely against the things I believe in. Please don't try to make me take sides, because I can't. I love all of you; I can't stab any of you in the back."

Imogene touched Susan's bent head briefly, then let her hand drop. "I only hope Cord has the same reluctance to hurt you, but I can't believe it. I don't want you to be caught in the middle, but it seems that you'll have to be, if you won't take sides. He'll smash anything that gets in his way."

"That's a chance I'll have to take," Susan whispered. She'd already accepted the risk she had to face in loving Cord; what else could she do?

The next morning she went to church as usual, but she couldn't keep her mind on the sermon. Imogene, sitting beside her, was quiet and withdrawn, not entering into conversation before the services began, her gaze fixed on the minister, but Susan felt that Imogene wasn't really concentrating on the sermon either. Preston had shadows under his eyes, and to Susan's concerned eye he seemed to have lost a little weight, though she'd seen him only two days before. The strain was telling on him, but he managed to smile and greet everyone as normal. Susan wondered if Imogene had told him anything that had been said the night before, then decided that it wasn't likely. Imogene was too reserved to cry on anyone's shoulder, even her own son's.

Susan declined Imogene's invitation to Sunday dinner and went home to prepare a light meal of a crisp salad and potato soup. The spring day was too beautiful to sit inside, so she took her needlepoint out on the patio and worked on it for a couple of hours. She was outwardly serene, but she was aware of the coiling tension inside her as she sat and listened for the sound of a car coming up her long driveway. Would Cord drive over today? The thought made her breath catch. He would take her upstairs to her bedroom, to the bed where no man had ever slept, and on the cool, pristine sheets he would blend his body with hers.

She closed her eyes as desire built in her, making her lower body feel heavy and tight, and painfully empty. Surely he would come; surely he could hear her silent call for him.

Stately, towering thunderheads began to march in from the west, and the wind developed a brisk chill, but still she sat there until the first fat raindrops began to splatter on the patio tiles. Gathering her needlework, she ran for the sliding doors and slipped inside just as the weather broke and the rain became a downpour, filling her ears with a dull roar. A sharp crack of thunder made her jump, and she hastily pulled the curtains over the glass doors, then moved around and turned on lights to dispel the fast, early dusk.

It was after eight o'clock that night before she admitted that he wasn't going to come, so she locked up the house and readied herself for bed. The storm had passed, but the rain continued to fall, and she lay awake for hours listening to the hypnotic patter, wishing that he was in bed beside her, warm and virile. The big house was silent and empty around her, emptier even than it had been after Vance's death, and that was strange, because Vance had lived here, and she had memories of him in every room. But Vance was gone, and Cord's personality was too strong to fight.

Because the day was so muted and gray when she woke up in the morning, and because she felt so depressed at not having seen Cord, Susan made a determined effort to cheer herself up. She chose a dark red silk sheath for work, and belted it with a snazzy wide black belt that she'd never worn before. A short black jacket pulled the outfit together, and Susan arched an inquiring eyebrow at her own reflection in the mirror as she leaned forward to put on her earrings. The sharply stylish woman in the mirror didn't quite look like Susan Blackstone, who usually preferred more conservative garments. But then, the Susan Blackstone who had looked in that mirror the Friday before had never spent the day making love with Cord Blackstone. She was gambling for the first time in her life, and the stakes were higher than she could afford. A woman who would risk her heart, knowing from the outset that the odds in her favor weren't too good, couldn't be as staid and conventional as Susan had always thought herself to be.

She kept her cheerful demeanor in place all day long, but after she got home and had eaten the dinner Emily prepared, after Emily had gone to her own house, she waited hopefully until long after dark, but still she didn't hear anything from Cord. A chill began to tighten her muscles. If the day they had spent together had meant anything to him at all, why hadn't he made any effort to see her again? Had it just been a...a convenience for him? A casual sexual encounter that he wouldn't think of again?

She thought of driving out to Jubilee Creek, but the lateness of the hour and the steady rain dissuaded her. Surely tomorrow she'd hear from him.

But she didn't, and the hours dragged past. She called Information to see if he'd had a phone installed, but they had no listing in his name. She could no longer even keep up the pretense of being cheerful, and her face was tight with strain, an expression that was duplicated on Preston's face. Susan knew that he had extended himself to the limit, liquidating assets to replace the money in Cord's account, and she wanted to ask him if he needed help, but an intimate knowledge of Blackstone pride kept her from making the offer. He'd refuse, and even if he later changed his mind, if things became desperate enough that he would want to accept her help, he wouldn't mention it to her.

Thursday afternoon she drove out to Jubilee Creek, but there was no sign of Cord. She looked in the windows and could see no lights, no dirty dishes, no clothing strewn about. She tried both the front and back doors, and found them securely locked. The thought that he might have gone permanently made her sag against the door, and bitter tears of regret seared her lids before she forced them back; not regret for what had happened, but regret that she'd had only that one day in his arms. She should have had more! It wasn't fair to give someone a brief glimpse of heaven, then draw heavy curtains over the scene! Where Cord was concerned, she wanted it all: all of his smiles, his kisses, his company every day. She wanted to be the one to calm his anger or incite his passion. She wanted to wake up beside him every morning and look at his sleepy, beard-stubbled face, and at night she wanted to lie close against his tall, hard body.

Of course, she could just be borrowing heartache; the cabin hadn't been emptied, so she had to assume that he would be returning. It was just... Why couldn't he have let her know that he was leaving, or when he would be back? Would a phone call have been so difficult for him to make?

But those were the conditions she'd set: He wasn't to tell her anything. Her eyes widened in realization. What if his absence had something to do with Imogene and Preston? They were convinced that he was scheming against them, and though she had defended him, suddenly she was unsure. What did she know about him, other than that he was so exciting and dangerous that he made her heartbeat lurch out of rhythm every time she saw him? He was a hungry, demanding lover, but considerate in controlling his strength and handling her carefully. He danced with wild grace, and his body was laced with the scars that a warrior collected over the years. She loved him, but she was painfully aware that he kept most of himself hidden away. If he had lived by the law of fang and claw, could she expect him to do anything other than strike back at people who had wronged him? Was she a fool to trust him? She'd always thought that a trainer who walked unarmed into a cage with a snarling tiger was extremely foolish, but she had been just as foolish. Suddenly she knew that Cord was more than capable of taking revenge; he could raise it to the level of fine art.

The next day Preston came into her office and dropped tiredly into the comfortable chair next to her desk. "Well, I've done it," he said in a voice hollow with exhaustion. "I've stretched myself to the limit, but Cord has been repaid in full."

She was overcome with sympathy for him, looking at the dark shadows under his blue eyes. "I wish you would let me help—"

"No, thanks, sugar." He managed a slow smile for her. "It wasn't your doing, so you shouldn't have to pay. Now that the debt is covered, if you don't want to lease the ridges to him, you don't have to. I've pretty well blocked any move he can make to cause trouble about the money; I've even paid him interest."

"I wish you could talk with him and settle your differences," she said wistfully. "It's not right for a family to tear itself apart like this. All of that happened so long ago; why can't you put it in the past?"

"There's too much resentment, on both sides," Preston replied. He stretched his long legs out in front of him and crossed them elegantly at the ankle. "We never got along, for one reason or another. That thing with Judith Keller just topped it off, as far as he was concerned. And as far as I'm concerned..." He gave her a direct look. "As long as you're interested in him, I have to hate his guts."

Susan blushed, distressed at causing him any pain. "Don't feel like that, please. Don't add to the trouble. I can't stand the thought of being a bone of contention between the two of you."

"But such a sweet, lovely bone," he teased, his blue eyes lightening momentarily. He really was an extraordinarily good-looking man, she realized with some surprise, slim and elegant, with a smooth style that sometimes made him seem misplaced in this century. But Preston wasn't out of place; he was supremely suited for his occupation. He was cool, level-headed, and fair in his practices. He was also completely out of his league in fighting Cord, because he lacked the ruthlessness that had kept Cord alive in a lot of dim back alleys.

The light had already faded out of Preston's eyes. "Do you see him often?" he finally asked, his tone gruff as he struggled to hide his emotions.

It was only the painful truth when Susan replied, "No, not often at all." In moments of mental detachment she was astonished at the way she had given herself to a man whom she didn't know that well, hadn't seen that often, and who was a direct threat to her way of life. Then the memory of the heat of his kisses would banish her detachment, and she would no longer wonder at the way she had lost herself in his arms. He wasn't a man who inspired a sedate love; he evoked the deepest, wildest passions a woman's heart was capable of feeling.

Preston sat there, a frown puckering his brow as he thought. After a moment he said, "I'd like for him to know that the money has been repaid. Will you tell him for me?"

"If I see him again," Susan agreed steadily. "I don't know where he is." The bald confession stabbed her as she realized anew how empty she felt at the thought that she might not see him again.

Preston sat upright. "Has he left town?"

"I don't know. But I haven't seen him for a week, and he's not at the cabin."

"He's either gone again, or he's making some sort of move against me," Preston muttered absently, tapping his fingertips on the top of Susan's desk. "Let me know if you hear from him." He got up and left her office, still preoccupied with the news that Cord had dropped out of sight.

After a moment Beryl appeared with an armload of correspondence to be signed, pulling Susan away from the chasm of loneliness, but inside herself she was aware that she had only stepped back, not walked away from it entirely. It was still there, cold and black in its yawning emptiness, a bleak, bottomless pit where she would fall forever, locked away from the fire of the man she loved.

Chapter 8

Just as she turned into her driveway a swiftly moving thunderstorm
swept in from the Gulf, and it threatened to drown her as she dashed
the short distance from her car to the covered side patio. Emily met
her at the door with an enormous towel, having seen her drive up.
Just as Susan stepped out of her soaking shoes and wound the towel
around her hair, the rain stopped as swiftly as it had come, leaving
only the cheerful dripping of water from the trees and the eaves of
the roof. A split second later the thundercloud was gone and the
sun was shining merrily on the wet landscape, making the raindrops
sparkle like diamonds. Susan gave Emily a rueful look. "If I'd
waited in the car for a minute, it would've been over with and I
wouldn't have gotten soaked."

Emily couldn't suppress a chuckle. "If you wanted predictable
weather, you'd live in Arizona. Go on upstairs and get dried off,
while I finish your dinner."

Fifteen minutes later Susan was downstairs again, helping Emily
put the finishing touches on the small but tasty meal she'd prepared.
Emily watched her set a single place on the table, and the older
woman's protective instincts were aroused. Putting her big spoon
down with a thunk, she braced her hands on her hips. "I'd like to
know why you've been eating alone every night, instead of letting
Cord Blackstone take you out."

Susan flushed, not certain how to respond. Because it was what
she feared most, she finally said, "Just because he passed out on
the couch and spent the night here doesn't mean he's interested—"

"Baloney," Emily interrupted in exasperation. "I've got eyes,
and I saw the way he was looking at you the next morning. You

were looking back at him the same way, and don't try to deny it. Then he went upstairs with you, and it was quite a while before he came down.''

"I don't know where he is," Susan admitted helplessly, staring down at the table. "He's not at the cabin. He hasn't called; he didn't even tell me he was leaving, or where he was going. For all I know, he won't be back.''

"He'll be back, mark my words." Emily sniffed. "He's not used to accounting for himself to anyone, but if he had it in mind to leave for good, he'd have let you know.''

"You knew him when he was a boy," Susan said, looking up at Emily with the hunger to know more about him plain in her eyes. "What was he like?''

Emily's care-worn features softened as she looked at the pleading face turned up to her. "Sit down," she urged. "I'll tell you while you're eating.''

Susan obeyed, automatically eating the tiny lamb chops and steamed carrots that were one of her favorite meals. Emily sat down at the table across from her. "I loved him as a boy," she said, turning her mind back over twenty years. "He was always ready to laugh, always up to some prank, and it seemed like he was more relaxed at my house. He never fit in with the people his parents expected to be his friends, never really fit in here at all, and that just made him wilder than he naturally was anyway, which was wild enough. He was always ahead of everyone else, stronger than anyone else his age, faster, with better grades, more girlfriends. Even the older girls in high school were after him. Everything came so easy to him, or maybe he made everything come to him; I've never seen anyone more stubborn or determined to have his way. Thinking back on it, I know that he had to be bored. Nothing challenged him. He pulled off every wild stunt he could think of, but he had a golden touch, and everything always worked smooth as silk for him. I've never seen anything like his luck.''

Susan's breath caught at the image Emily had given her, of a boy growing up too fast, without any limits to guide him. He wouldn't accept any limits, she realized. He'd been propelled by the extraordinary combination of genes and circumstance that should have made him the prototypical Golden Boy, with all the comforts and privileges of wealth and class: handsome, unusually intelligent, athletic, gifted by nature with charm and grace. But his restless, seeking mind had soared beyond that, driven him to test the limits of chance. He had pushed and pushed, seeking a boundary he couldn't push beyond, until he'd gone too far and been driven away from his home.

There had been dark years in Cord's life, times when he'd been close to death, when he'd been cold and hungry, but she couldn't imagine him ever being frightened. No, he'd face everything that came his way, the mocking twist of his lips daring everyone and everything to do their worst. The remaining vestiges of the Golden Boy had been obliterated by the harshness of the life he'd led. Perhaps he had money now, perhaps he lived comfortably, but it hadn't always been so, and his senses were still razor-sharp. She thought of the scars on his body and her heart twisted.

"Everyone acts as if he's a wild animal," she said painfully. "Why are they so afraid of him?"

"Because they don't understand him. Because he's not like they are. Some folks are afraid of lightning; some think it's beautiful. But everyone's cautious around it."

Yes, he was as wild and beautiful as a bolt of lightning, and as dangerous. She stared at Emily, her eyes glistening with tears. "I love him."

Emily nodded sadly. "I know, honey, I know. What are you going to do?"

"There's nothing I can do, is there? Just...love him, and hope everything works out."

A foolish hope, doomed from the start. How could it work out? It was impossible to hold a bolt of lightning.

He was gone, and every minute seemed to drag by, rasping on her nerves. An hour was a lifetime; a day, eternity. No book, no gardening, no sewing, could ease her bone-deep sense of yearning. All she could think of was Cord, overwhelming her with his reckless charm and the impact of his forceful sensuality.

If only he was with her! In his presence she wouldn't care about Preston, or Imogene, or whatever was going on. In Cord's arms, she wouldn't care about anything. She could lose herself in him, and count the loss well worth the cost in pain. She loved him simply, completely, and she had to follow only the dictates of her emotions.

She slept restlessly that night, and was jerked out of sleep a little after midnight by a boom of thunder that rattled the windows. Susan lay snugly in her warm bed, listening to the lightning crackle; then a hard, driving rain began to pound against her windows and the wind picked up. Deciding she'd better turn on the radio and get a weather report, she sat up and turned on her bedside lamp. When she did, another pounding reached her ears and she paused, a small frown touching her brow. Then it was repeated, and she jumped out of bed. Someone was trying to beat her door down.

She grabbed her robe and raced down the stairs, turning on lights as she went. "Who is it? What's wrong?" she called as she neared the door.

A deep laugh answered her. "The only thing that's wrong is that you're on that side of the door and I'm on this one."

"Cord!" Her heart jumped into her throat and she fumbled hastily with the lock, throwing the door open. He sauntered in, as wild as the night, and as dangerous. The wind had tumbled his dark hair into reckless waves, and his pale eyes were glittering. He brought the fresh scent of rain in with him, because the wind had blown a fine mist of moisture over him. He was dressed in a conservatively cut, dark business suit, but the coat was hanging open, his tie was draped around his neck, and his shirt was open to the waist. The suit couldn't disguise the desperado that he was, and her mouth went dry with longing.

Unthinkingly, she clutched at his sleeve. "Where have you been? Why haven't you called? I've been so worried—" She stopped, suddenly realizing what she was saying, and stared up at him with eyes full of vulnerability.

"Uh-uh," he crooned softly. "No questions, remember? I'm not telling you anything, not where I was, or when I'll be going again." A savage enjoyment lit his face as another crash of thunder reverberated through the house, and his teeth flashed in a grin. "I like storms," he murmured, taking a step toward her and lacing his arm around her waist in an iron embrace. "I like making love while it rains."

Something was wrong; she couldn't quite catch her breath. She stared up at him dazedly, and she clutched his lapels for support. "I was just going to turn on the radio to get the weather report," she stammered.

He grinned again. "Thunderstorm warning, with possible high winds," he said, pulling her closer until she was pressed full against him. "Who cares?"

The gleam in his eyes was still interfering with her breathing. "When...when did you get back?" she asked, hanging suspended over his arm, her feet having somehow lost touch with the floor. "Or is that another off-limits question?"

"Tonight," he answered. "I was driving home, thinking about how dead tired I was, and how good it would feel to fall into bed. Then I thought how much better it would feel to fall into bed with you, so here I am."

"You don't look tired," she observed cautiously. He didn't. He looked as if he could rival the storm for energy. He was almost burning her with his touch.

"Second wind," he said, and kissed her. His approach was direct and without hesitation, and he kissed her for a long time. She clung to him, first to his lapels; then her clutching fingers somehow found their way to his shoulders, and finally her arms were locked around his neck. He lifted her and started up the stairs, leaving all the lights on behind him, because that was the last thing on his mind.

He set her on her feet in her bedroom and watched her with lazily hooded eyes as he stripped his tie from around his neck and tossed it carelessly over a chair. The tie was followed by his coat; then his shirt was pulled free of his pants and discarded. When he kicked off his shoes and leaned down to pull his socks off, Susan swallowed at the sight of his half-naked body, so sleek and powerful, and she untied the sash of her robe and removed the garment, folding it over the chair. She could feel his eyes on her, on the ice pink nightgown that half revealed her body.

He dropped his pants and left them lying on the floor. His only remaining garment was a pair of jogging-style shorts, dark blue silk with white edging, which did nothing to hide his arousal. A thunderbolt of excitement raced through her as he nonchalantly stepped out of his underwear and came toward her, as naked and powerfully beautiful as an ancient god.

Quickly she raised the hem of the nightgown over her head and drew it off, the silk whispering over her bare skin. His look of hunger became almost fierce as he reached for her. When he placed her on the bed, Susan reached out for the lamp and he halted her, his hard fingers closing around her wrist.

"Leave it on," he instructed in a voice gone gravelly rough. "I thought of this all the time I was gone. I'm not going to miss seeing one minute of it."

She couldn't help the blush that tinted her breasts and spread upward to her cheeks, and he found it fascinating. Without a word he took her in his arms.

Their loveplay extended as he explored her body as thoroughly as if he'd never made love to her before, had never spent a lovely sun-drenched day sprawled across a bed with her. When she was writhing against him in frantic need, he paused for a moment to reach for his pants, and Susan realized what he was doing. Without a word, he assumed responsibility for their lovemaking. Then he turned to her and swiftly moved between her legs, sliding into her so powerfully that moans of pleasure were wrenched from both of them. His patience was at an end, and he thrust strongly, his rhythm hungry and fast. Susan wound her legs around him and absorbed the power of his thrusts with her eagerly welcoming body, so dizzy with pleasure at being in his arms again, kissing him, giving herself to him in the most intimate act between man and woman, that he couldn't leave her behind in his relentless quest for pleasure. The powerful coil that had been tightening within her was released suddenly, and her entire body throbbed with the pulsating waves that raced down her legs to curl her toes and spread upward through her torso in a splash of heat. She heard the wild cries that were ground out through his clenched teeth, felt him arch into her helplessly; then it was suddenly quiet again as the storm passed and he let himself down to lie on her in contented exhaustion.

After a moment he sighed and carefully eased himself from her, rolling over on his side. Susan touched him, her fingers gentle. "This might not have been necessary," she murmured. "I...I'm not sure I can get pregnant. Vance and I never used any protection, but I never got pregnant. I'm very...erratic."

He closed his eyes and a tiny grin touched his mouth. Relaxing, he threw one arm behind his head. "Somehow, that's not very reassuring. I get the feeling that if there's any man walking this earth who could get you pregnant, I'm him. We took a big chance last week, but we'll be more careful from now on." He opened one eye a slit and pinned her with the narrow ribbon of his gaze. "Let me know if it's too late to be careful, or if we hit it lucky. As soon as *you* know."

"Yes," she agreed, sinking down onto the pillow and closing her eyes as contentment claimed her. It felt so natural to be in bed with him, talking about very intimate things, feeling the heat of his body so close to her. She nestled closer to him and rubbed her face against the hair of his chest, feeling the soft curls catch at her eyelashes.

He drifted into sleep with her lying against his side, but woke when the storm, forgotten in their own storm of loving, renewed itself with a snap of lightning so close that the thunder was simultaneous, and Susan sat upright in bed at the unmistakable sound of a limb splitting away from a tree and crashing to the ground. Before she had time to voice her alarm, he seized her from behind and tumbled her back to the mattress.

"Just where do you think you're going?" he growled with mock roughness.

"The trees—" she began, and just then the lights flickered and went out.

"Oh, hell," he said into the sudden darkness. Another bolt of lightning flashed to earth and the eerie blue-white light illuminated the room. He was sitting up, too. "Where's a flashlight and the radio?"

"There's a flashlight in the top drawer of the nightstand," she said, pulling the sheet up around her as the damp chill of the air reached her. "The radio is downstairs in the den."

"Battery?"

"Yes." She listened as he fumbled around in the nightstand, finally locating the flashlight and clicking it on, the beam of light dispelling the darkness. He swung his long legs out of the bed.

"I'll bring the radio up here. Sit tight."

What else could she do? She pulled her knees up and rested her chin on them, her eyes on the storm erupting right outside her windows. It was loud and magnificent, full of fury, but she mourned the damage to the enormous old trees that surrounded the house. If one of the trees came down it could take the roof of the house off and crush the walls.

Cord came back into the room, the battery-powered radio in his hand. He had it turned to a local Biloxi station. Placing the radio on the nightstand, he clicked off the flashlight and got into bed with her, pulling her down to nestle in his arms.

In only a few moments the amused drawl of the radio announcer was filling the room. "The thunderstorm warning for the Biloxi area has been canceled. I guess those folks at the weather bureau haven't looked out their windows lately. Now, this is what I call *rain*. There aren't any reports of any serious damage, though several power outtages have been reported, and there are some signs blown down. Nothing major, folks. We're in touch with the weather bureau, and if it turns serious—"

Cord stretched out a long arm and turned the radio off, silencing the announcer in mid-sentence. "It's already passing," he murmured, and she noticed that the lightning was indeed less intense, the thunder growing more distant. The lights suddenly blinked back on, blinding both of them with their unexpected brilliance.

He laughed and sat up. "I was going to stay with you as long as the power was off," he said, getting out of bed and reaching for his underwear.

Bewildered, Susan sat up too, staring at him. He pulled on his underwear, then his pants, before she spoke. "Aren't you staying?"

"No." He slanted her a look that was suddenly cool and remote.

"But—it's so late, anyway. Why drive to Jubilee Creek—"

"Three reasons," he interrupted, a harsh note entering his deep voice. "One, I like to sleep alone. Two, I really need the sleep, which I wouldn't get if I stayed here with you. Three, Emily didn't turn a hair at finding me asleep on your couch, but finding me in your bed is something else entirely."

A hard, cold pain struck her in her chest, but she looked at him and saw the way he'd closed himself off, and she summoned all of her strength to give him a smile that wavered only a little. "Are you worried about your reputation?" she managed to tease. "I promise I'll take the blame for seducing you."

Her attempt at lightness worked; he smiled, and sat down on the side of the bed to cup her soft cheek in his palm. "Don't argue," he murmured. But when he was that close he could see her pain, though she was doing everything she could to hide it, and his level brows pulled together. He wasn't used to explaining himself, or talking about his past at all, but he found himself trying to explain his actions for the first time in years. The urge to take the uncomprehending pain out of those soft blue eyes was almost overwhelming. "Susan, I don't feel comfortable sleeping with another person, not anymore. I've spent too many years guarding my back. I may doze off after making love, but I don't fall into a deep sleep. Some part of me is always alert, ready to move. I can't rest that way and I'm really tired tonight; I need some sleep. We'll go out for dinner tomorrow night...make that tonight, since it's almost morning. Seven-thirty?"

"Yes. I'll be ready."

He winked at her. "I won't mind if you aren't dressed."

As he finished dressing, Susan watched him and hugged the sheet up over her nudity. She bit her lip, trying to force her own feelings away so she could consider his. She'd sensed that he was uneasy about allowing himself to relax when anyone else was with him, and she knew that her vision of him leaving his women alone in their beds had been an accurate one. *His women.* She had joined them, that long line of women who had held him in their arms for a taste of heaven, then lain weeping in their cold beds after he had gone. Yet she wouldn't have turned him away, wouldn't have missed her own chance at heaven. If she could turn time back, she would go with him that first night she'd met him, and not waste one moment of the time she had with him.

He completed dressing and reached for his coat, then leaned down to give her a swift kiss. Susan dropped the sheet and rose up on her knees, entwining her arms around his strong neck as she lifted her mouth. He paused, looking down at her gentle mouth, already pouty from his kisses; her eyes were serene pools, with thick black lashes drooping in a drowsy, unconsciously sexy manner. She was a naked Venus in his arms, soft and warm and feminine, and his hands automatically sought her curves as he kissed her long and hard, his tongue deep within her mouth. Despite his weariness, desire hardened his body, and it was all he could do to pull away from her.

"You're going to be the death of me," he muttered, giving her a look that she couldn't read before he left the room. Susan remained on her knees until she heard the sound of the front door closing; then she sagged down on the bed, fighting the hot tears that wanted to fall. For a moment she'd sensed that he'd been tempted to stay, but only to slake the urges of his amazingly virile body, not because he trusted her, not because he felt he could sleep in her arms. She knew that she could have touched him, wriggled herself against him, and he would have tumbled her back down to the mattress, but that wasn't what she wanted. That hot, glorious madness that seized her at his lightest touch was wonderful, but she wanted more. She wanted his love, his trust.

The tiger is a majestic beast, savagely beautiful and awesome in its power, but it's locked alone in its majesty. The beautiful tiger is solitary, hunting alone, sleeping alone. A tiger mates, and for a time is less alone, but the moments of physical joining are soon gone, and the tiger once again roams in solitude. Cord was a tiger in nature, and after mating he had gone to seek his bed apart from every other creature on earth, because he trusted no other creature.

She pounded her fist on the mattress in mute frustration. Why couldn't she have fallen in love with a man who *liked* cuddling up and falling asleep, a man who hadn't spent years of his life kicking around the globe in a lot of God-forsaken places, who did all the normal things like going to work during the week and cutting the grass on weekends? Because, she interrupted her own thoughts fiercely, a man like that wouldn't be Cord. He was wild and beautiful, and dangerous. If she had wanted a man who wasn't all of those things, she'd have fallen in love with Preston long ago.

She lay awake, her eyes on the ceiling as the hours slid past and dawn came and went. Part of her was hurt and humiliated that he had come to her for sex, then left as soon as he was satisfied, but another part of her was glad that he had come to her at all, for any reason. Certainly, if he made love to any woman, she wanted it to be herself. She wanted to believe that he felt something for her besides physical desire, but if he didn't, she would try to use that desire as a base to build on. As long as he came around at all, she still had hope.

*   *   *

She was taken by surprise the next afternoon when sudden cramps signaled that their reckless day of lovemaking hadn't borne fruit; she'd been feeling listless all day, but credited that to her lack of sleep the night before. She was further surprised when she burst into tears, and it wasn't until that moment that she realized she'd been unconsciously hoping that Cord's seed had found fertile ground. She almost hated her body for being so unpredictable, so inhospitable; she wanted his child, a part of him that would be hers forever. She wouldn't use a pregnancy to chain him to her, ever, if he wanted to go, but how she would love a baby of his making! Her arms ached at the thought of holding an infant with soft dark hair and pale blue eyes, and their emptiness haunted her.

She was pale and shadows lay heavily under her eyes when Cord arrived to take her to dinner; she told him immediately that he had no need to worry about a pregnancy, and almost winced at the relief he didn't bother to hide. Despite that, they had a pleasant dinner, and after eating they danced for a while to some slow, dreamy forties-style music. He'd taken her to a restaurant in New Orleans where she'd never been before, and she liked the place-out-of-time atmosphere. He knew that her energy level was low, and she thoroughly enjoyed the way he coddled her that evening. She drank a little more wine than she was accustomed to, and was floating slightly above the earth as he drove her home in the sleek white Jaguar that he had arrived in, though she had expected the red Blazer. The man has style, she thought dreamily, stroking her fingers over the leather of the seats. In the light of the dash his face was hard and exciting, the virile brush of his moustache outlining the precision of his upper lip. She reached out and let her fingers lightly trace his mouth, causing his brows to arch in question.

"You're so beautiful," she murmured huskily.

"Feel free to admire me any time you like, madam," he invited formally, but the wicked, sensual glint in his eyes was anything but formal as he glanced at her. She was a little high, her eyes filled with dreams, and he knew that she would come willingly into his arms if he stopped the car and reached for her right then. He shifted uncomfortably in his seat as his body reacted to his thoughts. He wanted her, but he knew that she didn't feel well, and he wanted her to enjoy their lovemaking as deeply as he did, not just allow her body to be used for his pleasure. He thought of how she looked in the throes of passion, and desire slammed into his gut so hard that he jerked in his seat. When this was over, when he had accomplished all that he wanted, he promised himself that he'd take her on a long vacation, maybe a cruise, and he'd make love to her as much as he liked. He'd satisfy his craving for her once and for all, sate himself on her slim, velvet body that was so surprisingly sensual. Her sensuality was so unconscious, so natural, that he sensed she wasn't even aware of it. A perfect lady, he thought, until he took her in his arms; then she turned into a hot, sweet wanton who took his breath away.

He didn't plan any further into the future than that; Cord had learned not to make long-range plans, because they inhibited his ability to react to circumstances. When some people formed plans in their minds, they locked their thoughts on course and couldn't deviate from them, couldn't allow for unforeseen interruptions or detours. When Cord plotted his course of action, he didn't tie himself down; he always allowed for the possibility that he might have to jump to the left instead of to the right, or even retrace his steps entirely. That flexibility had kept him alive, kept him in tune with his senses. In that way, he was a creature of the moment, yet he always kept his goal in mind, and changing circumstances only meant that he would have to reach that goal by a different route. He was usually prepared for anything and everything, but when he'd returned to Biloxi he hadn't been prepared for the primitive desire he would feel for a woman who had one foot in the enemy camp and seemed determined to keep it there. To the victor belonged the spoils, and he looked at Susan with hard determination; when he had won, she would be his, and he would force all thoughts of her in-laws out of her head. He wouldn't allow her any time to think of anyone but him. The savagely possessive need he felt for her had forced him to adjust his actions, but in the end...in the end, everything would be just like he'd planned it, and Susan would be his, on his terms.

Susan sensed the control he exercised when he kissed her lightly and left her at her door; she was too tired, too sleepy from too much wine, to try to understand why he left so abruptly. She only knew that she was disappointed; she could have made a pot of coffee and they could have sat close together and watched the late news, just as she and Vance had often done....

But Cord wasn't Vance.

Susan stood in the darkened foyer and looked around at the beautiful, gracious home Vance had built for her. The light she had left on at the head of the stairs illuminated the pale walls and the elegant floor-to-ceiling windows, the imported tiles of the foyer. Her home was warm and welcoming, because it was a home that had known love, but now she stood in the darkness, surrounded by the things that Vance had given her, and all she could think of was another man. Cord filled her days, her nights, her thoughts, her dreams. His pale lodestone eyes compelled her, like the moon silently controlling the tides. She tried to visualize Vance's face, but the features refused to form themselves in her mind. He had taught her about love; his tender care had helped shape her into a warm and loving woman, but he was gone, and he had no more substance for her than that of the drifting mist. *Vance, I really did love you,* she called out to him silently, but there was nothing there. Vance was dead, and Cord was so vitally alive.

Instead of going up to bed she went into the den and turned on the lights, then walked unerringly to the precise spot in the bookshelves that held a small album, though it had been at least four years since she'd looked at it. She took down the leather-bound volume and opened it, staring at the pictures of Vance.

How young he looked! How fresh and gallant! She saw the familiar mischievous sparkle in his blue eyes, the rather crooked smile, the strong Blackstone features. She traced the lines of his face with one gentle finger, seeing the resemblance he bore to Cord. He looked much the way she imagined Cord would have before experience had worn away his youthful wonder at the world, before all his ideals had been blasted out of existence. "I loved you," she murmured to Vance's smiling face. "If you could have stayed, I'd have loved you forever."

But he hadn't, and now Cord had stolen her love like the renegade he was.

Gently she replaced the album and left the room, walking slowly up the stairs to her empty bed, her mind and her senses filled with the memory of the night before when Cord had swept in with the rain, wild and damp, the air about him almost crackling with the heat of his passion. She hadn't even thought of denying him, even though he'd disappeared for a week without a word of warning. She'd simply undressed, so eager for his touch that she wouldn't have protested if he'd taken her there in the foyer.

She creamed the makeup off her face, closing her eyes slightly to combat the faint giddiness caused by the wine. How passionate he'd been the night before, and how considerate he'd been this evening. She tried to convince herself that he cared for her, but the thought kept coming back that he hadn't wasted any time getting away from her after driving her home. And the night before, he'd left after making love to her. He only wants me for sex, she silently told her reflection, and shut her eyes tightly against the words. It had to be more than that, because she wasn't sure she could keep from falling apart if it wasn't.

Chapter 9

By the time another week had come and gone, Susan was convinced that she knew nothing about Cord. He was the most enigmatic man she'd ever met; just when she'd decided that he was only using her as a convenient sexual outlet, he confounded her by taking her out every evening, wooing her with wine and good food, and dancing with her into the wee hours of the morning. Dancing with him was special. He was the most graceful man she'd ever known, and he enjoyed dancing. Between them, rituals of dancing were both flirtation and foreplay. She could feel his powerful body moving against her, sending her senses tumbling head over heels, and the unabashed response of his body told her that he was reacting the same way. Held in his arms, she felt secure, protected, locked away in their private world. She could have dreamed her life away in his arms.

He was a gentleman in every sense of the word, tenderly solicitous of her, courting her in a manner so old-fashioned that it stunned her even though she deeply enjoyed every moment of it. He gave her the grace of a few days' privacy, then brought his abstinence to an end with hungry impatience; instead of kissing her gently good-night, as he had been doing, he picked her up and carried her to her bed. When he left several hours later she lay sprawled nude on the tangled sheets, too exhausted to get up to find a nightgown or even pull the sheet over herself. She slept with a heavenly smile on her passion-swollen mouth.

The nights that followed were just as passionate, and she should have been wilting from lack of sleep, but instead she was radiant, full of energy. She sailed through the hours at work, too immersed in her own happiness to really pay attention to Preston's growing depression, knowing that when the night came she would be in Cord's arms again.

Her happiness made the blow, when it came, just that much more cruel. She was going over a productivity report from the small electronics plant they owned when Preston appeared at her office door. Susan looked up with a ready smile, but the smile died when she saw the taut expression that had made his face a gray mask. Concern snapped her to her feet, and she went across the room to him, taking his arm. "What is it?"

He stared at her for a minute, and she silently reproached herself for not having paid more attention to him this past week. She'd known that something was bothering him, but she hadn't wanted anything to dim her happiness. Her selfishness made her writhe inside.

Wordlessly, he extended the papers in his hand. Susan took them, her brow wrinkling as she stared at them.

"What is this?"

"Read it." He moved over to a chair and lowered himself into it, his movements slow and jerky, strangely uncoordinated.

She flipped through the papers, reading slowly. Her eyes widened, and she read them over again, hoping that she hadn't understood correctly, but there was no way to misunderstand. The meaning of every word was perfectly clear. Cord had bought up an outstanding loan against the Blackstone Corporation and was calling it in. They had thirty days to pay.

Almost suffocated by the thick sense of betrayal that rose in her throat, she dropped the papers to the top of her desk and lifted her stunned gaze to Preston. She couldn't speak, though she wet her lips and tried to force her throat to form the word. How could he have done that?

"Well, now you know where he went on that mystery trip," Cord said bitterly, nodding towards the papers. "Dallas."

She braced one hand flat on the desk, trying to support herself as acid nausea rose in her throat. She conquered the moment, but she couldn't conquer the pain that threatened to bend her double. Why had he done it? Didn't he realize that this hurt her as much as it did Preston? This wasn't just Preston he was striking at; he was threatening the entire corporation, her livelihood as well as the livelihoods of thousands of workers who depended on their jobs to put food on the table. He had to know, so the only supposition she could reach was that he simply didn't care. After the week she had spent with him, the passion she'd shared with him, the brutal realization that it all meant nothing to him was like a slap in the face, and she reeled from the impact of it.

"I thought we were protected against this sort of thing." Lifelessly, Preston stared at the floor. "But he found a way, and he's bought up the loan. He's called it in. God knows where he got the money to buy it up, or even how he knew where to go—" He broke off suddenly, his blue eyes narrowing as he stared at Susan with bitter accusation.

For a moment she didn't read the expression on his face; then her eyes flared with understanding. She went even whiter than she had been. How could he so readily believe that she would betray them to Preston, after all she had done to try to convince Cord not to seek revenge? But why not? Why should Preston trust her? Cord didn't trust her, despite the passionate devotion she revealed every time she gave herself to him.

"How can you believe that?" she choked. "I haven't told him anything."

"Then how did he know?"

"I don't know!" she shouted, then stopped, pressing her hands against her mouth, aghast at her loss of control. "I'm sorry. I didn't tell him; I swear I didn't."

His blue eyes were suddenly sick, and he drew a deep, shaking breath. "My God, he's got us fighting each other," he said miserably, getting to his feet and coming around to her. He took her in his arms and held her tightly to him, rocking back and forth in a comforting motion. "I know you didn't tell him; you don't have a deceptive bone in your body. I'm sorry for being so stupid. I'm rattled, Susan, he's trying to bankrupt us."

The evidence lay on her desk, so she couldn't even try to deny it. She pressed her face into Preston's shoulder, vaguely aware that she was shaking. The awful thing was that, even with her knowing that Cord was capable of being so ruthless and devious, the aching, burning love she felt for him didn't diminish at all. She had known the chance she was taking in mating with that human tiger.

How long they clung together like frightened children trying to comfort each other, she didn't know. But gradually she calmed, and their embrace loosened.

There were things to do, strategies to plan. "How badly will we be weakened?" she asked in a voice that was flatly calm.

Preston's arms dropped away completely, and he turned to drag a chair around so he could sit beside her at her desk. "Dangerously. He couldn't have timed it better. At the moment, our cash flow is restricted because we've invested so heavily in projects that won't begin paying for at least another year, possibly two years. You handled the paperwork on the laser project in Palo Alto, so you know how much we've sunk in that one project alone.''

She did. ''Then what about our personal assets? If we liquidate, we can raise enough money to cover the loan—''

He was shaking his head to stop her, and he smiled wryly at her. ''How do you think I raised the money to repay him for the money we used?''

She sat back, stunned. How neatly Cord had boxed them into a corner! He must have been planning this all along. First he had threatened to bring charges against Preston for stealing, then he had sat back and done nothing, giving Preston time to replace the amount taken, knowing that Preston would have to stretch himself thin to cover that much at one time. He had maneuvered them like pieces on a chessboard.

Still, she cast around for a solution. ''Imogene and I can cover it. We have stocks we can sell, and property in prime locations—''

''Susan, stop it,'' he said gently. ''Mother and I were both involved in using Cord's money, and we both had to sacrifice to replace it. She's stretched as thinly as I am, and you can't handle this all on your own. You wouldn't have anything left if you did.''

Susan shrugged. The thought of being penniless didn't bother her. ''If we can hold on for a year, two years at the most, then the corporation would be safe. That's what matters.''

''Do you really think I'd let you sell off everything Vance gave you? From the moment he married you, he worked to make certain you'd always be comfortable, no matter what happened. He cherished you, and I won't let you undo all of the things he did for you.''

''If we can stay out of bankruptcy, everything can be replaced.''

''Covering this loan won't guarantee that. What if he buys up another one? He's obviously got money behind him, enough money to destroy us if he wants to keep pushing. If he buys up another loan, we end up in the bankruptcy courts, even if you do sell everything you own to cover this one.''

Preston's logic was irrefutable, and she went cold to the bone. ''Then there's nothing we can do?''

''I don't know. We're going to have to consider everything. The damnable part of it is, he has a stake in this corporation himself, and that isn't stopping him. He'll take that loss in order to get back at me. I can't believe he went this far. I know he hates me, but this is...this is crazy!''

It was unnerving to think of someone so determined, so ruthless,

that he would go against his own best interests in his quest for
revenge. He was tightening the screws, pushing, enjoying tormenting Preston. He'd said that he wanted to make the other man squirm.
He might have reason enough for the way he felt; she could only
guess at the hellholes he'd been in since he'd been turned away by
his family, though she had seen the marks they had left on his body.
But no matter what the past had been, it was time the senseless
hurting was ended. It had gone on long enough, tearing families
apart, creating bitter enemies of the same blood. She wanted to take
Cord by the neck and shake him until he'd regained his senses, and
for a moment she could almost smile at the image of herself shaking
someone who was almost a foot taller than she was, and who out-
weighed her by about a hundred pounds.

She was exhausted when she went home that day. They had spent
the hours pouring over financial statements, marshaling their forces
to meet this challenge. Preston was a superb corporate tactician, but
she'd never before realized the extent of his subtlety and expertise.
He knew exactly how much they could sacrifice without dealing
themselves a mortal blow, and he'd set the wheels in motion to
liquidate the assets he thought the corporation could spare.

She was late getting home, but Emily was waiting for her with
a hot meal, which the older woman made certain she consumed.
Somehow, Emily always knew when Susan was tired or depressed,
and she would dispense an extra measure of coddling, but not all
her tender concern could erase the tension from Susan's face that
night. Thinking that all of her nights out with Cord might be tiring
Susan out, Emily asked, "Are you going out with Cord again tonight?"

Susan started at hearing the name that had been reverberating in
her thoughts. "Oh...I don't know. He said he might be over later
tonight. He had to drive to New Orleans to take care of some business." She felt sick at the thought. What sort of business? Finding
another nail to drive into the coffin of Blackstone Corporation?

"Well, I think you need to get more sleep than you've had this
past week," Emily scolded. "You look like a dishrag. Send him
home early if he does come over."

Somehow, Susan managed a smile for the woman, grateful for
her concern. "Yes, I will." She loved him, but right now she
couldn't be with him. She had the feeling that if she looked over
her shoulder, she'd be able to see the handle of the knife that was
sticking in her back.

Perhaps he wouldn't come. She hoped he wouldn't. She was too
tired, too hurt, to raw from the knowledge of his betrayal. But why

kid herself? He wouldn't see it as a betrayal, because he'd never promised her anything. All he had given her was the coin of physical passion, not a hint of commitment beyond the moment.

She hoped he wouldn't come, yet she wasn't surprised later that night to hear the rumble of the red Blazer that he used for his casual driving. She'd begun to think that she was safe for the night; it was after nine o'clock, and she'd been thinking about taking her bath and going to bed. But now he was here, and she stood in the den, her heart beginning to pound in apprehension. She felt sick; her hands were cold and clammy, and she pressed them against her skirt. How could she face him? Why couldn't he have waited until tomorrow, when she might be calmer?

The doorbell rang, but still she stood rigidly in the middle of the floor, unable to force her legs to move. Cold dread rippled down her spine. Seconds ticked past, and the doorbell began an insistent peal as he jammed his finger onto it and held it there. It wasn't until he began to pound on the door with enough force to rattle it on its hinges that she managed to move, her legs shaking. She crept into the foyer and released the bolt on the door.

The door crashed open under the impact of his fist, narrowly missing knocking her down. Cord loomed over her, his face dark and savage. He seized her by the arms, his fingers biting into her soft flesh. "Are you all right?" he bit out. "The lights were on, but when you didn't answer the door I thought something must be wrong. I was going to go around and break out the glass in the sliding doors—" He never finished the sentence, instead pulling her to him with one iron arm locked around her waist, his other hand cupping her chin and turning her face up to him. He bent his head and his mouth closed over hers, hard, hungrily, and for a moment she forgot everything. She was swamped by the exciting maleness of his scent, the coffee taste of his mouth. She clung to him, her fingers digging into the heavy muscles of his back as she rose on tiptoe to fit herself to him.

His desire rose swiftly, launched from the perfect condition of his superb body. Before she could think, he had lifted her off her feet and started up the stairs, after kicking the door shut. Feeling the last vestiges of control slipping away from her, Susan freed her mouth from his and gasped, "Wait! I don't—"

He caught her mouth again, his tongue plunging deep inside, stifling her desperate words as he placed her on the bed. If he had released her then, stepping back to remove his clothes, she might have had a chance, but he stayed with her. He covered her, his mouth taking hers with hard, deep kisses, while his hands delved under her skirt and peeled away her underwear. Stunned by his urgency, after a moment she forgot about the rift between them and held tightly to his neck, her slender body arching to him as he parted her thighs and fit himself between them. He paused a moment to adjust his clothing and insure her protection, then thrust deeply into her, the impact of his body making her jerk.

She wasn't the only one taken by surprise by his urgency. Cord had been unpleasantly surprised by the desperation that had knotted his stomach when she hadn't answered the door, and he'd had a vision of her sprawled lifeless at the foot of the stairs. Or someone could have broken in on her, and raped her before killing her. That last thought had made the hair on the back of his neck lift up, and he had been snarling silently as he pounded on the door. Then it had opened and she'd stood there, pale and silent, but obviously healthy, and his desire had bloomed with his relief. He had to have her right then, bury himself in her and satisfy his body as well as his mind that she was still there, still healthy, and still his. The taste of her, the silken feel of her under his hands, the intimate clasp of her body, were all that could drive the fear from his mind. He luxuriated in his possession of her, feeling her response building and the tension in her growing tighter, and the knowledge that she wanted him, that he could satisfy her, was a pleasure as great as that he was taking from her soft flesh.

Susan heard the soft little whimpers in the back of her throat, but she was powerless to stop them, powerless to control her body. She reached blindly for satisfaction, her fingers clenched in his hair, her body arching up to meet his. He was crushing her, yet she didn't feel his weight; his heavy shoulders and chest were holding her down, yet she was soaring high and free, everything forgotten except for this moment in time. She was completely physical, yielding to his rampant masculinity and demanding that he give her all of himself.

He caught her legs, pulling them high to coil them around his back, and the whimpers turned into sharp, breathless cries. Deliberately he paced his movements, keeping her on the edge but not allowing her to go over it, not wanting the act to end. His strong hands on her hips controlled her, guided her, held her when she would have taken over the rhythm he'd set. She clenched her teeth on the agony of pleasure that boiled in her; then suddenly it was too much to be held in, and she heard the words of love that she gasped, the words that she'd always longed to say but had held inside.

A rumble in his chest and the tightening of his hands on her flesh signaled the end of his control, and he began to thrust hungrily into her. Instantly an incredible heat exploded inside her, washing through her with ever-widening waves, making her shudder beneath him. She sank her teeth into his shoulder in an effort to control the sounds she was making, and the primitive, sensual act pushed him over the edge. Short, harsh cries tore from his throat as his satisfaction thundered through him, and he clasped her to him with a wild strength that made her gasp for breath, as if he could meld her flesh with his for all time. When he'd finished, he slowly relaxed until he lay limply on her, his body still quivering with small aftershocks. She smoothed his sweat-damp hair, her fingers gentle on his moist temple. His hot breath seared her throat, and she felt the flutter of his eyelashes against her skin as he began to doze.

But he lay there for only a moment before rousing himself and gently moving from her. He rolled heavily onto his back and lay there, one brawny forearm thrown over his eyes.

Susan lay beside him, tension and dread growing in her again now that the appetites of her body had been satisfied. She should never have let that happen, not tonight, not when she had so much on her mind. And she had told him that she loved him. He couldn't have misunderstood her; it seemed to her that the words still lingered in the air, echoing with ghostly insistence. Would he say anything, or would he just ignore what she'd said? He hadn't asked for any commitment from her any more than he'd offered one. He probably wasn't even surprised; it couldn't be the first time that a woman in his arms had cried out that she loved him.

Caught in her misery, she was only half-aware when he left the bed. The sound of running water caught her attention, and she opened her eyes to look at him through the open door of the bathroom as he stood drinking deeply from a glass of water. His strong brown throat worked as he appeased his thirst. He'd already straightened his clothing, she saw, and her hands clenched into fists. He'd be leaving now that his sexual appetite had been satisfied.

He came back and stood over her, his level dark brows lowered over eyes so pale and fierce that she almost flinched from them. "You scared the hell out of me," he said flatly. "Why didn't you answer the door?"

Restlessly, she sat up, and flushed wildly when she saw that her skirt was still tangled above her waist. Quickly she fumbled with the cloth, straightening it and pushing it down to cover her nakedness, an act that sparked a flash of fury in his eyes. But when she darted a glance up at him, she saw only the same iron implacability that had been there before as he waited for an answer. Pushing her tumbled hair back from her face, she said in a dull tone, "You bought up a loan against us and called it in."

Silence lay thickly between them for a long moment; then he sliced it by saying harshly, "You're not involved in that."

A laugh broke from her throat, a laugh that was almost a sob, and she got quickly to her feet, leaving the bed where she had given herself to him so thoroughly. For a moment she feared her legs wouldn't hold her, but after an initial wobble she regained control of them and moved a few paces away from him. "I have to be. You know that everything is tied together. If you attack them financially, you're attacking me financially. If you bankrupt them, you bankrupt me."

"You don't have anything to worry about. I'll take care of you."

The cool arrogance of his words almost made her choke, and she whirled on him in disbelief. "Is that supposed to make it all right? You'll reduce me to a...a kept woman, and I'm supposed to be grateful?"

One dark eyebrow quirked. "I don't see your problem," he said, and added with casual cruelty, "after all, you said that you love me."

She winced, unable to believe he'd attacked her so soon, even though she'd put the weapon in his hand. Suddenly she was too close to him, and she put the width of the room between them, withdrawing from him as far as she could. She bent her head, unable to look at him and face the contemptuous knowledge that she knew must be in his eyes. "Would you...would you actually push us all into bankruptcy just to get back at Preston? Even knowing that a lot of other people are involved, that they'd lose their jobs?"

"Yes." His voice was hard, as hard as he was, and the last vestige of hope died in her. Until then there had been one small shred of faith left; she had been able to hope that he was only punishing Preston and would stop before things went too far.

"You'd be hurting yourself!" she cried. "How can you do this?"

He gave a negligent shrug. "I've got other things to fall back on."

She'd begged before, with no result, but now she was reduced to doing it again. "Cord, stop this! Please! Don't push it until it's gone too far. When will you be satisfied? After you've ruined us all, then what? Will it have brought Judith back to you?"

His face turned into stone, and his eyes narrowed. Wildly, goaded by her own pain, she lashed out at him, sensing that she'd found a way to wound him. "You're just trying to ease your own guilt about Judith, because of your part in what happened to her—"

With a growl he strode across the room, seizing her before she could dart to the side and avoid him. His hands bit into her shoulders and he shook her lightly. "Shut up about Judith! I made a mistake in telling you about her, but you'll be making an even bigger one if you ever mention her to me again. For the last time, stay out of this."

"I can't. I'm already in it." She stared up at him with eyes so huge that they eclipsed her entire face, eyes so filled with pain that any other woman would have been weeping uncontrollably. They were going to destroy each other, Cord and Preston, and she was helpless to stop it. There could be no winners in this family war, because when the bond of common blood goes bad, it causes a rift that can never be healed. She saw the chasm that was already widening between herself and Cord, and she wanted to scream out in desperate protest, but there was nothing she could do. She held herself rigidly in his painful grip, trying to control the shrieking agony that was tearing her heart apart.

His grasp on her eased, and he stroked his thumbs over the fragile ridges of her collarbones. "You're too soft for this," he murmured to himself; then he eased her back into his embrace, shifting his arms to hold her against him. She was silent, letting herself rest against him because she hadn't the strength to deny herself what she feared might be the last time he'd hold her like this. He bent his head to press his warm lips into the sensitive curve where her neck met her shoulder, and a delicious shiver ran over her body. Just like that, with only a casual caress, he was able to make her want him again. She loved him too much, too dangerously, because she could hold nothing of herself back. There was no way she could protect herself.

"Don't go back to work," he instructed softly, brushing his lips against her hair. "Stay at home, and stay out of this. Vance left you secure, and whatever happens to Preston won't affect you at all." His big hands stroked slowly over her back and shoulders, their effect on her hypnotic. "You said that you love me; if you do, you won't take his side against me."

For a moment, for a weak, delicious moment, she wanted nothing more than to do just as he said, to let his hard embrace protect her and make her forget all other considerations. Then she stiffened and slowly pushed herself away from him, her face taut and pale.

"Yes, I love you," she said quietly, because there was no use in trying to hide it from him any longer. How could she deny it, when her body told him the truth every time he touched her? "But I have to do whatever I can to stop you from bankrupting the family."

His eyes narrowed. "You're choosing him over me?"

"No. But I think you're wrong in what you're trying to do, and if you won't stop, then I have to help him fight you."

Black fury gathered in him, sparking out of his pale eyes, but he held it in. "Is it asking too much for you to trust me in this?" he rasped, watching her carefully.

"The same way you trust me?" she shot back. "You told me yourself, just a moment ago, that you're trying to bankrupt us! Is that supposed to reassure me?"

He gave a derisive snort, the fire in his eyes turning to ice. "I should've known! You spouted that garbage about loving me, *then* you asked me so sweetly to ease up on Preston. You're good in the sack, baby, the best I've had, but you don't have that kind of hold on me."

"I know," she whispered blankly. "I've always known that. But I wasn't trying for any emotional blackmail. I think...I think you'd better go."

"I think you're right."

As he moved past her, she blinked at him with eyes suddenly blurred by a film of tears. He was going, and she knew he wouldn't be back. "Goodbye," she choked, feeling herself shatter inside.

He gave her a grim look. "It's not goodbye, not yet. You'll be seeing me around, though you'll wish you weren't." Then he was gone, lightly taking the stairs with graceful bounds. Slowly she followed him, and she reached the door in time to watch the red flare of the Blazer's taillights disappear as he rounded a curve. She shut the door and locked it, then methodically moved about and made certain the house was secure for the night. She even sat down and watched the late movie until it went off, then realized that she hadn't absorbed any of it. She didn't even know the name of it, or the names of the actors. She hadn't been thinking of anything, just sitting there, her mind numb. She wanted it to stay numb, because she knew that when the numbness wore off, she was going to hurt more than she could bear.

She went through the motions of going to bed; she showered and put on her nightgown, moisturized her face, neatened up her bedroom and put her discarded clothing in the laundry basket. Then she lay in bed until dawn, her eyes open and staring at the ceiling. He was gone.

He was gone! It was a litany of pain that echoed through her endlessly, an inner accompaniment to the gray, dreary days that followed. The sun could have been shining; she simply didn't know. But she couldn't see any sunshine, and she functioned only through instinct and sheer grim determination. She'd kept going after Vance's death, and now the same steely determination kept her upright even when she wanted nothing more than to collapse in a corner of her bedroom and not ever come out again.

She'd had to accept the bleak truth of Vance's death because she had seen his lifeless body, had buried him. It was worse with Cord. He was gone from her, yet he seemed to be everywhere. They met at several functions, and she had to act as if it didn't almost double her over with pain to see him. He was usually with Cheryl, of course, though she heard that he wasn't limiting himself to the other woman. She had to see him, had to listen to him say all the polite things while his icy eyes cut her, had to watch him slide his arm about Cheryl's waist, had to imagine him kissing the other woman, touching her with his hot, magic fingers, drawing her beneath him in his big bed at the cabin.

To stay sane she drove herself at work every day, working longer and longer hours, working frantically with Preston in an effort to raise enough cash to pay off the loan without seriously weakening the corporation. It was an impossible task; they both knew that if Cord chose to attack them again, they wouldn't be able to meet his demands.

Quietly, without letting Preston know, Susan sold some prime property in New Orleans that Vance had left her and added the proceeds to their cash fund. Preston would have died rather than let her sell off any of her personal property, though she knew he'd been heavily liquidating his. Sometimes, when she thought about the fact that Cord was deliberately forcing them to sell off land that had been in the family for generations, she hated him, but always that hate was mingled with love. If she hadn't loved him so much, she wouldn't have felt so betrayed by his actions, wouldn't have been so deeply angry when she saw Preston, without complaint, destitute himself personally in order to keep the corporation out of bankruptcy.

This had shaken Imogene, too, to the very basis of her foundations. Since the night she and Susan had argued so violently, she had been a little quiet, as if some of the spirit had gone out of her. Perhaps she had sensed then that she couldn't fight Cord, that by the very act of returning he had won. Always before, Imogene had been actively involved in any corporate decisions, but now she let Preston and Susan carry the weight. For the first time she was showing her age.

At last it was done. They had enough to cover the loan, and though Susan and Preston shared a moment of relief, it wasn't without worry. They had used every ounce of spare reserve they had, and another blow would be too much. Still, the relief was strong enough that they celebrated in the French Quarter that night, in a far noisier restaurant than the one Cord had taken her to. But she was glad of the noise and distraction, and for once she ate a good meal. In the time since Cord had sauntered out of her house she'd lost several pounds that she hadn't been able to spare. It was as much overwork as depression, or so she told herself every morning when she frowningly examined herself in the mirror, noting that her clothing was too loose to fall correctly on her increasingly slender body.

On the drive home Preston startled her by apologizing. "You've broken up with Cord because of this, haven't you?"

There was no denying it, no use in concocting a lame excuse that they simply hadn't gotten along, so she simply murmured, "Yes," and let it go at that.

"I'm sorry." He cast her a frustrated glance. "I should be glad, because I didn't like you being with him, but I'm sorry that you've been hurt. I didn't want you in the middle like this."

"I made my decision. He insisted that I choose sides, and I simply couldn't watch him cost a lot of people their jobs without trying to do something about it."

"I hope he knows what he's lost," Preston said violently, and returned his attention to his driving.

Even if he knew, he wouldn't care, Susan thought dully. He certainly wasn't pining away for her; he looked better every time she saw him, his hard, dark face becoming darker as the late spring sun continued to bronze him. Had he finished clearing off the land down by the creek? Was he doing any more work on the cabin? When he had pushed her out of his life, he had left her lost and desolate, without any emotional focus. She wondered if the rest of her life would be like this, a dull misery to be endured as she went through the motions of living.

Chapter 10

If she had known what awaited her when she walked into the office three days later, she would never have gone. Beryl was already there and had a fragrant pot of coffee brewing. "Good morning, Beryl. Is Mr. Blackstone in yet?"

"No, not yet. Do you want a cup of coffee now?"

Susan smiled at the young woman. "I'll get it. You look like you have enough to handle right now," she teased, nodding at the stacks of paperwork that littered Beryl's desk.

Beryl nodded ruefully. "Don't I, though? Mr. Blackstone must have worked until midnight last night. He left all of this, and enough tapes on the dictaphone to keep me typing through the weekend."

"Really? I didn't know he'd planned to come back to the office last night. He left when I did, and I can't think of anything that would have been so urgent."

She poured herself some coffee and carefully balanced the cup as she went into her office, keeping a cautious eye on the sloshing liquid. She placed the cup on her desk and walked around to pull the curtains open, letting the brilliant morning sunlight pour into the room. The day was hot already, with a sultry feel to it that had dampened the back of her neck with perspiration even before she'd left the house that morning. She was beginning to think of taking a vacation, finding a beach somewhere and doing nothing more strenuous than lying in the sun. Somehow, sweating on the beach didn't sound nearly as hot as sweating at work.

After fingering the blossoms of her favorite geranium, she went back to her desk and sat down. It wasn't until then that she saw the thick manila envelope lying there with her name printed on it in big block letters. Frowning, she opened the sealed envelope and pulled out a sheaf of papers. On top was some sort of legal document, and she turned it around to read it.

Immediately she went deathly white, not having to read further than the front page to know it for what it was. Cord had bought up another loan and called it in.

My God, he was going to do it. They couldn't weather this. They couldn't pay, and the shock waves he was going to make would reverberate throughout the corporation and the banks they were involved with. Their credit would be ruined. They simply couldn't pay this and keep operating.

Where was Preston? She wanted to run to him, wanted to hear him say that he would be able to work another little piece of magic and somehow come up with the money they needed. It was selfish of her, and she controlled the urge. He would have to know, yes, but let him have a few more hours of peace, of not knowing.

How had the envelope gotten on her desk? The office was always locked when they left, and Preston had worked late the night before....

Then she knew, and she felt sick. Preston already knew about the loan, and he'd left the envelope on her desk.

She flipped through the legal document, and behind it she found a letter to her, in Preston's handwriting. His usually elegant style was a scrawl as if the letter had been written in agitation, but the writing was unmistakably his. She read the letter through carefully, and when she was finished she let it fall to the floor, tears searing her eyes.

If Cord had wanted only to defeat Preston, he'd won. Preston had gone. His letter was both defeated and desperate. He'd done all he could, but he couldn't fight Cord any longer. Perhaps, if he left, Cord would let up. By taking himself out of the picture, Preston hoped that Cord would cease his vengeance.

Cord had had the legal paperwork delivered to Preston at home, by special messenger, an act that chilled Susan with its calculated cruelty. Preston had then returned to the office, methodically finished all the work currently on his desk, left the letter for Susan, and disappeared.

She couldn't blame Preston for leaving; she knew that it was his last-ditch effort to save the corporation, to keep Cord from putting it under. He hoped that when Cord found that Susan was running the corporation he wouldn't call in the loan, knowing that his prime target had fled and that now he was attacking only a woman he'd previously been very interested in.

As if that would stop him! Susan thought despairingly. Then her spine stiffened. As if she would run crying to him now, asking him to have mercy on her!

She'd begged him before, for Preston's sake, for everyone's sake, and he'd turned a cold shoulder to her. She wouldn't beg him for herself now.

Susan didn't recognize the fierce anger that seized her, but she wasn't going to just give up. If she had to fight him until she didn't have a penny left, then that's what she would do.

She picked up the telephone and quickly punched out a number. She wasn't surprised when Imogene answered herself.

"Imogene, do you know where Preston is?" she asked directly, not wasting time with polite greetings.

"No. He only told me that he was going." Imogene's voice sounded tired and a little thick, as if she'd been crying.

"Do you know why he left?"

"Yes. I tried to talk him out of it, but he wouldn't listen. He just wouldn't listen," she sighed. "He thinks that this is the only way he can get Cord to stop. What...what are you going to do? Are you going to see Cord?"

"No!" Susan said violently. She inhaled swiftly, searching for control and finding it. "I'm not going to tell him anything. I'm going to fight him with everything I have, and I need your help."

"Help?" Imogene echoed blankly. "What can I do?"

"You've been involved with this corporation for years. You have a lot of contacts, and you know everything that's going on even if you don't come to the office. There's too much to do on an every-day basis for me to handle it by myself and fight Cord, too. Will you come? Do you want to fight him?"

There was a long silence on the other end of the phone, and Susan waited tensely, her eyes closed. She really needed Imogene's help. She didn't fool herself that she'd be able to carry on for long by herself. The burden would break her. But Imogene hadn't been herself, and she wasn't sure what her mother-in-law would do.

"I don't want to fight him," Imogene finally said softly. "This insanity has gone on long enough. If I thought it would stop him, I'd sign everything I own over to him this minute just to bring peace to our family. I have to share in the responsibility for this mess, and I'm not proud of it. I shouldn't have turned on him; he's family, and I forgot that. I regret it so much now, but regrets don't do any good."

Susan's heart sank. "You won't help?"

"I didn't say that. I'll be there as soon as I can get myself ready and make the drive. But it's not to fight him, dear. It's to help you, and to do what I can to keep the corporation out of bankruptcy. That's the only important thing now, and when it's over, I'll crawl on my hands and knees to Cord if that will satisfy him and stop this war.''

The thought of proud Imogene being willing to humble herself in such a way left Susan fighting back tears again. ''I'll be waiting,'' she whispered, and hung up the phone before she embarrassed herself by sobbing into it.

If she had worked before, it was nothing compared to the way she drove herself now. She arrived in the office shortly after dawn and often remained until nine or ten in the evening. On the surface, it didn't seem possible that she would be able to meet Cord's demands, but she didn't give up. Imogene was on the phone constantly, calling in favors, trying to arrange a loan that would keep them going. But even old friends were suddenly wary of the Blackstone Corporation, for the business grapevine was remarkably sensitive, and word had filtered through that they were on shaky financial ground. Their common stock was trading hands rapidly, and in desperation Susan put some of her own stock up for sale. Preston and Imogene had already sold some of their stock in order to replace the money they'd embezzled from Cord, hoping to buy more when their cash flow had improved. But Cord had kept them on the ropes and hadn't let the pressure ease at all. At least the price of the stock was holding up, due to the brisk trading, but Susan knew that she had to take even more desperate measures.

She had stock in other companies, blue-chip investments, and ruthlessly she turned them into cash. She kept it secret from Imogene, knowing that Imogene would be as horrified at the idea, as Preston had been. Imogene was holding up wonderfully, attacking the work with increased vigor, and as she settled into it she began to display a wonderful panache for the job. Susan didn't want to do anything to throw the older woman back into the mild depression that had held her in its grip lately. She knew that Imogene worried about Preston and fretted over the absence of her only living son; that burden was enough.

Every morning when Susan looked in the mirror she realized anew that she was living on her nerves, and sometimes she wondered how much longer she could keep going. The shadows under her eyes seemed to have become permanent fixtures that she carefully disguised with makeup. She always left the house now before Emily arrived, and she was too tense to prepare breakfast herself and eat it. There was always a meal left for her when she got home at night, needing only to be warmed, but more often than not Susan was too exhausted to eat it. She was existing on pots of coffee and hasty bites taken out of sandwiches, sandwiches that were seldom finished and instead left to grow stale while she worked.

The steamy weather further sapped her strength, the heat and humidity weighing her down like a smothering blanket. She couldn't sleep at night, even with the air-conditioning on, and she would lie watching the flash of heat lightning, hoping that the bursts of light meant thunderstorms and rain, but the clouds never came and each day dawned hotter than the one before.

Lying on her bed in the thick, humid nights, the light cover kicked down to the foot of the bed because even a sheet was too oppressive, she thought of Cord. During the day she could resent him, hate him, fight him, but when the nights came she could no longer hold the memories at bay, and she would hug her pillow to herself, keening her pain almost soundlessly into the pillow. He had been on that bed with her, his dark head on the other pillow; he had wrapped her graceful legs around him, linking her to him with a chain of flesh while he drove deeply into her body and her heart. She wanted him so much that her entire body ached, her breasts throbbing, her thighs and loins heavy with need. She wanted just to see him, to watch his beautifully shaped mouth quirk into one of those devastatingly wicked smiles. Whenever she dozed she dreamed of him, and she would jerk herself awake with a start as she reached out for him. Sometimes the impulse to go to him was almost too strong to ignore, and in the hot, heavy nights she suffered alone.

She heard, through the grapevine of gossip that always yielded an astonishing amount of information, that Cord was gone again, and this time she didn't wonder if he'd ever come back; now she wondered what new weapon he was readying to use against her. No, not against *her* personally, but against them all in general. Though she wasn't able to pinpoint the exact date when he'd left, she knew that it was about the same time Preston had gone; it was possible that he didn't know Preston had bowed out and left the corporation in her lap. As far as all their acquaintances were concerned, Cord was on a business trip. That was the tale she and Imogene had decided to put out, rather than trigger a flood of gossip that would grow larger and wilder with every turn.

Despite everything, when the grapevine informed her that Cord had returned, she didn't feel the dread that should have overwhelmed her. For a sweet moment of insanity she was simply glad that he'd returned, that he was once more close by geographically, if not emotionally. Somehow she felt that if he was at least in Mississippi, then it wasn't all over. When it was finished for good, he'd leave for good.

If she hadn't been so tired, so desperate, pushed beyond common sense, she'd never have considered the idea. But late one afternoon she thought again of the ridges. She hadn't slept at all the night before, with her thoughts whirling around in her mind like a rabid squirrel in a cage, until she felt as if her very skull were sore from being banged from within. The air conditioner couldn't handle the heat and humidity, and her lightweight tan suit clung to her sticky skin. She'd already shed the jacket, since it was late and everyone else had already gone home, but even the thin cotton camisole top she'd worn with the suit seemed to be restricting her. A distant rumble of thunder held out the hope of rain to a parched region, but Susan had ceased believing in the thunder's promise. It had proved to be deceptive too often lately.

She had done everything she could think of, and still she hadn't managed to scrape together enough cash to pay off the loan. She'd liquidated a large portion of her stock in Blackstone Corporation, all her stock in everything else, and had disposed of all of the property Vance had accumulated for her...all of it except for the land the house stood on, and the ridges.

The ridges. The thought of them was like a jolt of electricity, straightening her in her chair. *The ridges!* With their promise of oil or natural gas, they were a gold mine, and she'd had it under her nose all the time. The money she could get from leasing them would be enough to finish covering the loan, and in her exhaustion she thought that it would be only fitting that the money from the ridges be used to defeat Cord; after all, it had been the ridges that had brought him back to Mississippi in the first place.

In the back of her mind she knew it was odd that Cord hadn't pressed her about signing the lease, but she simply couldn't follow his reasoning. She loved him, but even after weeks of agonized wondering, she couldn't understand him.

The thought of the ridges gave her a spurt of strength, rather like a marathon runner's last desperate burst of speed. She would drive out to the cabin and offer the lease to Cord, and he could take it right now or leave it. If he didn't take it, then she'd lease the land to the first oil company she could interest in it, but she was going to give him the first chance at it. She knew that her excuse was flimsy, but suddenly she had to see him. Even if he were an enemy now, she had to see him.

Without giving herself time to reconsider, she locked the office and left the building. If she thought about it, she'd begin to worry, and she'd let the doubts change her mind. Her hands were trembling as she guided the Audi out of Biloxi. A distracted glance at the fuel gauge warned her to stop for gas, but even that small interruption in her progress was too much to tolerate. She thought she'd have enough gas to get home, and that was all she cared about at the moment. She'd worry about getting to work later.

The radio volume was low, but even the background noise was rasping on her nerves, and she snapped the radio off with a quick, irritable movement. It was so hot, and she felt so weak! A moment of dizziness alarmed her, and she turned the air-conditioning vents so the cold air was blowing right on her face. After a moment she felt better, and she urged the Audi to greater speeds.

The Blazer was parked under one of the giant oak trees that kept the fierce sun away from the front of the cabin, and the front door stood open. Susan guided the Audi to a hard stop in front of the porch, and as she opened the door to get out, Cord strolled lazily out of the cabin to lean against one of the posts that supported the porch roof. He had on boots, and jeans so old that one of the pockets was missing, and that was all. She looked up at him and her heart stopped for a moment. He'd begun to let his beard grow again, and the several days' growth of whiskers on his jaw made him look like an outlaw out of a Western. His hard, muscled torso was darkly tanned, his hair longer, and if anything, his pale eyes were even more compelling than she'd remembered. Her mouth went dry, and her legs wobbled as she went up the steps, clinging with all her strength to the rough railing.

She'd tried to imagine what his first words would be, and her imagination had supplied any number of brutal things that would wound her. She braced herself for them as his narrowed gaze went over her from head to foot.

"Come on in and have a glass of iced tea," he invited, his rough, callused hand closing on her elbow and urging her inside the cabin. "You look like you're about to melt."

Was that it? She had to swallow an almost hysterical giggle. After all her panic, he calmly invited her in for iced tea!

Somehow she found herself sitting at his table while he moved around the kitchen. "I was just about to eat," he said easily. "Nothing hot in this weather, just a ham sandwich and a tossed salad, but there's plenty for two."

She started. He wanted her to eat? "Oh, no, thank you—"

He interrupted her refusal by sliding a plate in front of her. She stared down at the ham sandwich, wondering if she could possibly swallow a bite of it, and his hand entered her field of vision again, this time placing a chilled bowl of salad beside the plate. A napkin and cutlery were placed by her hand, and a big glass of beautiful, amber tea over ice finished her instant meal. When she lifted her stunned gaze, she saw that he'd set the same for himself, and he draped his tall frame into the chair across from her.

"Eat," he said gently. "You'll feel better after you do."

When had she last had a meal, a real meal? The days had merged into one long, steamy nightmare, and she couldn't recall her last meal. Half-eaten sandwiches, coffee, and an occasional candy bar had constituted her diet since Preston had left. She began to eat slowly, and the crisp, fresh flavor of the salad, only lightly coated with tart dressing, was suddenly the best thing she could imagine eating. She savored every bite of it, and the cold tea seemed to cool her from the inside out. Because she'd been eating so little she was unable to eat all of the sandwich, but Cord made no comment on the half left on her plate. Instead he swiftly cleared the table, placing the dishes in the sink before coming back to the table and refilling her glass with tea.

"Now," he said, dropping into his chair again, "you don't look like you're going to pass out at my feet, so I'll listen to whatever you came to say."

Susan held the frosty glass between both hands, feeling the refreshing chill on her hot palms. "I want to talk to you about the ridges," she said, but her mind wasn't on her words. She was staring at him, her eyes tracing the lines of his features as if etching them permanently on her memory.

"So talk. What about them?" He folded his arms across his chest and leaned back, bringing his booted feet up and propping them on the chair beside him.

"Do you still want to lease them?"

His lids dropped down to hood his eyes. "Get to the point, Susan."

Nervously, she took a sip of tea, then fidgeted for a moment with the glass, returning it to precisely the same spot where it had been before, making certain that it matched the ring of water that marked its position. "If you want them, then lease them now. I've decided not to wait for the report from the survey. If you don't want the lease any longer, I'm going to lease them to some other company."

"Oh, I still want them," he said softly, "but I'm not going to give you any money on them right now. You'd run all the way to Biloxi to give the money to Preston, and I'll be damned if I'll give you a penny until this is all over. The money from the ridges is for you, to keep you in your accustomed style after Preston doesn't have a penny left.'' He gave her a cynical grin, one full of wry amusement at himself. ''I'll keep you in silk underwear, honey.''

Susan choked and jumped to her feet, her cheeks scarlet. ''Then I'll lease them to someone else!''

''I don't think so,'' he drawled, swinging his long legs to the floor and getting to his feet, moving gracefully to put himself between her and the door. ''If you think I've used every club I have against Preston already, then you're mistaken. If you lease that land to anyone else, I'll crush him, and you can bet your sweet little life on that.''

Susan drew back from him, stumbling a little as she tried to circle the table without turning her back on him. She was slowed by her exhaustion, and totally unable to react when he moved suddenly, cutting her off. His hands closed on her fragile waist, and he felt the slenderness of her under his fingers. His black brows snapped together in a forbidding frown. ''How much weight have you lost?'' he demanded curtly, glaring down at her.

Despite the tremors that quaked through her insides, Susan held herself stiffly. ''That's none of your business.'' Her fingers dug into his biceps as she tried to push him away, but he was as immovable as a boulder.

He held her with one arm and swept his other hand over her body, exploring her newly frail contours. He slid his hand over her hips and buttocks, her slender thighs, then up to rub gently over her breasts, making her cry out and writhe in a desperate attempt to escape him. He held her easily, his eyes blue with fury. ''What in the hell has he done to you?''

Shards of pain pierced her, and she twisted suddenly, a gasping cry breaking from her lips. She managed to break his grip, and she shoved herself away from him, her face pale, her hair straggling out of its once-tidy knot. She hurt so much, and she was so desperate, that she screamed at him, ''He hasn't done anything to me! You've done it; you've done it all! You're not crushing him, you're crushing *me!* He left—'' Horrified at what she was saying, she stuffed her hand into her mouth to stop the mad tumble of words, her eyes huge and so dark they were almost black as she stared at him.

If he had been angry before, he exploded now. Hammering his fist on the table with a force that upset her glass of tea, he roared, ''What do you mean, 'He *left?*' That damned weasel!''

''He's not a weasel!'' She'd been pushed too far to be wary of his temper, to even consider the questionable wisdom of defending

Preston to Cord. "He left because he hoped you'd stop when you
saw that you weren't hurting him any longer! He's trying to save
the corporation, save thousands of jobs—"

"You mean he thought you'd come running to me with the information that you were trying to do it all on your own, and I'd
back off. Damn you, Susan, why didn't you do just that? Why have
you driven yourself into the ground like this?"

"Because I think you're wrong! Preston isn't using me as a sacrificial lamb; if you'd stop hating him long enough, you might see
that he's not the same person he was years ago. You can try to ease
your own guilt by making him pay, but you're wrong to do it!"

"Is that why you've run yourself half to death, to show me how
wrong I am?"

He was never going to listen to reason. The realization slapped
her in the face, and she reeled from the force of it. "No," she
whispered. "I've run myself half to death trying to keep a corporation alive. I don't sleep because I lie awake trying to think of a
way to raise money, and I don't eat because I don't have the time
to spare." She'd gone completely white now, her eyes blazing at
him. "I've sold everything I own, except my house and the ridges,
trying to stay afloat. Do you want them, too? Or maybe the keys
to my car? Or how about my record collection? I've got some real
golden oldies—"

"Shut up!" he thundered, reaching out a hand to catch her.

She twisted away, unable to bear his touch. "Leave me alone,"
she said rawly, then almost ran out of the cabin and tumbled into
the Audi. Slamming the door, she savagely turned the key in the
ignition and the engine caught immediately, but when she put the
car in gear it gave a shuddering jerk and died. "Don't do this to
me," she said through gritted teeth, turning the key again. The
motor turned over but didn't catch, and in horror her eyes flew to
the fuel gauge, where the needle bumped against the E. "Damn
you!" she shrieked at the car. "Don't do this to me!" She began
to pound on the steering wheel with both fists, screaming, "Damn!
Damn! Damn!" with every impact, and tears burst from her eyes.

"Susan!" The door was wrenched open, and Cord caught her
wrists, hauling her out of the car. "Susan, stop it! Settle down,
honey, just settle down. Don't fly apart like this. Let me see if I
can get the car started."

"You can't," she blurted, pulling her hands free to bury her face
in them and weep uncontrollably. It was just too much. She, who
always controlled her tears no matter how much she hurt, had dis-

solved into sobs because she had run out of gas. "The gas tank is empty."

He slid into the driver's seat, keeping one long leg on the outside of the car, as he turned on the ignition and checked it for himself. Sighing, he got out of the car and closed the door. "I'll drive you home."

"I don't want you to drive me home!" She turned to walk down the slope and he made a grab for her, hauling her back just as an enormous clap of thunder shook the earth. She jumped, startled, looking up at the horrendous black cloud that had suddenly taken over the sky. A brisk wind had begun blowing, but she hadn't noticed it until then. As they both looked up, the first enormous raindrops splattered them in the face with stinging force, and Cord put his arm around her, hustling her up on the porch just before the heavens spit open and dropped a deluge so thunderous that they had to shout to make themselves heard.

"You can't walk home in this," he yelled, bending down to put his mouth close to her ear. "We'll wait until it lets up; then I'll take you home."

Despairingly, Susan looked at the gray curtain of rain. Already it had turned the area around the cabin into a shallow river as the water ran down the slope, rushing downward to the creek. She knew that it would splash up to her ankles, and gave in to his opinion that she couldn't walk home. But neither could she stay here, so close to him, in the cabin where they'd made love the first time. Her nerves were at the breaking point. "I want to go home!" she half screamed at him. "I'm not going to stay here! I simply won't!"

A look of savage impatience twisted his face; then he brought himself under control by sheer effort of will. He caught her arm and dragged her into the cabin, slamming the door shut in an effort to close out the roar of the rain.

"All right, all right!" he snapped. "We're going to get soaked just getting into the Blazer, you know."

"I don't care." Obdurately she stared at him, and he stared back at her in frustrated furry, but evidently he saw something in her face that made him hesitate. She had no idea how frail she looked, or how deeply the shadows of exhaustion lay under her eyes. He shoved his hand through his too-long hair, making the silky strands tumble down over his forehead.

"I'll pull the Blazer up as close to the porch as I can," he muttered. "There's a newspaper on the table in front of the fireplace; put it over your head and make a run for it. But I warn you, it's not going to do much good against this downpour." He stalked to the cabinet and pulled out a plastic trash bag, then disappeared into the bedroom. Susan remained where she stood, feeling icy chills race over her body, too dispirited to wonder what he was doing. He came out a moment later wearing one of those disreputable T-shirts that hugged his magnificent body so faithfully. He had the trash bag folded and tucked under his arm, and a battered khaki-colored base-ball-style cap was jammed on his head. He looked as stormy and furious as the cloud outside.

Without speaking to her, he went out on the porch, and she fol-lowed him. He didn't bother with the steps; he walked to the end of the porch nearest to the Blazer and paused a moment to stare in disgust at the pounding rain. Then he leaped off the end of the porch, and was in a dead run by the time his feet hit the ground. As depressed as she was, Susan watched him in admiration, ad-miring the speed and grace of his powerful strides. He looked like a linebacker closing in on a pass receiver, every movement pur-poseful and deadly.

A bolt of lightning, blindingly white, snapped to the ground close to the creek, and the ear-splitting crack made Susan shriek and jump back as the entire earth shook. The tiny hairs on the back of her neck lifted at the electricity that hummed through the air, and sud-denly she realized how powerful this storm was, how dangerous it was to be out in it. The limbs of the giant oaks were waving back and forth as the trees bent before the onslaught. She wanted to call Cord back, but he was already in the Blazer; she heard the engine roar into life, and the headlights came on. She stumbled back into the cabin to get the newspaper he'd indicated, only to find that the storm had blotted out the lingering twilight and it was so dark inside the cabin that she had to switch on a lamp to find the newspaper.

Her fingers trembled as she turned the light off again. As Cord maneuvered the Blazer up close to the porch, inching it between her car and the steps, the headlights threw twin beams of light through the open door, illuminating the wet floor where the gusting wind had blown the rain across the porch and into the house. She touched her hair and found it was damp, and her clothes were equally damp; she hadn't even noticed that she'd been getting wet.

He blew the horn, and she started. Why was she standing there in the dark? Quickly she crossed the room and struggled out onto the porch, the wind making a strong effort to push her back inside. It took all her strength to tug the door closed, and the newspaper she held over her head was blown uselessly to one side. She grabbed it with both hands and held it; without giving herself time to think, she dashed down the steps, splashing in icy water that was over her ankles. She was soaked through to her skin immediately, and she gasped at the iciness of the rain. Cord had leaned over to open the door of the Blazer for her, but when she let go of the newspaper with one hand to reach for the hand that he extended to her, the paper was promptly whisked away and the deluge struck her unprotected head. The Blazer sat so high on its huge wheels that she couldn't jump up in it, so she caught the edge of the seat in an effort to haul herself up. Cord cursed, the word drowned out by the pounding rain, and leaned over to catch her under the arms. He lifted her bodily inside, then leaned in front of her to slam the door shut.

"There's a couple of towels in the trash bag," he informed her curtly, sliding back under the steering wheel and putting the vehicle in gear.

She pulled one of the towels out and patted it over her bare arms and shoulders, then blotted her dripping hair. That was the best she could do, and she stared in dismay at the soaked seats and floorboards of the Blazer. "I'm sorry," she choked, realizing now that they should have remained at the cabin until the storm had passed.

Rain still glistened on the rock-hard planes of his face, and drops were caught like liquid diamonds in the black silk of his beard. He pulled the soggy cap from his head and dropped it on the seat between them. In silence she offered him the towel, and in silence he took it, rubbing it over his face and head with one hand as he eased down the driveway.

The headlights caught the swirling, muddy waters of Jubilee Creek as they crossed the small bridge, and she was frightened at how high the water had risen in the short time it had been raining. Cord gave the water a grim look. "I hope I can get back."

He had to keep both hands on the wheel to hold the Blazer steady against the gusts of wind that pushed at it; one particularly strong gust pushed them so far to the side that the two left tires left the road and dug into the soft earth on the side. Cord wrestled them back onto the roughly paved secondary road, but they could proceed at nothing more than a crawl. The headlights did no good against a blinding curtain of rain, and the windshield wipers, though going full speed, couldn't keep the windshield clear.

Making a sudden decision, he glanced at her and pulled the Blazer over onto the side of the road, then cut the ignition. As the engine died, the roar of the rain hitting the metal top sounded even louder. He'd turned off the headlights but left the dashlights on, and in the dim glow she turned frightened eyes on him.

"I can't see to drive," he explained. "We're gong to have to wait until this blows over."

She nodded and clasped her hands tightly in her lap, staring out through the windshield. She couldn't see anything; the darkness was absolute, the rain cutting them off from everything else, isolating them in the small sanctuary of the Blazer.

Seconds ticked past and became minutes; if anything, the rain fell harder. Cord turned on the radio, but the static was so bad that they couldn't make out what the announcer was saying, and he snapped it off again. Out of the corner of his eye, he caught her shivering, and he reached out to touch her chilled arm.

"You should have said something," he scolded, and started the motor, then flipped the heat switch to high.

The blast of warm air felt good on her feet and legs, and she slipped her icy feet out of her soggy shoes to stick her toes up close to the vent.

Silence thickened and grated on her nerves. "It's been a long time since I've seen it rain like this," she ventured, if only to break the quiet.

He drummed his fingers on the steering wheel.

She controlled a shiver. "Why did you start letting your beard grow again?"

"Because I don't like to shave."

The curt sentence slapped at her, and she winced. So much for conversation. She hugged her arms around herself, for the first time thinking of the suit jacket she'd left in her car, as well as her purse. She'd been acting like a wild woman, so desperate to get away that she hadn't given a thought to anything else.

A metallic sound began to reach her ears, just barely detectable above the pounding of the rain. She sat up straighter and cast a puzzled glance in Cord's direction, to find that he was listening too. "What is it?"

"Sleet."

No sooner were the words out of his mouth than the sound of the sleet began to intensify. He turned off the motor, his eyes alert and wary.

"The thunder and lightning are further away," Susan said hopefully, not admitting until that moment that she was a little frightened.

"Shhhh," he cautioned, his head turned slightly in a listening position. He reached out and caught her hand, his hard fingers wrapping securely around hers. Susan caught her breath and listened, too, becoming more uneasy as she realized what they were listening for. The sleet stopped, then abruptly the rain stopped, leaving behind a silence that was broken only by the dripping of water from the battered leaves of the trees.

It was the silence, the utter stillness, that was so unnerving. There was a tense, heavy waiting quality to the air, making it difficult to breathe, or perhaps she was simply too frightened to draw in a deep breath. She was clinging so hard to his hand that her nails were sinking into his flesh. "You can see to drive now," she said nervously.

He slid across the seat until he was pressed warmly against her, his body heat making a mockery of the soggy condition of his clothes. He put his arm around her shoulders in a comforting gesture and briefly pressed his lips to her temple. "We'll wait a minute," he told her mildly. "We won't be able to hear it coming if the motor is running."

Susan shivered and closed her eyes. "I know." Her every muscle was tight, her heart pumping faster. The quiet before the storm wasn't just a cliché, it was a reality. As a native of the warm southern climes where the heated Gulf bathed the region in warm moisture, triggering wild and magnificent storms whenever a cooler system from the west swept in to collide with that warm, damp blanket of air, Susan knew all too well the lethal power of the twisting tornadoes that were spawned out of the towering thunderheads. She knew all the signs, the warnings, and as a child had been drilled in school in the best way to survive a tornado. The Number One Rule: Don't get caught by one.

"If we think we hear something, get out of the truck as fast as you can," Cord instructed quietly. "There's a small ditch on the left of the road; it's probably full of water, but that's where we'll go anyway."

"Okay." Her voice was strained but calm, and she rolled down her window a little, making it easier to hear. Only the dripping of the water, splattering down on the undergrowth, reached her ears.

The first hailstone hit the windshield of the Blazer with such force that they both jumped, and Susan bit back a shriek. Cord uttered a short, sharp expletive, then anything else he might have said was drowned out as golfball-size hail began to pound the Blazer, ripping the leaves of the trees to shreds, taking small saplings completely down. The din was incredible. Susan felt that they were on the inside of a giant drum, with some maniac beating wildly on it. She tore her hand from Cord's grip and pressed her palms over her ears.

Then it was gone, racing away, leaving the ground covered with shimmering balls of ice, a deep rumble following after it.

With a quick, hard motion Cord reached over her and shoved the door open, then used his body to force her outside. He grabbed her around the waist, keeping her from falling as her feet hit the ice and skidded out from under her. She was barefooted except for her stockings, and the ice was unbearably cold, bruising her soft feet, but she knew that she had better traction without her shoes anyway. High heels would have been more than useless, they would have been dangerous, unsafe for picking her way across a road covered with ice balls. Heedless of the pain, she ran, hearing the rumble come closer, feeling the earth begin to tremble beneath them.

They splashed into the ditch, the freezing water taking her breath. There was an eerie yellowish cast to the sky, an absurd lightening of the night sky, and she was able to see the taut lines of Cord's face. With one hand on her shoulder he forced her to lie down in the ditch, and the rushing stream of water splashed up in her face, filling her mouth with the taste of mud. She spat it out and looked up at him, her eyes burning. If she had to die, then thank God it was with him. Then he was covering her, pressing her down deeper into the foul water, putting his body between her and the fury of the storm that was thundering toward them.

Somehow, it didn't seem quite real. Inside she was terrified, but on the outside she was not only calm but oddly detached. She felt the wind buffeting their bodies, so fierce and strong that the tumbling water was blown out of the ditch to splash across the field in tandem with the gargantuan rain that had begun slashing down out of the abruptly inky sky. It had been raining hard before, but that was nothing to the way it rained then. The water that had been blown out of the ditch was instantly replaced by the downpour. Her skin was bruised and stinging in a thousand places as small stones and debris were hurled through the air, and she could hear nothing but the roar of the enormous, thundering monster as it tore across the earth. She clung to Cord, her slender arms wrapped about his head in an effort to give him as much protection as she could, and her desperate strength was so great that he couldn't dislodge her arms to tuck her more securely under him.

A deep, bull-throated bellow of destruction assaulted her, and she screamed, a sound that went unheard in the greater scream of the storm. Cord's grip on her increased until she thought her ribs would snap under the force of it, and he pressed her harder, deeper into the ditch. She fought for breath, but couldn't drag any oxygen into her lungs, as the monster's suction pulled all the air away into its rotating, twisting maw. Her only thought was, I'm glad I'm with him.

She must have fainted, though she could never be sure. Certainly she was dazed by the storm, her senses scattered. One moment she was suffocating, feeling as if any moment the tornado would come down on them, and the next the world was strangely normal, even serene. It was still raining but it was a normal rain, as if the violence of a moment before had belonged to another world. There was no lightning, no thunder, no hail...and no wind. Cord was still lying heavily on her, his chest heaving as he too sucked in much-needed oxygen, his arms outspread and his fingers sunk into the mud as if he would physically anchor them to the earth with his own body. They remained like that for several minutes, lying in the ditch with the rain slanting down on them, as they tried to assimilate the fact that they were not only alive, but relatively unscathed.

Susan moved beneath him, turning her face into the hollow of his throat, and her fingers moved through his hair.

He rolled off her and sat up, his arm behind her as he eased her into a sitting position. "Are you all right?" he demanded hoarsely.

"Yes," she said, and was surprised to find that her throat was sore, her voice so husky that she could barely form the word.

They stumbled to their feet, clinging together, and Susan heard Cord swear quietly as he peered through the darkness and the rain, searching for the Blazer. "I'll be damned," he muttered. "It's turned completely around, and pushed off the road on the other side."

Susan put her hand over her eyes to keep the rain out and was finally able to make out the black bulk of the Blazer, further away now than it had been when they'd jumped out of it so long ago...or had it been only a few minutes ago? Cord must have eyes like an eagle, she realized, because she could tell only where the Blazer was, not what direction it was facing.

"It missed us," he said suddenly, with horse jubilation. "Look where it came across the road."

Following his pointing hand, she could make out a twisted, broken mass that was evidently an enormous tree, lying across the road. There was an odd, flashing illumination, so bright and blue white that it almost hurt the eyes to look at it. The falling trees had taken down the power lines with them, and now a live wire was lashing back and forth just above the ground, throwing sparks like a Fourth of July celebration. The tornado had dipped down to earth and exploded everything in its path, by passing them by no more than fifty yards.

Seeing her pick her way, limping, across the hailstones, Cord turned to her and swung her up against his chest. Susan felt as if she'd used her last reserves of strength, and she was just as glad to let him carry her; wearily, she let her head fall against his shoulder, and his arms tightened momentarily about her. He carried her to the Blazer, placing her inside it before walking around and vaulting into the seat behind the steering wheel. He turned the key in the ignition, and to her amazement the engine started immediately. He flashed her a quick grin. After the last hour it was a pleasure to have something going right. He changed gears, easing the Blazer along, the big tires churning in the mud until they gained the hail-slick surface of the road.

"We're going back to the cabin," he said, letting the truck move slowly to keep it from skidding on the ice. "I can't get you home until morning, when I can see how to pick my way around those trees and power lines that are down."

Susan didn't say anything, merely clung to the edge of the seat. She was certain the power would be off at the cabin, but he could build a fire, and the thought of being warm and dry again seemed like heaven. Her muscles were still tense, and she found she couldn't relax, her gaze fixed on the stabbing beams of the head-lights as they probed through the gray curtain of rain.

They reached the crest of the gentle incline that led down to the creek, and Cord brought the Blazer to a halt. "I'm going down to check the bridge," he said, and left the truck before she could cry out that she wanted to go with him. Somehow, she didn't want him out of her sight for even a moment.

He came back in only a few minutes, his face harsh in the blind-ing glare of the headlights. He got back into the Blazer. "The water's over the bridge; we can't chance crossing it. We have to spend the night in the truck."

Chapter 11

Susan bit her lip, thinking of the fire that had been warming her in her imagination. She was silent as he shifted into reverse and turned the Blazer around, then drove a little further back the way they'd come. Finally he pulled to the side of the road and parked.

She had been so frantic to get away from him, she thought dimly, but now she was glad that he was here, that he was all right. They had come so close to death…but what if only she had been spared? The thought of him lying dead from the brute force of the storm was unbearable.

Her shaking hand went to her dripping hair, and her fingers combed through it. The driving rain had evidently washed the mud out, but she found a few twigs that she pulled out and dropped to the floorboards. But what did it matter, anyway, if her hair was a mess? She began to laugh.

Cord's head jerked around at the sound, and he reached out to touch her shoulder. Susan covered her mouth with her hand, trying to stifle the unwilling mirth, but she couldn't. "Baby, it's all right," he murmured, sliding out from under the steering wheel and taking her in his arms. "It's over; you're all right."

The hard strength of him surrounded her, and Susan burrowed into it, her arms lacing around his waist. The strained laugher turned into choking, dry sobs, then slowly diminished as he continued to hold her, talking to her in a quiet, gentle voice, his hand stroking her head.

But her shaking didn't diminish, and finally his hand moved down over her bare shoulder and arms. "My God, you're freezing," he muttered, taking his arms from around her. He found the two

towels that he'd brought when they'd dashed through the rain from
the cabin to the Blazer, and wrapped one around her hair. "Get out
of those wet clothes," he ordered, but in a voice so calm and matter-
of-fact that she didn't balk. "There's a blanket in the back; I'll
wrap you up in it." He turned the heater on high.

Susan looked at him, her eyes enormous. "You need to get out
of your clothes, too; you're not impervious to cold, either."

The normal tone of her voice reassured him, and he flashed her
a grin that shone against the darkness of his growing beard. "I'm
warmer than you are, but I'll admit that wet jeans are damned uncomfortable." He peeled his T-shirt off over his head and wrung
the excess water out, then draped it over the steering wheel.

The sight of his bare, powerful torso agitated her, and she jerked
her gaze away, beginning to unbutton the flimsy camisole top while
he struggled to take off his boots in the limited space they had. Her
cold fingers wouldn't cooperate, and she had managed to get out
of only the camisole and the strapless bra she'd worn under it by
the time Cord had completely stripped and was wiping himself
down with the other towel.

When he'd finished, he came to her assistance, pushing her shaking hands aside. He dealt with her skirt, pantyhose and panties in
short order; then he dried her vigorously, the rough fabric of the
towel speeding her circulation and driving some of the chill away.

He reached in the back for the blanket, unfolding it and draping
it across the seat. He sat in the middle of it, then scooped her up
and placed her on his lap, and wrapped the rest of the blanket
around both of them like a cocoon.

Blessed warmth enveloped her, and Susan gave a blissful sigh,
cuddling against his amazing body heat. She felt suddenly peaceful;
they were completely alone and isolated from the world, at least
until morning. They were naked together, rather like Adam and Eve,
and for the moment she wanted nothing except that they be warm
and dry. Everything else could wait until morning. For now she was
in his arms, and the feel of him was heaven. The scent of his skin,
of his warm masculinity, both soothed and aroused her, and she
turned to press more fully into the hair-softened contours of his
hard chest.

Cord held her, his hands on her satin curves, his face troubled.
"I've never in my life been as scared as I was tonight," he admitted
in a rumble, his words startling Susan.

She lifted her head from his shoulder, her eyes wide with astonishment. "You?" she demanded, her voice rising in disbelief. "*You*

were afraid?'' That didn't seem possible. He had nerves of ice, an imperviousness to danger that both alarmed and reassured her.

''I kept thinking: What if I couldn't hold on to you? What if something hit you? If anything had happened to you—'' He bit his words off, his face growing darker.

Susan was stunned. ''But you were in danger too.''

He shrugged, utterly indifferent to his own fate. Perhaps that was how he faced all dangers, with complete unconcern, and perhaps that was why death hadn't found him yet. He didn't fear it, and therefore it didn't seek him. But he had been afraid for her.... Her mind stopped, almost afraid to take the thought any further. She simply pressed close to him once again, her hands clinging to his neck.

He rubbed his bristly cheek against her forehead, his hands tightening on her. ''Susan.''

She loved the sound of her name on his lips. With unconscious sensuality, she moved her breasts against him, the hair on his chest feeling like rough silk against her sensitive nipples. ''Ummmm?'' she murmured bemusedly.

''I want to make love to you. Will you let me?''

The thought, the rough thread of need in his voice, made her shiver in delight. She lifted her mouth to him, simply and without reserve, and he took it with a tender fervor. He kissed her for a long time, their tongues meeting in mutual need, while his hard fingers found her breasts and stroked them until they hardened and thrust out for his touch.

He lifted his head and gave a low, shaky laugh. ''Is that a yes?''

''That's a yes.'' Despite the weeks they'd been apart, the anger between them, she wasn't shy with him. She was his, in the purest sense, and always in his touch she had perceived his genuine pleasure, the care and concern he gave her. His passion might border on roughness in his urgency, but he never hurt her, and she knew that he never would. Her trust in his physical care of her was so great that despite the rift between them, she knew that she had nothing to fear from him. And for this moment, there was no rift, or pain or disagreement; all of that had retreated, and would arrive with the sunrise, but for now there was only the sweet fever between them.

She could have fought him, could have insisted that he preserve the distance between them, but in the aftermath of the storm, none of their reasons for argument seemed very important. She loved him; she didn't want to fight him. After what they'd just been through, she wanted only to hold him and feel his hard, warm flesh against her, reassure herself that he was unharmed. He was so infinitely precious to her that she didn't want to waste a moment of this time they had together by holding him off. She'd worried herself sick about their situation anyway, and it hadn't changed anything. Let the sunrise bring its troubles; she had the nighttime, and for now that was enough.

He was slow, and exquisitely gentle, using his kisses and the boldness of his stroking fingers to bring her to fever pitch before he stretched her out on the seat, his hard hands controlling her even when she reached for him, trying to pull him down to her. Susan writhed in blind delight, small cries escaping from her throat, her eyes tightly closed as her head rolled slowly back and forth. He was suckling leisurely at her breasts, his tongue curling around each of her aching nipples in turn, a caress that sent bolts of ecstasy shooting through her body. She was no longer cold, but burning with a radiant glow, her body arching up to his.

Deftly he moved her, rearranging her legs, and his mouth left her breasts to rail down her stomach, his beard softly rasping her satin flesh and making her gasp at the rough pleasure. His tongue found her navel and he kissed her, paying homage to her for a long, sweet moment before moving on to a richer treasure.

A startled cry tore from her when he claimed her with his mouth, kissing her deeply, making lightning forays with his tongue that pushed her toward the edge so swiftly she couldn't breathe. Then she forgot about breathing as her fingers tangled in his damp hair; he was killing her with pleasure, stabbing her to death with his devilish tongue, and she rushed to meet her small death. He held her securely until she was calm again, lying peacefully in his arms; it was several moments before she realized he was doing nothing but holding her.

"Cord?" His name was an expression of bewilderment. "What about you?"

"I'm all right." Very gently, he tilted her face up and kissed her. "It's just that I'm unprepared; I don't have any way to protect you."

His unselfish consideration jolted her, but the ecstasy he'd just given her wasn't enough. She didn't want just simple release; she wanted him, with all his delicious masculinity, his driving power, the very essence of the man. She reached out for him, her soft hands touching his face. "I want *you*," she said in a low voice. "Would you mind, very much, if we took the chance?"

A shudder rippled through him, and he moved swiftly to lie over her, parting her thighs and taking her, a groan of pleasure breaking from his lips. He held nothing back from her, his urgency communicating itself to her. He was shaking in a way she'd never seen before, and she tried to soothe him with her yielding softness. All too soon he was hoarsely crying out his satisfaction, then he sagged against her to rest.

After only a moment they were both shifting uncomfortably. During the heat of their lovemaking, neither had noticed their awkward positions or cramped limbs, but now they seemed to be fighting a tangle of gear shift, steering wheel, and door handles, all of which were in uncomfortable places. Cord chuckled as he tried to untangle himself from her and still manage not to maim himself.

"I think we'll be more comfortable in back; God only knows why we didn't get in back anyway."

With the back seat folded down they had considerable space, though still not enough for Cord to stretch out his long legs. He'd cut the motor, so they had to depend on the one blanket and each other for warmth, but now that Susan was dry she didn't feel the chill so much. They lay on half of the blanket, and he pulled the other half around them. Susan nestled in his arms, quietly happy. "I'm so tired," she murmured, then smothered a yawn. She didn't want to sleep, didn't want to waste any of the time they had together, but her body was demanding rest. The stress of the past weeks, the emotional tension and fear she'd experienced today, had all taken their toll. Her limbs felt as heavy as lead, and her eyelids simply would not stay open.

She yawned again, her eyes slowly closing. She put her hand on his chest, where she could feel the strong, steady beating of his heart. He was so big and tough; she felt infinitely safe and protected when she was with him. "I do love you," she told him quietly, not needing anything now beyond the telling of it. She'd just wanted to say the words aloud this once, when there was peace between them. It was a gift, a simple gesture from her heart.

"I know," he whispered against her temple, and held her while she slept.

He hadn't expected to sleep at all; his senses were too raw. He had been sure that he would feel the restlessness that always seized him if there were anyone else about while he slept. But the rain kept drumming on the roof of the Blazer, and the darkness enclosed them like a cave; he was warm and dry, and his body pleasantly satisfied. She was soft in his arms, small and delicate, so completely feminine that from the moment he'd met her he'd found himself tempering his strength lest he accidentally hurt her. This afternoon, when she'd been crying and beating on her steering wheel, he'd felt as if he'd taken a punch in the chest; she simply wasn't the weepy type, yet he'd hurt her enough to make her cry, and he hadn't meant to. He'd been infuriated to hear that Preston had run off and left her to shoulder everything, that instead of Preston knuckling under and sacrificing, it had been Susan. He had to end this, as soon as he could, for Susan's sake. She was at the end of her rope, physically and emotionally.

She loved him. Once a woman's offering of love would have made him impatient, restless to be gone. He couldn't offer anything in return, and he hadn't wanted the complications of clinging hands, teary scenes, or the incredible plots of revenge some women could concoct when they felt they'd been wronged. Judith's death had scared him deeply, left him so wary of being wounded like that again that he'd instinctively protected himself...until Susan. She'd gotten in under his guard, and because she didn't demand anything of him, he found himself giving more.

Still, he hadn't realized, until she'd practically ordered him out of her house and out of her life, just how close she'd gotten to him. He'd felt lonely, and he was a man who treasured his solitude. His healthy body had burned for sexual release, but other women seemed unattractive in subtle ways he'd never noticed before. He didn't want other women; he wanted Susan, with her serenity like a halo around her. Susan, who became a sweet, loving wanton for him, only for him.

Now she was in his arms again, pressed against his heart, just where she belonged. He moved drowsily, seeking a more comfortable position, and she moved with him, her soft hands holding him even in her sleep. It was the most uniquely satisfying experience of his life, and a slight smile touched his hard mouth as he went to sleep.

As often happens after a storm, the next day dawned sunny and warm, but without the suffocating humidity that had been weighing down on everyone. It was as if nature were pleased by the destruction it had wrought. Cord's eyes blinked open, and for a moment he stared at the expanse of innocent, deep blue sky. The interior of the Blazer had already heated under the morning sun, and a trickle of sweat ran down his side, tickling him. He twitched, and Susan stirred, stretching. He rolled to his side and watched as she slowly came awake, her eyelashes fluttering. The blanket fell away, revealing her slender bare body, her full, pretty breasts and succulent nipples. His loins tightened, and he put his hand on her hip. "Honey, we have to leave soon," he said huskily. "Before we go...?"

Susan heard the question, the intent in his voice, and she turned to him. "Yes," she said drowsily, reaching out for him.

He took her gently, slowly, holding the world at bay while they loved each other. When it was done he leaned over her, his weight supported on one elbow, his eyes very clear and demanding. "Stay with me. Don't go back to the office. I'll take care of you, in every way."

Tears blurred her eyes, but still Susan managed a smile for him. As the salty liquid seeped from the corners of her eyes, she said shakily, "I have to go back; I can't just turn my back and walk away from everyone who's depending on me."

"What about me? How can you turn your back on me?" His words hit her hard, and she flinched.

"I love you, but you don't *need* me. You want me, but that's entirely different. Besides, I don't think I have what it takes to be a mistress." She reached up and stroked his bearded cheek, her mouth trembling. "Please, take me home now."

Silently they dressed in their damp, incredibly wrinkled clothing, and Cord began the torturous drive, detouring time and again as their way was blocked by fallen trees or downed power lines. They passed utility crews who were hard at work, trying to get new lines up, and in some cases new poles. The sounds of chain saws split the peaceful morning air as men began cleaning up the debris. What was normally a fifteen-minute drive took well over an hour, but finally Susan was tumbling out the Blazer's door into Emily's arms. The older woman's worn face was tight with concern.

"My lands, just look at the two of you," she breathed, and tears sparkled in her eyes.

Cord managed his devilishly casual smile. "I think we look pretty good for two people who've been lying in a ditch." Actually, every muscle in his body was protesting, not only from sleeping on a hard, cramped surface, but from the beating he'd taken from the hailstones. For the first time he saw a bruise high on Susan's cheekbone, and he reached out to touch it with his thumb. She stood very still under his touch, her eyes filled with pain and longing.

Emily wiped her tears away, and hustled them both inside, bullying them shamelessly now that she knew they were safe.

"Both of you get upstairs right now and take a hot shower, and toss those filthy clothes out so I can wash them—"

"I'll be leaving in a minute," Cord interrupted her. "I've got to see if I can get to the cabin and check for damage. But if you have any coffee brewed, I'd appreciate some."

She brought him a cup and he sipped it gratefully, the hot liquid sending new life into his body. Susan stood watching him, her arms limp at her sides, wanting to do as he said and go with him, forget about everything. Without knowing that she had moved, she found herself in front of him, and without a word he set the cup aside and folded her tightly in his arms. He kissed her roughly, almost desperately, as if he would imprint his possession on her mouth, and as Susan clung to him she felt the acid tears burning down her cheeks.

"Shhhh, shhhh," he soothed, lifting his lips at the salty taste. With his fingertips, he wiped her cheeks dry; then he framed her face between his big hands and held it turned up so he could see into her drowning eyes. "Everything will be all right. I promise."

She couldn't say anything, so he kissed her again, then released her. He gave Emily a swift hug and left, not once looking back.

Susan jammed her fist against her mouth, trying to hold back the sobs that shook her, but they burst out anyway. Emily led her upstairs and helped her undress, then took away her soiled clothing and laid out fresh garments while Susan stood under the shower and cried.

She knew there were a thousand things that needed doing, but she couldn't summon any interest in any of them. She wanted only to curl up on her bed and cry until she couldn't cry any more. It was all just too much; she couldn't fight any longer. It was a measure of her willpower that she had controlled her tears by the time she left the bathroom; she sat down and dried her hair, then applied a careful blend of makeup to hide the traces of her tears. After dressing in the casual slacks and shirt that Emily had put out for her, she went downstairs for the meal that she knew Emily would have ready. She wasn't hungry, but eating was a necessity that she'd been neglecting lately, all to no good. She wouldn't be able to keep the corporation from bankruptcy, even if she divested herself of everything she owned except her clothing, then held a yard sale to get rid of even that.

She sat on the patio all day, soaking up the sun, dozing, thinking, but her thoughts only went in circles and produced nothing. She called Imogene and explained why she wouldn't be at the office that day; she had no idea when Cord would be able to get the Audi back to her, but she found that it was the one bright spot she could see right now: She would be able to see him again when he did bring it to her.

She was probably a fool not to have taken him up on his proposition, she thought tiredly. She should just forget about tomorrow, about all the duties and obligations that she'd always served; she should go with Cord and take what love she could get from him. He cared; she knew he did. Perhaps he didn't love her, but she knew that he'd offered her more than he'd ever offered any other woman, except Judith. Poor, hurt, confused Judith, who was now the point of all this enmity years after her death. Because everyone had failed her, because she'd died, Cord was trying to make it up to her now, to get revenge for her, and for himself, perhaps, so he could be at peace.

She'd told him that she didn't have what it took to be a mistress, but what did it take, really, except a woman in love? She thought longingly of spending every night with him, of traveling around the world beside him. She'd always been a woman who was happy with her hearth and home, but for Cord she would learn to wander, and lay her head on a different pillow every night if that was what he wanted.

It was only a matter of time, anyway, before the life she knew was all over. She had failed; she couldn't pay the loan.

When Cord still hadn't brought her car back by the next morning, Susan called and asked Imogene to pick her up; there was nothing more she could do, but she would continue to handle the office and make the myriad decisions that still had to be made every day. The ship might sink, but she wouldn't make a confused mess of it. Dignity and grace in defeat, that was the ticket.

Giving herself pep talks didn't help much. She was agonizingly aware that she'd lost on both sides. She'd tried to heal the rift in the family, but instead it had grown deeper. Cord might want her, care for her, but how could he ever trust her? He'd asked her to stay with him, but instead she'd given her aid to Preston. Knowing that Cord was wrong didn't ease the hollow ache inside her.

She had to face everyone at the office, where they had all somehow heard that she'd almost been caught in a tornado. Several tornadoes had ripped through Mississippi that night, and one close to Jackson had hit a residential area, leaving two people dead, but her acquaintances and employees were only interested in the local one, which had missed all the populated areas and destroyed only trees and newly planted crops. She managed to be very casual about it, and her lack of detail soon killed their interest.

When she went home that night she found the Audi there, and disappointment speared her. Why couldn't he have brought it when she would be home? But perhaps he was avoiding her. She stared at the car for a long moment before thanking Imogene for the ride.

Imogene reached over and patted her hand. "Is there anything I can do?'' she asked. ''Anything I can say to Cord? I know you're not happy, and I feel like it's all my fault.''

''No, it's not your fault,'' Susan denied, managing a smile. ''I made my own decisions, so I imagine I'll have to live with them.''

Emily was still waiting, and she made a pretense of cleaning up the kitchen while Susan ate, but Susan had a feeling that she had caught on to Susan's habit of disposing of the food instead of eating it. As she dutifully ate the last bite, Emily nodded in satisfaction. ''Cord told me to make certain you were eating. You're too thin. This business is tearing you apart, and I'm ready for it to end.''

''It won't be long,'' Susan sighed. She hated herself for asking, but she had to know. ''Did he say anything else?''

''He said he lost one of his trees, but it fell away from the cabin, and there's hail damage to the roof, but other than that everything came through the storm okay.''

''That's good.'' It wasn't personal news, but it was better than nothing. She refrained from asking if he'd looked tired.

Emily had just left when Imogene phoned. ''Susan, can you come over?'' she asked, urgency filling her voice. ''Preston's back, and he's found out something about Cord!''

''I'll be right there.'' Susan dropped the phone and ran to get her purse. Something about Cord? Her heart clenched. Had he done something illegal? Whatever it was, if there were any way, she'd protect him. No, it wouldn't be anything illegal; he was far too visible, and he made no attempt to disguise his identity. It was far more likely that he'd crossed some powerful people. Preston might plan on using his knowledge against Cord, but she'd make certain that Cord knew all about his plans.

As she drove over to Blackstone House she was hardly aware of the turns she took, or the speed at which she traveled. Her heart was slamming wildly in her chest, hurting her ribs. She'd been longing for Preston to come back, but now that he had she could only fear that he'd try to hurt Cord in some way.

Preston looked surprisingly normal when he opened the door to her as she ran up the steps. He was casually attired; his tan was deeper, and he looked relaxed. He was startled when he saw her. ''Good Lord, Susan, you've lost a good ten pounds. What've you been doing?''

She brushed his comment aside. ''It doesn't matter. What have you found out about Cord?''

He ushered her into the den, where Imogene was waiting, and waited until she was seated before speaking. ''I've been doing some detective work while I was gone,'' he explained. ''I wanted Cord

to think that I'd chickened out so he wouldn't make any attempt to
cover his tracks. It worked, thank God. He must've thought he'd
won without a real battle.''

''I doubt that,'' Susan interrupted. ''He didn't know until the day
before yesterday that you'd gone.''

He frowned. ''But why? Didn't you tell him?''

Susan's eyes widened, and she sat up straight. ''That's what you
wanted me to do, wasn't it? You dumped all of that on me, thinking
I'd run straight to him and beg for mercy. He said that was what
you were doing, but I didn't believe him.'' She stared at him, her
eyes clear and accusing, and he shifted uncomfortably.

''What else could I think?'' he tried to explain gently. ''Are you
saying that I completely misread the situation?''

''I don't know; I haven't any idea how you read it.''

He turned away from her distinctly chilly gaze. ''Anyway, I went
to New York. I'd noticed that the prices of our stock had remained
high despite the rumors that had to be going around, so it followed
that someone was buying. I suspected then, but I wanted to be
certain. Cord has been buying up all the stock that came on the
market. He's not pushing the company into bankruptcy; he's been
pushing us into selling stock, which he's been buying. He's mounting a takeover!''

A takeover! For a moment Susan was dazed; then a spurt of
admiration for Cord's nerve made her laugh. ''A takeover!'' she
giggled, clapping her hands. ''All of this for a takeover!''

''I don't see that it's so funny.''

''Of course you don't! After all, *I'm* the one who's been selling
stock in an effort to raise money to pay off that loan!''

Imogene went white. ''Susan! Your own assets!''

Preston stared at her; then he swore quietly, and rubbed his eyes
in a disbelieving manner. ''Susan, we talked about that. I told you
not to liquidate anything of yours.''

''You also walked off and left me in a sink-or-swim situation,''
she pointed out. ''I thought I had a company going under; I didn't
know it was just corporate games! The stock isn't all that I've
liquidated.''

He looked ill. ''My God, you've done all that...and he had no
intention of calling in that loan. He just wanted us to panic and sell
enough to give him a majority. Susan, how much did you sell?''

''Nine percent.''

''That still leaves you six percent. I have eleven percent, and
Mother has eleven. Twenty-eight percent total. Cord has, I think,
twenty-six percent. We still have a majority.''

"If this takeover doesn't succeed, he may still collect on that loan," Imogene pointed out, but Cord shook his head decisively.

"No, that would be killing his own source of income. It didn't make sense from the beginning that he'd hurt himself financially just to get back at me, but I thought that maybe he did hate me that much. Then when the stock sold immediately whenever any shares went on the market, I began to think that it was something else entirely he was after."

"Why didn't you tell me?" Susan inquired. "Never mind; I know the answer to that. You didn't trust me because I was seeing Cord, and Cord didn't trust me because I was helping you."

"I'm sorry," he said softly. "I had no idea it would be this hard on you. I swear, I'll replace everything you sold."

She dismissed that with a wave of her hand. "It doesn't matter." She just wanted it over with.

Preston decided not to pursue the issue, because she was looking tired and dazed. "I drove out to see Cord as soon as I got in this afternoon," he continued. "I called a board meeting for ten in the morning, and this will be put to a vote. He'll have to take his chances on snapping up any more stock before we get to it, so he knows his game is up."

It had all been just a game. That was all she could think of that night. Just a game.

She didn't know how all the shares had been originally divided: when she'd married Vance, she'd known only that the family had owned fifty-one percent of the stock, and the rest of it was in others' hands. Others owned chunks of shares, but with the majority in family hands it hadn't mattered. Imogene had owned fifteen percent, Preston fifteen percent, and Vance fifteen percent. Susan had inherited Vance's shares. That had left six percent of the family majority, which she had always assumed was scattered around to distant cousins. She hadn't known of Cord's existence until the day he'd come back; he'd been gone for so long that no one talked about him. But now it was evident that he'd owned the remaining shares.

Preston and Imogene had both sold four percent of their stock in order to cover what they'd used of Cord's money; that gave Cord fourteen percent, assuming that he'd bought it, which he must have done. She'd sold nine percent, giving him twenty-three percent. If he had twenty-six percent, he'd bought some common stock as well, and possibly had acquired voting proxies from other stockholders. Preston also had voting proxies. It was all just a game of numbers, nothing else. If anything, the corporation was stronger, since Cord had essentially paid off an outstanding debt. The family now owned fifty-four percent of the stock. Everything was just fine.

Now Cord's reassurances made sense. He'd known that the company was in no danger of bankruptcy, but he hadn't trusted her enough to tell her what was going on, just as Preston hadn't trusted her enough to tell her his suspicions. She'd tried to be a mediator, and instead had become the sacrificial goat.

She was glad that the morning would bring the end to it. She was tired of games. They seemed to be fine for everyone except the goat.

Chapter 12

Of the five people in the boardroom the next morning, Cord looked the most relaxed. He was dressed impeccably in a summer-weight pin-stripe suit, the cut of which had a definite European flair. His growing beard gave him a raffish look that kept the suit from being *too* impeccable, but then his rampant masculinity allowed him to wear anything with elan...or wear nothing at all, her imagination whispered, conjuring up a vision of how magnificent he was in the nude.

Imogene was calm, almost remote. Preston was all business. Beryl looked as calm as ever. On the other hand, Susan felt disoriented, and none of the familiar boardroom rituals or words made any sense. She darted another glance at Cord, only to find him watching her, and he gave her a slow wink. Was he that unconcerned about the outcome? Was that elaborate scheme nothing more to him than another way of irritating Preston? If so, his practical joke had been enormously successful.

She was so detached that she missed what they were saying. It wasn't until she caught a surge of anger that she was able to gather her senses and pay attention.

"This is my birthright," Cord was saying, his tone hard and his eyes cold. "It took me years to realize that, but I'm not giving it up. I decided to fight for it, and there won't be any compromising."

"That's your loss," Preston said crisply. "Shall we put it to the vote?"

"By all means."

Cord sat there, so confident, but then it wasn't in him to be any other way. He had to know that he hadn't enough to best their combined shares, but that knowledge couldn't be read in his face.

He'd been shoved out of the family circle. What was in his mind now, when victory danced before him? Thoughts of revenge? Or just a determination to be in that family once again, wanted or not? To assume responsibility for what was his, to finally settle in his home?

"I vote yes," Cord drawled easily, and Susan jerked her thoughts back.

Imogene sat quietly, not looking at either Preston or Cord, but how else could she vote? She wouldn't vote against her own son. "I vote nay," she finally said.

"I vote nay," Preston followed promptly. "Susan?"

He was sure of her, Susan realized. She looked at him, and found him watching her impatiently, the gleam of victory already in his eyes. What a shark he was! He was a perfect chairman, conscientious and bold, and able to use guerrilla tactics when they were called for.

There was nothing for her to read in Cord's eyes. He simply waited. He hadn't contacted her, hadn't tried to persuade her to vote in his favor. Why should he? She'd come down solidly on Preston's side in every skirmish. No wonder he didn't trust her! He would be a good chairman, too; he'd shown his expertise in gathering enough money to mount this campaign.

"Susan!" Preston prodded impatiently.

Trust has to start somewhere, she thought painfully. Cord was so used to guarding his back that it was second nature to him now. "I vote yes," she said in a low tone, and total silence descended on the room, except for the quick rasp of Beryl's pencil across the pad as she recorded everything.

Preston looked to be in shock; he was pale, his mouth compressed to a thin line that was bracketed on each side by grooves of tension. The meeting was quickly adjourned, but only Beryl left the room. Everyone else remained in their seats; perhaps even Cord was stunned by the turn of events. Susan's motives were too murky for her to explain them even to herself, but she was aware, deep inside, of a feeling that she simply couldn't fail him now. If he had lost, he wouldn't have returned to being an absentee board member, his shares automatically voted by Preston; Cord entered a fight to win. He would have gone on and on, and the conflict would have continued to tear the family apart and drain the company. Let it end, even if she made herself an outcast with Preston and Imogene. Why not? She was tired, too tired to really care, and she was doubly bitter at being played with so callously by both Cord and Preston. She'd just been a pawn in their games, moved around according to their whims, and kept in the dark by both of them.

Imogene leaned forward, clasping her hands on the table. "Let it end," she said quietly, looking from her son to Cord and back. "We were a family once; I'd like us to be one again. I was wrong for my part in it, and if you can possibly forgive me, Cord, I'll be very grateful." The steel that was an inherent part of her personality shone clearly out of her gray eyes, and in that moment Susan knew that she'd never liked or respected her mother-in-law more.

Without waiting for an answer from Cord, Imogene turned her determined regard to Preston. "I know this will be difficult for you; you've been an outstanding chairman, and it won't be easy for you to turn over the reins. But I'm asking you to do it without bitterness, and to do whatever you can to ease the transition. Cord is family; he's as much a Blackstone as you are. I hope you're big enough to let this end now, before it totally destroys us. People have already been hurt, and others will be if this continues. Susan was the only one of us with enough sense to realize that from the beginning. If you won't stop it for yourself, then stop it for me...and for her. God knows she's paid enough for your enmity."

Susan flinched, hating to have her feelings dragged out in the open like this. She sat very still and pale, her eyes focused on her hands. Now it was up to them to either settle their differences or draw new battle lines. Either way, she'd withdrawn from combat, retreated to lick her wounds. She was simply too tired to care any longer.

Cord sat with an abstracted frown on his brow, his gaze turned inward to long ago, when he'd first become enemies with his cousin. "I always envied you," he said absently, reviewing his memories. "Everything always came so easily to you. Vance was a hard act to follow, but with you... My God, when you were around, I became invisible. Everyone watched you."

Cord stared across the length of the table at his cousin, his dark face hard and expressionless. What he thought of Preston's admission was impossible to guess.

Giving an unbelieving little shake of his head, as if he couldn't quite take in how far their enmity had taken them, Preston straightened his shoulders and looked at Cord directly. "When I was sixteen I started dating Kelly Hartland, and I fell hard for her. You were just starting your sophomore year in college, and I suppose to a high school girl that was irresistible. You came home for a weekend, met Kelly at a party, and just like that she dropped me flat."

A startled look flared in Cord's eyes. "Kelly Hartland? A little strawberry blond cheerleader type? I can barely remember her. I dated her a couple of times, but it was nothing heavy."

"It was for me. I hated you for taking her away from me when you obviously didn't care about her. At sixteen I thought she was the love of my life. When your affair with Judith blew up in your face, I saw a way to get back at you, and I took it. I'm not proud of it, but there's no way to undo it."

Cord inhaled deeply, and even without looking at him Susan knew that the mention of Judith was lashing at him, uncovering the deep pain and guilt he felt at the way she'd been treated. Yet the bonds of common blood, weakened by years of bitterness and hatred, were reaching out again, and the two men looked at each other, seeing their common heritage in each other's face. The serrated edge of pain rasped in Cord's voice when he spoke. "Judith was my wife. We were married after we left here; she died the next year. I could've killed you for what you did to her." A crystalline sheen was suddenly in his eyes. "I'm guiltier than anyone else for what happened to her." Even now, he was bitterly angry at the way she'd died, her spirit gone, her laughter stilled.

Silence fell, and suddenly Susan couldn't bear any more. Without looking at anyone, she pushed her chair back and got to her feet, walking out swiftly before she could be called back. Her chest was aching, yet she didn't think she could cry. The time for that was past.

Her senses were dulled as she went to her office, walking past Beryl who looked up eagerly, full of questions, but Susan didn't see her. She felt chilled to the bone, so cold that she could never be warm again.

All of this had been because of women who had long ago faded into the mists of the past. There was a certain irony in her own situation; did either of them want her for herself, or merely because each thought the other wanted her?

She had barely moved away from the door after closing it when it was thrust open again, and Cord loomed behind her, so close that she felt oppressed by his size, and she moved instinctively away from him. At her action, his eyes narrowed, and he closed the door behind him.

"Why did you leave the meeting?" he asked evenly.

"I'm going home." Her legs felt wooden as she walked to her desk and retrieved her purse, tucking it under her arm. She avoided his gaze and moved to the side to step around him.

He took one stride and stood in front of her, blocking the door.

"I need you here, Susan. You know it won't be easy, making the transition. Up until now only the family has been involved, but now everyone else will have to be informed and dealt with. I need your help. You can do more with a look than most people can manage with a baseball bat."

"If I hadn't thought you could handle it, I wouldn't have voted for you," she said tiredly. "Please, let me by."

"Why did you vote for me? Everyone else was as surprised as I was." He put his hand on her bare arm, the warmth of his fingers searing her, seeking a response, some sign of the quiet radiance he associated with her.

Susan couldn't give him one. She simply stared woodenly at the light gray fabric of his suit. "I'm tired; I want to go home," she repeated.

He looked at her pale, tense face, seeing the shadows around her eyes, and though all of his instincts screamed against letting her slip away now, it was obvious that she was almost at the breaking point. "I'll drive you home."

"No." Her reply was immediate, and firm.

He bit back a curse. "All right, if you don't want me to drive you home, I'm sure Imogene will—"

"I drove myself here; I can drive myself home. I'm not going to tangle with any power poles."

Forcing himself to compliance, he said, "All right. I'll come by tonight—"

"No," she interrupted, looking at him now, pain and betrayal plain for him to read in her eyes. "Not tonight."

It was a hard battle that he fought with himself, evident in the grim set of his jaw, the drumming of the pulse in his temple. "We have to talk."

"I know. Maybe later; I don't think I can handle it right now."

"When?"

She managed a shrug, but her lips were trembling. "I don't know. Maybe six or seven years."

"Hell!" he roared, his control shattered.

"I'm sorry, but that's the way I feel! Please, just leave me alone! I don't have anything else you want, anyway; you've already got my stock and my vote." She pushed past him, ducking her head to keep from looking at him. She just watched her feet, mentally commanding them to function. She left the building, and the hot Mississippi sun burned down on her, blinding her momentarily with its brilliance. She blinked and fumbled in her purse for her sunglasses, finally extracting them and sliding them on her nose. The sun felt good on her chilled skin, she noticed dimly. She would go home and sit on the patio in the sun, and sleep if she could. That was the most ambitious plan she could make at the moment, with her mind so dulled by pain.

She drove home slowly, carefully. Emily, bless her, didn't ask any unnecessary questions. Moving like an automaton, Susan shed her dress and slip, and peeled the hot pantyhose away from her legs. The freedom afforded her by an old pair of shorts that she usually wore only while gardening, and a plain white sleeveless blouse with the tails tied in a knot at her midriff, made her breathe easier for the first time in days. It was over. She had lost more than anyone else, but she could rest now.

She pulled a chaise longue out into the full strength of the sun and lay down, letting the heat begin the healing process in her exhausted body. Her eyelids each weighed a thousand pounds; she was unable to keep them up, and after a moment she stopped trying. She dozed in the sun, her mind blank.

Emily woke her once with an offering of iced tea, which Susan accepted gratefully. The chill was gone now, and she felt pleasantly hot, her skin damp with perspiration. She drank the tea, then turned over on her stomach and slept again. During the worst of the heat Emily came out and pulled the big patio umbrella into position to shield Susan, then went back in to finish the chores Cord had set for her.

Susan awoke late in the afternoon and wandered in to eat the light salad and stuffed tomato that Emily had prepared. Her eyes were still heavy, and she yawned in spite of everything she could do to prevent it.

"I'm sorry," she murmured. "I'm still so tired."

Emily patted her arm. "Why don't you go watch the evening news? Just put your feet up and relax."

"That's exactly what I've been doing for *hours,*" Susan sighed, but it was still an outstanding idea.

It was inevitable that she'd go to sleep in front of the television. Her last memory was of a stalled low pressure system on the weather map.

She was stiff when she woke, and she stretched leisurely, trying to ease the kinks out of her back and legs. Her lashes fluttered open, and she stared straight into Cord's eyes.

With renewed energy she sat up abruptly. "What are you doing here?" she demanded, her eyes wide, the haunted look creeping back into them.

"Waiting for you to wake up," he returned calmly. "I didn't

want to startle you. Now I'm going to do exactly what I wanted to do the first time I saw you.''

She pressed herself back into the corner of the couch, watching him warily as he approached and leaned over her. ''What was that?''

''Throw you over my shoulder and carry you off.'' He gripped one of her wrists, gave a gentle tug, and to her astonishment she found herself being hoisted over his shoulder. He settled her comfortably, one arm locked around her legs to hold her steady, while he patted her bottom with the other hand.

Dizzily she grabbed at his belt loops to anchor herself. ''Put me down!'' she gasped; then, as he moved deliberately around the room, switching off the television, turning off the lights, she said. ''What are you doing?''

''You'll see.''

It wasn't until he carried her outside into the warm, fragrant night air that she began to struggle, kicking futilely against the band of his arm. ''Let me down! Where are you taking me?''

''Away,'' he answered simply, his boots crunching on the gravel of the drive. In an effort to see Susan braced her arms on his back and raised herself, looking over her shoulder. His Blazer was sitting there, and he opened the door, then very gently lifted her off his shoulder and placed her on the seat.

''Emily packed your clothes,'' he informed her, leaning in to kiss her sweetly astonished mouth. ''I've already put them in the Blazer. Everything's taken care of, and all you have to do is ride. I still have that blanket in the back, if you'd rather sleep,'' he finished huskily, his tone telling her how clearly he remembered the last time he had used it.

Susan sat in dazed astonishment as he shut the door and walked around to the driver's side. He was really kidnapping her, with Emily's cheerful aid! She supposed she should feel more indignant, but she still felt slow and drowsy, and it just didn't seem worth the effort to protest.

When he slid under the steering wheel, she asked quietly, ''How did you know I wouldn't try to run while you went around to get in?''

''Two reasons.'' He started the motor and shifted into reverse, turning to look over his shoulder as they backed up. ''One, you're too smart to waste what little energy you have in a useless effort.'' He braked, then changed to first gear and smoothly let out the clutch, his powerful legs working. ''Two, you love me.''

His logic was iron-clad. She did love him, even though she was still trying to deal with the hurt he'd inflicted. She supposed that she could best describe her feelings as those of being ill-used, shuffled about with little regard in the high-stakes game he and Preston had been playing.

Cord slanted her a searching look. "No fervent denials?"

"No. I'm not a liar."

The simple dignity of her statement, coupled with her listlessness, shook him to the core. She loved, but without hope. He felt as if a flame that had been given into his care was flickering on the brink of extinction, and it would take tender nurturing to bring it back to full strength. His first thought, when she'd left the office earlier in the day, had been to give her time, let her rest and recover her strength, but as the day wore on he'd been seized by an urgent need to do *something,* to bring her back into the circle of his arms where she belonged. His arrangements had been hurriedly made, as he swept all obstacles and protests out of his path.

He'd thought she would sleep, but she sat very still and erect in the seat, her eyes on the highway. When he'd gone past every destination that she'd guessed, she finally asked, "Where are you taking me?"

"To the beach," he answered promptly. "You're going to do nothing but eat, sleep, and lie in the sun until you gain back the weight you lost and lose those smudges under your eyes."

Susan pondered his answer for a moment, since they were evidently not going to the stretches of beach that she was familiar with. She sighed. "Which beach?"

He laughed aloud, a rare sound. "I'll narrow it down to Florida for you. Does that help?"

She did sleep, finally, before they reached their destination. In the early hours of the morning Cord pulled the Blazer up to a darkened beach house and put his hand on her shoulder to gently shake her awake.

The house was right on the beach, and the luminescent Gulf stretched out before her as far as she could see. The white sand of the Florida panhandle looked like snow in the faint starlight. When she climbed from the Blazer, the constant wind off the gulf lifted her hair, bringing with it the scent of the ocean mingled with the fresher scent of rain.

It was a basic Florida beach house, built of whitewashed cement blocks, with large windows and low ceilings. Following Cord as he moved through the house turning on the lights, she saw a small, cheerful kitchen in yellow and white, a glass table in an alcove, with a ceiling fan above it, and a living room with white wicker furniture; then Cord led her to a small white-painted bedroom. He brought in the single suitcase Emily had packed for her and placed it at the foot of the bed.

"Your bathroom is through there," he said, indicating a door opening off the bedroom. "I'll be in the room straight across the hall, if you need me for anything."

Of all the things she had considered since he'd put her in the Blazer, that she would be going to bed alone wasn't one of them, yet that was exactly what happened. He kissed her on the forehead and walked out, closing the door behind him, and she stood in the middle of the room, blinking her eyes in astonishment.

But the bed beckoned her, and she took a swift shower, then crawled naked between the sheets, too tired to see if Emily had packed a nightgown for her.

Over breakfast the next morning, a meal that he cooked before awakening her, she commented, "You know, this isn't very wise behavior for a man who's just taken control of a firm. You should be in the office."

He shrugged and liberally spread his toast with jelly.

"There's wise, and then there's wise. I think I have my priorities in the right order."

Pursing her lips, Susan carefully cut her toast into thin strips. She wasn't quite certain why he'd brought her to the beach, but her questions could wait. She'd slept until she was almost dopey, and consequently she was rested for the first time in weeks. She didn't think she could handle any personal questions right then, but there were a lot of things she wanted to know.

"You had it all planned out before you came back, didn't you?"

He glanced up, his blue eyes glittering as the morning sun fell on his face. "It all depended on the first step. When I put pressure on him, he had to sell off stock and weaken himself financially in order to replace the money that he'd taken in order for any of it to work. He literally financed my takeover; the money that he replaced was used to buy up the first loan. Then, when that loan was paid, I used the money again to buy up the second loan."

His nerve and gall were truly astonishing, leaving her shaking her head in awe. "You don't have any other money to back you?"

"Of course, I have money," he snorted. "I'm a hell of a good gambler, regardless if it's cards, dice, horses...or oil. I've lost my shirt a few times, but more often than not I come out on top."

"Oil?" she asked blankly. "You wanted to lease the ridges yourself? You weren't acting for any company?"

He shrugged, his powerful shoulders rippling under the light blue polo shirt he wore. "The ridges were a smokescreen," he admitted. "They were a way to put pressure on Preston; I wanted him to refuse to lease them to me, giving me an excuse to use my lever against him."

Susan remembered feeling, at the time, that he'd deliberately pushed Preston into refusing; he'd manipulated them all like a master puppeteer, and they'd danced whenever he pulled the strings. "So there's no oil in the ridges? No wonder you weren't in any hurry to sign the leases!"

"I didn't say that." He reached out and put his hand on hers. "Stop butchering that slice of toast and eat it," he commanded. "Haven't you received the geological survey you ordered?"

"No, not yet."

"Well, the part about the oil is true, or at least there's a good chance of either oil or natural gas."

She ate a piece of toast, and fiddled with another one until she looked up and saw him glaring at her. She hastily took a bite, then put the remainder on her plate. "I'm really not very hungry. I'm sorry."

"That's all right. You'll get your appetite back soon." He rose and began to clear the table; when Susan moved to help him, he stopped her with a lifted hand. "Whoa, lady. Put that plate down. You're not to do any work."

"I'm fairly certain I'm still strong enough to carry a plate," she informed him mildly.

"Sit down. I think I'm going to have to explain the rules to you."

At the mock sternness in his voice, she sat down like a naughty schoolgirl, her hands clasped on her knees. He sat down in the chair opposite her and explained the situation to her slowly and carefully. "You're here to rest. I'm here to take care of you. I'll do the cooking, the cleaning up, everything."

"How long will heaven last?" she asked, and for the first time a tiny smile lit her face, catching his eye like a ray of sunshine after a storm.

"As long as it takes," he replied quietly.

He was serious. The next few days passed leisurely, even monotonously, but after the stress of the last weeks, that was exactly what Susan needed. Time was measured only by the rising and setting of the sun. At first she slept a lot, as much from mental fatigue as any physical tiredness. She didn't occupy her thoughts with tormenting questions of "What if?"; her mind was curiously blank, as if it were just too much trouble to think about anything.

She rested, she ate, she slept, all under the mostly silent guardianship that Cord offered.

She not only slept alone, she was completely undisturbed, and as she regained her strength she began to wonder about that. It was a sign of her returning vitality that she wondered about anything, but she was young and healthy, and the coddling she'd been receiving was rapidly restoring her strength. Her depression and fatigue had been feeding on each other, and with the weariness banished, the uncharacteristic depression began to lift. It was almost like rebirth, and she quietly enjoyed it. But she knew that it was also obvious to Cord that she was feeling much better, and every night she expected him to come to her bed. When he didn't, she had the panicked thought that perhaps he didn't want her any longer; then she realized that he was waiting for her to make the first move, to indicate that she was ready to resume their relationship.

Uncertainty kept her silent. She wasn't certain that it was what she wanted; she still loved him, but there was still that lingering sense of betrayal that she couldn't shake, and she knew that as long as she had doubts about him she had to hold herself aloof. Nor did she want simply to resume an affair; she wanted far more from him than that. She wanted his love, his legal commitment, and, if possible, his children.

The fifth night they were at the beach house a thunderstorm blew in from the Gulf and dumped its fury on them, rattling the windows with its booming claps of thunder. Susan awoke with a start, a cry on her lips, as for a confused moment she thought a tornado was bearing down on her. Then she realized where she was and curled up under the sheet, listening to the drumming rain against the window. She'd never been frightened of storms in the past; in fact, she rather enjoyed the display of power and grandeur, as long as it didn't escalate into a tornado. She would forever have a healthy respect for those snaking, dancing storms.

Her door opened abruptly, and Cord stepped into the room, his nakedness revealed in the flashes of lightning.

Susan stared at him, feeling the tart taste of desire on her tongue, the slow, heated coiling in her abdomen and thighs.

"Are you all right?" he asked softly. "I thought you might be nervous, after the tornado."

She sat up, pushing her tousled hair away from her face. "I'm fine. I was a little startled when it first woke me, but I'm not frightened."

"Good," he said, and started to leave the room.

"Cord, wait!" she called, not planning to say the words, but they burst out of her anyway. He hesitated and turned back to her, standing silently, waiting. "I think it's time to talk," she ventured.

"All right." He moved his shoulders in a strange manner, as if bracing himself. "I'll go put on some pants and be back."

"No." Again she stopped him, holding her hand out to him. "There's no need, is there?"

"I didn't think so," he returned. "But I wasn't sure how you felt."

"I feel the same... Please, sit on the bed." She moved to one side and pulled the covers about her waist, sitting up in the circle of them.

He dropped down to her bed, confiscated one of her pillows and stuffed it behind his back, stretched his long legs out on the mattress and turned on the lamp. "If we're going to talk, I'm going to be comfortable, and I want to be able to see you."

She tucked her legs under her Indian-style trying not to stare at the wonderfully masculine form sprawled in front of her. She couldn't imagine a man made any more beautifully. Every time she saw him, she only admired him the more; he seemed to improve with age. But his body was distracting her, and she forced herself to look at his face. The small, knowing, infinitely pleased smile that lurked on his lips made her flush; then she laughed a little at herself. "I'm sorry. You have a knack for making me blush."

"*I* should be blushing, if I'm reading your mind correctly."

He was, and they both knew it. She quickly sought control, and found it. This was far too important for her to let herself be sidetracked. "Before I say anything else, we might as well get one thing out of the way. I love you. If you can't deal with that, if it makes you uncomfortable, then we have nothing to talk about. You might as well go back to your own room."

He didn't move an inch from his comfortable position. "I've known for some time," he said, his eyes darker than she'd ever seen them before. "I knew the first time I made love with you. If you hadn't loved me, you never would have stripped for me like that, or put yourself in my hands so completely."

"But you couldn't trust me? You left me in the dark, knowing how much I was worrying, how it tore me apart to have to fight you." A jagged edge of pain tore into her again just at the memory, and she drew a quick breath, fighting to keep from falling apart, but still the hurt was evident in her voice.

"In my defense, let me say that I hadn't expected you. You blindsided me, sweetheart, and I've been floundering ever since. Except for my parents, I can't say that I've ever known anyone I could trust until I met you, and so many years had passed since I'd been able to turn my back to anyone that I couldn't let myself believe it. You defended Preston so stubbornly, even though you said you loved me; how could I be sure you wouldn't run and tell him immediately if I let it slip that I wasn't trying to bankrupt the company, only to pressure him into selling enough stock for me to have the majority?''

"Don't you see?" she cried. "I defended Preston *precisely* because I thought you were trying to bankrupt him to get revenge for Judith!''

"No, I wasn't after revenge, though I wanted him to think so. I'm far too guilty myself to have any right to take revenge. But the way things were when I left...honey, you have no idea how bitter and violent it had become. I wanted to come back home, and I knew the only way I could do it was from a position of power. I didn't want to simply live in the area again; I wanted to be accepted, to be a part of what I'd had before, when I was too young and too hot-headed to appreciate it.''

"And if you'd told me all that, you thought I'd still ruin it for you?'' she asked, blinking back tears.

He cupped her cheek in his palm, his fingers caressing her jaw. "Don't cry," he murmured. "I told you, I'm out of the habit of trusting people. I've spent a lot of time in dives and jungles and back alleys that—well, never mind. But, damn it, you know I never planned for you to be the one to sell! I never thought he'd dump it all on your shoulders, but he's a smart bastard, I'll say that for him. His idea almost worked. If I'd known that *you* were the one being beaten down, I'd have stopped on the spot. It was your own stubbornness in not telling me that kept things going for so long, that gave me enough time to buy the stock I needed.''

"Along with my vote," she reminded him thinly.

"Yes, along with your vote." He watched her intently, reading the myriad expressions as they flitted across her lovely face. She looked incredibly sexy, he noticed, with her hair all tousled and her eyes still heavy-lidded, her skin softly flushed from sleep. The dark shadows were gone from beneath her eyes, and the soft curves of her breasts shone beneath the thin silk of her nightgown, with her small nipples pushing against the fabric in an enticing manner that made him want to lean forward and take them into his mouth, silk and all. He felt it again, that punch in his chest, and he realized anew that she lit his life like an eternal candle, pure and white. If that serene flame ever went out he'd be doomed to darkness for the rest of his life.

"I was wrong not to trust you," he said softly. His voice went even quieter, so deep that it rumbled in his chest. "I knew that you loved me, and it was almost too much for me to believe. I was afraid to believe. My God, Susan, don't you know? Don't you have any idea what you do to people? Everywhere I turned, there were people falling all over themselves to please you, to get you to smile at them, to have your attention for just a little while. Even Imogene would fight her weight in wildcats for you! If I'd let myself believe that sweetness was all mine, then found out that it wasn't, I couldn't have handled it. I had to protect myself by not letting you get too close."

Susan stared at him, bewildered by his words. "People fall all over themselves for me? What do you mean?"

She truly didn't know, he realized, had never noticed the effect her radiant smile had on people, or the almost inevitable softening that crossed their faces whenever they talked to her. My God, he had a treasure that men would fight for, possibly kill for, and she didn't even know her own power, which he supposed was part of her elusive, but hauntingly sweet charm.

"Never mind," he told her gently. She wouldn't believe him even if he told her. "The important things is, do you love me enough to forgive me?"

"I have to," she replied obliquely, but the truth was plain in her eyes. She had to forgive him, because when she searched down to the deepest recesses of her heart, she loved him too much not to forgive him anything.

Very tenderly, he reached out and caught her waist, drawing her out of her tangle of covers and pulling her atop him, resting her weight on his chest. "I'm glad," he said gravely, his diamond-eyes so close that she could see her own reflection in the dilated blackness of his pupils. "Because I love you so much that I think I'd go crazy if you sent me away."

Susan's eyes widened, and her heart gave a great bound, then resumed beating with thuds that hammered against the delicate cage of her ribs. "I...what?"

"I said, I love you," he repeated, sliding his hand up her back in a slow, heated caress. She quivered, tried to speak, but her trembling lips couldn't form the words, and instead she gave up and dropped her head to his shoulder, her hands holding tightly to him. He folded her to him, pressing her soft, deliciously feminine body against his. Sudden tears, hot and acid, burned his eyes. He'd almost lost her, almost let her love slip away from him, and the thought tormented him.

"I love you," he said again, this time whispering the words into the dark cloud of her hair. The searing tears slid down his hard, sun-browned cheeks, but he wasn't aware of them. His world had narrowed to the wonder he held in his arms, the slim, delicate body that held such sweetness and gallantry, such an endless capacity for love, that he was staggered by it.

Susan drew a little away from him, her heart stopping when she saw the wet tracks on his face, and in that moment she knew beyond doubt that he loved her. He was looking at her with a deep, consuming love that he made no effort to hide. The last of his bitterness was drained away in the salt of his tears, the last grief and guilt he felt for Judith. She put her cheek against his, rubbing the wetness away.

Knowing that she would never refuse him, that what they felt burning between them needed to be consummated, had to be sanctified by their union, he rolled and deftly placed her beneath him, his legs parting her thighs. He rose to his knees and lifted her nightgown, then drew it over her head. After tossing it away, he regarded her slim beauty for a moment, then let his weight down on her. He kissed her fiercely, then drew back with masculine satisfaction stamped on his bearded features. "I'm going to marry you."

Again shock reverberated through Susan, but now it was a joyous shock, as at last she began to believe what was happening to her. She looked up at him, and suddenly a smile curved her lips. Just like that; it wasn't a proposal, a question, but a statement. He was going to marry her, and she'd better not try to argue with him about it!

"Yes," she said, then caught her breath as he entered her. Her moistly yielding body accepted him without difficulty, the sweet honey of her flesh welcoming him. He moved against her, probing slowly, and he groaned aloud in pleasure.

Then he raised himself on his elbow to look down at her, his gaze burning with desire. "It might be a good idea if we get married as soon as possible," he murmured. "After the night in the Blazer, you could well be pregnant."

"I know." She slid her hands over his shoulders to his neck, and smiled up at him. "I hope so."

An answering smile touched his lips. "Just to be on the safe side, let's do it again." He kissed her again; then their bodies began to move in unison, with a passion that was wild and tender and sanity-destroying, their love binding them together with an electrically charged force field of devotion. What had begun with a dance on a crowded ballroom floor had become a sensual dance of love, sanctified by the tears of a hard man who'd had to learn how to cry.

Epilogue

Cord lay heavily on her, sweetly limp after the whirlwind of their lovemaking. Susan nibbled on his shoulder, and he put his hand in her hair to pull her head up. He began kissing her again, slow, drugging kisses that lit the fires between them again, fires that burned higher and hotter than ever after a year of marriage. Just as he began moving within her, a faint, fretful cry caught their attention, a cry that quickly escalated into an all-out bellow.

He cursed luridly as he slid off of her. "She's got the most incredible timing!" he grumbled as he stalked naked from the room, outrage evident in every line of his powerful body.

Susan pulled the sheet up over her nude body; she was cool without the heat of him next to her. A slow, gentle smile touched her lips as she envisioned the scene in the next room. Cord might grumble and grouse, but he'd melt as soon as he set eyes on his tiny daughter, who had just learned how to blow bubbles. As soon as she saw her father, she'd stop her bellowing, and her arms and legs would go into overtime as her entire body wriggled in delight. She'd treat him to her entire repertoire of accomplishments, from kicking to blowing bubbles, and he'd be lost in adoring admiration. Alison Marie was a four-month-old tyrant, and she had Cord wrapped completely around her dainty finger.

It was a good thing they'd gotten married so swiftly, because within a month it had become evident that Susan was indeed pregnant. Cord had teased her before Alison had been born, insisting that if the baby were a girl, he was going to name her Storm, and if it were a boy, it had to be called Blazer. She'd been a little worried at how he would accept fatherhood, but she'd worried over nothing. No man could have been more delighted over his child.

She prepared herself to nurse the baby, and in a moment Cord came back into the bedroom, cradling Alison in the curve of his strong arm and crooning to her as her plump little hands waved in the air, trying to catch his beard. "We're going to have to trade her in for a model that doesn't leak," he said, getting back in bed, still holding Alison, while Susan stuffed a pillow behind her back.

When she took the baby, he moved to put his arm around her, holding her so most of her weight rested on his chest. "Look at that little pig," he drawled, as the baby latched onto the milk-swollen nipple with starving ferocity. He was fascinated by everything about her, and had been from the moment he'd known of Susan's pregnancy.

Despite it being her first child, she'd breezed through the months with almost boring ease. She'd had little morning sickness, no cravings, and had carried the baby easily. Her biggest problem had been Cord, who had hounded her if she even tried to change a light bulb. She had Alison with a minimum of fuss, and Cord had been there to hold his daughter, who weighed in at a tiny five pounds and two ounces.

Now his big hand touched the small, round head, smoothing the black curls that covered it. She opened her eyes briefly, revealing pale blue irises surrounded by a ring of darker blue. She was his image, and he adored her. But the delights of her mother's breast occupied her at the moment, and she closed her eyes again, suckling vigorously.

Soon she slept again, and Susan's nipple slipped from the relaxed rosebud mouth. "I'm going to have to wean her soon," she sighed.

"Why?"

"She's starting to teethe."

He laughed softly, sprawling naked on the bed. "Dangerous, huh?"

"Extremely." She carried Alison back to the nursery, and stood for a moment holding the infinitely precious little bundle in her arms. The baby grunted as she was placed on her stomach, but a tightly curled fist brushed her mouth and she latched onto it in her sleep, sucking noisily on her knuckles.

He was waiting for her when she came back into their bedroom, and he drew her back down into his embrace. Susan curled against him, placing her head on the broad, hairy chest. Being married to him was better than she'd dreamed, because she'd never thought that her restless renegade would have been so content.

He and Preston had reached a truce, a working relationship that allowed peace between them. Preston remained as president of the company, because his experience and ability were too good to waste. Cord's own daring and verve had blended with Preston's attention to detail, and together they were creating a company that was innovative but not reckless, sure-footed but not too cautious. The challenge kept Cord fascinated, and at night he came back to her arms, which was all she'd ever asked of heaven.

He reached out and clicked off the lamp, yawing in the sudden darkness. He settled her in his arms, in their sleeping position, and she nuzzled her mouth against his flesh. Just as she'd dreamed months ago, sleeping with him every night was deeply satisfying. They talked in the darkness, sharing the things that had happened to them during the day, planning what they wanted to do together. His hand moved lazily over her soft body, then found her breasts and became more obvious in his attentions.

"Susan? Do you think she'll wake up this time?"

Susan laughed, winding her arms around his neck. Her beloved desperado, her darling renegade, still swept her away into his dark, magic world of love.

*   *   *   *   *

Golden Lasso
Fern Michaels

Chapter One

Janice Warren shook her shining chestnut curls with a mixture of sadness and relief as she scrutinized the legal paper before her. The stiff, crackling letter, if she was interpreting it correctly, held the answer to her and Benjie's future.

"What's wrong, Jan?" the little boy in the bulky wheelchair asked fearfully, not understanding his sister's sudden silence. "Did the doctors say something scary about me? Is that why you look so funny?"

"Of course not, silly," Janice soothed, wiping the tears from her eyes. "This letter is going to make everything right for you and me. Do you remember Dad's brother? Uncle Jake? He owned the ranch in Arizona." At Benjie's nod, she continued, "Well, he left the Rancho Arroyo to me, and I'm going to share it with you. That's the happy part. The sad part is that Uncle Jake died and no one notified us. The letter says that he wanted a simple funeral. Uncle Jake was like that—fiercely independent."

With nine-year-old logic, Benjie asked, "How come he left the ranch to you? Didn't he have any children of his own?"

"Uncle Jake's wife died when she was very young and they had no children. I guess we're the last blood relatives and Uncle Jake was big on family." Janice blurted over a sob, "Oh, Benjie, do you know what this means? We can go to Arizona and begin a whole new life. I remember your doctor telling me there was a marvelous clinic in Phoenix that specializes in problems like yours. We've never been able to afford it; but now, since we'll be living close by, we can! You can go there and they'll help you and pretty soon..."

"I'll be able to walk again!" Benjie shouted happily, tossing his dark tousled head, his blue eyes shining.

"With God's help, that's exactly what's going to happen. I can't wait to see you out there playing Little League ball with all of the kids again. And you will," Jan said with determination. "I'll see to it if I have to work twenty-four hours a day to make it come true."

"What about your job here and that boyfriend of yours, Neil Connors—the one who doesn't like me?" Benjie asked curiously.

"Benjie!" Jan cried in surprise. "What a terrible thing to say. What makes you think Neil doesn't like you? And as for my job— pooh, I didn't like it anyway."

"I heard Neil say you were going to be saddled with me for the rest of your life, and he didn't plan on taking on a kid brother. I heard him," the little boy said past a lump in his throat.

"Well, if you heard that then you must have heard my reply. You did, didn't you?" she asked anxiously, her green cat's eyes studying her brother.

"No, I didn't hear what you said. I sort of...I thought Neil might tell you to put me in an orphanage or something."

Jan was off the chair and kneeling in front of Benjie. "Hey, this is Jan, your big sister. I thought we had an agreement that if something was bothering one of us we could talk it out. How could you think such a thing? I told Neil that you and I were a team, and if he didn't want to be part of that team, then that was his problem. I told him when Mom and Dad died in that car crash and you managed to survive I swore that I would take care of you for the rest of our lives. I meant it, Benjie. All we have is one another, now that Mom and Dad are gone. And now that Uncle Jake is gone too, we're all that's left of the Warren family. We have to stick together. You're such a good little kid putting up with me and never complaining when other kids are out there playing and having a good time. You're going to play, too—you have my word on it. When we get to Arizona, you'll get lots of fresh air. There'll be horses and treatments at the medical center, and at night you're going to be so tired you'll sleep better than ever. What do you say partner? Is it a deal?" Jan asked huskily as she hugged the little boy.

"You bet! When are we going to leave? What about my school-work?"

"We'll leave at the end of the week. Tomorrow is going to be a very busy day. There're only three weeks of school left before summer vacation, and I doubt if it will be a problem since you're a straight A student. I'll make the plane reservations this evening and start packing our gear. We'll just close up the house and decide later if we're going to keep it or sell it."

"Tell me about the ranch, Jan. Did you ever see it?"

"Once, when I was about your age, maybe a little older. It's great, Benjie," Jan said enthusiastically. "The main building is made from logs and there're all kinds of planters with bright flowers at the windowsills. There were separate cabins for the guests—a dozen or so, if I remember correctly—and each of them is on what Uncle Jake called a trail that branches off the main path. He wanted his guests to have privacy so they're sort of scattered. When it was in season, he would have big barbecues, where he roasted a whole steer, and then have a square dance. The guests would wear cowboy outfits, and there was an old Indian who played the guitar. At that time he had a lot of really good horses that he kept for his own pleasure and others that were for his guests to ride. All of the people who worked for Uncle Jake seemed to love him because he really cared about them. It was homey and cozy, and I guess that's what I liked about it. Mom and Dad went there on their honeymoon, and I guess that makes Rancho Arroyo special, too. I hope we can make a go of it—I don't know the first thing about running a dude ranch. This letter," Jan said, tapping the legal paper, "says the reservations for the guests have all been confirmed and we're starting off with a full guest list. The first party of guests arrives the day after we do. Our worries are over, little brother," Jan cried exuberantly. "I'm going to pack some of my things now. Do you want to come upstairs or would you rather watch television?"

"I'm going to work on my model and sort of listen to the TV if that's okay with you."

"Sure. If you want me, just holler," Jan said, running lightly up the stairs. Once she was inside her room she unfolded the letter from Uncle Jake's attorney and reread it. It was the last paragraph of the letter that bothered her. The printed words sent a chill down her spine as she reread the ominous-sounding words.

At the moment I doubt there is much cause for alarm; however, I feel that I must alert you to the fact that a new dude ranch, owned by Derek Bannon, had just been opened in the same vicinity. It caters to the entertainment crowd and its specialty appears to be a Las Vegas atmosphere. Your Uncle Jake was concerned up until the end about the effect of such a place on his little enterprise. However, he believed that family atmosphere and good home cook-

ing at Rancho Arroyo would win out. I want you to be aware, Miss
Warren, that while all the reservations have been confirmed, there
is nothing that says a guest can't change his mind once he sees the
glittering Golden Lasso. I want you to be prepared for any and all
emergencies.

I feel it is imperative that you visit my office as soon as possible
upon your arrival, as there are many facets of the business that need
discussing.

Jan folded the letter carefully and placed it in the zipper com-
partment of her handbag. The Golden Lasso. A man named Derek
Bannon. Jan's stomach curled into a hard knot. Suddenly, she was
afraid. Could she handle it? She had to, for Benjie's sake and for
her own. She had wept so bitterly that day at her parents' grave site
when she promised to take care of Berjie. She wouldn't let a man
named Derek Bannon upset her plans—not now, not when Benjie's
welfare was at stake.

From time to time, as Jan busily packed and sorted and then
discarded, she caught a flash of her reflection in the long mirror in
her room. Was that grim, tight jaw hers? Of course it was—she
was being threatened by an unknown named Derek Bannon. She
could feel it, almost taste it. Benjie's future was being threatened
more than her own. But now it was time for her to call the airlines
and make their reservations. And she did it with all the calm she
could muster. The die was cast. She would make a go of the ranch;
she had to. Now she had to call Neil and tell him what was happening.

After putting the receiver back in its cradle, Jan applied a light
layer of makeup around her eyes and then deftly added a little color
to her cheeks. She couldn't give way to her feelings now, especially
not in front of Benjie and Neil, who, rocked by the news that she
was leaving, was due to arrive any moment now.

But it was Benjie with whom Jan was concerned. The youngster
was so attuned to her feelings he could sense immediately if something was wrong. She had to think positively and act confidently in
front of the little boy.

With trembling hands, she ran a brush through her short-cropped
chestnut curls. She frowned at the smattering of freckles that ran
across her nose and then winced as she thought of the effect the
Arizona sun would have on those hated freckles. Her mother's comforting words, "Jan, don't worry about your freckles. With those
gorgeous emerald eyes of yours, no one will ever notice them,"
didn't help now. Twenty-one-year-old women weren't supposed to
have freckles. Neil always poked fun at her freckles, but in a nice

way. She supposed she would miss Neil when she went away, but Benjie was more important to her than romance. Not that there was much romance—not with her obligations to be both mother and father to Benjie. But still, Neil had always been in the wings waiting for her to have time for him.

Jan scowled. Romanticizing already? Face the truth, she told herself. Neil is great; he's nice to me, and he's always ready to give me a hand when I need it. He has a good job and he'd good-looking—a great catch, as the other girls in the office had told her. But somehow Jan couldn't stir herself up over a great catch. And the fact that she was willing to drop everything and go out to Arizona was proof enough to her that Neil just wasn't that important in her life.

There were times when she had thought he was about to ask her to marry him. But something always held him back. There were times, also, when Jan was so tired and disgusted with trying to make ends meet and taking care of Benjie that she knew that if Neil had only said the word she would have married him in a minute. It would be nice to have someone to lean on, she thought. But then, at other times, when she seemed to have control of the situation and she was well rested, she knew that marrying Neil would be a mistake. There was something lacking in their relationship, something she sensed in Neil that didn't appeal to her. Or was it because she knew Benjie didn't like him?

Neil Connors wasn't the kind of man who could make the earth move under her feet, Jan decided. At best, Neil might be able to move a small hill.

Jan descended the stairs calmly. It was time for Benjie's medicine and his snack before bed. She watched him toil away with his model and marveled at the child's patience. He held the tweezers and the tiny sticks that held pinpoints of glue on the end and matched them perfectly. He looked tired, poor little kid, and yet he never complained. He just sat and waited till she had time for him. He looked just like their father with his crisp, dark hair and bright blue eyes. Even now, at the age of nine, he had their father's chin, complete with a small cleft. He was bright and precocious with a delightful sense of humor. She loved him dearly. He was all she had left, and there was nothing or anyone who was ever going to change that. Not ever.

Benjie was at the kitchen table, his wheelchair pulled up close against the edge, when the doorbell rang insistently. Neil. Jan opened the door and in he stormed.

"What do you mean you're going off to Arizona?" he demanded, pushing his fingers through his thick blond hair.

"Just that," Jan railed. "And if you'll give me a minute, I'll explain it all to you. Come on into the kitchen and say hello to Benjie. I was just going to put him to bed. I'll pour you a cup of coffee."

Jan turned back to the kitchen, Neil hot on her heels. "Explain!" he demanded again, not bothering to answer Benjie's polite "Hi."

As Jan poured his coffee, she began to explain, feeling her patience fail. Was Benjie right about Neil not liking him? She shrugged and handed Neil his coffee. "C'mon, Benjie. Ready for bed? I'll be right back, Neil. Make yourself at home."

"Can't he get into bed on his own, for chrissakes?"

"Yes, he can," Jan bristled. "But when you were nine years old, didn't you like to have someone tuck you in?"

Jan returned from the downstairs den, which had been made over into a bedroom for Benjie. "Whatever you do, keep your voice down," she told Neil. "He's going to find it difficult enough to get to sleep."

"Yeah, yeah, okay. Now, what's this all about?"

Slowly, Jan explained, watching the look of disapproval deepen on Neil's face.

"You mean you're just going to go out there and take over and run that place?" He laughed harshly. "What do you know about running a dude ranch?"

"Nothing. No more than I knew what it was to run a house and take care of a little boy," she retorted sharply. "But I learned real fast. And I don't think the idea is so ridiculous. I'm not stupid, you know."

"I never said you were stupid, Jan. Just inexperienced. Naive. You're going to lose your shirt—you know that, don't you?"

"Thanks for the vote of confidence. No, I don't know that I'll lose my shirt. There are people out there, Neil—my uncle's staff— who know all about running the ranch. And am I or am I not one of the best darn bookkeepers you know? I'm halfway through my courses to become a certified public accountant, and that takes brains, whether you like to admit it or not."

"All right, so you're not stupid. But going off to Arizona this way is! What about your life here? This house? Your job?" He slammed his coffee mug down onto the table, sloshing coffee onto the checkered cloth.

"In that order? My life in Arizona would be a change from the humdrum life I live here. The house? I was hoping you'd keep an eye on it for me. My job? I've already told you I'm not stupid. I can always find a job. But what's most important to me is Benjie. There's a clinic out in Phoenix that was recommended to me months ago, but I couldn't afford it. Now Benjie will have the opportunity to go there and be helped.''

"So that's who's behind all this. That kid.'' Neil stood up abruptly and put his cup in the sink.

"Benjie is my brother, Neil, not 'that kid.' And no, he's not behind this. I would have taken this opportunity anyway. Benjie only validates my reasons for moving on this so quickly. I'm sorry you feel this way, Neil. I was hoping you'd cheer me on.''

Neil looked at Jan, an expression of exasperation on his face that clearly stated that this was the dumbest move she could make. "Write out a list of instructions about the house. I'll take care of it for you. When did you say you were leaving? Don't bother telling me—I don't want to know. Leave the list of instructions in your mailbox. Goodbye, Jan.''

Without turning around or saying another word, Neil pushed open the kitchen door and stalked out. Jan sat down moodily. Whatever reaction she had expected from Neil, this definitely wasn't it.

Jan was thrilled by the attention Benjie received on the plane from the stewardesses. On boarding, the pilot had handed the little boy a pair of plastic wings, and at the last moment he had fastened them to Benjie's polo shirt. Benjie had beamed his thanks, and from time to time Jan watched him touch the pin during the long trip.

Benjie was happy and amenable to this change in their lives, trusting Jan to take care of him. For a moment tears blinded her. She knew she was guilty of being too maternal, too protective of him. She was going to have to let go in degrees. In New York it had been hard, but now that they were going to the wide-open spaces, perhaps she could manage to bring herself to relinquish her hold and let others have a chance at getting to know the little boy. He needed friends—good friends—who would love him as she did. They were making the right move, Jan told herself determinedly— she was sure of it.

Besides, the house in upstate New York would be there for them if things didn't work out. Her cushion, so to speak. Now, with the income from the ranch, she wouldn't have so much difficulty meeting the taxes and insurance payments. And the money for Benjie's treatments wouldn't be so difficult to come by. She admitted she had become bone tired from holding down two jobs: her regular one at the dairy, where she was a bookkeeper, and her evening job as a receptionist at a health spa. Benjie's care hadn't presented a problem because he was at school all day while she worked at the dairy, and then at night he had been allowed to come with her to the health spa. Still, he had gotten to bed late, and more times than she cared to remember, they had eaten cold suppers from her lunch bag. But he had thrived and hadn't lost weight, and that was important, according to his doctors. What Benjie needed was her love and the security only she could provide.

Other niggling little thoughts plagued Jan as she stared out at the fluffy clouds far below them. What about me? the contrary little voice demanded. When am I going to have a life of my own? A chance to go out on dates or just for a simple dinner? For the past two years she hadn't even been able to accept an invitation. It was no wonder Neil had been so grudging of Benjie. What kind of date was it to sit and watch television after Benjie went to bed? And she had always been firm about ushering Neil out at the stroke of eleven. She didn't have much going for her either way she looked at it.

Dreamily, Jan closed her eyes and let her mind wander. It must be wonderful to be in love and thrill to another's voice. To know that the person loves you as much as you love him. Would she ever have the time to find that elusive thing called love? Would she ever be free to accept that love? She was almost twenty-two and so far it hadn't found her. She admitted she wanted to be swept off her feet. She wanted, yearned, to feel someone's arms around her, and she wanted to be kissed till she was left breathless and wanting more.

A sound of light laughter, feminine and crystal-sounding, captured Jan's attention. Across the aisle sat a fashionably slim, stylishly dressed woman about Jan's age. Her long, slim legs were crossed, and when she turned her head Jan saw that she was very pretty. The man sitting beside the woman seemed very attentive and kept glancing at her appreciatively as he spoke to her. Whatever he had said to her seemed to strike her as amusing and she laughed again, a light-hearted, abandoned sound that wrenched at Jan's heart. How long had it been since she had been carefree and laughed that way?

"...but I'm going to be married before the month is out. Do you think it would be right if I met you for a drink?" The woman's voice was light and teasing as she flirted with the good-looking, massively built man beside her. "It was only coincidence we took the same flight to Phoenix.... And my fiancé is rather jealous..." The rest of her statement was lost in the sound of the jet engines.

Jan watched the girl across the aisle covertly, a frown of scorn drawing her finely arched brows together. She didn't think much of any girl who could so lightheartedly announce that she was engaged to be married and at the same time flirt so blatantly with the first stranger she met on a plane. A jealous, green monster nipped at Jan's sense of propriety. Some girls just seemed to have it all— money, looks, someone who loved them—and still it didn't seem to be enough. A sudden rush of pity for the girl's fiancé forced Jan's pretty mouth into a thin, straight line.

"As long as you promise to behave yourself," the girl in the aisle warned. "I don't suppose a little drink would hurt anyone. I'll be at the Golden Lasso..." Again her words were drowned out as she turned her head away.

At the mention of the Golden Lasso Jan jumped to attention. Over the top of Benjie's head she took another long look at the girl and sighed. Women as beautiful as that always had men dancing attention around them, she concluded. Jan stiffened her back and sat up straighter in her seat. This was definitely none of her business, and she should be thinking about the kind of reception she would find at Rancho Arroyo and in what condition she would find it.

"I think we're going down," Benjie said, his eyes wide as he stretched to peer out the window. "Look, Jan, the seat belt sign just went on. Is someone going to meet us?"

A knot formed in the pit of Jan's stomach. This was the beginning of a new life for the both of them. She was the new owner of Rancho Arroyo. Boss lady. She could handle it—she would have to. Taking a deep breath, she leaned back and readjusted her seat as the stewardess requested. Quickly, she pressed the button on Benjie's seat, raising it to a full sitting position, and smiled at how happy he was. She had originally thought he would be terrified of flying. But nothing could have been farther from the truth. Benjie took to flying like a duck to water.

As the airport came into view and she felt the jar of the mechanism lowering the landing gear, Jan said a silent prayer that the Rancho Arroyo would be a happy place to make their new home and that the medical center in Phoenix would be successful in helping Benjie to walk again. She was tempted to utter a small plea to grant her wish for love and romance and then changed her mind. That would be almost too much to wish for.

Once on the ground, Jan peered around the airport baggage area searching for a person who looked like they might be looking for her. Surely, Uncle Jake's attorney had told someone at the Rancho that Benjie was in a wheelchair. If they didn't recognize her, Benjie was certainly visible with his hundred-watt smile.

Chapter Two

"Miss Warren? It is Miss Warren, isn't it?" a drawling voice inquired.

"I'm Jan Warren. Are you from Rancho Arroyo?" she inquired of the tall, slim man in the tight Levis who was towering over her.

"You've got it, and this little guy must be your brother. Andy Stone," he said, holding out his big, sun-bronzed hand to Benjie, who shook it manfully. "See that man over there?" he asked, motioning to a tall, dark-skinned man standing near the luggage carousel. "That's Gus and he's full-blooded Cheyenne Indian. He's the man who's going to take your baggage to the van and then we're all going to the ranch for a proper welcome."

"Wow! A real Indian!" Benjie cried excitedly.

Jan smiled, "Thank you for that, Andy Stone. I really appreciate it." She handed him the baggage tickets.

"He looks like a nice little kid and it must be rough being glued to a chair like that. I have a little brother in Montana who isn't much bigger and I...what I mean is... Heck, ma'am, I'm just rattlin' on. But your little brother is going to be around people who really care about young ones."

Jan smiled brightly and alleviated Andy's embarrassment. "Look, Andy, there's a man who seems to be trying to get your attention."

Andy tilted his head and looked in the direction Jan was indicating. His mouth tightened and his eyes narrowed. "That's Derek Bannon—he owns the Golden Lasso. There must be someone important on this plane if he's here to meet him personally. You might as well know now before someone else tells you—he's approached everyone who works at the ranch to come and work for him. Some of the people he asked directly and others he sent his business manager around to them. I was one of the ones he approached directly. I turned him down flat. It was hard because he offered me quite an increase in wages. But I liked your Uncle Jake. He took me in and gave me a job when I needed it, and I don't forget that quickly. Looks like Bannon's coming over here. Let me handle it. Later, when you're up on all the goings on, you can take a shot at him yourself.''

Jan was bewildered. Fifteen minutes on the ground and already she had a problem. Instinctively, she trusted Andy Stone. Her own gaze narrowed as she watched the tall, muscular Derek Bannon make his way through the milling passengers who were waiting for their luggage. He was tall—taller than Andy Stone—and he wore his extra flesh well. There was nothing lanky about Derek Bannon. He maneuvered himself gracefully, like a cat, and his low Western boots had just the right amount of shine to them. His Levis fit to perfection as though they were tailor-made, as did the shirt he wore, open to reveal a massive, sun-bronzed chest. There was a slight curl to his crisp, black hair and just a trace of gray at the temples. Steely blue eyes stared at her and through her, making her feel uncomfortable.

''Have you given my offer any more thought, Stone?'' he asked Andy in a deep voice that seemed to come from somewhere in his chest. His eyes, however, were on Jan.

''Not today, I haven't. I've been a little busy. This is Janice Warren, the new owner of Rancho Arroyo, and her brother, Benjie.''

''Miss Warren, a pleasure.'' Jan knew he noticed that she hadn't extended her hand, and after a moment he turned his attention to Benjie. He held out his hand and Benjie grasped it and shook it heartily. ''Benjie, is it? How old are you?'' Derek Bannon asked.

''Nine on my last birthday, sir.''

''Isn't it time you were called Ben instead of Benjie?''

Benjie flushed and stared at Jan and then at Andy Stone.

''But that's my name. My mom and dad gave it to me. They're dead and I can't change it, can I, Jan?''

''If you want to. Your real name is Benjamin and Benjie is just a nickname, like Ben. You don't have to decide right now, Benjie, and it isn't important. Is it, Mr. Bannon?'' she asked in a cold tone that told the man it was none of his business what her brother's name was.

Derek Bannon shrugged. "Perhaps we'll see one another again."
With a curt nod, he weaved his way through the milling crowd.

"What a strange man," Jan said in a puzzled tone.

"He's more than strange, Miss Warren. He's a hard man to fight,
and believe me when I tell you you have a fight in store for you.
He wants your ranch and he's not going to stop until he gets it."

"I like him," Benjie chirped. "I liked the way he didn't stoop
over and pretend I was a little kid. And I liked it when he said I
should be called Ben. I liked him," Benjie said emphatically.

"Well, will you look at that!" Andy said in surprise, pointing to
a group of men. "That's the entire Bison football team, and I guess
they're staying at the Golden Lasso." Benjie's eyes boggled at the
sight, and Jan didn't miss Derek Bannon wave his hand in the little
boy's direction.

Jan tugged at Andy's arm. "Why does Mr. Bannon want my
ranch?"

"Beats me, Miss Warren. All I know is he wants it. He was
forever palavering with your uncle, and as far as I know Jake turned
him down each time."

"Is our ranch a threat to the Golden Lasso?" she asked fearfully,
afraid now that all her wonderful dreams were going up in smoke.

"I can't see how. Our clientele is different. We cater to families
with children. Good home-cooked food, fresh air, and family-type
entertainment. Bannon, on the other hand, is all glitter and frills.
He's got show girls at the Lasso that would put some of those Las
Vegas girls to shame. I don't mind telling you the people around
here were just a mite disturbed over the whole thing. But then they
all settled down nice and quietlike when they saw the Golden Lasso
held pretty strict standards."

"Why would Mr. Bannon want to open a resort way out here in
the first place? Why not Las Vegas?"

"Derek Bannon inherited the land from his father. Over two
thousand acres. The only piece he doesn't own is the five hundred
acre spread the Rancho Arroyo is on. Your Uncle Jake won that
piece in a poker game from Bannon's father. He wants it back.
Unless you're one hell of a poker player, I don't hold out much
hope for you. Money talks, and Derek Bannon talks big. But for
what it's worth, I'm on your side, Miss Warren."

"If you're on my side, then I want you to call me Jan. Is it okay
if I call you Andy?"

"It's a deal, Jan. Looks like Gus is getting restless; I'd better get
these baggage claims over to him. Then what do you say we mosey
on back to the ranch?" He swaggered, pretending to be a cowboy,

much to Benjie's delight. "Gus, now—he doesn't talk much, but he listens. There isn't much that goes on around here that he doesn't know about. A body would be hard pressed to try to pull the wool over his eyes," Andy said softly to Jan before he left to help Gus with the bags.

"Andy," Jan stopped him in midstride. "Did Derek Bannon try to wean Gus away too?" she asked anxiously.

"You used the right word. Try was what he did. Gus listened and didn't utter a word. Oh, he was polite about it. After Bannon had his say, Gus just spit tobacco juice in the road and moved on. It's just a guess on my part, but some of the other hands back at the ranch figure that Bannon wanted to exploit the fact that Gus is Cheyenne. You know—dress him up in feathers and paint or something."

While Andy took Benjie over to the luggage carousel, Jan scanned the airport. Her eyes immediately fell on the escalator, where she saw the girl who had sat across from her on the plane. Now that she was standing, Jan could get a good look at her. The first thing she noticed was that she was alone; apparently, she had said her goodbye to the man seated beside her on the plane. Second, Jan could see what a terrific figure she had. Tall, slim, and willowy, wearing a clingy jersey dress that set off every curve to an advantage. And her shoes! Just how some women learned to walk in those sky-high creations was beyond her.

Suddenly, it seemed as though the girl spotted someone, and before the escalator touched bottom she lifted her arm and waved in excited greeting. As lightly as a dancer, she was off the escalator and skipping across the floor right into Derek Bannon's arms.

Jan was staggered. The girl had spoken about being engaged to be married. Could her fiancé be Derek Bannon? From the way he was hugging her—swinging her up off the floor and twirling her around—it must be. For an instant, Jan felt smug. Well, Mr. Bannon, it seems as though Rancho Arroyo isn't the only thing you can't put your brand on; your little girlfriend was making a date with another man. But the thought had a bitter taste.

Benjie demanded her attention. "Hey, Jan! Come on! Andy's bringing the van around to the front. Let's not keep him waiting!"

During the ride to the Rancho, which was about forty miles outside of Phoenix, Jan was entranced with the countryside. She remembered the beauty of the desert from her last visit to Arizona, but it hadn't seemed so majestic through the eyes of a little girl. Now she could view the shifting sands and the arrow-straight road with amazement that so close to a burgeoning city there could be such wilderness. Low mountain ranges lifted the horizon, and in the late afternoon the sun painted myriad color schemes from dull reds to vibrant purples with each scheme punctuated by black shadows and low-growing scrub. There was peace here—Jan could feel it—and she knew it was a sight she could enjoy for the rest of her life. Instead of becoming tired, her eyes picked up every nuance of color and symmetry. Gus, too, seemed intent on the scenery. Since climbing into the van beside Andy, his gaze never strayed from the window except to glance at Benjie to see how he was faring during the ride.

From the interstate highway Andy pulled onto a secondary road following a beaten signpost that pointed the way to Rancho Arroyo. "It's about four miles after turning off the interstate. That's where your property begins. From there, on our own road, which we maintain, it's another two miles. Think it's too far from civilization for you, Jan?"

"There were some days in the big city, Andy, that I thought the moon wasn't far enough away. Where's the Golden Lasso from here?"

"Well, you follow this secondary road for about eight or nine miles, and you can't miss it. It's only about two and a half miles as the crow flies, though. The roads are indirect to say the least."

Jan watched through the windshield and gained her bearings. They had headed west out of Phoenix and now were heading north. As Andy turned into the private road leading to the ranch, Jan's heart pounded with excitement. And when they at last pulled through the split-rail fence and she saw the low, flat buildings of her new home, she nearly shouted with joy. It hadn't changed. It was still the same. And she loved it.

"This is really beautiful." Jan drew in her breath. "I had remembered it being this way, but I was afraid to see that perhaps it had become run down with use and age. You see," she offered Andy by way of explanation, "it's been a long time since I was here. Not since I was a child not much older than my brother. It's just perfect." She eyed the colorful window boxes. "I know we're going to be happy here, don't you, Benjie?" But Benjie was off, his chair skimming over the smooth flagstone patio, Gus close behind.

"Don't worry about the boy—he's found himself a guardian. Gus loves kids, although you'd never think if from his rough exterior. Come on inside and meet your staff." Andy held the screen door open.

The dimness inside startled Jan for a moment after the bright light of day. But she recovered quickly and took in everything around her. The heavy pine tables were polished to a high gleam and the long, low leather sofas and armchairs looked inviting. The plank wood floor was buffed to a patina and Indian print scatter rugs seemed to follow the traffic flow and make intimate little conversation areas, almost like rooms within the room. The ceiling was rough adobe sectioned off by rough-hewn beams, and the far walls of the lobby were covered with used brick on which were hung gleaming brass plaques that offset the huge round wagon wheel chandelier with its brass lanterns. And everything sparkled—not a hint of dust anywhere, not even on the various plants and ferns showcased against the walls and positioned around the vast room. Off to one side of the door was the desk, and behind it the numerous nooks and crannies for mail and keys. Behind the desk was a door, and through it she could see a small, cozy office with one window that looked out on the corral. Her office, Jan told herself—her very own office.

She didn't hear the woman until she was standing beside her; she was wearing leather moccasins. Jan was looking down at the oval braided rug and knew it was handmade.

"You like." It was a statement, not a question. "I make it many years ago for your Uncle Jake."

"This is Delilah, Gus's wife. Don't ask me where she got the name." Andy grinned.

"Hello, Delilah." Jan smiled. "I understand you're our chef."

"I cook, I clean, and I do everything. You like my name, Delilah? I pick myself. Gus no Sampson, but I am Delilah," the woman chortled.

Jan liked her immediately. She was small and round as a ball with shiny black eyes and a wealth of braids arranged on her head in a coronet. Deep laugh lines etched Delilah's face, and Jan thought her one of the most beautiful women she had ever seen. "I like your name very much. It shows you have character," she told Delilah seriously.

"You see," Delilah said, poking Andy in the ribs. "One smart lady, Jake's niece. But you skinny like stick," she turned back to Jan. "One week, two, and I make you like Delilah." Jan pretended mock horror as Andy swooped her out of the lobby.

"Bannon offered Delilah a fantastic sum to come and work for him," Andy said sourly.

"But you said Gus turned him down. Surely Delilah wouldn't go without her husband."

"I hate to be the one to tell you this, but we only have Delilah's

word that she's married to Gus. Gus doesn't commit himself one
way or the other. Every now and then Delilah gets it into her head
to try to make Gus jealous. He yanks her hair and gets her back in
line until the next time. But she loves bangles and beads, so keep
it in mind. You can buy a lot of doodads with the kind of money
Bannon is tossing around."

"I'll keep it in mind. Let's do the tour so I can go into the office
and get familiar with the way things have been done around here."

"If those books are anything like the way your Uncle Jake did
everything else, you'll find them in top order. I thought maybe
you'd wait until that lawyer from Phoenix came down to give you
a hand with them."

"Don't worry about me, Andy. I've been a bookkeeper since I
graduated from business college. I think I can handle them. Then
you do know where they're kept?"

"Sure, everybody knows. There's a safe behind the desk and the
combination is the numerical value of the word *Jake* in the alphabet.
You know, A is the number one and so on. So working left, right,
left, it's 10-1-11-5."

Jan smiled up at Andy. "Is there anything you don't know about
the Rancho Arroyo?" She laughed.

"Oh, I suppose there's a few things." He seemed embarrassed
and pulled the brim of his Stetson low over his eyes.

"Seems like my Uncle Jake trusted you, Andy Stone. And I'm
giving you fair warning—I'm going to trust you too." Seeing a
flush of color creep up from his shirt collar, Jan changed the subject.
"Are you sure Benjie is okay?"

"He's fine. By now he probably has every ranch hand on the
place eating right out of his hand. Little kids are kind of hard to
resist around here, and he's automatically special if Gus adopted
him."

They followed the main path down to the first trail leading to the
cabins, where she followed Andy across the planked verandas and
stepped inside. Every modern convenience had been installed in the
cabins: air-conditioning, tiled baths—even a little efficiency kitchen.
Some of the cabins were one-bedroom, but most were two-bedroom
affairs, capable of housing a family with children. And each was
furnished in Western flavor with heavy oak pieces and bric-a-brac
and were kept in A-1 condition.

"There's a lot of work that goes into housekeeping around here.
Who does it all?" she inquired.

"There's four women who come in on call when they're
needed," Andy explained. "They live on the outskirts of Phoenix

and make the drive in every morning. As for repairing fences and the like—you know, roof repair and painting and taking care of the stables and horses—that's what the ranch hands do to keep themselves busy. They're a good bunch of guys, Jan, and I know you'll like them. Between myself and Gus, we handle things during the offseason. Right now, you've got a full crew working for you. Delilah has two girls to help her in the kitchen and she rides herd on them. Come one, I'll take you down to the corral where you can meet the hands. On the way we can stop at the swimming pool.''

By sundown Jan had taken her tour and had a bath and a cup of coffee. She pored over the account books until her eyes ached. Everything was right side up. Now all she had to do was keep it that way. A small cash flow, an emergency fund, a filled reservation list, and a storeroom full of every supply known to man—she couldn't ask for more.

At first she had been surprised and then relieved to discover that liquor was not served on the ranch. Applejack and a liberal dose of that potent liquor called white lightning was kept in the locked storeroom, and each had a label that stated it was the property of Gus: "Keep Hands Off.''

After dinner she took Benjie and settled him down in bed after his long, exciting day. With guests arriving in the morning, she wanted to be fresh and clear-headed when she handed over the first key to her first guest. She couldn't wait and she knew she would have trouble dropping off to sleep. She only hoped that thoughts of Derek Bannon and his faithless fiancée didn't keep popping into her head the way they had all during the day.

Chapter Three

Jan watched the sun come up from her room in the lodge. The sight was breathtaking. Only once before had she seen anything its equal and that had been a sunrise in Key West, Florida. She toyed briefly with the idea of waking Benjie and quickly negated the thought. There would be other days, other sunrises, for the little boy to see.

Benjie occupied the room adjoining hers on the second floor of the lodge. He had been as thrilled with his room as Jan had been with hers. She loved the dark mahogany furniture and the tall, heavy-paneled chifforobe that stood sentry just outside her private bath. Even here there was a flavor of days gone by. The floor was covered with an Indian patterned rug, and the walls were covered with a small-scale print of cranberry on federal blue paper. The bedstead was huge, and she had found the night before that she had had to literally climb into it. But the mattress was firm and the sheets smelled sweet, and she had almost immediately dropped off to sleep.

As Jan made up the bed and smoothed the dull cranberry comforter, which doubled as a spread, she wondered how she could feel so comfortable in a room completely devoid of the frills and ruffles she had had back home in New York. This room was handsome, almost masculine, the only feminine items being the Victorian globe lamps on her night tables. But comfortable it was, and it seemed to fit her new way of life. There was an austerity about it that seemed to compliment her new position of authority.

Jan washed and dressed herself in a comfortable pair of jeans and a long-sleeved blouse. As she stepped into a pair of wedge-soled clogs, she vowed to buy herself a pair of Western boots, and almost giggled at the thought. She didn't want to seem like a week-end cowboy, but she knew that the boots would do double duty against the hard-packed roads and trails leading to the various cab-ins. She would be covering a lot of territory on foot each day and she needed serviceable shoes.

She raked a brush through her chestnut curls and blessed the fact that her hair was naturally curly and, worn short, didn't require much attention. She'd be too busy from now on to fuss with elabo-rate hairdos. A last look in the pier glass, and Jan appreciated the fact that her jeans were well worn and didn't look new, as though she were contriving to look the part of a ranchowner. She liked the way they felt against her skin and admired the way they fit. They had been worth every saved penny she had paid for them.

A glance at her watch and she sighed. She would have to awaken Benjie and get him ready to come downstairs. It seemed a shame to wake him from his sound sleep, but there was no help for it. Benjie required a considerable amount of diligence to get him out of bed, washed, dressed, and into the wheelchair. After she had him ready, Gus would come up and carry him down the stairs to his chair. It hadn't been so long ago since Benjie hadn't been able to do anything for himself, but since he had gained the strength to maneuver on crutches, things had improved. But he still needed help in pulling up his trousers and tucking in his shirt. Jan smiled. Soon, with heaven's help and a lot of work, Benjie would be totally self-sufficient; but, she reminded herself, he would probably still need help to get him to wash behind his ears.

Breakfast was a perfunctory affair, with Jan being too nervous to eat more than a few bites of toast and drink several scalding sips of the best coffee she had ever tasted. She itched to get behind the desk in the lobby and wait for the Marshall family, which was to arrive at 10:00 A.M. She had it all planned. First she would greet them and register them in the large book on the desk. Then she would personally escort them to Cabin Six on Wayward Trail. She hoped they would like the seclusion and the scent of scrub pines that surrounded the three-room cabin. And after that she would drive into the Phoenix Medical Center with Benjie for his first treat-ment. She knew that was going to work out right also. It had to—it just had to!

Before leaving New York and on the advice of Benjie's physi-cians, she had phoned the Phoenix Medical Center and spoken to Dr. Rossi, who would take over Benjie's case. In her suitcase up in her room was Benjie's medical file, which she would give to Dr.

Rossi. There had been a lot of preparation involved in having her
brother continue therapy in Phoenix, and it was important that he
not miss his first appointment.

A cup of lukewarm coffee at her elbow, Jan waited at the desk,
her patience barely under control. It was now after eleven and Andy
still hadn't returned with the Marshalls from the airport. She looked
around the inviting lobby and was suddenly apprehensive. Surely
nothing was wrong, but if the Marshalls didn't arrive soon, she was
going to have to leave with Benjie for Phoenix.

She saw the dust and then heard the van. Even to her inexperienced ears, it sounded as though something was wrong. It hadn't
coughed and spit like that yesterday when Andy and Gus picked
them up at the airport in the minibus they used to transport guests
to and from the city.

Andy looked disgusted when he ushered the Marshalls into the
lobby with their luggage in tow. While Mr. Marshall filled out the
registration card, Mrs. Marshall oohed and aahed over the plants
and copper and brass and kept rein on her two precocious little
daughters. Andy took Jan aside and whispered. ''There's something
wrong with the van. I'm going to have to call a mechanic out from
town to take a look. Usually Gus tinkers with the wheels, but this
is something with the transmission. We might have to tow it into
the garage. We can use the pickup truck around the ranch so we
aren't entirely without transportation. Hopefully, the mechanic can
repair the van before tomorrow, when the other guests arrive. If not,
we'll have to hire a limousine. Sorry.''

''But, Andy, I have to take Benjie into Phoenix for his first therapy session this afternoon. Can I use the pickup? What about a
taxi?''

''I don't recommend the pickup. It's old and it's been patched
up so often with spit and prayers, it's apt to conk out on you two
miles down the road. A taxi is out unless there's a fare coming in
from the city. I guess you're going to have to cancel the appointment. I'm sorry, Jan. Where do you want me to take the Marshalls?''

''Cabin Six on Wayward Trail. There must be something I can
do,'' Jan almost wailed. She had forgotten that she wanted so desperately to take the first guests to their cabin but it was too late.
Now all she wanted was to get Benjie into Phoenix.

''Perhaps I can be of some help. I couldn't help overhearing. I'm
going into Phoenix and would be more than happy to take Ben with
me,'' Derek Bannon said quietly.

Jan was stunned by his sudden appearance. Where had he come

from and what did he want? He looked so physically fit, Jan felt weak and ineffectual beside him. His tan was just the right blend of bronze and gold, making his blue eyes brighter by contrast. Again, she was uncomfortable with his nearness. Should she accept his offer to take Benjie into Phoenix. Would he feel imposed upon? Would it make her indebted to him? Especially when he discovered that Benjie's therapy sessions took over an hour and he would be obliged to wait. She decided she would hold her answer until she discovered what he really wanted. "Is there something I can do for you, Mr. Bannon? I know you didn't come here just to offer us a ride into Phoenix."

Derek Bannon's blue-eyed gaze was openly amused and faintly mocking. "As a matter of fact, I did come here on business. I never beat around the bush. I want to buy Rancho Arroyo from you."

"I never beat around the bush either, Mr. Bannon. Rancho Arroyo is not for sale. Today, tomorrow, or any other day."

"Name your price, Miss Warren, and I'll have a check drawn within the hour," Derek Bannon said arrogantly, ignoring her reply.

Anger shot through Jan. "From reports I hear about your establishment I know that Rancho Arroyo couldn't compare to that glittering palace, and why you would make an offer for this ranch is beyond me. I plan to run this ranch and make a go of it. It's my and Benjie's home now, and one doesn't sell one's home on a whim. It's not for sale, Mr. Bannon," Jan said coldly.

"Everything is for sale if the price is right," Derek answered without emotion. "It might interest you to know that I was negotiating with your uncle, and we had about come to terms before he passed away. As I understand it, he died within minutes of suffering the heart attack. It was his intention to turn the ranch over to me."

"That's not the way I heard it. My people tell me my uncle rejected all three of your offers, and this makes your fourth rejection. Rancho Arroyo is not for sale, and, contrary to your opinion, everything and everyone does not have a price. Including me."

Derek Bannon leaned over the desk, the masculine scent of his after-shave making Jan's senses reel. He was so close Jan could have counted his eyelashes. Gently, he cupped her face in his hand and drew her closer to him. She knew his lips were going to touch hers, and she made no move to withdraw. Instead, she stared deeply into his eyes, aware of the intensity she saw there. It was a light kiss, feathery and fragrant, and left her feeling awkward and wanting more. This time she did withdraw. "Kissing me, Mr. Bannon, is not going to get me to sell you this ranch. At the risk of repeating myself, I can't be bought." To her own dismay, her voice sounded breathless and husky, betraying the fact that she was more affected by his kiss than she cared to admit.

Derek Bannon's eyebrows lifted and a wry smile touched the corners of his mouth. "Everyone and everything has a price. One just has to find it. Now, do you want me to take your brother to Phoenix or not? I'm leaving almost immediately."

"I can't be ready that soon," Jan said curtly. "I'll have to find another way to get into the city."

"You didn't understand me. I didn't ask you to go. I offered to take your brother. Dusty Baker, the running back on the Bison football team, has to have hydrotherapy on his knee. I thought your brother would enjoy riding along and meeting Dusty. I'll wait for him while he has his treatment and bring him home safe and sound."

Tears burned Jan's eyes, turning them into glittering shards of green glass. "Benjie isn't for sale either, and I think it's rotten of you to try and get to me through a little boy."

"It doesn't matter to me what you think, Miss Warren. I offered to do you a favor. Take it or leave it," Derek Bannon said coolly, his eyes shooting white sparks of anger.

Jan knew she had no other choice. Benjie's appointment was important and she couldn't just cancel it because everything hadn't gone according to plan. Benjie propelled his chair through the lobby, and she watched as his eyes lit up at the sight of Derek Bannon. "Benjie, Mr. Bannon has offered to take you to the medical center along with one of the football players. Do you think you can handle it?"

"Wow! Sure, Jan. Really, Mr. Bannon, just you and me and one of the Bisons?"

"Dusty Baker," Derek replied, watching Jan's face.

"Dusty Baker! Jan, did you hear that? Gosh, he's my favorite player! Is it all right, Jan? Huh?" Benjie literally glowed with excitement.

Jan couldn't find her voice, but she nodded her agreement. "Just remember, Mr. Bannon," she finally managed through clenched teeth, "Benjie is a little boy who has gone through traumas even an adult couldn't handle. You hurt him in any way and you'll answer to me."

"That sounds like a threat and unworthy of such a pretty lady." Derek smiled.

"That's not a threat, Mr. Bannon, that's a promise."

Derek laughed, a rich, booming sound that seemed to fill the room and bounce off the walls. "I make it a practice never to offer advice, but I'm going to make an exception this time. Don't ever threaten me, or you might get more than you bargained for. And stop smothering the boy with your frustrated maternal instincts. He's going to have to make the best of whatever life has in store for him. Find yourself a cat and take your frustrations out on it.''

"You...you arrogant, insufferable..."

"You ready, Ben? My car is out front. I'll meet you there," Derek said, striding through the open doors.

Benjie sensed Jan's intention of helping him. "I can do it, Jan. If Mr. Bannon thought I needed help, he would have offered. I can do it," Benjie insisted manfully as he turned the chair and expertly propelled it through the doorway without touching the wooden frame. "What did I tell you?" he called over his shoulder.

"Yes, I see," Jan said weakly. "I'll be right down with your medical file. Don't leave without it." Quickly, before she could change her mind, Jan ran up the stairs and dug into her suitcase for his records, then raced down the stairs.

Outside, Benjie was already situated in the car, his wheelchair folded in the back seat. She handed Benjie the manila envelope and turned to Derek Bannon. "You don't know the name of Benjie's doctor or where he's supposed to go."

Walking toward her, he grasped her arm and almost dragged her back into the lobby. He stood facing her, hands on hips, a look of disgust on his face. His voice was laced with sarcasm when he spoke. "Miss Warren, don't ever take me for an idiot. There's only one doctor at the center who can give the therapy your brother needs. And he's the same doctor Dusty Baker must see. I happen to know Dr. Rossi personally, and he mentioned to me that your brother was coming in for treatments. He felt it would be convenient for him if Dusty came in at the same time."

Again the words stuck in Jan's throat. He was insufferable. It had been natural for her to offer instructions as to where and whom Benjie was to see. After all, Derek had just popped in out of nowhere and had taken matters into his own hands. He certainly seemed like a man who had all the answers—and then some.

It took Jan the better part of an hour to get her emotions under control. There was no point in denying that Derek Bannon had an effect on her. He made her aware of the fact that she was a woman, a woman with feelings that had been submerged too long and were now creeping to the surface. She felt suddenly alive and vibrant. She liked the feelings and wondered what it would be like to be held in his strong arms and to feel his heart beating against hers and to know a deeper kiss than the feathery touch he had pressed upon her.

Jan felt herself blush. What was wrong with her? Derek Bannon was engaged to be married to that beautiful woman she saw on the plane. And what kind of person was he to kiss her and stir these emotions in her when he had promised himself to another woman?

And what kind of woman was Derek's fiancée to have someone like Derek Bannon dancing on a string while she amused herself with other men? A fool, that's what she is, Jan thought hotly. Derek Bannon was the kind of man to answer most girls' prayers, and there was his fiancée playing him for the fool. Or was that the normal way of doing things in that kind of glittering, glamorous society that the Golden Lasso suggested? Was that the kind of morals those rich and beautiful people had? Well, it wasn't *her* way— not in the least. If she ever pledged herself to someone, she'd never amuse herself with flirting with other men. And she'd never, never be attracted to a man like Derek Bannon, who probably collected women the way other men collected stamps.

Why did some men think they were so clever? Didn't Derek realize she saw through his little plan? He would try to make her brother his ally, his friend, and he would state his demands again, once he had the boy wrapped around his little finger. Well, he wasn't going to get away with it. This was one of Benjie's relationships that she was going to nip in the bud.

The remainder of the afternoon was spent in meeting the house-maids and inspecting the linens and supplies. When she visited the stables, she developed a particular affection for a mare named Soo-chie. She promised herself she would brush up on her riding techniques and take the gleaming palomino out for a canter at the first possible opportunity.

From time to time Jan heard the Marshall children squeal in delight over their father's antics in the swimming pool. When she glanced at her watch again, she was appalled to see that it was after four o'clock. Benjie should have been home by now. Each session was only an hour. A smidgeon of worry shot through Jan. What if Derek Bannon had forgotten the little boy and left him there at the medical center? What if they had had an accident? What if...what if...scurried through her brain until she gained control of herself. Her face flushed a brilliant scarlet. Derek Bannon was a responsible man, and he truly liked her brother. Whatever else he may be, he was reliable, and she knew she could trust him with Benjie's care and safety.

Jan was busily working her way down to her third fingernail

when she heard the high-pitched whine of Derek Bannon's sports car. She waited a second and then walked out onto the front veranda. The sight of Benjie's weary face went straight to her heart. Poor little guy, he looked so beat, and she hadn't been with him to help, if not with physical support, at least to cheer him on. Quickly, she opened the car door, intending to scoop Benjie into her arms and croon over him as their mother would have done.

"Don't! Ben can manage." It was an iron command, an order not to interfere. Jan stepped back in alarm, fearful that something was wrong with Benjie. Her eyes pleaded and implored the man in front of her to say something to reassure her. He said nothing, did nothing. Instead, he waited for Benjie to look up.

"What do you say, Ben? We can do it two ways. I can help you or you can help yourself," Derek said quietly, but encouragingly.

Benjie grinned. "If you push the chair closer, I think I can handle it, Derek."

Bannon gave the chair a little nudge with his foot and waited. The little boy slowly maneuvered himself to the edge of the car seat, his lower lip caught between his teeth. He slipped and Jan made a move to reach out a supporting hand. Derek Bannon caught her arm in a viselike grip and held firm. Benjie righted himself and slipped into the chair. "I did it!" he cried jubilantly.

Jan was suddenly aware that the man hadn't released his hold on her arm, although his grip had loosened. She liked that touch and hated the man. He was sadistic. "That was a brutal thing you just did," she hissed. "He's such a little boy, and he's absolutely exhausted. Why couldn't you help him or, at the very least, let me help him?"

"He didn't need any help. Leave him alone before you destroy him." Without another word, Derek slid behind the wheel of his car. His powerful hand moved effortlessly over the gear shift as he expertly reversed the sports car. "By the way, Dr. Rossi suggests you give him a call the first of next week. Benjie has a pamphlet describing the exercises he's to work on before his next visit to the center. And I suggest you get him out into that swimming pool. It's the best thing for him."

Benjie called, "Thanks, Derek. Thanks for taking me to the hospital."

Derek Bannon waved without turning around to acknowledge the boy's goodbye. He was insufferable!

"I'll bet you're starved. How about a snack like we used to have at home. Tea, cheese, and crackers?"

"I'm not hungry. Derek and Dusty took me for tacos and I had two with a malted. Isn't he great, Jan? And Dusty Baker is a super guy—just the way he looks on television. He didn't talk to me like I was a little kid. We talked about plays and signals and he said I knew a lot about football. Derek is going to take me to the field behind the Golden Lasso to watch the Bisons work out tomorrow. He said you could come along if you wanted. I told him you hated football and wouldn't want to come. You don't, do you?'' he asked anxiously.

Jan felt deflated, and defeated by Derek Bannon. And yet Benjie, who was usually so reserved with strangers, liked him. Maybe she was missing something.

"Look what Derek gave me," Benjie said pridefully, rummaging in his jeans pocket. "Four tickets to the Bisons salute dinner. I'm not sure what a salute dinner is, but Derek said I should get you to bring me. Can we go, Jan? Huh?''

Jan inspected the white cards with the gold engraving. "Benjie, these tickets cost one hundred dollars each! I can't afford to buy them.''

"They're free, Jan. Dusty gave me two and Derek gave me two. The other two are for Andy and Gus.''

"We'll see," Jan said, not wanting to make a decision at the moment.

But Benjie was not to be put off. "Don't, Jan. Just say yes or no. I don't like it when you tell me maybe," he said quietly.

"My 'maybes' never bothered you before," she answered tartly, knowing who she had to thank for Benjie's sudden independent behavior. "I want to remind you that you're only nine years old, and I'm the one who is taking care of you. It has to be my way, not Derek Bannon's way. Do you understand?''

"I understand, all right. I understand that you don't like Derek. Well, that's okay, too, because I heard him say he didn't like you. He told Dusty Baker you were on the verge of being a frustrated old maid," Benjie said with all the force he could muster. Mouth pressed into a grim line, he turned the chair and headed down the driveway.

Tears trickled down Jan's cheeks as she watched Benjie's slow progress in search of Gus. Things were falling apart, and they had only been on the ranch for twenty-four hours. What had she done to deserve those biting comments from Benjie? All she wanted was to love him and see that he was well again. Hadn't she given up two years of her life for him since he had been injured? And Derek Bannon swoops into their lives and it's all for nothing. Now I'm not good enough for Benjie. Whatever I can do, Derek Bannon can do it better. "In a pig's eye!" Jan snarled as she stamped her foot on the blacktop. "No way, Mr. Bannon!"

Still smarting from Benjie's comment on being an old maid, Jan made her way to the tiny mailroom and began to sort through the mail. She was just on the verge of taking it back to her office when Delilah intercepted her. The little Indian woman was carrying a large wicker basket. "This come for you on a special truck. Man wait for money. Says is five dollars and two cents."

"Are you sure it's for me? I didn't order anything. What is it?" Jan asked as she dug into petty cash for the money to give Delilah.

"How should I know? You open, we both see." Delilah waited patiently. "Will you open before I pay man or after I pay man?"

"I'll wait for you to pay him," Jan muttered. "I have no idea what it could be. I'm certain I didn't order anything."

It was Delilah who finally opened the wicker basket lid. She cocked her head to one side and peered into the basket, her shoe button eyes merry and full of mischief. "This funny present. I think you get stung. Is not worth five dollars and two cents. Must be tax, too?" she said authoritatively.

Swallowing hard, Jan moved nearer the basket and looked inside. A cat! Of all the unmitigated gall! Arrogant, know-it-all playboy! And she had paid money for it! He was cheap in the bargain!

Delilah's eyes widened. "You want cat? We have many for free in barn. You think maybe this is special cat?" she asked inquisitively.

"Nope. This is your run-of-the-mill, everyday alley cat, and from the looks of things she's about to bestow a blessing on us. Here, Delilah, you can have it," Jan offered generously.

"You pay, you stuck with present. Even for free, I don't want it. Maybe in New York you pay for cat. Here is free. You make little mistake but all right. Next time you look inside before you pay," Delilah indulged.

"There isn't going to be a next time. I should take this cat to the Golden Lasso and demand that...that..."

"He good-looking man, no? He make me itch all over." Delilah giggled as she waddled from the room. In spite of herself, Jan laughed. She would send Derek a thank you card that would set his teeth on edge. Better yet, she would send him the whole kit and kaboodle after the litter arrived.

Before getting into bed that night, Jan penned off a letter to Neil telling him all about Rancho Arroyo. She carefully omitted the fact that the minibus was out of order and that she had had a confrontation with the owner of the Golden Lasso, who was a stiff competitor for business. She did describe the landscape and the wonderful condition of the lodge and the cabins and the beautiful Arizona sunshine. Silently, Jan crossed her fingers and hoped that the trouble with the minibus and the disarming situation with Derek Bannon weren't an omen of things to come.

Hastily, before she was tempted to confide in Neil, she licked the envelope and pressed it shut.

Chapter Four

Jan saddled Soochie and rode out past the ranch into the wild terrain. Paying careful attention to the direction she was taking, she watched for the blazed trail and fence posts that would lead her around the entire circumference of Rancho Arroyo.

It was a beautiful day and promised to be hot, with the sun scorching down on the parched land. Yet there was beauty to be found here, so different from the verdant appeal of the Catskill Mountains with which she was so familiar. Here the eye could stretch, following the low, uninterrupted land right out to the horizon, where, in the distance, purple mountains stood sentinel and lifted the eye to the vibrantly blue sky. It was still early—hours before the heat of the day—and Soochie seemed grateful for her escape from the corral.

Relaxing in the saddle and instinctively trusting Soochie's temperament, Jan gave the palomino free rein. There was time to enjoy her new home now that everything seemed to be running smoothly—on the surface at least.

Andy had taken the guests on a ride into the desert and wouldn't return until well after sunset. A campfire and a sing-along was planned for them before their return to the ranch. She made a mental note to be on hand for the nine o'clock pool party, complete with Delilah's scrumptious buffet goodies.

However, Jan was aware of vague undercurrents that had recently reared their ugly heads. A mantle of worry settled over her slim shoulders as she dismounted and tied Soochie's bridle to scrub pine. She sat down on the hard-packed earth and munched on the cheese and crackers she had thought to bring along. Andy's grim words that the van could not be repaired without a major overhaul on the transmission had been the last thing she wanted to hear. But when the mechanic discovered a cracked engine block, the world seemed to come to an end. The ranch would have to buy a new minibus. Momentarily, she had panicked. To pay cash or take it on time payments was a difficult decision. She had finally opted for cash because the dealer was offering her a sizable discount if she took it that way. Her small cash reserve was now seriously depleted. And if Andy was right about the air-conditioning unit in the lodge going on the fritz, she was going to have another gigantic bill facing her very soon. She couldn't very well expect her guests to eat in a hot, stuffy dining room and her guests wouldn't expect it either.

Jan leaned back against an outcropping of rocks, her hands trembling. Was it the bills or was it the fact that two of the ranch's prospective guests had changed their minds about staying at the Rancho Arroyo once they saw the glittering Golden Lasso? There had also been three future reservations for large families that were also canceled. At the moment they weren't in any serious difficulty and could weather the storm, but if there were any further cancellations, the ranch could bury itself in the red side of the ledgers. A devastating thought, especially since Benjie would soon be ready for his third treatment.

And to make matters worse, while the guests professed to adore Delilah's cooking, Jan had noticed that most of them preferred dressing up and going to the Golden Lasso for dinner and entertainment, leaving their children behind for her and her staff to tend to. There wasn't a thing she could do about it. And all the food that Delilah prepared was wasted because there was no one to eat it. Jan groaned and her stomach churned at the thought of the colossal waste of food every day. From the looks of things, there wasn't going to be any profits for a long time to come.

And then there was Derek Bannon. Each time she saw him she felt more drawn to him and more confused than ever. Clucking mother hen indeed, she sniffed. A lot he knew and what business was it of his anyway? He'd just better not think he was going to make any decisions where Benjie was concerned. She was his own sister and she knew best.

Tears of self-pity burned her eyes and she brushed them away with the back of her hand the way Benjie did. It seemed she was doing an awful lot of crying lately. Maybe I am a frustrated old maid, she thought sadly. A man kisses me and I go all to pieces. As if that kiss meant anything to me. I've got other things to think about. Like earning a living for myself and Benjie. There's no time to become attracted to anyone—especially not a man like Derek Bannon.

Jan was about to gather up the crumpled cheese and cracker wrappers when she noticed her feet were in shadow. She had been so involved in her thoughts she hadn't heard him approach.

"Littering, Miss Warren? And trespassing," Derek Bannon said mockingly.

Jan was acutely aware of her position: sprawled on the ground, her legs wrapped in faded jeans and tucked beneath her like a yogi. She felt the trail of scarlet begin in her neck and work its way up to her cheeks. Her hateful freckles must be lighting up like neon lights, she thought inanely. She should say something—anything—to wipe that know-it-all smile off his face, but the words stuck in her throat. Scrambling to her feet and belatedly remembering the papers in question, she bent over like a child who had been severely reprimanded and stuffed the cellophane into the pocket of her jeans. She was humiliated and embarrassed and knew Derek was reveling in it. She hadn't seen the girl astride the cinnamon-colored horse waiting behind the scrub. Jan's eyes widened. It was the girl from the plane—Derek's fiancée.

The girl sat upon her horse looking like a model with her precision-cut clothes molding her slim body. She sat comfortably in the saddle as though she were born to it, and the soft, white Stetson was worn on the back of her head with just the right amount of ebony hair showing in front.

Jan had envied the girl on the plane, had been shocked to learn in the airport, that she was Derek's fiancée, and now she knew she could hate her—especially when she called to Derek in a low and husky voice.

"Andrea, I'd like you to meet our new neighbor. Miss Jan Warren," he said coolly, "who owns the Rancho Arroyo. This is Andrea, my..."

Before Derek could complete the introduction, the girl's eyes widened. "Really! So you're Jake Warren's niece. And is Ben your son?"

Jan stared first at Andrea and then at Derek. "Yes," she answered airily. "I really am. And as for Benjie, I'm more what some people would call his clucking mother hen," Jan snapped as she slid her foot into the stirrup.

At first Jan thought she had imagined it, but Derek was grinning at her. "Touché," he said softly.

"I'm sorry if I trespassed and I did clean up my litter, so I presume I'm free to leave.'' It was plain to see Derek was enjoying her discomfort.

"Don't move, either of you," he said suddenly in a strangely hoarse whisper.

Jan looked in the direction of Derek's gaze and then she saw it at the same time Andrea's horse bolted and raced off. A coiled rattler had crept out from beneath the rocks. She gulped and tried to swallow as she watched Derek rein in her horse and lead it carefully away.

"Aren't you going to kill it?'' she asked hesitantly, fighting back her own urge to bolt and run.

"You may have noticed, I don't make it a practice to carry my six-shooter,'' he answered sarcastically. "Besides, the Western rattler is an endangered species, and for the most part they're more frightened of us than we are of them.''

A shudder ran through Jan. "I'm afraid of snakes and bugs,'' she babbled. "Thank you. Andrea—is she all right?''

"Andrea was born to the saddle. By now she's back at the Golden Lasso with a Bloody Mary in her hand. Here, let me help you—you look a little shaky.''

"I'm all right,'' she snapped as she threw her leg over the saddle horn to slide to the ground. If there was one thing she didn't need at the moment, it was Derek Bannon's help, for that would require that he touch her, and then she would fall into his arms, weeping with fright.

She fixed a deliberate haughty expression on her face and slid from the saddle. Soochie sensed the change of weight upon her back and daintily backed up, throwing Jan off balance. Derek reached out his long arms and drew her against him.

Suddenly, she felt safe, protected, and it was with great difficulty that she forced herself to pull away from his grasp. She couldn't allow this arrogant man to see what he did to her.

"Your palomino is still a little skittish; give her a few minutes before you try to ride her,'' Derek said softly as he lowered his gaze to meet hers.

His blue eyes, shaded by the brim of his Stetson, had a hypnotic effect on Jan. It seemed, when she looked up at him, that all she could see was the blue sky framing his powerful shoulders and his face. Soochie was forgotten and the world seemed to tilt, and, like a moth to flame, she was drawn into his arms. For a long moment he looked down into her upturned face, and Jan was tingling with expectancy. His hand cupped her face, his long fingers coming to rest on her neck beneath her ear. Finally, at last, and with determination, he brought his face closer, touching his lips to hers. With an urgency that left her breathless, his arms closed around her, holding her against his lean, hard strength, and his mouth becoming more demanding, crushing hers, insistently summoning a response.

Derek Bannon filled her world. The sheer strength of the man, the wide width of his shoulders, the flaming touch of his mouth on hers became her existence. There was no world, no anything, beyond the reach of his arms and the touch of his lips. He was gentle, he was insistent, he was demanding, he was tender.

A rush of emotions pummeled her senses and the earth seemed to move beneath her feet. Jan clung to him, lifting her face to his, answering his demands, filling her own. He brushed the hat from her head, and his hands were in her hair as his mouth sought hers.

Jan felt her sensibilities leave her, and in their place, from somewhere deep within, came an answering response. As though of their own volition, her arms sought the rippling muscles of his back, the narrowness of his waist. Her thighs pressed against his, feeling their strength through the fabric of her jeans. He was no longer kissing her, and she was aware that his breath came in sharp rasps that matched her own. A deep sound of pleasure escaped him as he began to trail his lips along her neck and then down to the cleft between her breasts. Jan clung to him, welcoming him, pressing herself closer.

Derek Bannon smiled down at her. "Tell me you didn't like that."

Jan bristled, and with a huge effort she managed to regain control of herself. "Oh, I liked it, all right," she managed to say tremulously, "but you kiss like you do everything else—to perfection. The next time—if there is a next time—try putting some emotion into it. We clucking mother hens not only want, we demand, warmth and feeling. And, Mr. Bannon, I'm still not for sale and neither is my ranch."

Derek's face was set into grim, hostile lines. "Perhaps there's something lacking in you, Miss Warren. I've kissed many women, and you're the first who has complained."

"I'll just bet you have—kissed lots of women, that is," she snapped, thinking of Andrea. "And that makes you one up on me because I haven't kissed many men. But I do know what I like and what I don't like. Perhaps the reason no one has ever complained is because they're like you. Peripheral, without depth, no emotions. In short, Mr. Bannon, I find you sadly lacking."

Quickly, she mounted Soochie and dug her heels into the ani-

mal's flanks, riding off and leaving a stunned and angry man looking after her.

Soochie seemed to be aware of the emotions that embroiled her
young rider. Jan's trembling hands couldn't control the reins, making the palomino skittish and unruly. How in the world had she
managed to let him kiss her? And where in the world had she
mustered up the nerve to say the things she had said? The full
weight of the situation descended on her, seeming to block out the
sun and chill the air. Liar. Jan Warren is a liar, a small voice hissed.
You loved it, you loved every minute of it and you know it. Liar.
Liar! You just didn't want him to know that he shook the earth
beneath your feet.

Jan's backbone stiffened and she railed against the small voice.
"He deserved it!" she shouted to the sky. "He's going to marry
Andrea, and he thought he could play his games with me! He deserved it!" Still, on the long ride home Jan couldn't seem to erase
the memory of his lips on hers or the way his hands touched her
hair. And the soft sound of pleasure that came from him when his
mouth found the soft flesh between her breast came back to her.

At Rancho Arroyo Jan was greeted with a broken air-conditioning
unit and a mean, angry Gus, who was stomping around the lobby
as though he wanted to kill. Benjie was watching the man with
wide eyes, uncertain if he should maneuver his chair out of Gus's
way or not.

"What's wrong? Will someone tell me what's happened? If
whatever it is is going to cost me money, please, tell me gently.
Where's Delilah?"

"That's what the problem is," Benjie whispered. "She quit and
went to work for Derek at the Golden Lasso. She just left a little
while ago. You should have asked her to stay," the little boy accused the tall Indian.

Gus continued his parade around the lobby, stopping once to light
a foul-smelling pipe. He puffed furiously as he stomped out his
anger.

"If Delilah is gone, who's going to prepare the buffet table for
the pool party?"

"There isn't gong to be any pool party tonight, so we don't have
to worry about the buffet," Benjie volunteered. "One of the ranch
hands drained the pool and forgot to turn the water back on."

Jan sat down and wished she smoked so she could light a ciga-
rette. Instead, she jumped back up and headed for the storeroom
and uncapped a jug of Gus's white lightning. She took one gulp
and recapped the bottle. She waved away the fumes and thought

that flames were going to shoot from her mouth any second. When nothing happened, she locked the storeroom and made her way back to the stiflingly hot lobby.

"Well, Gus, aren't you going to go to the Golden Lasso and fetch Delilah back where she belongs?" Jan asked irritably, her throat burning from the alcohol.

Gus favored her with a withering glance and continued his furious pacing.

"Why?" Jan asked, throwing her hands helplessly in the air. "How could you let her go like that? The ranch is without a cook and I can't even begin to cook for all these guests. Gus," she implored, "we need Delilah."

"Delilah said Gus doesn't make her itch and she's tired of not listening to him. She said he never says anything," Benjie offered sadly, knowing he was going to miss the little round woman who made apple tarts for him with globs of icing on top the way he liked them.

"Then I'll go myself and get her," Jan said huffily. "I appreciate her even if you don't, Gus."

"Mr. Bannon won't give her back to us. Delilah said he was going to lock her in his kitchen and never let her get away. That's what she said," Benjie said at Jan's look of disbelief. "Honest."

"Where's the pickup? I'm going to get her, and when you see me again, Delilah will be with me. You can count on it or my name isn't Jan Warren. Will you come with me, Gus?" He just continued with his furious pacing, which was becoming wilder by the moment. "Well, if you won't come with me, do you have a message to her you want me to deliver?"

"Yes," Gus replied. Jan was dumbfounded. She had been at the ranch over a week, and it was the first time she had heard him actually speak. "Tell her I'm not itchy," he said in perfect English.

"That's just exactly what she's going to want to hear," Jan said stormily as she flounced out of the lobby and went in search of the battered pickup truck.

She seethed all the way to the Golden Lasso. More than one scathing look was shot her way in the parking lot of the Lasso. The truck was definitely not Lasso material among the Cadillacs and Continentals, not to mention the Mercedes that peppered the ample parking area. Jan looked around and made her way to the back of the club. No sense causing more of an uproar by going in the front door. She flinched when she remembered Andrea's perfect attire. The Lasso's hired help probably dressed better than she was at the moment.

Jan found the kitchen by the aroma. Delilah must be making her specialty—corn bread with raisins. She stood for a moment and watched the small woman wipe at her eyes from time to time. Quietly, Jan opened the door and stood a moment till Delilah recognized her. "Delilah, please, you have to come back to the ranch. I'll pay you whatever Mr. Bannon is paying you. You can't let me down now. There's no way I can possibly cook for all the Rancho's guests. If you stay here, I'll have to send them here and refund their money."

"I make promise to Mr. Bannon. I give my word," Delilah said defiantly.

"That's wrong, Delilah. You gave me your word when I came to the Rancho that you would stay and work for me. If it's Gus who's bothering you, you have something you better learn right now. He will not come over here to get you. He belongs at the Rancho, and if you stay here he's...he's going to get another...well, what he's going to do is find himself a...a girlfriend, and then where will you be?"

"You think Gus do that?"

"Pirating my help, Miss Warren?" a cold voice inquired.

"Actually, you could say I was pirating my help *back* again. That was a pretty shabby, shoddy thing for you to do, Mr. Bannon. Your tactics are definitely to the left of Attila the Hun," Jan said in a furious, choked voice.

"A simple business proposition. I offered Delilah money and she accepted. What's wrong with that?"

"There's nothing wrong with a simple cut-and-dried business arrangement, but it didn't happen like that and you know it. You're trying to put me out of business and it isn't going to work. I'm not selling and that's final!"

"My dear Miss Warren, think whatever you will," Derek Bannon quipped. "You're trespassing for the second time today."

"Yes, I know, but I came to talk to someone. So I consider it fair for me to be standing in your kitchen. Delilah, are you coming with me?"

Delilah looked uncertain, and from Jan's vantage point it looked like Derek Bannon was going to win. Jan felt desperate. "Delilah," she pleaded, "think of Benjie. What's he going to do, Delilah? He's such a little boy and he needs you. I need you."

"Okay, I come," Delilah said, taking off her apron. Without a backward glance, she followed Jan from the spacious kitchen. Jan allowed herself a smirk as she sailed past the astonished Derek Bannon. "And that's what I call fair."

Jan backed the pickup from the parking slot and headed for the highway. She took her eyes from the road a minute to look at Delilah. "I'm glad you're coming back with me."

Delilah shrugged. "I thought Gus come for me. I not plan on staying there. At Rancho I big boss in kitchen. At Golden Lasso, many cooks. Chefs, they call themselves." Delilah sniffed her disapproval of their self-appointed titles.

Jan was silent on the drive back to Rancho Arroyo, grateful that she had succeeded in getting Delilah to come back to work. And then it hit her. It had been too easy. Men like Derek Bannon always won. If he had wanted to keep Delilah, he would have kept her, and no amount of pleading on her part would have changed things. Men like Derek Bannon did not get where they were in the business world by being nice to their competitors. Suddenly, she felt like a fool. She had been maneuvered by an expert, and she had fallen for it. He was giving in graciously now; later, when she was lulled into a false sense of security, he would strike another blow in his quest for her property. Her hand trembled on the steering wheel. She felt uncertain, betrayed somehow. The only certainty on the horizon was that Derek Bannon wanted her ranch, and if he had to ruin her in the process, he would. Jan shivered in the hot, dry air. If that was so, then she would go down fighting. Derek Bannon would at least know he had picked a formidable adversary. She had to wait and play the waiting game just as Bannon was doing. Who would win? A fine bead of perspiration dotted her brow as she drove. She knew in her heart who was going to win, and all she could do was mark time.

Chapter Five

Although the picturesque facade of Rancho Arroyo pleased the eye, it was the *inner* working of the small complex that threatened to be the undoing of Jan Warren. The new car dealership kept reneging on delivery of the promised van, offering instead vague excuses, and the bills for the rental limousine Jan was forced to use kept mounting. The air-conditioning unit in the main lodge had to be replaced, and, to add insult to injury, the main generator gave out, and though the backup unit functioned, it failed to do the job efficiently, to the guests' acute discomfort.

The swimming pool had been inactive for three days, and the guests were becoming hostile, threatening to leave at a moments' notice. Her pleas that the filtering system was being cleaned and water pressure was low fell on unforgiving ears. All the guests cared about was the 105 degree temperature and how were they to cool off with the air-conditioning working on a hit-or-miss basis. There was no longer any cash flow and the small savings account had dwindled alarmingly. Food was being bought sparingly and paid for just as sparingly. Benjie's hospital bills were mounting faster than she could count. She was being beaten before she started. There was no way she was going to run this ranch by herself.

Jan gathered the mail and retired to her office. Slumping down in the swivel chair, she swung her booted feet on top of the desk. Lord, she was tired—more tired than when she had been holding down two jobs with a house to clean and meals to cook. It must be the heat, she told herself, plus the fact that she wasn't sleeping well.

Wearily, she massaged her temples, willing the approaching headache to evaporate. She felt like crying. No, she wanted to throw a furious tantrum. She wanted to kick and yell and scream and break things, then to cry stormily and get it all out of her system. But she couldn't do that, now that she was an adult. A pity—she would have felt so much better.

Jan pulled a piece of stationery out of her desk drawer and began to scrawl off a note to Neil. As she wrote she wondered how she could so blithely lie about how things were here at the Rancho Arroyo. Lies, all lies, she told herself. Even if she hadn't come right out and said that things were marvelous and wonderful and that she was making money hand over fist and that she was certain to make a success of the business, she had lied by omission. Consciously, she had worded her letters so they skirted the issue. She hadn't told Neil that the minibus had broken down, she had instead led him to believe that she had ordered a new minibus because there was enough capital in the ranch's account and because of a whim.

While she told him of Delilah and Gus, she had done it to describe their colorful characters. She hadn't told him that she was worried sick that her cook would stomp out and go over to the Golden Lasso and that nothing in this world—not even Gus—could bring her back again.

The taste of the glue on the back of the stamp was bitter. She applied it to the envelope and slammed her fist down on it. She'd prefer to die rather than tell Neil that she couldn't handle managing the ranch. That would be tantamount to admitting she was stupid, and she knew that Neil was not gentleman enough to refrain from saying "I told you so!"

Frowning, Jan told herself that she wasn't lying to Neil; she was merely dreaming aloud.

To Jan's weary mind and body it was inevitable that Derek Bannon should be entering her office. She didn't move but deliberately reached for a Coke bottle and took a long drink. Now what?

"I've come to make you another offer for this property," Bannon said, seating himself across the desk from Jan. His easy familiarity annoyed Jan. She took another gulp of the lukewarm soda and set the bottle down with a thump. "It's not for sale," she said curtly.

"Why?" The question sounded obscene to Jan's ears, and she momentarily saw red. How dare he come here and harass her like this? Who did he think he was?

"Because I said so. You look like a reasonably intelligent man, Mr. Bannon. Why do you refuse to accept my decision not to sell? Why are you harassing me like this? The ranch is not for sale, period."

"If you keep on like you've been going, you'll have to file for bankruptcy soon. Is that what you want? I'm willing to pay you three times what this property is worth. You're being very foolish in rejecting my generous offer.''

"Why? Why are you offering me three times what the ranch is worth?'' Jan asked coolly. "Nobody throws away money like that—not even rich people. Tell me why you want this ranch so badly. Your club seems to be a thriving place and equal to Las Vegas, if one is to believe my guests. What could you possibly want with this little place?''

Derek Bannon ignored the pointed question. "Shortly before your uncle's death we were in serious negotiations concerning this ranch. He agreed to sell at my price. I feel that you should honor his decision,'' Derek said harshly.

"I have only your word for that, Mr. Bannon. No one around here seems to know anything about your negotiations other than that you were here trying to pressure a sick old man. If I knew in my heart that what you say is true, I would sell you this ranch, but since I don't know for sure, I can't do it. My uncle had a will drawn up leaving me this property. It seems to me if he had any intention of selling Rancho Arroyo to you, he would have changed his will.''

"Your uncle was not a sick old man as you imply. He was a sharp, intelligent businessman, and, let me tell you, I met my match while we were discussing terms. He knew exactly what he was doing. Why he agreed to sell I don't know. The day before he died he called me at the club and made an appointment to see me the following afternoon to finalize the deal. As you know, he died shortly after awakening.''

"It's a pig in a poke, Mr. Bannon. Proof. If you can give me proof, then I'll sell—not a minute before. Now if you'll excuse me, I'm rather busy.''

"I can see that you're busy,'' Derek Bannon said mockingly, his white teeth gleaming against his bronzed tan. "I'm giving you until August first to take advantage of my offer and after that it's withdrawn. If you file for bankruptcy, you lose everything. Think about that before you make any rash decisions,'' Derek said, getting up from the chair. Before she knew what he was doing, he swept her feet off the desk and stood towering over her. "Ladies,'' he said coldly, "never sit with their feet on a desk.''

"What you mean is Andrea would never sit with her feet on a desk,'' Jan said spitefully. Now why had she said that? Her cheeks flushed and she was very aware of Derek's mocking eyes as he strode from her office. "I'm taking Ben back to the club with me,'' he called over his shoulder.

She should stop him, say something to prevent the hold he had over the boy. But how could she deprive her brother of the one main pleasure he had—seeing the Bisons work out in the field belonging to the Golden Lasso? It rankled her that Benjie had taken to the muscular man and was now calling him Derek. What did they do over there for hours on end? She admitted that she was jealous of the man's attention to her little brother, wishing secretly that it was herself he was courting.

Benjie arrived home shortly after four in the afternoon in the company of Dusty Baker. From her position behind the desk in the lobby Jan watched as Dusty opened the car door and pushed the wheelchair as close as possible for Benjie to maneuver. He tousled Benjie's hair and then followed him into the lodge. Jan smiled as Benjie introduced the famous ball player.

"I've heard a lot about you," Dusty said, indicating Benjie, who was grinning from ear to ear. "This," he said holding out a sealed envelope, "is your invitation to the Bisons' testimonial dinner. It's this evening at eight. Formal dress."

"I almost forgot," Jan apologized. "Thank you for reminding me."

"Don't thank me—thank Derek Bannon. He said he would have my scalp if I didn't deliver this when I brought Benjie home."

"Have you known Mr. Bannon long?" Jan asked pointedly.

"Sure have. He's a great guy. When his father died, he took over the club, and, let me tell you, he's one heck of an owner—just like his father. He never interferes with the managers, and when he does offer advice, he knows where he's coming from. This testimonial and vacation for the club is a treat for us. He picks up the tab once a year. I've gotta get back now. See you this evening. Hang tough, Benjie," he said, ruffling the little boy's hair a second time.

"I have to wear a shirt and tie—Andrea said so," Benjie said happily. "What are you going to wear?"

"Didn't Andrea tell you what I should wear?" Jan snapped irritably.

"No. Was she supposed to? She's wearing a dress that doesn't have straps and has a slit up the side. I saw her show it to Derek and he said it was...it was...sen...sensational. Do you have something that's sensational?"

"I'm afraid not, Benjie. There hasn't been much money lately to buy sensational clothes."

"That's what I told Derek," Benjie said offhandedly, maneuvering the chair through the lobby. "I'm going out to see how the work on the pool is coming."

Sensational, huh? Jan muttered as she ripped open the invitation. Hmm. According to the invitation, she and Benjie were to sit with Derek at his table. There was no mention of Gus or Andy, and yet Benjie was given four tickets. It made no difference, since neither Andy nor Gus expressed a desire to attend the festivities. She and Benjie would have to wing it on their own. At that moment she would have sold her soul to have a gorgeous dress to wear for the evening's entertainment. It was a night out—her first real one in over two years. It would be whatever she made it, good or bad. Clothes didn't necessarily make the person, but they sure helped.

How was she going to sit at a table with Derek Bannon and not show how uncomfortable he made her. She would blush like a schoolgirl every time she remembered how he held her, crushing his lips to hers. That heady, wonderful experience had made her aware that she was alive and that her adrenaline flowed like everyone else's. How? She just might be able to carry it off if Benjie chattered away all night long. A twenty-one-year-old woman depending on a nine-year-old to carry off an evening. It was a disgusting thing to want or even expect. "Well, Mr. Bannon, what you see is what you get," she muttered to the empty room. Hair! She had to do something about her hair, she thought wildly.

Jan checked the kitchen to be sure Delilah had everything under control. From there she checked out the work going on poolside and was reassured that by nightfall the filtering system would once again be operational and the pool ready for use by morning. She stood watching Gus give a group of youngsters a lesson in using a lasso. She whirled around in time to see a rather matronly-looking woman slide off a horse into Andy's outstretched arms. For the moment everything was under control.

A long, luxurious bubble bath later, Jan stepped from the tub and wrapped herself in a bright lemon bath sheet. She squinted down at her feet and decided not only on a manicure but a pedicure as well. The creamy mulberry nail lacquer went on smoothly, pleasing the excited girl. She had to look her best in case she found herself next to the ravishing Andrea in her sensational dress. How could she ever hope to compare to someone as gorgeous as Andrea? "I can't," Jan said dejectedly, sitting down on the edge of the tub while she fanned her nails in the air.

Her nails dry, Jan went through her closet slowly and methodically, searching for something to wear. There wasn't a lot to choose from. When she had bought clothes in the past, she had bypassed all the frivolous evening wear in favor of tailored suits and dresses she could wear to work or, if the occasion warranted, dress up with a colorful scarf or belt. There were two long dresses that were on the serviceable if not outdated list. Thoughtfully, Jan pulled a black sheath with a high mandarin collar from the hanger. It was too plain and there was nothing to dress it up with. Certainly a belt would add nothing and the high collar couldn't take a scarf. She shrugged and slipped into the dress and stood staring at her reflection. Maybe when she had her makeup on it would look better. Before she could change her mind she reached down and ripped the side seam of the gown to above the knee. A little flash of leg never hurt anyone. She had good legs—why not show them? Quickly, she threaded a needle and stitched up the seams so the frayed edges wouldn't show. Again she walked to the mirror and moved this way and that. It still needed something. Whatever it was, she didn't have it, so she would have to be content with the dress the way it was.

Jan slid her feet into wispy black sandals with spiked heels and immediately felt dressed. She toiled painstakingly over her makeup, diligently trying to cover the freckles across the bridge of her nose. Her attempt was less than successful. Well, she had tried—what more could she do? Derek Bannon probably wouldn't even notice her—especially with Andrea around.

Jan transferred the contents of her shoulder bag into a slim black envelope of a purse and left the room to wait in the lobby for Benjie. She hoped Gus had made him clean his ears. How good it was to see Gus take over the personal care of the little boy. Derek Bannon was right again. Benjie seemed to be thriving with all the male attention he was getting—especially from Gus.

Jan whistled playfully when Gus pushed the chair into the lobby. Benjie grinned. "You look...sensational, doesn't she, Gus?" The old Indian grinned and nodded, showing strong white teeth. Delilah took that moment to pass through the lobby and inspect them.

"You need something," she said, tilting her head to the side like a bright, precocious squirrel. "You wait, I get." She was back moments later with a heavy silver and turquoise pendant. "White Antelope, Gus's great-grandfather give to him. Is made for woman of beauty." Before Jan could say a word, Delilah had the heavy silver chain around her neck. Gus nodded his approval while Delilah beamed her pleasure.

"It's gorgeous, Delilah, and just what the dress needed. Now I feel dressed."

Delilah laughed. "Is good—you make Mr. Bannon itch much. But," she said, wagging a plump finger in the air, "you no let him scratch. You understand what I say."

"I understand, Delilah." Jan laughed. "Gus, you are driving us in the rented limo, aren't you? If we show up in the pickup, I'm afraid we'll be shown the back door. Gus certainly isn't big on words, is he?'' Jan whispered over her shoulder to Delilah.

''Not many words, no. He do other things good,'' Delilah said, closing the lobby doors behind them.

Aside from the day she had flown down the road and circled back around to the Golden Lasso's kitchens to retrieve Delilah, Jan had never really seen Derek's glittering establishment. She'd heard reports of its elegance from the guests staying at the Rancho who had gone for dinner at the Lasso, but nothing anyone said prepared her for what she found.

Even the tarmac in the parking lot glittered with iridescent chips of vermiculite and that twinkled under the old-fashioned lamps like stars. There was a flavor of the Old West that was defined in the lighting and split-rail fences that were painted white. It was almost like taking a step backward into the past, but instead of wagon wheels, old ox harnesses, and bleached bone steers' skulls that one expected to find, the Golden Lasso had such ornate and antique decorations that would have been quite at home even in the sophisticated society of a city like San Francisco. There was nothing of the Old Frontier here. Instead, it was a shrine to the Victorian era, complete with gaslights and overembellished furnishings of dark mahogany and trappings of rich turkey red. While the decor could have easily become overdone and gauche, it was a marvel of good taste.

The floor of the main dining hall, except for the dance area, was carpeted in thick, Oriental-style carpeting of reds and blacks and golds. The tables were covered with lace cloths and the chairs were upholstered in a dark red tapestry. Mirrors—hundreds of them, all framed in gilt—reflected the massive chandelier hung in the center of the room, and its crystal lights danced over the silver bowls filled with roses.

Benjie seemed oblivious to all this elegance, and Jan supposed it was because of his frequent visits. She noticed that the main dining hall opened onto several small rooms, all decorated on the theme of the elegant Pullman cars that had carried passengers from the East into the world of the New Frontier. Each room was narrow, and the tables nestled against the walls, which were hung with rich brocades. Even the lights hung along the walls were gimbaled, making one almost think they could swing gently with the rocking of the train. The ceilings were paneled in gleaming dark wood, and at the far end of each ''dining car'' was a glass and mirrored bar.

"This is really something, Benjie." Jan let out her breath in a silent whistle.

"Yeah. Didn't I tell you?"

"No, as a matter of fact, you didn't." Jan frowned, wondering what else Benjie had failed to mention.

"Well, if you think this is something, you should see Derek's apartment. Wow!"

"I didn't know you'd been to Derek's apartment. I thought you just came here to watch the Bisons practice on the back field."

"Yeah, I do that too. But the day Derek wanted me to meet Andrea he took me into their apartment. I got to really look around because Andrea was in the shower and we had to wait for her," Benjie said with all the innocence of a nine-year-old.

Jan looked at Benjie sharply. He had said "their apartment" and that Andrea was taking a shower. The statement seemed to throw her off balance. In spite of the fact that Derek and Andrea were engaged to be married, she hadn't thought of them as living together. This new realization struck a nerve in Jan, and she felt herself blushing. Derek and Andrea could do whatever they wanted and it didn't mean anything to her, but when she thought of his arms around her and his mouth on hers, she died a little inside. What a fool she was, and what a bounder Derek was. He had committed himself totally to Andrea, and yet he wanted to play his little games with Jan. Fool, fool, she cursed herself. And you let him do it, and, more to your stupidity, you loved it.

"Hey, Dusty!" Benjie called to the tall, well-built man across the room who was motioning for them to join him at his table. "Come on, Jan. There's Dusty. We're going to be sitting with him at Derek's table."

Jan's feet moved like lead weights across the floor. The last thing in this world she wanted was to be here, in the Golden Lasso, about to sit down to a night's celebration with Derek Bannon and Andrea. Benjie maneuvered his chair over to the table where Dusty Baker waited and pulled up to the space where a place had been set minus a chair.

"Hi, remember me? I'm Dusty Baker." He extended a beefy hand that swallowed Jan's. "As I said earlier, I've heard a lot about you, Miss Warren, and all of it's good. Ben knows how lucky he is to have you for a sister. Isn't that right, Ben?" He smiled affectionately at the boy.

"You bet, Dusty. Where's Derek?"

"Oh, he's seeing to some last-minute details. It's still early—he and Andrea will be here soon." Dusty held a chair and waited for

Jan to seat herself. Then he walked around to the other side of the table and sat down.

"Is this your first visit to the Golden Lasso, Miss Warren?" Dusty asked as he stirred the ice in his glass.

"Please call me Jan. And yes—I've never been here before. It's really something."

"It sure is. Andrea had a lot to do with it. She's an interior decorator, and she's outdone herself with the Lasso. It's been covered in quite a number of magazines, but I don't suppose you're the kind of girl who reads those kinds of books."

Jan blushed. It was obvious that the kind of magazines he was referring to were the girlie magazines that depicted nude women. Also, there was something about the way he mentioned Andrea. With a kind of proprietorial pride that denoted something more than a casual friendship. Dusty turned to motion to the waiter and Jan suddenly recognized his broad shoulders and the set of his head and immediately knew that Dusty Baker was the man on the plane who had joked and quipped with Andrea and made a date for a drink. As much as Jan was inclined to like the football player, she wondered what kind of man would try to make a date with his friend's fiancée. What kind of people were these who had no respect for friendship and loyalty and faithfulness? Even Derek—about to be married to Andrea—had made advances in Jan's direction. And gullible little fool that she was, she had allowed it.

Dusty ordered a drink for Jan and turned his attention back to Benjie, who preened with delight. Jan decided that whatever else she thought about these people, they certainly were kind to Ben, and that should redeem them at least a little bit.

The dining room began to fill and every so often Benjie would wave across the room at another of the Bisons. As he did, Dusty told Jan their names. Many of the players were accompanied by their wives and children, and Jan saw that many of the boys around Benjie's age waved their greetings.

"Pretty soon Ben will be out there with the other kids, running and swimming, won't you Ben?" Dusty asked.

"You betcha! Dr. Rossi says I'm coming along real fine. Isn't that right, Jan?"

"That's what the word is, Benjie. But there's still a lot of hard work ahead of you." Dusty turned to greet someone, and Benjie pulled on Jan's hand, making her lean over to hear him whisper.

"Jan, just for tonight, couldn't you call me Ben? I don't want everybody to think I'm still a baby."

Jan was almost speechless. Derek Bannon's influence over her brother was becoming insufferable. But when she looked into Benjie's eyes, she saw that this was very important to him. "All right, Ben," she whispered in return, "but I'm warning you—every time I have you alone, I'll still call you Benjie."

"Aw, Jan, that's okay for when we're alone. But not when there's somebody around, okay?" he pleaded.

"Okay," she assured him, "but don't blame me if I forget once in a while. You've been my little brother Benjie for a lot of years."

Dusty Baker rose to his feet and turned toward the entrance to the dining room. Andrea walked across the room, and, just as Benjie had predicted, her dress was sensational. A long, sleek, shimmering red that was slit from the hem practically up to her waist. It outlined every curve and line of her body, and the strapless bodice accented the smooth, flawless skin on her shoulders. The only jewelry Andrea wore was long, dangling earrings, which Jan supposed were real diamonds. Everything else about Andrea appeared to be real—why not her jewelry? Jan sighed to herself.

"Ms. Warren, this is Andrea..."

"We've met," Jan interjected hastily. She couldn't bear to hear Dusty Baker say "Derek's fiancée."

Feeling awkward and out of date in her black sheath gown, Jan accepted Andrea's welcome through stiff lips. Although Andrea's attitude seemed friendly enough, Jan couldn't seem to bring herself past the green-eyed monster to accept Andrea as a friend.

"Can you sit down with us now, honey?" Jan heard Dusty say to Andrea, and immediately she bristled at the familiarity of his tone and the pet name he used.

"I think I've done everything that needed doing." Andrea sighed wearily. "These affairs take more out of me than you could know, Dusty. Derek is settling some disagreement in the kitchen. He'll join us shortly. That is, if the chef doesn't quit and he has to broil the steaks himself." Andrea laughed, Jan supposed, at the vision of Derek, complete in chef's hat, bustling about the kitchen. Jan saw the way the girl touched the sleeve of Dusty's jacket and the way her fingers lingered there just a little too long. There was definitely more to this relationship than met the eye.

Andrea began talking to Benjie and offered him the dish of celery sticks and olives that the waiter had deposited on their table. Jan was suddenly jealous of the easy repartee Andrea had with Benjie, and she even thought she saw Benjie blush under the lovely girl's attentions.

"You know, I've always wanted a little brother," Andrea told

Benjie. "Big brothers can sometimes be a pain in the neck. They're always telling you what you can and can't do and when to do it."

Benjie laughed. "Jan's not like that—she's the best sister a guy could have. She lets me by my own man, don't you, Jan?"

Looking at Benjie with a wide-eyed amazement, Jan managed to force a smile. His own man indeed!

Jan reached for a large black olive and clumsily dropped it onto the table and watched as it rolled across the cloth onto her lap. "Lose something, Miss Warren?" Derek had come upon her so unexpectedly that Jan nearly toppled her drink.

Muttering some inane remark, Jan found the olive in the folds of her skirt and dropped it into the ashtray. She knew her face was red and that her hand trembled when she picked up her glass.

"I'm glad you brought Ben tonight," Derek said conversationally.

Jan nodded. He was glad she brought Ben—not he was glad *she* had come. As Derek moved to take the chair beside her, Jan concentrated on sipping her drink. At all costs she wanted to disguise the fact that every fiber of her being was totally conscious of his presence. She picked up the faint aroma of his after-shave and the sleeve of his tuxedo jacket brushed her shoulder as he sat down. She saw his hand, sun bronzed and masculine, against the white lace of the tablecloth. Her emotions rushed away with her, and once again she was alone with him on the desert and those capable-looking hands were in her hair and on her back, holding her close, pressing her against his magnificent length. The scent of his after-shave came to her on a wave of remembered desire as it filled her senses and she remembered the taste of his lips on hers. Stop it! her mind screamed. You can't do this to yourself! There he is, right now, this minute, joking with the girl he's going to marry. But if he really loved Andrea, her heart whispered, would he have kissed you that way?

Before she was faced with answering her own question, soft music began playing from the violin of the strolling musician and the waiters were carrying in the trays of shrimp cocktail, which signaled the beginning of the meal.

Dinner was excellent and the table conversation exceedingly pleasant. In spite of herself, Jan relaxed and found she was enjoying every minute of the evening. Benjie—or Ben, as he now preferred to be called in public—was on his best behavior, and Jan was proud that she had instilled in the boy a good amount of table manners. Derek, especially, was particularly attentive to Benjie and herself, and no mention was made of his offer to buy the Rancho, for which

Jan was grateful. Even Andrea was gracious and didn't seem to mind the attention Derek was paying to Benjie and herself. But when Jan dropped her napkin and bent to retrieve it, she understood why. Beneath the cover of the lacy cloth, Dusty and Andrea were holding hands! Right there under Derek's eyes! Practically.

After her discovery of Andrea's fickleness, Jan found it increasingly difficult to be more than barely polite. After several tries, Andrea ignored Jan altogether, behaving as though she wasn't even there. It was to the men at the table that Andrea directed her attentions, and it wasn't long before all three of them, Benjie included, were eating right out of her hand.

After dinner the Bison players assembled at the long table at the head of the room, where a podium and microphones were already set up. The testimonials were gracious and even amusing, and Benjie listened and applauded and laughed at inside jokes that Jan couldn't begin to fathom. But Benjie was enjoying himself and that was all that mattered.

When Dusty Baker stepped up to the podium to receive his award, Andrea clapped long and hard. Stealing a glance at Derek, Jan noticed that he didn't seem to mind at all that his fiancée seemed to be the man's biggest fan. Finally, unable to bear another moment of the duplicity of Derek and Andrea, she asked to be excused for a breath of fresh air. Without waiting for an answer from either Derek or Andrea, Jan stood from the table and walked across the crowded room to the doors she knew led to the garden. As she left, she was aware of Derek's glance piercing her back.

Like the parking lot, the garden was lit by tall, romantic gaslights, illuminating the paths and shrubbery in a warm, yellow glow. Shadows were accentuated and the pathways shimmered with metallic chips. Everything about Derek's Lasso was indeed golden.

At a sound behind her, Jan turned on her heel and for some reason wasn't surprised to see that Derek had followed her.

"Must you always come creeping up on me?" she demanded.

"Must you always walk around in a daze, Jan?" he replied.

"Lately, it seems as though every time I turn around, there you are," she said hotly. "Why don't you go back inside and join Andrea? She must be wondering where you've gone."

"Andrea can take care of herself. Besides, she has Dusty for company, not to mention Ben." His tone was offhanded and his mouth twisted into a wry smile.

What kind of man was he? How could he speak so offhandedly about Andrea being with Dusty Baker, and what was he doing out here in the garden with her. If he cared so little about the girl he

was engaged to marry, Jan knew that he would care even less for
her. She straightened her back and squared her shoulders.

"I came out here to get away from the crowd and for a breath
of fresh air. And you, Mr. Bannon, are creating a crowd out here
in the garden, and whenever you're around I find that the air is
anything but fresh." Her tone was haughty, her eyes cold and dis-
approving, but it seemed that nothing she could say would daunt
Mr. Derek Bannon.

Derek's eyes narrowed, and in one step he was against her, holding her fast to his lean, hard body. His lips were hot and wine
scented as they pressed against hers. She could feel her lips part
beneath his as she struggled to free herself, as though fighting for
her life. Derek held her closer, enveloping her within the strong
fold of his arms.

Weakened by conflicting emotions, Jan ceased her struggles. Derek's answer was a renewed ardor as he held her and pressed long,
passionate kisses to her mouth. She felt his hands on her hair, on
her breasts, on the small of her back, and reaching lower.

Resistance lost, she felt herself melt into him as though becoming
a part of him. Her arms reached around his neck, her mouth was
pliant and yielding to his. A spectrum of newfound desires coursed
through her body as she clung to him, offering herself to his caresses, submitting herself to his demands.

Suddenly, violently, she fought his advances. What was wrong
with her, submitting to Derek Bannon this way? If *he* couldn't remember that he was engaged to Andrea, *she* could!

Jan lashed out blindly, her hands beating at his broad chest and
reaching for his mocking face. Fury inflamed her cheeks and shame
and humiliation at what she had allowed to happen brought hot tears
to her eyes.

"You devil!" she shouted. "Keep your hands off me!" She
lashed out again, aiming for the cold blue eyes that seemed to burn
through her, turning her veins to ice.

Derek sidestepped her flailing arm, caught it by the wrist, and
pulled her against him, holding her there in his iron grip.

All the weariness of the past weeks overcame her. Dry, wracking
sobs of frustration caught in her throat. She was the vanquished, he
the victor. Let him do with her what he would, then just leave her
alone to crawl somewhere to hide.

Closely pressed against her, he held her; Jan's lips were burning
from his kisses and an involuntary trembling took hold of her.
Through their light clothing, she could feel the massive muscular
strength of him as he molded her body to his.

Feeling his lips part from her, Jan opened her eyes and could read the desire in his. His caresses became more intimate, and again Jan surrendered herself as though all her energy was anticipating a most unexpected pleasure.

Abruptly, he pushed her away from him with such a force her teeth rattled. His eyes avoided hers; the pain of rejection pricked her eyelids. In a gruff voice he commanded, "Go home, Jan." Silently, he turned and stalked away from her.

Humiliation swallowed her and a bitterness rose to her throat. He had used her, and she, heaven help her, had helped him—enjoyed it, loved it! And now he was through with her as though she were a cast-off shoe.

Oh, how I hate him! she cried silently. I hate him! But, realizing the truth for what it was, she sobbed, "Heaven help me, I love him. I love him!"

Chapter Six

Jan refused to glance in the mirror the morning after the testimonial dinner for the Bisons. How could she have made such a fool of herself? How could she have allowed herself to be drawn into Derek Bannon's arms and enjoy it? Gus must have thought her a raving idiot when she had run across the parking lot to where he waited in the rented limo and tearfully choked out the order to get Benjie out of the dining room; they were going home!

Why did Derek Bannon have this invisible hold over her? What was there about the man that made her heart pound and her senses reel? She had been in the presence of other men who were almost as handsome as Derek. Good looks and fancy clothes didn't account for the way he made her feel. She thought to herself, I can't be in love with him! I don't want to be in love with him! "I can't handle this," she cried in a broken voice. I have to see to Benjie and the Rancho, and I don't need all this emotional turmoil in my life—especially not now.

She looked around the room wildly, as though hoping some answer was going to leap out from the four walls and make everything all right. It was a new day; she had to get on with everyday living and not think about Derek Bannon and how he made her feel. It was an impossible order, and she recognized it for what it was. She could no more stop thinking about Derek than she could stop breathing.

He had given her till August 1 to decide about selling Rancho Arroyo. He was right about one thing; it would be better to sell the ranch than to file for bankruptcy and lose everything. And that was where she was headed eventually. The bills would mount and the

ranch would be sold to cover the bills. And one thing was certain—
on the open market, with her back to the wall, she wouldn't get
half what Derek was offering for the ranch.

If she sold the ranch now, she could bank the money for Benjie's
education and go back to New York to the big old house. Big old
house. Maybe the bank would give her a loan if she put up the
house as collateral. Aha! Derek Bannon didn't know about the
house back east. How long did it take to get a loan? If she went to
the bank today, she could at least set the wheels in motion. All the
papers from her parents' estate were in a manila envelope in the
office safe. She would take everything with her and hope the bank
would realize what a valuable property she held title to. If it took
only two or three weeks, she felt confident that she could stall off
the creditors for at least that long. However, she thought morbidly,
perhaps that would be a mistake. If guests kept canceling their reservations and moving over to the Golden Lasso, she would be pouring money down the drain.

If there was only someone to talk to, to go to for advice, to
confide in. There was no one. She had only herself to depend on.
Perhaps the banker would help her. If she was lucky, the loan officer
might be able to advise her.

Three hours later, Jan exited the bank feeling more morose than
when she had entered. While friendly and helpful, the loan officer
had not been overenthusiastic about making her a loan. He used
words like sizeable and pointed out that she was a novice to this
sort of business and that there was the competition of the Golden
Lasso to consider. His voice had dropped a degree when he said
that appraisal took several weeks and one simply did not hurry a
bank. Everything in good time. He would call, he told Jan, when
he saw tears trickle down her cheeks. "If he had just patted me on
the head, I would have felt better," Jan mumbled as she hailed a
cab to take her out to the medical center.

Dr. Rossi's youth and exuberance were evident when he told her
of the progress Benjie was making in his physical therapy. "Dusty
Baker and Derek Bannon have had a great deal to do with that
progress. You have those men to thank for Ben's positive attitude,
Miss Warren. And, of course, your own patience and work in helping Ben perform his daily exercises."

Jan bristled. If there was one thing she didn't need right now, it
was another Derek Bannon fan.

"Ben thinks a great deal of Derek," Dr. Rossi went on to say.
"With his encouragement, I predict that Ben will be walking very
soon."

"Dr. Rossi, I'm so happy! That's fantastic news! I'm so grateful.
I had no idea things would progress so quickly." Jan smiled. Benjie's happiness depended upon his walking again, and anything that
made Benjie happy was good for her, too.

"A positive attitude and hope are something we here at the medical center never discount. As a matter of fact, we depend on them.
I just wish all our patients responded as well as Ben."

Outside his office Dr. Rossi's receptionist told Jan that the billing
office would like her to stop by and see them. Jan smiled nervously
and stepped out into the corridor. She didn't know if she was happy
or sad. Certainly happy that Benjie was doing so remarkably well,
but sad that she had to see about paying the bill. Would they refuse
to treat Benjie once they discovered that she couldn't meet the full
responsibility of the bill? There was no decision to be made. If it
came down to Benjie, she would sell the Rancho to Derek Bannon
if the bank refused to give her a loan. She wouldn't lose sight of
the fact that Benjie came first.

Surprisingly, the woman who was in charge of the billing office
understood her problem and worked on it accordingly. "It's not the
center's policy to deny help to those who can't afford to pay. We
have a very wealthy patron here in Phoenix who donates often and
handsomely. You can pay when you're able, Miss Warren. Just fill
out this pledge form. Actually—" the woman smiled "—it's not
even a pledge. Mr. Bannon said it was important for people to feel
that they weren't charity cases. And do you know, he's right?" the
woman beamed. "Even several years after treatment, many of our
patients continue to pay on their bills. Even if it's small amounts
at first. So everyone benefits from Derek Bannon's generosity—the
clinic and the new patients."

Jan left the credit office in a daze. Derek Bannon certainly was
an enigma. No two people saw him in the same light. How could
a kind, wonderful, generous person as the woman in the credit office
described set out to ruin a poor girl from New York who only
wanted to set the Rancho on a paying basis to support her brother
and herself? And how could such a philanthropic, humane man
stand in the wings like a vulture waiting for her to go bankrupt so
he could snatch up her property?

A quick glance at her watch told her it was almost noon and time
for lunch. She looked around for a suitable restaurant, but the only
thing in sight was a cocktail lounge that had a sign proclaiming
they served businessmen lunches. Why not? The next bus back to
the ranch wouldn't leave till two fifteen, so she had plenty of time.
Jan decided to treat herself.

"A vodka and tonic. And I think I'll have a Waldorf salad," she said bravely to the waitress. She hated eating alone, and when the occasion came up, she never ordered a drink, thinking all eyes were on a solitary woman eating and drinking by herself. For the moment she felt the need of the artificial stimulation to get her mind in gear again. Why did Derek Bannon always toss her a curve? Just when she thought she had him figured out, he did something to confuse her and make himself look like the proverbial knight in shining armor.

"Drinking alone, Miss Warren?" a cool voice demanded. Jan almost choked on the liquid in her mouth. Maybe if she ignored him he would go away. But men like Derek Bannon never went away. It was impossible to ignore such a masculine presence. Setting her glass down with expert precision, she stared at the man who was seating himself opposite her.

"Permit me to recommend the baked sole." Jan said nothing. "Have you given my offer any more thought?" Derek Bannon asked quietly.

"Yes." She deliberately avoided saying more.

"What's your decision?"

"I haven't decided. You said August first. I'll give you my decision then." Their eyes locked, and it was Jan who flushed and lowered her gaze, remembering how his eyes had softened as he stared into hers right before she melted into his arms. Was he remembering, too?

"I meant it when I said I would withdraw the offer at that time," Derek said coolly.

"I'm sure you did. Your offer was more than generous. Why can't you understand how important it is for me to keep the ranch? I have to try to make a go of it. You can't possibly need it. You appear to be very wealthy, and your club must be making you a handsome profit. My ranch isn't an eyesore that would offend your guests, so if you would level with me, I might be more amenable to your request. Wanting something just for the sake of wanting it is not reason enough. You might have been born with a silver spoon but I wasn't. I've worked since I was sixteen, and for the past two years I've held down two jobs, seven days a week, to be sure Benjie got the best I could give him. This, Mr. Bannon, is my best, and I can't let you take it from us. No, that's not right—I *won't* let you take it from us. If you'll excuse me, I have to get back to the bus station."

Derek Bannon stared at the tight-lipped girl who was sliding out of the booth. "I'm going back to the Lasso. If you want a ride,

you're welcome to come with me." Jan ignored him as she laid
some bills on the table and paid for her uneaten meal. There was
no way she could handle the ride back to the ranch sitting next to
Derek Bannon. Right now it was all she could do to hold the threatening tears in check. She was through the revolving door and hail-
ing a cab before Derek could get out of the booth. "And I'll bet
that's the first time one of your women ever refused you anything,"
she muttered to herself.

Jan's bus was already boarding when she climbed from the cab.
Derek Bannon wheeled his sports car in front of the bus and came
to a screeching halt. Jan didn't look in his direction but immediately
took her place in line.

"This is ridiculous. I'm going right by the ranch. If you take this
bus, you have to walk from the highway to Rancho Arroyo. Stop
being so silly and come with me," Derek said, taking her posses-
sively by the arm. Jan pulled away, his touch, like a firebrand,
scalding her bare arm.

"I'm taking this bus. I came on the bus and I'm going home on
the bus. It's not my fault that you don't understand the word no.
No, Mr. Bannon, I do not want a ride home. And," she said tartly,
"you can just come by the Rancho and pick up that cat you had
the gall to send me."

"Is this man bothering you, Miss?" the bus driver demanded
gruffly.

"He certainly is. He tried to pick me up in a coc...restaurant."

"Beat it, buddy, and leave the young ladies alone or I'll have to
call a policeman. You good-looking playboys are all alike. You see
a pretty face and you think all you have to do is move in. Take
that fancy rig of yours out of here right now so I can get this bus
moving."

Jan was delighted at the look of acute discomfort on Derek's
face. Two put-downs in the space of five minutes. She smiled win-
ningly and waved a jaunty salute. She shuddered at Derek's cold,
unreadable face. He looked as though he wanted to murder someone. Serves him right, Jan thought as she leaned back in her seat.

When Jan left the bus on the highway, she almost expected to
see Derek waiting for her, and she was disappointed that he wasn't.
The heat was unbearable and before she was halfway home she
wished she had accepted his offer. Her sandal straps were rubbing,
and she knew she would have king-size blisters the moment she
removed her shoes. She could feel her makeup run, and she knew
her hair was wet and tangled, hanging limply to her head. She didn't
know when she had ever felt so miserable.

When Jan hobbled up the flagstone walkway leading to the kitchen, she thought she was going to faint. Delilah clucked over her like a mother hen, bathing her face in cool water and then wrapping her blistered feet in an herb-scented cloth. A frosty glass of lemonade was placed in her hand to be refilled twice. "Where's that weird cat that came in the mail?" Jan demanded petulantly.

"Not one cat anymore. Nine cats now," Delilah said, pointing to a spot near the open-hearth fireplace in the gigantic kitchen.

"Remarkable," Jan said through clenched teeth. "He's sadistic, Delilah. Do you have any idea how much it's going to cost to feed nine cats?" Delilah shook her head mournfully. "A lot, a fortune. I can't afford it. Tomorrow I'm mailing them back to him C.O.D."

"You much mad at Mr. Bannon?" Delilah inquired, a frown on her face. "You much mad because he kiss you or because he no kiss you? He kiss good, no?"

"He kiss good, yes," Jan giggled. "Too good."

Delilah waddled over to the stove. "Much good kiss, so you send back cats. Not good sense," she muttered as she stirred a bubbling pot on the stove.

Chapter Seven

As always, after being in Derek Bannon's company, Jan felt inadequate. This was the third time he had reduced her to a mass of silly putty. She must be doing something wrong. It wasn't her fault she didn't know how to act around people like Derek and the beautiful Andrea. She admitted that she hated the word *homespun,* but that's exactly what she was—a down-home country girl. And while she hadn't just dropped off the watermelon truck, she was incapable of playing in Derek Bannon's league.

And on top of that was the niggling suspicion of why Bannon wanted her property. What possible use could he make of it? Why wouldn't he say why he wanted it?

Somehow Jan managed to work her way through the day without any mishaps of any kind. Things were running smoothly for a change and she wanted to enjoy the calm atmosphere, if not to revel in it. Derek Bannon was the stuff dreams were made of and that's where she would relegate him in her mind. She would allow herself the luxury of thinking of him only when she drifted off to sleep. If she allowed him to get under her skin, she couldn't function. Delilah was right—he made her itch.

The day's work behind her, Jan watered the tubs of flowers around the pool and then sat down to relax with a cold glass of ginger ale. She felt good, knowing she had worked a full day and somehow managed to cope and make everyone happy. She deserved this brief respite before putting Benjie to bed.

Delilah seemed always to be the bearer of bad tidings, and this time was no different. Jan watched her approach the pool area, her bright eyes searching out Jan in the dim lantern light. "Bad news," she said matter of factly. "Andy break leg here, here and here. Three places," she said, holding up three plump fingers. "I call ambulance."

"What?" Jan exclaimed, jumping up from the chaise longue. "How...never mind." If there was one thing she didn't need, it was one of Delilah's explanations. "Where is he?"

"On floor in bunkhouse. He dreaming and fall out. Simple."

Jan was sure Delilah was right. Anything more would have been too confusing. Now what was she going to do?

"Andy, are you all right?" she asked, bending over the lanky man.

"Yeah, I'm okay, but the leg is busted in three places—at least, that's what Delilah said. I'm embarrassed," he said, gritting his teeth in pain. "I don't know how it happened. One minute I was asleep dreaming about all those lovelies over at the Golden Lasso and *wham,* I was falling out of the bunk. I tried to grab the rail and that's all I remember."

"Delilah called for the ambulance; it's on the way. Here, let me put a pillow under your head. Do you want me to have Gus ride along with you to the hospital?"

"I'd appreciate that, Jan. Listen, do you think you could do me a favor and not...what I mean is, people might think..."

Jan grinned. "I'll tell them you did it in the line of duty. Don't worry about it. Do you think some brandy might ease the pain? I'm afraid to give you anything else."

"I get," Delilah said, waddling off to fetch the brandy.

"Did Delilah check your leg?"

"Are you kidding? She just looked at it and then went, '*Tsk, tsk, tsk,* is broke, three places.' When she says something, you can count on it."

"Amazing," Jan said, shaking her head.

"That she is. Your uncle regarded her as a real treasure."

The brandy arrived at the same time the ambulance did. The attendants vetoed the brandy, to Delilah's annoyance. She fixed her shoe-button eyes on the youngest attendant and said, "You stupid— brandy make him sweat. Where you learn medicine, Sears Roebuck? *Tsk, tsk, tsk,*" she muttered as she downed the fiery liquid and waddled back to the kitchen.

The young attendant looked at Jan and shook his head. "His leg is broken in three places—please be careful," Jan pleaded.

"How do you know his leg is broken in three places?" the older man asked.

"I just know." Not for the world would she admit that she was taking Delilah's word for the three breaks in Andy's leg.

Andy winked at her; he wasn't about to tell them either. His look clearly stated, "Why shake up medical science?"

By the time she checked on Benjie and found him propped up in bed with a Hardy Boys book, she was bone tired. She felt a tug at her heart as she looked at the little boy. How game he was; he never complained and he always had a smile for her. He looked wan and tired, though.

"Benjie, how do you feel?"

"I feel tired, but it's a good tired. Dr. Rossi and Derek say so. Dr. Rossi said I was making...re...remarkable progress and Derek said he was proud of me. Dusty Baker said so, too. You shouldn't worry about me, Jan—the guys are taking good care of me. Aren't they the greatest?" he asked happily.

Jan nodded. "If they're making you happy, then, yes, they're the greatest," she said, bending over him to give him a good-night kiss. "Ten minutes and lights out. Tomorrow is another day."

"Jan, would you like to go on a picnic to Rattlesnake Canyon with me and Derek. He said it was okay if you came along as long as you brought the food."

A sharp retort rose to her lips but Jan squelched it. "I'll think about it. Remember, ten minutes. Goodnight, Benjie."

"'Night, Jan," Benjie mumbled as he joined the adventuresome Hardy Boys in one of their wild escapades.

What kind of left-handed invitation was that? You can come along if you bring the food. She dutifully answered Neil's letter, the thought of the picnic continually on her mind. *Humph,* she sniffed as she got ready for bed. She was planning the menu as she drifted off to sleep.

The digital clock on the night table read 3:18 A.M. when she heard Benjie cry out. She lay quietly, waiting to see if the sound was repeated. It had been a long time since he had had nightmares. He wasn't crying; he was groaning when she reached his room and flicked on the light switch. "What's wrong?" she asked anxiously.

"My legs. They're all cramped up," Benjie cried. "They hurt, Jan. Make it go away!"

"I'll call Dr. Rossi. Do you want me to get Gus to come and stay with you while I make the call?"

"Gus went to the hospital with Andy and they aren't back yet." Benjie groaned. "Please, Jan, do something..." His words were stopped by the effort to grit his teeth and bear the pain.

Jan ran into her room and called the hospital only to find out that

Dr. Rossi had left for Tucson late that afternoon and wouldn't be back in his office until late the next day. Since it was an emergency, they would try to reach him and have him call her back.

"Jan, get Derek. He'll know what to do," Benjie pleaded. "He stays in the therapy room while I have my treatments."

"But, Benjie, Derek isn't a doctor..."

"I want Derek," Benjie said, crying now, tears streaming down his cheeks. "Please, Jan, please get him."

"Okay, okay, honey, I'll call him. I'll be right back." Jan raced down to the first floor and pounded on Delilah's door, waking her and instructing her to go to Benjie while she made the call.

The main switchboard at the Golden Lasso answered and rang Derek Bannon's apartment suite. The line was busy. Trying to control her panic, Jan asked them to please break into the line. It was an emergency with Ben Warren down at the Rancho Arroyo. The young man at the switchboard was sympathetic and came back on the line.

"I'm terribly sorry, but the phone must be off the hook. If I can reach someone, I'll have them go over to Mr. Bannon's apartment. You do understand that I can't leave the desk."

Jan slammed down the receiver. She would have to go to the Lasso and get Derek herself. She would have to use the pickup truck; the rented limo had been returned that afternoon. Taken back, actually—she forced herself to face reality.

Jan ground the gears in the old pickup as she raced up the road. She would bring Derek Bannon back to the Rancho if she had to drag him out of bed. Benjie had said something about his private apartment being somewhere near the tennis courts.

Halfway to the Golden Lasso, the pickup coughed and sputtered, and before she had gone another five hundred feet, it died altogether. Jan shifted into neutral and turned the key. Nothing. Twice more she tried. Again nothing. Climbing out from the truck, she slammed the door shut with a vengeance. Darn old dilapidated, confounded machine! Nothing worked. Nothing!

Now what was she to do? She was already halfway to the Lasso—turning back now would be foolish. She had to go on ahead. The night was chilly, as always in the desert. Her Western boots rubbed against the unhealed blisters. She had hurriedly pulled them on but hadn't taken the time to search for socks. At that moment she would have cheerfully given her back teeth for a skateboard.

By the time she reached the cobblestoned driveway to the Golden Lasso, she was perspiring with the effort of the walk. Her hair hung in limp strands about her ashy face. Her silk pajamas, emblazoned

with green turtles, was plastered to her body, and she was limping
from a bruise on the bottom of her sore feet. The thin robe that
matched her pajamas flapped about her like bat wings. Somewhere
along the way she had lost the belt. She wanted to cry, but she
couldn't afford the luxury. Instead, she sniffed, wiped at her mouth,
and headed for the rear of the Golden Lasso. If she couldn't find
Derek's apartment immediately, she would scream to raise the dead.
Someone would come running. She hoped.

Jan found the tennis courts and looked about for what might look
like private apartments. Someone was up—there was a light in the
window to the left of the courts. She squared her shoulders and
marched over to the door and rapped on it sharply. Andrea, clad in
a wispy affair of black lace, stood framed in the doorway, her eyebrows arched in amusement. "Jan, what are you doing here at this
hour?"

Licking her lips and swallowing hard, Jan replied, "I'm looking
for Derek...Mr. Bannon. Is he here? I must see him—it's very important. It's about Benjie...Ben. It's important." No one should
look that beautiful at four in the morning. Jan knew she was going
to cry.

Sensing her desperation, Andrea opened the door wider and ushered Jan into the living room. "I'll go get Derek; I'll be right back.
Can I get you something, Jan? Water?"

Wordlessly, Jan nodded her head. Her mouth was so dry and
parched, her tongue was thick and sticking to the roof of her mouth.

Andrea brought her a tall glass of iced water and said she would
go get Derek. Impatiently, Jan paced the apartment, oblivious to its
elegance and charm. All she knew was that Benjie was home and
in pain and needed her and that she'd been gone too long already.
Her pacing took her near a glass and chrome desk at the far end of
the room. On the desk were blueprints, and the lettering at the
bottom of the page stopped Jan in her tracks. "Rancho Arroyo—
Redevelopment."

Upon closer examination, Jan discovered the prints were indeed
of the ranch. There was the main lodge and along the trails the
twelve cabins and swimming pool...Derek Bannon certainly lost no
time. He was so confident that she would sell him the Rancho that
he'd already consulted an architect about redeveloping the site.
Reaching out to turn the page and try to discover exactly what
Derek Bannon intended to do with the property *if* she should sell it
to him, a voice startled her.

"Trick or treating, Miss Warren?" Derek Bannon said coolly.
"To what do I owe the pleasure of this visit at—" he looked at the

clock over the mantel "—four o'clock in the morning. Are those turtles?" he asked, touching the collar of the thin robe.

Jan was exasperated. "Yes, they're turtles and, no, I'm not trick or treating for Halloween. I need you to help Benjie. I don't know what to do for him and Dr. Rossi is in Tucson. Benjie has severe cramps in his legs. He's crying for you. Benjie never cries. Will you come?" she pleaded.

"Of course, I'll come. Where's your car? I'll follow you back."

"My pickup broke down when I was halfway here. I came the rest of the way on foot. I had no other choice. Your phone is off the hook!" she accused hotly, holding back the tears. "That's why I came in person—the switchboard couldn't get through."

Derek cast an angry glance at Andrea, who shrank from his silent accusation.

"Do you mind if I go back with you?" she said, the tears that had been held in check now running in rivulets down her cheeks. "But first I have to take these boots off—my feet are covered in blisters."

Derek stared at her for a moment before he scooped her up in his arms and carried her to his car. "You weigh about as much as a postage stamp. Do you eat?"

"Of course I eat," Jan muttered as she settled herself in the bucket seat. She tugged at the leather boots and could feel the skin leave the backs of her heels. She winced and then sighed with relief. She felt Derek's eyes on her, but she refused to look at him, knowing that if she did she would cry.

The ride was mercifully short, and Derek was hardly out of his car before he asked where he could find Ben.

"He's up in his room, second floor. Delilah is with him," Jan responded, climbing out of the low sports car, her feet aching.

Benjie was rolling around in his narrow bed, groaning with pain and biting his lip against crying out. When he saw Derek, his face lit up a bit and he tried to smile.

"It looks like you're having a problem," Derek said quietly, the low sound of his voice instilling confidence in both Benjie and Jan. "Jan, run a tub. Delilah, go to my car and get the bag out of the back seat and bring it here." Both women rushed off to do his bidding while Derek pushed up the little boys pajama legs. "You're going to feel this and it's going to hurt like the devil in the beginning. Can you handle it?" he asked as his strong hands massaged the boy's thin calf muscle.

Benjie dug his elbows into the mattress and gritted his teeth. "Boy, does that ever hurt."

"I know. Take a deep breath and let it out slowly. Count backwards from one hundred and make sure you don't miss any numbers. How's the water coming?" he called out to Jan.

"It's ready," Jan called, testing the water for just the right temperature.

"Good, I'll put him in the tub, and when your cook brings my bag in, take the jar of yellow ointment and warm it in a saucepan." Derek came to the bathroom door, his blue eyes serious and his tone very low and deep. "We have a tough night ahead of us Jan. It's going to be rough for Ben. We can do it, can't we?"

Jan looked up into his eyes. Derek instilled such confidence, such a positive attitude, it was little wonder that Benjie adored him. And the way he had said "us." "We've" got a tough night ahead of "us" warmed Jan and made her feel as though she wasn't alone.

Derek went back into the bedroom for Benjie and lifted him from the bed. "Hey, Jan," he called, just as she was about to head for the kitchen, "do you think you can change your clothes? When I was Ben's age, I wasn't allowed to have a pet, a real pet. So my parents compromised and let me have a turtle. I hated that turtle. I still hate turtles."

"What happened to it?" Benjie asked inquisitively as Derek lowered him into the tub.

"You won't believe this, but that turtle lived for twenty years," Derek replied before breaking into the misadventures of himself as a young boy and his detested turtle, who seemed to have no other purpose in life except to torment the young Derek. Jan could see him bent over the tub, rubbing Benjie's thin legs. A smile played about the corners of her mouth as she reached for her jeans and a pullover. She could change in the kitchen while the ointment was heating. She suspected she understood why Derek had wanted her to change out of the thin, silky, clinging pajamas.

All through the night Jan and Derek took turns massaging Benjie's legs. It was eight o'clock when Benjie was finally dressed in clean pajamas and sound asleep. Jan's arms ached as well as her head. She smiled wanly to Derek who put his arm around her shoulder.

"You did okay, Jan. Ben will be fine now. But the cramps will come again. It's part of the healing process. When they do, call me. I'll come over."

"You must be tired," Jan said. "Would you like some breakfast?"

"I thought you'd never ask. I'd like the biggest and best breakfast Delilah can dish up."

"Then that's exactly what you'll have. Let's let Delilah surprise us.''

Jan enjoyed watching Derek make a path through the bacon and eggs and weave his way through a stack of blueberry pancakes. She picked at her food, exhausted by the trials of the night. And into her head popped a vision of Andrea in her wispy black nightie. "I'm sorry if I interrupted your…your morning. As I told you, your phone was off the hook."

Derek frowned. "Sometimes Andrea is very careless. It won't happen again."

Jan was silent and sipped her coffee. What had she expected him to say? Benjie had already informed her that Andrea was living with Derek.

"Has Ben asked you about the picnic in Rattlesnake Canyon?"

Jan laughed. "In a manner of speaking. He said I was invited if I brought the food."

"Well?"

Suddenly uncomfortable under his scrutiny, Jan nodded.

"Just don't make peanut butter sandwiches. I hate them. Almost as much as I hate turtles," Derek said as he strode through the lobby.

"I'll remember that," Jan said, making a mental note to burn those pajamas the first chance she got. The second thing she would do was throw out all the peanut butter and jelly in the kitchen. It was a good thing Derek Bannon hadn't told her to jump from a second story window. She must be out of her mind!

Chapter Eight

Benjie's excitement was contagious; he was excited over the promised picnic with Derek Bannon. In spite of herself and her own confusion concerning Derek, Jan found she had to smile and was actually anticipating the day just as Benjie was. There wasn't any need to fool herself about Derek any longer. The few kisses had meant nothing to him, and she had to take the cue and not allow these strange emotions he aroused in her to take such importance in her life. Derek was probably sowing the last of his wild oats before he married Andrea. If she were fool enough to let him kiss her and fool enough to suppose—no, hope—that it meant anything to him, then she deserved whatever came her way.

It had taken a great deal of reflection and hard thinking to come to terms with how she felt about Derek Bannon. Now, after pondering the logic of it all, she knew that she had to accept the fact that she meant nothing at all to him. All the emotions were on her part. It was difficult to come to grips with something like that, but Jan resolved that when Derek married Andrea she wouldn't be left with a broken heart. Whatever it took to defend herself against the wonderful and stirring things he did to her whenever he was near, she would do it.

Jan busied herself in Delilah's kitchen under the little woman's watchful eye. Carefully, she packed the picnic basket with a wide assortment of food that had taken quite awhile for her to prepare. It was the usual kind of picnic food that she and Benjie always enjoyed. If it didn't meet with Derek's gourmet palate, then that was his problem. If she had to torment herself by going on this picnic, she was at least going to enjoy what she would eat.

A sudden disconcerting thought occurred to Jan. What if Derek had invited Andrea to go along with them? Jan groaned and snapped the lid of the picnic hamper closed. She could almost see the beautiful girl wrinkle her nose at the hard-boiled eggs and paper napkins. And fried chicken! In those perfectly manicured hands! Gracious.

What did Derek see in Andrea? It was true she was beautiful and glamorous and dressed like a fashion model, but she certainly didn't rain affection down upon Derek. And at the testimonial dinner she had actually had the gall to flirt and hold hands with Dusty Baker under the table. And what kind of friend was Dusty Baker to play around with Derek's fiancée? It was all too much. Jan decided she had heard of the jet set and that they played by a different set of rules, but she didn't have to like it and knew she could never be a part of it. Some small voice echoed: But you already are. You let Derek kiss you and stir up all those strange, yearning emotions. You're no better than Dusty Baker or Andrea or even Derek.

"Well, not any longer," Jan spoke aloud without realizing it. "Derek Bannon's kissing days are over," she said tartly, puzzling Delilah, who watched her as she marched out of the kitchen toting the heavily laden picnic basket.

"Here he comes, Jan," Benjie cried excitedly. "Right on time. Derek is right on time all the time. He says punctuality is the mark of a successful man. He's not like you, Jan. You're always late. Andrea is always late, too. Derek says she has to change her clothing six times before she makes a decision. I told Derek you don't do that, but you look in the mirror a lot, and he said, 'Same difference.'" Benjie babbled happily as Derek climbed from the car.

"Is everyone ready?" Jan strained her eyes into the bright sun to see if there were any other passengers in the high-axled four-wheel-drive station wagon. Maybe Derek got tired waiting for the sixth change and left without Andrea. Jan smiled. She would make an effort to be more punctual in the future. She lumped that thought into the same category as the turtles on her pajamas and throwing out the peanut butter and jelly. It was a stupid thought. It wouldn't make any difference what she did. Derek Bannon was getting married to someone else. And the thought was always with her that his deadline to sell the Rancho was bearing down on her with bared teeth. She felt a headache coming on and she knew that if she gave into it the day would be ruined for Benjie as well as herself. Why couldn't she just enjoy it for what it was and then forget about it? Because, she thought, as she watched Derek's broad back as he held the door for Benjie, I'm in love with him.

Derek moved to the side in time to see the flush creep up her cheeks. "You better bring a hat—this sun is brutal today." Jan walked back inside on trembling legs for the worn and battered Stetson she had confiscated from her uncle's belongings. She didn't like this feeling of being out of control and at some man's whim, and that's what it was. Why couldn't he look at her the way he looked at Andrea? Why couldn't he say nice things to her the way he said them to Benjie and Andrea? Why was he always so cool and mocking when he looked at her? Why should he be anything else? He was engaged to marry Andrea. He was definitely a male chauvinist like Neil. She squared her shoulders. Today she wouldn't let him get to her. She could be just as cool and just as mocking. The only difference was she would have to work at it, whereas with Derek Bannon it was a natural trait.

"Did you forget anything?" Derek asked casually, eyeing the picnic hamper.

"Gosh, no, Derek. Jan was up before the birds packing everything." Benjie grinned from his seat in the back of the car.

"Then I guess we're ready for a day in the desert. After you, Jan," he said, holding open the door. Jan nodded coolly and slid into the deep seat. Their eyes met as Derek moved to close the door. Jan felt the familiar flush and was the first to look away.

"Aren't we taking my chair, Derek?" Benjie asked anxiously.

Derek leaned over the back of the seat. "How would you manage it in the sand? If I thought you needed it, I would have put it in the trunk. I brought along a canvas chair and that spare set of crutches you leave at the Lasso. That should do it."

"If you say so," Benjie said happily, leaning back into the seat. "I'm ready if you are."

Jan, too, leaned back, determined to enjoy the drive into the desert. Somehow she managed to keep up her end of the conversation in a limited way, always aware of Derek's nearness. Each time his hand moved to the gear shift she thought he was going to touch her leg; instead, he shifted expertly, the muscles in his thighs tightening and relaxing as he let the clutch in and out. Her heart alternated between wild flutterings and heavy pounding. What was wrong with her? He had no right, she thought angrily, to have the power to make her feel this way, especially since he was soon to be married. Surely he knew she was attracted to him. Why did he insist on being with her and using Benjie as an excuse? Or was she the one who was using Benjie as an excuse?

"Penny for your thoughts," Derek said softly.

Startled, Jan turned from viewing the roadside and stared at Derek. She smiled sadly. "They were deep, dark, and dire, and I don't think you really want to hear them. Besides, I'd never let them go for a mere penny." Derek's eyes narrowed. He reached for the polished sunglasses on the visor and slid them on with one hand.

Jan sensed, rather than saw, the tightening of his shoulders. She grimaced as she turned to viewing the Arizona landscape. Benjie was chattering away and Derek was answering him. She was safe for a while longer before she had to contribute to the conversation. She should be thinking about what she was going to do when Derek's deadline to sell or not to sell the ranch was up. If she didn't sell out to him, she could be left with a white elephant. If she did manage to hold on and try to make a go of Rancho Arroyo, how could she live down the road from Derek Bannon and his wife, Andrea? She couldn't. There was no decision to be made. She wouldn't spoil the day for Benjie. She would tell Derek later, or tomorrow. She and Benjie would live in Phoenix until he completed his treatments at the center and then they would head back for New York. With the money from the sale of the Rancho, she wouldn't have to work so many hours to make ends meet. Somehow things would work out. The decision made to sell out to Derek, she felt drained, emotionally and physically. She risked another glance at Derek. He turned, his expression behind the polished glasses unreadable. She hoped he couldn't see the tears in her eyes. Impossible dreams were just that. Impossible dreams. This was reality and she had better learn to live with it.

The four-wheel drive station wagon bounced easily on its high axles, affording an overview of the land. Neither Benjie nor Jan had come so far into the desert before, and Derek obligingly pointed out the sights. Low hills stained a dusky purple because the sun hadn't risen sufficiently to illuminate them rose in the distance. Barrel cactus raised their thorny heads out of the hard-baked earth, and Derek made them laugh when he said he could imagine the plants with huge eyes staring out of their limbless bodies and watching the world go by.

Derek seemed to be looking for something as he slowed the vehicle and pulled over to the side of the road close to an outcropping of tall, spiky cactus. There among the thorns was the most beautiful pink flower Jan had ever seen. Derek explained it was a night-blooming cactus, and because the sun hadn't reached it yet, it was still open. The delicate pink petals moved slightly in the breeze, and Jan and Benjie watched, transfixed, as the sun slowly crept among the branches of the plant and the lovely flower closed upon itself.

Derek drove slowly, pointing out ferns and the different kinds of cactus and flowering bushes, explaining that when most people thought of the desert they thought of a barren waste. Nothing could have been further from the truth, Jan thought. Here was life and harmony. The hills dipped and gave way to the roads; mesquite and tumbleweed dusted the earth, and yuccas and boulders kept a companionable silence. And above it all was the sky, scrubbed and blue and relentless. In a few short weeks she had come to love the desert even more than she had loved the green mountains of upstate New York. And when she must leave Arizona, as she knew she must, she would remember and mourn.

"We're here," Derek announced, swinging the wagon into a driveway paved with gravel and cutting the engine.

"But this...where...I thought you said we were going to have a picnic in the desert," Jan said, looking around at the small adobe house with its red tiled roof that sat back from the driveway and was surrounded by lush foliage. "Where is this place?" she demanded, sensing a trick on Derek's part.

He laughed. "This is the desert. Ben's doctor Bob Rossi's idea of the desert. He calls it his oasis. How do you like it? There's a pool in the back, complete with a Jacuzzi for Ben. That's why I wanted to come here."

"How does he keep all the plants and trees? And roses!" Jan gasped.

"He was lucky and he tapped into an underground spring. Fantastic, isn't it? I've got the keys, if you want to go inside and freshen up."

"It's breathtaking! It rivals any garden back home," Jan said, climbing from the car, forgetting about Benjie as she examined first one colorful plant and then another. "And there's moss—I don't believe it!" she laughed, bending down to feel the velvety softness at her feet. "It's almost like back home with the trees and the roses! I can't believe the roses!"

"The place is for sale," Derek said quietly. "Bob Rossi is moving back to Rhode Island in October to open a clinic." Jan was too busy poking beneath the shrubbery to hear his words and missed Derek's sly wink in Benjie's direction.

The place was perfect and incredibly beautiful. Here was the majesty of the desert and the nostalgia of home. Here was the perfect blending of two opposite worlds, and she knew, without fail, that here she could be happy for the rest of her life.

"Where are we going to have the picnic? Are you going to carry Benjie? We should have brought his chair," she accused. "He could get around here," Jan said, motioning to the paved walkways.

Derek grinned and whistled sharply. A young boy of perhaps seventeen came around the side of the house leading a pony and cart. "Now if you had a choice, which would you prefer? A wheelchair or one of these?" Derek said, pointing at the pony cart.

"Oh, wow!" Benjie exclaimed as he peered out the car window. "Do I really get to ride in that?"

"All day, if you want. There's lots for you to explore. Nick will ride along with you on horseback to keep an eye on you. He'll be perfectly safe," Derek said sharply to Jan, who was about to protest.

Jan snapped her mouth shut and fumed. She hadn't been about to protest over Benjie's safety, but because it appeared that she was about to be left alone with Derek.

Nick lifted Benjie from the car and settled him comfortably in the pony cart. He handed the excited boy the reins and grinned down from his perch atop a tall roan horse. "The pony's name is Sally, and she works at two speeds. Slow and stop. Just hold the reins loosely, and she'll do all the work. I'll be right beside you."

"Gee whiz, this is great, isn't it, Jan? Boy, I wish I could ride a horse like you do." He looked up at Nick.

"If Doctor Rossi is taking care of you, you will. Five years ago I was sitting in that cart being pulled by a pony named Feather. If I can do it, so can you. Say *giddy-up* and Sally will take you wherever you want to go."

"Giddy-up, Sally," Benjie cried excitedly, his thin little hands shaking with the reins. Sally obediently trotted off.

"Hey, Nick," Derek shouted after them, "come back around noon and we'll have that picnic. I'm going to take Jan up into the hills to Prospector's Gap."

Nick signaled that he had heard and cantered beside the pony cart.

Derek grasped Jan's hand and led her around the house to the corral and barn. Two horses were already saddled and waiting.

As they rode side by side into the hills, Jan was once again aware of the beauty surrounding her. Derek pointed out a dry riverbed and said they were going to follow it into the hills, where she was certain to be surprised.

Long before they reached it, Jan could hear the joyous splash of water. The air became sweeter, more fragrant with greens, and lighter with moisture. As they rounded an outcropping of huge boulders, the sound of rushing water became louder. Eagerly, she dug her heels into her mount's flanks. When she saw it, she was overcome. Sunlight dazzled her and reflected off the waterfall in a crown of jewels. The pool into which the waterfall emptied played in the sunlight and winked back at the sun like a million Christmas tree lights.

Derek held back, watching the delight dance across Jan's features. There was no need for words; it was all there to be seen in her face. "You love the desert, don't you, Jan?"

"Oh, yes, I do. I never imagined that I would, but it's worked its magic on me."

"I wanted to bring you up here. It's one of my favorite places. Geologists say this used to be a rushing river that filled the whole valley. Now there's only this waterfall, which is fed by the underground springs and empties into the pool. The pool feeds that little brook, and I've heard it said that the brook weaves its way across the desert and all the way south to the Rio Grande."

Jan was mesmerized, and it was with regret that she followed Derek back down the hills to Bob Rossi's house. Time had flown, and Nick and Benjie were returning for the picnic. Derek turned the mounts over to Nick, who took them back to the corral to water them. He lifted Benjie's crutches out of the trunk space and help the boy down from the pony cart, positioning the crutches under his arms.

"Think you can make it, buddy?"

"Yeah, sure, Derek," Benjie answered. "Just lead me to the food! I'm starving!"

Around the back of the house was the swimming pool and a patio complete with picnic table and benches. After lunch they rested in the shade of the awning over the patio in companionable silence.

When Benjie began getting fidgety, Derek suggested Nick take him into the house and help him get into bathing trunks so he could benefit from the Jacuzzi.

While Nick and Benjie played a limited game of water polo with a giant beach ball, Jan and Derek prowled through the house. If possible, the house was lovelier on the inside than outside. The ceilings were high, allowing the hot desert heat to rise, leaving the cooler air below. Rafters and heavy beams were left exposed, and between them was plaster, roughened and swirled. The floors were red tiles and accented by frequent use of area rugs in wonderful patterns.

The house itself was larger than Jan had expected. Four bedrooms, den, living room, kitchen, dining room—each decorated uniquely and lovingly. "If I had a lot of money and didn't know what to do with it, I'd buy this place and live here forever and ever. I could paint and cook and just plain love it."

Derek smiled. "You really like it? You don't think it's too remote?"

"It wasn't too remote for Dr. Rossi, and he had to go into Phoenix every day. But I'm only dreaming—where would I ever get that
kind of money? And even if it were possible, where would Ben go
to school?"

"It's not as remote as you think," Derek explained. "This is
even closer to Phoenix than the Rancho or the Golden Lasso. I have
to confess, on the drive out this morning I took the long way around,
using secondary roads. I thought you and Ben would enjoy an early
morning ride. I could see you were nervous and tense when I picked
you up; I thought the ride would relax you."

"That it did. I used the time to straighten a lot of things out in
my head," Jan laughed merrily as Derek led her out onto the patio
again.

"I'm glad, Jan." Derek looked off to the pool, where Nick and
Benjie were having a rousing good time. "I'd better water and feed
the pony, Sally. Nick has spent his whole day with Ben and probably hasn't done it yet. Want to give me a hand?"

Jan followed Derek around to the barn, where the cool shadows
and fragrant straw beckoned them in from the bright sunshine.

Derek unhitched Sally and watered her. As she drank, he picked
up a curry comb and smoothed the coat on Sally's flanks. Jan
watched Derek's hands move over the animal in sure and gentle
strokes. For a fleeting moment, she imagined the feel of Derek's
hands on her own flesh and felt herself blush.

"I hope you have room for Sally and her little cart in your barn,
Jan. I intend to make a gift of her to Ben."

Everything inside of Jan railed against Derek Bannon. This would
be one more thing she would owe him. She could never have given
Benjie a surprise like owning Sally—never in her whole life. And
when she sold out the Rancho to Derek Bannon and eventually went
back to New York, what then? He had made himself a part of
Benjie's life, and she would have to cut him out. And he would
have to leave Sally behind, too. She would be the bad guy in
Benjie's eyes and he would never, ever forgive her.

Adrenaline shot through her and she became more angry than she
had ever been in her entire life. She backed off a step and looked
measuringly at Derek Bannon. "You are the cruelest man I've ever
met, and I hate you for it!" she hissed. "I know what you're doing,
and I'm the one who'll pay the price. I can never do the things
you've done for Benjie. How could you do this? He's just a little
boy and he loves you like a brother and he trusts you. When I take

him back to New York, I'll be tearing his heart out. You're thoughtless and insidious and I hate you!"

"New York? You're taking Ben back to New York? Why? He's
doing so well with his therapy..."

"Yes, back home," Jan snapped. "I've decided to sell you the
Rancho at the end of your deadline. August first. And when I do,
what do you think I'm going to do? Pitch a tent? Isn't this what
you've intended from the very beginning? Well, you can have the
ranch—for your original offer, not a penny more. I don't want anything from you, Derek Bannon. But," she said, pushing a finger
into his chest, her eyes spewing fire, "you're the one who's going
to tell Benjie, not me. I almost thought you were different there for
a while, but you're not. You're a user, Derek, and you prey on
women and little children. So buzz off, Derek Bannon, and leave
me and my brother alone," Jan cried, the tears running down her
cheeks.

"Jan..." She paid him no heed, turning on her heel to head out
of the barn. He caught at her arm and pulled backward. "Wait...you
don't understand..."

"I understand, all right. I understand more than you think. Get
away from me you...you...Arizona gigolo," she shouted, pulling
herself free.

She nearly escaped him, thought she had, and the door to the
barn was within reach, when she felt her ankles being swept out
from under her and fell backward into a stack of hay in one of the
stalls.

"Gigolo!" Derek shouted in rage, wrestling her onto her back
and staring down into her face. "Of all the stupid, stubborn
women..."

"That's it. Call me stupid. Well, I'm not stupid. I saw right
through you from the beginning. You're stupid for what you're
trying to do to my little brother! I'm one thing, but don't mess with
Benjie. He loves you, and when I have to take him away he's going
to be heartbroken."

Derek held her firmly, pressing her back into the fragrant straw,
a wry smile playing about his mouth. "And does his sister love
me?" he asked quietly.

"Love you!" she spit out. "I hate you! I wish I had never set
eyes on you. You're disgusting. What kind of man are you anyway?
I've seen the way you treat Andrea and here you are trying
to...to..."

"Seduce you?" he asked, laughing, pressing his full weight on
her to control her strugglings.

"Go away—leave me alone. But I'm warning you—I'm going to steal a page from your book and do as you suggested. You said I should let Benjie accept whatever life has in store for him. When he's devastated because of all this, I'll let him know exactly how you are. How dare you laugh at me?" Jan cried, gulping back the tears for a second time. "I'm warning you, get away from me," she said through clenched teeth as she was paralyzed into immobility as she watched Derek lean closer, holding her tighter, squeezing her between the haystack and himself.

"I mean it, get away from me. This is the last time I'm going to tell you…I'll scream." He lowered his head and covered her mouth with his.

There was no escaping him. He held her roughly, molding her body to his. Jan summoned all her determination to speak. "Leave me alone," she gasped as he lifted his mouth from hers. Her voice came out thin and weak—hardly the strong emotional statement that she had made to him a moment ago. But that was before he was looking at her as he was now. Before he had trapped her in his embrace and held her against him. So close, so very close.

Derek looked down at her and the world was in his eyes. Tenderly, he touched his finger to her chin, lifting her face to his. A tear slowly traced along her cheek, and he brushed it away. "You're trembling. Do I make you tremble, Jan?" His voice was soft and gentle, belying the strength in his arms. The sound of her name on his lips, the way he said it, sent a stirring through her veins. "Why do you think I'm such a dragon?" As if he hadn't expected her to answer, he pressed her head to his chest and held her, quieting her, soothing her, as though she were a wild colt.

Once again his finger tipped her face to his and he covered her mouth with his own, bringing her back in close contact with his lean, tall frame. Jan felt the hard, manly boldness of him, and she closed her eyes as his searing lips traced feathery patterns over her face and throat. His hands caressed her, leisurely arousing in her a varicolored array of emotions.

A warm, tingling tide of excitement and desire washed through her. Her mind whirled giddily and a soft sigh escaped her lips as she welcomed his kiss. Her trembling lips softened and parted as his mouth possessed hers. Her arms came around his back, aware of his strength and masculinity, and they held each other, offering to one another and blending together like forged steel. Their kisses became fierce and hungry, making them breathless.

Jan fought against the chaos in her mind. She should be fighting him, running away from him, raking her nails across his arrogant face. Instead, she lay back in his arms returning his kisses, bending her body against his, loving the touch of his mouth on hers, the touch of his hands on her neck, her throat, her breasts.

Clasping her tightly to him, as though he would draw her into himself, Jan felt the thunderous beating of his heart while her own pounded a new and rapid rhythm.

Their moment became an eternity before Derek loosened his hold on her. His eyes held her softly, with tenderness, and when he spoke, his voice was thick with emotion and husky with desire. "I'm not such a dragon, Jan. And I don't breathe fire on little boys or on their beautiful sisters."

Jan turned away, not able to bear the hurt she saw in Derek's eyes. She had hurt him cruelly when she had accused him of using Benjie.

Suddenly, as though a curtain had dropped between them, Derek regained his composure and usual cool tone. "I didn't mean for this to happen. I didn't want anything to spoil Ben's day."

Jan nodded in agreement, not able to face Derek. Benjie had been looking forward to this picnic, and the day was almost at an end. She didn't want to spoil it for him now any more than Derek did. He helped her to her feet and began to brush the hay from her back.

"I won't mention the pony to Ben. Perhaps you're right—I was being thoughtless." He took her arm and led her back to the patio, and Jan noticed a new, almost imperceptible possessiveness in the touch of his hand. And when he spoke to her the brittle tone of his anger was gone. While not exactly lighthearted, she heard herself reply in kind and she began to relax. Derek was as good as his word. Benjie's day wouldn't be spoiled by hidden currents of bitterness between them.

For the remainder of the day, Jan remembered the taste of his mouth on hers and the strange and wonderful emotions she had experienced in his arms. She basked in Derek's attention and reveled in the sound of Benjie's laughter. And at the end of the day, when they loaded into the car for the drive home, she was saddened that it had come to an end.

As Derek drove them home in the deepening twilight, Jan rested her head back against the seat and relived the moments she had shared in Derek's arms, and she knew with certainty that she would remember this day always.

Chapter Nine

Jan woke with a throbbing headache, knowing that the day was somehow going to bring disaster; she could feel it, sense it in every pore of her body. She felt drained as she swung her legs over the side of the bed. Drained and foolish. How could she have allowed Derek Bannon to do the thing he did—to kiss her like that, to touch her that way? She had behaved terribly, giving in to her emotions like some wanton hussy. "Oh, heaven," she cried, "how could I allow myself to..." It was over and done with. From this moment on she would make sure she was never within a mile of him. She would let an attorney handle the sale of Rancho Arroyo, and she would never have to come in contact with him again. At the end of the month she would be back in New York and all of this would be behind her. A brief interlude in her life—no more and no less. She could do it; she had no other choice. If she had to, she would work day and night, twenty-four hours a day to make up to Benjie the loss he was going to feel when Derek Bannon was no longer around to serve as a big brother to him. Surely the little boy would understand—or would he?

The cold, bracing shower helped a little in brightening her spirits and so did the bright tangerine pullover. However, Delilah's gloomy countenance in the kitchen dampened her fledgling spirits. "Don't spare me—just tell me what's wrong," Jan muttered as she sat down at the wide, butcher-block table with a cup of coffee.

Delilah stood with her hands on her ample hips, her dark eyes sad and gloomy. "Is bad. Freezer ruin all food—Gus throw out now."

"What?" Jan exploded, knocking her coffee cup onto the pol-

ished floor. "How could the freezer be broken? And what happened
to the emergency generator? It can't be broken; the food can't be
spoiled—it just can't be. Tonight is the going-away party for our
guests. Are you sure, Delilah?"

"Yes, the fuses blew. No power all night. You have to cancel
party. Or you go to town and buy more food. Guests expect big
wing ding; you promise on brochure. Everybody dress up and have
good time. No good time," she said, shaking her black braids.
"You have big problem."

The sound of Benjie's chair caught Jan's attention, and she immediately began to pour cereal into a bowl. Her hand trembled and
she dropped the spoon as she set the dish in front of Benjie. He
waited patiently for another moment and then gulped the sugary
flakes as if he was in a hurry. "Why don't you call Derek and ask
him if the guests can have dinner at the Golden Lasso? He told me
he always keeps six tables in reserve for special guests. Do you
want me to ask him?"

Jan stared at the little boy without seeing him. It was a solution.
But where was she to get the money to pay for the night's entertainment? "No, don't ask him. I'll think about it. Is Dusty Baker
taking you to the hospital or is Derek doing the driving?"

"I never know. Whoever shows up," Benjie said blithely as he
put the chair in motion. "I'll see you this afternoon."

"Okay, Benjie. Have a good day." Jan sighed. It was the perfect
solution, if Derek agreed. Maybe there would be some advance
reservation checks in the mail, and she could make some kind of
deal with him. And you weren't going to go within a mile of him,
a niggling voice harassed. Sometimes we all have to do things we
don't want to do, she answered herself.

By late morning the mail had arrived with a fifty-dollar check
for a deposit for a family of three due to arrive in three weeks. She
wouldn't be able to get inside the door of the Golden Lasso for
fifty dollars. Could she lay her pride on the line and ask Derek
Bannon for credit until the sale of the ranch went through? Oh, she
could ask him, and he would look at her with those mocking eyes
of his and be very gracious, not to mention condescending, and say,
yes, of course, he would help her out. He'd probably take it one
step further and pick up the tab himself, compliments of the Golden
Lasso. She didn't need his charity and she didn't want it. But the
guests—what was she to do?

Delilah was hovering, making Jan jittery to the point of explod-
ing. "When you make phone call to Golden Lasso?" Delilah demanded. "Is late."

"Look, if I go to the guests and explain the situation, maybe they'll understand. I can offer them a refund at some future date," Jan said, grasping at straws.

"*Tsk, tsk, tsk.*" Delilah clucked her tongue. "You no understand. No food for any kind of dinner. They pay and want to eat. You want guests to go to bed hungry? *Tsk, tsk, tsk.*"

Jan was outraged. "Are you telling me there's no food at all? Nothing! What about the refrigerator?"

"Wienies," Delilah said curtly. "We have one string of wienies. The rest is what we serve for breakfast."

Jan stared at the cook and trudged dejectedly to the office. There were no options, no choices. She would have to call Derek Bannon and plead her case. Each time she reached for the phone she withdrew her hand, and then the sound of the children in the pool stiffened her spine, and she would again reach for the phone, only to draw away. Thank heaven the guests were leaving, and the new batch wasn't due to arrive till Sunday. Instead of sitting here like some ninny, she should be making calls, canceling the other reservations. She couldn't put it off any longer. She had just dialed the first three digits of the Golden Lasso when Delilah ran into the office. "You come see. Now. *Tsk, tsk, tsk,*" she said turning and waddling back to the kitchen.

"Oh, please let there be water." What *else* could it be. Everything that could possibly go wrong had gone wrong. When she walked into the kitchen, there was food everywhere, packed in ice. Good enough for an army. "Where, who...how..." she said to a broad-shouldered man hefting a heavy carton.

"You Jan Warren?" At Jan's nod he handed her a slip of paper. Tears burned her eyes as she scanned the brief, curt note. "Ben explained. Call this Arizona hospitality or, if you prefer, one businessman helping another." It was signed simply: DEREK BANNON. Darn! He must want something in return. Her ranch. No, she had already told him she was going to sell it to him. Protecting his investment ahead of time, that's what he was doing. And humiliating her in the bargain. She would have felt better if she had asked and arranged the terms. This made it sound like a gift—charity, for want of a better word. She didn't need his charity or want it. Yet she had to accept it. And she had to call him and acknowledge his generous help. That was going to be harder to do than asking for his help the way she had originally intended. When it came to Derek Bannon, she was always on the receiving end of things.

Jan thanked the delivery men and started to help Delilah stack the meats into the large kitchen refrigerator. Delilah was right—

there was enough for an army. Evidently the illustrious Derek Bannon didn't want her weak from hunger when it came to signing on the dotted line. She hated herself for such opinions but didn't seem able to control her thoughts when it came to the owner of the Golden Lasso.

As soon as the cartons were emptied, Jan left the kitchen, needing no further reminders of Derek Bannon and wanting no more confrontations with her emotions. Perhaps a ride would clear away her headache—if not clear it away, at least reduce it to a dull ache. Delilah had things under control; Benjie wouldn't return for another three hours. She was more or less on her own. Gus was seeing to the freezer, and all the guests were doing their thing. She shook her head as she saddled Soochie and admitted to herself that she didn't like the feeling of not being needed. Everyone deserved to be needed. Why should she be any different?

Tugging on the reins lightly, she let Soochie have her head. The golden animal reared once and then headed for the open. Jan sat the horse with ease, reveling in the hot breeze the galloping animal created. She felt free, more free than she had felt since coming to Arizona. She rode for what seemed like hours before dismounting. She withdrew two apples from her saddle bags, gave one to the horse, and started to munch on the other.

She felt so tired and yet she had done nothing really physical since coming to this beautiful state. Mentally tired, she corrected herself. How terrible to be in love and not be able to do anything about it. It was such a devastating feeling. How could you love someone so much and not have the other person love you? Tears gathered and she wiped at them with the back of her hand. That was another thing—she had to stop this senseless weeping and wailing every time she thought of Derek Bannon. Crying never solved anything. All it did was give you the hiccups and red-rimmed eyes. She fixed her watery gaze on the quiet horse and muttered, "Emotionally, I can't afford you, Derek Bannon."

The hot Arizona sun, along with the horse's quiet grazing made Jan drowsy. The past day's tensions evaporated as she fell into a deep, restful sleep. She neither saw nor heard Soochie as she trotted off on her own to explore the terrain.

Jan woke, stiff and disoriented, from her sound sleep to see darkness falling. What happened? she wondered wildly as she struggled to her feet. She rubbed grit from her eyes, and gradually her eyes became accustomed to the indigo shadows around her. It took her seconds to realize Soochie was gone. She whistled and called the mare to no avail. How far had she come? She had ridden for over two hours and an hour of that had been fast, hard riding. To go it on foot, providing she didn't get lost in the darkness, would take her more hours than she could stand. The blisters on her feet were not healed sufficiently to make the long trek back even if she were wearing rubber-soled canvas sneakers. What time was it? How long had she slept? Surely by now somebody should be looking for her. When she didn't show up for the guests' farewell party, someone would start wondering about her whereabouts. Benjie. Benjie would worry and call Derek. But they didn't know which way she had come. All they would know was that Soochie was gone.

She couldn't sit here all night and do nothing. She had to move. She had to try to find her way back on her own. How could she have been such a fool as to let the animal graze and not tether it? Why did she always have to learn her lessons the hard way? She wasn't going to find any answers sitting here.

She started out, her head high and her shoulders straight. She trudged for hours under the full moon, wishing a tall, blue-eyed man named Derek Bannon would swoop down on her and carry her back to the ranch. She sighed wearily. At this point she would settle for Gus and a painted wagon. She was tired! She had to keep going and not think. One foot in front of the other, over and over. The blisters on the backs of her heels were sore and running. Disgustedly, she removed the offending sneakers and hurled them into the darkness. The moment she did she was sorry. Alone and lost in the desert was bad enough. Barefoot, it was intolerable.

Twice within minutes she stumbled and fell. She managed to get to her feet and start walking, only to fall into a crumpled heap. Bitter tears of frustration rolled down her cheeks. She couldn't give in, not now. The highway must be close. A while ago she thought she had heard the engine of a car, but it was too dark to see anything with the moon sliding behind a giant cloud cover.

It was the feel of the macadam road on her sore, bare feet that told her she had finally found a road. Where it was, she had no idea. She shivered violently as she tumbled down the road. She prayed silently that she was going in the right direction.

Jan raised her eyes and for the first time was aware that dawn was fast approaching. She had been stumbling along with her head down and her eyes closed. Now she would be able to see where she was. Hopefully, a car would come along and offer her a ride.

Jan heard a car and teetered on her feet in an effort to steady herself. She was so tired and numb from the night air that she fell, skinning her hands and knees. Angry beyond belief, she pummeled the road with her clenched, bleeding hands. Why wasn't someone helping her? She had to get up and walk. The car—it was stopping. "Please, don't let it be a mugger," she gasped.

The voice was angry and... What was that in the tone that reminded her of her father? Who cared? She was picked up in strong arms and carried like a baby. That was okay—she felt like a baby with the tears running down her face. She knew she was safe; she could feel it even if the voice was chastising her.

"You aren't safe to let loose, do you know that?" the voice was saying over and over. "Half the state is out looking for you. How could you be so thoughtless, so careless, and for heaven's sake, don't you care about that little boy back at the ranch who is crying his eyes out over you?" And then the arms tightened around her.

She burrowed her head in his chest and muttered. "I care, I really do. I knew you'd find me. I want to go home—my feet hurt." And then she was asleep.

Derek gently lowered the sleeping Jan into the depths of the bucket seat. A smile played around his mouth as he watched her curl into a ball and then sigh. He fastened her seat belt securely and climbed behind the wheel. Before he fastened his own seat belt he bent over and touched Jan's tousled hair. He kissed her lightly on the mouth and heard her murmur in her sleep, "I knew you'd find me." He whistled softly as he slid in the clutch and headed back toward Rancho Arroyo.

Chapter Ten

Leaning back against a nest of pillows, Jan contemplated first the gray, overcast day through her window and then her bandaged feet, which were propped up with cushions at the foot of her bed. She had been guilty of some foolish moves in her life, but getting lost and trekking through the desert all night long was, without a doubt, the most stupid to date. What did Derek Bannon think of her now? She moaned. He had been so angry with her, so upset with her stupidity. And then her falling into his arms with such abandoned relief! Jan cringed and tried to make herself invisible by hiding under the bedcovers. She couldn't hide from what she had done any more than she could forget what a fool she was. It was over, done, and she was safe once again in her own bed with a cup of black rum tea at her elbow.

"Tsk, tsk, tsk..." Delilah muttered as she waddled into the room to check on her impatient patient. Deftly, she replaced Jan's bandaged feet on the cushion and ordered her to remain in bed. "You have a visitor in the lobby. I bring him to see you—you don't get out of bed," she ordered as she exited into the hallway.

"No! Wait! I don't want... Oh...I don't want to see Derek," Jan yelped. "Can't you see I'm a mess? Just look at me! Delilah, please, don't bring him up here. Look at this...this...thing I'm wearing," Jan wailed, pointing to her oversized football jersey with the number 77 printed across the chest. "Delilahhhh!" she pleaded.

Delilah looked back and shrugged. "So, you number seventy-seven on list. Is funny nightgown but not my business," she shrugged again. "Your visitor not Mr. Bannon but lady in tight pants. I bring her tea and maybe cookies."

Jan's curiosity suddenly peaked. "What lady in tight pants? Are you sure it isn't Derek and you're only teasing me?"

"I sorry you disappointed, but I know lady when I see one. You want to see Mr. Bannon, I call Golden Lasso and tell him," Delilah clucked as she closed the door behind her.

Jan settled back against the pillows, her pretty features turned down into a frown. The visitor had to be Andrea—who else could it be? Beautiful, stunning Andrea. Jan slid beneath the covers and pulled them to her chin. She'd die before she allowed Andrea to see the football jersey that doubled for a nightgown, especially since she had seen the cloud of black lace that was part of Andrea's wardrobe. Darn! Why did these things always happen to her?

A cautious knock on the door alerted Jan to Andrea's approach. "Come in," she called weakly.

"I came as soon as Derek told me what happened. I'm so sorry about what happened to you last night. You must have been frightened to death. Do you have any idea how lucky you are that Derek found you? You could still be out there wandering. It was foolish, Jan, and it could have been a fatal accident. I hope you're more careful in the future."

Jan was puzzled. Andrea sounded so sincere, so concerned. Would she still sound that way if she knew that Jan, too, was in love with Derek? Not likely. "I realize what a fool I was, and you don't have to worry about me doing such a stupid thing again. I really did learn my lesson." In spite of herself, Jan found that she was warming to Andrea's sincere concern.

"We were all concerned about you. Especially your little brother. I can't tell you what the little guy went through when Derek had to tell him that they couldn't search for you during the night. You put Ben through a lot of anguish with your foolishness. Please." Andrea held up her hand to stifle Jan's protests. "I saw Ben and what he went through. He's told me about the accident that took your parents, and all he could think of was that something had happened to you, too! That was unfair, Jan, and Derek and I hope you'll take Ben's feelings into consideration in the future."

Jan bristled and she felt as though the hair at the nape of her neck was standing on end. How dare Andrea? How dare Derek? Who did they think they were? As if she had planned her bad luck the night before just to put Benjie through a bad time. If there was anyone in this world who could get Jan's back up, it was Derek Bannon and Andrea.

"This is hardly any of your business," Jan growled, her face stiffening into hard lines of anger.

"You're wrong, Jan. It is my business and Derek's too. We care about you and we love Ben." Exasperated, Andrea emitted a deep sigh. "Look, Jan, I didn't come here to stage an argument. I'd like us to be friends because we're neighbors, and we're so close in age a friendship would seem natural. But it's evident you aren't interested in my friendship, and I'm truly sorry for that. Derek's been pleading me to come over here and get to know you better. I tried to tell him you seemed less than receptive to the idea, and this will prove to him that I was right. However, just so my trip isn't wasted, I'd like to invite you and Ben to my wedding. It's the last Saturday in July. In the gardens at the Golden Lasso. I hope you'll put aside your hostility for me and bring Ben. I really want both of you to attend."

Jan couldn't believe what she was hearing. Derek had pleaded with Andrea to come over and try to be friends? After the times he had taken her in his arms, the way he had kissed her? He wanted her to be friends with his wife-to-be? Jan realized she was glaring at Andrea, who had turned her face away rather than subject herself to Jan's open hostility.

"Take care of yourself, Jan. Blisters can be a nasty problem. If there's anything I can do for you—"

Jan had turned her head away.

"I see. I don't know what I've done to make you feel this way about me, Jan. And I'm sorry." Not waiting for a reply, Andrea turned and left the room.

Jan sat and stewed until Delilah came back into her room. "Delilah. Do you know what she wanted?" Jan sputtered. "She had the gall to come here and rail me out for what happened last night. She told me what anguish I put Benjie through—as though I'd planned it! As though I wanted to scare the life out of him! And then, after telling me how stupid I was, she had the nerve to invite me to her wedding! Even after blaming me for the fact that she and I aren't friends!"

"Reason you're not friends is your fault," Delilah said calmly, puttering around the room with a tired old dust rag and flicking the cloth haphazardly over the surface of the furniture. "Sometime you have face like cigar store Indian. Much frown, much anger. Me, I think sometimes you scared, so I still like you. Other people, they don't understand like Delilah."

"Is that what you think?" Jan challenged.

"How else to think? That you really one nasty person? No, I think you scared sometimes," Delilah answered matter-of-factly, seeming to concentrate on flicking the dust cloth between the bottles of hand cream and perfume that dotted Jan's dresser. "You tell her that you go to wedding?"

"I did not! Why should I want to go to *her* wedding? I don't care that Derek told her to come here and make friends with me! And I don't care to go to the wedding!"

"Oh, sure. You only care that they very nice to Benjie. You only care that Mr. Bannon take Benjie to hospital for treatments. You only care that he come here at night to take care of boy because you can't. I see," Delilah said offhandedly, still busying herself with straightening the room.

Desperate to justify her decision without revealing the true reason to Delilah, Jan persisted. "What kind of people are they anyway? I have every reason to believe that Andrea is living in sin with—with—her fiancé. Just because they're going to get married now, is that reason enough for me to condone what they're doing? And to bring Benjie to that wedding?"

"Is reason enough because Mr. Bannon is good to you. You think somebody live in sin? Big deal!" Delilah snorted, stuffing the dust cloth into her apron pocket and coming to stand at the bedside. Her hands were propped on her hips and her shoe-button eyes snapped with anger. "You look at me, I live 'in sin' with Gus for forty years. Is nothing wrong with me. Is nothing wrong with Gus. We get married, we have plenty wrong. He tell me what to do and I have to do it. Now we live in sin. When I tell him, 'Buzz off, you old Indian,' he listens. I marry him and he stick like fly to honey. Is good for some, is not good for others. You not judge other people, Miss Warren. I go get you something to eat. Later I give you advice."

Delilah left Jan alone in the room, and the hard sound of the closing door announced the woman's anger. Jan pummeled her pillows. Maybe she really was "one nasty person," as Delilah had said. But how could she go to the wedding and watch the man she loved marry someone else? What kind of people were they? What kind of man was Derek Bannon? There he was about to marry Andrea, and yet he seemed bent on seducing Jan. And Andrea—openly flirting with Dusty Baker at the testimonial dinner! And on the plane! What kind of marriage was Andrea going to have? Maybe they were planning on having one of those open marriages. Well, she wasn't going to get involved. Never! A fresh wave of tears drowned out her hiccups as she continued to pound her pillows with a vengeance.

Nearly an hour later, exhausted from her crying, Jan dried her eyes and sat up in bed to gulp some coffee from the breakfast tray

Delilah had set on her nightstand. The coffee was less than steaming, but it made little difference—she couldn't taste it anyway.

Within the past hour Jan had reached a decision. There was an old saying that when you were down and out the only way to go was up. Perhaps some people were cut out to be martyrs, but she wasn't one of them. People got married every day of the week; some of them lived happily ever after and some didn't. When she got married, if she ever did, she would live happily ever after because she wouldn't marry anyone who didn't love her as much as she loved him. How could that—that weasel kiss her until her teeth rattled and then go off and marry someone else? She sniffed and blew her nose with gusto.

The next step was to get out of bed—gingerly, of course—and hobble around and see to her business. Life didn't stop just because you were laid up in bed and were moaning about fate and the way the cards were being dealt. She would spend the rest of the day on the veranda at the back of the lodge with a tall glass of lemonade and the ledgers from her office. And she would try to force her thoughts to remember the finer details of the blue prints she had seen in Derek Bannon's apartment the night she had gotten him to help her with the sudden, terrifying cramps that had plagued Benjie. She had a right to know what Derek Bannon was planning for the Rancho Arroyo.

Climbing out of bed was less painful than she had imagined. Delilah's poultices were working their magic. She dressed in Levis and a colorful sleeveless blouse. Her feet were tender but not too painful, and she noticed the cane Delilah had brought for her so she wouldn't be putting her full weight on her blistered feet. Jan felt decrepit, old beyond her years, as she made her way down the stairs and through the lobby out to the veranda. Gratefully, she dropped into a wicker chair and winced with relief. She wasn't going to be doing much walking in the next few days, that was for sure.

By midafternoon Jan was certain of one thing. She was on the verge of bankruptcy. With the payment from the guests that were due within a few days, she would just be able to meet her expenses. That was providing nothing else went wrong.

Jan had just closed the last ledger when Delilah came to the door and motioned to the phone she was plugging into a jack on the veranda. "For you. They say they call from bank." Jan picked up the receiver, her heart leaping wildly.

"Janice Warren," she announced in her most businesslike tone.

"Miss Warren, this is Michael Davis at City Trust. The bank has approved your application for a loan using your house in New York as collateral. If you would care to stop by the bank sometime tomorrow, we can set the wheels in motion, and I can guarantee you'll have your money within ten days.''

"Why, thank you, Mr. Davis," Jan said coolly, fighting to keep her excitement from creeping into her voice. "I'll come by tomorrow afternoon."

She was solvent again, or would be in ten days. Now she didn't have to sell out to Derek Bannon, who seemed all too greedy for her land. She wouldn't have to go back to New York and lick her wounds. She could stay in Arizona and so could Benjie. And the first thing she was going to do was hire reliable help to get this business off the ground in the proper manner. She would take a few business courses at night in the off season and learn whatever there was to learn about managing a resort. With just one phone call her world was right side up again. If Derek Bannon would call and say he decided not to marry Andrea, her life would be perfect. She stared at the black phone, willing it to ring, willing it to be Derek.

When the instrument shrilled, Jan's heart almost jumped from her chest. It couldn't...it couldn't...it must be! "Hello," she said cautiously, breathlessly.

"It's Neil, Jan."

"Neil! What a nice surprise," Jan stuttered, regaining her composure. What a fool she was to think that her prayers would be answered and that the voice she would hear would be Derek's. "How nice of you to call," she choked into the receiver. "How are you? How's the house? Nothing wrong, is there?" she asked anxiously. Just what she would need. She could imagine the old house in New York burning to the ground and then the bank refusing her the loan.

"I'm fine," Neil answered in brisk tones. "And your house was fine when I saw it this morning. I'm not in New York, Jan. I'm here in Arizona. I decided I couldn't live without you and here I am. Tell me how to get to the ranch, and I'll soon be walking through your door."

Jan was stunned. Neil in Phoenix? He couldn't possibly have chosen a worse time to pay her a visit. "How...how nice," she said, trying for a light tone. "It's very simple. Take the Interstate east and watch for the signs about thirty miles out. They point the way to Rancho Arroyo and the Golden Lasso."

"Gotcha," Neil assured her. "Tell me you missed me as much as I missed you. I'm going to sweep you right off your ever-lovin' feet. You got that?"

"Yes, I heard you. Neil, you should have told me you were coming so I could have prepared," Jan said tartly.

"And spoil the surprise? No way! I knew you'd be eager to see me right about now. I purposely planned it this way. From now on I'm not letting you out of my sight. And look, Jan, do us both a favor and keep the kid out of sight for a while. We have a lot of catching up to do. By the way, how is the kid?" Neil asked as an afterthought.

Jan's jaw tightened. "If you mean Benjie, he's fine. He's making remarkable progress with his therapy. I thought I told you that in my letters."

"Great, just great. Remember now, I want to spend my time with you, not the kid. By the way, I quit my job. I'm going to help you out there at the ranch. I've decided we're a team and teams work together. See you in a little while."

Jan looked at the phone and winced. Team. He quit his job. He wanted to spend all his time with her. She shrugged. At least she'd have an escort to Andrea's wedding and wouldn't look like an unwanted old maid. Jan shook her head. What was wrong with her? Was she crazy? What did it matter whether or not she had an escort? To save face? What face? Derek Bannon certainly wouldn't be impressed; he'd be too busy with Andrea on their wedding day.

An hour later Jan watched from her chair on the veranda as Neil careened around the circular driveway on two wheels, finally bringing the rented Pinto automobile to a grinding halt. Jan shivered and frowned. What was wrong with Neil? Didn't he realize there may have been guests or children who could have been hurt by his reckless driving. Jan's frown deepened. She hadn't liked Neil's "surprise" visit, and the idea that he quit his job gave her cause for concern. What did he have on his mind? What was she going to do with him during his visit?

She watched with a kind of detached interest as Neil hopped from the car, resplendent in cowboy attire that some fast-talking salesman must have palmed off on him. No one dressed that way! Certainly no one here in Arizona. Perhaps on the backstage lot of a Hollywood studio Neil's outfit would have seemed natural, but certainly not here! Talk about Rhinestone Cowboys! Jan giggled as she likened Neil to a cross between Tom Mix and Gene Autry. If he said, "Howdy, pardner," she would laugh in his face.

Neil was up on the veranda, teetering on his high-heeled boots, before she could blink an eye, and he was sweeping her off her feet. "Howdy, pardner. What say we mosey out to the old corral and snatch a few quick kisses?"

"Neil, put me down! We don't have a corral, and we don't 'mosey' anywhere. We walk or we use the pickup. I'm not in the mood for kisses, quick or otherwise. You're behaving like Benjie. Now put me down!" she squealed.

"You haven't changed. I was just having a little fun," Neil said loudly. "I thought you'd be glad to see me."

"I am glad to see you, Neil. It's just that you're so exuberant. Sit down here—let's talk. What made you decide to come out here? Vacation?" she asked, mentally crossing her fingers. "What ever possessed you to quit your job? I thought you liked it! Who's looking after the house? You did make arrangements, didn't you?"

"Of course I did. My Aunt Mary is going to stop by there several times a week to check on things. As for my job, it was boring me to death, and all the challenge was gone. It was time to start looking around, so here I am. Why do I have the feeling you aren't happy to see me? I haven't seen you smile yet?"

Jan managed a wan smile for his benefit. "I guess I'm just a little tired. I've been working pretty hard lately, and I haven't had too much time to sit around and relax. We're taking a breather before another wave of guests descends on us. It's not easy running a dude ranch."

Neil rolled his eyes. "I saw the sign at the turnoff for that Golden Lasso. You never mentioned it in your letters. I'll bet it gives you a run for your money. It looks like a swinging place to me. Who owns it?"

"I do," said a voice from the screen door leading onto the veranda. Derek held the screen door open for Benjie and then stepped into the porch himself. Jan swallowed hard as she watched Benjie maneuver himself along on his crutches. The boy was looking in stark amazement at Neil, and it was apparent he wasn't pleased with Neil's turning up on the doorstep.

"Neil Connors," Neil said, introducing himself, holding out a too starkly white hand. Derek looked at the hand a moment and then covered it with his.

"Derek Bannon," Derek said curtly.

"Derek owns the Golden Lasso and the Bison football team," Benjie offered proudly, "and he introduced me to all the players. Dusty Baker is a good friend of mine, too."

"How are you, kid?" Neil asked, stepping over to and putting his arm around Benjie. The boy shrugged off his arm and moved out of Neil's reach. It was apparent Benjie wanted nothing to do with this interloper.

"Neil is a friend of mine from New York. He'll be staying with us for a while," Jan said softly, mostly for Benjie's benefit.

"We're engaged to be engaged, if you know what I mean," Neil said brashly, winking at Derek Bannon.

"Neil!" gasped Jan in exasperation. "We're not engaged!"

"Not right this minute, maybe, but we will be. Why do you think I came out here? You aren't getting away from me again. Nice meeting you, Banyon," Neil said jovially, as he took Jan's arm to lead her into the lobby.

"His name is Bannon, not Banyon," Benjie cried with a catch in his voice.

"See you tomorrow, Ben." Derek nodded in Jan's and Neil's direction and left the veranda, his back stiff and straight.

"Listen, little fella, it was rude of you to do that. Don't you ever correct your elders. And don't ever embarrass me like that again. You mind your manners and we'll get along just fine." Neil scolded through tight lips.

Benjie stared at Jan a moment and then headed for the kitchen and some of Delilah's cookies and buttermilk.

Jan's shoulders ached with tension. She should have defended Benjie right then and there, but somehow the words didn't come. The little boy had given her every opportunity to come to his defense and put Neil in his place and she had failed. Jan knew she had trouble and his name was Neil Connors.

"Who was that guy, anyway? What's he doing with your brother? Looks like one of those aces to me."

"He introduced himself to you. His name is Derek Bannon and he does own the Golden Lasso and the Bison team, just as Benjie told you," Jan retorted curtly. "I don't have to explain anything to you, Neil. Derek Bannon happens to be a very nice person. He's gone out of his way to take Benjie to the Phoenix Medical Center every day. Benjie is crazy about him."

"Yeah, and why are you so defensive of him?" Neil demanded, watching Jan very closely.

Jan hedged. "Am I? I told you, I think he's a very nice person, and he's been great with Benjie."

"Well, if he's been going out of his way to take the kid into the city for his treatments, I can relieve him of that chore right now. I'll take the kid from now on. That way you won't feel obligated to him."

"I don't feel obligated. He takes Benjie because he wants to take him. He offered—I didn't ask."

"I've seen guys like him before and believe me, they never do anything without a reason. Especially lugging some lame kid around. I'm a guy. I should know. You've always been such a babe in the woods, Jan. From now on just leave everything to me."

Jan turned in a fury and lashed out. "Don't you ever call Benjie a lame kid again. And I don't need you to tell me about men like Derek Bannon. Let it drop, Neil, before we say things to one another that we'll regret later. If you don't like Derek, keep your thoughts to yourself. Benjie likes him and so do I."

It was immediately apparent to Neil that he had overstepped the bounds in Jan's private life, a life that somehow involved Derek Bannon. "Okay, sorry if I offended you. If you and your brother like him, then I'm certain he's a great guy. End of matter, subject dropped." Neil grinned as he put his arm around her shoulder to draw her closer. "Look, how about a tour of the ranch?" Noticing her cane for the first time, he asked, "What's wrong?"

"My feet are a little tender. I've acquired some nasty blisters. It's not serious, just uncomfortable. I'll have Gus show you around and assign you a cabin."

"You mean I don't get to stay here in the lodge? That's where you stay, isn't it?" Neil leered.

"That's exactly what it means. Paying guests stay in the cabins. You *are* a paying guest, aren't you?" Jan challenged.

The leer vanished, replaced by a look of stunned surprise. He recovered quickly and grinned. "You didn't think I was going to freeload, did you?"

Again Jan hedged. "Can you ride, Neil?"

"I'm not an expert, but I've ridden the trails in New York the same as you. I think I can manage. Bring on your old Indian guide," he joked.

Jan turned and Gus was waiting patiently, just as he did everything. Benjie must have told the Indian about their new guest.

"Well, I'm ready if you are," Neil said, perching a ten-gallon hat on his head, covering his golden hair. He seemed uncomfortable with the hat, just as he seemed unfamiliar with the studded Western-cut shirt and narrow slacks that were stuffed into handsome Western boots that were too obviously new. Jan fought back a giggle at the ridiculous sight he made and even Gus turned his head. But not before Jan saw the wicked grin that ripped across the Indian's usually solemn visage.

Neil turned to follow Gus and then wheeled back toward Jan.

"You didn't say how you like my Western togs. What do you think?"

"Neil, I can truthfully say those are the fanciest duds I've yet to see around here."

"Thought you'd like them. See you later."

Delilah stood framed in the doorway to the kitchen. *"Tsk, tsk, tsk.* Your friend smell like vanilla pudding," she chirped.

"What do you think of him, Delilah?"

"I tell you, that man very pretty. Maybe turn some girls' heads, but not mine. That man not make me itch, he give me rash!"

Jan's giggle turned into helpless laughter, doubling her over. "He's not so bad when you get to know him," she gasped between bouts of hilarity.

"That why you laugh at friend?" Delilah said tartly as she shook her head, a perplexed expression on her face.

"Okay, okay, I shouldn't laugh, but he actually thinks that's the way cowboys dress. With bangles and beads. I can't help it. I think it's so funny!"

Delilah held her hands over her ample belly and joined in Jan's laughter. "I see but I not believe. First time I see Gus laugh in many years."

Jan dressed for dinner in a raspberry silk shirt and tan slacks. She added a belt of natural twine braid and stepped back to admire the effect. She wasn't going anywhere but to the dining room in the lodge so it didn't really matter how she looked. Neil never noticed other people's clothes, and right now he was overly impressed with his own flamboyant "togs," as he called them. Neil probably thought of himself as a dandy, but once the ranch hands got a look at him, they'd know him for what he was. A dude. A genuine, bona fide eastern dude.

How had Derek looked when he saw Neil on the veranda with her? Angry, amused, startled? He looked, she decided, as though he was barely controlling his anger. Serves him right, she mused. Did Derek really think no other man in the world could find her attractive? And when Neil had made that brash statement about them being engaged to be engaged, what was the expression that crossed his face then? Jealousy? Jan sighed. The probability of Derek being jealous of Neil was so farfetched as to be ridiculous. At this point in time it made little difference. Derek was getting married at the end of the month, and Neil was going to save the day by escorting her to that wedding. Afterward, she would tell Neil there was no hope of furthering their relationship as he had implied.

If there was one thing she knew, it was that she would rather end up an old maid than settle down with Neil Connors. It would be like driving a wedge between herself and Benjie. There was little to say about the relationship between Neil and her brother. There was no relationship. Period.

If it was a spinster she was meant to be, then a spinster it would be. A vision of herself rocking sedately at the age of eighty-five with nothing to carry her through the days but the old memories of Derek Bannon kissing her and the feelings he evoked in her was such a vivid picture she winced. She clenched her small hands into tight fists and brought them crashing down onto her dressing table. The pain was welcome. If she wasn't careful, she could end up a basket case with Delilah spoon-feeding her.

With the aid of her cane Jan made her way onto the veranda to wait for Neil. Benjie was already there, watching a small portable TV that Gus had rigged for him. The small boy turned to his sister and with a break in his voice asked, "How long is he staying?"

Jan ruffled Benjie's hair and smiled. "Not long. I want you to be polite. I can't force you to like Neil, but I want you to be courteous. He is our guest. What are you watching?"

"It's an environmental program that Derek told me to watch. He said he thought I might find it interesting. He's really smart, Jan. He knows what I like and what I don't like. I don't even have to tell him. He's a super guy. He never gets mad and he always explains things to me. He explains even when I don't ask him questions. He listens to me and he hears what I say."

"You really do like him, don't you?" Jan said softly.

"You bet I do. Derek is my friend. He said he'll always be my friend, no matter what happens. And I can always count on him. That makes him a good friend, doesn't it?"

"I'd say so," Jan replied quietly. No matter what happens—now what did Derek mean by that? Probably his marriage to Andrea.

"You don't like him as much as I do, I can tell," Benjie complained.

"I like him, Benjie. It's just that with me it's different than it is with you. You're a little boy, Derek is a man. He relates to you differently that he does to me. I'm a girl." She smiled.

"Derek says some women are wily and tricky, and they like to manipulate men. That means to wrap them around their fingers. I had to get Derek to explain that to me because I didn't understand. He said that some women—like you, Jan—aren't like that at all. He said it's something dumb women have to practice."

Jan flushed. So Derek thought she was dumb and she hadn't

practiced enough. Of all the insufferable, egotistical men, he took the prize. "Is that what he said?" Jan muttered through clenched teeth.

"Yeah. But Derek likes ladies. He said they make the world go round."

Jan gulped. She had to put an end to this conversation and now, before Neil made his appearance. "What do you feel like having for dinner?" she asked lightly.

"A hamburger, french fries, and a Coke," Benjie said, rattling off his favorite menu, knowing full well he wasn't going to get it. "But, I'll settle for roast beef and baked potatoes. Delilah said that's what she was making. And strawberry rhubarb pie. She made an extra one for Derek. I'm going to give it to him tomorrow when he picks me up. It's his favorite."

"What's who's favorite, sport?" Neil inquired as he walked up to Benjie clad in another brand new set of togs.

"Derek likes strawberry rhubarb pie, and Delilah made an extra one for me to give him tomorrow," Benjie said curtly.

"Listen, sport, you won't have to do that. Now that I'm here I'm going to take you to the hospital for your treatments. It's the least I can do for your sister to show her my appreciation. Your friend Derek can have some time off. Sometimes squiring little kids around can be a real drag. Running that fancy hotel up the road must take a lot of time. I'm sure he'd appreciate the time off. It's settled then," Neil said, looking from Jan to Benjie. Both remained mute, stunned at his words. He did have a point, Jan thought. It was impossible to read Benjie's face as he stared at the small screen.

As far as Jan was concerned, dinner was a dismal affair. Benjie picked at his food and stirred it around his plate with the fork, making scraping noises on the plate. Jan ate little, watching Neil wolf down his food and go back for seconds. Somehow he managed to keep up a running conversation dealing with things he saw wrong and how they could be improved.

"The way I see it, you have a thriving little investment here, and with the proper management you could do a lot better, Jan. You could add at least another dozen cabins and make them closer together. Of course, you'll have to cut back on some of the nature trails and cut down some of the timber, but in the end your bank balance will win out."

"Environmentally, it's not a good idea," Benjie said hotly. "We have to keep the trees and the trails. If Uncle Jake wanted to build on, he would have. Even Derek said people are ruining this country just so rich men can get richer."

Neil's voice rose an octave. "And who is it that owns that glittering neon palace down the road? He must have cut down a good many trees to build that! What's good for him is only good for him and no one else."

"That's a lie!" Benjie said belligerently. Before Jan could gather her wits about her, Benjie had his wheelchair backed away from the table and was whizzing through the dining area and out the wide doors to the patio and pool area.

"Opinionated little bugger, isn't he?" Neil managed through bits of Delilah's pie.

"Why shouldn't he be? Derek Bannon is his friend and that means a lot to Benjie. You attacked Derek and he didn't like it, so he defended the man the only way he knew how. You're too blunt, Neil. And for the rest of your stay here I don't want you to antagonize him anymore. He has enough to contend with as it it."

"Okay, okay. If you want to coddle him that's your business. If you remember correctly that was our problem back in New York. You worry about the kid too much. I'm here now, and I want you to worry about me and show me some consideration. Listen, I have a great idea. Let's go to Bannon's place and make up for lost time. A few drinks and take in the floor show. If you're such a good friend of his, maybe the guy will pick up the tab and it won't cost us a cent. What do you say?"

"Not tonight, Neil. If you want, you can go. I wouldn't be able to dance with the blisters on my feet, and you know I'm a one-drink person."

"Would you mind if I go?" Neil asked hopefully.

"Of course I don't mind. I have a book I want to read, and Benjie and I try to spend some time in the evening together since he's at the hospital most of the day. You go ahead and have a good time. I'll see you in the morning."

"You're terrific. That's why I came here." He swallowed the last of his coffee and rose from the table. Bending over Jan, he gave her a slapdash kiss and was gone before she could speculate on his hasty behavior.

Delilah stood over the table with her hands on her hips, making it clear that she had something to say. It was also clear to Jan that the woman wasn't going to speak until invited. Whatever it was, it must be a shocker, Jan thought. "So say it already," she said wearily.

"Your friend is phony and a freeloader. Gus no like, Benjie no like, and I no like," she said forcefully. "He stay too long, I quit."

"He's just visiting for a while," Jan said hotly, hating herself for defending Neil. She didn't like him either; he didn't belong here, and if it came right down to the matter, she would rather go to the wedding alone than go with him. How had this happened? Why hadn't Neil called her first before making the trip? She couldn't dwell on the matter now. "We're just going to have to wing it for a while. You can't quit and you know it. Gus wouldn't let you. I'll keep Neil in line and see that he doesn't bother you. What makes you think he's a freeloader?" she asked curiously. "He's going to pay like any other guest."

"No see deposit in book for money. I check out his room," Delilah said slyly. "Much credit cards. No bank book. No cash money. Everything new, still tickets hooked on clothes."

"Shame on you, Delilah. You were spying on Neil. Don't do it anymore," she said sternly, trying hard not to smile at Delilah's indignation.

Delilah sniffed. "You see—he go to Golden Lasso and pick up...how you say...chick."

This time Jan did laugh and so did Delilah. "If he does it might be the best thing that happens around here. And I didn't have a chance to get a deposit from him. He just got here. We do take American Express, you know."

"For you, big problem," Delilah muttered as she started to clear away the dinner table. "Your friend a gigolo."

The frown on Benjie's sleeping face tore at Jan's heart. He didn't like Neil and he saw him as a threat to his and Jan's security. Somehow, tomorrow, she was going to have to try to make him understand that Neil was just visiting and nothing was going to come of his visit in the way of a romantic entanglement for herself.

Jan adjusted the thermostat on the air conditioner and straightened the covers. Benjie stirred slightly, muttering something indistinguishable in his sleep. She waited to see if he would wake, and when he didn't, she released a sigh of relief. Turning off the lamp, she closed the door softly behind her.

A quick glance at her watch told her Neil would be just about ready to leave for the Golden Lasso. If she stayed in her room, she could avoid a meeting with him and at the same time she could make the call to Derek she was dreading. There was no reason to put it off, no reason for her to dread telling the club owner that the bank had agreed to her loan application. As one business person to another, he should be happy that she wasn't going to go under and had another chance at making the Rancho Arroyo a paying proposition.

Was it the phone call she was dreading or was it the sound of Derek's voice that was making her stomach churn and her heart pound like a trip-hammer? Twice she picked up the receiver and twice she replace it. Her throat felt dry, so dry she could barely swallow. Maybe, if she cleared her throat and took a sip of water from the bathroom it would help. Nothing would help. Do it and get it over with and go on from there. How would he take the news, she wondered fretfully. Just how badly did he want Rancho Arroyo and for what? A vision of the blueprints on Derek's desk floated before her. The worst he could think was that she was wishy-washy and unable to make up her mind. So what if her credibility came under his close scrutiny. She shouldn't care, but she did, even knowing he was marrying Andrea. She cared; it was as simple as that.

Dial the number, a niggling voice urged. Dial it and say what you have to say and hang up. Do it! Jan dialed the number Derek had given her and waited. Six, seven rings—he must not be home. Eight. "Hello."

"Derek, this is Jan Warren. I hope I didn't take you away from anything. I was just about to hang up."

"Is something wrong? Is Ben all right?" Derek asked in concern.

"Benjie is fine; that's not why I called. I called to tell you that I won't be selling the ranch after all. I applied to the bank for a loan, and they called today to say my application was approved. I'm sure that you understand and you won't hold it against me if I have to go back on my word to you. I have to do what's best for Benjie, and staying here and trying to make a go of the ranch is what I have to do. Your offer was more than generous, but I want you to know that I would have sold it to you for the original offer. I wasn't trying to hold you up or gouge a higher price out of you. Your original offer was more than fair." Jan's hand was clutched so tight on the receiver her knuckles were white as she waited intently for his reply. The creak of the floorboard outside her room didn't register. Neil's shadow in the dim light also went unnoticed as Jan waited.

"I understand, Jan. In a way it was my own fault. I apologize for placing a deadline on the transaction. If you decide to sell at some later time, I hope you'll give me first consideration. And I do hope that you can successfully make a go of the ranch for your own sake as well as your brother's. Good luck."

Jan blinked and looked at the receiver, a foolish look on her face. He certainly had accepted the matter better than she could have hoped for. He was even gracious and he had apologized. And she had worked herself into a frenzy over the matter. Men! He was probably in some kind of tizzy with his fast-approaching wedding and had other things on his mind. Which, she thought tartly, just went to prove that he probably didn't want the ranch so much after all. It would have been just another investment to him. What did he care about her or the people who worked here? Investments, tax dollars, write-offs—that was all people like Derek Bannon thought of. Lust—she had to add lust to the list. And as long as she was making a list, she could add cheating on Andrea and heaven only knew what else. A philanderer, that's what he was. Well, she wasn't going to cry over Derek Bannon. Her days of crying were over. She was going to go on about her life without him.

Darn! She forgot to tell him not to pick Benjie up in the morning. She picked up the phone and then replaced it. She couldn't, she wouldn't, make the second call. She couldn't bear to hear his voice a second time in one night, and this time she would be the one who had to apologize. She would explain in the morning when he arrived for Benjie. It would be harder to do face to face, but she would do it. She wasn't a coward. Derek would be annoyed and justifiably so, but he would have to live with his annoyance. She had been forced to live with things over the past weeks that she didn't like and he could do the same.

While she prepared for bed and brushed her teeth, she wondered how long Neil was going to stay. She made a mental note to ask him point-blank on the morrow. She hoped she wouldn't be forced to ask him for an advance payment. Surely he would offer it on his own. He couldn't think he was a nonpaying guest. She would explain, and if he didn't like it, he, too, would have to live with his annoyance at her blunt business manner. She was in business to make money, not give it away. Neil was going to be a problem in more ways than one—she could sense it, feel it in every pore of her body. She would be diplomatic, of course, but she wouldn't beat around the bush with him. How had she ever seriously considered him a possible suitor? She shook her head wearily and slipped into her football jersey.

If she had anything to be thankful for this day, it was that she hadn't paid much attention to her feet. What with the news from the bank and Neil's appearance and Benjie's apprehensions, her feet had stopped hurting. Delilah's herbal bandages had worked their magic, she thought to herself as she slipped beneath the covers.

Jan tossed and turned in her sleep. On the brink of wakefulness, she thought she heard a sound outside her window. Groggily, she crawled from the bed and slipped open her window. She wiped her eyes, trying to clear them and to see into the inky darkness outside. Leaning over the sill, she was stunned at the sight that greeted her. Neil and a girl—obviously a showgirl from the Golden Lasso from the looks of her costume—were chasing around the perimeters of the swimming pool. From where Jan stood, she could make out the bare flash of long, silky leg as the girl scampered away from Neil. Eventually, she allowed Neil to catch her, and Jan flushed at the ardent kiss he was bestowing on the willing girl. His arms around her, he led her toward the trail that led to his cabin. His first night in Arizona and he had made a conquest. Suddenly, Jan hated him. She hated all men.

Slamming the window shut, she paced around the room. What she should do was march right over to Neil's cabin and tell him that she didn't run that kind of place and that if he wanted that kind of extracurricular activity he would have to go somewhere else. This was a family place! That was what she should do, but she wouldn't. But she was going to let him know what she had seen. She wouldn't put up with it—especially not around Benjie. If necessary, she would move Neil into the bunkhouse with the other hands for the remainder of his stay. Gus would keep him on the straight and narrow.

Jan tumbled back into bed. Move him out! By rights, she should throw him out! Out! Right off the Rancho! It didn't seem as though Neil was going to pay for his stay at the Rancho anyway. What did she have to lose?

Escorting her to the wedding so she wouldn't look like an undesirable old maid was no reason... "Oh, *no!*" Jan cried aloud. Here she was thinking she could hide herself from Derek and Andrea behind a seemingly interested suitor, and all the while that suitor was up at the Golden Lasso flirting with the showgirls. She would look more than ever like a fool! Jan's face became heated and red and she felt as though it could light up the dark corners of her lonely room.

Chapter Eleven

The following morning brought a fresh set of problems in the way of Delilah and Gus. When Jan entered the dining room for breakfast, Benjie was already seated at the table, his tight little face an indication of what the day was going to be like.

"Where's breakfast, Benjie? It doesn't smell as though anything is cooking," Jan said, a note of apprehension in her voice.

"That's because there isn't any breakfast cooking. We're having cold cereal and Gus is fixing it."

"Is Delilah sick? What's wrong?" Jan demanded, heading for the kitchen.

"I quit is what's the matter," Delilah announced as she pulled a heavy suitcase through the doorway.

"Why? What's wrong? What's happened this time?"

Delilah sniffed disdainfully and pranced for the lobby.

"Delilah, I demand an answer!"

The rotund woman turned and her dark eyes snapped at Jan. "You say living in sin is not good for young boy. You say it is wrong. Right? So I tell that old Indian that I want to marry, don't want to live in sin anymore."

Jan turned to Gus, who was pouring milk over Benjie's cereal. "And what did you say, Gus?" she asked, feeling more like a monkey in the middle by the moment.

"Darn fool woman," Gus growled. "She said she wanted to get married so I said okay. Now she's changed her mind. I won't ask her again."

"Not what he said at all," Delilah said angrily. "he say we have big Indian wedding. Humph! Me not stupid Indian woman. I know the law. Indian wedding not count for that!'' she snapped her fingers. ''Indian wedding is nothing. Must have license...everything! So I tell the old man Delilah only get married in Presbyterian church or nothing.''

''You're throwing away a chance for Gus to marry you because of that?'' Jan said incredulously. ''I thought you said you didn't want to get married. Something about a fly sticking to honey. Which is it?'' she asked wearily.

''So, I change my mind. Church wedding, marriage license, or nothing. Gus has one foot in happy hunting grounds. When he go, I want Social Security.''

''I don't believe this,'' Jan said, rubbing her temples wearily. ''Why can't you two get married because you love each other? Why do you have to put each other through all this torment?''

''I tell you if we marry we have problems,'' Delilah groaned.

''What's wrong with the Presbyterian Church, Gus?'' Jan asked.

''Indian wedding or nothing,'' the Indian answered flatly.

''No, you wrong. Presbyterian church or nothing,'' Delilah shot back hotly.

''Then it's nothing,'' Gus muttered, stalking from the room.

''Why don't you have them compromise and get married by the justice of the peace and have an Indian reception afterward?'' Derek asked as he walked into the dining room. Jan groaned in echo to Delilah's groan. Why did he always show up when she was in a spot? This time she was grateful for his advice. She didn't need a rebellious cook and a surly handyman.

''What do you say, Delilah? A justice of the peace sounds good to me. You give a little, Gus gives a little.''

''No problem with Social Security later on?'' Delilah demanded of Derek.

Derek grinned. ''No problem. I guarantee it.''

''Then it's settled,'' Jan said gratefully. ''All you have to do is decide on a date and that's it.''

''Is good thinking,'' Delilah said, waddling back to the kitchen pushing her heavy suitcase in front of her.

''Is Ben ready?'' Derek asked. ''I've got the car running.''

''I could eat a horse! Where's breakfast?'' Neil interrupted as he entered the room, rubbing his hands together briskly as though he were expecting to sit down to a long-awaited meal. ''Oh, Bannon, are you here to take Benjie? No need, old buddy. I'll be doing it from now on. Jan wanted to stop by the hospital and see one of her employees, and I offered to drive. Right, Jan? Get you off the hook, Bannon,'' he said loudly, slapping Derek soundly on the back.

Derek's eyes narrowed as he stared first at Neil and then at Jan.

Jan felt her heart race up to her throat, and she felt powerless to tear her gaze away from Derek's. She had to say something. Derek didn't wait. He turned on his heel and stalked out the door.

Feeling as though she'd been kicked in the stomach, Jan watched him leave. She had never seen Derek look at her like that, as though he hated her. And Benjie was avoiding her glance, his own mouth grim and tight. She might have one problem solved, but she had another now, a worse one.

"When do we eat? Who's cooking?"

"Whenever you want to eat, as long as you cook it, Neil. Delilah is taking the morning off. And from now on, Neil, you either get here on time for breakfast or you'll cook it yourself. Even when we're full with guests, breakfast is served between certain times. Anything else would be less than fair to Delilah. By the way, Neil, I'd like to have your American Express card so I can properly bill you for your stay here. Give it to me now so I can take care of the paperwork while you prepare your breakfast."

"My American Express card!" Neil said in surprise. "Do you mean you're really going to charge me for my stay here? And I still have to make my own breakfast? I came here, Jan, to see you, and I intend to help out in order to earn my keep." He laughed as he made his statements.

"I'm sorry, Neil. I don't operate a give-away establishment, and after today you'll have to move into the bunkhouse with the other hands. If it was a job you wanted, you could have said so from the beginning. Also, all hands eat in the kitchen; ask the men what time. You'll be sitting at their table from now on."

"Move me to the bunkhouse? But I like that cabin—it affords me privacy, and I won't be in your hair," Neil said, a note of panic in his voice.

"I'll just bet you like your privacy," Jan said tartly, remembering the scene below her bedroom window in the wee hours of the morning. "I'm sorry, but hands stay in the bunkhouse. Also, there are guests arriving in the morning. The cabins have been reserved. I can't let them down now. In case you don't understand, I'm in business to make money, not to give it away. That cabin has to be free to accommodate a guest."

"Is it reserved?" Neil demanded.

"No, not yet. But if I have an opportunity to take a reservation for it, I will."

"If that's the way you feel about it, here," Neil said, whipping out the plastic credit card. Jan accepted it and walked to the office, praying that the card was good. Neil was angry and behaving like a spoiled child. Her original instincts about him had been correct. He had thought he was going to be her guest in every sense of the word. What would he do and say when he realized that she had seen him bring the showgirl to his cabin? Somehow she knew he would try to weasel out of that, too.

Neil stayed in attendance while Benjie had his physical therapy as soon as he realized that was what Derek Bannon had always done. Benjie had protested, saying that it wasn't necessary, that he could make out just fine on his own. But Neil had insisted.

Jan took the opportunity to visit Andy Stone.

"Don't say it." The cowboy grinned as he watched Jan eye the apparatus that held his leg in its sling. "You aren't going to believe this, but I'm having the time of my life. There's this great little nurse on the three-to-eleven shift and she adores me. All she wants to do is give me sponge baths and back rubs. She says I'm her most willing patient."

"Just what I need, another wedding. Well, they say it always goes in threes," Jan grimaced.

"Who's getting married?"

"Delilah and Derek Bannon."

Andy laughed raucously. "Somehow I didn't think Delilah was his type!"

Jan laughed in spite of herself. "No, silly, not Delilah and Derek. Delilah and Gus and, of course, Derek Bannon."

Andy Stone whistled softly. "Derek Bannon is getting married? I didn't think there was a woman good enough for him. Surprises me that he's finally going to tie the knot. He's the sort of guy you always expect to end up a bachelor."

"Same difference. Marriage won't change anything for him."

"Aha, so that's the way the wind blows. You fell for the guy, right? Look, Jan, this is none of my business but you're real people. Down home. Bannon is in a different league. I'm real sorry you got hurt."

"Andy, I've known what you think of Derek right from the first time I met you at the airport. But, believe it or not, he does have his saving graces. Did you know he's been bringing Benjie in for his therapy almost every day. Not only that, but he saw Benjie through some pretty bad times. I walked into that whole thing with my eyes wide open. I've been hurt before and lived through it. What do you think about Delilah and Gus?" she asked, hoping to change the subject.

"I never thought she'd get married either. What did she do? Club Gus over the head? He's pretty set in his ways, Jan. Do you think he can handle a piece of paper that says he belongs to Delilah?"

"It was touch and go there for a while, but I think he's going to come around. Gus wanted an Indian wedding and Delilah was holding out for a Presbyterian church. I think they're going with the justice of the peace and then an Indian reception."

"When is the wedding? I hope I'm out of here. I want to give the bride away." Andy grinned. "Delilah's been good to me. Almost like a mother. You should have been there the day I tried to explain the Social Security system to her."

"Let me be the first to tell you that you got through to her loud and clear." Laughing and giggling, Jan explained about the meeting in the kitchen that morning. She felt happy sitting here with Andy, and it was with regret when an hour later she had to leave when the nurse said that visiting hours were over.

The ride back to the ranch was made in silence except for Neil's comments from time to time. Jan hated the sour look on Benjie's face and wondered if her own countenance was similar. This was best, she kept telling herself. Benjie had to be weaned from Derek's company sooner or later because when he got married he would forget the little boy. And, she thought bitterly, let's not forget the honeymoon. Benjie had said just a few days ago that Andrea said the honeymoon was thirty days in Europe. Wearily she closed her eyes. This was the best solution, the only solution, for both of them.

Her plan to hire summer college students to help at the ranch could now be put into effect. One of the stipulations for the job would be that Benjie be kept occupied. Hopefully, Benjie would be able to relate to the young people. If not, then she would have to come up with some other plan, but she would cross that bridge when she came to it. She was going to do the best she could by her brother and what more could anyone ask or expect of her?

"We're home Benjie. I'll get Gus to help you into the Jacuzzi for your thirty minutes."

"Help me out of the car, I'm tired." Benjie complained.

Jan frowned. He did look tired—as a matter of fact, he looked utterly exhausted. "Okay, I'll help you today, but after this you have to do it yourself. Is that understood?" Benjie ignored her as she and Neil struggled with his limp form. He made no effort at all to maneuver himself into his wheelchair.

The minuite he was out of sight Neil reached for Jan's arm. "I thought you said he was doing well and would be walking soon.

He looks the same to me and that therapy session was a waste of three hours. Are you sure you aren't pouring your money down the drain?''

"The doctor says he's coming along nicely, and I'm not concerned about spending the money for Benjie's treatments, so don't worry about it. Benjie's just tired—those therapy sessions are hard on him—and he still has the Jacuzzi to get through. He's doing remarkably well, and I have every confidence in the doctor's prognosis.''

"Exactly what is the doctor's prognosis?'' Neil asked intently.

"That with proper treatment over an extended period of time Benjie will walk again,'' Jan said curtly. "Why?''

"I'm concerned over the little tyke. After all, we may one day soon decide to take that fateful step, and I want what's best for the kid just as much as you do. I'm not callous, you know.''

"What fateful step are you talking about?'' Jan asked, remembering the girl from the Lasso in the pool area.

Neil appeared flustered. "You know—we're engaged to be engaged—that sort of thing. I'm certainly willing to marry you if you decide that it's what you want. I wanted to give you enough time to get Benjie squared away before I asked you for a commitment. We'll work something out. Later,'' he added hastily.

Jan pretended puzzlement. "Work something out. Oh, I see, you mean you'll try to fit me in between visits to the Golden Lasso and all those luscious beauties scampering around. Thanks, but no thanks. I really think it's my destiny to be an old maid. A rich old maid,'' she added viciously as she stormed into the lobby. Of all the gall. Did she wear some invisible sign that she was good enough for certain men when they didn't have anything better to do. Bitter tears of frustration burned her eyes at the thought.

Nonchalantly, she looked around. Neil hadn't even bothered to follow her inside to say something trite, as was his manner when she got the upper hand.

She felt angry and humiliated as she plopped down on the swivel chair behind the desk.

Delilah marched into the room, a broom in one hand and the mail in the other. She laid the mail on the desk and turned to leave.

"Delilah, I've been thinking. I don't think you should get married after all. Men are terrible and they take advantage of women. We don't do that to them. I want you to think about it some more before you decide for sure.''

Delilah's eyes widened. "First, you say live in sin no good; then you say marry and live happy life. Now you say sin okay. I want

Social Security and real wedding. Gus agree to all my demands. If I chicken out now, I make fool of myself.''

"Don't you see? That's the whole point. All we women ever seem to do is make fools of ourselves over men. Do you really want to get married or not? If you don't want to get married, then don't do it.''

"How else I get Social Security?''

"Didn't Andy explain to you that my uncle, and now I, pay your Social Security? You can collect on your own without marrying Gus. Look,'' Jan said patiently, ''all I'm trying to tell you is don't get married for the wrong reasons. If you love Gus and want to get married, that's fine. If you're marrying him for his Social Security, that's the wrong reason.''

"Gus have many...how you say...defects,'' Delilah said, comimg up with the right word. "He sometime drink too much and no good for much.''

"That's another thing. If he's drunk all the time, how do you handle it?'' Jan asked.

Delilah shrugged and grinned toothily. "For me no problem. I put him to bed and play with him later.''

In spite of herself Jan laughed. "Do what you want, Delilah, but make sure it's what you really want. And don't worry about your Social Security—it's all taken care of. Where are you going with that broom?''

"I chase Gus to help Benjie.''

"Why didn't you just tell him instead of going after him with the broom?'' Jan asked, knowing she wasn't going to like the answer.

"And have Gus think I not love him? Shame,'' she said, wagging her finger under Jan's nose. "Gus expect me to go after him. He like it when I chase him. Is love game we play. Like when you get lost in desert and Mr. Bannon come for you. Was big trick you play, no?''

"No, it wasn't a trick. I really was lost.''

"I hear that story before. All young guests that come to ranch do that so Andy go after them.'' Delilah sniffed as she marched from the room, the broom held straight in front of her.

Chapter Twelve

The days continued to pass, each of them bringing Jan closer to having to attend Andrea's wedding. There were, however, several distractions that proved to be welcome. Another wave of guests arrived at Rancho Arroyo. With the help of two part-time workers things were working out nicely. Andy would be home from the hospital in another week, complete with a walking cast. Although he would be unable to resume his strenuous activities, his advice and know-how would be invaluable.

Delilah had postponed her wedding plans, much to Gus's relief, and was spending whatever time she could steal away from the kitchen with Benjie. The youngster had become withdrawn and had regressed alarmingly, according to Dr. Rossi's latest reports. Jan had relinquished her care of Benjie to Delilah because the boy seemed to become even more sullen and uncooperative whenever she was around. As much as she wanted to believe that this was a temporary state of affairs between her brother and herself, Jan was plagued with concern.

As she took care of the paperwork at the desk in the lobby, Jan's eyes fell on the calender near her elbow. Her heart thumped painfully when the red circled date denoting the wedding date leapt out at her. She had neither seen nor heard from Derek since that morning in the kitchen when Neil told him he would be taking Benjie for his regular visits to the medical center. Out of sight, out of mind, she thought wistfully.

Even before she saw him, Jan picked up the heavy scent of Neil's cologne. He approached the desk and said encouragingly, "It's two o'clock. You are ready to go riding, aren't you?"

If there was one thing she didn't feel like doing, it was going riding with Neil, but she had promised and she would have to honor that promise. Besides, it was time she had a long talk with Neil and found out exactly what his plans were. The past few days everything concerning the tall blond man annoyed her, and she found herself hoping that each day would be his last on her Rancho. The thought made her feel guilty, and she smiled to let him know she was ready to leave with him. "I'm ready whenever you are. Benjie is in the Jacuzzi so I have a little free time."

"I knew that, so I saddled the horses and have them out by the paddock waiting for us. Come on, slowpoke, get a move on," Neil joked.

"You go ahead. I want to change into riding boots and I'll meet you in a few minutes." Neil banged out the screen door and Jan added a column of figures before she closed her ledger and headed toward the stairs and her room.

Looking neither to the right nor the left, Jan crossed the lobby and walked smack into Derek Bannon. It took only one glance for her to see that he was furious to the point of rage.

"You little fool, do you have any idea what you've done?" he demanded coldly. "Do you have any idea at all?"

"Let go of me!" Jan said, frightened by the viselike grip he had on her arm. "What are you talking about?"

"What am I talking about? Don't you know? Are you so blind and wrapped up in your rhinestone cowboy that you've lost sight of what's happening to Ben? Open your eyes! Look at your brother and tell me what you see!"

Frightened by his fury, Jan could only stare at Derek. She could feel her knees tremble and the pain in her arm from his grip was tooth rattling. "What are you talking about?" she repeated.

"I'm talking about Ben and the phone call I received from Dr. Rossi. He tells me Ben has regressed almost to the point he was at when he first began attending the clinic. He chewed me out for neglecting the boy. He also said that when I start something I should finish it and that I had no right to play around with a child's life. Are you listening to me, Jan Warren? Do you hear me? Dr. Rossi said Ben isn't responding to the therapy and he has no desire or will to walk again. He said Ben gave up. Now," Derek said angrily, shaking her arm so viciously that her head almost snapped, "I want you to tell me what's going on, and then I'm going to tell you what I'm going to do."

Jan was terrified both by his verbal and physical onslaught. "Dr. Rossi told me several days ago that Benjie had a setback. That he was regressing. He said he was optimistic and would continue with the treatments. Benjie is...Benjie isn't very happy. He missed you. I knew you would do this to him. You don't care about him. If you did, you would have come around to see how he was doing. Regardless of who takes Benjie for his therapy, you never should have deserted him the way you did. Also, I thought when you found out I wasn't going to sell the Rancho that you didn't want to be bothered with either Benjie or me. I thought..."

"Do me a favor, Miss Warren—don't think. I can't afford it when you think. From now on I'll be taking Ben for his treatments, and if that neon sign that poses as your engaged-to-be-engaged boyfriend interferes, his lights are going to be punched out! When I start something, I finish it. Now where the hell is Ben?"

"He's...he's out in the Jacuzzi. He still has five minutes to go and I think..."

"I've told you, don't think!" Derek snapped "Even Delilah has more sense than you do. Feebleminded..." The rest of his words were lost on Jan as Derek made his way to the pool.

Jan stood on the side and wanted to die at the look on Benjie's face when he saw Derek stoop down on his heels. "I knew you wouldn't forget me! What are you doing here? How come you came? How are all the guys at the Lasso? Gee, Derek, I missed you. How long can you stay?" Benjie babbled nonstop.

"Whoa. One question at a time. From now on I'm back to taking you for your therapy. What in the world made you think I could forget my good buddy? I had some business that needed my attention. I came to see you. The guys miss you, and Dusty said I was to bring you back for the barbecue tonight. I missed you too, Ben. So what do you say? Shake off the water—your time is up. Let's make tracks for the Lasso. There's a lot of your friends who are eager to see you."

"Just you and me, Derek?" Benjie asked hopefully as he waited for Derek's reply.

"You got it—just you and me. Andrea and the guys will be at the barbecue, but with a little luck we can shake them easily enough. Between the two of us, we should be able to handle it."

"Wow! I can't wait! Derek, I haven't been doing so good with Dr. Rossi. I didn't make any...progress since you left."

"I heard about it and I'm here to see that you get back on the track."

"I can't get out of the Jacuzzi by myself. I can't do anything by myself anymore," Benjie said quietly, his blue eyes solemn, the dancing lights that had been there when he first saw Derek extinguished.

"I guess I can help you this time around. Starting tomorrow, though, you're on your own."

Jan watched with a catch in her throat as Derek bent down and lifted Benjie from the Jacuzzi and wrapped the boy in a thirsty towel. Carefully, as though he were handling eggs, he settled the little boy in his wheelchair and bellowed for Delilah. "Dress him and bring him back here. Ten minutes," he thundered.

Derek Bannon made no move in Jan's direction but stood glaring at her in stony silence. His eyes clearly said all, and she knew the words. Hadn't she been saying them to herself over and over these past few days? She had neglected Benjie. She had refused to see what was happening to the little boy. She had been so wrapped up in the ranch and fending off Neil that she had neglected the most important person in her life. If it hadn't been for Derek, how long would she have allowed it to continue? She had no defense; there was no defense. Her shoulders drooped as she headed for Benjie's room.

As Jan turned and walked away, she had half expected Derek to call out to her, to rail her out, to yell and holler, but he hadn't. Why should he? There was no sign that he even knew she was visible.

Delilah was just wheeling Benjie through the door when Jan got to his room. Gus waited patiently for Delilah to help Benjie dress so he could carry him back down the stairs.

"I heard you were going to the Lasso for a barbecue. Have a good time, Benjie," Jan said, her eyes brimming with tears.

"Are you crying because I'm leaving?" Benjie asked in surprise.

"Heck, no. I think I have some kind of allergy."

"Yup," Delilah muttered from where she rummaged through Benjie's dresser for a shirt. "Me get allergy, too. Whenever the dude with the big hat come around. He make my eyes water, too," the woman sniffed.

"Derek says the desert is the best place for allergies. Derek is finished with his business and he's going to take me for my therapy again, starting tomorrow. It's okay, isn't it?" he said anxiously.

"You bet it is," Jan said, blowing her nose.

"Jan, if Derek asks me to sleep over, can I? He said there's a guest room and it's got my name on the door. Can I, Jan? I never did before, because I didn't want you to be alone. Your friend is here, so, if he asks me this time, can I stay?"

Jan was aware of two things—one, that Benjie really did care for her and was concerned about her, and the other, that he still never called Neil by name but always referred to him as ''her'' friend.

''I think it's a great idea. I know you're going to have a good time. Give me a call, though, just so I know your plans. Okay? I'll be fine. You'd better get a move on. I heard Mr. Bannon give you ten minutes and you're on overtime right now.'' Quickly, she gave Benjie a peck on the cheek.

Later, Neil found Jan leaning against the wall outside the kitchen door. Tears were streaming down her cheek, but he didn't seem to notice. ''Do you have any idea what time it is? I've been standing out there with two saddled horses for over half an hour and I feel like a fool! Are you going riding or not?'' he demanded arrogantly.

''Shut up, Neil. Shut up and don't say another word,'' Jan cried as she ran into the lodge and slammed the door shut behind her. Up in her room, she threw herself on her bed and buried her face in her pillow.

The soft, velvety night enveloped Jan as she strolled the grounds of the Rancho Arroyo. For the second time in days she made a decision to sell the ranch to Derek Bannon. She knew now she could never live in such close proximity to Derek and still survive emotionally. Today had been proof of that fact. Instead of calling Derek, she would write him a formal business letter and spell out the terms for him. She would be asking his original offer, not the elevated, inflated price he had offered when he thought she was being plain stubborn.

If Derek didn't want the property or had changed his mind, then she would have to sell it to someone else. Surely there were other businessmen who would be interested in the Rancho for investment purposes.

She would have to work something out with the hospital and Dr. Rossi as far as Benjie's treatments were concerned. Jan's anger rose and her sense of justice was assaulted. It was fine for Derek to storm into the ranch and tell her he was taking over Benjie's treatments again because she had sloughed off on her job. But what and who was going to take care of Benjie while Derek was away on his thirty-day honeymoon in Europe? I'll just bet he never gave *that* a thought, Jan sniffed.

A deep feeling of loneliness swept over her. Why couldn't someone fall in love with her and cherish her the way the heroes did in books? She wasn't ugly; she'd been told she had a pleasing personality. Was she unaware of something about herself that was a definite turnoff as far as men were concerned? Men, she said to herself. Be honest; when you talk about men, you're thinking only of Derek Bannon.

A deep sob rose in her throat and she squelched it immediately. No more crying, she told herself firmly.

How bright the stars were. It was a beautiful night, a night made for lovers and close embraces. Someday she would have another night like this and someone special to share it with her.

"Jan, I've been looking all over for you," Neil's voice called from somewhere deep in the shadows. "I want to talk to you."

From where she stood Jan picked up the excitement in Neil's voice. What now? she groaned inwardly.

Neil emerged into the flickering lights that surrounded the pool and motioned for Jan to sit down on a yellow chaise. "I have something I want to tell you," he said exuberantly.

"That's good. Because I have something I want to tell you," Jan said quietly.

"Whatever it is, it can wait. This is important. Jan, I want you to marry me! I've just discovered something that will make us millionaires. Are you listening?"

"Of course I'm listening, and so is half the Rancho. Lower your voice, please," Jan admonished.

Neil's voice dropped a tone. "Jan, don't sell the ranch to Bannon. I found out why he wants it. We can beat him to the punch and do it ourselves and make a fortune."

Jan laughed. He hadn't even bothered to wait for a reply to his marriage proposal. She raised her eyes heavenward and grinned. "This isn't exactly what I had in mind when I prayed for someone to love and cherish me," she mumbled almost silently.

"What did you say?" Neil questioned. "Never mind. Listen. Don't sell Bannon the Rancho."

"What? How did you know? I never told you Derek wanted to buy the Rancho..."

"I know, I know. I overheard you talking to him on the phone..."

"You what?" Jan hissed, starting to rise from her chair. "You spied on me? That's despicable..."

Neil pushed her back down onto the chaise. "Look, there's no time for that now. I know about it and that's all that counts. But don't do it, Jan. We'll take over his plans and make ourselves a fortune. Today I took a run over to the shopping center for some shaving supplies, and there's an architect's office right next to the drugstore. And whose car do you think was parked right outside? Your friend Bannon's. There were some rolled-up blueprints on the front seat and I sort of took a look at them. Don't worry, he doesn't know anything about it. I saw him go into the drugstore with Benjie.''

"You what?'' Jan demanded, fury lighting her eyes to shards of green glass.

"Shut up. Let me finish. I saw those blueprints, and believe me when I tell you that Bannon is out to steal this place right out of your hands. You can't sell it to him.''

"Don't you mean you spied on Derek Bannon, and you spied on me, too? You didn't just happen to see the blueprints—you spied. You should be ashamed of yourself!''

"Well, I'm not!'' Neil answered loftily. "It's Bannon who should be ashamed for what he's trying to pull over on you. Well, I won't let him do it to you, to us. I'll pull the rug from under him and we'll roll in clover from now on.''

"Neil, I don't love you. I don't want to marry you. Stop saying 'us.'''

Jan's words penetrated and made an impression. "Okay, then I'll be your business manager. We'll clean up,'' he said, rubbing his hands together. "Say, you didn't even ask what the plans were. Don't you care? Oh, I see. You really don't care and you'll leave it up to me.''

"You're right about one thing—I don't care. Listen, Neil, I'm selling the Rancho to Derek Bannon for his original offer. I have no intention of gouging him or keeping this place. I have to do what's best for Benjie and myself. I can't worry about you or Mr. Bannon. I really am tired, Neil, so, if you'll excuse me, I'll go up to bed and you can go back to the Golden Lasso and your nocturnal prowling. By the way, you're going to have to vacate the bunk- house. Andy Stone will be discharged from the hospital over the weekend, and he'll need his bunk. All the cabins are either filled or reserved, so you'll have to vamoose. You should be able to get a room at the Lasso. Sorry,'' she said, getting up from the chaise.

Neil appeared stunned but recovered rapidly. "I don't believe what I'm hearing,'' he snapped. "This guy is out to rip you off and you tell me to move out, when all I have is your best interests at heart? He's going to build some kind of treatment center for cripples like Benjie. How do you like that? If you keep this place and do the same thing, you could make a fortune. Do you know how easy it is to apply for federal aid? Everybody's got a soft heart when it comes to crippled kids. We could make a fortune just skimming off the top. You're a fool, Jan. I can't believe you're selling out! You could have a gold mine here. Open your eyes!''

Jan's face froze into shocked lines. Could she believe what she was hearing? One look at Neil's determined features told her. "You are the most despicable man I've ever known," she hissed. "You can't stand the sight of Benjie because he's disabled, and yet you'd make the Rancho into a treatment center for children just like Benjie and then steal from them! Get back under your rock, Neil. I want you to clear out of here before morning."

"Listen, Jan. I've put up with a lot from both Benjie and you, and I'm not going to let you go until you see things my way!"

"You don't know *my* way, Neil," she said savagely, lifting her hand and slapping him soundly across his hated face.

"Why, you little...!" Instantly, Neil was on his feet, dragging her up with him and holding her fast. "You love him, don't you? You think if you sell the Rancho to him that will make him come around. I've seen him at the Lasso. Women follow him as though he were the pied piper. He's the kind of man who takes everything and leaves nothing behind but tatters and frayed ends. You aren't his type." Neil's voice had become shrill.

Jan struggled for her release, her fingers curling into claws reaching for his face. "I know one thing, Neil—Derek Bannon doesn't steal. If his plan is to make a treatment center for handicapped children, it isn't with the intention of skimming off the top. Regardless of his romantic adventures, he's a man of honor and principle. But, then, you wouldn't know anything about that, would you?"

"You're not going to cheat me out of this, Jan. This is the chance of a lifetime, and you're not going to stop me!" Unleashing his rage, Neil tossed her backward, knocking her off balance and throwing her down into the chaise. She saw him lift his arm, his hand bunched into a fist, ready to strike her.

Suddenly, a figure stepped out from the path and seized Neil's arm. Derek Bannon. Neil turned with fury upon Derek, now aiming his blow upon him. Derek blocked, stopping Neil's fist in midair, and directed a well-placed blow to Neil's midsection. As Neil doubled over to clutch his stomach, Derek pounded his fist into Neil's face, knocking him backward onto the grass.

"Now, get up and get out of here; you heard the lady! And don't ever show your face around these parts again!" Derek's voice was harsh, filled with menace and fury.

Neil touched his hand to his nose and mouth, and his fingers came away stained with his own blood.

Stunned by Derek's sudden violence, Jan stood abruptly and loomed over Neil's reclining figure. "I've told you once and I'll tell you again—this time for the last time. Go back under your rock, Neil—that's where you belong.'' Unable to stomach the sight of him for another instant, she turned on her heel, squared her shoulders, and headed for the lodge.

Derek caught up with her on the veranda and held the door open for her. ''I just came by to tell you Benjie is staying the night with me. He's with Dusty and the guys right now. I tried calling you, but Delilah said you were outside somewhere. I came by hoping to find you.''

Why was he looking at her that way? Had he heard her defense of him to Neil? Or had he just happened upon them just as Neil was about to strike her? Even if he had heard, what difference did it make? It couldn't matter to him; he was going to marry Andrea in just a few days. ''Good night, Derek. Thank you for going to all this trouble to tell me about Benjie.''

''Jan, wait. I want to talk to you.'' Derek gripped her wrist, stopping her hasty retreat.

''Regardless of what you want, Derek, I've had enough. E-N-O-U-G-H! Go back where you belong and I'll stay where I belong.'' He reached for her, his hand cupping her chin, forcing her gaze to meet his. Desperately, Jan tried to avoid his penetrating stare. In agonizing defeat she knew she was helpless against him. Slowly— ever so slowly—she raised her eyes to meet his. The past few minutes had been too emotionally charged. She had discovered so much, and yet there were so many mysterious shadows remaining. She admitted it hadn't been so great a shock to discover what a heel Neil Connors was. Hadn't she always suspected it, based on the way he treated Benjie? And it hadn't really come as a devastating revelation to learn that Derek intended to use the Rancho Arroyo as a camp for handicapped children. Hadn't she learned about his generosity at the medical center? But, still, it was all becoming too much to handle. It was the havoc her own emotions created within her that was bringing tears to her eyes. Derek touched his finger to the glistening tear as it raced along her smooth cheek.

''You're coming with me,'' he stated simply, pulling her across the porch and pushing her into his station wagon, which was parked out in front of the lodge.

All the fight had gone out of her. Somehow she knew that her protests would fall on deaf ears, and she was so tired. So very tired. Drained emotionally. Obedient to his demands, she allowed herself to be put into the car and sat quietly as he climbed in beside her and spurred the engine to life.

The night was black, the only light coming from the headlights as they drove along the road leading to the interstate highway. Jan cowered against the door, too numbed to wonder where he was taking her, too defeated to even ask.

Just before the turnoff for the interstate, Derek swung the long station wagon onto a side road and parked. The lights from the dashboard struck his features, turning his eyes dark and delineating his chiseled jaw. His dark hair was tousled and falling across his forehead, lending him a boyish look. But his mouth was grim, tight—little more than a thin line of anger.

"Now will you tell me what this is all about? What goes on in that silly head of yours? Jan," he said in exasperation, "sometimes I feel as though we're so close. Then suddenly, without warning, something comes between us and I don't understand it. I know you feel something for me. You proved that the day we were in Dr. Rossi's barn."

Jan was silent, refusing to answer. What did he want her to do? What did he want her to say? He had no right to bring her here, to corner her, to demand she confess she loved him when in a few days he would be marrying someone else. Or was that his little game? Did his male ego demand she throw herself at his feet and plead and beg with him not to marry Andrea? Never! She warned herself. Regardless of how close and tempting those words were to her lips. She would never beg. How could he not know that his relationship with Andrea was the only thing that kept her from throwing herself into his arms and declaring her love?

"Jan?" His voice was so close it startled her. Suddenly his arms were around her, pulling her closer. His lips found the soft skin below her ear and his breath was warm and stirred her senses as he whispered, "Don't pull away, Jan..." and then his mouth covered hers and blocked out the universe.

Jan was moved by his plea. How could she deny him anything? This was Derek, the man she loved. She relaxed against him, her head tipped upward and resting against his shoulder. She felt the feather-light caress of his lips on her hair. "You always smell so sweet," he murmured as he bent his head, searching once again for her lips.

Her arms slid around him, aware of his hard-muscled torso against her touch. Unconsciously, her hands wound around him, hugging him closer. Derek kissed her, a warm, searching, drugging kiss, teasing Jan's senses and licking the flames of passion that were banked within her. Slow to passion, deliciously slow, touching, tender, loving, adoring...his lips traced a pattern that evoked her response.

His hands took possession of her, roaming lazily over her body, molding her to him. And he breathed her name, so softly she thought she had only imagined hearing it.

Her parted lips followed the strong line of his jaw and descended to the hollow of his neck. She gave herself up to the pressure of his touch on her body, feeling as though the world began and ended within the circle of his embrace.

The night was dark; the moment was rapture. Derek held her tenderly, quieting his passions, yet arousing her own. And when she felt his fingers fumbling with the buttons on her blouse, she made no protest. Being with him, loving him seemed the most natural thing in the world.

His touch against her skin ignited a spark that blossomed into a shower of flames. The sound of her name on his lips before he covered hers was as heady as imported brandy. And the air was sweet and the night was silent. Only the whisper of his name rode on the desert breeze.

And when he followed the curve of her chin along her throat and touched his lips to the hollow between her breasts, she arched her back, welcoming his touch. Within her burned the new sensation of an indescribable budding, a splintering emotion that swelled and bounded from deep within her.

When she heard it, she thought it was merely wishful thinking. But he said it again—this time louder, hesitantly, as though unsure of her response. "I love you, Jan."

The words that she longed to hear and should have made her the happiest woman alive instead broke the magic. Jan's spine stiffened and he sensed her immediate withdrawal.

Puzzled, he sat back, looking at her as she struggled with shaking fingers to redo her buttons. Softly, so softly she had to strain to hear him, he said, "I thought you wanted me to love you, Jan."

Jan's eyes flashed with fury. "To repeat one of your own phrases, Mr. Bannon, you shouldn't think! Now, take me home!"

She was angry, angrier than she'd ever been in her life. Derek had no right to do these things to her! He had no right to tell her he loved her—not with Andrea waiting for him up at the Golden Lasso!

Without another word, Derek started the car and expertly maneuvered it around and onto the secondary road leading to the Rancho. Although he was silent, when Jan sneaked a peek at him she saw his features were stricken. He gripped the steering wheel with a fury that whitened his knuckles. She couldn't think! She wouldn't think! She wouldn't be Derek Bannon's new plaything until something better came his way. And what of his wife-to-be? Jan never imagined that she would find cause to pity the beautiful Andrea, but at this moment that was exactly what she did.

A few moments later Derek drove the station wagon up to the front of the lodge. An instant before Jan found the door handle Derek turned to face her. His features were stiff with rage and his voice, when he spoke, was rife and menace. "Get out of my car, Miss Warren. I'll do my best to forget what a fool I made of myself tonight, and I hope you'll have the decency to do the same. Get out."

Jan was paralyzed by the menace in his tone and the naked hatred in his face. "Decency!" she cried. He had already turned his head away from her and his foot pressed the accelerator and revved the engine impatiently. Exasperated beyond words, Jan sprung from the car and slammed the door shut, hearing the window rattle and wishing it would shatter into a million pieces. It would be fitting. That's exactly what her heart felt like—as though Derek Bannon had crushed it in his hands and shattered it into a million pieces.

Chapter Thirteen

Jan descended the stairs early the next morning and pasted a stiff smile on her face. There was no sense in parading around with her heart on her sleeve for all the hands to see. The night had been interminably long and lonely. Thoughts of Derek kept turning over and over in her head, denying her peace and stealing her sleep. And when she did fall asleep, finally, it was only to awaken with a start, expecting to find him there beside her, whispering her name and holding her close. She must put it all behind her now, push it out of her mind and out of her life. But all through the night she heard him whisper, "I love you, Jan," and yet the dreaded vision of the naked hatred on his face as he ordered her out of his car returned to confound her.

Quickly, she entered the kitchen where Delilah was busy at the stove while the ranch hands stood in line waiting for her to drop a stack of wheat cakes onto their plates.

After saying good morning, Jan poured herself a cup of coffee and looked inquiringly at Delilah. "When did you start humming to yourself in the morning?"

"When your friend make tracks in the night."

"Neil?"

"*Tsk, tsk, tsk*—you have only one friend. Yes, rhinestone cowboy leave early this morning. Not even leave one rhinestone behind. Is good, yes?" Delilah grinned, showing her strong white teeth.

"Is good, yes," Jan mimicked. "But I'm not surprised. He received his walking papers last night."

"Yes. And also he got something else," Delilah said as she served another ranch hand. "Your friend got himself one swollen lip, two loose teeth, and banged-up nose. Right, fellas?'' She addressed the four men sitting at the long table, devouring her luscious wheat cakes.

"Right!" they called in unison.

Jan grimaced, Neil had lived with the hands and yet he had been unable to become friends with any of them. That had a lot to say about the man.

"Wonder who punched your friend out?" Delilah muttered. "Me? I not give him time of day."

Hmmm. I wonder." Jan pretended bafflement.

"Sometimes I think you maybe not so dumb as you look," Delilah said heartily. "You just take longer than most."

Jan gulped. "I'll take that as a compliment and leave the rest unsaid." She grimaced. "How's breakfast coming? Need any help?"

"No, you sit down and eat. You too skinny—like stick!"

Jan took her place at the table and picked at a breakfast plate that Delilah had put in front of her. Should she tell everyone that she was selling the ranch to Derek Bannon? Should she wait? No. It wouldn't be fair. It was important to everyone to know her plans so they wouldn't be left high and dry at the last minute. She was glad Benjie wasn't here to hear it like this. She would have to handle him very delicately when she broke the news.

When breakfast was over and some of the men broke out cigarettes, Jan called for their attention. "I have something to tell everyone and I hope you'll understand. You all know the unexpected expenses we've been faced with lately; it's been difficult keeping the ranch in the black. Matter of fact, there were several times I thought we would go under. Also, there's the competition from the Golden Lasso to contend with, and that's not easy. We just can't afford to offer the accommodations they offer there. So—" she took a deep breath "—I've decided to take Derek Bannon's offer and sell him the Rancho." There, she had said it, but she hadn't expected the crestfallen faces of her staff.

There was silence. Total and complete.

"Listen, everyone. It's not what you think. I haven't given up and I'm not selling out for a higher price. As a matter of fact, I'm accepting Mr. Bannon's first offer. I believe him when he said that Uncle Jake died before he could sign the necessary papers. But I do know this. He's going to need help. Mr. Bannon isn't just going to make this Rancho a part of the Golden Lasso and use it for his staff's living quarters. I've discovered he wants to open a treatment

center for handicapped children. He'll be needing all the help he
can get.''

"Miss Warren, is there anything we can do to help you change
your mind? We hate to see you leave and we'll miss Ben. We really
care about that kid, and you, too.'' It was the first time Gus had
said more than five or six words.

"Gus, no, I'm sorry. I just can't handle it financially. Sooner or
later it would have to come to this and it would have been even
more difficult. I've got to secure Benjie's future and I can't do that
if I have to file for bankruptcy. Understand? And I would appreciate
it if none of you mentioned this to Benjie. I'll find the right time
to tell him.''

There were mutters and finally agreements around the table. It
was heartwarming to know that in a few short months she had come
to be so well thought of at the Rancho. The atmosphere was dismal,
subdued to the point of a funeral.

Groping for something to lighten the mood, Jan turned to Delilah.
"When are you and Gus getting married?''

Delilah shrugged.

"What do you say we have the wedding here? You could invite
all your friends, and it would really be something for our guests to
attend. And the Rancho will empty out its food locker to feed everyone. What do you say, Delilah?''

"I say you too late. Gus and me get married yesterday afternoon
in Presbyterian church.''

Gus stood up from his place at the table and raised his coffee
mug. "To Delilah.'' He offered the toast to his new bride. Then,
in a most unexpected display of affection, he rounded the table,
caught Delilah in his arms, and squeezed her tightly. With a re-
sounding smack, he put a kiss on her chubby cheek. Everyone
praised Gus for his choice in women and immediately the mood
lightened.

Jan smiled brightly, but inside she was dreading the thought of
telling Benjie of her decision to sell the Rancho. He had come to
love these people just as she had. It was cruel, but, then, life was
cruel. She, too, had come to love someone, and she knew the pain
of not being able to be near him. She would weather it; she would
have to. And so would Benjie.

Jan closeted herself in her office to accomplish two things. One
was that she would manage to avoid Benjie's eyes when he returned
from the Golden Lasso with Derek; and, two, it would give her an
opportunity to discuss selling the Rancho with her uncle's lawyer.

As she was on the phone with the lawyer, she heard Derek's powerful sports car pull up the drive. Gus went out to help Benjie, who was looking marvelously improved. The boy was using his crutches again and he refused Gus's helping hand. Derek had remained in the car with the motor running. As Benjie waved goodbye, he shouted something that sounded like "See you at the wedding!"

For a moment Jan was so distracted that the lawyer had to repeat something twice before she heard him. "Just draw up the papers and I'll come into town next week to sign them. Anything, as long as it isn't necessary for me to come face to face with Derek Bannon."

If the lawyer thought this a strange request, he didn't say so, he just muttered something about wanting to play golf this weekend, and now he was going to have all this paperwork.

Jan buried herself in the ledgers and receipts and bills. A few minutes later, Benjie knocked on the office door and entered. "Hey, Jan, Derek's gonna pick me up to take me to the medical center in about two minutes. I asked him to wait around for me when he dropped me off, but he said he had something to do up at the Lasso. Why don't you come out and say hello to him when he comes for me?"

Jan looked up at Benjie's bright blue eyes. Derek Bannon had worked his magic on the little boy once again. "I can't come out, Benjie—I've got so much work to do."

"Aw, come on out, Jan. It won't take but a minute. Please, Jan?"

Unable to deny Benjie this one small request in the face of the news about selling the Rancho, Jan smiled. "Okay, sport. I'll wait on the veranda for you."

The midmorning air was already heavy and hot, but it was a balm to Jan, who, ever since Derek had dropped her off the night before, felt as though she could never be warm again. Benjie prattled something about the preparations for the wedding, and Jan only half listened, insulating herself against the pain. From Benjie's report, the florists were already decorating a small dining room that would serve as the chapel, and the cooks were preparing the most scrumptious food Benjie had ever seen. The boy's eyes widened as he described the ice sculpture of turtle doves that would be used for the champagne fountain. "It's really something, Jan. I bet you've never seen anything like it! Andrea says that the man had to come all the way from California to do it!"

Smiling stiffly, Jan tried to show enthusiasm for the news Benjie was reporting. The last thing she wanted to hear about was Andrea's wedding plans and the elaborate showing she and Derek were planning to make. *"I love you, Jan."* The words seemed to float on the desert wind. *"I love you, Jan."* The remembered tone of Derek's voice as he whispered those words sent Jan into a panic. Nervously, she turned to Benjie, asking him inane questions about the medical clinic, Dr. Rossi, the Bison football team—anything to blot out the wound of those words.

"What's the matter with you, sis? You're as jumpy as a cat on a griddle." Benjie questioned her, piercing her with his stare.

"Nothing," she snapped. "I thought you wanted me to come out here and keep you company. I'm keeping you company!" she insisted, hearing her own voice rise two octaves.

As though saved by the bell, Derek's car rounded the drive. He honked his horn and Benjie hurried out to the car on his crutches. "I won't be needing these before long," he called out to Jan. "Someday I'm just going to run off that porch and right over to Derek!"

The conviction in the boy's voice convinced Jan. If nothing else, she had to be grateful to Derek Bannon for her brother's bright prognosis.

The whole time Benjie was settling himself in the car, Derek kept his face turned away. It seemed as though Derek had spoken the truth about feeling like a fool the night before. Well, it served him right. But in her heart Jan knew there was no bigger fool than she. The sight of Derek's head turned away from her ate at her soul. She had to hurry the lawyer, do everything she could to facilitate the deal about selling the Rancho. She had to get away from here, away from the desert, away from Derek Bannon. Her heart beat thunderously in her breast, her breath caught in her throat, and tears stung her eyes. Heaven help her, whatever the man was, whatever he did, she loved him. *"I love you, Jan."*

The fickle desert wind had returned his words again. *"I love you, Jan."*

"Come on, Jan! You're gonna make us late!" Benjie admonished through the closed bedroom door.

"I'm coming. Just a minute!" she answered, desperately trying to keep her voice light.

"You said that ten minutes ago! Come on!"

"All right, all right! Just give me a few more minutes without your badgering. Now get away from the door and wait for me in the lobby. I'm hurrying."

Jan sighed deeply as she stroked the brush through her hair. She felt as though she were marching to her own execution. Today was going to be the worst day of her life. First, she was being forced to attend Andrea's wedding; and second, she was going to have to tell Benjie of her decision to sell the Rancho.

There was no avoiding it. The boy had to know. And the longer she put it off, the harder it would be on him.

Jan surveyed herself in front of the pier glass, checking her hem and the back of the pale blue linen dress she had decided to wear. If she had to watch the man she loved marry someone else, at least it would be while looking her best. Her cinnamon-colored hair shone, and there was just the right amount of color in her cheeks. The linen sheath dress hugged her hips and emphasized her long, lean legs. Satisfied that everything was where it should be, she hurried out of her room and down the stairs into the lobby.

Benjie emitted a long, low whistle, which caused Jan to raise her brows. "Where did you learn a thing like that?" she demanded. "Riding through town with Derek, no doubt." Her tone was harsher than she intended and Benjie looked at her curiously. "Don't look at me like that," she scolded. "You were the one in a hurry. Now, let's get going."

Even as they drove through the gates of the Golden Lasso, it was evident there was a festive note in the air. Garlands of flowers lined the drive, and crepe-paper wedding bells were entwined around the lamp posts. A parking attendant, resplendent in livery, claimed Jan's pickup truck and drove it around to the back lot. Benjie was impatient and became insistent when he heard the organ music coming from the small back dining room. "I told you you would make us late! Now hurry up or I'm gonna leave you here!"

The last thing Jan wanted was to have to enter the makeshift chapel all by herself, so she hurried behind Benjie, who was making fast tracks for the chapel.

Inside the chapel soft organ music played the Wedding March. The interior was decorated with hundreds of flowers and white satin ribbons. The center aisle had been overlayed with a white carpet that led to the makeshift altar where Andrea and Derek would pronounce their vows.

Jan's eyes became misty and her throat choked up. How could she sit here and watch Derek swear his love for Andrea when only a few days ago he had whispered those words to her. A great heaviness weighed on Jan's heart. Her impulse was to run—run away as fast and as far as she could. Instead, she sat there paralyzed, incapable of motion, knowing only that the one man she could ever love was standing there at the altar waiting for his bride.

"Derek looks great in his penguin suit, doesn't he?" Benjie whispered.

"What?"

"His tuxedo. Derek calls it a penguin. And, hey, doesn't Dusty look nervous?"

"Shh!"

The organist began the Wedding March again, and the outer doors swung open to reveal two pretty girls dressed in yellow and carrying baskets of flowers. Behind her bridesmaids, Andrea stood, awaiting her cue. Jan caught her breath when she saw the dark-haired girl, who was beautiful in her antique lace gown and fine Holland lace veil.

Suddenly, Derek was standing beside Andrea, murmuring something to her and giving her a slight chuck on the chin. Derek! What was he doing back there? He should have waited for Andrea at the altar!

Benjie was pulling on Jan's arm. "Jan, Jan. When you get married can I give you away like Derek's giving his sister away?"

The full import of Benjie's words didn't penetrate Jan's consciousness for a full minute. Giving his sister away? Andrea was Derek's sister? No! It couldn't be! Jan's thoughts raced backward, trying to remember who had told her that Derek was marrying Andrea. No one. No one had told her. Back, through the haze of the days...Andrea, sitting beside Dusty Baker on the plane, telling him that she was going to be married. That was a flirtation, a coyness. And that time at the Golden Lasso when Dusty Baker introduced Andrea and she had interrupted him, not wanting to hear the words "Derek's fiancée." Jan's eyes followed Andrea and Derek and jumped ahead of them to where Dusty Baker was waiting. Andrea was going to marry Dusty! That was why Derek hadn't been jealous at the tribute dinner. How could he be jealous of his sister?

Back again, to where she had seen Andrea hug Derek in the airport. What made her think it had been more than sisterly affection? Had hearing Andrea's words on the plane and her own instant jealousy of the girl colored everything she knew about the girl?

And of course Andrea lived with Derek. Where else should she live while waiting to be married? Andrea had had every right to answer the door in the middle of the night wearing her nightgown.

Fool! Fool! Fool! she cursed herself. Always jumping to conclusions. The agony she had caused herself thinking Derek was in love with Andrea. The pain she had inflicted on everyone because she had assumed that Andrea was going to marry Derek!

Derek! Jan's heart leaped in her breast. Derek had said he loved her. *"I love you, Jan."* Again she heard the words, listened for the warm timbre in his voice. Fool! Fool! What had she done? Her pride had kept her from discovering the truth. All those times when doubt had ruined what it was that she and Derek had between them, all she had had to do was say it. Tell him. Even if she had openly accused him of being engaged to marry Andrea while toying with her emotions—Derek would have laughed and then taken her in his arms and told her that she was such a silly because Andrea was his sister. His sister!

And Andrea, coming to see her when she was laid up with blisters on her feet and offering her friendship again. How many times had she insulted the unwitting girl by rebuffing her offers of friendship? Even now, she couldn't remember Andrea saying or doing one nasty thing to encourage Jan's hostility. No, it had all been Jan.

She covered her face with her hands to stifle her sobs. Benjie was embarrassed and she heard him whisper to someone: "Girls. They always cry at weddings."

Again the music reached a crescendo and filled the chapel with brightness. Andrea raced down the aisle with Dusty, her face as bright as the Arizona sunshine, and Dusty looking as proud as a peacock.

The wedding guests emptied out after the bride and groom, and Jan knew the impulse to turn and run. Fool! Fool!

Leaving Benjie behind, she followed the crush of guests out into the elegantly appointed lobby of the Golden Lasso. Tears streaming down her face, Jan longed for escape. Suddenly, she heard someone call her name.

"Jan!"

She turned to see Andrea standing on the stairs, looking down at her. "Jan! Catch!" The bridal bouquet flew through the air, and with the accuracy of the Bisons' quarterback, Andrea's toss went directly into Jan's arms.

Fresh tears stung Jan's eyes and, clutching the bouquet to her, she ran out of the Lasso and across the wide expanse of lawn. Over and over the words, "Fool, fool!" shrieked through her head, blocking out all other sound.

The remembered sight of the hatred on Derek's face swam before her. She could never make it up to him, not if she lived to be a hundred. The most wonderful man in the world had told her he loved her, and she had destroyed that love, crushed it beyond repair. "Fool! Fool!"

"I love you, Jan."

The words seemed to come from a distance, and yet they were

close enough to touch her heart. She turned and saw him walking toward her. Through the mist of her tears, she saw he was smiling. "I see you've caught the bridal bouquet. You know what that means, don't you?"

He was standing beside her, offering her his snowy handkerchief to dry her tears. "Weddings make me cry, too. Especially when it's not my wedding to you, Jan." His voice was gentle, quiet, almost somber.

"Derek, I've been such a fool...you don't know. I thought—I thought—"

She was in his arms, her heart beating fast against his. His eyes held the sky as he looked down at her and a smile played near the corner of his mouth. "Kiss me. Tell me that you love me. To coin a phrase, Jan—don't think."

And she didn't as he held her tighter and gently parted her lips with his own, robbing her mind of all thought except him.

* * * * *

Baby Blessed
Debbie Macomber

For
Cindy DeBerry, a steadfast friend through the years

Chapter One

"All right, I'll play your little game," Jordan Larabee said between gritted teeth as he paced the thick carpet in front of Ian Houghton's shiny mahogany desk. "Just where the hell is she?"

"I presume you mean Molly?"

Ian could be a real smartass when he wanted to be, and apparently he'd fine-tuned it into an art form since their last meeting.

"I might remind you Molly is *your* wife."

"She's your daughter," Jordan shot back. "It was you she went to when she left me."

Ian relaxed against the high-back leather chair, seeming to enjoy himself. An insolent half smile curled up the edges of his mouth. "It was my understanding Molly's leaving was a mutual decision."

Jordan snickered. "By the time she moved out there wasn't anything mutual between us. We hadn't spoken in days." The communication between them had died with their six-month-old son. The autumn morning they'd lowered Jeff's tiny casket into the ground, they'd buried their marriage, as well. For eight months afterward, they'd struggled to hold their lives together. But the grief and the guilt had eaten away until there was nothing left but an empty shell, and eventually that had crumbled and scattered like dust.

Ian stood, looking older than Jordan remembered. He walked over to the window and gazed out as if the view were mesmerizing. "Why now?"

"It's been three years," Jordan reminded him.

"I'm well aware of how long it's been," Ian murmured, clenching his hands behind his back.

"It's time I got on with my life," Jordan said coolly. "I want a divorce."

"A divorce," Ian repeated, and it seemed his shoulders sagged under the weight of the word.

"Don't tell me this comes as a shock. I should have filed years ago." Jordan paced the room with ill patience, the anger simmering just below the surface until it felt like a geyser about to erupt. His annoyance was unreasonable, Jordan realized, and directed more at himself than his father-in-law. He'd delayed this confrontation for longer than he should have, dreading it. The divorce papers were tucked away in his briefcase. All he sought was Molly's signature. After three years, he didn't anticipate Molly's objection. Actually he was surprised she hadn't taken the action herself.

Ian moved away from the window and glanced toward the framed picture on his desk. Jordan knew it was one taken of him and Molly shortly after Jeff had been born. He remembered it well. He was standing behind Molly, who held Jeff in her arms; his hand was braced on Molly's shoulder and the two of them were gazing down with wonderment and love on this young life they'd produced. Little did they know that their joy would soon turn into the deepest grief they'd ever experience.

"I'd always hoped you two would patch things up," Ian said, his words tinged with sadness.

Jordan pressed his lips together and buried his hands deep inside his pants pockets. A reconciliation might have worked earlier, but it was impossible now; the sooner Ian accepted that, the better. "I've met someone else."

Ian nodded. "I guessed as much. You can't blame an old man for wishing."

"Where's Molly?" Jordan wasn't enjoying this cat-and-mouse game any more than Ian. The time had come to cut to the chase.

"Manukua," Ian told him.

Jordan's head snapped up. "Africa?"

Ian nodded. "She's doing volunteer work with some church group. The country's desperately in need of anyone with medical experience, and working there has seemed to help her."

Jordan splayed his fingers through his hair. "How long has she been there?"

"Over two years now."

"Two years?" Jordan felt as if he'd taken a blow to the abdomen and slumped into a nearby chair. It was just like Molly to do something impulsive. Manukua had been in the news almost nightly, with accounts of rebel unrest, drought, disease and God only knew what else.

"I've done everything I know how to convince her to come home," Ian said, sitting back down himself, "but she won't listen to me."

"What's the matter with her?" Jordan demanded.

"The same thing as you, I suspect," Ian said without rancor. "You buried yourself in your work, and she's dedicated herself to saving the world."

"Any fool would know Manukua's not safe," Jordan protested heatedly, furious with his soon-to-be ex-wife.

Ian nodded, agreeing with him. "She claims otherwise. Apparently she's working in a hospital in Makua, the capital, for two weeks out of the month. Then she commutes into the backcountry to a medical compound for another two weeks."

"Is she crazy, traveling outside of the city?" Jordan demanded. He wished Molly was there so he could strangle her himself. He was on his feet again, but didn't remember standing. "The woman should have her head examined."

"I couldn't agree with you more. Something's got to be done." He grinned and reached for a Cuban cigar. "As far as I'm concerned, you're the man for it."

"Me? What the hell can I do?" Jordan asked, although he was fairly certain he already knew the answer.

For the first time Jordan read a genuine smile in the older man's eyes. "What can you do?" Ian repeated meaningfully. "Why, Jordan, you can go get her yourself."

It was the evenings that Molly loved best, when the compound slept and the night slipped in—silent, cool and welcome. She sat outside on the veranda and drank in the sounds, allowing them to soothe her exhausted body and spirit. The news from headquarters in Makua had arrived earlier that evening and it hadn't been good. It never was. Each report, no matter where or when she was in the backcountry, seemed filled with dire warnings and evil threats. That evening's communication had been no different, with a lengthy account of political unrest in the capital city and the threat of a rebel attack. Headquarters asked that she and Dr. Morton be prepared to evacuate at a moment's notice. The identical message came through on a regular basis and had long since lost its urgency. At the end of the week they'd return to Makua the same way they did every month.

The black stillness of the night was filled with gentle sounds from the water hole just outside the compound walls. The savanna was a refuge for the dwindling animal population. The drought had taken a dramatic toll on wildlife, just as it had on the natives.

Just a week earlier Molly had witnessed a small herd of elephants tramping across the dry plain, stirring up a haze of red dust. They were moving, looking for a more abundant water supply, Molly guessed.

A hyena yipped in the night, and she smiled softly to herself. Additional sounds drifted toward her as the antelope and other beasts made their way to the water's waning edge to cool their thirst. Over time and with patience, Molly had become adept at identifying each species. She'd discovered, contrary to popular belief, that lions didn't roar so much as cough. She'd hear the king of beasts and then the night would go quiet as his intended prey silently slipped away from the water's edge.

Leaning back in the white wicker chair, she stretched her arms high above her head and stared into the heavens. The sky was illuminated with an incredible display of stars, but she would have sold her inheritance for the sight of a water-fat rain cloud.

Unfortunately the sky was disgustingly clear. Molly couldn't look into the night without experiencing a twinge of sadness. Somewhere in a world far removed from what was her life now remained the husband she'd abandoned and the son she'd buried.

She tried not to think about either, because doing so produced a dull, throbbing pain. And pain was something she'd spent the past three years running away from, until she was breathless and emotionally exhausted from the effort. The gold wedding band on her finger felt like an accusation. She wasn't even sure why she continued to wear it. Habit, she suspected, and to ward off any who thought she might be interested in romance. She wasn't.

Familiar footsteps sounded behind her.

"Good evening," Molly greeted her associate. Dr. Richard Morton was well past the age of retirement, short, bald and lovable, but he didn't know how to stop working, not when the need remained so great. Molly, who was slender as a reed, stood nearly a head taller. With her short blond hair and deep blue eyes, she caused something of a sensation with the black African children.

"Why aren't you asleep?" Molly asked her friend. By all rights they should both have fallen into bed exhausted.

"I haven't figured that out myself," the physician said, settling into the chair next to her. "Something's in the air."

"Oh?"

"I've got a feeling about this last message from Makua."

"You think we should leave?" Richard couldn't have surprised her more. Her companion had never revealed any signs of being anxious for their safety in the past, even when the radio messages had sounded far more urgent.

Richard shrugged and wiped a hand down his face. "I don't know, but something tells me this time is different."

This past week had been hectic with an outbreak of influenza, and they'd both been working grueling hours, often as many as eighteen a day.

"You're overly tired," Molly suggested, searching for a plausible excuse for his qualms.

"We both are," Richard murmured and gently patted her hand. "Go to bed and we'll talk about this some more in the morning."

Molly followed his advice, taking a few extra moments to stroll through the pediatric ward. The nurse on duty smiled when she saw who it was. The walk through the children's ward had become something of a ritual for her.

Silently moving between cribs, Molly stopped to check if each child was breathing. This was the legacy SIDS had given her. It was as though she anticipated that terrible scene replaying itself over again with another child in another time and place. The fear never left her. The fear of losing another child had taken up residence in the deepest roots of her heart.

Once she was assured all was well, Molly made her way into her own tiny room, not bothering to turn on the light. She undressed and slipped between the cool sheets, closed her eyes and dreamed of what her life would have been like if Jeff had lived.

"I'm sorry I'm late," Jordan said, kissing Lesley's cheek before pulling out the chair and sitting down at the table across from her. Each time Jordan was with the accomplished architect he was struck by her charm and beauty. "How long did I keep you waiting this time?" he asked as he unfolded the pink linen napkin and placed it on his lap.

"Only a few moments."

He was a full fifteen minutes late, and knowing Lesley she'd arrived five minutes early, yet she didn't complain. This was one of the things he liked best about her. She understood his preoccupation with work, because she was often deeply involved in a project herself.

Jordan reached for the menu, scanned the contents and quickly made his choice, setting it aside.

"Don't keep me in suspense," Lesley said. "Tell me how the meeting with Ian went."

Jordan shrugged, not sure he wanted to talk about Molly or Ian just yet. He found it awkward to be discussing his wife with the woman he intended to marry. There'd been a time when he'd hoped he and Molly might be able to salvage their marriage. But as the weeks and months slipped past and neither of them seemed inclined to breach the silence, Jordan lost hope for a reconciliation.

"Everything went fine," he said, reaching for the wine list, studying the different choices.

"You don't want to talk about it, do you?" Lesley said after a moment.

"Not particularly."

"All right...I can understand that," she said, and although he could read the disappointment in her voice he knew she wouldn't pursue the issue further. This was something else he appreciated about Lesley. He'd known her for years and couldn't remember her so much as raising her voice, even once.

In the past year they'd started working together on a large construction project on Chicago's east side. She was the architect and he was the builder. Heaven knew he wasn't looking for another relationship. Falling in love a second time held no appeal.

Ian was right when he claimed Jordan had buried himself in his work after Jeff's death. He went from one project to the next with barely a breath in between. He didn't know what would happen if he ever stopped—he didn't want to know.

"I realize this is difficult for you," Lesley said in that soft, sultry voice of hers. "But you must know what an awkward position this puts me in. I can't continue to date a married man."

"I do understand."

"Nor do I want to force you into a divorce when it's something you may not want."

Jordan frowned. This ground was all too familiar, and he wasn't thrilled to be traipsing over the same worn path. "The marriage is dead." If he'd said it once, he'd said it a hundred times.

"You told me that in the beginning," Lesley reminded him, "but we've been seeing each other steadily for six months and in all that time you didn't once mention divorcing Molly." This sounded faintly like an accusation.

"I should have filed years ago."

"But you didn't."

Jordan didn't need Lesley to tell him that.

"Do you know why?" she pressed. Generally she was willing to let sleeping dogs lie, but not this evening.

"I was too busy," he said, a bit more heatedly than he intended. "Besides, I assumed Molly would see to it."

"She didn't file for a divorce, either, you'll notice," Lesley felt obliged to point out to him. "Have you stopped to consider that?"

He nodded, and motioned for a waiter, who promptly appeared and took their order. Jordan asked for a bottle of chardonnay and for the next five or so minutes he was preoccupied with the opening and tasting of the wine. Jordan hoped Lesley would drop the subject of Molly and the divorce, but he doubted she would. Her pretty brown eyes were aimed at him with the same gentle persuasion he'd witnessed the night she'd first announced she couldn't continue to date a married man. Rather than lose her, he'd agreed to start the divorce proceedings.

"You're still in love with her, aren't you?" Lesley pressed in that delicate way of hers. She was rarely angry at him, unlike Molly who took delight in igniting his ire. Lesley was subtle and concerned. Whatever her methods, they worked wonders on him.

"It's perfectly understandable, you realize," Lesley continued.

"To love Molly?" He couldn't believe she was suggesting such a thing.

"Yes. What happened to the two of you is tragic."

A pain tightened in his chest. "She blamed herself," he whispered, his hand gripping the wineglass with unnecessary force. "With all her medical training she seemed to think there was something she could have done to save him."

He'd argued with her until he had no voice left. It hadn't helped matters that he'd left the house when she and Jeff were still asleep. Apparently Jeff had stirred and cried out, but it was early yet and, thinking she'd get a few more moments sleep, Molly had ignored the lone cry. It was the last sound their son had ever made. Molly had woken an hour later to discover Jeff dead.

Jordan looked at Lesley and blinked, wondering if what she suggested was true. Did he still love Molly? He'd never faulted her for what happened to Jeff, but she'd readily accepted the blame herself, despite everything he said and did.

But did he love Molly? Jordan asked himself a second time. He didn't know. So much of what he felt toward her was tangled up in his feelings for his son. He'd loved Jeff more than he thought it was possible for a man to love his child. He'd grieved, in his own way, until he had nearly killed himself, working all hours of the day and night. In some way he suspected he had died. Part of him had departed with his son.

If Jordan had learned anything from his limited experience as a father, it was that he would never be vulnerable to this kind of pain again. This was Lesley's great appeal. She didn't want children, either. They were perfect for each other.

"I don't mean to pressure you with these uncomfortable questions," Lesley continued in soft, caring tones.

"You're not," Jordan said. The loss of his son wasn't a subject he'd ever feel comfortable sharing. But if he was going to join his life with Lesley's, Jeff was a topic they needed to talk about.

The waiter delivered their salads, and Lesley, who sensed his mood perfectly, left Jordan alone with his thoughts.

At some point this evening he'd need to tell Lesley he was going to Manukua after Molly. He didn't relish the task.

He'd like to wring Molly's pretty neck for this. Why couldn't she have gone to some tropical island and set up a medical clinic? Oh no, she had to throw herself into one of the world's hottest trouble spots. It would be just like her to get herself killed.

Ian hadn't fooled him, either. Molly's father was worried sick about her himself, and Jordan had fallen right into the old man's capable hands, coming to see him when he did. Talk about crummy timing. He should get some kind of award for that.

"Molly's in Manukua," Jordan announced to Lesley without warning.

"Manukua," Lesley repeated in an astonished gasp. "What in the name of heaven is she doing there?"

"She volunteered with some missionary group."

"Doesn't she realize how dangerous it is?" Lesley set her fork aside and reached for her wineglass. Jordan wished now that he'd taken more care breaking the news to her.

"I'm going after her." He didn't mention that Ian was pulling every string he had to get Jordan a visa. By hook or crook he was going to Manukua, even if he had to be smuggled into the country.

"You." Lesley's eyes went wide, and when she set the glass down the wine sloshed over the edge. "Jordan, that's ridiculous. Why should you be the one? If she's in any danger, then the State Department should be notified."

"Ian's aged considerably in the past three years and his health is too fragile for such a strenuous journey. Someone's got to do something, and soon, before Molly manages to get herself killed."

"But surely there's someone else who could go."

"No one Molly would listen to."

"But...what about your work?" It was rare to see Lesley so flustered.

"Paul Phelps will take over for me. I shouldn't be gone long— a week at the most."

"What about the necessary papers? My heavens, no one travels in and out of Manukua these days...do they? I mean, from what the newspeople are saying, the country's about to explode."

"Ian's making the arrangements for me. He'd intended on making the trip himself, against his doctor's and everyone else's advice. Listen, Lesley, this isn't anything I want to do. Trust me, if I was going to take a week away from the job, Manukua would be the last place I'd choose to visit."

"I understand, Jordan," she said, her hand reaching for his. "This is something you have to do."

Jordan's relief was so great his shoulders sagged with it. He hadn't been able to put his feelings into words, but Lesley had said it for him. Perfectly. It was something he needed to do. This one last thing before he said goodbye to this woman and their marriage. He considered going after Molly a moral obligation. To her and to Ian. To the man who'd given him advice and financial backing when he'd started out in construction. To the man who'd given him his daughter. Giving Molly back to Ian seemed a small thing to do by comparison.

"When do you leave?" Lesley asked, and Jordan noticed that her voice was shaking slightly, although she struggled to disguise it. Jordan was grateful she didn't attempt to talk him out of it, or to convince him of the danger he was placing himself in for a woman he intended to divorce.

"The first part of the week."

"So soon?"

"The sooner the better, don't you think?"

Lesley nodded, and lowered her eyes. "Just promise me one thing."

"Of course."

"Please be careful, because despite everything, I love you, Jordan Larabee."

Molly woke to the sound of gunfire echoing in the distance. She sat up in bed, but it took her a moment to orientate herself. Tossing aside the thin blanket, she climbed out of bed and quickly dressed. The rat-a-tat sounds seemed closer now and a shot of adrenaline propelled her into action.

Dawn had just come over the hill and Molly could see people

running in several different directions at once. Pandemonium reigned.

"What's happening?" Molly demanded, catching an orderly by the shoulders.

Large brown eyes stared into hers. "The rebels are coming. You must go...now," he said urgently. "Very fast, do not wait."

"Dr. Morton?" Molly pleaded. "Have you seen Dr. Morton?"

He shook his head wildly, then broke away, running toward the row of parked vehicles.

"Richard," Molly shouted. She couldn't, wouldn't, leave without her friend. His sleeping quarters were across the compound from her own, but making her way across the open area was nearly impossible. Sounds came at her from every direction. People were shouting in more languages than she could understand. Fear was like an animal that clawed at her legs, nearly immobilizing her.

"Molly, Molly." Her name seemed to come from a deep valley. She whirled around to find Richard Morton frantically searching the crowd for her.

"Here," she shouted, waving her hand high above her head.

She had to fight her way to his side. Briefly, they clung to each other.

"We have to leave right away. Mwanda has a truck waiting."

Molly nodded, her hand gripping Richard's. They'd been fools not to heed headquarters' warnings. She'd worked with these people for two years and found them to be gentle, peace-loving souls. The dangers of a coup had seemed like distant threats that didn't affect her, but she was wrong.

"What about the sick?" Molly pleaded. Richard was on one side of her and the six-foot Mwanda on the other.

"We will care for them," Mwanda promised in halting English. "But first you go."

Richard and Molly were literally tossed into the truck bed. They huddled in the corners and waited for their escape, although only God knew what they'd meet along the way.

The truck fired to life. Molly swore the old camouflage contraption had served in Africa during World War II. She was convinced God and Mwanda were the only ones who kept it running.

A tall, thin Manukuan boy vaulted toward the truck, speaking furiously in his native tongue. Over the past couple of years, Molly had picked up a fair amount of the language, although she wasn't as fluent as she would have liked. The cold hand of fear settled over her as her mind translated the frantic words.

Her gaze met Dr. Morton's and it was plain he understood the message, as well.

They couldn't leave now. It was too late. The countryside was swarming with rebel troops, bent on hatred and vengeance. Many innocents had already been murdered.

Richard and Molly were trapped inside the compound.

Mwanda turned off the engine and climbed out of the truck. His eyes were empty as he helped the two climb down from the back.

"What will we do now?" Molly asked.

Richard shrugged. "Wait."

Wait for what? was the immediate question that came to Molly's mind. For death, and pray that it would be merciful? She doubted that there was any real chance of rescue now. If they were captured, what they might do to her as a woman didn't bear thinking.

So this was how it was to be for her. Surprisingly she wasn't afraid. The fear left her as quickly as it came, replaced with an incredible sense of calm. If the rebels broke through the compound, they weren't going to find her cowering in some corner. They'd find her doing what she did each and every day, helping her patients.

"I believe I'll do my rounds," Richard announced, his voice shaking slightly.

"I'll come with you," Molly said.

Her partner seemed pleased to have the company and offered her a shaky smile.

Mwanda shook his head and, with a resigned shrug of his shoulders, moved away. "I go back to kitchen," he announced with a wide smile. Two of his teeth were missing, but Molly doubted that she'd ever seen him smile more brightly. Or bravely.

Clinging to routine was of primary importance to them; although the thread of normalcy was fragile and threatened to break at any moment, it was all they had to hold on to.

The sound of gunfire continued to sound in the distance, creeping closer, bit by bit. Radio communication with Makua had been severed, so they had no way of knowing what was happening in the capital city. For all Molly knew, the entire country had been taken over.

It was the not knowing that was the worst. Several of their patients left, preferring to take their chances on reaching their families. Richard tended to those who were too sick to walk away from the compound. Several attempted to convince Molly and Richard to leave with them, but they refused. This was where they belonged.

This was where they'd stay. Within minutes, Molly was shocked to realize there was only a handful of natives left.

Molly prayed for their safety, but there was no way for them to know how long they'd be safe behind the protective walls of the compound.

It could have been minutes, but it might have been hours later, when Molly heard the unmistakable sounds of a helicopter. It circled the compound, but she couldn't read any markings on it, so she wasn't sure if it was friend or foe.

The chopper hovered, then slowly descended. The noise was deafening, and the wind strong enough to stir up a thick layer of red dirt that cut visibility down to practically zero.

From the snatches of color she did manage to glimpse, she saw soldiers leap from the helicopter, dressed in full battle gear. Guerrillas, she suspected.

Molly remained in the pediatric ward, empty now. The door burst open and she faced a soldier with a machine gun. The guerilla stopped when he saw her, then shouted something over his shoulder. Molly straightened her shoulders and waited, not knowing for what.

A few seconds later another man burst into the room, nearly tearing the door off its hinges in his rush. Bracing herself against the rails of a crib, she met the angry eyes and realized they were hazel. And amazingly familiar.

"Jordan?" she whispered, looking up into the tight features of her husband. "What are you doing here?"

Chapter Two

"We're getting the hell out of here," Jordan said, convinced his heart rate was in excess of ninety miles an hour. From the aerial view he'd gotten from the helicopter, the rebels looked to be less than two or three miles outside of the medical compound and were quickly gaining territory. It was likely they'd move in on them at any minute.

"What about Richard?" Molly cried. "I can't leave without him."

"Who?" Jordan argued, gripping her by the upper arm and half lifting, half dragging her toward the door. Zane, and the men his mercenary friend had hired, surrounded the helicopter, their machine guns poised and ready.

"Dr. Morton," Molly shouted to be heard above the roar of the whirling blades of the helicopter. "I can't leave without Richard."

"We don't have time," Jordan argued.

With surprising strength, Molly tore herself away; her eyes were bright with fire as she glared at him. "I refuse to go without him."

"This is a hell of a time to be worrying about your boyfriend, don't you think?" Jordan snapped, furious that she'd be concerned about another man when he was risking his damn fool neck to save hers.

"I'll get him," Molly said, surging past him. Before Jordan could stop her she was gone. The helicopter blades stirred up a thick fog of dust and smoke. Bedlam surrounded them. An ominous crackling noise could be heard in the distance. More than once Jordan had asked himself what craziness had possessed his wife to put herself into this situation. Molly wasn't the only one—he was stuck in

Manukua, as well, and wishing the hell he was just about anyplace else.

Jordan's area of expertise lay in constructing high-rise apartments and office buildings. Guerrilla warfare was definitely out of his league and the very reason he'd contacted Zane Halquist.

"Molly," he shouted, shaking with urgency, "there isn't time."

Either she didn't hear him, or she chose to ignore his frantic call. It came to him that he should leave without her. He would have, too, if he'd known he could live with himself afterward. This woman was going to be the end of him yet. Jordan had never thought of himself as a coward, but he sure as hell felt like one now.

An explosion rang in his ears, the blast strong enough to knock him off-balance and jar his senses. He staggered a few steps before he caught himself. He shook his head, hoping that would help bring order to his thoughts. It didn't.

Zane shouted something to him, but with his ears ringing, Jordan didn't have a prayer of understanding him. He shook his head to indicate as much, but by that time it wasn't necessary. The man he'd trusted, the man he'd freely handed several thousand American dollars, raced toward the waiting copter with two or three of the other soldiers.

Jordan's heart slammed against his chest when he realized what was happening. They were leaving him, Molly and a handful of mercenaries behind.

Jordan hadn't finished cursing when he saw Molly with an elderly man on the far side of the compound. She held her hand to her face to protect her eyes from the swirling dust. She stood frozen with shock and regret, he guessed, as she watched the helicopter lift and speed away.

The man who'd found Molly in the nursery grabbed Jordan by the elbow, jerking him out of his momentary paralysis. "Take the woman and hide," he instructed roughly.

Jordan's instinct was to stay and fight. He wasn't the type to sit contentedly on the sidelines and do nothing. "I'll help," Jordan insisted.

"Hide the woman first."

Jordan nodded and ran as if a machine gun were firing at his heels. He raced toward Molly, and she ran toward him. He caught her just as she stumbled and fell into his arms.

She clung to him and Jordan wove his fingers into her hair, pressing her against him. His heart pounded with fear and adrenaline.

Jordan had never been more angry with anyone in his life, and at the same identical moment he was so grateful she was alive he felt like breaking into tears. It amazed him that it had been more than three years since he'd last held her and that she fit like a comfortable glove in his embrace.

"Where can I hide you?"

She looked up at him blankly, then shook her head. "I...I don't know. The supply house, but wouldn't that be the first place anyone would look?"

Jordan agreed with her. "There isn't a cellar or something?"

"No."

"Then don't worry about it. If the rebels make it into the compound, they'll check every outbuilding. I'll take you and Dr. Morton to the supply hut."

"What about you?" She clenched his arm with a strength he found amazing, as if he were her lifeline.

"I'll be back later."

Her hands framed his face, and she blinked through a wall of tears. "Be careful please, be careful."

He nodded. He had no intention of sacrificing his life. Hand in hand they ran for the supply house. Jordan glanced around for Dr. Morton and saw that the men had taken Molly's friend under their wing and were hiding the elderly physician themselves.

The supply hut was locked, but luckily Molly had the key. Jordan quickly surveyed the grounds, wondering exactly how much protection this ramshackle building would offer her. If the rebels broke into the compound, he needed to be in a position where he could protect her.

The sound of gunfire rang in the distance, sounding like the cap guns he'd played with as a boy. Only this was real.

"Keep your head down," Jordan instructed, closing the door after her. "I'll be back for you as soon as I can." He noticed how pale and frightened she was, but that couldn't be helped. He probably didn't look much better himself. His last thought as he left her was that anyone going after Molly would need to kill him first.

Terror gripped Molly at every burst of a machine gun. She was huddled in the corner, hunched down, with her back against the wall, her knees tucked under her chin. Her hands covered her ears, and she gnawed on her lower lip until she tasted blood. The room was pitch-dark with only a thin ribbon of light that crept in from beneath the door.

Footsteps pounded past the storehouse and she stopped breathing for fear the rebels had succeeded and broken into the compound.

The worst part of this ordeal was being alone. She wouldn't be nearly as frightened if Dr. Morton was with her. Or Jordan.

Nothing in this world could have shocked her more than her husband bursting into the nursery, armed with a rifle and dressed as if he were part of Special Forces. He'd served in the military, but that had been years earlier, when he was right out of high school.

She didn't know what craziness had possessed Jordan to risk his life to save her. It might sound ungrateful, but she'd rather he'd stayed in Chicago. He was furious with her, that much she'd read in his eyes, but then his anger wasn't anything new. In the end, before she'd moved out, their marriage had deteriorated to the point that they were barely on speaking terms. It hadn't always been like that. Only after Jeff had died... She forcefully pushed thoughts of their child from her mind. Early on in their marriage they'd been so deeply in love that Molly would never have believed anything would ever come between them.

Death had.

The grim reaper's scythe had struck and his blade had fallen directly between them, separating them in the most painful of ways, by claiming their six-month-old child.

Molly had no idea how much time had passed before the door opened. Panic gripped her as she squinted into the light, but she relaxed when she realized it was Jordan.

"What's happening?" she pleaded, eager for news.

"The hell if I know." He abruptly pulled the door closed after him. The room went dark once more and he lit a match that softly illuminated the compact quarters. He leaned his rifle against the wall and sank down onto the dirt floor next to her. She noted that his breathing was heavy. His shoulders heaved several times before he exhaled sharply and relaxed. "Knowing Zane, he'll do everything he can to come back for us, but there are no guarantees."

"Who the hell is Zane?"

"An old friend," he said, "you don't know him. We met in the Army years ago."

The room was pitch-black once more. His shoulders pressed against hers, and some of the terror and loneliness left her at his closeness. "What about the rebels?" She needed to know where they stood, or if there was any chance of them getting out of this alive. Death didn't concern her, but how she died did.

"Apparently Zane and the others have been able to hold them off, for now at least, but there're a thousand unknowns in this. Everything's quiet for the moment, but I don't expect that to last."

She nodded, although there wasn't any way he had of seeing her. "What are you doing here in Manukua?" The question had burned in her mind from the moment he'd stormed into the compound as if he were Rambo on the loose.

"Someone had to do something to get you out of here. Ian's worried sick. If you want to risk your own foolish neck, fine, but you might have waited until your father was too senile to know or care. He'd never recover if anything happened to you."

The words were thrown at her, an accusation, sharp and cutting in their intensity.

"I certainly didn't know anything like this was going to happen," she snapped back defensively.

"You might have opted to volunteer for someplace other than Manukua," he said between clenched teeth. "Why couldn't you be content dispensing medication to school kids? Oh no, that would have been too simple. What'd you do, look for the hottest trouble spot on the world map and aim for there?"

He was stiff and distant. It pained her to realize that, within five minutes of seeing each other after three years apart, they were arguing.

Molly knew that at some point in the future she'd need to talk with Jordan, she just hadn't suspected it would be here in Manukua, surrounded by rebel troops.

"I'm sorry you're involved in this," she said softly, and despite her best efforts her voice was swamped with emotion. Her words came out sounding as if she were standing at the bottom of a deep pit.

"It isn't your fault I'm here. I volunteered to come." The anger was gone out of his voice, as well, and she sensed his regret for his earlier outburst.

"H-how have you been?" she asked softly. It seemed insane that they would sit on the hard dirt floor of a run-down shack and exchange niceties. Especially when they were in danger of being attacked by rebel soldiers any minute. But Molly sincerely wanted to know how his life had been going these past few years.

"Busy."

"Are you still working twelve-hour days?"

"Yeah."

Molly figured as much. Jordan had never allowed himself to grieve openly for Jeff. He'd buried himself in his work, effectively closing himself off from her and from life. Not that she'd been any saint. After Jeff had died, she'd been consumed with guilt and was so emotionally needy a thousand Jordans couldn't have filled the void her son's death had left in her life.

As the weeks and months wore on after the funeral, Molly had become continually more lethargic, while Jordan took the business world by storm. Within eight months he was Chicago's golden boy, with his hand in three major construction projects. Meanwhile, Molly had trouble finding the energy to climb out of bed in the morning.

A gunshot echoed like cannon fire and Molly jerked instinctively.

"Relax," Jordan advised. "Everything's under control."

He couldn't know that, but she appreciated the reassurance. "I feel like such a fool," she admitted, pressing her forehead to her knee.

Jordan placed his arm around her shoulders and brought her closer to his side. His shoulder was rock hard, but his comfort was more welcome than a goose-down pillow. It was hard to imagine how two people who had desperately loved each other had grown so far apart. In all her life, however long or short it was to be, Molly didn't ever expect to love anyone as much as she had her husband and her son. It seemed vitally important Jordan know this. She couldn't leave matters as they were between them. Not when she'd been given the opportunity to make things right. The words felt like a huge lump in her throat. "If...if the worst does happen, I want you to know I'll always love you, Jordan."

He went still and quiet, as if he wasn't sure how to deal with her confession. "I've tried not to love you," he admitted grudgingly. "Somehow I never quite succeeded."

Another gunshot sounded, and in a knee-jerk reaction she burrowed deeper into the shelter of his arms. She trembled and Jordan increased the pressure, holding her tightly against him.

Burying her face in the hollow of his neck, she breathed in the warm, manly scent of him. Jordan said nothing, but continued to hold her as his arm gently caressed her back.

It had been so long since she'd been in her husband's arms, so long since she'd felt loved and protected. She might never have the opportunity again. This time together was like a gift God had given them both. Tears welled in her eyes and spilled down her cheek.

"Molly, don't cry. It'll be all right, I promise you."

"I'm not worried," she lied, "you're here and you always did love playing the role of the hero."

He brushed the hair away from her temple, his touch gentle and reassuring. She wanted to thank him for being here with her, but couldn't find the words to adequately express her gratitude.

Kissing his neck seemed the natural thing to do. She slid the tip of her tongue over his flesh, reveling in the salty taste of him. She felt him tense, but he didn't stop her, nor did he encourage her.

Her palm was pressed against his heart and his pulse beat in strong, even thuds, the tempo increasing when she opened her mouth against the strong cord of his neck and sucked gently.

"Molly," he warned hoarsely, his hands gripping her upper arms as if to push her away. He'd done that often enough after Jeff's death, as if his desire for her had died with his son. Perhaps not physically, but emotionally.

"I'm sorry..." she whispered, but before she could say anything more, his mouth was on hers, hot and compelling. His kiss was so fierce that her breath jammed in her throat and her nails dug into his shoulders.

Molly knew that it was crazy for them to get involved in something like this now, but it didn't stop her from responding, didn't keep her from moaning in abject surrender. She returned his kisses with a wildness that had been carefully hidden and denied for three long years.

Jordan stroked her breasts, his touch feather light, as if he were afraid of what would happen if he allowed himself to enjoy the fruits of her body. Her nipples quivered until they hardened and throbbed for his touch. Molly needed him as she had rarely needed anyone. Her fingers awkwardly reached for the buttons of her blouse, unfastening them in haste and peeling it off her shoulders. Jordan helped her remove her bra and groaned hoarsely as her breasts spilled into his waiting palms.

"Molly..."

"Love me," she pleaded softly. "One last time...I need you so much."

His mouth fastened on her nipple with greedy passion. Wild sensation shot through her and she buckled at the mixture of pleasure and pain. He feasted on one nipple and then the other, suckling and bunching her breasts together while his mouth created a slick, well-traveled trail between the two hardened peaks.

"This is nuts." Jordan sighed, but he didn't reveal any signs of putting an end to it.

"The world is crazy," she reminded him and finished undressing.

His hand moved lower, caressing her smooth abdomen and flat stomach, edging downward until he reached the soft patch of hairs between her thighs. He flattened his hand there as if to absorb the pulsations that rocked her. It was as though the years apart had vanished like mist. They were well acquainted with each other's bodies and used that knowledge to drive one another to a fever pitch of desire and need.

Seated, he positioned her on top of him. The sounds outside the supply shed were lost to the thunder of her heart echoing in her ears and the soft moaning sounds working their way up the back of her throat.

They were on fire for each other as he slowly lowered her onto the swollen strength of his manhood. His hands dug into her hips as she swallowed him with her own moist heat.

Molly gasped with pleasure, thinking she would die with it. Her head fell forward, her hair spilling wildly over her face.

It had been so long, so very long, since they'd last made love. A sob of welcome and regret was trapped in her chest as Jordan worked her against him, setting the cadence for their lovemaking.

A few moments later Jordan growled, then panted as if struggling for control. His breath came in short, uneven gasps as she rotated her hips against him, tormenting him the same way he was her. His hands closed over her buttocks, controlling her thrusts, setting the rhythm, increasing the pace.

Danger surrounded them, the threat of death was very real, but there wasn't room in her mind for anything more than the wonder of their love, and the need they were satisfying with each other.

She cried out as her body reached its climax and Jordan clamped his mouth over hers, swallowing her cries of exultation and joy. Pleasure burst gloriously inside her even as the tears rained unheeded down her face.

Jordan responded with one savage thrust as he reached his own peak. Trembling, they clung to each other. Molly was sobbing softly against his shoulder and his arms were wrapped securely around her.

They didn't speak. There was no need; words would have been superfluous just then. Gently he kissed her, once and then again, not with passion but with thanksgiving. Molly returned his kisses with the same heartfelt gratitude.

Jordan helped her dress and held her close for several moments afterward. When he released her, she felt his reluctance. "I have to go," he told her.

"Where?" she cried, not wanting him to leave her.

"I'll be back as soon as I can," he promised, kissing her. "Trust me, Molly, I don't want to leave you, but I've already stayed longer than I should have."

"I understand." She tried to hide, without much success, the panic she felt.

He brushed his hand against her temple, running his fingers down the side of her face. "I won't be long, I promise."

She knew he didn't want to leave any more than she wanted to see him go, but it was necessary. For the safety of them both.

Once she was alone, Molly shut her eyes and prayed God would protect her husband. She'd lost track of time and didn't know if it was afternoon or evening. The light coming from beneath the door seemed less bright, but that could be her imagination.

Jordan returned several hours later with blankets and food. Although she hadn't eaten all day, Molly wasn't hungry. Only because he insisted did she manage to down the MREs, meals ready to eat, he brought with him. Leave it to a man to think of food at a time like this. Jordan ate ravenously, while she picked at her food.

"What's happening around the compound?" she asked, finishing off a piece of dried fruit.

"It's secure for now."

"What about Dr. Morton?"

"He's safe and asking about you." He spread the blanket over the dirt floor. "Try and get some sleep," he advised. "Here." He wrapped his arm around her shoulders and brought her close to his side, but something was different. His hold wasn't as tight nor as personal as it had been earlier.

"Jordan," she asked, nestling close. "Are you sorry about what happened before? Neither of us planned on making love and, well, I thought it might be troubling you."

"No, I don't regret it." His answer sounded oddly defensive. "But I should."

"Why? Good grief, we're married."

He didn't answer her right away. "It's been three years. A lot can happen in that amount of time."

"I know."

"I'm not the same person anymore."

"Neither am I," she agreed.

After the hellish fighting of the day, the night seemed relatively peaceful. The sounds of silence were welcome ones. For the first time since Jordan had made love to her earlier, she felt safe and protected. Whatever happened didn't matter as long as she was in his arms.

Molly's breasts inadvertently brushed against the hard wall of his chest and Jordan's breath caught. It seemed several moments passed before he breathed again.

He kissed her once, softly, experimentally, then again and again, each kiss gaining in length and intensity. He slid his mouth from

her lips across her cheek to her ear, taking the lobe between his
teeth and sucking gently. Molly gasped as the tingly sensation rippled down her spine.

Jordan chuckled softly. "I wondered if that had changed."

"Two can play that game, buster." She climbed into his lap and
placed her head against his shoulder. Wrapping her arms around his
neck, she spread a series of soft kisses along the underside of his
jaw, using her tongue to tease and entice him. She didn't need any
lights to know the effect she was having on him. Jordan couldn't
disguise his growing need.

He kissed her then as if he were starving for her. His tongue
alternately plundered and caressed her mouth while he locked his
arms around her waist and her back. It was as if Jordan never
intended on letting go of her again. It was a feeling Molly could
learn to live with.

She met his hunger with her own and soon their passion became
a raging fire that threatened to consume them both. Their bodies
had found satisfaction in each other only hours earlier and yet it
wasn't adequate to quench the long dry spell away from each other.

They couldn't take off their clothes fast enough, removing only
what was necessary. Jordan spoke, but Molly found the words strangled and incomprehensible. Not that it mattered; nothing did just
then, except each other.

Their desire for one another was urgent and frantic, and Jordan's
strength might have bruised her if she had been aware of anything
beyond her own tortuous need. As had happened earlier, Molly
found her deliverance first and buried her face in the warm hollow
of his neck. Soon afterward Jordan's body shuddered and she felt
his throbbing release deep inside her body. She moved against him,
her thighs clenched as she milked him in a driving dance of ecstasy.
The melting sensation increased her own lingering enjoyment.

Molly didn't know how much time elapsed before her breathing
returned to normal.

"I can't believe this," Jordan murmured between soft, gentle
kisses.

"Who would have thought we'd experience the most incredible
sex of our lives in a supply hut in Africa?" she whispered. If the
soldiers burst in and gunned her down right then and there, Molly
decided she'd die a happy woman. She doubted that either of them
could have mustered the strength to put up much of a fight.

"You're smiling?" Jordan asked, pushing the hair away from
her face.

"You would be, too, if you experienced anything close to what I just did."

"Trust me, I'm smiling."

"You know what I was thinking," she said, then yawned loudly. "What?"

"I just realized I'd really like to come out of this mess alive."

"So would I," Jordan said adamantly.

That hadn't been entirely true for Molly. She didn't actively think about death, but she hadn't much cared what happened, either. One way or the other it hadn't seemed to matter. It did now, and she had Jordan to thank for that.

"Do you think you can sleep now?" he asked, his hands stroking her back.

She nodded. "What about you?"

"Yeah, for a while. I've got the second watch. My feeling is we'll know more about what's going to happen in the morning."

Nestled against him, warm and snug, Molly felt herself drifting off. Sleep would have been impossible earlier, now it came to her like an unexpected gift.

Sometime later, she felt Jordan leave. He kissed her softly before slipping out of the storehouse. She didn't remember anything else until he returned. He climbed beneath the single blanket and lay down beside her, gathering her close. His arm slipped over her middle and cupped her breast. Molly felt his sigh as he relaxed and she smiled softly to herself. It was almost as if the past three years hadn't happened. It was almost as if they were young and in love all over again. Almost as if Jeff hadn't died.

Molly woke to the unmistakable sound of gunfire. It was close. Much closer than before, as if a war had erupted outside the door.

Jordan bolted upright and reached for his weapon. "Stay here," he ordered and was gone before she could protest.

Molly barely had time to gather her wits when the door to the shed was thrust open. Jordan stood framed in the light. "Come on," he shouted, holding out his hand to her. "Zane's coming and this time we're going with the chopper."

Molly was so relieved that she would have gladly kissed Jordan's friend. He was coming back! She could hear the chopper more distinctly when she moved outside of the supply shed. She was greeted with a whirlwind of dust and grit. Doing what she could to protect her eyes, she hunched forward and, with Jordan's arm around her waist guiding her, ran for all she was worth toward the deafening sound.

Dr. Morton climbed into the helicopter after her, looking shaken and exhausted. He offered her a weak smile and gently patted her hand as he moved to the rear of the aircraft. Molly waited for Jordan, but he didn't board with the other soldiers.

"Where's my husband?" she demanded.

"He's coming. Don't worry, Jordan can take care of himself." He guided her firmly but gently out of harm's way.

"Jordan," Molly shouted, near frantic. The chopper was filling up with people and she couldn't find her husband. Pushing her way past the others, Molly was sobbing when she saw him. He was walking backward toward the chopper, his gun raised and firing at what she could only guess.

The chopper started to lift.

"Jordan," she screamed, although there wasn't a prayer he could hear her. "For the love of God, hurry."

Some part of her must have reached him because he turned abruptly and ran like she'd never seen him sprint before, racing toward the chopper. The minute his back was turned three rebels appeared from around the end of the hospital. Two men fired machine guns from the door of the chopper while Zane helped lift and drag Jordan aboard. He collapsed once inside, pale and bleeding heavily from his shoulder. He hand clenched his wound and the blood oozed between his fingers.

Molly fell at his side, weeping. "You've been hit."

He smiled weakly up at her, then his eyelids fluttered closed. He'd passed out cold.

Chapter Three

Jordan felt as if his shoulder were on fire. The pain seared a path through his mind, catching hold of him and guiding him out of the comfort of the black void.

He opened his eyes to find Molly and her physician friend working over him. Bright red blotches of blood coated the front of her blouse and he guessed it was his own. She seemed to sense that he was awake and paused to look toward his face.

"You're going to be fine," she assured him when she realized he'd regained consciousness. But Jordan wasn't so out of it that he didn't recognize the cold fear in her eyes.

"Liar," he said, and the lone word demanded every ounce of strength he possessed. Even then his voice was little more than a husky whisper.

Molly held his hand between her own, her eyes bright with tears. "Rest if you can. Zane said we'll be to Nubambay soon. There's an excellent hospital there."

"Nubambay," he repeated weakly.

"Don't worry, the country's government is safe and sound."

He attempted a smile.

"I won't let anything more happen to you, Jordan, do you understand? It's over now."

He closed his eyes, tried to nod, but it required more energy than he could muster. The pain in his shoulder increased and he gritted his teeth with the agony. Then gratefully everything started to go black. Jordan welcomed the release, sighing as the bottomless void settled over him.

When he awoke again, the first things Jordan saw were an IV

bottle and stark white walls. The antiseptic scent assured him he was in a hospital.

He blinked and rolled his head to one side. Molly was asleep in the chair next to his hospital bed. How she could rest in a molded plastic chair was beyond him. She'd curled up in a tight ball, her feet tucked beneath her. Her head rested against her shoulder and a thick strand of beautiful golden hair fell across her cheek. With her pale blond hair and bright blue eyes, she must have caused a stir with the children of Manukua, he mused, especially if they'd never seen a white woman before.

Molly was a natural with children, Jordan remembered. Once she found it in her heart to forgive herself for what happened to Jeff, there was a chance she'd marry again and have the family she'd always wanted.

A weight settled over his chest, as heavy as a concrete barricade. He'd done his stint with this fatherhood business and wasn't willing to take the risk a second time.

Lesley had agreed there would be no children. He was convinced they'd find their happiness together.

Molly was a different kind of woman. She was a natural mother, and in time she would be again. Jordan remembered when they'd first brought Jeff home from the hospital. He'd been afraid to hold their son for fear he'd inadvertently do something to hurt him.

By contrast Molly had acted as if she'd been around infants all her life. She'd laughed off his concerns and taught him what he needed to know, insisting he spend part of each day holding and talking to Jeff. Soon he was as comfortable as she was and the nightly sessions he spent with Jeff had been the highlight of his day. Jeff had been a happy baby with a budding personality.

Then he was gone.

Unexpectedly he'd been ripped from their lives without rhyme or reason, leaving behind a burden of grief and anger that had crippled them both. What an unfortunate legacy for such a cheerful, good-natured baby.

Jordan forced himself to look away from Molly. He closed his eyes and with some difficulty brought Lesley's face to his mind. Sweet, kind Lesley. A fuzzy image drifted carelessly into his conscious, followed by a deepening sense of guilt.

He'd made love to Molly, not once but twice. A momentary lapse in good judgment he could explain away, but not two such breaches. Not that he was obliged to explain anything to Lesley. She wasn't the type to ask, and he sure as hell wasn't going to volunteer any confessions.

"Jordan?" His name came to him softly, tentatively, as if Molly were afraid to wake him.

He rolled his head toward her. "Hi," he said, and realized his mouth felt as if someone had stuffed it full of cotton balls.

"How are you feeling?" She stood by his side and gently stroked his forehead.

"Like hell."

"Are you thirsty?"

He nodded. It surprised him how well she anticipated his needs.

"Here." She poured him a glass of ice water and brought it to him with a straw. She held it to his mouth and he drank greedily, letting the cold water quench the bulk of his thirst.

"All right," he said, relaxing against the pillows once he'd drank his fill. "Let's talk about the bullet. How much damage did it do?"

"There were two and both of them were clean hits. Luckily there's no bone damage. It's going to hurt like hell for a while, but you'll recover. Think of this time as a long overdue vacation."

"This may come as something of a surprise," Jordan said, having trouble hiding his agitation, "but if I'm going to vacation I'd prefer a nice peaceful Caribbean island instead of fighting off rebels bent on mayhem."

"I couldn't agree with you more. I could arrange for us to fly to the Virgin Islands. A couple of weeks there soaking up the sun and the sand would do us both good." Her eyes brightened with the idea. He could almost see the little wheels churning in her mind, stirring up some romantic fantasy she was dying to live out.

Jordan closed his eyes. He'd walked into that one all by himself and had sank to his thighs in the thick mud of the past. There wasn't anyway in hell he could spend two weeks in paradise with Molly when he fully intended on going through with the divorce.

"How soon can I travel?" he asked roughly.

"A couple of days. You're weak now because of the blood loss, but with the proper rest you'll regain your strength soon enough."

"I have to get back to Chicago. I don't have time to lollygag around some beach."

"All right."

Jordan heard the hurt and disappointment in her voice and felt like a jerk. That compounded with everything else left him feeling sick to his stomach. He never intended to make love to Molly; he never intended on getting shot up, either.

"How soon can I get the hell out of here?" he wanted to know next. The question came out sounding gruff and impatient. He felt both. The sooner he could make the break between him and Molly the better. Unfortunately he'd ruined any chance of making it a clean one.

"You should be released the day after tomorrow," Molly told him. "I've booked a hotel room and will call and arrange the flight back to the States if you want."

"I want." Jordan couldn't put it any more bluntly than that.

Molly walked over to the window and gazed out. She crossed her arms and waited a couple of moments before asking, "Why are you so angry?"

"Maybe it's because I've got two bullet holes in my shoulder. Then again it might be because I was forced to fly halfway around the world to get you when you should have had the common sense to leave on your own. It's you who's got the death wish, not me."

"I didn't ask you to come," she flared.

"No, your father did."

"Next time I suggest you stay at home," she said heatedly as she walked past the bed. She moved so speedily that he felt a draft.

"Next time I will," he called after her, his voice little more than a thin reed of sound.

Jordan didn't see her again until it was time for him to be released from the hospital. Zane stopped in later, but Jordan wasn't in the mood for company. The two shook hands and Jordan didn't expect to see his friend again.

Molly was at the hospital a number of times. He heard her talking to the doctor outside his room once and she stopped in to sit with him when he was sleeping. He wasn't sure how he knew this, he just did.

Jordan wasn't a good patient in the best of times. He was convinced that by the time he left Nubambay Hospital the staff was more than ready to be rid of him. Not that he blamed anyone. He'd been a rotten patient; he knew it and regretted it.

Molly was waiting for him outside the room with a wheelchair.

"I'll walk," he insisted.

"Jordan, for the love of heaven, be sensible."

He threw her a look that told her if he had any real sense he would have stayed in Chicago.

The cab ride to the hotel seemed to take hours. By the time they arrived he was exhausted, much too tired to complain that she'd booked them in one room. At least there were twin beds.

Molly ordered lunch from room service and they ate in silence. Jordan didn't plan on it, but he fell asleep afterward and woke up two hours later.

Molly was gone, which was just as well. He was uncomfortable around her. If he wasn't such a coward he'd talk to her about the divorce and get it out in the open the way he'd originally intended. Somehow it didn't seem the right thing following their night in the supply shed. Their lovemaking episodes had definitely put a chink in that plan. He didn't know what the hell he was going to do now.

Sitting on the end of the bed, Jordan carefully worked one shoulder and then the other. Pain ripped through him and he gritted his teeth. The medication the doctor gave him was in the bathroom and he walked in there without thinking.

He realized his mistake the moment he stepped over the threshold. Molly was in the shower, standing under the spray of warm water and lathering her torso. The muted glass did little to hide her lush figure from him. Her creamy, smooth skin glowed and her breasts stood out proud and regal, her nipples a deep rose color beaded against the force of the water. She lathered the washcloth and rubbed it over her stomach and lower between her legs, parting her thighs.

Jordan's breath caught in his throat, and he reached out and gripped hold of the sink. He was instantly aroused. This had to be some sort of punishment God had seen fit to place upon him for his many sins.

The view of his wife hypnotized him, and for the life of him Jordan couldn't force himself to look away. He could barely control the need he felt to touch her and taste her again. It was impossible for reality to live up to the memory of her in his arms, her legs wrapped around his hips. He meant to turn and walk out as abruptly as he'd entered, but his legs were heavy and rooted him there.

"Jordan?"

"Sorry," he muttered, feeling like a schoolboy caught with his hand in the cookie jar, "I didn't mean to interrupt you."

"It's no problem." She turned off the water and reached out and grabbed a towel, taking it into the shower with her.

Jordan stood transfixed, unable to manage more than the simple breath, as she dried her arms and breasts. Something was very wrong. Jordan was a strong-willed man. He wasn't easily tempted by the flesh. The past three and a half years of celibacy were testament to that.

Somehow he managed to make it back into the other room. He literally fell into a chair and turned on the television. A full five minutes passed before he realized the broadcast was televised in French.

A couple of minutes later, Molly strolled barefoot out of the bathroom, dressed in a thick, white terry-cloth robe. She toweled her hair dry and wore a silly grin as if she were fully aware of the affect she had on him. Apparently she enjoyed seeing him suffer.

"Did you need a pain pill?" she asked ever so sweetly.

Jordan shook his head and concentrated on the television screen as though he understood every word spoken.

Jordan had behaved strangely from the moment they'd left the medical compound in Manukua. Matters weren't any better now that they were on the flight headed back to Chicago.

Molly didn't know what to make of his irrational behavior. One moment he was looking at her as if he was counting the minutes before he could charm her into his bed and the next he growled at her.

Okay, she reasoned, so he had been wounded. He was an injured beast. Depending on his mood, she didn't know whether to comfort or clobber him. One minute he was sullen and uncommunicative, and the next witty and warm. Almost warm, she amended. Jordan had never been a personable kind of man. He was too direct and blunt for that.

He fidgeted in the cramped airline seat next to hers, trying to find a comfortable position. The pain pills would have helped him relax, if he'd agreed to take them. Molly had given up suggesting as much. The looks he sent her were enough to tell her exactly what he wanted her to do with the pain medication. He was a damn stubborn fool, and if he hadn't risked his life to save hers, she'd have told him so.

The newsmagazine Jordan was reading slid from his lap onto the floor. Molly retrieved it for him and he immediately crammed it into the pocket of the seat in front of him, bending it in half, then stuffing the excess pages down with a force strong enough to cause the seat to rock.

"Now, now," Molly said under her breath.

Jordan muttered something she preferred not to hear, then glanced at his watch, something he did routinely every five minutes or so. She thought to remind him of the old adage of a watched pot not boiling, but strongly suspected he wouldn't appreciate her pearls of wisdom.

An eternity passed before the plane touched down at O'Hare International. She was home and the joy that swelled in her chest was testament to how glad she was to be back.

Customs seemed to take forever. Her father was waiting for her, looking older than she remembered. His face lit up with a smile when she appeared and he held his arms open wide the way he had when she was a little girl.

"Daddy," she said, hugging him close. Unexpected tears welled in her eyes and, embarrassed, she wiped them aside. She clung to him, drinking in his love. She may be a mature woman, but she'd never outgrow her need for her father's love.

"It's about time you came back where you belong," Ian chastised, and wiped the moisture from his eyes. He hugged her again once more, then wrapped his arm around her waist.

Jordan shifted his weight from one foot to the other. He hated emotional scenes, Molly knew.

"Thank you," Ian said, breaking away from her and shaking Jordan's good hand. It took him a moment or two to compose himself before he was able to continue. "I might have lost my little girl if it hadn't been for you."

"It was no big deal," Jordan said as if he'd done nothing more than walk her across the street. A fuss would embarrass him, and so she discounted his heroism.

A porter walked past with Jordan's luggage and Jordan glanced outside, obviously eager to be on his way. His gaze met Molly's and in it she read a multitude of emotions. Relief that they were home and safe, regret, too, she suspected. His defenses were lower, dulled by pain and fatigue. He couldn't disguise his feelings from her as easily as he had in the past.

"Take care," Molly said, taking a step toward him before she could stop herself. She longed to press her hand to his cheek and thank him herself, as if it were possible to ever adequately express her appreciation. She longed to kiss him, too, to prove what they'd experienced had been as real as it had been right.

He nodded. "I will. I'll call you later in the week," he promised.

Molly had to bite her lip to keep from telling him not to work too hard. A gunshot wound wasn't a simple injury and it would be weeks, possibly months, before he regained the full use of his arm. She bit her lip; Jordan wouldn't have appreciated the admonition.

He turned abruptly then and followed the porter outside.

Molly watched him go. She'd lived apart from Jordan for three long years, considered their life together forever gone, destroyed by grief and pain. This week had shown her the impossible. This week proved beyond a shadow of question that Jordan continued to love her. Just as she did him.

He wasn't happy about it, she mused sadly. She sincerely doubted that he knew what he was going to do. For now he was as confused and uncertain as she was herself.

* * *

Molly woke with the sun rippling across the cherry-wood dresser in the bedroom that had been hers as a young girl. She lay on her back, her head cradled by thick feather pillows, and reveled in the abundant comforts of home.

She wasn't a teenager any longer, but a woman. A married woman. The thought produced a small frown. Some decisions had to be made regarding her relationship with Jordan, but neither of them were ready to make those. Three years seemed plenty of time to decide what they were going to do with their relationship. In their case it wasn't.

Molly dressed in a sleeveless summer dress she found in the back of her closet. A pretty white-with-red-dots concoction with a wide belt.

Her father was sitting at the breakfast table with the morning newspaper propped up against his glass of freshly squeezed orange juice. It seemed little had changed in the years she'd been away.

"Morning," she said, kissing him on the cheek and pouring herself a cup of coffee.

"Morning" came his absent response.

"I see you still read over the financial section first thing every morning."

"I'm retired, not dead," he said with a chuckle. "Semiretired. I got too bored sitting at home, counting my money."

"So you're working again."

"Don't fuss," he said, his eyes not leaving the paper. "I go into the bank a couple of days a week. The staff there are kind enough to let me keep my office, so I go down and putter around and they let me think I'm important. I know otherwise, but I don't let on."

Molly smiled, pulled out a chair and sat down. Her father had always been big on formality. Lunch and dinner were served in the dining room on Wedgwood china and Waterford crystal. Breakfast, however, was taken in the kitchen at the round oak table that sat in a comfortable nook where the sunlight spilled in and splashed around them.

Molly reached for a blueberry muffin and the pitcher of orange juice. "Dad, did Jordan sell the house?"

Her father lowered the paper, folded it in fourths and set it beside his plate. "Not to my knowledge, why?"

She shrugged. "I was curious."

He studied her for a long moment. "I take it the two of you didn't get much chance to talk."

Peeling the paper bottom away from the muffin, Molly shook her head. "Not really." Her words were followed by a short silence.

"I see." Molly raised her gaze to her father. He sounded down-right gleeful, as if this small bit of information were cause for celebration.

"What's the grin all about?" she asked.

"What grin?" His eyes went instantly sober, then round with innocence.

"Don't play games with me, Dad. Does Jordan have something to tell me?"

"I wouldn't know," he said and the edges of his mouth quivered ever so slightly. "Now," he added in a whisper.

Molly stood and set the napkin on the table, frowning. "Something fishy's going on here."

"Oh?"

She'd forgotten what a little devil her father could be. She walked over to the patio doors, crossed her arms and tapped her foot while she thought of the unexpected turn of the morning's events.

"Can I have the car keys?" she asked, whirling back around, her decision made.

Her father held them out in the palm of his hand, grinning broadly. "I won't expect you home for lunch," he said and reached once more for his morning paper.

It was ridiculous to show up on Jordan's doorstep before ten. Especially when he'd so recently arrived back from Africa. Unsure how to proceed, Molly drove to their favorite French bakery for croissants. To her surprise and delight, the baker, Pierre, recognized her. He called to her and hurried around the glass counter to shake her hand.

"I gave up hope of ever seeing you again," he said in a heavy French accent. He poured her a cup of coffee and led her to one of the small tables in the corner, in front of the long row of windows. "Please sit down."

Molly did, wondering at this unusual greeting. He set the coffee down and his assistant delivered a plate of delicate sweet rolls. The aroma was enticing enough to cause a weight gain.

"Our daughter's baby died the same way as your son," he said, and his eyes revealed the extent of his sadness. "Amanda put her little girl down to sleep and Christi never woke. It's been several months now and still my daughter and her husband grieve, still they ask questions no one can answer."

"The questions never stop," Molly said softly. Nor does the grief, but she didn't say that. It grew less sharp with time, the years dulled the agony, but it never left, never vanished. The pain was there, a constant reminder of the baby who never grew up.

"Our daughter and son-in-law blame themselves...they think they did something to cause Christi's death."

"They didn't." Molly was giving the textbook response, but in her heart she knew differently. The medical community had no cut-and-dried answers. Physicians offered a number of theories, but nothing concrete. There was no one to blame, no one to hold responsible, no one to yell and cry at, or take out their grief upon.

With nowhere else to go, the pain, anger and grief turned inward. It had with Molly, until she bore the full weight of the tragedy upon her thin shoulders. Over the months, the burden of it had maimed her. By the time she moved out on Jordan, she was an emotional wreck.

"They need to talk to someone who has lost a child the same way," Pierre said, "before this unfortunate death destroys them both." He stood and took a business card from the display in front of the cash register. Turning it over, he wrote a phone number on the back side.

Molly accepted the card, but she wasn't sure she could make the call. There were others this young couple could speak to, others far more qualified to answer their questions. Another husband and wife who'd walked over the fiery bed of coals and come out on the other side.

"Please," Pierre said, folding his much-larger hand around hers and the card. "Only someone who has lost a child can understand their pain."

"I...don't know, Pierre."

His eyes boldly met hers. "God will guide you," he said. "Do not worry." He brought her a sack with the croissants and wouldn't allow her to pay for them.

Molly left, not knowing what to do. If she hadn't been able to help herself or Jordan, how could she reach another grieving couple?

Jordan's truck was parked outside their home. So he hadn't sold the house. This small bit of information lifted her spirits. She didn't put much significance in his keeping the two-story house, but knowing this one piece of their marriage was intact was just the incentive she needed to propel her to the front steps.

This was the first time she'd been back and she wasn't sure if she should knock or simply walk inside. It was her home, or at least it had been at one time. Ringing the doorbell was the courteous thing to do.

It took Jordan an inordinate amount of time to answer. He opened the front door with a bathrobe draped over his naked shoulders. His hair stood on end and he blinked as if afraid she were an apparition.

"Before you chew my head off," she said, remembering what a grouch he was in the morning, "I come bearing gifts."

"This better be good," he said, eyeing the white sack.

"Pierre's croissants," she informed him.

He grinned, opening the screen door. "That's good enough."

The house was exactly as she'd left it. Sort of. The furniture was arranged in the identical pattern. Jordan hadn't updated the carpet or the drapes. Everything was as she'd left it except there were blueprints and files stacked in every conceivable corner.

"I see you still bring your work home with you," she commented dryly.

"Listen, if you came to lecture me, you can go right back out that door. Just leave the croissants—I deserve that much for answering the doorbell."

"Never mind," she said, leading the way into the kitchen. This room wasn't much better. Luckily she was familiar enough to know where he kept the coffee. She put on a pot, then brought down two black mugs embossed with silver—Larabee Construction.

"Hey," she teased, "you're in the big time now. When did you give up the pencils and go for the mugs?"

Jordan frowned at her and it was obvious he had no intention of answering her question. Molly found his surly mood entertaining. She waited until the coffee had filtered through, poured him a mug and carried it over to the table, where he'd planted himself.

He wolfed down two croissants before she managed to get hers out of the bag. The return of his appetite encouraged her. The temptation to ask him about his medication was strong, but she resisted, knowing he'd consider the query some sort of intrusion on his privacy.

"Dad asked me if we'd had a chance to talk," Molly said evenly, carefully broaching the subject.

Jordan stopped eating and his gaze narrowed.

"Was there some particular reason he seemed so curious about us talking?"

He took his own sweet time mulling over the question. Molly didn't press him, didn't force the issue. She knew Jordan well enough to realize that when and if he offered an explanation it would be in his time, not hers, and certainly not her father's.

The doorbell chimed once more. Jordan growled, stood and answered it. Paul Phelps, his job superintendent, casually strolled inside and paused when he saw Molly. His face lit up in a broad grin.

"Molly. Damn but it's good to see you." He walked over and gave her a bear hug. "You're a sight for sore eyes."

Molly had always enjoyed Paul, who was more friend than employee. "How's the family?" she asked.

"Brenda had another girl last year," Paul boasted proudly.

"Congratulations."

Jordan's employee turned to her husband. "I saw a truck parked outside and wondered if you'd gotten back," Paul said conversationally and helped himself to a cup of coffee. "What the hell happened to your arm?" he asked Jordan, gesturing toward the sling.

"Nothing a little time won't fix," Jordan muttered. "If a parade's going to march through here, I might as well get dressed." He didn't look happy about it, but Molly welcomed the time alone with Paul.

"How's he been?" she asked as soon as Jordan had vacated the room.

Paul shrugged. "Better the last year or so since he..." He stopped abruptly and glanced guiltily toward Molly. "Since, well, you know, since he hasn't been killing himself working every hour of the day and night."

"If this house is any indication, that's exactly what he has been doing."

"What happened to his shoulder?" Paul asked, and Molly wondered if it was a blatant effort to change the subject.

"He was shot," she said, "twice."

"Shot." Paul damn near dropped the coffee mug.

"It's a long story," Molly said.

"Longer than either of us has time to explain," Jordan said gruffly, appearing in the doorway. From the frustrated look in his eyes, Molly realized his dressing was more than he could handle alone. He needed help, but she doubted that he'd ask for it.

Paul glanced from one of them to the other, then set the coffee cup down on the counter. "I can see you two have lots to talk about. It was good to see you again, Molly. Damn good. Don't make yourself a stranger now, you hear?"

She nodded and walked him to the door. He seemed anxious to make a clean getaway, but she stopped him, her hand at his elbow. "What is it everyone's trying to hide from me?"

Paul looked decidedly uncomfortable. "That's something you'd better ask Jordan."

Molly fully intended on doing exactly that. Her husband's eyes met hers when she walked back into the kitchen. She read a certain look about him, one she didn't freely recognize. It seemed to be a mixture of determination and regret. One of anger and pride.

"Tell me," she said without emotion.

His eyes briefly left hers. "There was more than one reason I went to Manukua," he said evenly. "You're father asked me to bring you home."

"And?"

"And," he said, taking in a deep breath. "I came to ask for a divorce."

Chapter Four

Molly felt as if the floor had collapsed beneath her, sending her crashing into space.

Divorce.

Jordan had come to Manukua to ask her for a divorce.

Since Jeff's death Molly had learned a good many things about emotional pain. The numbness came first, deadening her senses from the rush of unbearable heartache that was sure to follow. Only later would she expect the full impact of Jordan's words to hit her. For now she welcomed the protection.

"I see," she managed, closing her eyes. She'd made such an unadulterated fool of herself, suggesting they vacation together on a tropical island as if they were lovers, as if their marriage had been given a second chance. Her face burned with humiliation, but she resisted the urge to bury her face in her hands. "You might have said something sooner, before I made such a fool of myself."

"If anyone's a fool, it's me." Jordan's voice was filled with self-condemnation.

"No wonder you were in such a rush to get back to the States." It all made sense now, a painful kind of logical sense.

"I didn't mean to blurt it out like that." He walked to the far side of the room, his shoulders slumped with regret.

"I'm glad you did. Good heavens, who knows how long I would have continued making a complete ass of myself." Another thought occurred to her. "My father knows, doesn't he?" An answer wasn't necessary. Paul did, as well. That explained the awkward way he'd answered her questions and his hasty exit.

"I know what you're thinking," Jordan muttered.

"I doubt that." How could he when she didn't know herself?

"You're wondering about what happened between us in the supply shed." His mouth tightened as if he dreaded bringing up the subject. "If you're looking for an apology I can't give you one. It happened. It shouldn't have, but it did, and I'm not sorry."

"I'll admit it was a curious way of saying goodbye," she said with a small, short-lived laugh. She appreciated his honesty, knowing what it had cost him. "I...I don't regret it, either."

"I never meant to hurt you."

"I know." Her feet felt as heavy as concrete fence posts. Walking to the front door required an incredible effort. She paused, her back to him when the realization hit her like a sledgehammer against the back of the head. "You've met another woman, haven't you?"

He didn't answer right away, in fact it seemed to take him a good long while to formulate a reply. Long enough for her to turn around to face him, preferring to hear the truth head on. His eyes firmly held hers. "Lesley Walker."

The name slid over the surface of Molly's memory and caught. "The architect?"

"We worked together a good deal over the past year."

She nodded. Other than the name, Molly had no clear picture of the woman. "She must be very special." Otherwise Jordan wouldn't love her.

"Damn it all to hell," Jordan exploded, his one good fist clenched in a tight knot at his side. "You don't need to be so damned understanding. I should have told you up front. Instead I left you hanging, thinking there might be a chance for us, when there isn't. You have every right to be angry. Throw something," he shouted, reaching for an empty vase, "you'll feel better."

She smiled and shrugged her shoulders. "You mean, you'll feel better." She removed the vase from his hand and set it back down. "Don't look so concerned. I was the one who walked out on you, remember?" Her hand trembled slightly as she opened the front door. "Whatever arrangements you make are fine. Just let me know when you need me to sign the papers."

Jordan would rather have taken another bullet than have Molly look at him the way she had when he'd announced he wanted a divorce. First her eyes had widened, as she dealt with the shock his words inflicted, then they'd gone dull and empty. It was all he could do not to reach for her with his one good arm and comfort her.

He never meant to tell her about Lesley like that, hurling the words at her without warning. He'd wanted to sit down and explain that he hadn't intended on falling in love again. It had happened. But his good intentions had taken a greased track straight to hell.

Following the doctor's instruction to sit at home and rest lasted all of an hour. He needed to get down to the job site. He needed to talk to Paul. He needed to escape his own thoughts before he questioned what he was doing. What he really needed, Jordan decided, was to have his head examined.

Lesley caught up with him at the job site. He'd been back nearly twenty-four hours before he thought to contact her. Blaming Molly for that seemed the appropriate thing to do, but he couldn't honestly do so. At the moment he wasn't keen on seeing any woman, even Lesley.

"I can't believe you're working," she said, stepping into the construction trailer, looking as wholesome and sunny as a spring day. Her eyes lit up with concern when she saw his arm in the sling. "I went to the house first. Shouldn't you be in a hospital or something?"

"Probably," Jordan muttered, allowing her to kiss his cheek.

Paul took one look at him and made a convenient excuse to leave. Jordan didn't need to ask his friend's opinion; it was there for him to read in Paul's eyes.

Jordan didn't need his best friend in order to feel guilty. After the morning confrontation with Molly, no one could make him feel more of a heel than he already did. If someone gave out awards for jackasses, he'd win first place, hands down.

"How did everything go in Manukua?" Lesley asked.

"Great."

"Molly wasn't hurt?"

"No." He made his responses brief, hoping she'd quickly realize he wasn't in the mood to talk.

"How did you feel seeing her? I mean, it's been a long time, certainly you must have felt something."

"I did."

The pain in his shoulder increased and he slumped into a chair and closed his eyes until the worst of it had passed.

"Jordan, are you all right?" Lesley pleaded. "When you phoned, you said it was nothing. You've been badly injured."

"It's little more than a flesh wound." Another understatement, but he didn't want her gushing sympathy all over him. She'd make him sound like some hero, and he wasn't.

"How long will you have to wear the sling?"

"As long as it takes," he answered shortly.

If he wasn't in such a crappy mood, he'd appreciate what a beautiful woman Lesley was. He wasn't likely to meet another like her. She understood his need for work and was ambitious herself. They were a perfect match. An ideal couple. It was time to cut the ties that bound him to Molly. Past time.

"I realize this probably isn't a good time to ask this, but did you get a chance to mention the divorce to Molly?"

Talk of the divorce left an ugly taste in his mouth. He ignored the question, stood and pretended to be involved in the blueprints.

"Naturally you didn't get a chance to talk to her, not with the country involved in a revolution," Lesley said, answering her own question. "You were lucky to get out with your lives."

"I talked to her about it this morning," he told her impatiently. "She's agreed. There won't be any problem."

Lesley went still. "I know this was difficult for you, Jordan."

She hadn't a clue, but surprisingly neither had he. A divorce seemed the natural progression for him and Molly. It was the right thing to do, but Jordan hadn't anticipated the bad feelings that came over him when he announced he formally intended to end their marriage.

"Are you having second thoughts?"

Lesley had a way of reading him that was sometimes intimidating. Was he? "No," he said without pause. The time for second thoughts was long gone. "I want the divorce," he assured her.

Larry Rife wasn't keen on divorce cases. He took them on occasionally, but generally only for a change of pace. He'd met with Jordan Larabee three or four times now and his client had assured him this was a friendly divorce. There was no such animal, but Larry didn't see the point of saying so. Larabee and his wife would discover that soon enough on their own, he suspected.

From what Larry understood, Mrs. Larabee had yet to retain her own attorney, and had indicated she saw no need to do so. Apparently she'd read over the agreement he'd drawn up and was satisfied with the settlement offer her husband had proposed.

That of its own was highly unusual, but then little about this divorce was normal. Larabee had bent over backward to make this as simple and easy for his wife as possible. Frankly, Larry couldn't help being curious what had gone wrong in their marriage.

His intercom beeped, and his secretary said, "The Larabees are here to see you."

Larry stood when the couple entered. He exchanged a courtesy handshake with Jordan, and everyone was seated. Larry couldn't help being curious about Larabee's wife. She was a pretty thing, young and fragile looking. But then appearances were often deceiving. A delicate woman wouldn't have spent the past two years as a nurse in Manukua.

Larry reached for the file and addressed the question to Molly. "Have you had the opportunity to read over the settlement offer?"

"Yes, I have," she answered in a thin voice. "And I found Jordan to be more than generous."

"It's highly unusual for you not to have an attorney look this over on your behalf," Larry felt obliged to explain. He wasn't entirely comfortable with this aspect of the divorce. It wasn't necessary, of course, but he had a certain responsibility to her.

"I don't see why. There's nothing here I take exception to, and I can see no reason to prolong the proceedings."

"As long as you understand the terms of the settlement."

"Everything is perfectly clear to me."

Larabee was unusually quiet. "He's right, Molly. It might be a good idea if you had your own attorney look it over."

"If that's what you want, but I don't see why I should. You want your freedom. You've waited long enough."

Larabee crossed his legs in what seemed a nervous movement. "I don't want you to feel that I've cheated you in any way."

"That's the last thing I need worry about with you. You've been overly generous. Why don't we leave matters as they are?"

"You're sure?"

"Positive."

She was so serene about this. Larry couldn't remember any couple who were so caring about each other over the details of a divorce. He flipped through the file for some clue of what had gone so wrong between two decent people.

"There are no children involved," he muttered to himself.

"No children," Jordan answered, although it hadn't been poised as a question.

"There was a child," Mrs. Larabee added, and Larry swore the color of her eyes changed when she spoke. When she walked in the door, he'd been struck by their clear shade of blue, but when she mentioned the child, they darkened to stormy pale agony. "A son...he died of SIDS. His name was Jeffrey."

Jordan said nothing

Larry made a notation in the file. It was all coming together for him now. The divorce wasn't based on the usual grounds. It was rooted in grief. The pain of their loss was less when they were apart because then they could pretend to forget.

"Did you need me to sign something?" Molly Larabee asked,

breaking into his thoughts. She sounded eager now, wanting this over as quickly as possible.

"Yes, of course." Larry took out the papers and then handed her a pen. "I'll file these papers this afternoon. The divorce will be final in sixty days."

"That soon?" Jordan asked.

"That long?" was his wife's question.

Larry studied the couple sitting across from him. Over the years he'd seen far too many divorces where the couple literally hated each other by the time they filed the final papers. It was disconcerting to represent two people who continued to deeply love each other.

Sitting beneath the weeping willow tree seemed the appropriate thing to do after the meeting with the attorney. Molly hadn't anticipated the emotional toll the appointment would take on her. She was grateful her father was away for the afternoon, because she needed this time alone to sort through her emotions.

She expected tears. None came. How could she weep for a marriage that had been dead all these years?

The spindly limbs of the weeping willow danced in the wind about her feet. With her back braced against the tree trunk, she stared at the meticulously kept gardens that had been her mother's pride and joy. But her mother, like Jeff, like her marriage, was dead and forever gone.

In the week since Jordan had delivered the news, Molly had made discreet inquiries about Lesley Walker. Everything she learned about the other woman was positive. Lesley was a talented architect with a promising future. She was young, energetic and well liked. As difficult as it was for Molly to stomach, Lesley was exactly the type of wife Jordan needed.

Admitting that produced a sharp pain. A knot formed in her throat and the tears that had been bottled up inside her rolled freely down her face.

"I wondered if this was where I'd find you." Her father's voice sounded from behind her.

Molly hastily wiped the moisture from her face. "I thought you were going to be away for the afternoon."

"I was," Ian Houghton said, awkwardly sitting down on the grass next to her. He looked out of place in his expensive Italian-made suit. "But I got to thinking you might be feeling a little blue after signing the final papers."

"I'm fine."

Ian handed her his crisp white handkerchief. "So I noticed." He placed his arm around her shoulders and rested his chin on the top of her head. "You used to come here when you were a little girl. The gardener's been telling me for years I should have this old tree removed, but I could never find it in my heart to do it, knowing how much you love it."

"I'm glad you didn't."

"Things aren't as bleak as they seem, sweetheart. Someday you'll look back on all this and the pain won't be nearly as deep."

Her father had said something similar after Jeff died and she hadn't found that to be true. The ache would never leave her.

"Would you rather Jordan had never been a part of your life?" Ian asked.

Her first instinct was to tell him yes, she wished she'd never met Jordan, never loved him, never given birth to his son. But it would have been a lie. Jordan was her first love, her only love, and how could she ever regret having had Jeff? It wasn't in her to lie, even to herself.

She'd failed Jordan, Molly realized, and he'd failed her. They'd been equal partners in the destruction of their marriage.

He was the first one to recognize and act on the truth. He was the first one to step out and make a new life for himself. He'd always been stronger than she was.

"I remember when Jeff died," her father said with some difficulty. It was hard for him to talk about his only grandchild. "Grief leaves one feeling hopeless. It turns you hollow inside and makes you wonder about God."

Molly was well acquainted with the toll grief demanded. "Whenever I'm hurting that badly I ask myself why God doesn't do something," she added.

"He does, but we're in too much pain to realize it."

Molly knew that, as well.

Now, nearly four years after losing their son, Jordan was moving ahead and she needed to take that first tentative step herself. "I'm going to find myself an apartment," she announced with newfound commitment.

"There's no rush," Ian was quick to tell her.

"It's time I got on with my life."

"Like Jordan?" her father questioned.

"He's right, Dad. I shouldn't have buried my pain. Heaven only knows how long I would have stayed in Manukua if it hadn't been for the revolution. I was hiding from life and, you know, it got to be downright comfortable."

"I realize I'm being selfish, but I hate to see you move out so soon."

Molly hugged her father, grateful for his love and support. He was all she had left in the world now. It was the same way it'd been from the time she was eleven, just the two of them.

Once Molly made up her mind what she was going to do, it didn't take her more than a week to find a job and an apartment. She moved several pieces of furniture from Jordan's, along with a number of personal items.

She made sure she stopped over at the house when there wasn't any chance of her running into him. For courtesy's sake, she left him notes, listing what she'd taken. She also gave him her new address.

The duplex she'd rented was in a friendly neighborhood and offered her a small yard. Molly enjoyed roses and was looking forward to planting several varieties once she was completely settled.

The apartment was roomy with two large bedrooms, a nice size kitchen and a comfortable living room. It wasn't home yet, but it would be once she had everything arranged the way she wanted. Compared to her quarters in Manukua, the duplex was a mansion. The best part about her new home was that she wasn't far from Lake Michigan and her work at Sinai Hospital.

Molly was dressed in cutoffs and a sleeveless T-shirt, placing books inside the bookcase, when the doorbell rang. She wiped the perspiration from her brow with the back of her arm and stood.

A dizzy sensation sent the room into an awkward tailspin and she collapsed onto the sofa, taking in deep, even breaths. A moment passed before the world righted itself once more.

The doorbell chimed a second time, with short, impatient bursts. No one she knew rang a bell like that except Jordan Larabee.

Standing, she composed herself as best she could and opened the front door. He had a box braced against the side of the duplex, holding it beneath his one good arm and having difficulty doing so. "It took you long enough," he complained gruffly.

"Sorry," she said, opening the screen door and stepping aside. Jordan walked in and literally dropped the box down on the carpet next to the one she was unloading into the bookcase.

"You forgot this," he said.

The dizziness returned and Molly slumped onto the arm of the sofa and pressed her hands against her face, waiting for the whirling sensation to taper.

"Are you all right?" Jordan demanded, and his brow folded in half with his concern. "You're as pale as a sheet."

"I...don't know. I must have gotten up too quickly. Everything started to spin there for a minute...I'm fine now."

"You're sure?"

"Listen, Jordan, I'm a registered nurse. I may not know a lot about some things, but I do know when I'm healthy and I tell you I'm fine."

"Good." He stuffed his hand in his pants pocket and walked around the room, surveying the duplex. "What does Ian think about all this?"

"My moving? Well, he'd rather I stayed with him the rest of my life, but I'd prefer living on my own." She surveyed the contents of what he'd brought and didn't find anything that warranted his visit. She would have picked it up the following day, or whenever she made her next trip over to the house.

Jordan strolled into the kitchen. "Do you mind if I get myself something to drink?"

"Sure." Apparently there was something more on his mind than helping her move, otherwise he wouldn't be making excuses to stay. "There's lemonade in the refrigerator. I'm afraid I don't have anything stronger."

"Lemonade's fine." He brought down a glass from the cupboard. It was a beautiful crystal one they'd received as a wedding gift from her Aunt Thelma a thousand years earlier. He paused, his hand cupped around the base of the glass.

Molly folded her hands together and moved one step forward. "I hope you don't mind that I took those glasses...they weren't specifically listed in the agreement. I didn't think it'd matter."

"Why should I care about a few glasses?"

"You looked as if you might object."

"I don't," he admitted gruffly. "I was just thinking about the last time we used them...Christmas, wasn't it?" he stopped abruptly and shook his head. "Never mind, it isn't important." Taking the glass with him, he moved into the living room and sat down on the sofa, balancing his ankle across the top of his knee. He stretched his arm out across the sofa top and appeared to be at ease.

Molly felt anything but relaxed. She sat on the ottoman opposite him, her hands pressed between her knees, waiting. Clearly there was something on his mind, something he wasn't having an easy time saying.

He took a sip of the lemonade. "How have you been?"

"Fine, and you?"

"I can't complain."

"How's the arm?"

The sling moved against his chest. ''It's getting better every day. I should be able to get rid of this thing by the end of the month.''

''Good.''

Silence.

Molly had forgotten how loud silence could be between two people. It rang in her ears until she would have welcomed earplugs.

Briefly she wondered how long it would take him to get to the meat of the conversation, to break down and tell her what he intended.

''Was there some reason you wanted to talk to me?'' she asked when she couldn't tolerate the quiet a second longer. It angered her that she had to be the one to press the issue.

He dropped his leg and leaned forward, bracing his good arm against his elbow. ''The divorce will be final within the next couple of weeks.''

Molly didn't need him to tell her that. ''So?'' She didn't mean to sound flippant, but she didn't understand his point, if he was making one.

''Are you happy?'' He rubbed a hand down his face, as if he wanted to start over again and didn't know where to begin. ''Damn, I'm making a mess of this. Listen,'' he said and vaulted to his feet. Jordan had never been able to sit in one place when something was troubling him.

''You want to know if I'm happy?'' she asked, wanting to help. ''Do you mean am I happy about the divorce?''

''Hell, I don't know what I want you to tell me. I have this incredible sense of guilt over God knows what. Coming here like this doesn't make a damn bit of sense, but something inside me isn't comfortable ending our marriage without…without what?'' He answered his own question with another, clearly confused.

Jordan turned and their eyes met. She read his bewilderment and knew she'd experienced those same feelings herself, and like him, had been unable to put them into words.

''I guess in some ways I'm looking for you to absolve me,'' he said with a short, mocking laugh. ''The problem is I don't know what it is I want you to forgive.''

''The divorce makes me incredibly sad,'' she admitted in a whisper. ''I don't blame you, Jordan, and I'm not angry with you if that's what you're thinking.''

''Maybe you should be. Did you ever think of that?''

Molly took a moment to carefully examine her feelings. She wasn't angry now, but that didn't mean she wouldn't be in the

future. All the emotions tied into the divorce and their time together
in Manukua hadn't been fully processed.

"Give me time," she suggested with a weak smile.

"There's something you should know," Jordan said, and his
shoulders heaved as if this was difficult for him to admit. "Lesley
and I have never been lovers."

"Jordan, please, that's none of my business." She stood and
walked over to the bookcase, examining the even spines of the
volumes she'd recently placed inside.

"I know that. The fact is, it embarrasses the hell out of me to be
talking to you about my relationship with another woman. God
knows I've committed my share of sins, but adultery isn't one of
them."

Their conversation was growing decidedly uncomfortable. "You
asked me if I was happy," she said, throwing his question back at
him. "That's what you really came to find out, and I'll tell you."
She brushed the hair away from her face and held it there. "I'm
ready to resume my life. I'm completely on my own for the first
time…Africa didn't count. I have a new job I start first thing Monday morning. Am I happy? Yes, I suppose I am, but I'm not sure
what happy means anymore. I haven't known since Jeff died."

Jordan's jawline went white. He seemed to need some time to
compose himself. "Why is it every conversation we have boils
down to Jeff?"

"He was our son."

"He's dead," Jordan shouted.

"That's the problem in a nutshell," she shouted back, and her
voice trembled so badly she wondered if he'd been able to understand her. "You want to pretend Jeff never lived. You wanted to
destroy his pictures and ignore the fact we had a child. I can't do
that. I'll never be able to do that. Jeff was a part of you and a part
of me and I refuse to deny he lived." She was sobbing now and
made no effort to disguise her tears.

"How long will it take for you to forget?" Jordan demanded
furiously. "Five years? Ten? When will it ever end? Tell me."

His words exploded like firecrackers dropped into the middle of
the room.

"How long will you continue to grieve?"

Squaring her shoulders, Molly met his angry glare, her fists knotted at her side.

"When are you going to start? When will you stop denying we
had a son? When will you be willing to own up to the fact Jeff
lived?"

Jordan didn't answer, not that she expected he would. He headed for the door and nearly removed it from its hinges as he stalked outside.

Molly was trembling so much she had to sit down. She pressed her hand over her mouth to hold back the anguish that threatened to swallow her. Her stomach cramped and she knew she was going to lose her lunch. She barely made it into the bathroom in time.

Her queasy stomach didn't go away. The following morning, she woke with a headache and had to force herself out of bed. By noon she felt a little better, well enough to meet her father for lunch.

She arrived at the restaurant to find him seated and waiting for her.

"Molly, sweetheart, I'm so pleased you're feeling better. Is it the flu?"

"No," she said, wrinkling up her nose. She reached for the menu. "It's Jordan. We argued and, well, it left me terribly upset. I'm fine now."

"What did Jordan say that troubled you so much?"

"Dad," Molly chided, loving the way his voice rose with indignation as if he were ready and willing to make her husband pay handsomely for distressing her. "It's over and forgotten. The divorce will be final soon and then we'll never need have anything to do with each other again." She made a pretense of studying the menu.

The waiter arrived before she could make her selection. Her father however had already made up his mind. "I'll have a bowl of the French onion soup," he said, spreading the napkin across his lap.

The waiter looked to her expectantly. Molly's stomach heaved and she placed her hand to her abdomen at the unexpected tumult. "I'll...I'll have a salad ... spinach salad." Her voice trembled and a paralyzing kind of numbness settled over her. She closed her eyes. There'd only been one other time that the mere mention of French onion soup had made her instantly ill.

"Molly?" Her father's concerned voice sounded as if it came from a long way off. "Is something wrong?"

She managed a weak nod. "Something's very wrong. Oh, Dad, I don't know what I'm going to do." Tears flooded her eyes and she hid her face in her hands.

"Sweetheart, tell me." He gently patted her forearm.

When she could, Molly lowered her hands away from her face. "I'm...pregnant."

Chapter Five

Dr. Doug Anderson walked into the cubical, reading Molly's chart. Her gaze scrutinized him carefully, although she already knew the answer. She was pregnant. Not a shred of doubt lingered in her mind. When she was first pregnant with Jeff, she'd suffered the same symptoms. The bouts of morning sickness and the decreased appetite were signs she could reason away, but not the sudden and violent aversion to French onion soup.

"Well, Molly," Doug Anderson said cheerfully, smiling at her. "Congratulations are in order. Your test is positive."

"I guessed as much." She looked away, fighting down the flood of emotions. Tears were close to the surface along with the almost irresistible urge to laugh. She had an incredibly awkward sense of timing. Each emotion was foreshadowed with a growing sense of fear.

"Molly, are you all right?"

She gestured with her hands, not knowing how to answer him. "I'm afraid, Doug, more afraid than I can ever remember being." She'd lost her son; she didn't know if she could bear to relive the nightmare a second time.

Doug pulled out a chair and sat down. "You aren't going to lose this baby to SIDS," he said, sounding remarkably confident.

"You can't guarantee that." She was a medical professional herself and knew the statistics well. Crib death is the major cause of infant death in the United States. She didn't need anyone to tell her that one out of every five hundred babies dies mysteriously, for no apparent cause. She was also aware that the chance of losing a second child to SIDS was so infinitesimally small that it shouldn't warrant her concern. But it did.

How could she not worry? It wasn't humanly possible.

"It's more than that," she whispered, fighting hard to keep her voice from shaking. "Jordan and I are divorcing. It'll be final soon."

Doug looked as if he wasn't sure what to say. "I didn't know."

Molly didn't want to rehash her marital troubles, especially with someone who was familiar with Jordan. "I realize I'll need to tell him about the baby." The prospect filled her with a deepening sense of dread. An uneasiness settled on her like an anchor hitting the bottom of the sea.

"He'll want to know," her physician added. "It could make a difference."

Molly agreed with a nod. Doug seemed to think the news might have some effect on the divorce proceedings, but Molly sincerely doubted that. Jordan was involved with Lesley. He was the one who wanted out of the marriage. Oh dear heaven, this complicated everything.

Doug gently patted her hand and asked, "Is there anything I can do for you?"

"No, but thanks for asking."

"I'd like you to make an appointment in two weeks."

"All right," she said, knowing she sounded like a robot. That was the way she felt, as if the simplest movements demanded a major effort.

Molly didn't know how much time passed after Doug left the cubical and she found the energy to move. Although a part of her had accepted the information that she was indeed pregnant, another equally strong part of her had dallied in the comfort of denial. That luxury had been taken away from her. She was carrying Jordan's child. Soon her womb would stretch and fill to accommodate this new life they'd created.

Naturally she had no option but to tell Jordan. The task, however, held no appeal.

She returned to her apartment, changed into shorts and a sleeveless top, poured herself a glass of iced tea and sank into her chaise longue on her sunlit patio. She needed to review her options. Getting in touch with her emotions proved difficult. She couldn't seem to get past the nearly suffocating fear of losing a second child.

She'd barely had time to assimilate all the changes a baby would bring into her life when the doorbell chimed, scattering her thoughts like marbles against a hardwood floor.

She opened the front door to find Jordan, dressed as if he'd recently walked off the job site, still wearing his hard hat. He wore a frown as if he were displeased about something.

"Hello, Jordan." For one wild moment, her heart went into a panic, fearing that he'd somehow learned about the pregnancy. It didn't take her that long to realize he wouldn't be nearly this calm if that were the case.

"Do you mind if I come in for a moment?" he asked.

"Please." She held open the screen door for him, all the while wondering at the purpose of his visit. If they were to make the break, she'd rather it was clean. Having him repeatedly pop in unannounced didn't sit well. Apparently it didn't with him, either, because he looked about as comfortable as a voodoo doctor in a Methodist prayer meeting.

"Would you like a glass of iced tea?" she asked. He looked tempted, then shook his head.

"Listen, I thought I should clear something with you."

"About what?"

"Kati's wedding."

Her cousin's wedding was scheduled for that Saturday.

"She sent me an invitation," Jordan went on to say. "I'm fond of Kati and, frankly, I'd like to go. But I won't. Not if it'll be awkward for you."

"Jordan, for heaven's sake, don't be ridiculous. Of course you should go. Kati's been half in love with you for years. There isn't any reason why you shouldn't go."

He rubbed his forearm across his brow and lowered his gaze. "I was thinking about asking Lesley to join me."

The other woman's name pricked at her pride, but Molly would have rather walked across a bed of hot coals than let Jordan know. "Are you asking my permission?"

"In a way, yes," he said, which was a concession coming from him.

"We're getting divorced, remember?"

"I'm trying to be as up front with you as possible," Jordan said, his voice elevated as though he were struggling to maintain his composure. "The situation might be awkward and it seemed only fair to give you notice."

"My family will find out about the divorce eventually. Now is as good a time as any to get it out in the open."

"If you'd rather I didn't invite Lesley, then…"

"Jordan, please, you've got to make that decision yourself. Don't ask me to do it for you."

"I don't want the wedding to be uncomfortable for you."

"Stop worrying about me."

"It's your family."

"Do you think the divorce will come as a shock to my relatives?" she asked, forcing a short laugh. "We've been separated for three years."

He nodded, but he wasn't happy with what she'd had to say. It came to her that she should tell him about the baby right then and be done with it. The sooner she let him know, the better it would be for everyone involved.

Jordan walked over to the front door, his hand on the knob. "I'll see you Saturday afternoon, then."

"Jordan." His name had a frantic edge to it and he turned around immediately.

"Yes."

She looked at him, debating if she should tell him about the baby and instinctively knew she couldn't. Not yet. She needed time to come to grips with the news herself before she confronted him. When she told Jordan, she'd need to be strong and confident, and right then she was neither.

"Nothing," she said, offering him an apologetic smile. "I'll see you Saturday."

Jordan was fond of Kati. She was by far his favorite of Molly's cousins, and since she'd specifically sent him a wedding invitation he felt honor bound to attend the gala event.

There was more to his determination to attend this family function than sharing in Kati's happiness, Jordan was forced to admit.

True, this wedding was an excellent means of broadcasting his divorce from Molly. He would use this social event to introduce the woman he intended on marrying, but there was more to it than that. It was his way of proving to himself that the marriage, the relationship, was completely over, completely dead.

Inviting Lesley had been a calculated risk on his part and Jordan had heavily weighed the decision. If he attended the wedding alone, it was a foregone conclusion that one or more of Molly's aunts would take it upon themselves to speak to him and possibly Molly about the breakup of their marriage.

By bringing Lesley with him, he was making a statement to all those concerned that the divorce was imminent. Any well-meaning advice at this late date would be lost on him and Molly.

The decision made, he picked up Lesley, who he swore never looked better. She was a lovely woman and she deeply cared for him. They would make a good life together. Jordan didn't know why he found it necessary to remind himself of that so often. He'd be glad when this divorce business was over and done with. He found the whole process distasteful.

For some unknown reason, he couldn't make himself stop feeling guilty. Hell if he knew what he had to feel guilty about. Molly was the one who'd abandoned him. She'd been away three long years.

All right, so he'd made an ass of himself in Manukua, but given the circumstances, that was forgivable. As for the divorce, he'd bent over backward to be fair in his settlement offer. More than fair. All he was asking for was his freedom. There wasn't a reason in hell he should feel the way he did.

"You're looking thoughtful," Lesley commented as they drove to the church.

Lesley often sensed his mood. She knew him well. He reached over and squeezed her hand. "I was just doing a little thinking."

"About what?"

"Our own wedding," he lied, and the words nearly caught in his throat. "We should start making the arrangements soon, don't you think?"

Her hesitation surprised him. "I'm not in any rush and I don't think you should be, either."

"Why not?"

"Jordan, a divorce takes time."

"Four lousy weeks!"

"I don't mean legally, I mean personally. You're going to need to grieve the loss of your marriage before we can start making any wedding plans ourselves."

"Grieve the marriage," he repeated impatiently. What did she think he'd been doing the past three years. There was nothing left to mourn. It was dead, and he had no intention of digging it up and examining it all over again.

"You'll understand more once it's final," Lesley added with a soft sigh.

He didn't know what had made her such an expert on the subject and bit his tongue to keep from saying so. The last thing he wanted to do was argue, especially now.

"Fine, whatever you say," he muttered as they approached the church.

Finding a parking place proved to be a bear, and his mood hadn't improved by the time the ushers seated them on the bride's side of the church. The first person he saw, two rows up from him and Lesley, was Molly. She was wearing a pretty outfit with a red blazer and a pleated red-and-white flowered skirt. He remembered the suit from years earlier and how she'd struggled to fit back into it after Jeff had been born. It fit her just fine now. Just fine.

Thankfully they didn't need to wait long before the organ music filled the sanctuary and the bridesmaids ceremonially marched down the center aisle. Jordan stood with the others when Kati approached on her father's arm.

Uncomfortable emotions began to stir awake memories of his and Molly's wedding. Dear sweet heaven, they'd been so deeply in love. They were young, younger than they should have been, and crazy about each other.

Jordan vividly recalled when Ian had escorted Molly down the same church aisle and how he'd stood at the front of the altar waiting for her, thinking he'd never seen a more beautiful woman in his life. He remembered the vows he'd spoken that day and how his voice had wobbled with the intensity of what he was feeling. He'd meant every word.

Molly had looked up at him, her eyes filled with devotion as she'd repeated her own vows. Jordan could remember thinking he'd rather die than stop loving her.

The years hadn't changed that. He did love Molly. Not in the same way he had the day they'd married. He'd been little more than wet behind the ears. Over time his love had matured and grown. He remembered when Jeff was born...

His thoughts came to a slow, grinding halt, and he gave himself a mental shake, refusing to drag his son into this.

Everyone sat back down and Jordan was grateful. Not because standing had become a burden, but the change gave him the opportunity to focus his attention on the bride and groom and push the memories of his own long-ago wedding to the farthest corner of his mind.

That, however, proved to be impossible. Kati and Matt seemed intent on everyone joining them as they exchanged their vows. Lesley reached for his hand, and for the briefest of moments he was surprised to realize she was with him. It shocked him to look down and find another woman other than Molly standing at his side. To his credit, he recovered quickly.

Jordan tucked Lesley's hand around his elbow and patted it, hoping to reassure her of his devotion. He did care for her, but he didn't love her, not with the magnitude with which he'd loved Molly.

He didn't appreciate the track down which his thoughts were leading him. Of course he loved Molly, he reassured himself.

They'd been married—and would be for another four weeks. They shared a history together. What Lesley had said earlier about needing to grieve their marriage made sense. He wasn't sure he needed to wear sackcloth and ashes, but a certain adjustment in thinking would be necessary.

Before he realized what was happening, Kati and Matt were involved in a deep kiss to the approval of their guests. Smiling, the two hurried down the aisle together, arm in arm, their happiness glowing as bright as the noonday sun. Molly and he had been that happy once, a long time ago.

The reception was held at the country club, the very same one where he and Molly had held their own wedding reception. Jordan hadn't made the connection until they arrived. He wished now that he'd mailed Kati her gift and left it at that.

The valet parked his car, and Jordan and Lesley walked through the clubhouse and onto the lush green grass where the dinner and dance were being held. The yard was beautifully decorated with Chinese lanterns and round tables and white wooden chairs. The food was exquisitely displayed on long linen-covered tables beneath the white canopies.

By then he was beginning to have second thoughts about the wisdom of following through with this. He decided to drop off his gift, congratulate the newlyweds, make his excuses and leave.

"Jordan Larabee, my goodness, is that you?"

He found himself face-to-face with Molly's Aunt Johanna. He loved her dearly, but the woman was a born meddler. "Aunt Johanna," he said, hugging her briefly. When he finished, he placed his arm around Lesley's shoulders. "I'd like to introduce you to Lesley Walker, my fiancée."

Aunt Johanna giggled as if she'd heard a joke. "How can you be engaged when you're married to Molly? Why that's downright amusing. You'd think it was April Fool's Day instead of May."

Jordan wished he'd thought to warn Lesley. "Molly and I are divorcing," he explained. "And I've asked Lesley to be my wife."

Aunt Johanna's face turned a bright shade of pink. "Oh, Jordan, I'm so very sorry to hear that. I mean it's sad for Molly, but good for…oh, dear," she said, pressing her hands to her face. "I seem to be making a mess of this."

"There's no need to apologize," Lesley said, her natural graciousness taking over. "It was an honest mistake."

Jordan was grateful by how well she handled the uncomfortable scene.

"It was good to see you again," Molly's aunt said, making a hasty exit.

"I'm sorry," Jordan whispered. And he was. He should have warned her about what to expect and wanted to kick himself for being so insensitive to her feelings.

"Jordan, it wasn't that big a deal."

"We'll make our excuses and leave."

Lesley placed her hand on his arm. "We most certainly will not. Leaving now will embarrass poor Aunt Johanna and leave Molly to make lengthy explanations. The last thing she needs is to explain what you were doing here with another woman."

Lesley was right. "We'll stay no more than an hour, though, agreed?"

"Perfect," Lesley said, brightly smiling up at him. "It's going to be all right, darling, I promise."

Lesley wasn't one to use affectionate terms and having her do so now came as something of a surprise. It wasn't until later that he realized she was staking her claim on her territory. That pleased him. Lesley wasn't immune to a few pangs of jealousy.

Jordan was even more surprised to realize he wasn't exempt from being visited by the green-eyed monster himself. Only the source was Molly. Once the meal was served by waiters in white jackets, the band struck up and the space was cleared for dancing.

Jordan had originally intended to stay for the first few dances, the traditional ones between the bride and groom, but before he knew it he was on the dance floor, enjoying himself with Lesley.

He couldn't remember the last time he'd let go like this. It surprised him to realize how good it felt to throw back his head and laugh.

Then he saw Molly, dancing.

The sight of her in the arms of another man had a curious effect upon him. He felt like he'd been slapped alongside of the head. The mental punch was powerful enough to leave his ears ringing.

He didn't give any outward indication of what he experienced, although he made an excuse to leave the dance floor soon afterward.

"Don't tell me you're tired already," Lesley complained. "We were just getting started."

"I need something to drink," Jordan said, reaching for a champagne glass from a waiter's tray as he walked past. He preferred red wine to bubbly champagne, but it was any port in a storm and he felt as if he'd been hit by hurricane-force winds.

It took some doing to divert his gaze away from Molly and her partner, and focus his attention on Lesley instead. He didn't recognize the tall, good-looking man with his soon-to-be ex-wife. He held her in a possessive way that tightened Jordan's jaw.

Thankfully there were plenty of acquaintances to renew, plenty of people to occupy himself with until he decided what he was going to do. If anything.

Carrying his champagne glass with him, Jordan circulated the area, introducing Lesley and doing his damnedest to ignore the fact his wife was in the arms of another man.

"Hello, Jordan, it's good to see you."

"Ian," Jordan said, courteously inclining his head. "Have you met Lesley Walker?"

"Hello, Lesley," Ian said, taking her hand and raising it to his lips. His father-in-law had always been a consummate charmer, and within a relatively short while had Lesley eating out of his palm.

Lesley must have guessed that Ian had something private he wanted to say because she mumbled something about powdering her nose and quietly slipped away.

"You're looking good," Ian said and slapped him across the back. "Back to a hundred per cent after your little adventure, I see."

Jordan frowned. "I'm fine. Get to it, Ian."

"Get to it?" The old man did a fair job of pretending.

"Say what it is you want and be done with it," Jordan advised.

Ian looked downright amused. His eyes were bright with a touch of irony as if it was all he could do not to laugh outright. "I don't have anything important to say," Ian murmured, but the edges of his mouth quivered. "That might not be the case with my daughter, however. When was the last time you talked to her?"

"This week, why?"

"Why?" Ian said, breaking into a ready smile. "You'll need to ask her that."

"I will." This was just the excuse Jordan had been looking for. He set his champagne glass aside and walked onto the dance floor. Molly's eyes widened with surprise when he tapped her partner on the shoulder. "I'm cutting in," he said without apology and a sorry lack of manners. And proceeded to do exactly that.

"Jordan," she said, staring up at him, "that was downright rude."

He didn't have a word to say in his defense, so he let the comment drop. "What's your father grinning ear to ear about?" he demanded.

Molly's gaze darted away from his. "Nothing," she answered

smoothly. "You know my how my dad gets this way sometimes. If...he's troubling you, I'll be happy to say something to him."

She did a commendable job of disguising whatever it was she was feeling. Jordan might have believed her if he hadn't felt her stiffen in his arms the moment he mentioned Ian.

"Tell me."

"There's nothing to tell."

"You're sure?"

"What could I possibly have to say at this late date?"

She felt damn good there, in his embrace, and after a little while he forgot why he'd asked her to dance and enjoyed the simple pleasure of holding her.

"It was a beautiful wedding," he said as means of carrying the conversation.

"It reminded me a little of our own." He knew the minute she admitted that, Molly regretted it. "The comparison is inevitable really. The same church...our reception was held here, too, remember? We were about the same ages, too, and we invited so many of the same guests."

"Don't worry, I know what you're saying." It made sense she'd noticed the same things he had. The same brooding emotions.

Jordan wondered what she'd been thinking while Kati and Matt exchanged their wedding vows. He wondered if she remembered how his voice had wobbled or how her eyes had filled with tears. Did the memory of how desperately they'd been in love come back to haunt her, as well?

"It's a beautiful wedding," she said after an awkward moment.

"Real nice," Jordan agreed.

The music stopped and he had a difficult time dropping his arms and stepping away from her.

"You'd better get back to Lesley," she whispered, lowering her gaze.

Lesley. He'd damn near forgotten her. "Yeah. Your dance partner's tossing daggers my way, as well." It was a weak attempt at a joke. A weak attempt of getting the information he wanted about the other man.

Molly was kind enough to smile. "David's not like that."

"Who is he?" Jordan asked, hoping to sound casual and approving.

"David Stern. Dr. David Stern. He works at Sinai. We met last week."

"He's your date," Jordan said, stunned by the realization. Talk about being obtuse! He hadn't noticed Stern at the church, but that was understandable. His gaze hadn't filtered past Molly in her cheery red suit and broad-rimmed white hat. It hadn't occurred to him to notice the man who was standing next to her.

"Not really," Molly was quick to tell him. "David's a family friend of Matt's. I didn't realize he knew Matt, and David didn't know Kati was my cousin. We'd both talked about attending a wedding on Saturday without realizing it was the same one."

"I see," Jordan said stiffly. He didn't like Stern. Dr. Stern, he corrected.

"Lesley looks very nice," Molly said, glancing behind him.

"Have you talked to your Aunt Johanna lately?" Jordan said as they walked off the dance floor. He was making excuses to linger and knew it, although he didn't understand why he found it necessary. Nor did he want to know.

"Apparently she wasn't aware we're divorcing," Molly said, answering his unspoken question. "You needn't worry, the word will get around fast now. Aunt Johanna is the family gossip. Everyone who's even distantly related will hear the news by nightfall." Her smile was forced, but only someone who knew Molly well would see through that. "I hope she didn't embarrass you."

"No," Jordan muttered. "What about you?"

"Not in the least. It's better if people know as soon as possible, don't you think?" She seemed eager to leave now, looking around as if she were trying to locate her precious David.

"I'd better get back to Lesley," he said, making his own excuses. "It was good dancing with you again."

"You, too." How polite they sounded, as though they were little more than strangers. That was the way it would have to be, he told himself. They had no future, only a sorry, pain-filled past.

Jordan's gaze followed her as she moved across the dance floor. Instead of finding her date, she took the most direct route to her father's side. Even from this distance he could see that she was irritated with Ian. His father-in-law took her chastisement with a grain of salt, reaching for a glass of champagne halfway through her tirade.

Apparently there was something more to the lazy, I-know-something-you-don't smile Ian wore. Jordan wondered what the hell it was, but he had a sneaking suspicion he'd find out soon enough.

Monday morning Jordan got a call from Larry Rife. "I just got the court docket, and the final hearing is set for Thursday afternoon."

"That soon."

"Count your blessings," Rife went on to say. "If Molly had wanted to, she could have tied you up in court for years."

"But it hasn't been the full four weeks yet?"

His lawyer hesitated. "Are you sure you want to go through with this?"

"Yes, I'm sure," Jordan snapped. "Fine, I'll be in court on Thursday afternoon. What time?"

Larry told him. Jordan stared at the telephone receiver for a long time afterward. Thursday afternoon would be the end of his marriage. Thursday afternoon some judge he'd never seen would pound his gavel and his life with Molly would end.

He waited until he suspected she would be home from work before he dialed her phone number. She answered on the third ring; her voice was reed thin as if she were ill and struggling hard not to show it.

"It's Jordan," he announced. "What's wrong? You sound like you're sick."

"I'm fine."

She sure as hell didn't sound like it. "Have you got the flu?"

"Something like that."

He would have liked to question her more, but wasn't sure how to pursue it. "I got a call from Larry Rife this afternoon," he said, getting to the purpose of his call. He didn't relish this task. "The divorce will be final on Thursday."

"Will I need to be in court?"

"No. Not unless you want to be."

"I don't."

"I was the one who filed, I'll go. Do you want me to call you afterward?"

She hesitated as if this was a momentous decision. "That won't be necessary. Thursday it is, then. Thank you for letting me know."

It seemed crass to tell her she was welcome. Crass to thank her for the good years they'd shared. Now didn't seem the time to tell her how sorry he was about Jeff, or mention how badly he'd failed them both.

He'd assumed getting the divorce was a formality. All that was required of him was his signature. No one had told him it was like having his arms torn off and that it would leave him feeling as if he were sitting on a pile of rotting garbage. It wasn't supposed to be like this.

"Goodbye, Molly," he said after a moment.

"Goodbye, Jordan." Her voice quivered and he knew she was

experiencing the same things he was. They shared the same pain, the same deep sense of loss.

From Thursday onward it would be like that song Molly sometimes sang. She'd be someone he used to love.

"Jordan," she said quickly as if she were afraid he'd already hung up the phone. Her voice rang with a note of panic.

"Yes," he said softly, reassuringly.

An eternity passed before she spoke. "Nothing."

"Molly, listen, I know we're divorcing, but if you ever need me for anything…"

"Thank you, but that won't be necessary."

"I see." He didn't have any reason to be hurt by her words, but he was.

"I didn't mean that the way it sounded," she said softly, regretfully. "Thank you for the offer, Jordan, I appreciate it. If you ever need me for anything, don't hesitate to call."

"I won't." Although he doubted that he would. "Goodbye," he said a second time and gently replaced the receiver before she could echo the sentiment.

For reasons Jordan didn't want to analyze he didn't have the heart to hear her say the words a second time.

Chapter Six

"If you don't tell Jordan before Thursday afternoon, I swear I will."

"Dad!" Molly argued, so frustrated she wanted to weep. "This is none of your business."

"I'm making it my business!" He stood and walked around his bulky desk until he stood no more than a few feet from where she was sitting. They rarely disagreed, and when they did Molly could generally reason with her father. Not this time.

"Jordan has a right to know he's going to become a father."

"I'll tell him in my own good time," Molly insisted.

"You'll tell him before Thursday," Ian pressed.

"Do you seriously believe Jordan will call off the divorce?"

"Yes."

"The baby isn't going to make any difference in how he feels about Lesley. He wants his freedom...my pregnancy isn't going to stand in his way."

"We'll see, won't we?"

Ian was serious; if she didn't tell Jordan she was pregnant, he'd take on the task himself. She almost wished she could let him. Walking over to the phone she punched out the number she knew so well. Jordan answered abruptly on the second ring.

"Are you alone?" she asked brusquely.

"Yes, why?"

"I'm coming over."

"Now?"

"Yes, I'll be there in ten minutes," she said and slapped down the receiver. Her father smiled approvingly until she walked over to the liquor cabinet and took out a full bottle of his favorite Kentucky whiskey.

"Where are you taking that?" he demanded.

"To Jordan, he's going to need it."

Her father chuckled and escorted her to the front door, opening it for her. "Give me a call later."

"You're a conniving old man."

"I know," Ian Houghton said, beaming her a wide smile. "How do you think I got to be bank president?" The sound of his amusement followed her out the front door.

By the time Molly pulled into the driveway of the home she'd once shared with Jordan, she'd changed her mind no less than three times. She might have done so again, if he hadn't immediately opened the door and stood on the porch and waited for her.

"What's going on?" he asked.

Molly didn't answer him. Instead she walked into the house and headed straight for the kitchen and brought down a thick glass tumbler. Next she walked over to the refrigerator, opened the freezer door and filled the glass with ice. She poured Jordan a stiff drink and handed it to him.

"What's that for?" he asked, frowning.

"You might want to sit down."

"What the hell's going on?"

Molly had thought she could do this unemotionally, but she was wrong. She was shaking like meadow grass stirred up by the force of high winds.

"If you won't sit down I will," she announced, slumping into a chair. She set the whiskey bottle on the table, and it made a loud clanking noise that echoed through the kitchen.

"What's gotten into you?" Jordan insisted. He pulled out the chair across from her. "I realize this divorce thing is more emotionally wrenching than either of us expected."

Her eyes started to water. "This doesn't have to do with the divorce."

"Why else are you here?"

"Oh, honestly, Jordan," she said impatiently, "don't be so obtuse."

"Obtuse? About what?"

She had an aversion to coming right out and telling him. "Think about it," she suggested, gesturing wildly with her free hand. The other continued to hold the bottle.

"I am thinking."

What she needed was a stiff drink of that whiskey herself, but she couldn't, not when she was pregnant.

"Care to join me?" Jordan asked, bringing down a second tumbler.

"It isn't a good idea for me now. Trust me, it's tempting, I could use the courage."

"It's probably better that you don't. You never could hold your liquor."

"Great, insult me."

He stared at her as if he hadn't seen her in a long while, as if studying her would tell him what it was he didn't know.

"We made love in Manukua, remember?" She waved the whiskey bottle at him, hoping to jolt his memory.

"Yeah, but why bring it up now?" As soon as the words left his lips, he made the connection, falling back into the wooden chair. Slowly his eyes linked with hers. His went wide and then narrowed as he reached for the tumbler and drank down a big gulp. He pressed the back of his hand to his mouth the same way she had and briefly closed his eyes. "You're pregnant."

"Nothing gets past you, does it?" she said mockingly.

"How long have you known?" Why he found that so important, she could only guess.

"A couple of weeks."

"It's taken you until now to tell me?"

She recognized the tone of his voice. His anger simmered just below the surface. Outwardly he was as calm and collected as the next man, but the deep, almost imperceptible inflection of his voice gave him away.

"Sure," she cried, "blame me. I didn't get pregnant all by myself, I'll have you know. Oh no, you had to come after me like Indiana Jones, sweep me into your arms and make mad, passionate love to me."

"I didn't plan for that to happen," he said in his defense.

"Are you saying I did?"

"No," he shouted and wiped his hand down his blood-drained face. He reached for the whiskey and refilled his glass. "What are you going to do?" he asked, not looking at her.

"About what?"

"The pregnancy?"

"That's a stupid question to ask. I'm going to have this baby, raise him or her and live long enough to be a problem to my grandchildren. What else is there to do?"

Jordan propped his elbows against the tabletop. "What about the divorce?"

"I don't see where this pregnancy should make any difference. Lesley will understand." Although Molly would have thoroughly enjoyed being a bug on the wall when he broke the news to his faithful fiancée.

"You might have said something sooner, don't you think?" he flared. His eyes glared at her accusingly. "You knew on Saturday, didn't you? That's what your father was hinting about. Who else did you tell—your good friend Dr. Stern?"

"Leave David out of this."

"So it's David now instead of Dr. Stern."

"Listen, Jordan, I've done my duty and told you about the baby. I realize it's a shock...it was a shock to me, too, but this needn't change anything. You can go about your merry way and do as you damn well please."

Jordan scowled back at her. "You might have given me some warning. I don't know what the hell I'm going to do."

"Might I suggest—nothing?"

"No," he growled.

"Here," she said, handing him the whiskey bottle. "When you've had time to think this through, give me a call and we can talk this out in a more reasonable fashion."

Reasonable fashion!

It was just like Molly to waltz into his home, the night before the divorce was due to be final, and casually announce she was pregnant.

Jordan was furious. He reached for the tumbler, and the ice clanked against the sides of the glass as he jerked it toward his mouth. At least she had the foresight to realize he was going to need a good, stiff drink to help him deal with this.

Pregnant.

He had to give Molly credit. She had an incredible sense of timing. Leave it to his wife to drop a bombshell at the worst possible moment.

A baby.

Jordan's hand tightened around his drink. Sweet heaven, how could this have happened? If it wasn't so incredulous, he'd laugh. Weeping, however, seemed far more appropriate.

Molly had had time to adjust to this news. He hadn't. Frankly, he didn't know that he ever would. Dealing with the possibility of losing a second child was beyond his scope of endurance.

His hand was shaking and Jordan realized it had nothing to do with the amount of alcohol he'd consumed. He'd never been fond of whiskey, Kentucky smooth or otherwise.

He was frightened. So damn frightened he shook with it. Give him a band of machine-gun toting rebels any day of the week. Another gunshot wound was preferable to the risks involved in loving another child.

The grandfather clock in the living room signaled the time, reminding him there was only a matter of hours before he stood before a judge.

"Thank you so much for meeting with me," Amanda Clayton said when Molly joined her on the wooden bench in Lincoln Park. She was a petite thing, young with thick dark hair that naturally curled under at her shoulders.

Pierre had gifted Molly with a dozen or more croissants over the past few weeks in an effort to encourage her to meet his suffering daughter. Molly had finally agreed, but she wasn't sure she would be able to say anything that would help.

Although the day was cloudy and overcast, Amanda wore sunglasses. Molly wasn't fooled, the glasses were an effort to disguise the blotchy red eyes from the ever-ready flow of tears.

"How long has it been?" Molly asked gently.

"Christi died six months ago yesterday. How...how about you?"

"Jeff's been gone almost four years now."

"Four years," Amanda echoed, then added softly. "Does it ever get any better? Does the pain ever go away?"

"I don't know." Molly had been uncomfortable about this meeting from the first. How could she possibly help someone else when she hadn't been able to help herself? "I can get through a day without crying now," Molly told her.

"How...how long did that take?"

"Two years."

"What about your husband?"

"How do you mean?"

"This seems so much harder for me than it does Tommy. I can't even talk about Christi with him because he thinks we should forget, but how am I supposed to forget her?"

"You can't and you won't. You're husband's hurting, too, but men have a far more difficult time expressing their grief. My husband never cried, at least not when I could see him." She knew Jordan had grieved in his own way, but never openly and never with her.

"What...what did you do with Jeff's things? I know this must sound stupid, but what am I supposed to do with Christi's clothes and her toys and the special things we bought for her? Do I just pack those away as if she'd never lived? Or do I leave them out?"

"I don't know," Molly answered sadly.

"What did you do?"

Molly knotted her hands into tight fists. "A few days after we buried Jeff, my...husband went into our son's bedroom, closed the door and packed up all his things to give to a charitable organization."

Molly vividly remembered the terrible argument that had followed as she fanatically sorted through the boxes removing the precious items that had marked Jeff's all-too-short life. She'd managed to salvage his baby book, a hand-knit blanket and his baptismal gown. A rattle, too, and a few other things that were important to her.

Their argument had scarred their marriage. It was as though Jordan believed if he could cut out every piece of evidence that Jeff had lived, then the pain would stop. They'd each dealt with their grief in different ways. Molly had clung to every memory of Jeff. While Jordan had systematically pushed their son out of his life.

This was what had driven them apart. In looking at Molly, Jordan was forced to remember his son. In looking at Jordan, Molly was forced into dealing with Jeff's death.

"Tommy thinks we should sell the house."

"Do you want to move?" Molly asked gently.

"No. Tommy feels that there was something in the air that caused Christi to die. He believes the same thing will happen if we have another baby, but I love our home, and the neighbors have been wonderful. I don't want to move where I don't know anyone. I talked to the doctor about it and he's assured me nothing in the environment was responsible. Besides," Amanda added, "I don't have the energy it would take to find a new home and then pack up everything we own. It's all I can do to get from one day to the next."

Molly understood that, as well. For weeks after Jeff died it was all she could manage to get out of bed in the morning and dress. By contrast, Jordan was up at the crack of dawn and didn't return until long after the dinner hour.

Work had been his release, his salvation. There hadn't been any such relief for Molly, not until she realized she couldn't continue to live with Jordan.

"Eventually I went back to work," Molly said, remembering

how it had taken eight long months for her to function again. "That helped me more than anything, although I don't think it was a solution. At least when I was working I didn't dwell on 'if only.'" She dragged in a deep breath, knowing only someone who'd suffered these kinds of regrets would understand. "You see, I'm a nurse, and as a medical professional I couldn't keep from blaming myself. I should have known…I should have been able to do something. Jeff woke that morning and cried. I…I wanted to catch a few minutes' extra sleep and so I stayed in bed. By the time I climbed out of bed…" It wasn't necessary to finish.

"Tommy and I woke before Christi and he wanted to go in and get her up, but I told him to let her sleep while I went in and took a shower. Only she wasn't sleeping," Amanda said, her voice cracking, "she was dead."

Molly reached for Amanda's hand and gently squeezed her fingers.

"I lost more than my baby when Christi died," Amanda whispered brokenly. "I lost my faith, too. I don't attend church services anymore. I don't want to believe in a God who allows children to die."

Molly had made her peace with God early in the grieving process. She'd felt so terribly alone and needed Him so desperately. "I can't believe God caused Jeff's death, but I know He allowed it."

Amanda reached for her purse. "Would you like to see Christi's picture?"

"Very much," Molly said.

Amanda opened her purse and handed her a small padded photo album. Christi had been a beautiful baby with a head full of dark, curly hair and bright blue eyes. "She looks like such a happy baby."

"She was. I sometimes wonder…" Amanda didn't finish. She didn't need to; Molly understood. She'd wondered herself what Jeff's life would have been like had he lived. Her own life, and Jordan's, too, would have been drastically different. It was as if the world had spun off its axis early one Saturday morning nearly four years ago.

"I have to get back to the hospital," Molly explained. They'd already talked much longer than what she'd expected.

"I'm glad we met."

"I am, too. I don't know that I helped you."

"But you have," Amanda assured her. "More than you realize. Would it be all right if we got together again sometime. I know it'd help my husband if he could talk to yours."

"I'm sorry," Molly said, struggling now to keep her voice even. It was the first time she'd ever spoken the words aloud. "Jordan and I are divorced."

"Oh, I'm so sorry."

Molly stared into the distance until she'd composed herself enough to respond. "So am I."

She should probably do something wild and expensive, Molly decided when she got off work that afternoon. It wasn't every day a woman got divorced. Surely the occasion called for a shopping spree or a lengthy appointment with a masseuse. A divorce demanded more than a hot-fudge sundae, or even a banana split.

Molly had almost reached her car when she heard someone calling her name. She turned around to find Dr. David Stern briskly walking toward her.

"Hi," he greeted breathlessly. "I was beginning to think I wasn't going to catch you."

"Hello again." She was mildly surprised he'd been looking for her. They'd danced a few times at Kati and Matt's wedding, and ate together on the lush green lawn, but she hadn't talked to him after Jordan had been so rude.

"I was hoping I could convince you to go out to dinner with me tonight," David said. He was tall and burly. A few of the staff members referred to him as Dr. Bear, not because of his temperament, but for his size.

"Tonight," she repeated.

"I realize it's short notice, but I'm on call the rest of the week. We could make it another night if that's more convenient, but it never fails. If I've got a date, someone decides this is the night they're going to hurl themselves off a cliff." His grin was wide and boyish.

Molly had liked him the moment she'd watched him comfort an elderly patient. David might be as big and burly as a bear, but he was as gentle as a newborn kitten when needed.

"I'd enjoy dinner with you very much," Molly told him. "But not tonight."

"You've got other plans?"

"In a way. My divorce was final this afternoon and, well, I was thinking I should do something…extravagant. I don't know what yet. Something reckless."

"Hey, some would say dinner with me was downright daring."

Molly was sorely tempted to accept the invitation, but she wasn't ready to date again, not so soon. In addition, there was the baby.

Not every man would be thrilled to date a pregnant woman. "I don't think I'd be very good company."

"I understand," he said, and although he sounded disappointed he offered her a warm smile. "If you need to talk to someone, give me a call." He reached for his prescription pad from his jacket pocket, wrote out his home phone number, peeled off the sheet and handed it to her.

"Promise me one thing," he said, "don't sit around home alone and mope. I'll be in all evening if you want to talk. If nothing else, I've got this great joke book and I can read it to you over the phone."

Impulsively Molly hugged him. She could use a friend just now.

A few minutes later, Molly walked into her apartment and closed the door. The sun had broken through the afternoon clouds and the sky was a polished shade of blue. Funny how bright everything could be when she was weathering a fierce emotional storm. The least it could do was drizzle. A downpour would have been more appropriate.

The phone rang and Molly swerved around to look at it. Perhaps it was fanciful thinking on her part, but she half hoped it was Jordan calling to tell her how the final divorce proceedings had gone. That wasn't likely, however, and she knew it.

"Hello."

"How are you?" It was her ever-loving father.

"Fine."

"You didn't call me," he chastised her. "How did your talk go with Jordan?"

"It went. He wasn't overly pleased, as you might imagine."

"Did he change his mind about the divorce?"

"No." Some small part of her had hoped he would, although she'd never have verbalized as much to her father. Had only now admitted it to herself.

All Ian's talk had ignited a spark of hope, however futile, that her marriage could be saved. But Jordan was involved with Lesley now. It made sense that he was looking to sever his ties with her.

"You told Jordan about the baby, didn't you?"

"Yes."

"And he still went through with the divorce?" Ian's elevated voice revealed his shock. "I thought..." He hesitated, recovered quickly and when he spoke again he was calm and collected. "How are you taking all this?"

"I'm fine." If it wasn't for the baby, Molly would make a point of getting good and drunk, which would take, at most, one margarita. For all the reassurances she offered, she was mildly surprised to discover it was true. She was going to be all right.

"What are you doing?"

"You mean right this minute?" She returned her father's question with one of her own.

"I don't think it's a good idea for you to be alone at a time like this."

Molly smiled, loving him for his concern. "I've already turned down one invitation for dinner. I prefer my own company. I was thinking of ordering myself a decadent pizza, soaking in a hot bubble bath and being especially self-indulgent for the next few hours."

"I can come over, if you want."

"Dad, I'm a big girl. I'll be fine."

It took her a good five minutes longer to assure him of that. When she hung up the receiver, Molly stood there for a few moments, attempting to connect with her feelings. The afternoon had been spent assuring everyone how well she was taking this divorce business.

Really, what else was there for her to do? Pound the walls and weep with frustration? Wallowing in regrets and recriminations was damn draining. She'd spent the past eight hours on her feet and lacked the energy for a lengthy pity party, especially when it would be so sparsely attended.

In the end, Molly changed into her most comfortable pair of shorts and propped her bare feet against the ottoman. She leaned back and drank a glass of iced tea in front of the television while she listened to the evening news.

The tears that silently crept from the corners of her eyes came unbidden and unwelcome. Rubbing the moisture from her face, she reached for a tissue and blew hard. Her emotions were always close to the surface when she was pregnant, and this was an emotional day.

She certainly wasn't going to beat herself up over a few maverick tears. If she needed to cry over this divorce, then she gave herself permission to do so.

Apparently she needed to cry.

"Oh damn," she said, angry with herself, and reached for the tissue box. It hurt, far more than she'd expected it would. Jordan was free to marry Lesley and live happily ever after with someone else.

Resting her hand on her stomach she closed her eyes. At least she wasn't walking out of this marriage empty-handed. This pregnancy was Jordan's final gift to her.

Determined to ignore her need to weep, she reached for the phone and ordered a deep-dish sausage pizza with extra cheese. Despite everything, she found she was ravenous. Crying demanded a lot of energy and if she needed to fuel those tears, then what better way than with a Chicago pizza?

Her doorbell chimed forty-five minutes later. Carrying a twenty-dollar bill with her, Molly opened the front door to discover Jordan standing on the other side.

His hands were buried deep in his pockets and he looked as if he wanted to be anyplace else but where he was. "You're crying."

She mocked him with a smile. "I never understood why you wanted to be a builder when it's obvious you would have made such a great detective."

He ignored her sarcasm. "Are you going to invite me in or are you going to make me stand on your porch all evening?"

She held open the screen door for him.

He stared at the twenty-dollar bill clenched in her hand. "What's the money for?"

"I thought you were the pizza delivery boy."

Jordan's frown deepened. "Pizza gives you heartburn."

Molly found it ironic that he would remember something like that and not her birthday. "I take it there's a reason you wanted to see me."

He nodded and walked over to the sofa. "What the hell's been going on in here?" he asked when he noticed the discarded tissues. It did look as if she'd held a wake, and in a manner of speaking she had, but it wasn't something she wanted to share with her husband.

Ex-husband, she reminded herself.

"I've got a cold," she lied, grabbing the tissues, wadding them up into one tight ball and holding it with both hands.

"Sit down," he ordered.

"Is there a reason I should?" Jordan looked about as friendly as a porcupine.

"Yeah, I think we should discuss the...pregnancy."

"The word isn't all that difficult," she muttered under her breath, just loud enough for him to hear.

Several uncomfortable moments passed before he spoke. "You're making this damned near impossible."

She was behaving like a shrew, but he'd interrupted her. She was grieving their disillusioned marriage and it was entirely unfair that he should interfere. Especially now, when her pizza was about to be delivered.

No sooner had the thought skipped through her mind when the doorbell chimed. It was the delivery boy.

"Do you mind if I eat while you talk?" she asked. She couldn't see any reason to let the pizza go cold.

Jordan wasn't overly pleased with her request, but he agreed with a hard nod of his head. Molly brought out a plate and dished herself up a piece. She was about to offer him one, when he spoke.

"Do you plan on eating that all by yourself?"

"That was my original intention. You're welcome to some, if you'd like."

Apparently he liked, because he got himself a plate and joined her on the living room floor. They sat, Indian style, knees touching, with the steaming pizza between them.

"You were saying?" she prodded when he didn't immediately resume their discussion.

"I talked to Larry Rife first thing this morning about the pregnancy."

"I bet that surprised good ol' Larry."

"Larry nothing," Jordan snapped. "I wish you'd thought to say something to me."

"Come on, Jordan. You can't tell me the possibility never crossed your mind."

He glared at her. "It never crossed my mind. I assumed you were on the pill."

Molly laughed outright. "Why in the name of heaven would I be taking birth-control pills? I hadn't slept with a man in years."

"All right, you've made your point." He reached for a napkin, wiped his hands clean and set the dish aside. "It was downright stupid of us both, and now we're left to deal with the consequences."

Molly set her own pizza aside, her appetite gone. Her baby wasn't a consequence. Jordan made the pregnancy sound as if it were something unpleasant and best ignored. That irritated her. In fact, it infuriated her.

"Larry's arranging for child-support payments to be sent on a monthly basis."

"I don't want anything from you, especially your money."

"That's too bad, because it's already been arranged."

"Fine." She'd let his money accumulate interest in the bank.

"You'll need to let me know who your physician is, too."

"Why?"

"I changed medical insurance a couple of years back and the physician has to be on their approved list."

All this talk about insurance plans and the like confused her. "I went back to Doug Anderson. I always liked him despite what you say about his golf game. Besides, he spent a lot of time with me after Jeff died."

Jordan flinched at the mention of their son's name, and her heart softened. The wall of tears returned and she reached for a paper napkin and held it against her mouth while she battled for her composure.

Jordan reached out as though to comfort her and stopped himself. Slowly he lowered his arms to his sides. "I'm sorry, Molly, more sorry than I can say."

"Just be quiet," she sobbed. "You aren't supposed to be gentle."

He reached for her then, taking her in his arms and holding her against him, letting his body absorb the sound of her cries. How long he simply held her, she didn't know. She should break away, but she couldn't make herself do it.

"I don't think I've slept two winks since you told me about the pregnancy," he whispered.

"You're right...I should have said something right away."

"I can't deal with another baby, Molly. I'm sorry, but I just can't. I'll do what I can to help you through the pregnancy, but I don't ever want to have anything to do with the child."

His words hurt like fire and she jerked herself free of his arms. "Don't worry, you're free now. You've taken care of your responsibilities. I'm sure Lesley's been waiting for this day for a good long while." That was an incredibly bitchy thing to say, she realized, but didn't care.

"What's Lesley got to do with this?"

"You're free," she said, dramatically tossing her arms into the air.

"The hell I am."

"You went before the judge, didn't you?"

It took him far longer than necessary to answer. "As a matter of fact, I didn't."

Chapter Seven

"You mean to tell me we're not divorced?" Molly cried, vaulting to her feet. Here she'd been going through a ritual of grieving. She'd buried her face in a sausage and extra-cheese pizza, and sniffled her way through an entire box of tissues, as she confronted her pain. It had all been for naught.

"We aren't divorced," Jordan said as if he regretted every minute that had passed since he'd made his decision.

"Why aren't we?"

"Because you're pregnant," Jordan returned forcefully.

"So? You just got done saying you didn't want to have anything to do with the baby."

Jordan stuffed his hands in his pockets, and his gaze averted hers. "The pregnancy makes a difference. It's reasonable to wait to refile the papers until after the baby's born. Another few months won't matter one way or another, will it?"

Molly didn't answer him. She sincerely doubted that Lesley would feel that way, but then it wasn't her place to point that out.

An awkward silence fell between them. "How are you feeling?" Jordan asked after what seemed like an inordinately long while. He seemed so ill at ease that it was all she could do not to say something to reassure him.

"I'm fine."

"Morning sickness?"

She shrugged. "A little."

"What about the afternoons?"

So he remembered the afternoon bouts of nausea she'd suffered when she was first pregnant with Jeff. "Some, but not as bad as it was...the first time."

He nodded and took his hands out of his pockets.

Molly pushed the hair away from her face. The muggy heat felt stifling. It didn't seem right for them to be sitting in her living room, discussing her pregnancy on the heels of the details of their divorce.

"I don't know how to act around you anymore," she whispered. "You aren't my husband, and yet we're married. I'd made my peace with the divorce and now we aren't divorced. What exactly are we, Jordan?"

The question seemed to cause some internal deliberation. "Couldn't we be friends?"

Molly didn't know how to answer him. Friendship implied camaraderie and rapport, and she wasn't sure they shared that anymore. It implied an ongoing relationship, and being vulnerable to each other.

"Remember how we assured Larry this was going to be a friendly divorce," Jordan prompted.

"That's the problem," Molly said, laughing softly. "The divorce is more friendly than the marriage."

Jordan laughed, too, and it helped ease the tension between them. He sat down on the other end of the sofa.

"A few months won't make any difference," he said, almost as if he were speaking to himself. "Lesley won't mind."

"I'm sure you're right," Molly said, although if she were Lesley she'd have a whole lot more to say on the subject.

"When will you be seeing Doug again?"

"Late Monday afternoon."

"So soon?"

"He wants to closely monitor this pregnancy because I've just come out of Manukua." That and the fact they'd lost Jeff, but that much was implied.

"I see," Jordan commented. "Is his office still downtown?"

Molly nodded.

"That's my project going up, two blocks over. I'll be there Monday afternoon. Why don't you stop by afterward and let me know what the doctor has to say."

"All right," Molly agreed, "I will."

Jordan tried not to think about Molly all morning, but she was like a bad penny, turning up in his thoughts, plaguing him with memories of how good their lives together had once been. All that had changed with Jeff.

He couldn't think about his son and not experience anger. An anger so deep it bordered on rage. Over time Jordan had focused his wrath in just about every direction. At first he blamed the medical profession, Jeff's pediatrician, Molly and finally himself.

If only he'd he gone into Jeff's bedroom that morning. Instead he'd left the house and damned Molly to the agony of finding the body of their lifeless son.

Jordan's fists clenched at his side as the fury worked its way through him. His breathing was hard and heavy and his heart felt like a rock pounding against his ribs. Within a few minutes the anger passed the way it always did, and the tension eased out of his muscles.

Now Molly was pregnant again.

Jordan had delayed the divorce, and even now he wasn't sure why. Molly was right. The baby wasn't going to change anything. Seven, eight months from now it would be born.

It.

He was more comfortable thinking of Molly's pregnancy as an it. Dealing with a tiny human being that cried and laughed and smiled when he recognized his daddy was beyond Jordan's capabilities. He'd keep his distance, Jordan promised himself. He planned never to see this baby, never to hold it, never to love it. But for Molly's sake and perhaps his own, he'd do what he considered best for now.

After Molly's baby was born, Jordan fully intended on having the final papers processed. Then he'd marry Lesley.

He felt better. His life was neatly arranged, tied up in a colorful bow. He was in control again.

He glanced at his watch and exhaled slowly. He was meeting Lesley briefly, returning some blueprints to her office. He wasn't looking forward to this because sure as hell she was going to ask about the divorce.

When he hadn't been plagued with thoughts of Molly, Jordan had been stewing about what he was going to tell Lesley. The truth, of course. But he needed to couch it in a way that assured her of his commitment. Now, however, felt wrong. He'd prefer to give it a few days and sort through his feelings.

If luck was with him, Lesley would be busy and he could hand over the papers to her secretary and make a clean escape. But Luck, the fickle lady she was, hadn't smiled on him in years.

As it happened, Lesley had stepped outside her office and was talking to her secretary when Jordan arrived. He was cursing his fate when she looked up and beamed him a delectable smile.

"Jordan, come and have a cup of coffee with me."

"Sure." For show he looked at his watch, hoping to give the impression he had another appointment and could only manage a few minutes. He followed her into her office, his heart heavy. This could well be the most difficult conversation of his life.

He liked the way Lesley had decorated her office with oak bookcases and a matching drafting table. One thing he could say about Lesley, she had exquisite taste.

"So," she said, automatically pouring him a cup of coffee. "How did everything go in court yesterday afternoon?"

There wasn't any way to say it other than straight out. Perhaps he should reconsider his tactic. He borrowed a trick from Molly instead. "You'd better sit down."

"Sit down?" She raised her eyes from the glass coffeepot until they'd connected with his. "Something's wrong?" she asked and walked around to her side of the desk.

"Not exactly wrong." For all his advice about sitting, he found it necessary to stand himself. "I got a bit of a shock the other night."

"Oh?"

He paused, then decided the only way to say it was straight out. "Molly's pregnant."

"Pregnant?" Lesley made it sound as if she'd never heard the word before. "That must have been a surprise. Who's the father?"

"Ah..." He would have told her then, if she'd given him the chance.

"I imagine it's that doctor friend of hers you mentioned. The one who was with her in Manukua?"

He stiffened and met her gaze straight on. "No. I am."

The mug in Lesley's hand started to shake and coffee splashed over the sides until she managed to set it down on her desk. She sank, slow motion, into her chair.

"I know this is a blow, Lesley, and I can't tell you how sorry I am."

"You and Molly...I see."

Witnessing the pain in her eyes was almost more than Jordan could look at. "I don't have any excuses. It happened while we were in Manukua, while we were held down by the rebel gunfire. We hid in a supply shed and for a time I didn't know if we were going to make it out alive."

"That's your excuse?" she asked, and her voice wobbled with indignation.

"Lesley, I couldn't be more sorry. I wouldn't hurt you for the world."

"Funny, you've done a surprisingly good job of it." She reached for her coffee in an effort to mask the tears that brimmed in her pretty dark eyes.

Jordan couldn't remember feeling more of a heel. Without trying he'd managed to offend the woman he cared enough about to want to marry.

"You didn't go through with the divorce, did you?"

It surprised him how well Lesley knew him. "No, not yet. I felt it was better to wait until after the baby was born."

"I see."

"I don't blame you for being upset," Jordan said, leaning toward her, his hands clenched together. "I wouldn't blame you if you threw me out that door and said you never wanted to see me again, but I hope you won't. My marriage is dead..."

"Apparently not as dead as I once believed," Lesley said, her voice trembling.

"A baby isn't going to solve the problems between Molly and me. If anything, this pregnancy complicates the issues. We're both having to sort through a lot of emotional garbage."

"What about the child?" Lesley wanted to know. "How do you feel about...having a child?"

His hands tightened until his fingers ached. "I never wanted another family. It was understood from the moment we discussed marriage that there wouldn't be children. That hasn't changed. Neither Molly nor I had much say about this new life. She seems to have adjusted to the news without much trouble, but I...frankly, I don't ever plan on seeing the baby. Naturally I'll support the child financially, but I refuse any emotional involvement."

Lesley's lips quirked upward in a brief smile; at least, Jordan suspected it was a smile. "Jordan, it would be impossible for you not to love this child."

His spine stiffened. Another Jeff. Never. "You can't love what you don't see," he told her confidently.

"You already love this child, otherwise you would have gone through with the divorce," Lesley argued gently. "A pregnancy wouldn't have mattered if you honestly believed you could turn your back on the child."

"It was Molly I couldn't walk away from," he countered. As soon as the words escaped, he realized the profound truth of them, and how deeply they had wounded Lesley. "She had a difficult pregnancy the first time," he added quickly, wanting to undo the damage, already knowing it was too late.

Lesley stood and walked to the window, her back to him. He noticed how rigid she stood, as if she were fighting back the pain. She crossed her arms, her elbows jutting out. "You still love her."

"No," he denied quickly, then added in a thin spiderweb of a voice, "Yes, I suppose I do." He waited, hoping Lesley would turn around, but she didn't. "Don't condemn me for that. Molly was...is my wife. A man doesn't forget his first love."

He saw Lesley's hand move to her face and he realized she was wiping the tears away. It pained him to know he'd hurt her so deeply.

"You might think this an asinine question, but would you be willing to wait for me to divorce Molly?" he asked. "It shouldn't be any longer than a few months. Nothing has to change for us unless you want it to." He'd been as honest with her as he could be, and he hoped she'd take that into consideration.

"I ought to throw you out that door, just the way you suggested."

"But you won't," he coaxed, feeling confident she would have by now, if that had been her intention.

"I...don't know what I should do. Then again, it should be crystal clear," she said with a laugh that sounded more like a sobbing hiccup. "I need time to think this through."

"All right. How long?" They were scheduled to attend a cocktail party with a group of investors over the weekend. Important investors. Even if they didn't arrive together, avoiding each other would be impossible.

"I can't give you an answer to that," Lesley said. "But I will promise to call you once I make up my mind."

Molly stood in line at the hospital cafeteria, deciding between the egg-salad sandwich and the chicken salad, when David Stern cut in front of her.

"Hello again," he said, grinning as he slipped the orange plastic tray next to her own. "I've been waiting to hear from you."

Molly felt mildly guilty for not searching him out, knowing that was what he expected. She liked David, but she didn't want to mislead him into believing they could become involved.

"Care to join me for lunch?" he asked.

"I'd care a whole lot," she joked.

He paid the cashier for her sandwich and milk, plus his own much-larger lunch, and then wove his way between crowded tables to the patio outside.

Molly followed him, grateful he'd chosen to eat outdoors. She loved the sunshine. She set her tray down on the round glass table, under the sheltering shade of the blue-and-yellow umbrella.

"What decadence did you fall into the other night?" David asked.

"A sausage and extra-cheese pizza," she said, opening the wax-sealed milk carton and pouring it into a glass.

"That sounds pretty tame to me. Surely a divorce rated a double Scotch on the rocks."

"I shouldn't drink now," she returned automatically. Her hands froze on the milk carton as she raised her gaze to David's. He might as well know. Her pregnancy wasn't a secret. "I'm pregnant."

David took the information in his stride. "Does your ex know?"

"Yes. It was a shock for us both, but he paid me back in spades."

"How's that?" David asked as he dumped half the pepper shaker on his tuna salad.

"He had his attorney withdraw the divorce petition. I drowned my sorrows in pizza, and cried me a river, only to discover we're still married."

"He wants to reconcile?"

It wasn't polite to laugh, but Molly couldn't help it. "Nothing that drastic. He felt, for whatever reason, that we should wait until after the baby's born. I don't know how his fiancée is going to take this, but that's his problem."

"He's engaged?"

Her life sounded as if it came straight out of a soap opera. "From what I understand, she's perfect for Jordan." Molly raised her sandwich to her mouth. "As you can see I'm not exactly a prime candidate for a relationship. I'd suggest counseling for any man who wanted to become involved with me."

David laughed. "You sound like you might be needing a friend."

That was the word Jordan had used, too. Why was it every man in her life suddenly wanted her for a friend? She might as well get used to it. There was only one thing about which Molly was completely certain. She never intended to marry again.

"You're right," she admitted, "I could use a friend."

"So could I," David said, centering his attention on his lunch. "My wife died the first part of January. We'd been married fifteen years."

"David, I'm sorry, I didn't know."

"She'd been sick with cancer for several years. In the end death was a blessing and came as a friend. We both had plenty of time to adjust to the inevitable."

"Can one ever prepare themselves for the death of a loved one?" Molly questioned, curious. As a nurse, she'd seen death countless times. She'd watched patients struggle and hold on to life until their knuckles were raw from the battle. Yet others gracefully slipped from one life into the next with little more than a token resistance.

"I thought I was prepared," David said quietly, painfully, "but I wasn't. Certainly I didn't want Joyce to suffer any longer. What surprised me was the desperate loneliness I experienced afterward. That lack of connection with one other human being." He stopped eating and reached for his glass of iced tea.

David had walked through the same valley she had, where death cast its desolate shadow. That was what had attracted her to him and why she'd felt an instant kinship with him.

"It's taken me several months to come to terms with Joyce's death. I'm not looking to involve myself in a relationship, if that concerns you. All I want is a little companionship, and it seems to me we're really after the same thing. Just maybe we could help each other."

Molly's eyes met his. "Just maybe we might."

Jordan's pickup was parked outside the house when Molly pulled in behind it and turned off the engine. It might have been better if she'd phoned, but she had agreed to stop off following her appointment with Doug Anderson. Only it was much later than what she'd told him.

It felt strange to ring the doorbell to the home that had once been hers, then stand outside and wait for Jordan to answer. Odd and awkward. She wished now she'd phoned instead. She couldn't be friends with Jordan. Cordial, yes, but their pain-filled history precluded being bosom buddies. She appreciated his concern, but it would probably be best for them if they kept their distance.

When he answered the door Jordan's eyes revealed his surprise at seeing her. The first thing Molly thought was that Lesley was with him and her unannounced arrival would embarrass them all.

"Have I come at an inconvenient time?" she asked, "because I can leave."

"Don't be ridiculous," Jordan answered. He must have recently gotten home himself because he was dressed in his work clothes— khaki pants and a short-sleeved shirt.

"I can quietly leave if...someone's with you."

"I'm alone," he said, drawing her into the house. "What happened? When you didn't show, I contacted Doug's office and got his answering service."

"He was called into the hospital for a delivery. I had to reschedule my appointment. I tried to reach you, but you've got a different cellular number now."

"Damn, that's right. Here, let me give it to you."

"That's all right, " she said, holding up one hand. "It isn't necessary." Carrying his mobile phone number around with her was too intimate, too familiar.

Jordan looked surprised by her refusal. "You might need it sometime."

"I...I can always contact your office. They should be able to reach you for me, shouldn't they?"

He shrugged as if it made no difference to him one way or the other, but it did, and she could tell that her refusal had offended him.

"How are you?" he asked, after a short delay.

He wasn't comfortable asking about the baby, she realized, but his question implied his concern. "Healthy as a horse. The morning sickness isn't nearly as severe this time." But she wasn't feeling all that terrific, just then. It was funny how the afternoon bouts of nausea continued to plague her.

He didn't respond, but opened the refrigerator and brought out a pitcher of iced tea. Without asking, he poured her a glass and added a teaspoon of sugar just the way she liked it.

"I thought I'd stop by and explain why I didn't do so earlier," Molly said, positioning herself so that the breakfast counter stood between them. "I...won't stay."

"All right, if that's what you want."

Her stomach rolled and pitched and she felt terribly ill all at once. "Would it be all right if I sat down for a minute."

"Of course." Something in her voice must have relayed how ill she was feeling because he took her by the elbow and guided her into the family room.

Sitting helped slightly, and she took in several deep, even breaths. Unfortunately it wasn't enough. She shot up and raced for the bathroom and promptly lost her lunch.

When she finished, Jordan was there with a wet washcloth.

"I'm sorry," she whispered, feeling incredibly weak and close to tears. Once again, her awkward sense of timing had clicked into place.

"You don't need to apologize," Jordan told her, gently guiding her back to the upholstered chair. He brought her a glass of water and she drank thirstily. Jordan stayed by her side, and it seemed he wasn't sure what he should do.

Resting her head against the back of the chair, Molly closed her eyes. "I'll be all right in a minute," she said.

"Relax," Jordan instructed.

Molly felt him place a thin blanket over her. Her mind was drifting into a lazy slumber. She tried to tell herself it wasn't a good idea for her to doze while she was at Jordan's house, but it demanded far more effort than she could muster to pull herself back from the edge of sleep.

Jordan sat across from Molly, watching her while she napped. Dear heaven, she was beautiful. His heart ached as he studied her, hoping she could rest.

The awkwardness between them troubled him. He knew he was to blame and that Molly was protecting herself from any further heartache.

He'd been an ass about the pregnancy. Over the past week he'd made several attempts to reconcile himself to the fact he was going to be a father again. It hadn't worked. His instincts told him to run as fast as he could in the opposite direction.

Molly had his deepest admiration for her bold-faced courage. Dear God, how he wished he could be different. How he wished he could feel the elation he'd experienced when they first learned she was pregnant with Jeff. But that pleasure had been stripped from him the day Jeff had perished.

From the moment Molly told him she was going to have another child, all he'd known was fear. It was like a second skin that clung to his every thought, dictated his actions and taunted him with the feeling nothing in his life would ever be right again.

He longed to give Molly the emotional support she needed and deserved through this pregnancy. But he didn't know if that was possible. This child, innocent and fragile, left him weak with anxiety. Weak in other ways, too, until he damned himself for the coward he was.

A strand of blond hair fell across her pale skin. Jordan yearned to tuck it behind her ear, to hold her head against his chest and wrap her in his arms. He didn't examine his feelings too closely because if he did he might remember how incredible their night together in Manukua had been.

It had been like that in the beginning, after they were first married. Their need for each other had been insatiable, their happiness had brimmed over into every aspect of their lives.

He needed to move away from Molly, Jordan realized, otherwise he'd quickly become trapped in the maze of happy memories.

Cooking dinner seemed the solution, so he moved into the kitchen and brought out a package of steaks. His culinary skill was limited, but he barbecued a decent steak. Salads weren't that difficult, either. He brought the prepackaged lettuce from the refrigerator, a tomato and a green pepper. He chopped the vegetables, feeling especially creative. Every now and again, his gaze involuntarily drifted to Molly.

He must have been glancing her way more frequently than he realized, because the knife sliced across the end of his index finger. A rush of bright red blood followed.

"Damn," he muttered at the unexpected pain. The cut was deep and bled freely. Turning on the faucet, he held his finger beneath the running water and noticed it turn a light shade of pink.

"What happened?" a groggy Molly asked.

"Nothing," he snapped.

"You cut yourself." She was standing next to him. "Let me see."

He jerked his hand away from her. "I told you it's nothing."

"Then let me take a look at it," she insisted. She turned off the water and reached for his wrist, holding it tightly while she wrapped his hand in a clean kitchen towel.

"It's not that bad," Jordan maintained, feeling foolish. It was his own damn fault for being careless.

"You'll live," she agreed. "I'll put a bandage on it and you'll be good as new within a week." She opened the cupboard by the kitchen sink and brought down the bandages, carefully wrapping his index finger in gauze and tape. When she'd finished, she kissed the back of his hand.

The kiss, simple as it was, rippled through him. Unprepared for the impact of her touch, he drew in his breath sharply. Somewhere in the farthest reaches of his mind, the pleasure gripped hold of him and refused to let go. It had been like this in Manukua when she'd placed her arms around his neck and her breath came hot against his throat.

When he dared, he lowered his gaze to Molly's and found that she was staring at him. Her eyes were a reflection of his own, filled with doubt and wonder.

Neither of them moved, neither breathed. It was as though they were trapped in a time warp. He needed to kiss her. Not wanted. *Needed.* He couldn't think about this feeling, couldn't analyze it, knowing that if he did he'd lose courage.

He reached for her and she came into his arms like a soft kitten, purring. She parted her lips to him and trembled as her feminine body adjusted to the hard length of his.

He kissed her again and the pleasure of holding her was his undoing. He trailed his lips down the side of her neck, his tongue dipping into the hollow of her throat.

She might have protested, but he cut her off with the hunger of his kiss, backing her up against the kitchen counter. What had started out gentle and exploratory had quickly altered to a frenzy of need. As his mouth worked against hers, his hands bustled, unfastening the front of her blouse, until he could fill his palms with the weight of her breasts.

"Jordan?" She breathed his name. She had a way of saying it that was unlike anyone else, all breathless and needy. The only time she said it in just that way was when she wanted to make love. It hadn't been so long ago that he'd forgotten.

He moved his hands to her hips and held himself against her, letting her feel the strength of his need. She moaned and met his kiss with a desperation and insistence that was as powerful as his own.

Where he found the strength to break away, Jordan didn't know. "Not in the kitchen," he muttered on a thick guttural sound. He lifted her into his arms and carried her into the family room and placed her on the sofa. His breath was thin and his heart scampered wildly. They were crazy, the pair of them together like this, but he didn't care.

Gently he settled over her, careful to position his weight in such a way not to hurt her or the baby. Her breasts were fuller than he recalled, soft and round. Her nipples pearled up at him and, unable to resist, he locked his lips around one and sucked gently.

Molly buckled against him, and he smiled at the pure glory he experienced, loving her like this. When he lifted his head, he discovered that her eyes carefully studied him, looking for some kind of confirmation, he guessed. With his eyes still on hers, he lowered his mouth to hers.

"I want you," he whispered. His thigh eased hers apart and she let him, welcomed his body as it nestled snugly over her own.

"I know." The words were slow and thick. "I want you, too."

His hands returned to her breasts and she wantonly arched herself against his palms. Her sweet lips were close to his, too close to ignore, and he kissed her, probing his tongue deeply inside her mouth. It swirled over hers in an erotic mating that left them both panting and breathless.

Molly whimpered, sounding very close to tears, and in that moment Jordan died a little. He'd missed her so much, needed her and wanted her and had denied it, hiding his love behind a wall of fear.

Her arms circled his neck and he felt the wetness of her tears. He wanted to tell her how sorry he was, and couldn't, for the lump in his throat. Instead he kissed her gently, lovingly. He kissed her in all the places he'd missed, under her chin, behind her ear and at the edges of her mouth. She clung to him as if he were her source of life.

"I love you," Jordan whispered. "I never stopped, not for a moment."

"What about the baby?"

His world crashed at his feet and shattered in small pieces. "I don't know...I just don't know."

The phone rang then, slicing the moment wide open like a hunting knife ripping through fragile cloth.

"Ignore it," Jordan said.

"No," she insisted, "it might be important."

Nothing was more important than her in his arms, but the phone rang again, sounding urgent. Against his better judgment, he moved away from Molly and reached for the receiver.

"Hello," he barked, irritated at the intrusion.

"Jordan." It was Lesley.

Jordan closed his eyes and groaned.

"Jordan, are you there?"

"Yes." It was all he could do to manage the one word.

"Is something wrong? You don't sound like yourself."

Chapter Eight

"Lesley," Jordan stated, and out of his peripheral vision he caught a glimpse of Molly leaping off the sofa. Quickly she righted her clothes, her movements filled with righteous indignation.

"I thought you'd want to know," Lesley said when he didn't continue.

"Know?"

"What I've decided," Lesley continued.

"Yes, of course." Jordan cupped his hand over the mouthpiece of the receiver. "Molly, wait," he pleaded. They needed to talk, needed to discuss what had happened and make some sense of it.

Molly hesitated.

"Molly's there now?" Lesley asked.

"Yes, listen, could we talk later?"

"That sounds like it'd be for the best. Tomorrow morning?"

"Sure...sure." All he wanted to do was get off the phone. His main concern was keeping Molly with him, until they'd had a chance to talk this out. It was just like her to run. Just like her to leave him grappling with regrets.

"At ten?"

"Fine. I'll see you then." Jordan replaced the receiver just as Molly walked past him on her way to the front door. "Molly, please wait," he called, nearly stumbling in his rush to reach her before she escaped.

She stopped, her purse clenched against her stomach, for protection, he guessed. Her eyes were leveled at his chest, her breasts heaving slightly in her rush to get away.

"Please don't go. Not until we've had a chance to talk this out."

"No," she answered stiffly. Her eyes, which only moments earlier had been warm with passion, stared back at him empty in an effort to conceal her distress.

"Dammit, Molly, don't do this."

"Me? I'm not the one with both a fiancée and a wife. As far as I'm concerned you've got one too many women. I don't want to see you again, Jordan. I'll have my father notify you when the baby's born and you can have Larry petition the court. All I ask is that you notify me when the divorce is final." Her voice rocked with the strength of her emotion.

"How can you walk away like this after what happened? What nearly happened," he corrected.

"Easy. We've been married and, well, I guess you could say we fall into an old habit. It didn't mean anything, how could it, when you plan on marrying Lesley. We're human, aren't we? It was just one of those things. It happened, and I don't think we should put any credence to it."

"Habit?" Jordan repeated. "You don't honestly believe that."

"Come on, Jordan," she said and laughed, but the sound of her amusement was hollow and tinny. "We used to make love on that old couch more often then we ever did on the bed upstairs."

Jordan couldn't disagree with Molly. But kissing her, tasting her, wasn't habit. It had been a rediscovery, a reawakening. He wasn't ready to excuse it away, nor was he willing to leave matters unsettled between them.

"It was far more than habit and you know it," he argued.

Molly sighed with bleak frustration. "I'm not going to stand here and fight with you. If you don't buy my explanation, then make up one of your own. One you're comfortable with." She met his gaze steadily, conviction flashing from her beautiful blue eyes. "What I said stands. I don't want to see you again. Please don't make this any more difficult than what it already is."

"If you're worried about Lesley, then..."

"I'm not going to discuss Lesley with you or anyone else."

"It's over between Lesley and me," he said, then realized Molly had walked away. He debated if he should run outside and try one last time to reason with her.

His relationship with Lesley had been a mistake. Jordan didn't know what had taken him so long to realize it. He wasn't entirely sure why he'd ever gotten involved with her. Loneliness, he suspected. He'd been separated from Molly for three long years and his life was empty.

One night, after a couple of drinks, he'd performed a two-bit self-analysis and decided he was over Molly, over Jeff and wanted out of the marriage. He was looking to break new ground in a relationship that wasn't weighted down with grief so heavy it had nearly buried them both.

Jordan felt tired and old and the emotional resilience he'd once prided himself on was long gone. The stark truth was he'd never stopped loving Molly. As hard as he tried, he couldn't make himself not care about her. Oh, he'd managed to convince himself he had for a time, however brief, when he first started dating Lesley. That theory had been blown to hell in a supply hut in Manukua.

The situation might have righted itself naturally if it weren't for the pregnancy. The icy cold fear he experienced each time he thought about this new life they'd created had left him trembling. But then he'd be divorced by now if it weren't for the pregnancy. He didn't know if this new baby was a blessing or a curse.

One thing he did know. He wasn't ready to be a father again.

He didn't know if he'd ever be ready. Or if he wanted to be.

Jordan walked outside, hands in his pockets as he strolled toward Molly. He was willing to swallow his pride in order to keep her with him until they could settle this.

"You're running away again," he said. It was what Molly had done after Jeff had died and now she was guilty of it again, claiming she didn't want to see him anymore.

"I'm running away *again?*" Her eyes filled with fury and were impacted straight at him. "Are you seriously suggesting I was running away when I moved out? Did it ever occur to you, Jordan Larabee, that you all but pushed me."

"That's not true," he answered heatedly, struggling to hold on to his temper.

"You couldn't stand to look at me because every time you did…"

"You cried and cried and cried. Dammit, Molly, all you did was mope around the house, sobbing from one room to the next for weeks on end. Jeff was the center of every thought, every conversation. Did you think if you cried long enough and hard enough it would bring him back?"

"I was grieving."

"You didn't have the common decency to tell me you were leaving. I walked in the house and found a stupid note posted on the refrigerator door. You couldn't have told me face-to-face?"

"Why should I? We hadn't talked in weeks. The only reason I left a note," she said, throwing back her head and glaring at him, "was because I feared it'd take a month for you to notice that I'd moved out."

"I handled Jeff's death in my own way," Jordan shouted.

"You handled nothing. You wanted me to pretend he'd never lived...you wanted me to continue as if nothing was wrong. I couldn't do it then and I refuse to do it now."

"You're doing it again," he shouted, "throwing Jeff in my face. You're using him as a weapon to beat me up, to tell me how wrong I've been."

"You're the one guilty of repeating the same mistakes," she said, throwing the words at him as if they were steel blades. "You want to pretend this baby isn't alive, either." She flattened her hand over her stomach and her eyes brimmed with tears. "I find it ironic that you accuse me of running away when that's what you've been doing for nearly four years."

Jordan knotted his fists, fighting down the rage. "For once you're right. We have no business seeing each other any longer. By all means, let's not make the same mistakes again."

"That's perfectly fine with me. Go back to sweet, understanding Lesley," Molly suggested, reaching her car. "I'm convinced you're exactly right for each other."

The following morning, Jordan met with Lesley. He wanted to be gentle with her, and sincerely hoped he could break off their unofficial engagement in such a way that left her with her pride intact.

Following his argument with Molly, his nerves were raw. He felt edgy, impatient and so damn weary. He sat up most of the night thinking, not that it had done the least bit of good. In the morning, he felt as if he were walking in a haze. The sensation reminded him of when he'd woken in the hospital after being shot. Drugged, thwarted, restless.

"This time hasn't been easy on either one of us, has it?" Lesley commented, automatically bringing him a cup of coffee. He sat in the leather chair across from her desk and thanked her with a smile. It was going to take a hell of a lot more than caffeine to get him through this ordeal.

"I've done some heavy soul-searching the past couple of days," Lesley said evenly, taking the seat behind her desk. He noticed that she avoided looking directly at him, and guessed she was as uncomfortable as he was.

"What did you come up with?" Jordan asked, sipping his coffee. To his surprise the hot liquid helped clear his head.

"Mostly, I realized that I've been playing a fool's game," she admitted nervously. "You're in love with Molly. I should have realized it when you decided to go after her in Manukua yourself. When you came back, I knew immediately matters between us were different, but I didn't want to own up to it. Then...then at her cousin's wedding, I saw the two of you dancing. It should have been abundantly clear then. You might have said something, Jordan, and spared me this."

She had every right to be angry. Jordan had no defense.

"When I learned Molly was pregnant and you decided to hold up the divorce...well, that speaks for itself, doesn't it?"

"I didn't mean to hurt you." How weak that sounded.

Her hands cradled the coffee mug and she lowered her gaze, taking a moment to compose herself, before she continued.

"I realize now that I was willing to marry you for all the wrong reasons. We'd worked together for several years and were comfortable together, but there's never been any great passion between us. I was willing to marry you, Jordan, because I so badly want to marry. For years I've struggled to build my career and then I woke up one morning and realized how desperately lonely I was. I wanted a loving relationship, needed one."

"We were both lost and lonely souls," Jordan interjected.

"I...know I agreed there wouldn't be any children, but I was hoping you'd change your mind later. Talk about living in a fool's paradise."

"I'd like it if we could find a way to remain friends."

Lesley nodded. "Of course. I'm not angry—at least, not at you. You're a good man, Jordan, and I'm hoping you and Molly can work everything out."

"I'm hoping we can do that, too." But it wasn't likely, not now. He stood and set the coffee mug aside. "There's someone out there for you, Lesley. You'll meet him, and when you do you'll know."

October was Molly's favorite month of the year. The winds off Lake Michigan were warm yet, swirling up orange and brown autumn leaves while she walked along the redbrick pathways of the neighborhood park.

At four and half months, her baby was actively making himself known, stretching and exploring his floating world.

Molly hadn't seen Jordan since that last fateful afternoon six weeks earlier. He hadn't made an effort to contact her, and she certainly had no plans to see him. Not after the terrible things they'd said to each other.

In the intervening weeks, Molly was struck by how different she felt. About herself. About life.

At first she assumed it was Chicago that had changed. It had taken her several weeks to realize the Windy City was the same and she was the one who was different.

The years she'd spent in Manukua, she'd been hiding in the shadows of yesterday. Resting in the shade of her loss had become comfortable. It had become home. Ever since she'd discovered her son dead in his crib, she'd been trapped on a treadmill that continually revolved around the heart-wrenching events of that single Saturday morning. She'd examined those final hours, those final words, those final acts, until the darkness took over and the sum of her life had narrowed down to one single thread of light. She hadn't moved forward since.

Until now.

She'd stepped forward into the sunlight. She'd leaped back into life and experienced joy and laughter once more. Only now could she look with gratitude at the happiness Jeff's short life had given her. The innocence of those few precious months they'd shared would always be with her. The memories of holding him against her breast and feeding him, so pure and perfect. And loving him beyond reason.

God had smiled on her again and she'd been given another child to love. She wanted to laugh when she recalled how shocked and unhappy she'd been when she first realized she was pregnant. She wasn't unhappy now. This baby had filled her life with purpose, had given her a reason to look forward to each new tomorrow.

"I thought you were going to wait for me," David said breathlessly, racing up to her, wearing his blue-and-silver nylon jogging outfit. He slowed his steps to match hers, stopped and braced his hands on his knees while he caught his breath. "How do I look?" he asked, anxiously glancing her way.

"Like an Olympic athlete," she said, lying through her teeth.

David would have laughed if he'd had the energy, Molly guessed. "That's what I like most about you," he said, gasping for breath, "your ability to lie so convincingly."

Molly smiled, squinting into the sunlight.

"How about something to drink," he suggested.

"Sure."

He walked with her to a café across the street from the park and ordered café latte. They sat at one of the outside tables. The umbrella was folded closed and multicolored leaves danced around their feet.

"I've got two tickets for *Les Miserables* for Saturday evening," David mentioned casually, after sipping from the hot drink.

It wasn't the first time he'd hinted that he'd like to take her out. Until now, Molly had declined, but the little-boy expectant look in his eyes caught her attention. She hated to disappoint him.

David had become a good friend in the past six weeks. They'd never officially dated—Molly was uncomfortable with that—but they often walked in the park and occasionally their schedules coincided so they ate lunch together in the hospital cafeteria. But that had been the extent of it.

Molly feared that if she openly dated David, the hospital staff might assume David was her baby's father, and she didn't want to burden him with gossip.

"I'm starting to show just a little," she said, answering his suggestion with a comment.

"Does it bother you to be seen in public with me?"

She laughed softly and shook her head. "No, of course not."

"Then why the hesitation. These are great tickets."

David deserved her honesty. "I'm afraid someone might assume you're the father and I don't want to do anything to taint your reputation."

David laughed outright at that. "I've been waiting for years for someone to taint my pristine reputation. Come on, Molly, let's live dangerously. You'll love the play, and we both deserve a night out, don't you think?"

"We do?"

"I just finished a seven-minute mile, and I told myself when I could do that I was going to treat myself to something special."

"You mean the play?"

"No," he said, reaching for her hand. "A date with you. You'll go with me, won't you?"

Although she wasn't convinced she was doing the right thing, Molly agreed. She was lonesome, and David was her friend.

Jordan wasn't keen on attending this silly play from the first. He'd purchased the tickets six months earlier because Lesley had told him how badly she wanted to see *Les Miserables*.

He'd phoned and reminded her about the tickets, intent on asking her if she wanted the pair herself. It was the first time they'd talked, outside of business, in six weeks. She was the one who suggested they attend the play together, and Jordan figured he owed her that much. Perhaps he'd agreed because he was so damned lonely.

The past six weeks had been difficult. Molly had asked not to see him, and he'd abided by her wishes. That was the end of it, except that he continually toyed with the thought of making one last ditch effort to settle their differences.

He hadn't, for a number of excellent reasons. All right, one excellent reason.

Molly was right.

He'd been running, just the way she claimed. He'd submerged himself in calm, cool waters of denial, refusing to deal with Jeff's death or accept this new life Molly's body was nurturing.

He picked Lesley up at seven and whistled appreciatively when he saw her. She was dressed in a beautiful dark blue full-length silk dress that did wonders for her. The material moved over her hips like a second skin.

"You look fabulous," he said, but even while he was speaking his mind drifted to Molly. She was nearly five months' pregnant by now. Her stomach would be swelling, and the pregnancy would be apparent.

He shook his head in an effort to free himself from thoughts of his wife. He was going to enjoy himself this evening, put his troubles behind him and remember there was a beautiful woman on his arm, who was his friend.

They arrived at the Shubert Theater in plenty of time. Jordan was buying a program when he spotted Molly in the middle of the lobby.

His heart skidded to a sudden halt. She was laughing, her eyes bright with happiness, and Jordan swore he'd never seen anyone, anything, quite so beautiful. She wore a simple white dress with gold sequins along the bodice and hem. The gown wouldn't have looked more elegant on a French model.

Her hair was longer than he remembered. She'd tucked it behind her ears, the length bouncing against the tops of her bare shoulders. Her earrings were a dangly gold pair he'd given her the first Christmas they were married.

Jordan didn't know how long he stared at her. Several moments, he suspected. It took that long for him to notice Molly wasn't alone. A tall sturdy-set man stood at her side. Recognition seized Jordan. Molly was with the same man she'd danced with at Kati's wedding.

She'd had the gall to hurl Lesley in his face while she was involved with someone else herself. Deep, dark emotion bubbled in his soul. It demanded every shred of decorum he possessed not to storm over to her side and cause a scene.

Getting a grip on himself proved difficult, and several minutes passed before he returned to the seat where Lesley was waiting for him.

A few minutes later, Lesley turned, looked at him and whispered, "Jordan, for the love of heaven, what's wrong?"

"Nothing."

"Then why are you so tense?"

"I'm not," he denied sharply. It was apparent he wasn't going to be able to disguise his irritation. "Excuse me a moment," he said as he jerked himself out of his seat.

"Jordan," Lesley said anxiously, "the play's about to start."

Jordan ignored the comment. Thankful he was on the aisle seat he all but raced back to the lobby. Not that he had an iota of an idea what he intended to do once he was there.

The minute he entered the vestibule, Jordan recognized his mistake. Molly was still there with her doctor friend at her side.

She glanced up just then and their gazes collided like giant cymbals. The impact was enough to knock the breath from his lungs. He fully suspected Molly had experienced the same phenomenon. She looked up at her date, gently placed her hand on his forearm and apparently excused herself.

David Stern's eyes sought Jordan out, but he refused to meet the other man's gaze. Instead he centered his concentration on Molly, who was stepping toward him. Her fingers nervously adjusted the strap of her evening bag at her shoulder.

Within seconds they faced each other. Silence followed silence like waves pounding the shore, crashing one after another.

"Hello." It was Molly who spoke first.

"Molly." Burying his hands in his tuxedo pockets became necessary, otherwise he feared he'd drag her into his arms.

Silence again, as he absorbed the sight of her. "How are you feeling?"

"Very well," she told him. She flattened her hand over her stomach and he noticed for the first time the soft swelling there. She was showing. The pregnancy wasn't obvious, but noticeable. "How about you?"

He shrugged. "You look good."

She smiled, lowering her lashes, uncomfortable with his compliment. Only moments earlier he'd wanted to ring her scrawny neck, and one look, one soft whisper, and he was willing to eat out of her hand.

"You seeing much of the good doctor?" His gaze briefly left her to rest on the man waiting impatiently for Molly to return to him. He clenched his back teeth in an effort to resist saying something he shouldn't, although heaven knew he would welcome the opportunity to get face-to-face with the other man.

"Not much. How's Lesley?"

Jordan wondered if she'd seen them together. "She's fine."

The orchestra started to play and once again Molly lowered her lashes. "David and I had better find our seats. It was good to see you again."

His hands remained in his pants pockets and hardened into fists in a desperate effort to contain himself from behaving like a fool. "It was good to see you, too."

"I hope you enjoy the play," she added softly and turned away from him.

He didn't know why Molly continually walked away from him. Every time she did, he felt as if she took a part of his heart with her.

He waited until his wife and Dr. Stern were completely out of his line of vision before he returned to his seat. The play was probably one of the best known and loved of all time, but it couldn't hold Jordan's attention. He doubted that anything could have.

Somehow, through the course of the evening, he managed to say all the right things, comment on the play, even laugh over a joke Lesley made. At intermission he slipped away on the pretense of getting them two glasses of chablis, but in reality he stood alone and waited, hoping for another glimpse, another look, at Molly and her rounding tummy.

He didn't find her again in the crowded lobby. His disappointment was keen when he returned to his seat. The strength of his feelings for her frightened him. The last time they were together they'd come within a heartbeat of making love. He wanted her, needed her, beneath him, making love with him, whispering sweet promises in his ear. He wanted her cuddled against him asleep. He wanted to watch her wake up and smile that dulcet, sexy smile of hers when she found him looking down on her. He wanted her to raise her arms up to him and welcome him into her heart.

How Jordan managed to sit through the remainder of the play, he never knew. A hundred times, possibly more, he toyed with the idea of seeking Molly out and insisting she leave with him, right then and there. Without explanation, without excuse.

He drove Lesley home, battling back a shipload of remorse because he couldn't get away from her fast enough. As always, she was warm and generous and understanding.

Jordan had never thought of himself as an obstinate man, but he had no other accounting for the length of their separation. Now it might be too late. He might have lost her to another man. The thought flashed like quicksilver through his mind, torturing him with the unknown.

There was only one way to find out.

He'd ask.

Two days later, Jordan walked into Ian Houghton's office and shook hands with his father-in-law.

"It's good to see you," Ian said, gesturing toward the high-back leather chair across from his desk. "To what do I owe this unexpected pleasure?"

Ian was always the gentleman, but Jordan knew the old man well enough to recognize the glee in his eyes. Ian had been waiting for this day for a good long while.

Jordan couldn't see any reason not to cut to the chase. "I want Molly back. Is it too late?"

Ian opened his desk drawer and took out a fat Cuban cigar. He offered one to Jordan, who declined. Naturally Ian was going to drag this out as long as he could. He reached for his lighter and the flame curled around the end of the cigar.

"Too late?" he repeated, after taking several puffs of the cigar. "I don't know. You'll have to ask Molly that, not me."

"I saw her Saturday night."

"She was with David?"

Jordan nodded. He almost added how beautiful he'd found her and knew if he did he'd be playing right into Ian's hands. His father-in-law already had the advantage, and Jordan wasn't willing to add to it.

"Has she been seeing a lot of the physician?"

Ian exhaled a puff of thick smoke and the scent of tobacco filled the office. "Not to my knowledge, but my daughter doesn't discuss these things with me."

Jordan was disappointed. He was hoping Ian could tell him more about Molly's relationship with the other man. If he was too late and she was in love with David, he'd be forced to make his peace with that. But if he stood a chance with her again, even a small one, he'd glom on to it and do his damnedest to make their marriage work.

"What about the baby?" Ian asked. "From what Molly said, you don't want to have anything to do with the child."

Jordan didn't respond. Not because he didn't like the question. He didn't have an answer to give the older man. He rubbed his hand down his face and relaxed against the soft leather cushion. "I don't know."

Ian was quiet for a moment before he spoke again. "Did you come here looking for advice?"

"No," Jordan said stiffly, then realized his pride hadn't served him well thus far. "But if you want to offer me some, I'll listen."

Ian arched his thick eyebrows and grinned. "I suggest you make up your mind about the baby before you approach Molly. What you've got here, son, is a package deal. Nothing on this good earth will ever separate my daughter from her child. Not even you, and God knows she loves you."

That tidbit of information should have encouraged Jordan, but it didn't.

He stood, his thoughts as tightly knotted as a tangled gold chain. He desperately wanted Molly. He couldn't bear the thought of loving another child.

He left the office without a word to Ian and stepped outside and walked past his car. He kept on going, block after block, mile after mile. Each step against the pavement moved him forward, but did nothing to solve the dilemma of his heart.

He needed Molly.

But not the child.

Jordan knew the truth of what Ian had told him. Molly and the baby were a package deal. It wasn't one without the other, but the two of them together.

Jeff's chubby happy face, cheerfully smiling at him, returned to haunt Jordan. The pain that sliced through him with the memory was sharper than any physical agony he had experienced. Physical pain he could handle, but not this unending emotional torment.

All at once Jordan was tired. Overwhelmed and lost. He felt as if nothing were real anymore. He continued to walk, but he moved in a haze from one block to the next with no real destination in mind. At least, he didn't realize he'd set his course until he stepped off the curb and crossed the street. Molly's duplex was three doors down.

"Make up your mind about the baby before you approach Molly." Ian's words echoed in the deepest recesses of his heart as he stepped up to her porch.

He didn't have anything to offer Molly, nothing he could say—only that he wanted her, needed her back in his life. Other than that he was as lost now as he had been when he approached Ian.

He had to see her or go insane. Had to know if she still loved him. Had to know if there was one chance in a million that they could mend the rift between them.

He didn't remember ringing the doorbell, but he must have, because the next thing he knew Molly was standing directly in front of him. A thin mesh wire of the screen door was all that separated them.

"Jordan, what are you doing here?" She studied him and he was unable to disguise the murky emotions churning in his mind.

She was shocked to see him and it showed in her eyes. She was dressed in jeans and a loose-fitting shirt. His gaze fell to her waist and he noticed the snap of the jeans was undone to make room for the baby.

The baby.

"Come in," she said, holding open the door for him. His gaze didn't budge from hers.

"Are you alone?" he asked, psychologically distancing himself from her because of the power she wielded. One look, one word, could devastate him.

Molly eyes rounded with surprise. "Yes."

He stepped inside the duplex and closed the door. He studied Molly, wondering what he could possibly say to her that would make a difference.

"Why are you here?" she asked, standing no more than two feet from him.

"Are you in love with him?" Jordan blurted out.

"With David? No, not that it's any of your business."

His heart raced like that of a gazelle's in a dead run. He briefly closed his eyes.

"Why?"

Jordan wasn't a man who trusted words. They had failed him in the past, failed him now when he needed them to explain why he'd shown up on her doorstep, miles from where he'd left his truck. He'd come to her without a single, plausible excuse.

"Jordan," she whispered, her face revealing her confusion.

For hours he'd been numb, walking, thinking, lost in a maze of the impossible. Now Molly was standing within reaching distance and he could feel again. He desperately needed to feel again.

His eyes held hers. "I'm sorry, Molly," he whispered. "So damn sorry." The words barely made it past the knot in his throat. There was more he wanted to say, needed to say, but couldn't.

He watched the tears fill her eyes and her bottom lip start to tremble as she struggled not to give in to the emotion.

Jordan wasn't sure who moved first, him or her. It didn't matter. Within the space of a single heartbeat they were in each other's arms. He felt her tears that coursed unheeded down her face, then wondered if they were his own.

With a deep-seated groan, Jordan kissed her.

The kiss was like fire, a spontaneous combustion. She tasted of honey and passion, and it was impossible to tell which of the two was more potent.

Jordan backed her against the door and she gasped softly when he thrust his tongue deep inside her mouth, stroking and teasing, enticing and mating, until her gasp became a whimper that trembled gently from her lips.

By some fate he found the strength to tear his mouth from hers. His chest was heaving; hers was, too, as he looked down on her. Her hands gripped his shirt and she stared up at him, her mouth parted and moist. Already her lips were slightly swollen from the fierce hunger of his kiss.

"Tell me to leave, Molly. Order me out of here, otherwise I won't be able to keep from touching you. I need you too damn much."

He watched her carefully, knowing the impossibility of what he was asking, praying she wanted him as urgently as he wanted her.

Gradually—he could almost see the wheels of her mind working—a smile formed, starting at the edges of her mouth and working its way to her eyes.

"Are you going to make love to me?" she asked.

He closed his eyes and groaned. "Yes. God, yes."

"What about Lesley?"

He was tugging the shirt over her head with fingers shaking in his need to hurry. "I broke it off six weeks ago."

"You did?"

"Yes." He tossed the shirt aside and freed her breasts. Next his hands were at the zipper of her jeans. She laughed softly and kissed him, using her tongue in ways that caused his knees to buckle.

"What took you so long to come back to me?" she whispered.

Chapter Nine

Jordan lifted Molly into his arms and carried her down the short corridor to her bedroom. He kicked open the door and placed her on the bed. She smiled up at him, her body humming with need. Her jeans were unzipped and she awkwardly slipped them over her hips and down her legs while Jordan undressed with equal haste.

When he was free of the restricting clothes, he joined her on the bed and kissed her. Molly moaned as he rolled onto his back, taking her with him. His tongue plundered her mouth and he buried his hands deep into her hair, holding her prisoner.

It had been so long since he'd touched her like this. Her nerve endings fired to life; the flames of her need raced over her skin until she couldn't bear to hold still. Moving her hips even slightly stroked the swollen heat of his erection until it throbbed and pulsed against her.

Jordan groaned and held her, his fingers like vises against the sides of her face, as his eyes burned into hers. His chest heaved as though it demanded every ounce of strength he possessed not to flip her onto her back right then and there and bury his body in hers.

He seemed to be asking her something, or wanting to, but held back as if afraid.

"Jordan?" His name was a breath of sound and need and love. "Love me," she whispered. "Just love me."

He briefly closed his eyes. "I do." His hands caressed the bare roundness of her hips, then swept down the backs of her thighs. Slowly, careful not to place his full weight on her, he reversed their positions so that he was sprawled across the top of her. His eyes burned into her as he eased her thighs apart and, with a provocative, unhurried ease, positioned himself to enter her.

Molly closed her eyes as the moist tip of his manhood parted the folds of her womanhood. Her breath went shallow as she waited. He held himself stiff and still; much more of this and he'd drive her to the brink of insanity. She arched her hips upward, taking him by surprise. "Jordan...don't stop, oh, please."

He moaned and filled her. Molly's groan of pleasure mingled with his as she was enveloped in the hot, moist pleasure of his lovemaking. He gave her a moment to adjust to him and eased still deeper until he was wholly within her.

Only then did he stop. Only then did she resume breathing. Only then did she look up at him, knowing he'd read the love she'd tried so strenuously to hide.

A lone tear rolled from the corner of her eye onto the pillow. Soon her gaze was blurred and Jordan's face was obliterated from her. Bending forward he kissed her. Gently. Sweetly.

Molly curled her legs around his back and laced her arms around his neck and kissed him, her heart bursting with love, until the texture of the kisses changed from tenderness to hunger to raw hunger.

Jordan began to rock against her, his need fierce and primitive, setting a pace so fast and furious that it was akin to being trapped in a rowboat in the middle of a wild winter storm. All Molly could do was cling to him and pray they survived.

With each thrust the tempo increased until Molly was convinced he would propel them both straight off the bed. Not that she would have cared. She panted and whimpered and eventually cried out as her body raced breathlessly toward searing, total completion. When it came, her nails dug into his shoulders as her world shattered into a thousand glorious pieces of light.

Jordan groaned and threw back his head, his eyes tightly closed, and joined her, pumping his body into hers again and again until they were both too weak, too spent, to continue.

Jordan went still and hid his face in the curve of her neck, and the only sound that shattered the silence was that of their breathing.

Jordan woke sometime later, with Molly asleep in his arms. He moved onto his side so he could study her, but he kept her within the wide circle of his arms, unwilling to be separated from her. If he were to die right then, Jordan decided, he would leave this life a happy man.

Never again would he attempt to convince himself he could live without her. That was a fool's game, which he was destined to lose, and he'd learned his lesson well.

He reached out and brushed a strand of hair away from her cheek and noted the track the tears had taken down the side of her face.

Unable to stop himself, he leaned forward and ever so lightly kissed her temple. She stirred and smiled before she reluctantly opened her eyes.

The smile was what did it, that sexy, womanly smile of hers. It created an instant and undeniable hunger within him. He kissed her lips, outlining their shape with his tongue, dipping it erotically into her mouth every now and again.

"Hmm, that feels good," she whispered, wrapping her arms around his neck.

He gathered her close, cradling her in his arms. "You cried," he whispered close to her ear, not understanding her tears. Then again he did. He experienced gratitude, an indebtedness to God for giving him this second chance with Molly. He wasn't going to waste it. Not again.

"I...never thought we'd make love again," she whispered, brushing the hair away from his face. Her gentle hands trembled.

Like Molly, Jordan was caught in the force of a strong, emotional upheaval. His arms circled her waist and they clung to each other.

He could account for every minute of the past three years they'd spent apart. He didn't know what it meant to waste an afternoon, or even an hour. He'd driven himself and his employees hard, tasted the high of success, damning the emotional and physical cost. Anything that would allow him to escape the crippling sense of loss that overwhelmed him every time he thought about Jeff and the breakup of his marriage.

His son was gone, ripped from his arms and his heart, but he still had Molly. And heaven help him, if he lost her, too. He was convinced he'd shrivel up and die. That's exactly what he had been doing in the three years since she'd moved out. Dying. A little more each day, with a pain so profound that it hollowed out his heart.

He wanted this marriage. Needed this time with her. Needed Molly and the healing touch of her love. Their lovemaking had expanded his need. Her touch, her kiss, her generosity, had given him a fresh breath of life. A taste of what their marriage had once been.

Jordan wanted it back. All of it.

He could think of no way to tell her this and so he kissed her. She made a soft, womanly sound that was half whimper, half moan as his hand reached for her breast. His thumb grazed her nipple, which puckered instantly. Smiling at the power he evoked over her body, Jordan fastened his mouth to her breast and sucked gently. He was rewarded with a fractured sound of pleasure as she arched her back off the bed.

Paying equal attention to the other breast produced the same reaction, only now a small cry tumbled from her lips. He felt her shudder of pleasure and continued lavishing attention on her breasts and her mouth.

He'd thought to tease her with the sinfully delicious things he could do to make her want him, but in the end it was Jordan who suffered. Molly looped her leg over his, parting her thighs until his pulsating staff was poised at the opening of her silken heat. He jerked his hips forward, but she moved at precisely the same moment, denying him entrance.

"Molly, for the love of heaven." His hands reached for her waist, dragging her forward. How she managed to maneuver herself on top of him, Jordan was never to know. By some trick, she deftly rolled him onto his back, then gracefully settled her body on top of his, swallowing him whole in one swift, downward movement.

The pleasure was so sharp he nearly passed out with the sheer unexpected nature of it. His hands clenched at her hips to guide and control her movements, but she laughed saucily and gently removed them.

"Hold on, cowboy," she whispered, and her legs tightened against his sides.

Jordan was soon caught up in the wildest ride of his life. She straddled him as though he were a wild bronco, one hand braced against his chest, the other against the headboard as if she were afraid of losing her balance. Her movements were frenzied and wild as she rode him straight into the gates of the keenest pleasure he'd ever known. He buckled against her, arching his back and hips, panting and pleading until she'd milked him dry. Only when she'd given, and taken, everything she wanted did she slow her movements. Panting, she lay down on top of him and buried her moist face against his equally sweat-drenched neck. Simultaneously their chests rose and fell together as the sound of their breathing splintered the silence.

Jordan looped his arms around her and would have released a primal shout of joy, but he hadn't the strength left to do anything more than breathe. And hold this magnificent woman he loved.

Both physically and emotionally drained, they slept again. Jordan woke when the room was pitch-dark, feeling utterly content and satisfied. After three long, loved-starved years, they had a lot of time to make up for, but it didn't need to be done in the space of one night.

Jordan reluctantly eased himself out of Molly's arms, intent on finding himself something to eat. If they were going to continue this kind of physical endurance test, he needed fuel. A peanut butter and jelly sandwich, anything.

"Jordan?" Molly's whisper followed him to the bedroom doorway.

His heart clenched at the dread he heard in her voice, as if she were afraid he was leaving her, sneaking away while she slept. Nothing could be further from his mind.

"I'm hungry."

He heard her soft laugh. "Little wonder." The bed creaked as she climbed off the mattress, reached for something to cover herself with and joined him. Jordan had felt no such compulsion to dress and stalked bare-assed into the kitchen. That room was dim, the moon the only source of light, but when he opened the refrigerator the glow filled the room.

Jordan noticed that Molly had chosen to dress in a long T-shirt that adequately covered her torso and reached the top of her thighs. She looked very much as though she'd spent the past four hours in bed, her eyes hazy with satisfaction, her smile seductive and wanton.

"What are you looking at?" she muttered.

"You."

"I...I'm a mess."

"No," he corrected. "I was just trying to decide if I had enough stamina to ravish you again, right here in the kitchen."

Her smile widened, and she blushed prettily. "It wouldn't be the first time you had your way with me in a kitchen."

Jordan's mind grabbed hold of the memory of the early days of their marriage when they'd made love in every room of the house, and he grinned broadly.

"Let's eat. I'm hungry, too."

"There's nothing here," Jordan complained when he examined the refrigerator's contents.

"I've been so tired lately that it's easier to open up a can, or pop something in the microwave."

Jordan knew Molly worked long, grueling hours at the hospital and wanted to ask her to quit, but he hadn't the right. Soon, once they'd settled matters, he'd see to it that she didn't work, not unless she wanted, and then he'd prefer if she did so on a volunteer basis.

He was a rich man and there wasn't any reason for her to put in such long hours.

He searched the cupboard next and found a can of peaches in heavy syrup.

"I'll scramble us some eggs," Molly offered.

"Nice idea, but I didn't see any eggs," Jordan said as he ran the peaches under the can opener. The grinding sound filled the silence. He tossed the lid in the garbage, dug into the can with his fingers and produced a slice of peach that he hand-fed to her.

The juice ran down Molly's chin as she ate the fruit. Jordan lapped it up with his tongue, catching the juice just before it dripped onto her shirt. The temptation to kiss her was strong, but he knew the way he was feeling, it wouldn't stop with a kiss.

He fed himself the next slice.

"Jordan," Molly whispered excitedly, her eyes widening. "Feel." She reached for his free hand and pressed it against the small swell of her tummy. "The baby just kicked."

Jordan felt as though she'd thrown ice water in his face. The shock of it rippled over him, and his breath froze in his lungs.

The baby.

Dear sweet God, the baby. For these few idyllic hours he'd managed to effectively push the memory of this second child from his mind.

"Here's your daddy," Molly was chirping softly, unaware of the downward spiral of emotion Jordan was experiencing. He knew he wouldn't be able to hide it much longer. He wanted to jerk his hand away, but she held it flat against her abdomen, her palm pressed against the back of his.

"Molly."

"Did you feel him?" she asked, looking up at him expectantly. The joy drained like fast-flowing water down a sink when her eyes connected with his. She released his hand, but Jordan had the impression she wasn't aware of what she was doing.

Without another word, she turned and marched down the hall.

"Molly," Jordan pleaded, following her, although he didn't know what he would possibly say if she did decide to listen to him.

She gathered up his clothes from the floor, jerking them off the carpet, wadded them in a tight ball and then thrust them into his arms.

"I'd like to talk about this," he said calmly.

"Go ahead." She wrapped her hands around her waist, balanced her weight on one foot and tapped the other in an impatient tempo.

"I'm afraid, Molly."

"Do you think I'm not?"

"It's different for you. The baby's a part of you. Flesh of your flesh...but it's not the same for a man."

"A lot of things are different for a man, aren't they?"

Jordan didn't have an answer to give her. He didn't want to argue with her, didn't want this beautiful time together to end with them hurling ugly words at each other.

"I'm trying, Molly, give me credit for that."

She, too, must have felt the need to preserve what they'd shared. Their peace was fragile and easily destroyed. Molly was as aware of it as he was and seemed equally reluctant to ruin it with another argument.

"Be angry with me in the morning," he suggested. "Hate me then, if you must, but for now let me hold you and love you." He dropped the clothes on the floor and stepped toward her. He was afraid to reach for her, convinced she'd push him away. When he gathered her in his arms, she held herself still. Her arms hung lifelessly at her sides, but gradually he felt the tension ease from her limbs.

"Wait until morning to be angry," he urged softly.

Eventually they returned to the bed and they lay together silently for what seemed like hours. She was cuddled close to his side and they held on to each other as if they heard the high winds of an approaching storm.

"What time is it?" she whispered.

Jordan glanced at the illuminated dial of his watch. "A little after midnight. You'd better get some sleep." One of them should, he mused. For his own part, he didn't want to waste a single minute on sleep.

Molly reached down and covered them with a blanket. It looked for an instant as if she meant to roll away from him, but he reached for her and dragged her back to his side.

"I have tonight," he reminded her. "You can regret it all in the morning if you want, but for the next several hours pretend it doesn't matter, all right?" His hand cupped the fullness of her breast and he experienced a sense of power at the ready way in which her nipple beaded against his palm.

Molly said nothing.

Jordan slipped his hand lower, past the T-shirt to her silky thighs, worming his way between them. She kept her knees tightly clamped together until his finger found her feminine opening and he knew the reason. He grinned. Already she was moist and eager for him.

"I have this theory about regrets," he whispered, working his finger against her pleasure points until her breathing had gone deep and heavy. He all but flipped her onto her back and entered her in one, swift motion. He hesitated until she opened her eyes and glared up at him, openly challenging him.

"If you're going to regret this night," he said with a taunting smile, "let me make it worth your while."

He made love to her slowly, over and over again, until he was convinced they'd both die of pleasure before they lived long enough to rue this one night.

Molly waited for Amanda outside of the secondhand furniture shop early Saturday afternoon. Amanda parked her truck next to Molly's and they both opened their doors and climbed out simultaneously.

When she stepped onto the sidewalk, Amanda's eyes beamed with pleasure. "My goodness, you're showing."

"You can tell?" Molly cupped her hands under her enlarged tummy, making the swelling more pronounced. She looked up at her friend expectantly. "I'm nearly five months now."

"You look wonderful," Amanda said, smiling. "I could be jealous. You're obviously one of those women who positively glow when they're pregnant. Not me. I went through the entire nine months looking like I needed a blood transfusion. If I had any color at all it was a faint tinge of green."

Molly laughed.

"How are you feeling?" Amanda asked.

Molly shrugged. "I've felt better." She hadn't been sleeping well, but she couldn't blame the baby for that. It'd been five days since she'd last seen Jordan, and had yet to decide how she felt about their interlude. She wanted to deny how much she'd enjoyed their lovemaking, but couldn't. He would call her a bald-faced liar and he'd be right. Molly swore that if she hadn't already been pregnant, the night would have produced triplets.

When Jordan did scrounge up the gumption to contact her again, a lot would depend on the mood she was in. Either she'd slam the door in his face, or throw her arms around his neck and drag him back to her bedroom.

He must have intuitively known how ambivalent she felt because he'd completely avoided her. One thing was certain, she wasn't going to seek him out.

"I appreciate you helping me with this," Molly said, leading the way into the shop. She'd purchased the crib a week before, but didn't have any way of getting it to her duplex. Amanda had kindly offered the use of her truck.

"No problem," Amanda returned graciously. "You've helped me more than you'll ever know. It feels good to be able to lend you a hand."

With the help of the shopkeeper, they loaded the crib into the bed of Amanda's truck. Molly led the way to her apartment and together they set it up in the spare bedroom. Since Molly intended on painting the crib, she'd spread newspapers and plastic over the carpet.

"Stay and have some tea with me," Molly offered when they'd finished.

"You're sure you have the time?"

"Of course." She was anxious to get going with the painting, but delaying the project another half hour or so wouldn't hurt.

"I talked to Tommy about us having another baby," Amanda said, while Molly filled up the teakettle and set it on the burner.

"What did he say?" she asked, curious if Amanda's husband felt the same way as Jordan.

"He wants to wait a while first."

"How long?"

"Another six months."

"How do you feel about that?" Molly asked.

Amanda lowered her gaze, then shrugged. "In my heart I know another baby will never take Christi's place, but my arms feel so empty."

Molly understood what her friend was saying. Her arms had felt empty, too. That was why she'd volunteered to work in Manukua. She'd been willing to travel anywhere in the world, endure any hardship, if only it would ease the ache in her soul.

"Do you think that's what concerns Tommy?"

"I don't know. He's afraid we'll lose a second baby too, and I don't think either of us would survive that."

"I...didn't think I'd survive losing Jeff," Molly said, and in some ways she continued the struggle and would for a very long time.

"We agreed that I could go off the pill in three months. It took me six months to get pregnant the first time. The way we figure it, the timing should be about right."

The kettle whistled and Molly removed it from the red-hot burner.

"How's Jordan?" Amanda asked timidly. "Listen, you don't have to talk about your husband if you don't want. It's just that...well, I can't help being curious, especially since he's decided to delay the divorce until after the baby's born.''

"He's fine I guess. I...he stopped by last week.''

"He did?'' Amanda asked excitedly. "Remember when you told me about seeing him at the play? Something about the way you looked when you mentioned him struck me. You're still in love with him, aren't you?''

There wasn't any use in denying it, so she nodded.

"I knew it,'' Amanda said triumphantly. "What did he want?'' She edged closer to the table, then seemed to realize Molly and Jordan's relationship wasn't any of her business. "You don't need to answer that if you don't want.''

"Apparently he's broken off his relationship with Lesley,'' Molly supplied.

"Hot damn!''

"He'd like a reconciliation...I think.''

"Double hot damn!''

"But he's still having trouble dealing with my pregnancy.''

Amanda's shoulders slumped dramatically as the air rushed from her lungs. "He's afraid. Tommy and I are, too. It's only natural, don't you think?''

"Perhaps, but it's more than fear with Jordan. He's petrified.'' Molly didn't know what Jordan expected of her anymore. It wasn't as though she could ignore their child. "He's terrified of having any feelings for this child,'' Molly continued. "I think he's convinced the minute he does that something will happen. He keeps everything bottled up inside. He always has...even with Jeff.''

"I feel sorry for him,'' Amanda said thoughtfully. "He must be miserable, loving you the way he does.''

They were both miserable.

Molly poured the tea and the two women chattered for fifteen more minutes. Although they were very different, they'd bonded as friends, both having shared the same heart-wrenching tragedy of losing a child to SIDS.

As soon as Amanda left, Molly changed clothes and got out the paint she'd purchased earlier in the day. She put on an old dress shirt of Jordan's, rolled up the long sleeves and paused to study herself in the mirror.

"Stop kidding yourself,'' she muttered. Choosing to paint in Jordan's shirt had been a deliberate and willful act. As completely illogical as it was, she felt close to him in this shirt. Years earlier, when they'd been innocent of all that was to befall them, it had been a favorite of hers.

She'd stolen it from his closet when she'd taken her things from the house and moved them into the apartment. For a short time afterward, she feared he'd ask her about it. As the weeks passed, she realized he had so many shirts he wouldn't miss this one.

Wearing it now, while she painted the baby's crib, had been a blatant effort to feel close to him. To bring him closer to her and their baby. In this shirt, she could pretend his arms were around her. In this shirt, she could defy the past.

She was stirring the paint with a flat wooden stick when the doorbell chimed. Feeling thwarted and impatient, she pushed up the sleeves and marched into the living room.

The last person she expected to find on the other side of the door was Jordan. His arms were filled with two heavy brown sacks, and his eyes scooted to hers as if he wasn't sure what to expect.

"I come bearing gifts," he said with a brief, beguiling smile.

"What kinds of gifts?" she asked, crossing her arms, trying to decide what she should do. By all that was right, she should close the door in his face, but she couldn't make herself do it.

"Dinner, with all the fixings," he said. "All your favorites."

Her heart seemed to melt in her breast. "Southern-fried chicken, potatoes and giblet gravy?"

"Or a mild variation thereon."

Molly threw open the screen door. "Come right on in."

Jordan chuckled. "You always could be bought with food."

"If you plan on staying more than five minutes," she warned, "then I suggest you start cooking."

His grin grew broader. Molly followed him into the kitchen and quickly discovered he'd brought far more groceries than necessary for a single meal. He made two additional trips to his car to haul in more groceries.

"I don't mean to be nosy," he said, loading cans into her cupboards, "but where'd you get that shirt?"

Molly's eyes grew round with feigned innocence. "This old thing?"

"It looks amazingly like one of mine."

She fluttered her long lashes. "Are you suggesting I stole it?"

He turned and faced her, hands on his hips. "I am."

She lowered her gaze demurely. "Did you miss it?"

"No, but I've got to tell you, it never looked that good on me."

Molly laughed and, with a turn of her heel, left him and resumed her task in the baby's bedroom. She could hear Jordan working in the kitchen, humming softly to himself as he went about preparing their dinner. Not that it would require any great skill. The deli had already roasted the chicken, which he was attempting to pass off as southern fried, and the mashed potatoes and gravy looked suspiciously as if they'd come from a fast-food restaurant.

No more than fifteen minutes passed before Jordan joined her. He watched her dip the brush in the enamel and spread it evenly over the wood. Molly waited for him to say something, and he didn't for the longest time. She paused in her task and glanced up at him.

"Is it a good idea for you to be painting in your condition?" he asked.

"It's perfectly safe. I asked the man at the hardware store." If he was so concerned, she had an extra brush. She waited, but he didn't volunteer and she didn't ask.

"How was your week?" he asked, and the question was full of implication. It would have been easier to traipse across a mine field than answer it, Molly decided.

Molly reviewed her options. She could lie and tell him everything was just great when she'd been restless and miserable. Or she could admit she hadn't slept a single night through because each time she closed her eyes she remembered how good it had felt to cuddle in his arms.

"I don't know how to answer that, Jordan," she said when she realized it was impossible to be completely honest and keep her pride intact.

"Did you think about me?"

She dipped the brush in the paint and hesitated. "Yes." Turnabout was fair play. "Did you think about me?"

"Every minute of every day. It took me until this afternoon to work up the courage to come back and try again. I never know what to expect from you."

She couldn't deny what he was saying. "Why do we say the things we do?" she asked sadly. "We've both been hurt so badly, and still we do and say such terrible things to each other?"

"I don't know, Molly. All I do know is that I love you."

Under any other circumstances that would have been enough. More than enough. But she wasn't the only one involved. A new life blossomed and grew within her. A new life that couldn't be ignored.

"Say something," Jordan urged, walking toward her.

She hung her head, knowing the instant she mentioned the pregnancy it would erect a concrete wall between them.

Jordan placed his index finger beneath her chin and raised her head until their eyes met. Then, ever so gently, he lowered his mouth to hers. The kiss was long and sweet and potent.

He unfastened the opening to her shirt and cupped her breasts. "Does this bra have to stay on?" he whispered.

"Not particularly."

"Good." He fumbled with the closure at her back that released the front. His hands scooped up the weight of both breasts and he moaned and feasted on each nipple in turn.

Molly didn't know what was keeping her upright. Certainly it wasn't her legs. They felt as if they should have collapsed ten minutes earlier.

Jordan kissed her again and reached for the snap of her jeans. "I didn't stop thinking about us, and how badly I want to make love to you every night for the rest of our lives."

"I...I don't know if this is a good idea," she said, garnering the fortitude from somewhere to offer resistance, even if it was only token.

"I know what you're thinking," Jordan countered, his hands and mouth working their magic on her. "You're wondering if all we share is fabulous sex."

Molly's eyes flew open. That wasn't anything close to what she was thinking.

"Maybe we do," he answered, nibbling her ear, using his tongue to probe and flicker over the sensitive skin. "I don't care anymore."

Molly pushed herself free of his arms. "You think all we share is sex?" she repeated, outraged that he would even suggest such a thing. "What about our son, several years of marriage and this pregnancy?" she cried. "Are you saying the only reason you married me was because I was a good lay?"

Molly didn't give him the time to answer. She'd forgotten the paintbrush in her hand, but she remembered it now. Heavy with paint, it dripped onto the back of her hand. Stepping forward, she slapped the paint-soaked bristles across the front of his shirt several times.

"That's what I think of that," she cried.

Chapter Ten

Molly clamped her hand over her mouth, unable to believe she'd actually painted the front of Jordan's shirt. He held up his arms as if he expected to take flight and stared down at his front with a look of horrified surprise.

"Oh, Jordan, I'm sorry," she muttered, setting aside the paintbrush. She reached for a rag, but it soon became apparent that her efforts were doing more harm than good.

"You...painted me."

"You deserved it," she returned, smothering a laugh. As far as she was concerned, Jordan Larabee should be counting his blessings. He was downright lucky that she hadn't taken the brush to his face. To suggest their entire relationship revolved around sex still rankled.

"You might apologize yourself," she suggested while he peeled off the shirt, being careful to avoid spreading the wet paint across his arms and torso.

"All right," he agreed, handing her the damaged shirt, "perhaps I was wrong."

"Perhaps?" She braced her hand against her hip and glared at him, her eyes filled with challenge.

Jordan's Adam's apple bobbed in his throat as he swallowed tightly, holding back a laugh. Apologies had never come easy to him, she realized, and generally he disguised them with humor.

"I was wrong," he muttered, his eyes growing serious, but only momentarily.

She rewarded him with a smile and carried his shirt to the mini washing machine, which was tucked neatly away in a kitchen closet. It was one of those compact washers with the dryer below.

"Don't worry, it's a water-based enamel," she told him, turning the buttons and setting the washer. At the sound of water filling the machine, she turned to him. True, her reaction to his outrageous suggestion had been instinctive, but it was also funny.

Their gazes met and held.

Having her estranged husband walk around her home bare chested offered more of a temptation than Molly was willing to admit. She'd never openly say as much, but Jordan had one fine chest. His shoulders were well muscled and his stomach flat and hard.

"Wait here," she instructed, walking back to her bedroom, removing the old shirt she wore as she progressed. She delivered it to him minutes later, almost hating to part with it. Unfortunately she didn't have anyone to blame but herself.

"Thanks," he mumbled, donning the shirt.

While he was buttoning it up, Molly lowered her gaze. She couldn't look at him and not remember their recent night together. She recalled how she'd felt lying with him, her ear pressed against the wall of his chest. The even, rhythmic beat of his heart had lulled her to sleep, lulled her into believing that there was hope for them, for their wounded marriage.

Molly was well aware of the mistakes she'd made. She deeply regretted them and wanted to right the wrong she'd done to Jordan. If that was possible. Molly was convinced their relationship would always be strained until Jordan properly grieved for Jeff.

They were stuck, traversing down the same dead-end road, and would be until they'd made their peace over the loss of their son. Then and only then would Jordan be free to move forward and accept the baby she was nurturing beneath her heart.

Molly waited until they were sitting across the table from each other, their paper plates piled high with the goodies Jordan had brought with him.

Molly dipped her fork in the steaming heap of mashed potatoes and gravy. "I'd like for us to talk, Jordan. Really talk."

"All right," he agreed, but she heard the hesitancy in his voice.

"I love you so much and this awkwardness between us is hurting us both."

Jordan lowered his fork to the table. His eyes filled with tenderness. "I love you, Molly, so damn much. I can't believe I allowed all this time to pass. I should have gone after you the day you moved out. My foolish pride wouldn't let me."

"I should never have left the way I did. Those days after we buried Jeff were so bleak. I wasn't myself, and I didn't know if I would ever be again.

"I felt like I was walking around in a haze. I was insane with grief and I couldn't make myself snap out of it. You were right when you said all I did was cry."

She hesitated, waited a moment, then continued. "I realize now how terribly depressed I was, but I didn't know it then. I don't think anyone really did."

"I should have helped you."

"You tried," Molly whispered, fighting back tears. "But you couldn't help me. I doubt anyone could have." In retrospect, Molly believed she had probably been close to being institutionalized, and perhaps she should have been.

They each made the pretense of eating, but neither one appeared to have much of an appetite. They didn't speak again, each trapped in the memories of those bleak, pain-saturated months following Jeff's death.

Molly finished her dinner first, dumping her leftovers into the garbage can beneath the sink. "Thank you, Jordan, you're a fabulous cook," she said in an effort to cut through the tension.

"Anytime." He smiled, but his eyes revealed the lack of any real amusement. He stood and carried his plate to the sink, as well.

"Would you like a cup of coffee?" she offered.

"Please."

Her back was to him as she reached for the canister and dumped the grounds into the paper-lined receptacle. The coffee dripped into the glass pot before she broached the subject of their son a second time.

"We need to talk about Jeff."

Her words staggered into the silence.

"Why?"

"I believe it will help us now." She turned around to face Jordan.

He was standing not far from her. Two mugs sat on the kitchen counter where he'd placed them. His hands were clenched at his sides, his knuckles white.

Pretending they were having a normal, everyday conversation, she reached for the mugs and filled them. Jordan joined her at the table. She sat down, propped her elbows against the table and held the mug to her lips. Slowly she leveled her gaze to him, waiting for him to respond.

A full five minutes passed.

"We had the same problem before," he said, sounding perfectly natural. "Jeff is dead—talking about him won't bring him back."

"That's true," she responded evenly. Molly wasn't fooled. Jordan's back was ramrod straight, and it was a credit to the mug maker that the cup withstood the tightness of his grip. She knew the heat from the coffee must be burning his palms, but he seemed unaware of it. "No amount of discussion will resurrect our son," she said, even as the pain sliced open her heart. It still hurt to talk about Jeff, especially with Jordan.

"Then why insist upon dragging that dear boy back into our lives? He's gone, Molly. As painful as that is to accept, he's never coming back."

"Do you think I don't know that?"

"I don't know what you think anymore."

She needed to tread carefully, Molly realized, otherwise they'd fall into the identical trap as before and their discussion would disintegrate into a bitter shouting match. That had been their pattern three years earlier, before they'd blocked each other completely out.

She rested her hand against the soft bulge of her tummy. As she suspected, Jordan's gaze followed the movement of her arm. He quickly looked away.

"I'm pregnant with another child," she said softly.

Jordan kept his eyes trained across the room as if he couldn't bear to be reminded of this second pregnancy. "This child has nothing to do with Jeff."

"That's where you're wrong. This baby has everything to do with Jeff. For nearly four years you've tried to pretend our son didn't exist. You don't want to talk about him. You destroyed every piece of evidence he lived. It isn't as easy as that, Jordan. Jeff was our son and he's indelibly marked our lives, the same way this baby will."

"Listen, Molly, I'm not going to let you force this baby on me," he said, his control snapping. "The pregnancy was a mistake. It should never have happened."

"I refuse to believe that," Molly said as unemotionally as she could, although pain and anger simmered just below the surface. "If it hadn't been for this baby, we'd be divorced by now and you'd be engaged to Lesley. This child is a blessing."

The truth hit her then with as much shock as when she'd walked into Jeff's bedroom that fateful morning. She raised her eyes to Jordan and stared at him as the pain whirled around her like dust in a freak storm. "Maybe I am nothing more to you than a good lay," she choked out.

"No." Jordan's argument was immediate and strong. "That's not true. I love you, Molly. I've never been able to stop loving you."

She so desperately wanted to believe him that she couldn't make herself do otherwise. Her breath was shallow and her lower lip refused to still as she struggled with the effort not to weep. How she managed to hold on to her composure she didn't know. "My baby isn't a mistake, Jordan, not to me."

He didn't respond.

Her hand trembled as she raised it to her face, to brush away a strand of hair that had fallen over her eye. "I'm hoping we can both be mature enough to accept each other's difference of opinion."

"I didn't mean to hurt you," he whispered.

She lowered her head and a tear fell and splashed against the tabletop. "I know."

His hand reached across the table for hers. His fingers locked around hers, his grip tight. "I'd better go."

Just the way he said it made her suspect he wouldn't be back anytime soon. Even knowing that, she couldn't bring herself to suggest he stay.

Jordan was about to walk out of her life and she was about to let him. Another tear fell and bounced against the table, followed by another and then another.

Jordan stood, his gait quick and purpose filled. Abruptly he paused in the doorway leading to the living room, his hands knotted at his sides. He was there for so long that Molly raised her gaze to him. His back was stiff, his shoulders tense.

"Can I come see you again?"

Tightness gripped her throat and when she spoke her voice squeaked as if it badly needed to be oiled. "All right."

He left then and Molly wondered if they were both prolonging the inevitable.

Sometimes loving each other wasn't enough.

Perhaps the kindest thing she could do was cut her losses now and set them both free.

Jordan sat in front of a set of blueprints, drinking a beer. His mind wasn't on his construction company and hadn't been from the moment Molly sashayed her way back into his life. The woman would be the death of him yet.

He hadn't left her apartment more than two hours ago and already he was wondering how long it'd be before he could manufacture an excuse to see her again.

He'd managed to hold off for a week and it'd nearly killed him to stay away that long. He sincerely doubted he'd last another seven-day stretch without being with her, without holding and kissing her again. The woman was an addiction. He could live without lovemaking, but he couldn't live without her. Not again.

Jordan wasn't a man who felt inept around women. He knew he was reasonably good-looking and that women generally found him appealing. He had a nice personality, and the fact he owned a successful business didn't hurt him any.

It wasn't anything he wanted to brag to Molly about, but he could have found plenty of solace after she'd moved out on him, if he'd wanted.

He hadn't.

That was the crux of the problem. He'd never wanted another woman from the moment he'd met Molly Houghton, fresh out of college. He knew the moment they were introduced that this woman with eyes the color of a summer sky would greatly impact his life.

For a time he'd convinced himself that he cared for Lesley, and he had, as a friend. But they'd never been lovers, never shared the deep love and intimacy that had been so much a part of his relationship with Molly. He'd attempted to fool himself into thinking he could put his marriage behind him and make a new life. Lesley had fallen into the scheme herself, eager to marry. She'd admitted as much herself.

Jordan sipped from the beer, wrinkled his nose and set the bottle aside. He didn't like beer, had never liked beer. The only reason he kept it on hand was for his project superintendent, Paul Phelps, who sometimes dropped by the house.

Come to think of it, the last time Jordan had indulged in a beer had been when he and Molly had last lived together and had disagreed over something. He tossed the bottle into the garbage and watched the liquid spill against the plastic lining.

Maybe Molly was right.

She seemed to think all they needed was for him to feel the pain of losing Jeff. Which left him to wonder what he'd been doing for the past four years.

Molly was wrong. He hadn't denied Jeff's existence. He couldn't. He wasn't sure what she wanted, or if he was capable of doing it. Yes, he had disposed of Jeff's personal effects in a timely fashion, but he'd done so in an agony of grief, believing it would be easier for them to deal with their son's death if they weren't constantly being reminded of what they'd lost. In retrospect he could understand why it had been a mistake. They'd both made several blunders in the frantic days following their son's funeral.

For all the unknowns Jordan faced, there were an equal number of facts he did recognize. Molly's pregnancy leaped to mind bright as the noonday sun, blinding him with the glare of truth.

He'd longed to push all thoughts of this baby from his mind and his heart, and to some extent he'd succeeded. But he was well aware that his marriage was doomed beyond hope if his attitude didn't change, and change fast.

He hadn't seen Molly in a week and even in that short time he noticed the subtle changes in her body. It was easy to deny the baby when all evidence of its existence was quietly hidden from view. The baby was making itself more and more evident as time progressed. Within a few weeks Molly would be wearing maternity clothes, and every time he looked at her he'd be reminded of the child.

He rubbed a hand down his face. Despite what Molly claimed, he couldn't force himself into believing this pregnancy was anything but a mistake.

The thought of Molly pregnant deeply depressed him. Needing to escape, Jordan reached for his jacket and left the house. He was in his truck, driving with no destination in mind, before he pulled off the side of the road and parked. There wasn't anyplace he could run. There wasn't anyplace he could hide.

He turned off the engine and, gripping the steering wheel, closed his eyes and desperately sought a solution. He waited several moments for his breathing to relax and his racing heart to return to an even, slow pace.

The temptation to turn his back on the entire situation was strong. He could move his company to another city, and escape his troubles. The Pacific Northwest strongly appealed to him. Within a few years he could establish himself in Seattle, or maybe Portland. Molly could continue to live here in Chicago and come visit him on weekends. He'd find someone she trusted to leave the baby with. Molly might object, but...

The sheer idiocy of the idea struck him all at once and he expelled a giant sigh and restarted the truck. His thoughts as troubled as when he left, Jordan returned to the house.

He sat down in front of the television, and it was a long time before he moved. When he did, it was to turn off the set and go to bed, knowing he'd solved nothing.

"Dad," Molly said as he led her by the hand into her childhood bedroom. "What did you do, buy out the store?" Her mattress was heaped with every conceivable piece of clothing the baby would possibly need, in addition to a car seat, stroller and high chair.

"You said you didn't have anything other than the crib."

"I certainly didn't expect you to go out and buy it."

"Why not? I'm a wealthy old man, and if I can't indulge my grandchild, then what's the use of having all this money."

"Oh, Daddy," she said, throwing her arms around his neck. He, at least, shared her excitement over the baby. It was all becoming so much more real now that she could feel the baby's movements. "Thank you."

"It's my pleasure."

Molly and her father spent the next hour examining each and every item he'd purchased. She held up a newborn-size T-shirt and nearly laughed out loud. "Can you imagine anybody this tiny?"

"That's what I said to the salesclerk."

There were several blankets, all in pastel colors.

"Have you had an ultrasound yet?" her father asked, sounding eager.

"I've had two." Dr. Anderson was being extra cautious with her and this pregnancy, looking to reassure her as much as possible.

"And?" her father prompted.

"If you're waiting for me to reveal the baby's sex, I can't. I told Dr. Anderson I didn't want to know. It doesn't matter to me if the baby's a boy or a girl." She patted her tummy as she realized that in all this time Jordan hadn't once inquired about the baby's sex, although she'd mentioned the ultrasound. He didn't want to know because he wanted nothing to do with their child.

Generally she tried not to think about Jordan in connection with the baby because it resulted in a lengthy bout of unhappiness.

"From that frown you're sporting, I'd say you're thinking about Jordan," her father suggested, breaking into her heavy thoughts.

Molly nodded.

"How are matters between the two of you?"

"I don't know." Rather than raise her parent's hopes for a reconciliation, Molly had decided to play it safe.

"You're seeing him on a regular basis now, aren't you?"

Molly nodded, holding one of the receiving blankets against her front before refolding it and placing it inside the protective covering. "At first he made a point of stopping by once a week and it's more often now."

She wouldn't be all that surprised if Jordan showed up at her apartment after she arrived home. She hoped he would because she was going to need help carrying all the things her father had bought into the house.

"Come downstairs and have a cup of tea with me before you drive home," Ian coaxed.

Molly followed him down the stairs. As she moved down the steps she realized she could barely see her toes. She wasn't a full six months' pregnant and already she was experiencing some of the minor discomforts of the third trimester. Her feet swelled up almost every day now and she'd decided to request a schedule change for part-time employment after Thanksgiving.

"You haven't mentioned your friend Dr. Stern lately," her father said casually. "How's he doing?"

"Just great. We had lunch together last week, and he was telling me about a woman he recently met through a colleague of his. They seemed to hit it off and he's taking her to dinner this week." Molly smiled to herself as she recalled their conversation. David had sounded as excited as a teenage boy about to take his father's car out for the first time. Molly was pleased for him.

David had been a good friend and just exactly what she'd needed those first few weeks. They'd had plenty of in-depth discussions since the day they bumped into each other at her cousin's wedding. He called her occasionally still, but he'd moved on to greener pastures and it was just as well.

"He's a good man," her father commented, carrying the tea-filled china cups to the kitchen table. He chuckled softly. "Jordan came to me, you know."

"No, I didn't."

Her father sprouted a sly smile. "He was afraid it was too late and you and David were already in love."

"When was that?"

Ian cocked his head at an angle as he mulled over his answer. "I can't rightly remember, but it was several weeks back now. It was like someone had hit him over the head with a hard object. Don't misunderstand me, I'm downright fond of Jordan and think of him as a son, but there are times I'd like to slap that boy silly."

"Let me hold him down for you," Molly volunteered, not expecting her father to hear. Apparently he did because he chuckled.

"How's he treating you?"

"With kid gloves." She didn't want to say too much for fear Ian might decide to take matters into his own hands. Jordan had made progress. Not much, but he was trying. She had to believe that or she wouldn't be able to continue seeing him.

"I love him, Dad."

"I know, sweetheart, and he loves you. Somehow I don't think even he realizes how much." Deep in thought, her father sipped his tea. "Be patient with him, Molly."

"I'm trying, Dad. So is Jordan."

"Good."

Ian helped her load the car, and before she left his house Molly phoned Jordan.

"Hello," he answered gruffly on the second ring.

"Hi," she said. It was the first time she'd phoned him, preferring for him to set the course of their relationship. She felt self-conscious now and wished she'd waited to contact him until after she'd arrived home. As it was, her father was standing no more than five feet from her, grinning from ear to ear.

"Molly. I stopped by earlier and you weren't home."

"I'm not home now." So she'd guessed right. Jordan had sought her out. He'd taken her to a movie on Saturday and brought Chinese takeout with him when he stopped by the house Sunday afternoon. Monday he was going out of town for a brief business trip, and he told her not to expect to hear from him.

"Where are you?"

"My dad's. Listen, he went on a shopping spree and I'm going to need some help unloading my car. Can I bribe you with the offer of dinner?"

"I'll be there in five minutes."

"Jordan, your house is a good ten minutes from mine, in light traffic."

"I know that. I intend to speed. I've missed you, woman. In fact, I think we should give serious consideration to moving back in together, this going back and forth is ridiculous."

Molly's heart cheered at the news, but she didn't agree one way or the other. It was much too soon, but the suggestion was downright tempting.

Jordan was waiting for her in front of her apartment when she arrived. She'd barely had time to put the car into Park when he opened the driver's door and all but lifted her out of the car.

Not giving her time to protest he hauled her into his arms and kissed her as if they'd been apart for months instead of days. The kiss was wet and wild and when he finished Molly was clinging breathlessly to him. She was convinced holding on to him was the only thing that kept her upright.

Jordan buried his face in her neck. "I don't think it's a good idea for you to look at me like that."

"Like what?" she asked in a voice that grew progressively more reedy.

"Like you can hardly wait for me to take you to bed."

Molly blushed profusely, because that was exactly the way she felt. They hadn't made love in weeks, not since the night they'd spent together while she'd wrestled with regrets.

The subject had been on both their minds since that night. Molly couldn't have Jordan touch her and not want him to continue. She was certain he experienced the same physical pull she did. They were young, in love and very human.

The lovemaking had always been good between them, and after their one unforgettable night of passion Molly knew it could easily become dangerously addictive, again.

Jordan knew it, too. Molly was convinced of that. Like her, he was also aware they weren't going to solve their differences on top of a mattress. So they'd both avoided anything but the most innocent of touches. The heated kiss had been a slip on both their parts.

Reluctantly Molly eased herself out of his arms, but it felt cold and lonely outside the circle of his love. "I'll unlock the door," she said, hurrying away from him.

Jordan opened the backdoor of her car and piled his arms full of sacks. "What is all this stuff?" he asked, following her up the brick walkway that led to her half of the duplex.

Molly didn't answer him right away and steered the way into the dark house, turning on the light switches as she went. She paused in the baby's bedroom. She'd decorated it with love and care, anxious for his or her arrival.

"Dad's anxious to be a grandfather again" was the only explanation she gave.

Jordan paused in the nursery doorway, his arms loaded with sacks. For a long moment he didn't step beyond the threshold. Molly turned and waited, her heart pounding like a brass drum, echoing in her ear. After what seemed like an eternity, he came into the room and dropped the packages into the crib, and hurried back out.

Together they must have made five trips or more.

"It looks like he bought out the store," Jordan complained as he brought in the box that contained the high chair. Molly was hoping Jordan would agree to assemble it for her, but she'd broach the subject later.

"Dad's getting excited." So was she, but she found no such enthusiasm in her husband.

Jordan nodded, and decisively closed the door to the nursery. It clicked closed, as though he were shutting all thoughts of their baby off, as well.

Discouraged, Molly went into the kitchen. She didn't want to argue with him, not tonight. She was tired and she'd missed and needed him.

"Do you need help with dinner?" he offered.

Molly shook her head. Hoping inspiration would strike as to what she would cook for dinner, she opened the refrigerator door and gazed inside.

"I meant what I said earlier." Jordan spoke from behind her. His arms came around her and settled lazily over her breasts. "It's crazy for us to live apart when we're husband and wife. I want you in my home and in my bed. I love you, Molly, and you love me."

"I...don't think it's a good idea. Not yet."

Somehow he'd managed to unfasten her blouse and his hands roved freely over the fullness of her breasts. Molly closed the refrigerator door and, against every dictate of her will, her eyes drifted closed. Her nipples were so hard they pulsed, but that wasn't the only part of her that was affected by his touch. The lower half of her body felt incredibly heavy and moist.

She rotated her buttocks against his front and with one swirl of her hips felt him grow hard. A lengthy list of seductive promises were hidden beneath a single layer of tight denim.

Jordan turned her around and kissed her, backing her against the refrigerator door.

"I...was going to cook dinner."

"Later," he said between heated kisses.

Molly was having trouble keeping a clear head. When she found the strength, she pulled her mouth free from his and panted. "You must be starved by now."

Jordan directed her lips back to his. "You haven't got a clue how hungry I am." He hiked up her skirt until it was gathered like a drawn drape at her waist. Silencing any chance of a protest with a kiss, his hands found their way inside her lace-lined panties.

She knew what he intended to do, and she was intent on letting him, when the baby kicked strong and hard. Jordan must have felt it, too. It would have been impossible for him not to have experienced the sharp, swift motion.

He went still and then expelled his breath in a deep, harsh breath. His head fell forward until he'd braced his forehead against her shoulder.

"Jeff used to do that, too, remember?" It was risky mentioning their son.

Jordan nodded. Easing himself away from her, he righted her clothes and even managed to offer her a shaky smile.

"What was it you were saying about dinner?"

Chapter Eleven

Dipping the crisp dill pickle into the butter-brickle ice cream, Molly swirled it around and carried the coated pickle to her mouth. After she sucked off the ice cream, she repeated the process.

Wearing her robe and shorty pajamas, she stood in the kitchen, depressed and miserable. She hadn't heard from Jordan in three days. Three of the longest days of her life.

He'd helped her unload her car and stayed for dinner, but quickly made an excuse to leave almost immediately afterward. She hadn't seen hide nor hair of him since. Not so much as a phone call.

Something had been troubling him from the moment he'd held her and felt the baby kick. He'd done a good job of trying to hide his distress, but Molly knew. Until that evening, he'd tried to ignore the fact she was pregnant. He couldn't overlook it any longer, however. Not with the evidence so evident!

Molly gently patted her swollen abdomen. The time had come for Jordan to make his decision about her and the baby. Perhaps that was what had kept him away.

The imaginary drumroll had started for them and their marriage. Jordan had to decide what he wanted. It was either love and accept this child or—God, please, no—go through with the divorce. It pained Molly that it seemed to be such a hard decision.

Glancing at the phone, Molly wavered as she toyed with the idea of contacting him herself. She didn't want to lose Jordan, not when they'd worked so hard and covered so much ground. She refused to give up without making one last effort herself.

Swallowing her pride was difficult, but too much was at stake to let a little thing like her ego stand in her way. She'd battled with her pride all too often and regretted it later. If it came down to losing Jordan she didn't want to look back and wish she'd made one simple phone call.

Her hand tightened around the receiver as she dialed his number.

Jordan answered almost immediately as if he were sitting next to the phone, anticipating her call.

"Hello," she said softly.

"Molly." He seemed surprised to hear from her, but the inflection in his voice told her he was pleased.

"I hadn't heard from you in a few days," she said.

"I've been busy."

"I thought that must be it."

He hesitated as if he wanted to say more, then apparently changed his mind.

"How are you?" she asked when there didn't seem anything else to say.

"Good. How about you?"

Molly decided to plunge right in, head first. "The baby and I are doing great."

"I'm glad to hear that."

"I've gotten everything put away in the nursery now. It's organized and ready for when I come home from the hospital." Enough, she wanted to shout. She hadn't meant to stuff the subject down his throat.

"So you've been busy, too."

"Yeah," she said. Closing her eyes, she leaned her shoulder against the wall. "I miss you, Jordan."

He expelled his breath on a lengthy sigh. "I miss you, too."

"Come see me," she whispered, closing her eyes. She needed him with her, yearned for the feel of his arms around her. She longed for him to pick up where he'd left off the last time he was with her.

"You want me to drive over now?" The word contained an element of surprise and reluctance.

"Yes." She decided he needed a bit of incentive. "I'm wearing my baby-doll pajamas." Molly wasn't certain why she found it necessary to tell him that. At one time the black silky top had been Jordan's favorite. It seemed they made love every time she wore them. She'd put them on that evening, wanting to feel close to him, to remember the love they shared.

He hesitated. "Molly, I don't think my coming is such a good idea."

Her eyes flew open with hurt and disappointment. "Why not?"

Once more it seemed to take him a long time to respond. "If I do, we're going to end up making love."

The time to be coy had long passed and Molly smiled softly to herself. "I know."

"You're sure about this?" His voice trembled slightly.

Molly wasn't sure of anything these days. "I'm sure I love you. Is that answer enough?"

Her words seemed to convince him. "I'll be there before you know it."

Molly barely had time to put away the pickles and the ice cream when the doorbell chimed. She hurried to the front door, checked to be sure it was Jordan and then, her hands trembling with eagerness, let him inside.

"Hello," she said, smiling up at him. "You didn't take long."

"No man would with the invitation you just offered."

She laughed and lowered her gaze. "No, I suppose you're right." She was hoping he'd take her in his arms, kiss her until she was senseless and then carry her into the bedroom and make wild, passionate love to her. His reluctance did little for her self-confidence.

"You've got something on your chin," he said, rubbing his thumb over the offending spot. He frowned. "What is that?"

"Ice cream... I was eating it with a pickle and I guess it was messier than I realized." She glanced down at her top and found a couple of spots where the ice cream had dripped.

"How the hell do you eat ice cream with a pickle?" Jordan asked, as if he'd come all this way from his house to hers for a demonstration.

"I'll show you." She walked back into the kitchen, removed both items from the refrigerator and scooped up a dollop of ice cream on the end of the dill pickle. "Generally you need to soften the ice cream in the microwave first, but once you do that it works great. Do you want to give it a try?"

"Why not?" he asked, his eyes smiling.

If she didn't know better, Molly would think he was stalling for time. Her choice of dessert had never overly concerned him before now.

She swirled the pickle around the edge of the ice-cream container and hand-fed it to Jordan. His brows arched upward with surprise. "Hey, it isn't bad. This isn't butter brickle, is it? You hate butter brickle."

"I used to. About a week ago I got this craving for it. I've always heard about pregnant woman getting cravings, but this is the first time it's happened to me."

Jordan lowered his gaze to her protruding stomach. Any increase in her girth since their last meeting would be infinitesimal, but the way he studied her suggested that she'd swollen up like a hot-air balloon.

Feeling self-conscious, Molly tugged the silk robe closed and tied the loop around what had once been her trim waist. Her slender figure was far from svelte these days.

"It wasn't your work that kept you away these past three days, was it, Jordan?" she asked softly.

"No."

At least he was honest enough to level with her.

"I've been doing some thinking," he admitted.

"And?" she prompted when he didn't immediately continue, eager to hear if he'd found any solutions.

"Would you mind if we sat down?" he asked, glancing toward her sofa.

"Of course not." She followed him into the other room and they sat together. Curling her feet beneath her, she leaned against him and smiled softly when he lifted his arm and lovingly placed it around her shoulders.

Molly all but sighed aloud at the warm comfort she felt as he brought her into his arms. She cozied up to him and leaned her head against his chest. It didn't matter if they talked or not, she was content.

He kissed the crown of her head. "I've missed you something fierce."

"Why did you stay away?" The last time they met, he'd asked her to move back into the house with him; now she had to phone and almost plead to see him. What a difference a few days could make.

"I can't think when we're together," he admitted, then added with heavy reluctance, "I needed time to give some thought to us and the baby."

"I assumed as much. Did you come up with any solutions?"

"No."

"I haven't, either." She raised her arms and looped them around his neck. Using her tongue and her mouth, she made lazy circles against his skin, loving the taste and feel of him. She concentrated her attention at the hollow of his throat, gently sucking and kissing his skin. It'd been so long since they last made love and she needed him.

"Molly." Her name was little more than a whispered plea.

"Hmm?" Using the moist tip of her tongue, she worked her way up the underside of his jaw, creating a slick trail that led a meandering path to his lips.

They kissed and it was deep and heady. She sighed as Jordan's hands pushed aside her robe and found her breasts. They'd filled out with the pregnancy and overfilled his palms. Her nipples pearled into tight nubs under his loving attention.

"This isn't going to solve anything," Jordan whispered huskily.

"I'm tired of looking for solutions. I want to make love." She seldom played the role of the aggressor, but when she had in the past, Jordan had enjoyed it as much as she.

Kissing him in the ways she knew he loved, she crawled onto his lap, straddling him with her knees. Freeing his tie, she pulled it loose from the restriction of his button-down collar and tossed it aside. Next she worked free his shirt buttons. The entire procedure had been accomplished with her mouth slanted over his and his hands kneading and molding her breasts.

Jordan stretched out his arm for the lamp and fumbled until he found the switch. Murky shadows blanketed the room and the only sound that could be heard was the mingling of their moans and sighs.

It was while she was on her husband's lap, greedily kissing him and removing his clothes, that their baby decided he intended on becoming a soccer star. The first fluttering of movement they both ignored, but that quickly became impossible as he kicked and prodded against Jordan's tight chest.

Smiling, Molly eased her mouth from Jordan's and sat back. She rested her hands on top of the budding mound of her tummy that was their child. "He's so strong."

Jordan closed his eyes and leaned his head against the back of the sofa.

Molly reached for his hand and pressed it against her stomach. He didn't offer any resistance, which greatly encouraged her. Gradually he opened his eyes and straightened.

"You're going to love him, Jordan," she said softly, wanting to reassure him. "You won't be able to stop yourself."

Again he didn't respond.

"I love you," she whispered, speaking to both the father and the child.

Jordan gently eased her off his lap, stood and paced the room. His steps grew quick, his distress gaining with each stride. "This isn't going to work."

"What isn't?" she asked, her gaze following him as he moved

from one end of the room to the other like a confined tiger. Turn, pace, turn, until it was all she could do not to yell at him to stop.

He paused and looked at her in the dim light. "I can't make love to you."

Molly settled back in her seat and wrapped her dignity around her as if she were dressing herself in a mink stole on the coldest night of the winter. "Why not?"

"I don't mean to hurt you, Molly." He repeatedly rubbed the back of his neck, while avoiding looking at her. Much to her irritation, he resumed the incessant walking.

"Tell me," she insisted. Anyone else would have left it at that, saved themselves the humiliation, but she had to know. She demanded to know.

"This embarrasses the hell out of me. It happened the other night, too," he said, as if making a confession. "I can't look at you and not want to make love, but the minute I feel the baby move my desire is gone. It's the same way now. I love you, Molly. God help us both, but right now I'm physically incapable of making love to you."

Molly wasn't sure what she'd expected, but not this. Never this. He was telling her he found her ugly and unattractive. His words hurt as if he'd cut her with a razor blade.

Silence fell as he waited for her to respond.

It took Molly several moments to recover. "Well, that answers that, doesn't it," she said, hoping to hide the extent of her pain. "I don't have a single argument, do I? My figure certainly isn't what it once was."

Climbing off the sofa, she reached for the lamp and turned the knob. Light spilled into the room. Molly would have sold her inheritance not to be wearing these sexy pajamas. She felt like an elephant who'd, by some miracle, managed to stuff itself into a bikini.

Gripping hold of the front of her robe, she walked over to the door and opened it for Jordan. "I'm sorry you have to leave so soon."

"Molly, don't send me away. Not now. Not like this."

She should be awarded a medal for keeping the tears at bay. Holding her chin high and proud, she slowly turned her head so their gazes met. "Please, Jordan, just go."

"The problem's mine, Molly, not yours. You're beautiful. I'm the one who needs help. Let's talk this out."

"Everything's been said a thousand times," she whispered

through her pain. "I believe you said it best. This isn't going to work."

Jordan impatiently rammed his fingers through his hair. "I shouldn't have said anything, but sooner or later you were going to suspect something was wrong."

Molly could sympathize with him. He'd backed himself into a corner, but that didn't make any difference. It would always be like this with him. Jordan wasn't going to change and she was living in a fool's world if she continued to believe otherwise.

"You once suggested the only good thing between us was the sex... I was quick to take offense," she reminded him, her voice heavy with sadness. "But now I realize you could be right." This last part was the most painful. "Now that I don't...turn you on, so to speak, there really isn't anything left between us, is there?"

"Molly, that's not true."

"Maybe," she agreed. "Then again maybe not." All she could be sure of at the moment was that she wanted Jordan out of her home. If he didn't leave soon, she'd be in serious danger of an emotional breakdown. Her pride was already in shreds, and she didn't relish the thought of humiliating herself further.

"You'll give me a call?" he asked when it became apparent she wasn't going to change her mind. She stood like a bouncer holding open the front door, waiting for him to vacate her apartment.

"I don't know," she whispered, although she seriously doubted that she would. It probably would have been best to tell him that, but she didn't want to invite additional arguments.

He paused, his eyes connecting with hers before he left. In him she read regret and pain and a mixture of several other emotions. She trained her eyes to stare straight through him, hoping he'd read her lack of emotion for blatant indifference.

Of one thing Molly was certain. She'd never be indifferent to Jordan Larabee.

A week passed and Jordan wasn't sure what he expected from Molly. He'd insulted her, wounded her pride and just about ruined whatever hope there was of salvaging their marriage. Whoever was credited with saying honesty was the best policy had never been married, he decided.

He phoned her countless times in an effort to undo the damage, but Molly had taken to screening her calls with the answering machine. He'd stopped by her apartment so often the neighbors had started waving when they saw him. But he hadn't found the courage to confront her, especially when she'd made it plain she wouldn't welcome him after their last meeting.

Damn, but he'd really messed matters up this time.

Nothing short of a blowup with Molly would have led him to visit his father-in-law. Ian Houghton would take sheer delight in knowing Jordan had made an ass of himself for the umpteenth time. But then Jordan should be accustomed to Ian's belligerent attitude by now.

His father-in-law was smoking one of his king-size Cuban cigars, looking downright pleased with himself, when Jordan joined him in his den. Book-lined walls sat behind him and must have recently been waxed. The scent of lemon oil permeated the air along with the fragrant aroma of rich tobacco.

"Jordan, it's good to see you," Ian said as he stood to greet him. The two men exchanged handshakes.

"You, too." Jordan helped himself to a chair and rested his ankle against the top of his knee, hoping to give a carefree, relaxed impression.

"My guess is that you're here to inquire about my daughter?"

"What makes you think this isn't a social call?" Jordan asked.

Ian laughed. "I know you too well for that. You don't make social calls. If you've taken the time and the trouble to come see me, it has something to do with Molly."

"Don't be so sure. I might be here about money." He'd come to Ian to discuss financing often enough when he was first starting up his construction company. The older man's assistance had been invaluable. He and Molly had spent many an evening with Ian going over the details of a construction project. Molly had never complained and often curled up with a book in this very room while the two men talked business. Jordan missed those times and the closeness the three of them shared.

Jordan met Ian's look. With a knowing smile, his father-in-law puffed at his cigar. "You've got more money than you know what to do with these days. It's not money you're after, it's Molly."

It wouldn't do any good to ease his way into the conversation, Jordan realized. "All right, if you must know, this does have to do with Molly. We had a falling out."

"About what?"

He felt fool enough already without explaining the details. "I insulted her."

Ian relaxed against his leather chair and smiled broadly. "Hell hath no fury like a woman scorned."

"If I wanted to listen to proverbs I'd be reading *Poor Richard's*

Almanac. I'm here for advice. I don't want to lose Molly. I love her.''

"And the baby?"

Jordan had wondered how long it would take Ian to bring up the pregnancy. "In time I'll grow accustomed to the baby."

Ian's eyes grew dark and serious. The smile Jordan had found irritating seconds earlier folded closed. Ian's eyes sharpened. "My daughter isn't having just any baby, Jordan Larabee, that's your seed she's carrying. It's damn well time you accepted some responsibility."

Jordan stiffened, disliking Ian's tone. "I told Molly from the first that I'd assume complete financial responsibility for the child."

Ian's eyes narrowed as he directed the full force of his outrage on him. "I'm talking about emotional responsibility. Do you think you're the only one who's ever lost a baby? Enough is enough. It isn't any wonder Molly's having medical problems."

Immediate fear stabbed him. "Molly's having problems."

"From what I understand she hasn't been to work all week."

"What's wrong?" Jordan was on his feet by now and unwilling to play a game of cat and mouse while Ian beat him up with the information. He'd ring the old man's neck if Ian didn't tell him and soon.

"You needn't worry, it's nothing serious."

"What's wrong with her?" Jordan demanded, more strenuously this time.

"You'll have to ask my daughter. She gets downright feisty when I do the talking for her," Ian said nonchalantly, then lazily puffed his cigar. Jordan swore the old man did it to hide a smile.

Jordan paced to the other side of the room. "She doesn't answer my calls."

"You might want to visit her."

"Has she been in to see Doug Anderson?" Jordan demanded. The physician was a longtime friend of his, although they hadn't seen each other in several years. Jordan's company had been involved in the construction of the medical building where Anderson practiced.

"I don't know, Jordan. You'll have to ask Molly that yourself."

Jordan glared at his father-in-law and his blatant effort to get him to visit Molly.

"She only tells me a little of what's going on in her life," Ian argued. "My guess is that she has seen the doctor. If she did go, I imagine it's because she's more worried about the baby than herself."

The temptation to drive over to her apartment and find out for himself exactly what was wrong strongly tempted Jordan. He would have if he believed it'd do any good. The minute Molly learned it was him, she simply wouldn't open the door. The woman had a stubborn streak that rivaled his own.

Before he jumped to conclusions, Jordan decided to contact Doug Anderson himself and find out what he could. He left Ian, and sat in his truck and called Doug from his cellular phone.

"Jordan Larabee, my goodness, how long has it been?"

"Too long," Jordan answered, talking inside his truck, parked in front of Ian's house. "I understand Molly's your patient?"

"Yes. I know this bout of flu has been difficult for her, but it's nothing to be worried about. I've given her some medication and suggested she gets lots of rest."

"You're sure it's just the flu?"

"Fairly certain. I've treated several cases in the past couple of weeks with similar symptoms."

"Would you care to get together for a drink?" Jordan asked. "I know it's short notice, but there're a few matters I'd like to talk over with you."

"Sounds like a good idea. Come by the house, why don't you. Mary would love to see you. In fact, she's been wanting to ask you about a contractor. We're looking to have a house built this summer."

Forty minutes later Jordan pulled up in front of Doug and Mary Anderson's three-story brick home.

Mary answered the doorbell and greeted him like a long-lost relative. Jordan regretted having allowed their friendship to lapse. He'd always liked Doug and Mary and couldn't remember the last time he'd talked to them. After Jeff died, and Molly moved out, there hadn't been any room in his life for anything other than work.

Mary insisted on feeding him dinner. Jordan had forgotten how good it was to sit down at a table with friends. The Andersons' three boys were all teenagers. They were tall, good-looking youths, busy with their own lives. Judd at eighteen was the oldest. He was in the kitchen briefly, grabbed a chicken leg off the platter, kissed his mother's cheek and left, claiming he needed to study for an important test with Angela. Peter and Adam had eaten earlier, following football practice, and after shaking hands with Jordan, disappeared.

Jordan found it was almost painful to watch Doug and Mary with their three sons. This was what it would have been like with him and Molly had Jeff lived, he mused. In his mind's eye he could picture his son, wrapping Molly around his little finger, interrupting her scolding with a peck on the cheek and a promise to be home before ten. He could see himself handing his son the car keys so he could study for a test with a girl named Angela.

Following dinner, Doug and Jordan had coffee in front of the fireplace. "I'm worried about Molly," Jordan admitted. "We haven't been on the best of terms lately." He hesitated, then willingly added, "Mostly that's my fault. I've been something of a heel over this pregnancy."

"It's difficult, I know."

Jordan was sure Doug had plenty of experience with couples who'd lost infants to SIDS, but only someone who'd lived through this agony could fully appreciate it.

From what Molly had told him, Doug was closely monitoring this pregnancy. He was pleased his friend had taken special care with her, although he was fairly certain Doug would have done so with any patient who'd previously lost a child.

"I remember how I felt when we learned Mary was pregnant after we lost Joy."

Jordan's head snapped up, certain he'd misunderstood. "Joy?"

"We lost a daughter to SIDS nearly twenty-three years ago. I thought you knew."

Jordan shook his head. Perhaps he did remember Doug and Mary saying something to him at Jeff's funeral, but he'd been in such a state of confusion and pain that it hadn't clicked.

"She was only three months old," Doug added. "It nearly destroyed Mary. Trust me, Jordan, I've walked in your shoes. In some ways I've been in Molly's, too. Because we're both in the medical profession, I know the torment of doubts she suffered. I felt there must have been something I should have done, should have known. After all those years in medical school, and I couldn't save my own child."

"How long did it take to get over it?"

Doug sipped from his coffee. "I don't know that I can answer that, not in months or years at any rate. We both got on with our lives, but we waited nearly five years before we decided to have Judd. In many ways it took me longer to come to terms with Joy's death than Mary."

"Molly seems to have dealt with it better than me." This was the first time Jordan had openly discussed Jeff with anyone other than his wife.

"It takes a man longer to process the grief," Doug said. "We aren't as likely to let go of our emotions. I envied Mary her ability

to cry. Men have a far more difficult time expressing their feelings.''

"How did you feel when you learned Mary was pregnant with
Judd?'' Jordan had scooted forward in his chair, anxious to learn
the answer.

"Scared spitless. I'm not going to tell you it was easy for either
one of us, but it was time to move forward and we both knew it.
Molly's going to do just fine with this child, and so are you.''

Jordan wished he were as confident as his friend.

"By the way,'' Doug said casually, "I've taken two ultrasounds
of the baby now. Molly's been adamant about not wanting me to
tell her the baby's sex, but if you're curious I'd be happy to let you
know.''

Jordan felt the weight of indecision shift from one shoulder to
the next. He couldn't help wanting to know, but at the same time
he wasn't sure he did. "All right,'' he found himself agreeing, "tell
me.''

"You're going to have a little girl.''

A daughter.

For some reason, certainly not one he could explain or understand, Jordan had assumed their baby was a boy. Molly had always
referred to her as "him,'' and he'd believed she'd said so know-
ingly.

"Congratulations,'' Doug said, beaming him a wide grin.

"Thanks,'' Jordan mumbled. His hand was shaking when he set
down the coffee mug.

A daughter.

One that resembled Molly with bright blue eyes and pretty blond
hair. His heart clenched with such a powerful surge that it was all
he could do not to place his hand there and hold on to the incredible
sensation. He didn't know that he could name this emotion, but
whatever it was, all he could say was that the power of it was
tremendous.

"Have you decided on names yet?'' Mary asked, joining them.

Jordan looked at his friend's wife as if seeing her for the first
time. "No,'' he whispered.

He stood, and set the coffee aside.

"A daughter,'' he repeated. He kissed Mary on the cheek, shook
hands with Doug as if he were pumping a well for water and let
himself out the front door.

So many emotions were coming at Jordan that he didn't know
which one to deal with first. He'd just made one of the most profound discoveries of his life.

He wanted this child, wanted her so much it was all he could do not to stand in the bed of his pickup and scream it to the world.

Secondly, he felt like the biggest fool that had ever walked the face of the earth. He'd behaved like a first-rate heel for months. It was a miracle Molly had put up with his stupidity this long. He didn't deserve her, but by heaven, he vowed, he'd find a way of making it up to her.

Jordan resisted the urge to drive directly over to Molly's apartment. He'd give her adequate time to recover from the flu, and then they could sit down and talk this out.

When he walked into the house he saw that the message light on his answering machine was flashing. Praying that Molly had deemed to return his calls, he pushed down the button.

"Jordan, it's Larry Rife. Your office gave me this number. I hope you don't mind me calling you at home, but this is important.

"It's after six now, and I'll be leaving here soon. I got a call from Molly. She asked me to petition the court for a date so the final divorce papers could be filed.

"I thought you'd decided to wait until after the baby was born. I'm confused, but Molly was adamant she wanted to go through with the divorce. Give me a call first thing in the morning if you would. Thanks.''

Chapter Twelve

Molly had endured a full week with the worst case of flu in recent memory. The only time she'd been out of the house in five days had been to see Dr. Anderson who offered her sympathy, advice and a mild prescription to see her through the worst of the stomach cramps.

The virus wasn't the only thing keeping Molly down. She'd cried herself a bucket of tears since her last confrontation with Jordan. Her frustration with him that swept through her was far stronger and more debilitating than any virus. Every time she thought about these past few months, she suffered an emotional relapse.

Their marriage was over.

The time had come for Molly to quit kidding herself. For days she'd lain on the sofa and stared into space, reliving the past six months with its tumultuous ups and downs.

She'd almost believed it was possible for them. The bitter disappointment was a difficult pill to swallow when they'd both wanted to salvage their relationship.

Contacting Larry Rife was difficult. She'd barely been able to speak. Her weak voice trembled when she told him the reason for her call. Several times she'd had to stop and compose herself before continuing.

Larry had attempted to persuade her to wait, but she'd insisted. She wanted the divorce over with before she gave birth. That was important to her. Jordan had repeatedly told her he intended to emotionally distance himself from their baby. It would be better, she decided, to completely isolate their child from Jordan with his current attitude. She'd seen no evidence that it would change. The baby deserved better. For that matter so did she.

Having made the phone call, she was left to face the taunts of regrets and doubts. They sat beside her like Job's friends, one on her left, the other on her right, all the while mocking her. She refused to give in to the weakness of tears. She'd shed all she cared to in the past several months.

Now was the time to heal. The time to rejoice in the birth of her son or daughter. The time to pick up the pieces of her life and move steadily forward.

The phone rang and she tensed. Over the past week Jordan had repeatedly called, but she wasn't emotionally or physically up to another confrontation with him. The answering machine had collected his messages. As the messages accumulated, she heard his anger and frustration, followed by his insistence that she have the decency to return his calls. Then he stopped phoning. Abruptly.

The answering machine picked up the call on the fifth ring. Molly tensed until she heard the attorney's voice come over the line.

"Molly, it's Larry Rife. I wasn't able to get hold of Jordan, but I left a message on his machine. I'll get back to you as soon as I've talked to him. I don't suspect that'll take long. If you have any questions, give me a call here at the office. And, Molly—" he paused momentarily "—if you want to change your mind, all you need do is say so. I'll wait for your instructions."

So it wasn't Jordan who was calling. Well, according to Larry, Jordan knew that she intended to go through with the divorce. Or he would shortly. Personally, she didn't want to be around when he heard the news. His temper was infamous.

Molly spent the night on her sofa. The effort it demanded to get up and make her way down the hallway to her bedroom was more than she could muster.

She woke around six and felt wretched, but she wasn't sure if her condition was more physical or emotional. Possibly a combination of both.

She showered, washed her hair and changed clothes. By the time she finished, she was so weak she needed to sit down. Her knees shook and she pushed the wet strands of hair away from her face, pondering just how long it would take to get rid of this bug and resume her everyday life.

The flu, she realized, would gradually work its way through her system, but the deep, brooding sense of loss she experienced over her marriage would require a much longer healing process.

Around eight, Molly managed to eat a piece of dry toast and

weak tea. She propped her back against the end of the sofa with a
thick pillow and reached for the television controller. It was a sorry
day when she resorted to filling her time tuning in to talk shows.
Several of her friends were addicted to them, but personally Molly
didn't understand what society gained by listening to people who'd
claimed they'd talked to aliens and now wanted to marry their pets.

Just when she was comfortable the doorbell chimed, catching her
off guard. A glance at the wall clock told her it was barely nine.
The buzzer sounded a second time.

The impatient beeps assured it was none other than Jordan. No
man on earth rang a doorbell quite like he did. He was always in
a hurry and detested having to wait.

"I know you're in there," Jordan shouted from the other side of
the door. "Open up."

"Go away," she called back, "I've got the flu."

"I'm not leaving until I've talked to you, so either let me in or
call the police right now, because I'll bash in your door if that's
what it takes."

The man had no sense. Molly threw aside the comforter and
ambled toward the door. Her back ached and she pressed her hand
to the small of her spine. She wasn't physically up to a showdown
with Jordan, but she had few options. It was face him now or do it
later. She preferred to have this scene over with as soon as possible.

She unlocked the door. "It'd serve you right if I did phone the
police," she mumbled.

He marched into the duplex like a storm trooper seeking revenge.
He was halfway into the living room before he whirled around. His
teeth were clenched and the sides of his jaw were white. His eyes
were as angry as she'd ever seen them.

"I take it you've talked to Larry."

"Not yet. I decided to have this out with you first."

"I suggest you talk to Larry."

The anger left his eyes as if he were seeing her, really seeing
her, for the first time. His fists relaxed and fell slack at his sides.

Molly knew she looked dreadful. It wasn't as if she'd spent the
past week at a health spa receiving beauty treatments.

"How are you?" he asked.

Molly closed the front door and leaned against it. "I've never
felt better," she lied.

"Sit down," he urged. He moved to help her back onto the sofa,
but she pulled away from him, avoiding his touch. She clung to her
dignity as if her sanity depended on it, and in many ways it did.

"You wanted to say something," she pressed, willing him to get this over with quickly.

He waited until she'd seated herself and pulled the thick comforter over her legs. For having threatened to bust down her door, now that he had her attention, Jordan didn't seem to know what he wanted to say.

"I had a long talk with Doug Anderson last night."

Of all the things she expected, this came as a surprise. She wasn't sure if he was inviting comment, but she had none to give.

"Mary had me over for dinner," he elaborated. "I saw their three boys."

Molly looked up at him, wondering exactly where this conversation was leading.

He stuffed his hands deep inside his pockets. "I talked to your father, too."

"You certainly made the social rounds."

He smiled briefly at that.

This time the silence was initiated by him. It stretched and stretched, wearing so thin Molly was convinced it would soon break and shatter their taut, courteous discussion.

"Doug and Mary lost a daughter to SIDS over twenty years ago," Jordan said, his voice low and steady. "I wasn't sure if you knew that or not."

"We've talked about it several times." She didn't dare look at Jordan. The minute she did she'd realize how deeply she loved him. It was difficult enough to accept that their marriage was over without being reminded how much the divorce was going to hurt. Jordan had a way about him, a way of turning her will. Even one glance was too risky.

"Larry's message was waiting for me when I got home."

Her gaze was level with his hands. She watched, mesmerized by the expression she read in their movements. First he clenched them, then seemed to force himself to relax. He wiggled his fingers, then clenched them again.

"I can't think of a solitary reason why you should delay the divorce," he surprised her by saying. "I've given you plenty of reasons to wish you'd never met me."

Loving him the way she did, Molly couldn't make herself regret their years together. He'd given her two children, and if for nothing more than Jeff and the life she carried within her now, Molly would always be grateful.

"Jordan, please, I don't have the strength to argue with you. I've made up my mind. Nothing you say now is going to change it."

"I love you."

She closed her eyes. "Love isn't always enough. Please don't make this more difficult than it already is."

"You're sure this is what you want?"

Molly closed her eyes and nodded.

"I don't have the right, but I'm going to ask one small favor of you. Wait." She started to object, but he stopped her. "All I'm asking for is a few months."

"No," she said immediately, "I can't..."

"Until after the baby's born."

For her own peace of mind, Molly didn't know if she could delay it any longer.

"Please," he added almost under his breath.

She'd anticipated his anger, but not this. He seemed almost humble. To the best of her memory, she couldn't remember Jordan asking anything of her. The temptation to give in was strong, like the pull of the tide. It wasn't fair that he solicit this kind of decision now.

The hands that had clenched and unclenched moments earlier flexed and fidgeted before turning palms up as if to silently plead his case.

"On one condition," she said when she found her voice.

"Anything."

"I'll agree to wait, if you don't make any attempt to see me again. It's over as of now, Jordan. I won't make it legal until after the baby's born, because that seems to be important to you, but that's all I'm willing to concede."

"But, Molly..."

"I'm serious, Jordan. Either you agree or I'll go through with the divorce as soon as Larry can arrange a court date. If you attempt to break your word, I'll contact Larry immediately."

What seemed like an eternity passed before Jordan responded. "If that's your one request, then I don't have any choice but to agree."

Molly was feeling wretched, as if she was about to lose her breakfast. "I think it would be a good idea if you left now."

"Can I get you anything?"

"No." She wished he'd hurry. "Please just go."

He turned and walked toward the door, then turned back. "Do you have any names picked out for the baby?"

"Yes." But she didn't understand his sudden curiosity.

"Would you mind telling me?"

"I...I wanted Richard for a boy. I'd like to name him after Dr.

Morton. He's back working in Manukua, by the way. He's the kindest, most gentle man I've ever known and he'd be thrilled to pieces to learn I'd named *my* baby after him." She made sure he heard the inflection in her voice.

As far as Molly was concerned, he'd relinquished all rights to their child. The baby was hers and hers alone.

"What about a girl's name?" Jordan pressed.

"Bethany Marie." If Jeff had been a girl they'd planned on the name Lori Jo. They'd sorted through name books for weeks before arriving at a final decision.

Jordan smiled briefly. "That has a nice sound to it. Are you naming her after anyone in particular?"

"Marie's my mother's middle name, and I've always liked the name Bethany."

"I do, too," he said and opened the door.

It seemed to take him a long time to walk away from her. The minute she could, Molly tossed aside the covering and rushed into the bathroom. She didn't know if she'd taken a turn for the worse or if this sudden bout of vomiting was the result of yet another nerve-wracking encounter with Jordan.

A month passed and Jordan didn't hear a word from Molly. Not that he expected he would. But he'd hoped. He'd prayed.

Thanks to Ian and Doug he received regular updates on Molly's condition and savored each report about Bethany Marie's progress. He drilled Doug with so many questions that his friend had eventually handed him a textbook on what to expect the last trimester of pregnancy. Jordan read through it twice.

Thanksgiving was lonely as hell. He flew to Arizona and spent the holiday with his mother, who'd retired there several years earlier. She was pleased and excited to have him. He hadn't been to visit her since Jeff had been born. His life was too crammed full of activity and work to bother with a little thing like maintaining a relationship with his mother. His father had died years earlier while he was in high school, and his sister lived in Oregon.

When he arrived at his mother's home, one of the first things Jordan noticed was a framed photograph of Jeff on top of the television. It disconcerted him so badly that he had to ask her to put it away.

He felt badly about that later, when he returned to Chicago, to an empty house and an emptier life. Molly and tiny Bethany had been constantly on his mind. He wondered how they'd spent the holiday and was tempted to contact Ian and ask.

He rummaged around the house and resisted the urge to phone
Ian, knowing he'd made a regular pest of himself recently. He was
tired from the weekend travel and the craziness that was involved
in flying over a holiday.

He listened to the messages on his telephone answering machine.
Nothing important. No one he need call back. No word from Molly.

Walking up the stairs, Jordan passed the room that had once been
Jeff's nursery. He hadn't been in the bedroom in more than four
years. Not since the day he'd stripped away everything that had
been their son's. Not since he'd attempted to wipe out every piece
of evidence that Jeff had ever lived.

The fight he'd had with Molly that terrible afternoon would forever stay with him. And her, too, he speculated. He'd carried down
the baby furniture and she'd come crying after him, begging him
not to give Jeff's things away. She was rooting through the boxes,
sobbing hysterically, when the truck driver arrived for the charity
pickup.

The man had sat down on the steps with Molly and talked to her
in gentle tones. Jordan had stood in the doorway demanding that
the agency remove everything. It appalled him now that a stranger
had been more sensitive to Molly's pain than he'd been.

Some force he couldn't name directed him to Jeff's room now.
He turned the handle and walked inside. The floor was bare. As
were the walls. The one item that remained was Molly's rocking
chair.

He'd forgotten about that. She used to nurse Jeff by the fireplace
in their bedroom. After he died, she'd moved the chair into his room
and sat in there alone for hours on end.

Oftentimes he'd come home from work and find her sitting in
that very chair, staring into space, tears streaking her face. He
guessed she'd spent the entire day there.

Stepping into the bedroom, Jordan sat down in the chair. It
creaked as it accepted his weight. He placed his hands over the
wide arms and gently rocked back and forth. He closed his eyes
and recalled Molly holding Jeff to her breast, talking softly to their
son while she gently rocked. Sometimes she sang to him in a beautiful, lyrical voice that vibrated with her love.

It was like a childhood remembrance—something that had happened years and years earlier. A dream from his youth.

Jordan thought again about Doug and Mary Anderson's three
sons, and how he pictured Jeff as a young adult, had he lived.

"You're going to have a sister," he whispered.

He pressed his lips together, the sound of his own voice shocking him. It was the loneliness, he decided, that had caused him to talk to a baby who was long dead, long buried, long grieved.

"I have a younger sister," Jordan whispered, then surprised himself by laughing out loud. "She was a pest from the moment she was born. The very bane of my existence until I was a high school senior." He stopped rocking, remembering how fortunate he'd been to have a younger sister who was an "in" for him with the sophomore girls.

Caught up in the memories of his childhood years, Jordan glanced out the window to the manicured grounds of their yard. Perhaps he was overly tired from the trip, he didn't know, but he'd like to have something to blame for what happened next.

In his mind's eye he saw his seven-year-old son racing around, flying a kite. Bethany, who was barely old enough to stand, was reaching toward the sky, laughing with glee. The vision left him as quickly as it came.

He was going insane, Jordan decided. Perhaps he already was.

He didn't know what was happening to him, but all at once his chest felt as if he were being shoved against a concrete wall. His heart thudded like a huge stone. He felt every beat as it pounded and pulsed.

Hot, blistering tears filled his eyes.

A man doesn't cry... A man doesn't cry...

Apparently whoever was supposed to listen, wasn't. Huge sobs racked his shoulders. He hung his head, then covered his face, embarrassed, although no one could see him.

The tears stopped as abruptly and as unexpected as they came, replaced with a savage rage. The force of it threatened to swallow him whole. He'd carried it with him for years, Jordan realized, hauling it around with him like a heavy backpack.

Right or wrong, justified or not, he was furious. Jeff was gone and there was no one to blame. No one he could slam up against a wall and vent his fury upon. No one he could punish and send to jail to rot. And so he'd allowed it to weigh down his life, spitting and spewing with the least provocation.

He vented his anger now, because he hadn't allowed himself to do it back then. Hadn't given himself permission to grieve the way Molly had.

He was a man. A man didn't reveal his pain. A man didn't cry. A man buried his son and then went on with his life. A man held and comforted his wife. A man held his family together. That was what Jordan believed a man should do.

Only he was weeping now.

Weeping alone.

He was angry, and the force of his grief bled like a bad cut across his heart, leaving him yearning for one thing. The end. Deliverance.

For four senseless years, a thick rage had boiled just below the surface of his soul. The cost had been tremendous.

SIDS had taken far more than Jordan's perfect, innocent son. SIDS had robbed him of his wife and his marriage. In many ways, SIDS had claimed a part of his sanity.

Jordan was standing now, his fists clenched at his sides, the chair rocking behind him. He didn't remember coming to his feet. Falling back into the rocker, he closed his eyes and waited for his pulse to return to normal. The room was silent, all but for the heavy thud of his heart, which sounded like a cannon in his ears.

Jordan waited for a release, anything that would end this agony of pain. But he knew that if this catharsis didn't run its course, it would solve nothing. He had walked through the valley, and the only hope he had of reaching the other side was to continue along this same path. His only hope was the promise of the rainbow on the other side.

"I'm pregnant," Amanda announced when Molly answered the telephone. "I just killed a rabbit."

"Congratulations." Molly didn't have the heart to tell her they didn't test rabbits these days.

"Oh, Molly, I'm so excited I can barely stand it."

She wasn't generally emotional these days, not like she was when she was first pregnant, but she wiped a tear of shared happiness from her eye. "Does Tommy know?"

"Yes. I just called him at work and you know what he did? Oh, Molly, he's so sweet. He started to cry right there on the phone with everyone and his mother watching. Then I started to weep. My goodness, we're a pair. I can't remember when I've been so happy. Yes, I can...but this time, well, this time it's different."

"When are you due?" Molly asked. She was sitting on the sofa, her swollen feet propped up on the coffee table. She'd quit work the week before and had fully intended on putting away her Christmas decorations, but she hadn't found the energy. It would take her a couple of weeks, she speculated, to recoup from the business of the holidays.

"The doctor seemed to think mid-August. I can't believe I'm going to have to spend the hottest part of the summer pregnant. You'd think we'd know how to plan better, wouldn't you?"

Molly wondered if there was ever an easy time to be pregnant.

She had another three weeks left before her due date and she felt as big as a house. Ian had become a mother hen, calling her at all times of the day and night. Her father called, but not Jordan. She'd made it plain that she didn't want to hear from him, and apparently he'd accepted the wisdom of her decision.

Fool that she was, Molly couldn't keep herself from hoping he'd call. He'd sent her a Christmas gift by means of her father, and it had depressed her so that she'd wept for days afterward. Ian had wanted to call the doctor. He couldn't understand why a slinky pair of black baby-doll pajamas would upset her so.

She knew that Jordan had company for Christmas. His friend, Zane Halquist, the mercenary he'd hired to get her safely out of Manukua, had flown into Chicago and the two men had spent the holidays together. Molly would have liked to thank Zane herself, had she known he was in town.

Molly had gotten a long letter from Jordan's mother shortly before Christmas and was surprised to learn that he had spent Thanksgiving in Arizona. Martha Larabee told about Jordan asking her to put Jeff's picture away. Her mother-in-law wrote to let her know how badly she felt that she and Jordan hadn't been able to work matters out. She asked Molly to let her know when the baby was born and had mailed a beautiful hand-knit blanket as a Christmas gift.

"I'll save my baby things for you," Molly promised her friend.

"Thanks, but we have plenty of things from Christi."

Molly noted how much easier it was for Amanda to talk about the daughter she'd lost to SIDS now. It was easier for her to discuss Jeff, too. Together they'd found a support group for parents whose children had died and it had helped them both tremendously. Each time she attended a meeting, she thought of Jordan. It was painful, but she came away stronger and more confident.

"I haven't told my dad yet, so I'd better get off the phone," Amanda said.

"Of course. Give him my best."

"I will. And thank you, Molly."

"Me? I didn't do anything."

"You've been the best friend I ever had."

"You've been a good friend to me, too."

"You'll call me when you go into labor," Amanda coaxed.

Everyone seemed to think she was ready to pop. "It won't be for several weeks yet."

"But you'll phone me right away?"

"You're second on my list. My sweetheart of a dad insists on being first."

"Are you going to contact Jordan?"

Molly's gaze fell on the baby blanket his mother had sent. Jordan hadn't been able to bear to look at a framed photograph of Jeff. He wouldn't be able to deal with the labor and birth of this child.

"No," she said sadly. "He doesn't want to know."

"You're sure about that?"

"Positive. Now call your father with the good news and give him my love."

Pleased at her friend's news, Molly hung up the phone and walked into the kitchen. She felt good, but clumsy. As awkward as the broad side of a barn, but good. Although she seemed to require a nap every afternoon, she was full of energy now. After putting away the Christmas decorations, she phoned her father and invited him over for dinner.

Ian arrived promptly at six with a bouquet of flowers and a carton of milk. He patted Molly's tummy and commented on how "full" she looked.

Molly accepted his teasing good-naturedly, kissed him on the cheek and led him into the kitchen.

"How are you feeling?" he insisted on knowing, studying her with an eagle eye.

"I can't remember when I've felt better," she said with a smile, taking the casserole out of the oven and carrying it over to the table.

"I talked to Jordan today," her father commented nonchalantly, smoothing the napkin across his lap.

"Dad, I told you I didn't want to discuss Jordan." Molly had given up counting the ways Ian had of introducing her husband into casual conversation.

"He's worried about you."

"It's an unusually mild winter we're having, isn't it?" she said, setting the serving spoon on the steaming ceramic dish. She waddled over to the refrigerator and brought out the green salad she'd prepared earlier.

"He calls at least once a day to ask about you."

She noticed Jordan didn't inquire about the baby. Molly ignored him and dished up her salad, passing the bowl over to her father. She set the dressing bottle down with a thud. "I was thinking of planting red roses this spring. The same variety Mom loved."

"I was talking about Jordan," Ian returned stubbornly, setting the salad bowl against the table hard enough for it to make a clanging sound.

"I was talking about roses" Molly came back with equal stubbornness.

"He loves you."

"I love that rich deep color of red roses."

Ian slammed his fork down. "I don't know what I'm going to do with the pair of you. Jordan's just as stubborn as you are. Worse. I've told him a dozen or more times that I refuse to answer his questions. If he wants to know how you're doing, he can damn well ask you himself.

"You know what he does, don't you? He phones Doug Anderson right from my own home. When he hangs up, he repeats everything to me as if I needed a physician to tell me about my own daughter."

"Dad," Molly said gently, placing her hand on his. "It's over between me and Jordan."

"Damn fools," he muttered. "The pair of you."

Molly didn't argue. Personally she agreed with him.

It had started out as a perfectly normal January day. Jordan was on the job site talking over a supply problem with Paul Phelps when his beeper went off. Absently he reached for it, removing it from his belt, and glanced at the phone number being printed out across the miniature screen. His heart froze solid when he recognized the caller's number.

"Jordan," Paul's voice broke into his confusion. "What is it?"

"That's Ian. There's only one reason he'd contact me this time of day."

"Molly's having the baby?"

"That would be my guess." Jordan took off in a dead run for the construction trailer. A hundred times, possibly a thousand, he'd warned his crews to put safety first. At the moment, Jordan didn't care what the hell he tripped over as long as he found out what he needed to know.

He punched Ian's home number so hard he nearly jammed his finger. Then he waited. The phone rang a good five times before his father-in-law deemed to answer.

"Jordan, my boy," he greeted jovially, "it didn't take you long to get back to me."

"Where's Molly?" he demanded breathlessly.

"Molly? What makes you think this call has anything to do with my daughter?" He responded to his own sorry joke with a laugh.

"Damn you, Ian, if this is some sort of prank, I don't find it the least bit funny."

Ian's laughter died down. "As it happens, you're right. Molly's on her way to the hospital as we speak. She was adamant that you not know, but I decided otherwise. The problem with my daughter is that I've spoiled her. She seems to think I should do everything she asks.''

''Ian, is she all right?''

''I assume so. She sounded fine when she contacted me. A little excited. A little afraid. You are coming, aren't you?''

Now it was Jordan's turn to laugh. ''I wouldn't miss this for the world.''

Chapter Thirteen

Everything seemed to move in slow motion once Molly arrived at the hospital. The labor room nurse, Barbara, a middle-aged motherly type, was gentle and encouraging as she prepared Molly for the baby's birth.

By the time Molly was situated in bed, connected to the fetal heart monitor, she heard some type of commotion at the nurses' station. It was apparent her father had arrived and wanted to see her.

"That's quite some father you have," Barbara reported when she next came to check Molly. "He's demanding to know what's taking so long. He expected his grandchild to be here before now. He's convinced something has gone terribly wrong."

Ian had been away on a business trip when Jeff had been born and seemed to forget that these matters took their own sweet time.

"You better talk to him," her nurse suggested.

"By all means," she said, "send him in before he makes a genuine pest of himself." Molly couldn't help smiling. She was convinced the last time her father had been anywhere close to a maternity floor had been when she was born twenty-eight years earlier.

At the approach of a contraction, Molly laid her head against the thick feather pillow and breathed in deeply while rubbing the constricting tightness of her swollen tummy. The labor pains were gaining in intensity now, coming every three or four minutes.

Her concentration must have been more centered than she realized, because when she opened her eyes she found Jordan standing at her bedside, his face pale with concern.

Molly stared speechlessly up at him. It had been nearly three months since she'd last seen him, and she damned her fickle heart for the glad way it reacted. It took her a full minute to recover. "How'd you get here?"

"I drove," he answered with a saucy smile. "How are you?"

"Very pregnant." She thought this as good a time as any to remind him of the fact.

"So I see."

Self-conscious, she tugged the thin sheet up to her chin. "How'd you know I was here?"

"Your father phoned me."

Furious, Molly pinched her lips together, suppressing a tirade. Later she'd talk to Ian and let him know, in no uncertain terms, how displeased she was by his treachery. Her father knew she didn't want to see Jordan again. She couldn't have made her feelings any plainer.

"Where's my father?" she asked, looking away from him, simply because it was easier to remember that within a few weeks he would no longer be an important part of her life.

Jordan chuckled softly. "He lit up a cigar and was escorted from the hospital by two orderlies."

"Dad knows better than that."

"He's nervous."

"That's no excuse," she returned primly.

"Perhaps not."

Another pain arrived unexpectedly and Molly closed her eyes at the sudden sharpness she experienced.

"What's wrong?" Jordan asked, instantly sensing her distress. She shut her eyes and shook her head, not wanting to be distracted. Silently she sent loving thoughts to her baby, encouraging him or her through the contraction. Actually she was looking to reassure both the baby and herself. It'd been several years since she'd given birth to Jeff and she didn't recall the labor being quite this intense this soon.

When the pain passed, Molly opened her eyes and discovered Jordan was holding her hand between both of his. His eyes were warm and loving.

The temptation was strong to ask him to remain with her, to help her through this birth the way he had so lovingly stayed by her side when Jeff had been born.

"I don't know that you should be here," she said finally, wishing with all her heart he'd leave now before she broke down and begged him to stay.

"Why not? I was there in the beginning. It only seems fair that

I get to see the finished product. Besides there isn't anyplace else in the world I'd rather be,'' he told her, his voice even and strong. ''I love you, Molly, and I love our baby.''

Uncertain if she should believe him or not, Molly looked away. She was about to ask him to leave when another contraction struck. Tensing with the pain, she gritted her teeth.

Jordan spoke softly, encouragingly, helping her through the worst of it. When she opened her eyes, she found her husband had helped himself to a chair and had planted himself at her side. His eyes challenged her to send him away. His look told her he wouldn't go without a fight.

''I'm staying,'' he said, as if he needed to punctuate his determination. ''It's my right.''

''Why are you demanding parental privileges now? They certainly didn't interest you before.''

''I've learned some hard lessons these past few weeks. First and foremost you're right, Molly, I'm going to love our daughter...or son. I won't be able to help myself.''

''You're saying that because you know it's what I want to hear.'' Molly was afraid to believe him, afraid to put her trust in what he was telling her for fear he'd break her heart one more time.

''No, Molly, I've given a lot of thought to this. I already love Bethany...or Richard.''

Molly bit into her lower lip. She wasn't in any position to be making sound decisions. Jordan must have sensed her confusion because he brushed the hair from her forehead, bent forward and gently kissed her lips.

''Let me stay with you.''

Molly hadn't the strength to refuse. ''All right.''

As the hours and her labor progressed, Molly was forever grateful Jordan was at her side. He was a tremendous help. He encouraged her and rubbed her backside to soothe away the worst of the pain she experienced there. He cooled her face with a damp cloth and gripped her hand when the contractions were at their worst.

The pains were growing in intensity now. Jordan verbally charted the seconds for her in a calm, reassuring voice as the hard contractions gripped her body.

''You're smiling,'' he commented as he wiped the perspiration from her face with a cold washcloth. ''Care to let me in on the joke?''

''You want a little girl, don't you?''

''What makes you think that?''

''Oh, come on, Jordan, you couldn't be more obvious. You've

referred to the baby as Bethany several times. You haven't called him Richard once.''

"Would you mind a daughter?'' he asked.

Molly hadn't given the subject much consideration. She had no preference, she believed, but now she wasn't so sure. Deep in her heart she might be looking for a son to replace the one she'd lost. A son to ease the ache of her loss.

As soon as the thought moved through her head, Molly realized that wasn't true. No child could ever replace Jeff. He held his own, distinct spot in her heart.

"All I want is a strong, healthy baby,'' Molly answered.

"That's what I want, too,'' Jordan assured her.

Molly rolled her head to one side so she could look up at him. "Do you want this child?''

"Yes, Molly, I want this baby as much or possibly even more than I wanted Jeff.''

His words confused her and she wasn't sure she could trust him, especially since her nurse had recently been in to give her a shot. Barbara had claimed it would help relax her. "I want to believe you so badly,'' she whispered, "but I don't know if I dare.''

"Dare, my love,'' he whispered, kissing her temple.

When it came time for Molly to be moved from the labor room into the delivery room, Jordan left her. She tried to hide how disappointed she was that he'd opted to stay out of the delivery room, but couldn't.

"Don't look so down in the mouth,'' Barbara said, patting her hand. "Your husband will be right back as soon as he's changed his clothes.''

Molly all but wept when Jordan reappeared a few minutes later, donned in a green surgical top and pants. She didn't realize there were tears in her eyes until he lovingly brushed the moisture from her cheekbone.

"It won't be long now,'' he said, gripping her hand.

Once everyone was in place and situated, Molly heard Jordan and Doug Anderson chatting. She knew the two men were acquainted, but she hadn't realized they were such good friends. Leave it to Jordan to talk golfing scores with her physician. Both men were so involved in their conversation they seemed to have forgotten all about her and the baby.

"Push,'' Doug urged Molly at the appropriate moment.

"What do you think I'm doing?'' she snapped, then gritted her teeth and strained for all she was worth.

"I don't advise you to cross her just now," Jordan said to his friend.

"It isn't you who's down here giving birth to a watermelon, buster," she said testily to her husband.

"You're doing great, sweetheart."

This was hard, so much more difficult than what she remembered.

"Molly, look, you can see the top of her head." Jordan sounded as excited as if he'd won the lottery.

"It could be a boy," she reminded him.

"No way," Jordan said confidently, "that's the hair of a beautiful baby girl. No boy would be caught with soft blond curls."

"You don't know that she's going to be blond."

"Ah, but I do," he said, bending forward and whispering close to her ear. "Just like her mommy."

"It won't be long now," Doug told them both.

"You told me that an hour ago," Molly reminded him waspishly.

"It just seemed like an hour."

Molly glared up at her husband. "Do you want to trade places?"

Jordan's smile was wide and full. "Not on your life. I'm content with my contribution to this effort. In fact, I found it downright pleasing."

"Now isn't the time to joke, Jordan Larabee." No sooner had the words escaped Molly's lips when she felt a tremendous release followed by the husky cry of her newborn baby.

"Welcome to our world, Bethany Marie," Doug Anderson said.

"A girl. We have a girl," Molly whispered. A joy so strong it could barely be contained filled her. Her breathing went shallow and her heart pounded with the force of it. Tears flooded her eyes and ran unrestricted down the sides of her face.

"Come here, Daddy, and meet your little girl," Doug instructed Jordan.

Molly watched as her husband left her side. Bethany, who didn't appear to be the least bit delighted with her new surroundings, squalled lustily while being weighed and measured. Her tiny face was a bright red as she freely kicked her legs and arms.

The nurse wrapped her in a warm blanket and handed Bethany to Jordan who was sitting down. Molly watched her husband's face as his daughter was positioned in his arms. Jordan looked down on their daughter for several seconds, and then as if he were aware of Molly's scrutiny, looked up.

It was at that moment that Molly saw the tears rolling down Jordan's cheeks.

Jordan crying. It must be an optical illusion, Molly decided. She'd never seen Jordan weep. Not even when they'd buried Jeff.

The tears appeared to embarrass him as the nurse lifted Bethany from his arms and carried her over to Molly. Apparently worn out by the ordeal, Bethany nestled comfortably into Molly's embrace.

"She's perfect," Molly whispered when Jordan came over to stand by her bedside.

"So's her mother." Jordan bent in half and kissed them each on the forehead.

Molly didn't feel perfect. If she were capable of any feeling, it was exhaustion. Time had lost meaning and she hadn't a clue of whether it was afternoon or evening. For all she knew Monday could have leaked into Tuesday. It had been Monday when her water broke, hadn't it?

"You were so confident we were having a girl," Molly said to Jordan.

Her husband raised the back of her hand to his mouth and kissed it. "I have a confession to make."

Now, she mused, was not the time to make any confessions.

"I've known for weeks we were having a daughter."

"How?" she demanded. It wasn't possible.

Jordan's grin rivaled the piercing light of the delivery room. "Doug told me. You claimed you didn't want to know, but I felt no such restraint."

"You did know." She yawned loudly, barely able to stay awake.

"I love you, Molly, more right this moment than I believed it was possible to love anyone."

"I love you, too."

He brushed the hair from her face. "Go ahead and sleep—you're exhausted. We'll have plenty of time to talk later."

Molly was eager to comply. She sighed, completely and utterly content.

Molly might be exhausted, but Jordan had never been more wide-eyed and excited in his life. Ian was pacing the waiting room floor when Jordan arrived through the swinging doors, still in his surgical greens.

"Well, for the love of heaven, don't keep me in suspense any longer," Ian said impatiently. "I haven't been this nervous since Molly's mother went into labor."

"Mother and child are doing fine." It was payback time. For once Jordan had the information Ian wanted, but it wasn't in him to keep the older man guessing. Not when it was all Jordan could do not to shout out the wonderful news.

"Boy child or girl child?" Ian barked.

"You have a beautiful granddaughter."

"A little girl." Ian slumped down into a chair as if his legs had suddenly turned to rubber. "By heaven, a girl." He reached for his cigar in his shirt pocket and stuck it in his mouth. It looked as though Ian had taken to chomping on it to ease the tension and had chewed it down to a nub.

"Molly's fine?" he asked, looking up at Jordan.

"Sleeping. You can see her for a moment, if you want."

Recovering quickly, Ian stood and rubbed his hand down his face. "I don't know about you, young man, but I can't remember a more wretched night."

Jordan disagreed. This had to be one of the most fantastic nights of his life.

"I'm headed home, and the minute I arrive I'm pouring myself a stiff drink of Scotch." He looped his arm companionably over Jordan's shoulders. "Would you care to join me?"

Jordan was sorely tempted. "Give me a rain check. I think I'll stick around here for a little while longer. I want to watch Bethany receive her first bath. The nurse said she'd let me hold her again once they're finished."

Ian slapped his back affectionately. "What about you and Molly? Are you going to be all right?"

"I think so."

"Good." Having said as much, Ian left the hospital.

Jordan spent the next hour with his newborn daughter, then slipped into Molly's room. As he suspected, his wife was sound asleep. He intended on only staying long enough to be sure she was resting comfortably. There'd be time enough in the morning for them to talk. But he soon discovered he couldn't make himself walk away from her.

He felt extraordinarily happy. Tired, too, but unlike any other kind of exhaustion he'd ever experienced. Sitting beside her, he studied the face of the woman he loved. His heart was so full, it felt as if it would burst wide open.

He must have fallen asleep because the next thing he knew Molly's hand was on his head.

"Jordan," she whispered, sounding dreamy and vague, "what are you doing here?"

He'd rested his eyes for a few moments, he recalled, crossed his arms against the side of the bed and leaned forward, but he hadn't intended to rest more than five minutes.

"It seems to me," he said, yawning loudly, "this was where the conversation got started sometime yesterday afternoon. You asked me what I was doing here then, too."

Her smile was the most beautiful sight he'd ever seen, with the one exception of her holding Bethany while they were in the delivery room.

"How are you feeling?" he asked.

She didn't answer him. "You wept."

The display of tears embarrassed him, but he didn't regret them. They'd come of their own accord without him realizing what was happening. His emotions had taken control more than once in the past few weeks.

"I don't ever remember seeing you cry," she continued.

The strong male image had been too important for that. "I've done my fair share of weeping lately," he confessed, "sitting in Jeff's nursery and dealing with some deeply buried emotions."

Molly looked as if she were about to break into tears herself. They should be celebrating instead of crying, but he refused to chastise her for tears. Not when he'd done it so often in the past.

"I'm sorry, Molly, for being such a heel. Can you find it in your heart to forgive me?"

"Yes," she said, bypassing the tightness in her throat. "It's past and forgotten."

"I'll find a way of making it all up to you someday. I have a lot of ground to cover, starting from the moment you found Jeff's body until a few months ago."

She smiled through her tears. "I hope you're aware that could take some doing."

"You could sentence me to a life term."

"Consider yourself sentenced." She raised her arms and Jordan wrapped her in his embrace. He buried his face in her neck and drank in her love.

"You never tried to contact me," she whispered, "not even once."

"When?"

"These past few months. I needed you the most then."

"But you said you didn't want to see me!" He'd never understand a woman's mind. Staying away had been torment, but he'd had no choice but to abide by her wishes. Now she was telling him she'd wanted him.

"You won't have to worry about that happening again," he assured her. "I've got a life sentence and I'm not about to be cheated out of a single day."

Molly smiled softly and directed his mouth to hers. "The penalty should start soon, don't you think?"

Jordan laughed and then his lips met hers. He wondered if a single lifetime was enough time for him to properly love this woman.

* * * * *

Don't miss Silhouette's newest cross-line promotion,

Four royal sisters find their own Prince Charmings as they embark on separate journeys to find their missing brother, the Crown Prince!

The search begins in October 1999 and continues through February 2000:

On sale October 1999: **A ROYAL BABY ON THE WAY**
by award-winning author **Susan Mallery** (Special Edition)

On sale November 1999: **UNDERCOVER PRINCESS**
by bestselling author **Suzanne Brockmann** (Intimate Moments)

On sale December 1999: **THE PRINCESS'S WHITE KNIGHT**
by popular author **Carla Cassidy** (Romance)

On sale January 2000: **THE PREGNANT PRINCESS**
by rising star **Anne Marie Winston** (Desire)

On sale February 2000: **MAN...MERCENARY...MONARCH**
by top-notch talent **Joan Elliott Pickart** (Special Edition)

ROYALLY WED
Only in—
SILHOUETTE BOOKS

Available at your favorite retail outlet.

Visit us at www.romance.net

SSERW_T6

Rx

PRESCRIPTION:
Marriage

Back by popular demand!

CHRISTINE RIMMER
SUSAN MALLERY
CHRISTINE FLYNN

prescribe three more exciting doses of
heart-stopping romance in their series,
PRESCRIPTION: MARRIAGE.

Three wedding-shy female physicians discover
that marriage may be just what the doctor
ordered when they lose their hearts to three
irresistible, iron-willed men.

Look for this wonderful series at your favorite retail outlet—

On sale December 1999:
A DOCTOR'S VOW (SE #1293)
by **Christine Rimmer**

On sale January 2000:
THEIR LITTLE PRINCESS (SE #1298)
by **Susan Mallery**

On sale February 2000:
DR. MOM AND THE MILLIONAIRE (SE #1304)
by **Christine Flynn**

Only from
Silhouette Special Edition

Looking For More Romance?

Visit Romance.net

Look us up on-line at: http://www.romance.net

Check in daily for these and other exciting features:

View all current titles, and purchase them on-line.

Hot off the press

What do the stars have in store for you?

Horoscope

Hot deals

Exclusive offers available only at Romance.net

Plus, don't miss our interactive quizzes, contests and bonus gifts.

PWEB_T6

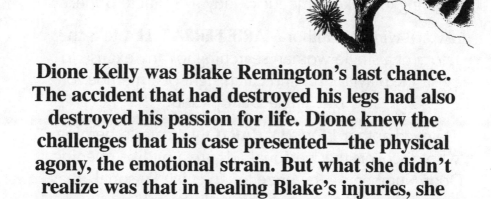